READER'S DIGEST
CONDENSED BOOKS

www.readersdigest.co.uk

The Reader's Digest Association
Limited 11 Westferry Circus
Canary Wharf London E14 4HE

For information as to ownership of
copyright in the material of this
book, and acknowledgments, see
last page.

Printed in France
ISBN 0 276 42621-5

READER'S DIGEST
CONDENSED BOOKS

*Selected and edited
by Reader's Digest*

CONDENSED BOOKS DIVISION
THE READER'S DIGEST ASSOCIATION LIMITED, LONDON

CONTENTS

Carmen Greer lives in fear of what her
violent husband will do to her when he gets
out of jail. She can't flee their isolated
Texas home with her daughter Ellie,
because he would be sure to hunt her
down. Then, by chance, she meets Jack
Reacher. He's ex-military, out of work, and
only too ready to help wherever he finds
injustice. An unforgettable thriller that
sizzles with Texan heat and suspense.

PUBLISHED BY BANTAM PRESS

When software billionaire Rex Wyman sets
up the world's most challenging sailing
race and personally enters his multi-million-
dollar super-yacht, he is confident that
Victory will win and provide a public
relations coup for his business empire. But
as the boats enter the wintry, storm-tossed
Bering Sea, it emerges that *Victory*'s sophisticated computer system is fatally flawed . . .
Vivid drama, set on the high seas.

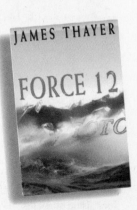

PUBLISHED BY MACMILLAN

THE OBSERVATORY 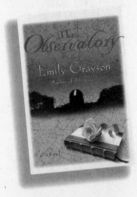 page 295

Emily Grayson

Liz Mallory and her beautiful, fiery sister Harper are twins, but their very different personalities and lifestyles have led them to drift apart. When tragedy suddenly strikes Harper's family, Liz feels compelled to help. In so doing, she meets and falls in love with astronomer David Fields, and her life seems set to take a completely new turn. A captivating story of passion and rivalry from a popular American author.

PUBLISHED BY WILLIAM MORROW, USA

THE FALLS  page 369

Ian Rankin

When Flip Balfour, daughter of one of Edinburgh's top bankers, disappears, Inspector Rebus is soon on the case. His first lead is a miniature coffin discovered at a waterfall close to Flip's parental home. Then his assistant, DC Siobhan Clarke, finds herself drawn into solving cryptic clues sent by someone calling themselves 'Quizmaster'. Tantalising suspense set in atmospheric Edinburgh, from Britain's foremost crime writer.

PUBLISHED BY ORION

echo burning

Lee Child

Ex-military policeman Jack Reacher needs a ride out of town and he's not choosy about where he finds it. So, when an attractive woman pulls her car over to offer him a lift, he doesn't waste time wondering why. Reacher's more than happy to go along wherever she's headed.

Which is how he finds himself passing through a lonely little township in Echo County, Texas, on the way to the Red House Ranch and a family torn apart by suspicion, jealousy and murder.

ONE

There were three watchers, two men and a boy. They were using telescopes, not field glasses. It was a question of distance. They were almost a mile from their target area, because of the terrain. There was no closer cover. It was low, undulating country, burned khaki by the sun, grass and rock and sandy soil alike. The nearest safe concealment was the broad dip they were in, a bone-dry gulch scraped out a million years ago by a different climate, when there had been rain and ferns and rushing rivers.

The men lay prone in the dust with the early heat on their backs, their telescopes at their eyes. The boy scuttled around on his knees, fetching water from the cooler, watching for waking rattlesnakes, logging comments in a notebook. They had arrived before first light in a dusty pick-up truck, the long way round, across the empty land from the west. They had thrown a dirty tarpaulin over the truck and pegged it down with rocks. They had eased forward to the rim of the dip and settled in, as the low morning sun dawned to the east behind the red house almost a mile away. This was Friday, their fifth consecutive morning, and they were low on conversation.

'Time?' one of the men asked.

The boy checked his watch. 'Six fifty,' he answered.

'Kitchen light on,' the man said.

The boy wrote it down. *Six fifty, kitchen light on.*

'On her own?' the boy asked.

'Same as always,' the second man said, squinting.

9

Maid prepares breakfast, the boy wrote. *Target still in bed*. The sun rose, inch by inch. Seven o'clock in the morning and it was already hot. By eight it would be burning. By nine it would be fearsome. And they were there all day, until dark, when they could slip away unseen.

'Bedroom drapes opening,' the second man said. 'She's up.'

The boy wrote it down. *Seven oh-four, bedroom drapes open*.

They heard the well pump kick in, very faintly from almost a mile away. A quiet mechanical click, and then a steady low drone.

'She's showering,' the first man said.

The boy wrote it down. *Seven oh-six, target starts to shower*.

The well pump clicked off after six minutes. The boy wrote, *Seven twelve, target out of shower*. Then: *Seven fifteen, probably dressing*. Then: *Seven twenty, probably downstairs, eating breakfast*.

'Stand by,' the second man said. 'A buck gets ten she goes out to the barn now.' It was a wager that nobody took, because so far four times out of four she had done exactly that.

She came out, dressed in a blue gingham dress, walked across the yard and heaved the barn door open.

Seven twenty-eight, comes out, goes to barn, the boy wrote.

'Here comes her ride,' the second man said.

Miles to the south, there was a dust cloud on the road.

'She's coming back,' the man said.

Seven thirty-two, target comes out of barn, the boy wrote.

'Maid's at the door,' the man said.

The target stopped at the kitchen door and took her lunch box from the maid. It was bright blue plastic with a cartoon picture on the side. Then she trotted out through the gate, to the shoulder of the road. The school bus slowed and stopped and the door opened. The target clambered up onto the step. The door closed and the watchers saw her corn-coloured head bobbing along level with the base of the windows. Then the bus moved away.

Seven thirty-six, target on bus to school, the boy wrote.

He closed his notebook and the watchers lowered their telescopes. Seven thirty-seven, Friday morning.

Seven thirty-eight.

SEVEN THIRTY-NINE, more than 300 miles to the northeast, Jack Reacher climbed out of his motel-room window. One minute earlier, he had been in the bathroom, brushing his teeth. One minute before that, he had opened the door of his room to check the temperature.

He had left it open, and the closet just inside the entrance was faced with mirrored glass, and there was a mirror in the bathroom on a cantilevered arm, and by a freak of optical chance he caught sight of four men getting out of a car and walking towards the motel office.

The car was a police cruiser. It had a shield on the door: at the top it said CITY POLICE, and there was a fancy medallion with *Lubbock, Texas* written underneath. All four men were in uniform. They had belts with guns, nightsticks and handcuffs. Three of them he had never seen before, but the fourth was familiar. He was a tall heavyweight with a gelled blond brush-cut above a meaty red face. This morning the face was partially obscured by an aluminium splint taped over a shattered nose. His right hand was similarly bound up with a splint and bandages protecting a broken finger.

The guy had neither injury the night before. And Reacher had no idea the guy was a cop. He just looked like some idiot in a bar. Reacher had gone there because he'd heard the music was good, but it wasn't, so he had backed away from the band and ended up on a bar stool watching a sports channel on a TV fixed high on a wall. The place was crowded and noisy. He got bored with the sports and turned round to watch the room.

The heavyweight guy was on his left. He was eating chicken wings. The wings were greasy and the guy was a slob. He was dripping chicken fat off his chin and off his fingers onto his shirt. But the best bar-room etiquette doesn't let you linger on such a sight, and the guy caught Reacher staring. 'You looking at me?' he said.

'No,' Reacher answered.

'Don't you be looking at me, boy,' the guy said.

Reacher turned his head and looked at him. Not to antagonise the guy. Just to size him up. He knew one day he would come face to face with his physical equal. With somebody who might worry him. But he saw this wasn't the day. So he just smiled and looked away again.

Then the guy jabbed him with his finger. 'I told you not to look at me,' he said, and jabbed. It was a meaty forefinger and it was covered in grease. It left a mark on Reacher's shirt.

'Don't do that,' Reacher said.

The guy jabbed again. 'Or what?' he said.

Reacher looked down. Now there were two marks. The guy jabbed again. Three marks.

'You deaf?' Reacher said. 'I told you not to do that.'

'You want to do something about it?'

'No,' Reacher said. 'I don't. I just want you to stop doing it, is all.'

The guy smiled. 'Then you're a yellow-bellied piece of shit.'

'Whatever,' Reacher said. 'Just keep your hands off me.'

'Or what? What you going to do?'

'Touch me again and you'll find out,' Reacher said. 'I warned you.'

The guy paused a second. Then he went for it again. Reacher caught the finger and snapped it at the first knuckle. Just folded it upwards like he was turning a door handle. Then because he was irritated he leaned forward and headbutted the guy in the face.

The guy thumped on the floorboards and Reacher used the sole of his shoe to roll him half onto his front. Then he nudged him under the chin with his toe to pull his head back and straighten his airway. The recovery position. Stops you choking while you're out.

He paid for his drinks and walked back to his motel, and didn't give the guy another thought until he was at the bathroom mirror and saw him out and about in a cop's uniform. Then he thought hard, and as fast as he could.

What to do? An angry cop bent on revenge could cause trouble. A noisy public arrest, for sure, maybe wild gunshots, definitely some fun and games in an out-of-the-way cell down at the station house, where you can't fight back without multiplying your original legal problem. Then all kinds of difficult questions, because Reacher habitually carried no ID and nothing except his toothbrush and a couple of thousand dollars cash in his trouser pocket. So he would be regarded as a suspicious character. Almost certainly he'd be charged with attacking a law officer. All kinds of witnesses would materialise to swear it was malicious and unprovoked. He could end up convicted and in the penitentiary, easy as anything. He could end up with seven-to-ten in some tough establishment.

So he put his toothbrush in his pocket, walked through the room and opened the window. Climbed out, closed the window and walked away to the nearest street. Kept walking until he was hidden by a building. He looked for buses. There weren't any. He looked for taxis. Nothing doing. So he stuck out his thumb. He figured he had ten minutes to find a ride before they finished at the motels and started cruising the streets.

THERE WERE THREE KILLERS, two men and a woman. They were based in Los Angeles, contactable through an intermediary in Dallas and a second cut-out in Vegas. They had been in business ten years, and they were good at what they did. A good team. And perfectly suited to it. Bland, forgettable, white, anonymous.

They travelled separately. One always drove and the other two flew, by different routes. The driver was one of the men. The car was rented at LAX arrivals. The licence and credit card used to obtain it were real, issued in a distant state to a person who had never existed. The driver was small and dark and had a rolling duffle, a carry-on and a harassed expression, same as everybody else.

He did the paperwork, rode the bus to the rental compound and found his allotted car. He dumped his bags in the trunk and drove out into the glare. He spent forty minutes on the freeways, making sure he wasn't followed. Then he ducked off into West Hollywood and stopped at a lock-up garage in an alley. He left the motor running while he opened the garage door, then opened the trunk and swapped his rolling duffle and his carry-on for two big valises made of thick black nylon. One was very heavy, and was the reason he was driving, not flying. It contained things best kept away from airport scanners.

He closed up the garage and settled in for the two-day drive to Texas. He wasn't a smoker, but he lit numerous cigarettes and flicked ash everywhere. That way, the rental company would have to vacuum the car thoroughly, spray it with air freshener and wipe down the vinyl. That would eliminate every trace of him later.

The second man was taller and heavier and fairer. He joined the end-of-the-workday crush at LAX and bought a ticket to Atlanta. When he got there, he swapped his wallet for one of the five spares in his carry-on and a completely different man bought another ticket for Dallas-Fort Worth.

The woman travelled a day later. That was her privilege, because she was the team leader. She was closing in on middle age, medium-sized, medium-blonde. Nothing special about her, except she killed people for a living. She used a forged MasterCard to buy her ticket.

After his second stop for gas on the first day, the driver made a detour into the New Mexico hills and changed the car's California plates for Arizona plates, which he took from the heavier valise. Back on the highway he drove another hour, then found a motel.

He made it to Dallas-Fort Worth at the end of the second day and parked in the airport long-term lot. Took his valises with him and used the shuttle bus to departures. Took the moving stairs straight down to arrivals. Lined up at the Hertz counter. Hertz, because they rent Fords, and he needed a Crown Victoria.

He did the paperwork, with Illinois ID. Rode the bus to the Hertz lot and found his car. It was the plain-Jane Crown Vic, in steel-blue metallic. He heaved his bags into the trunk and drove to a motel. Checked in, ate and slept. He woke early and met his two partners outside the motel at exactly the same moment Jack Reacher first stuck out his thumb, more than 400 miles away in Lubbock.

HE GOT A RIDE within three minutes. Even more surprising, the driver was a woman. Three minutes was the shortest interval between sticking out his thumb and climbing into a car he could remember.

He wasn't some dapper little guy, neat and inoffensive. He was a giant, six foot five, heavily built, close to 250 pounds, scruffy, unshaven, and his hair was a mess. Which was why he was surprised about the three minutes. And the woman driver.

He was hurrying south and west of the motel strip, his left thumb jammed out, when she pulled over and buzzed her far window down. 'Where to?' she called, like she was a cab driver, not a private citizen.

'Anywhere,' he said. He regretted it instantly. To have no specific destination usually makes things worse. They think you're some kind of aimless drifter, which makes them worried they might never get rid of you. But this woman just nodded.

'OK,' she said. 'I'm headed down past Pecos.'

'Great,' he said. He opened the door and slid inside. 'Thanks,' he said. 'You don't know how much I appreciate this.'

She pulled out without a word. Reacher glanced around inside the car. It was a Cadillac, two doors, but very fancy and clean as a whistle. There was a handbag and a briefcase on the back seat. The briefcase was open and there was a lot of paper stuffed in it, the sort of thing you see in a lawyer's office.

He twisted in his seat so he could look the woman over without staring straight at her. She was short and slim, dark-skinned, fine-boned. Maybe a hundred pounds, maybe thirty years old. Long black wavy hair, dark eyes. Mexican, he guessed. She was wearing a sleeveless cotton dress that finished above her knees. Not much to it, but it looked expensive. Her arms and legs were dark and smooth, like they had been polished.

'So, where are you headed?' she asked. Then she smiled. 'No, I already asked you that. You didn't seem very clear about where you want to go.' Her accent was pure American, maybe western. She was steering two-handed and he could see rings on her fingers. There was a slim wedding band and a platinum thing with a big diamond.

'Anywhere I end up,' Reacher said, 'that's where I want to go.'

She paused and smiled again. 'Are you running away from something? Have I picked up a dangerous fugitive?'

'I'm exploring,' he said. 'Like a tourist.'

'You don't look like a tourist. The tourists we get wear polyester leisure suits and come in a bus.' She smiled again. She looked good when she smiled, assured and self-possessed and elegant.

He was suddenly aware of his short answers, and his stubble and his stained shirt. 'You live around here?'

'I live south of Pecos,' she said. 'More than three hundred miles from here. I told you, that's where I'm headed.'

The woman slowed and made a shallow right, towards New Mexico, then a mile later a left, straight south, towards old Mexico. Her perfume was subtle, mixed into the freezing air from the dashboard vents.

'So is Pecos worth seeing?' Reacher asked in the silence.

She shrugged. 'I like it,' she said. 'It's mostly Mexican, so I'm comfortable there. Pecos grows the sweetest canteloupe in the whole of Texas. There's a rodeo in July, but you've missed it for this year. And just north of Pecos is Loving County. You heard of Loving County?'

He shook his head. 'Never been here before.'

'It's the least-populated county in the United States,' she said. 'Well, if you leave out some of the places in Alaska, I guess. But also the richest, per capita. Four hundred and twenty active oil leases.'

'Sounds like a fun place,' he said. 'Your family from Pecos?'

'No, California,' she said. 'I came to Texas when I got married.'

Keep talking, he thought. She saved your ass. 'Been married long?'

'Just under seven years.'

'Your family been in California long?'

She smiled. 'Longer than any Californian, that's for sure.'

They were in flat empty country and she eased the silent car faster down a dead-straight road. The instrumentation on her dashboard showed it was 110 degrees outside and 60 inside.

'You a lawyer?' he asked.

She was puzzled for a moment, and then she made the connection and craned to glance at her briefcase in the mirror.

'No,' she said. 'I'm a lawyer's client.'

'And what else are you?' he asked.

She paused a beat. 'Somebody's wife and mother,' she said. 'And somebody's daughter and sister, I guess. What are you?'

'Nothing in particular,' Reacher said.

'You have to be something,' she said.

'Well, I used to be things,' he said. 'I was somebody's son, and somebody's brother, and somebody's boyfriend.'

'Was?'

'My parents died, my brother died, my girlfriend left me.'

'I'm very sorry,' she said.

'Water under the bridge,' he said. 'It's not as bad as it sounds.'

'You're not lonely?'

He shrugged. 'I like being alone.'

She paused. 'Why did your girlfriend leave you?'

'She went to work in Europe.'

'And you couldn't go with her?'

'She didn't really want me to go with her.'

'I see,' she said. 'Did *you* want to go with her?'

'Not really, I guess,' he said. 'Too much like settling down.'

'And you don't want to settle down?'

He shook his head. 'Two nights in the same motel gives me the creeps.'

'So you *are* running away from something,' she said. 'Maybe you had a very settled life before and you want to escape from that.'

He shook his head again. 'The exact opposite. I was in the army all my life, which is very *un*settled, and I grew to like the feeling.'

She paused. 'How is a person in the army all his life?'

'My father was in, too. So I grew up on military bases all over the world, and then I stayed in afterwards.'

'But now you're out.'

He nodded. 'All trained up and nowhere to go.'

FORD BUILDS CROWN VICTORIAS in Canada, and almost all of them are sold to police departments, taxicab companies or rental fleets. Which makes private Crown Vics rarer than red Rolls-Royces, so the subliminal response when you see one that isn't taxicab-yellow or black and white with POLICE all over the doors is to think it's an unmarked detective's car. Or government issue of some other kind, maybe FBI, or Secret Service. That's the subliminal impression, and there are ways to enhance it a little.

In the empty country halfway to Abilene, the tall fair man pulled off the highway and headed through fields and past dense woods until he found a dusty lay-by. He stopped there, turned off the motor and popped the trunk. The woman zipped open the heavy valise and handed a pair of Virginia plates and a screwdriver to the tall fair man. He removed the Texas plates, front and rear, and bolted the Virginia issue in their place. The small dark man pulled the plastic covers off all four wheels, leaving the steel rims showing. He pitched the wheel covers into the trunk. The woman took four radio antennas from the valise, CB whips and cellular phone items. The cellular antennas stuck to the rear window with self-adhesive pads. She waited until the trunk was closed again and placed the CB antennas on the lid. They had magnetic bases. They weren't wired up to anything. They were just for show.

Then the small dark man took his place behind the wheel and headed back to the highway. A Crown Vic, plain steel wheels, a forest of antennas, Virginia plates. Maybe an FBI pool car, three agents inside, maybe on urgent business.

'WHAT DID YOU DO in the army?' the woman asked, very casually.

'I was a cop,' Reacher said.

'They have cops in the army?'

'Sure they do. Military police. Like cops, inside the service.'

'Were you a good cop?' she asked.

'I guess. They made me a major, gave me some medals.'

She paused. 'So why did you leave?'

'End of the Cold War, they wanted a smaller army, not so many people in it, so they didn't need so many cops to look after them.'

She nodded. 'Like a town. Population gets smaller, police department gets smaller, too. I live in a very small town. Echo, south of Pecos, like I told you. It's a lonely place. Not many inhabitants. But it's a county, too. No police department at all. Just the county sheriff.'

Something in her voice. He watched her out of the corner of his eye. She was pretty, but she was troubled.

'What was life like in the army?' she asked.

'Different,' he said. 'Different rules, different situations. It was a world of its own. Very regulated, but kind of lawless. Kind of rough and uncivilised.'

'Like the Wild West,' she said. 'I think you liked it.'

He nodded. 'Some of it.'

She paused. 'May I ask your name?'

'Reacher,' he said.

She paused again. 'Have you killed people, Reacher? In the army?'

He nodded again. 'Some.'

'There's a museum in Pecos,' she said. 'A real Wild West museum. Out back is Clay Allison's grave. You ever heard of Clay Allison?'

Reacher shook his head.

'They called him the Gentleman Gunfighter,' she said. 'There's a nice headstone, with ROBERT CLAY ALLISON 1840–1887 on it. And an inscription. The inscription says: HE NEVER KILLED A MAN THAT DID NOT NEED KILLING. What do you think of that?'

'I think it's a fine inscription,' Reacher said.

'There's an old newspaper, too,' she said. 'In a glass case. With his obituary in it. It says: "Certain it is that many of his stern deeds were for the right as he understood that right to be."'

'A fine obituary,' Reacher said. 'As good as you can get, probably.'

'Would you like an obituary like that?'

'Well, not just yet,' Reacher said.

She smiled. 'No, I guess not. But would you like to *qualify* for an obituary like that? I mean, eventually?'

'You want to tell me where this is heading?'

She pulled off onto the dusty shoulder.

'My name is Carmen Greer,' she said. 'And I need your help. It wasn't an accident I picked you up.'

'So why did you pick me up?' Reacher asked.

'I was looking for a guy like you,' she said.

'Why?'

'I must have picked up a dozen guys,' she said. 'And I've seen hundreds. That's about all I've been doing, all month long. Cruising around West Texas, looking at who needs a ride.'

'OK, Carmen,' he said. 'Tell me what's going on here, will you?'

'You ever had anything to do with lawyers?' she asked. 'They want a lot of money and a lot of time, and then they tell you there's nothing much to be done.'

'So get a new lawyer,' he said.

'I've had four,' she said. 'And they're all too expensive.'

'You're driving a Cadillac.'

'It's my mother-in-law's. I'm only borrowing it.'

'You're wearing a big diamond ring.'

Her eyes clouded. 'My husband gave it to me,' she said.

He looked at her. 'So can't he help you?'

'No,' she said. 'Have you ever gone looking for a private detective?'

'Never needed one. I *was* a detective.'

'They don't really exist,' she said. 'Not like you see in the movies. They just want to sit in their offices and work with their computers. I went all the way to Austin. A guy there said he could help, but he wanted to charge me ten thousand dollars a week.'

'For what?'

She shrugged the question away. 'So I got desperate. I was really panicking. Then I got this idea. I figured if I looked at people hitching rides, I might find somebody. One of them might turn out to be the right type of person, and willing to help me. I tried to choose pretty carefully. I only stopped for rough-looking men.'

'Thanks, Carmen,' Reacher said.

'I don't mean it badly,' she said. 'It's not uncomplimentary.'

'But it could have been dangerous.'

'It nearly was, a couple of times. But I had to take the risk. I figured I might get rodeo guys, or men from the oil fields. You know, tough guys, roughnecks, maybe out of work, with a little time on their hands. Maybe a little anxious to earn some money, but I can't pay much. Is that going to be a problem?'

'So far, Carmen, everything is going to be a problem.'

'I talked to them all,' she said. 'You know, discussed things, like we did. And none of them were really any good. But I think you are.'

'You think I'm what?'

'I think you're my best chance so far,' she said. 'Really, I do. A former cop, been in the army, no ties, you couldn't be better.'

'I'm not looking for a job, Carmen.'

'I figured that out. But that's better still. It keeps it pure, don't you see? Help for help's sake. No mercenary aspect to it. And your background is perfect. It obligates you.'

He stared at her. 'No, it doesn't.'

'You were a soldier,' she said. 'And a *policeman*. It's perfect. You're *supposed* to help people. That's what cops *do*.'

'If you need a cop, go to the county sheriff.'

She shook her head. 'No, I can't do that.'

Reacher said nothing more.

'I'm not crazy,' she said. 'It's just that I've dreamed about this for a month. It was a ridiculous plan, I guess, but there was always the chance it would work, and with you I think maybe it could, and now I'm screwing it up by coming across like a crazy woman.'

He paused a long time. Minutes. He could be sitting next to some cheerful trucker now, listening to rock'n'roll on the radio. On the other hand, he could be bruised and bleeding in a police cell, with an arraignment date coming up.

'So start over,' he said. 'Just say what you've got to say. But first, I could use a cup of coffee.'

FIFTY MILES SOUTHWEST of Abilene, on a silent county road, the Crown Victoria waited quietly on the shoulder. The driver had the door mirror racked out so he could see the road behind him. The view was clear for about a mile, back to the point where the blacktop and the sky mixed and broke into a silvery shimmering mirage. The driver focused on that distant glare, waiting for it to be pierced by a car.

The team was well briefed. They knew the car would be a white Mercedes, driven by a man on his own towards an appointment he couldn't miss. They knew the time of his appointment, and they knew his destination was thirty miles up the road, so simple arithmetic gave them a target time. A target time that was fast approaching.

'So let's do it,' the driver said. He took a ball cap from the woman. It was one of three bought from a souvenir vendor on Hollywood Boulevard. It was dark blue, with FBI machine-embroidered in white across the front. The driver squared it on his head and pulled the peak low. Kept his eyes on the mirror. 'Right on time,' he said.

The silver mirage was boiling and wobbling and a white shape pulled free of it and speared towards them like a fish leaping out of water. The shape settled and steadied on the road, moving fast. A white Mercedes roared past and the Crown Vic pulled out into its slipstream. The driver straightened the wheel and accelerated.

The Mercedes driver saw headlights flashing in his mirror and saw the sedan behind him. Two peaked caps silhouetted in the front seat. He dropped his eyes to his speedo, which was showing more than ninety. Felt a cold stab in his chest. Eased off the gas.

The sedan pulled alongside as he slowed and he saw three people, one of them a woman. Radio antennas all over the car. No lights, no siren. Not regular cops. The driver was waving him to the shoulder. The woman was pressing an ID wallet against her window. It had FBI in two-inch-high letters. Their caps said FBI. Serious-looking people, serious-looking squad car. He relaxed a little. The FBI didn't stop you for speeding. Must be something else. Maybe some kind of security check. He nodded to the woman, eased onto the shoulder and coasted to a stop. The Bureau car stopped behind him.

'Mr Eugene?' the woman called. 'Al Eugene, right?'

The Mercedes driver opened his door, slid out of his seat and stood up. He was around thirty, not tall, dark and sallow, soft and rounded. 'What can I do for you, ma'am?' he asked.

'Sir, can you spare us five minutes?' the woman asked. 'We have an FBI assistant director a ways up the road, needs to speak with you. Something urgent, I guess, or we wouldn't be here, and something pretty important, or we'd have been told what it's all about.'

Eugene looked at his watch. 'I have an appointment,' he said.

The woman was nodding. 'We know about that, sir. We took the liberty of calling ahead and rescheduling for you.'

Eugene shrugged. 'Can I see some ID?' he asked.

The woman handed over her wallet. It was made of worn black leather and had a plastic window on the outside. There was an FBI photo-ID behind it, laminated and embossed and printed with the kind of old-fashioned typeface the federal government might use.

'Up the road a piece?' he said. 'OK, I'll follow you, I guess.'

'We'll drive you,' the woman said. 'There's a checkpoint in place, and civilian cars make them nervous. We'll bring you right back.'

Eugene shrugged again. 'OK,' he said.

They all walked back to the Crown Vic. The driver held the front passenger door for Eugene. 'You ride up here, sir,' he said. 'They're listing you as a class A individual, and if we put a class A individual in the back, then we'll get our asses kicked, that's for damn sure.'

Eugene slid into the front seat. The driver closed the door on him and ducked round to his own. The tall fair man and the woman climbed into the rear. The Crown Vic eased onto the blacktop. Accelerated up to about fifty-five.

The driver slowed, hunting the turn he had scouted thirty minutes before. He spotted it and pulled left, crossed the opposite shoulder, and bumped down through a depression where the road was built up like a causeway. Then he slewed to the right, tight in behind a stand of tall brush. The man and the woman in the rear seat leaned forward and jammed handguns into Eugene's neck.

'Sit real still,' the woman said.

The driver got out and approached Eugene's door with a gun in his hand. He opened the door and jammed the muzzle into Eugene's throat. 'Get out,' he said.

Eugene got out, with three guns at his head.

'Step away from the car,' the woman said.

Eugene stepped away from the car. One pace, two, three.

The woman nodded. 'Al,' she called loudly.

Her two partners jumped away, long sideways strides. Eugene's head snapped round to face the woman. She shot him through the right eye. He went straight down. She stepped round him and crouched down to take a closer look. 'OK,' she said.

The two men took an arm and a leg each and dragged Eugene's body ten feet into the brush. They had found a narrow limestone cleft there, a crack in the rock maybe eight feet deep and a foot and a half across, wide enough to take a man's corpse sideways, too narrow to admit the wingspan of a vulture or buzzard. They manoeuvred the body until the trailing hand and foot fell into the hole. Then they dropped him. He wedged tight, about seven feet down.

The bloodstains were already drying and blackening. They kicked desert dust over them and swept the area with a mesquite branch to confuse the mass of footprints. Then they climbed into the Crown Vic and the driver backed up and swung up the slope to the roadway.

TWO

'I have a daughter,' Carmen Greer said. 'I told you that, right?'

'You told me you were a mother,' Reacher said.

She nodded at the wheel. 'Of a daughter. She's six years old. They called her Mary Ellen. Ellie, for short.'

'They?'

'My husband's family,' she said. 'The Greers. An old Echo County family. Been there since Texas was first stolen.'

'They named your kid?'

'I wasn't in a good position to stop it. We've been married less than seven years. So you can do the math. It explains why I wasn't in a good position. We got off to a bad start, me and his family.'

'What are they like?'

'They're what you might expect,' she said. 'Old white Texans, big money from way back, a lot of it gone but a lot still left, some history with oil and cattle. The father died some time ago, the mother is alive, there are two sons. My husband is the elder boy, Sloop Greer.'

'Sloop?' Reacher said. 'What's the other boy called? Yacht?'

'Robert,' she said. 'People call him Bobby.'

'Sloop,' Reacher said again. 'That's a new one to me.'

'New to me, too,' she said. 'I met him in California. We were in school together, UCLA.'

'Off of his home turf,' Reacher said.

'Correct. Only way it could have happened, looking back.' She squinted ahead into the glare of the sun. There was a bright shape up ahead. 'There's the diner,' she said. 'They'll have coffee.'

The diner sat alone on the side of the road in the centre of an acre of beaten dirt serving as its parking lot. There were two pick-up trucks, carelessly parked, far from each other.

She bounced off the road, parked and switched off the engine. Reacher opened his door. The heat hit him like a steelyard furnace. He waited for her and then they walked together across the hot dirt.

The diner had a tiny foyer with a rack of fliers about rodeos and gun shows. Inside the second door it was cold. There was a waitress sitting on a counter stool. Two men in separate booths, eating.

Reacher led Carmen to a booth at the far end of the room. He slid across sticky vinyl and tilted his head back into a jet of cold air coming from a vent in the ceiling. Carmen sat opposite.

She had spectacular dark eyes with long lashes and a slight tilt to them. High cheekbones framed by thick black hair. A rosebud of a mouth with a subtle trace of lipstick. Her skin was smooth and clear, the colour of weak tea, with a translucent glow behind it.

The waitress brought iced water and no conversation. Carmen ordered iced coffee and Reacher ordered his hot and black.

'My daughter doesn't look like she's mine at all,' Carmen said. 'Pink skin, yellow hair, a little chubby. But she's got my eyes.'

'Lucky Ellie,' Reacher said.

She smiled briefly. 'Thank you. Plan is she should stay lucky.'

The waitress brought their drinks.

'You told me to start at the beginning,' Carmen said. 'So I will. I loved Sloop once. He was big and handsome, and he smiled a lot. We were in school and we were young, and LA is a place where anything seems possible and nothing seems to matter very much.' She took a drinking straw from the canister on the table and unwrapped it.

'You need to know where I was coming from,' she said. 'I wasn't some Mexican worrying about whether the white family would accept me. I come from a thousand acres in Napa, we've been there for ever, we were always the richest people I knew. So I worried about what my folks would say about me marrying this gringo boy.'

He sipped his coffee. 'And what did they say?' he asked.

'They went insane.'

'So what happened?'

She sipped her drink through the straw. 'Well, I was pregnant,' she said. 'And that made everything a million times worse. My parents are very devout and traditional, and basically they disowned me.'

'So what did you do?'

'We got married. We lived a few months in LA, graduated, stayed there until the baby was a month away. But getting a job wasn't in Sloop's plan. College was four years of fun for him, then it was back to take over Daddy's business. His father was ready to retire by then. I didn't like that idea. I thought we were starting up fresh on our own, a new generation on both sides. I'd given stuff up and I thought he should, too. We argued. I couldn't work, because of being so pregnant, and I had no money of my own. In the end we couldn't make the rent, so he won, and we trailed back here to Texas, and moved into the big old house with his folks, and I'm still there.'

'And?' he asked.

'And it was a shock. All my life I'd been like a princess, and then I was just a hip kid among ten thousand others in LA, but now I was suddenly just a piece of beaner trash. They never said it straight but it was clear they hated me. I was the greaseball whore who'd hooked their darling boy. They were painfully polite, because I guess their strategy was to wait for Sloop to come to his senses and dump me.'

'But he didn't dump you, evidently.'

She looked down at the table. 'No,' she said. 'He didn't. He started hitting me instead. First time, he punched me in the face. He split my lip and loosened my teeth. He just lost it. But straight away he was full of remorse. He drove me to the emergency room himself, and the whole way he was begging me to forgive him. Then he begged me not to tell the truth about what had happened. He seemed really ashamed, so I agreed. But as soon as we arrived I started into labour so they took me straight to the delivery unit. Ellie was born the next day.'

Reacher watched her face. 'And then what?'

'Then it was OK,' she said. 'For a week, at least. Then he started hitting me again. I was doing everything wrong. I was paying too much attention to the baby, I didn't want sex because I was hurting from the stitches. He said I had gotten fat and ugly from the pregnancy. He got me believing it. For a long, long time. Two or three years, I thought it *was* my fault, and I tried to do better.'

'What did the family do?'

'They didn't know about it,' she said. 'And then his father died, which made it worse. He was the only reasonable one. Now it's just his mother and brother. He's awful, and she's a witch. And they still don't know. It's a big house. We're not all on top of each other. And it's all very complicated. He's too stubborn and proud to agree with them he's made a mistake. So the more they're down on me, the more he pretends he loves me. They knew I wanted horses, and he bought them for me, so he could look good in front of them. But really to explain away the bruises. He makes me say I've fallen off. They know I'm still learning to ride. And that explains a lot in rodeo country, bruises and broken bones.'

'He's broken your bones?'

She nodded. 'My left arm. My collarbone. My jaw. I've had three teeth reimplanted.'

'Why the hell did you stick around? Why didn't you just get out?'

'I could have gone if I'd left Ellie,' she said. 'Sloop told me if I left the baby he'd pay my fare any place I wanted to go. But how could I do that? So Sloop makes out this is my *choice*. Like I *want* it. So he keeps on hitting me. Kicking me. Humiliating me. Every day.'

He looked across the table at her, tracing his gaze over her hands, her arms, her neck, her face. The neckline of her dress had shifted, and he could see a thickened knot on her collarbone. A healed break, no doubt about it. But she was sitting absolutely straight, her head up and her eyes defiant, and her posture was telling him something.

'He hits you *every* day?' he asked.

She closed her eyes. 'Well, most every day. Not literally, I guess. But three, four times a week, usually. It feels like every day.'

He shook his head. 'You're making it up,' he said.

'Why do you say that?' she asked, quietly.

'Physical evidence,' he said. 'You've no bruising visible anywhere. And you skipped across that parking lot like a ballerina. So you're not hurting any place. You're not stiff and sore. If he's hitting you most every day, he must be doing it with a feather.'

She nodded. 'It happened for five whole years. Exactly like I told you. Most every day. But then it stopped, a year and a half ago.'

'What did it feel like?' he asked. 'Getting hit? Physically.'

She thought about it. 'Depends where,' she said.

He nodded. She knew it felt different in different places. 'The stomach,' he said.

'I threw up a lot. I was worried, because there was blood.'

He nodded again. She knew what it felt like to be hit in the stomach. 'So what happened?' he said. 'Why did he stop?'

'Can we go now?' she asked. 'We need to get back. It's a long drive.'

'I'm coming with you?'

'Please, Reacher,' she said. 'At least hear the rest of the story, and then decide. I can let you out in Pecos, if you won't come all the way to Echo. You can see the museum. You can see Clay Allison's grave.'

'OK,' he said.

THEY WERE ON A STRAIGHT deserted road, the sun dead-centre above them. Heading south and near noon, Reacher figured. At random intervals billboards advertised gas and accommodation miles ahead.

Carmen glanced across at him. 'Do you believe me yet?' she asked.

He glanced back at her. He had spent thirteen years as an investigator, and his natural instinct was to believe nothing at all. 'What happened a year and a half ago?' he asked. 'Why did he stop?'

She adjusted her grip on the wheel. 'He went to prison.'

'For beating up on you?'

'In *Texas*?' She laughed. 'In Texas a gentleman would never raise his hand to a woman. Everybody knows that. So if a greaseball whore wife dared to claim a thing like that, they'd lock *her* up.'

'So what did he do?'

'He evaded federal taxes,' she said. 'He made a lot of money trading oil leases down in Mexico. He neglected to tell the IRS about it. One day they caught him.'

'They put you in jail for that?'

'Actually, they try hard not to. A clean breast and a pay-back plan is what they're looking for. But Sloop was too stubborn for that. He made them dig everything out for themselves. He refused to pay anything. And all the money was hidden behind family trusts, so they couldn't just take it. It made them mad, I think.'

'So they prosecuted?'

She nodded. 'With a vengeance,' she said. 'Sloop's lawyer is his best friend from high school, and his other best friend from high school is the DA in Pecos County, but the IRS just rolled right over all of them. He got three to five years. The judge set the minimum at thirty months in jail.'

Reacher said nothing. She accelerated past a truck, the first vehicle they had seen in more than twenty miles.

'After the verdict came in they just told him to present himself at the federal prison the next morning. They didn't drag him away in handcuffs or anything. He came home and packed a little suitcase. We had a big family meal, stayed up kind of late. Went upstairs, and that was the last time he hit me. Next morning, his friends drove him to the jail, some place near Abilene. Minimum security.'

'Do you visit him?'

She shook her head. 'I pretend he's dead.' She went quiet, and the car sped on towards the haze on the horizon.

'Thirty months is two and a half years,' she said. 'I thought it safest to bet on the minimum. He's probably behaving himself.'

Reacher nodded. 'Probably.'

'So, two and a half years. I wasted the first one and a half.'

'You've still got twelve months. That's plenty of time.'

'Talk me through it,' she said. 'We have to agree on what needs to be done. Just theoretically for now, if you want.'

He shrugged. Then he thought about it, from her point of view. 'You need to get away,' he said. 'So, a place to live, and an income. Any big city. They have shelters. All kinds of organisations.'

'How do I get there?'

'On a plane, on a train, in a bus. Two one-way tickets.'

'I don't have any money.'

'You dress pretty sharp for a person with no money.'

'Mail order,' she said. 'Sloop's lawyer signs the cheques. So I've got clothes. But what I haven't got is cash.'

'You could sell the diamond.'

'I tried to,' she said. 'It's a fake. Stainless steel and cubic zirconium. The jeweller laughed at me. It's worth maybe thirty bucks.'

'There must be money in the house. You could steal some.'

'Then I'm a double fugitive,' she said. 'You're forgetting about Ellie's legal status. She's Sloop's child, too. The lawyers all warned me. If I transport her across a state line without his consent, then I'm a kidnapper. They'll put her picture on milk cartons, and they'll find me, and they'll take her away from me, and I'll go to jail.'

'So don't cross the state line. Stay in Texas. Go to Dallas.'

'I'm not staying in Texas,' she said.

She said it with finality. Reacher said nothing back.

'It's not easy,' she said. 'His mother watches me. That's why I didn't sell the ring, even though I could have used the thirty bucks. She'd notice and it would put her on her guard. So if one day money is missing and Ellie is missing, I might get a few hours' start before she calls the sheriff and he calls the FBI. But a few hours isn't much help, because Texas is big and buses are slow. I wouldn't make it.'

'Got to be some way,' he said.

She glanced back at her briefcase on the rear seat. The legal paperwork. 'There are lots of ways,' she said. 'Procedures, provisions, wards of court, all kinds of things. But lawyers are slow and expensive. There are *pro bono* people who do it for free, but they're always very busy. It's a mess. A big, complicated mess.'

'I guess it is,' he said.

'But it should be possible in a year. A year's a long time, right?'

'So?'

'So I need you to forgive me for wasting the first year and a half. It was all so daunting, I kept putting it off. You agreed, twelve months is plenty of time. So nobody could say I'd left it too late, could they?'

There was a beep from the dashboard. An orange light started flashing in the shape of a gas pump, right next to the speedometer.

'Low fuel,' she said.

'There's Exxon up ahead. I saw a billboard. Fifteen miles.'

'I need Mobil,' she said. 'There's a card for Mobil in the glove box. I don't have any way of paying at Exxon.'

'You don't even have money for gas?'

She shook her head. 'I ran out. Now I'm charging it all to my mother-in-law's Mobil account. She won't get the bill for a month.'

She steered one-handed and groped behind her for her bag. Dumped it on his lap. 'Check it out,' she said.

'I can't be poking through a lady's handbag,' he said.

'I want you to,' she said. 'I need you to understand.'

He zipped it open and a soft aroma came up at him. Perfume and make-up. There was a hairbrush, tangled with long black hairs. A nail clipper. And a thin wallet.

'Check it out,' she said again.

There was a dollar bill in the money section. That was all. A solitary buck. No credit cards. A Texas driver's licence, with a picture of her on it. There was a plastic window with a photograph of a little girl behind it. She was slightly chubby, with perfect pink skin. Shiny blonde hair and bright lively eyes. A radiant smile.

'Ellie,' she said.

'She's very cute.'

'She is, isn't she?'

'Where did you sleep last night?'

'In the car,' she said. 'Then I wait for the breakfast rush and wash up in some diner's rest room, when they're too busy to notice.'

'What about eating?'

'I don't eat.' She was slowing down, trying to preserve her gas.

'I'll pay for it,' Reacher said. 'You're giving me a ride.'

'OK,' she said. 'I'll let you pay. But only so I can get back to Ellie.' She accelerated again.

Reacher suddenly realised what he should do. 'Stop the car,' he said.

'Why?'

'Just do it, OK?'

She glanced at him, puzzled, but she pulled over.

'Now wait,' he said.

They waited until the truck she had passed came through. He unclipped his seat belt, squinted down and tore the pocket off his shirt. 'What are you wearing?' he asked.

'What? What are you doing?'

'Tell me exactly what you're wearing.'

She blushed. 'This dress,' she said. 'And underwear. And shoes.'

'Show me your shoes.'

She paused a second, then worked her shoes off. Passed them across to him. He checked them carefully and passed them back. Then he took off his shirt. Passed it to her. 'I'm getting out now,' he said. 'I'm going to turn my back. Take all your clothes off and put the shirt on. Leave your clothes on the seat and then get out, too.'

'Why?'

'You want me to help you, just do it. All of them, OK?'

He got out of the car and walked away. He could feel the sun burning his shoulders. Then he heard the car door open. He turned and saw her climbing out, barefoot, wearing his shirt. She was hopping from foot to foot, because the road was burning her feet.

'You can keep your shoes,' he called.

She leaned in and picked them up and put them on.

'Now walk away and wait,' he called.

She moved ten feet away. He stepped back to the car. Her clothes were neatly folded on her seat. He reached back and searched her handbag again, then the briefcase. Nothing there. He turned back to the clothes and shook them out. The dress, a bra, underpants. Nothing hidden in them. He laid them on the roof of the car and searched the rest of it. Under the hood, under the carpets, in the seats, under the seats, in the trunk, under the fenders. It took him twenty minutes. He found nothing, and he was prepared to bet his life no civilian could conceal anything from him in an automobile.

'OK,' he called. 'Get dressed now. Same routine.'

He waited with his back turned until he heard her behind him. She was holding his shirt. He took it from her and put it back on.

'What was that about?' she asked.

'Now I'll help you,' he said. 'Because now I believe you.'

'Why?'

'Because you really don't have any money,' he said. 'No credit cards, either. And nobody travels three hundred miles from home, not overnight, with absolutely no money. Not unless they've got big problems. And a person with big problems deserves help.'

They climbed back in the car and shut the doors. Then she manoeuvred back onto the road again.

'So, you've got a year,' he said. 'That's plenty of time. A year from now, you could be a million miles away. New start, new life. Is that what you want me for? To help you get away?'

There were buildings in the distance. Probably the gas station.

'Right now just agree with me,' she said. 'A year is enough. So it's OK to have waited.'

'Sure,' he said. 'A year is enough. It's OK to have waited.'

THE CADILLAC TOOK more than twenty gallons, which cost Reacher the price of a motel room.

'*Gracias, señor*,' Carmen said. 'Thank you.'

'Pleasure,' he said. '*De nada, señorita*.'

'You speak Spanish?'

'Not really,' he said. 'I served all over, so I can say a few words in a lot of languages. But that's all. Except French. I speak French pretty well. My mother was French.'

'So you're half foreign,' she said.

'Sometimes I feel a lot more than half.'

She smiled like she didn't believe him and eased back to the road. 'But you should call me *señora*. Not *señorita*. I'm a married woman.'

'Yes,' he said. 'I guess you are.'

She went quiet for a mile. Then she took a deep breath. 'OK, here's the problem,' she said. 'I don't have a year.'

'Why not?'

'Because a month ago his lawyer friend came out to the house.

Told us there was some kind of deal on the table. I don't know what exactly. My guess is Sloop's going to rat out some business associates in exchange for early remission. I think his other friend is brokering it through the DA's office.'

'Shit,' Reacher said.

Carmen nodded. 'I left it too late. A year and a half I was sitting around in a trap and now it's sprung shut and I'm still in it.'

Reacher nodded. 'So what's the progress on the deal?' he asked.

'It's done,' she said, in a small voice.

'So when does he get out?'

'Today's Friday,' she said. 'I don't think they can do it at the week-end. So it'll be Monday, I expect. A couple of days, is all. He's going to start it all up again.'

'Maybe he's changed,' Reacher said. 'Prison can change people.' It was a useless thing to say. He could see it in her face. And in his experience, prison didn't change people for the better.

'No, it's going to be worse than ever,' she said. 'I know it. I know it for sure. I'm in big trouble, Reacher. I can promise you that.'

'Why?'

'Because it was me who told the IRS about him,' she said. 'I knew how stubborn he was. I knew he wouldn't cooperate with them. Even if he didn't go to jail, I thought it might shake some money loose for me. And it worked real well, apart from the money.'

'How did you do it?'

'I just called them. They're in the book. They have a whole section to take information from spouses. It's one of their big ways to get people. Normally it happens during divorces.'

'Why haven't you gone ahead and *got* a divorce?' he asked. 'Husband in jail is grounds, right? Some kind of desertion?'

'It doesn't solve the problem with Ellie,' she said. 'It makes it worse. It alerts everybody to the possibility I'll leave the state. Legally, Sloop could require me to register her whereabouts, and he would.'

'You could stay in Texas,' he said again.

She nodded. 'I know I'm being irrational, but I can't stay here. It's a beautiful state, and there *are* nice people here, but it's a *symbol*. Things have happened to me here that I have to get away from.'

He shrugged. 'So what do you want me to do? Help you run?'

She said nothing. He fell to thinking about the potential target group she had outlined to him. Out-of-work rodeo riders and rough-necks. Men of various talents, but he wasn't sure if beating a federal manhunt would be among them. So she had got lucky.

'You need to get started right now,' he said. 'We should pick Ellie up and turn the car around and get going. Vegas, maybe, first stop.'

'And do what there?'

'Pick up some ID,' he said. 'Place like Vegas, we could find something, even if it's only temporary. I've got some money. I can get more, if you need it. Then maybe you should go back to LA. You could start building some new paperwork there.'

'No, I can't run,' she said. 'I can't be a fugitive. I can't be an *illegal*. Whatever else I am, I've never been an illegal. I'm not going to start being one now. And neither is Ellie. She deserves better.'

'You both deserve better,' he said. 'But you've got to do something.'

'I'm a citizen,' she said. 'I'm not going to give it up.'

'So what's your plan?'

'You're my plan,' she said.

Bull riders, roughnecks, a six-foot-five, 250-pound ex-military cop. 'You want me to be your *bodyguard*?' he asked.

She made no reply.

'Carmen, I'm sorry about your situation,' he said. 'But I can't be your bodyguard. Do you think I'm going to be with you twenty-four hours a day? Seven days a week? Making sure he doesn't hit you?'

No reply. A highway interchange sprawled across the landscape.

'It's ridiculous,' he said. 'What happens when I'm gone? Because sooner or later I'm going to be gone, Carmen. I'm not going to stay around. Face it, *nobody's* going to stay around. Not long enough. Not ten years. Or twenty, or thirty or however long it is until he ups and dies of old age.'

She drove onto the highway. 'I don't want a bodyguard,' she said.

'So what am I supposed to be for?' he asked.

She opened her mouth. Closed it again. Swallowed hard, and said nothing. He stared at her. Bull riders, roughnecks, an ex-MP. Clay Allison's grave, the inscription, the obituary in the newspaper.

'You *are* crazy,' he said. 'And you can forget about it.'

'I *can't* forget about it. I want him dead, Reacher,' she said. 'It's my only way out. And he deserves it.'

He shook his head. Stared out of the window. 'Just forget all about it,' he said. 'It's absurd. This isn't the Wild West any more.'

'I tried to do this right,' she said. 'Soon as his lawyer told me about the deal, I saw a lawyer of my own, and then three more, and none of them could do anything for me as fast as a month. All they could do was tell me Ellie traps me exactly where I am. So then I looked for protection. I asked private detectives. They wouldn't do anything. I went to a security firm in Austin and they said it would be six men and nearly ten thousand dollars a week. Which is the same as saying no. So I tried, Reacher. I tried to do it right. But it's impossible.'

He watched the highway. It was busy with traffic.

'So I bought a gun,' she said. 'It took all the cash I had.'

'You picked the wrong guy,' he said.

'But why? You've killed people before. In the army. You told me.'

'This is different. This would be cold-blooded murder.'

'Don't you take an oath or something? To protect people?'

'It's not the same,' he said.

'Please, Reacher. I've been through it a million times. I've examined all the options. And this is the only way. I *know* that. You haven't thought about it before. So I sound crazy and cold-blooded to you. But I'm not crazy or cold-blooded. It's just that I've had the time to reach the conclusion, and you haven't.'

'Whatever, I'm not killing a guy I never saw before.'

'He beats me, Reacher,' she said. 'Badly. Kicks me. He enjoys it. He laughs while he does it. I live in fear, all the time.'

'So go to the cops.'

'The cop. There's only one. And he wouldn't believe me. And even if he did, he wouldn't do anything about it. They're all big buddies. You don't know how it is here.'

Reacher said nothing.

'I'm desperate,' she said. 'You're my only chance. I'm begging you. Why won't you do it? Is it because I'm Mexican? You'd do it for a white woman? Like your girlfriend? I bet she's a white woman. Some guy was beating up on her, you'd kill him.'

Yes, I would, he thought. 'It's not the same,' he said again.

'What's her name?' she asked. 'Your girlfriend?'

'Jodie,' he said.

'OK, imagine Jodie getting beat up every day by some maniac sadist. She tells you all about it. What are you going to do?'

Kill him, he thought.

She nodded like she could read his mind. 'But you won't do that for me. You'd do it for the gringa, but not for me.'

It was true. He would do it for Jodie Garber, but he wouldn't do it for Carmen Greer. Why not? Because you can't force it. It's a hot-blooded thing, and you go with it. If it's not there, you can't go with it. Simple as that. He'd gone with it many times in his life. People mess with him, they get what they get. They mess with Jodie, that's the same as messing with him. Because Jodie *was* him. Or at least she used to be. In a way that Carmen wasn't. So it just wasn't *there*.

'It's not about gringas or Latinas,' he said quietly.

'So what *is* it about?'

'It's about I know her and I don't know you.'

'Then get to know me,' she said. 'We've got two days. You're about to meet my daughter. Get to know us.'

He said nothing.

'What do you want, Reacher? You want sex? We could do that.'

'Stop the car,' he said. 'I've had enough of this.'

She jammed her foot down hard on the gas. The car leapt forward. He glanced back at the traffic and knocked the transmission into N. The engine screamed. He hauled the wheel round against her grip and steered to the shoulder. The gravel bit against the tyres. He jammed the lever into P and opened his door. The car skidded to a stop and the speed washed away. He slid out and stood up. Felt the heat on his body like a blow from a hammer and slammed the door and walked away from her.

THREE

He was sweating heavily twenty yards after getting out of the car. And already regretting his decision. He was in the middle of nowhere, on foot on a major highway, and the slowest vehicles were doing sixty. Nobody was going to stop for him. The sun was fearsome and the temperature was 112 degrees. He had no water. If a state trooper didn't come by and arrest him for jaywalking, he could die out there.

He made it about fifty yards and stopped. Turned and stuck out his thumb. But it was hopeless. After five minutes, the nearest he'd got to a response was some trucker blasting his air horn.

He saw the Cadillac start up the shoulder towards him. He started walking back to it. He stopped alongside the car as she braked.

She buzzed the passenger window down. 'I'm sorry,' she said.

He got in.

'I'm very sorry for the thing about the sex,' she said. 'It was a crass thing to say.' Her voice went small. 'It's just that some of the guys I've picked up, I figured that was what it was going to have to be.'

'You'd have sex with them so they'd kill your husband?'

She nodded. 'I don't have anything else to offer.'

He said nothing.

'I'll let you out in Pecos,' she said.

He shook his head. He had to be *somewhere*. When you live on the road, one place is as good as another. 'No, I'll come with you,' he said. 'Hang out a couple of days. I'm sorry about your situation, Carmen. Just because I won't shoot the guy doesn't mean I won't help you some other way. If I can. And if you still want me to.'

She paused a beat. 'Yes, I still want you to,' she said.

CARMEN CAME OFF the highway just short of Pecos and speared south on a small county road which led down into total emptiness.

'Where will I be?' he asked.

'On the property. In the bunkhouse, I guess. They'll hire you for the horses. We're always a man short. You can say you're a wrangler.'

'I don't know anything about horses.'

She shrugged. 'Maybe they won't notice. They don't notice much. Like me getting beaten half to death.'

An hour later, they came up a long steep grade and turned out between two rock pillars on a peak and suddenly there was flat land below them as far as the eye could see. The road fell away and was crossed twenty miles ahead by another, just visible through the haze. The distant crossroads was studded with a handful of tiny buildings.

'Echo County,' she said. But she was looking at a tiny plume of dust on the road far below them. 'That must be the school bus,' she said. 'We have to beat it to town, or Ellie will get on and we'll miss her.' She accelerated down the grade. 'It's good of you to be coming,' she said. 'Thank you.'

'*No hay de qué, señorita,*' he said.

'So you do know more than a few words.'

'There were a lot of Spanish-speaking people in the army.'

'But you should call me *señora*. *Señorita* makes me too happy.'

She reeled in the bus and blasted past. Five minutes later they approached the crossroads.

There was a diner on the northwest corner. Diagonally opposite it was the school. On the southwest corner was a gas station. There were four other buildings, all one-storey, all plain concrete, all set back with rough driveways leading to them from the road. Houses, Reacher guessed. Their yards were littered with junk, children's bikes and tired automobiles on blocks and old living-room furniture.

Carmen drove past the school and U-turned across the road. She came back and stopped with the school gate close to Reacher's window. The bus came labouring down from the north and stopped on its own side of the road. The schoolhouse door opened and a woman stepped out. The teacher, Reacher guessed. She waved to the children. They spilled out in a long stream. Seventeen of them. Ellie Greer was wearing a blue dress. She looked hot. He recognised her from her photograph and by the way Carmen moved beside him. He heard her catch her breath and scrabble for the door handle.

She met her daughter on the beaten earth strip that passed for a sidewalk. She scooped her up in a wild hug. Spun her round. Reacher could see the child laughing and tears in Carmen's eyes. They came back round the rear of the car clutched tight together. Carmen opened the door and Ellie scrambled straight into the driver's seat. She stopped dead when she saw him.

'This is my friend Mr Reacher,' Carmen said. 'Say hello to him.'

'Hello,' Ellie said.

'Hey, Ellie,' Reacher said. 'Hop in the back and let your mom in out of the heat.'

Ellie scrambled into the back. Carmen slid in and shut the door.

'Mom, it's hot,' Ellie said. 'We should get ice-cream sodas.'

Reacher saw Carmen about to agree, and then he saw her glance back at her handbag and remember the lone dollar stashed inside it.

'Good idea,' he said. 'Let's get ice-cream sodas. My treat.'

Carmen pulled back through the crossroads and turned into the diner's lot. She parked in the shade against its north wall, next to the only other car in the place, a steel-blue Crown Victoria. Must be a state trooper's unmarked, or maybe a rental, Reacher thought.

The diner was empty, apart from a group Reacher took to be the Crown Victoria's occupants, a trio of ordinary indoor types, two men and a woman. The woman was medium-blonde and pleasant-looking. One guy was small and dark and the other was taller and fair. So the Crown Vic was a rental, not a cop car, and these guys were maybe some kind of sales team. He glanced away and let Ellie lead him towards a booth at the opposite end of the room.

She jumped up and scooted sideways over the vinyl seat.

Carmen smiled. 'I'm going to use the rest room. I'll be right back. You stay here with Mr Reacher, OK?'

The kid nodded and Reacher sat down opposite her. She was a living version of the photograph in her mother's wallet. Thick corn-coloured hair tied in a ponytail, incongruous dark eyes, a little snub of a nose. Her skin was impossibly perfect, like pink damp velvet.

'Where did you go to school?' she asked. 'Did you go here too?'

'No, I went to lots of places,' he said. 'I moved around.'

'You didn't go to the same school all the time?'

He shook his head. 'Every few months, I went to a new one.'

He saw her look beyond his shoulder, and turned to see Carmen on her way back, trapped temporarily by the sales people getting out of their booth. She waited until they had cleared the aisle and then she skipped back and sat down, all in one graceful movement. She pressed close to Ellie, hugged her one-armed and tickled her, and got a squeal in exchange. The waitress finished with the sales people at the register and walked over, pad and pencil at the ready.

'Three Coke floats, please,' Ellie said, loud and clear.

CARMEN DROVE BACK through the crossroads and past the school again and then more than sixty miles straight south.

Power lines looped rhythmically between weathered poles on the shoulder. There were oil pumps here and there in the distance, some of them working, most seized up and still. There were irrigation rigs on the western side of the road, silent and rusted because the winds had scoured the earth shallow. The eastern side was better. There were whole square miles of mesquite, and sometimes broad patches of decent grassland. Every ten or twelve miles there would be a ranch gate by the side of the road, with beaten earth tracks running through them into the distance. Some of them had names on them.

'Greer property starts here,' Carmen said. 'On the left. Next track is ours, about eight miles.'

There was a forest of oil derricks visible against the skyline, all surrounded by tin huts and abandoned equipment.

'Greer Three,' Carmen said. 'Big field. It made Sloop's grandfather a lot of money, way back.'

In the distance Reacher could see barbed wire change to an absurd picket fence, like something you would see in New England, but painted a dull red. It ran about half a mile to a ranch gate. Behind the gate was a big old house with a two-storey core and sprawling one-storey additions. There were barns and sheds clustered loosely around it. Everything was painted dull red.

She turned in under the gate. There was a name on it, high above their heads. It said RED HOUSE.

'Welcome to hell,' she said.

The house itself had a wide planked porch with wooden columns and a swinging seat hung from chains. Beyond it was a motor barn, but she couldn't drive down to it because a police cruiser was blocking her way. It was a Chevy Caprice, painted black and white, with ECHO COUNTY SHERIFF on the door. It was empty.

Ellie crawled through and knelt on the padded armrest between the front seats. 'Maybe a burglar stole my pony, Mommy.' She scrambled across Carmen's lap and scrabbled at the door handle. Jumped out of the car and ran across the yard, as fast as her legs would carry her.

Carmen unclipped her seat belt and swivelled sideways. She placed her feet on the dirt of the yard and stood up.

Reacher did the same on his side. 'Maybe they're looking for you. You've been away overnight. Maybe they reported you missing.'

She shook her head. 'They don't care where I am.'

The house door opened and a uniformed man stepped out onto the porch. The sheriff. He was about sixty and overweight, with thin grey hair plastered to his head. He wore a gun belt with a revolver in a holster. The door closed behind him and he turned towards his cruiser and stopped short when he saw Carmen.

'Mrs Greer,' he said.

'What happened?' she asked.

'Folks inside will tell you,' the sheriff said. 'Too damn hot for me to be repeating everything twice.'

Then his gaze settled on Reacher. 'And who are you?' he asked.

'I'll tell the folks inside,' Reacher replied. 'Too damn hot for me to be repeating everything twice.'

The sheriff gave him a long look, then dumped himself in his cruiser and backed out to the road. Reacher watched Carmen drive the Cadillac down the track to the motor barn. There were two pick-ups and a Jeep Cherokee in it. One of the pick-ups was recent, the other was sitting on flat tyres and looked like it hadn't moved in a decade. Beyond the building a dirt track looped off into the desert. Carmen walked back out into the sun.

'So where's the bunkhouse?' he asked.

'Stay with me,' she said. 'You need to meet them anyway. You need to get hired. You can't just show up in the bunkhouse.'

'OK,' he said.

She led him to the front door and knocked.

'You have to knock?' Reacher asked.

She nodded. 'They never gave me a key,' she said.

The door swung open. A guy was standing there, holding the inside handle. He looked to be in his mid-twenties. He had a big square face, with the skin blotched red and white. He was bulky with muscle turning to fat, and smelt of sweat and beer. He was wearing denim jeans, a dirty white T-shirt and a red baseball cap backwards on his head. A shock of hair spilled out, the same colour as Ellie's.

'Bobby,' she said.

His glance settled on Reacher. 'Who's your friend?'

'His name is Reacher. He's looking for work.'

'Well, come on in, I guess.' The guy turned back into the gloom.

Carmen followed, entering her home of nearly seven years like an invited guest. Reacher stayed close to her shoulder.

'Sloop's brother,' she whispered to him.

He nodded. The hallway was filled with expensive stuff, but it was all old, like they'd run out of money decades ago. Or else they'd always had so much that the thrill of spending it had long worn off. There was a huge mirror on one wall. Opposite it was a rack filled with six hunting rifles. The mirror reflected the rack and made the hallway seem full of guns.

The parlour had a big farmhouse table and eight wheelback chairs. One of the chairs was occupied by a woman. She looked to be in her mid-fifties. She was wearing tight jeans with a belt and a blouse with a Western fringe. She had a young woman's hairstyle, coloured a bright shade of orange and teased up above a thin face. She looked like a twenty-year-old prematurely aged by some rare medical condition. The woman turned to look in Reacher's direction.

'His name is Reacher,' Carmen said. 'I found him on the road. He's looking for work.'

'What can he do?' Her voice was like rawhide.

'He's worked with horses before. He can do blacksmithing.'

Reacher looked out of the window while she lied about his skills. He had never been closer to a horse than walking past the ceremonial stables on the older army bases that still had them.

The woman sketched a wave across the table. 'I'm Rusty Greer,' she said. 'Welcome to the Red House Ranch, Mr Reacher. Maybe we can find you work. If you're willing and honest.'

'What did the sheriff want?' Carmen asked.

'Sloop's lawyer's gone missing,' Rusty Greer said. 'He was on his way to the jail to see Sloop. Never got there. State Police found his car abandoned on the road, south of Abilene. Doesn't look good.'

'Maybe the car broke down,' Carmen said.

'Cops tried it,' Rusty said. 'It worked just fine.'

'Does it change anything?' Carmen asked.

'You mean, is Sloop still coming home?'

Carmen nodded weakly, like she was afraid of the answer.

'Don't you worry none,' Rusty said, smiling. 'Sloop will be back here Monday. Al Eugene going missing doesn't change a thing. The sheriff made that clear. It was a done deal.'

Carmen forced a trembling smile. 'Well, good,' she said.

'Yes, good,' her mother-in-law said.

'What do you suppose happened to him?' Carmen asked.

'How would I know? Some sort of trouble, I expect.'

'But who would make trouble for Al?'

'Somebody who buys them a big old Mercedes and gets sent to jail anyhow, that's who.'

'Well, who did that?'

'Anybody could have. Al takes anybody for a client. He has no *standards*. He's halfway to being plain crooked. Maybe all the way, for all I know. Three-quarters of his clients are the wrong sort.'

'You mean Mexican?'

'Well, tell me different,' Rusty said. 'Some Mexican boy gets sent to jail, he doesn't stand up and accept his punishment like we do. He blames his lawyer, and gets all his brothers and cousins riled up about it, and now you see how that turns out. Just like it is in Mexico itself. You of all people should know what it's like.'

'Why should I of all people? I've never even been to Mexico.'

Nobody replied to that. The room was quiet.

'You got an opinion here, Mr Reacher?' Rusty Greer asked.

'I'm just here to work, ma'am,' he said.

'I'd like to know your opinion, all the same.'

'Mr Reacher was a cop himself,' Carmen said. 'In the army.'

Rusty nodded. 'So what's your thinking, ex-army cop?'

'If there was trouble, maybe white folks made it,' Reacher said.

'That's not going to be a popular view around here, son.'

'It's not looking to be popular. It's looking to be right or wrong. And the population of Texas is three-quarters white, therefore I figure there's a three-in-four chance white folks were involved, assuming people are all the same as each other.'

'That's a big assumption.'

'Not in my experience.'

'Well, time will tell, I guess,' Rusty said. 'One or other of us is going to be eating humble pie.' She said it *paah*. The long syllable trailed into silence.

'Now, where's Sloop's little girl?' she asked, with an artificial brightness in her voice. 'The maid is ready to give the child its supper, so take it to the kitchen, and show Mr Reacher to the bunkhouse on your way.'

THE BUNKHOUSE was a two-storey building. The lower floor had sliding doors. There was another pick-up in there. At the far end was a wooden staircase leading through a rectangular hole in the ceiling. The air was hot and smelt of gasoline. Reacher used the staircase and came out on the second level. It was hotter still up there. No air conditioning, and not much ventilation. Apart from a closed-off area at the far end, which he guessed was the bathroom, the whole of the floor was one big open space, with sixteen beds facing each other eight to a side, with bedside cabinets and footlockers.

The two beds nearest the bathroom were occupied. Each had a small, wiry, muscular man lying on top of the sheets. Both men wore blue jeans and fancy boots and no shirts. Both had their hands folded behind their heads. They both turned towards the staircase as Reacher stepped up inside the room.

Reacher had seventeen years' experience of walking into a new dormitory and being stared at by its occupants. The way to do it was to just walk in, select an unoccupied bed, and say nothing. Make somebody else speak first.

He walked to a bed two places away from the head of the staircase, against the north wall, which he judged would be cooler than the south. In the past, in the army, he would have had a kitbag to dump on the bed as a symbol of possession. But the best he could do in this situation was take his folding toothbrush from his pocket and prop it on the bedside cabinet. As a substitute gesture, it lacked impact. But it made the same point. It said: *I live here now, same as you do. You got any comment to make about that?*

One of the guys hauled himself upright. 'You hired on?' he asked.

'I guess,' Reacher said.

'I'm Billy,' the guy said.

The other guy moved up on his elbows. 'Josh,' he said.

Reacher nodded to them. 'I'm Reacher. Pleased to meet you.'

'The Mexican woman bring you in?' Josh asked.

'Mrs Greer,' Reacher said.

'Mrs Greer is Rusty,' Billy said. 'She didn't bring you in.'

'Mrs Carmen Greer,' Reacher said.

Billy said nothing. The guy called Josh just smiled.

'We're heading out after supper,' Billy said. 'Bar, couple hours south. You could join us. Call it a get-to-know-you type of thing.'

Reacher shook his head. 'Maybe some other time, when I've earned something. I like to pay my own way, situation like that.'

Billy thought about it and nodded. 'That's a righteous attitude,' he said. 'Maybe you'll fit right in.'

THE MAID BROUGHT SUPPER. She was a middle-aged white woman. Supper was a pail of pork and beans, which she served into metal bowls. She handed out forks and spoons and empty metal cups.

'Water in the bathroom,' she said, for Reacher's benefit.

Then she went back down the stairs and Reacher turned his attention to the food.

'Hey, Reacher,' Billy called over. 'So what do you think?'

'Good enough for me,' he said.

'Bullshit,' Josh said. 'A hundred degrees all day, and she brings us hot food? I showered already and now I'm sweating like a pig again.'

Billy and Josh finished up and took clean shirts out of their lockers. Shrugged them on and combed their hair with their fingertips.

They clattered down the stairs and a moment later Reacher heard the sound of an engine starting up below. The pick-up, he guessed. He heard it drive away.

He piled the three used bowls on top of each other, with the silverware in the topmost. Threaded the three mug handles onto his forefinger and walked down the stairs and outside. The sun was nearly below the horizon but the heat hadn't backed off at all. He walked through the yard, skirted the porch and looked for the kitchen door. Found it and knocked. The maid opened up.

'I brought these back,' he said. He held up the bowls and the mugs.

'Well, that's kind of you,' she said. 'But I'd have come for them.'

'Long walk,' he said. 'Hot night.'

She nodded. 'I appreciate it,' she said. 'You had enough?'

'Plenty,' he said. 'It was very good.'

She shrugged, a little bashful. 'Just cowboy food.' She took the used dishes from him and carried them inside.

He turned away and walked out towards the road.

'Reacher,' a voice called.

Reacher squinted right and saw Bobby Greer in the shadows on the porch. He was sitting in the swing seat.

'Come here,' he called.

Reacher walked back and stopped at the porch steps.

'I want a horse,' Bobby said. 'The big mare. Saddle her up and bring her out.'

Reacher paused. 'You want that now?'

'I want an evening ride. And we need a demonstration.'

'Of what?'

'You want to hire on, you show us you know what you're doing.'

Reacher paused again, longer. 'OK,' he said.

'Five minutes,' Bobby said. He headed back inside.

Reacher headed to the barn. A demonstration? You're in deep shit now, he thought.

There was a light switch inside the door. He flicked it on and weak yellow bulbs lit the enormous space. The centre of the barn was divided into horse stalls, with a perimeter track lined with floor-to-ceiling hay bales inside the outer walls. He circled the stalls. Five were occupied. Five horses. All tethered to the walls of their stalls.

He took a closer look at each of them. One was a pony. Ellie's, presumably. OK, strike that. Two were slightly bigger than the other two. He bent down and peered up at them, one at a time. He knew it should be easy to spot a mare, but it wasn't. The stalls were dark and the tails obscured the details. In the end he decided the first one he looked at wasn't a mare. Wasn't a stallion, either. Some parts were missing. A gelding. He shuffled along and looked at the next. A mare. The next was a mare, too. The last, another gelding.

He stepped back to where he could see both of the mares at once. Which was bigger? The one on the left, he decided. A little taller, heavier, wider at the shoulders. The big mare. So far, so good.

Now, the saddle. Each stall had a post coming horizontally out of the outside wall, with a bunch of equipment on it. A saddle for sure, but also a lot of complicated straps and blankets and metal. The straps are the reins, he guessed. The metal thing must be the bit. It goes in the horse's mouth. The bit between her teeth, right?

He lifted the saddle off the post and opened the stall gate. The horse moved. Its ears went back and it swung its huge rear end towards him. He touched it on the side. It kept on coming.

Don't get behind it. Don't let it kick you. That much, he knew.

It was swinging sideways towards him. He met its flank with his right shoulder. Gave it a good shove. The horse quieted. He put the back of his hand near its nose. It was something he had seen at the movies. You rub the back of your hand on its nose, and it gets to know you. Some smell thing. The skin on its nose felt soft and dry.

'OK, good girl,' he whispered.

He lifted the saddle and dumped it on her back. Was it the right way round? Had to be. It was shaped a little like a chair. There was a definite front and a back. Straps hung down on either side.

'Not like *that*,' a voice called from way above him.

He spun round and looked up. Ellie was lying on top of the stack of hay bales, up near the roof, her chin on her hands, looking down at him. 'You need the *blanket* first,' she said.

'What blanket?'

'The saddlecloth,' she said.

'Ellie, does anybody know you're in here?' he called.

She shook her head, solemnly. 'I'm hiding.'

'You know how to do this horse stuff?'

'Of course I do. I can do my pony all by myself.'

'So help me out here, will you? Come and do this one for me.'

She scrambled down and joined him. 'Take the saddle off again,' she said. She took a cloth off the equipment post and threw it over the mare's back. 'Now put the saddle on,' she said.

He dropped the saddle on top of the cloth. Ellie ducked underneath the horse's belly and caught the straps. She threaded the ends together and pulled. 'You do it,' she said. 'They're stiff.'

He lined the buckles up and pulled hard.

'Not too tight,' Ellie said. 'Not yet. Wait for her to swell up.'

'She's going to *swell up*?'

Ellie nodded. 'They don't like it. They swell their stomachs up to try to stop you. But they can't hold it, so they come down again.'

He watched the horse's stomach. It blew out, bigger and bigger, fighting the straps. Then it subsided.

'Now do them tight,' Ellie said.

He pulled them as tight as he could.

Ellie had the reins. 'Take the rope off her. Just pull it down.'

He pulled the rope down. The mare's ears folded forward and it slid down over them, over her nose, and off.

'Now hold this up.' She handed him a tangle of straps. 'It's called the bridle.'

He turned it in his hands until the shape made sense. He held it against the mare's head and tapped the metal part against her lips. The bit. She kept her mouth firmly closed.

'Put your thumb in,' Ellie said.

'My thumb? Where?'

'Where her teeth stop. At the side. There's a hole.'

He traced the ball of his thumb sideways along the length of the mare's lips. The teeth stopped and it was just gum. He pushed and the lips parted and his thumb slipped in. Sure enough, the mare opened her mouth.

'Quick, put the bit in,' Ellie said.

He pushed the metal into the mouth.

'Now pull the bridle up and buckle it.'

He eased the leather straps up over the ears and found the buckles. There was a worn mark on the strap, which he guessed indicated the usual length.

'Now loop the reins up over the horn,' Ellie said.

He reckoned that the rein was the long strap coming off the ends of the bit in a loop, and the horn was the upright thing at the front end of the saddle. Ellie was busy pulling the stirrups down into place.

'Now lift me up,' she said. 'I need to check everything.'

He lifted her into the saddle. She checked the buckles. Tucked the loose ends away. Pulled the mane hair out from under the straps.

'It's OK,' she said. 'You did good.' He lifted her down. 'Now lead her out. Hold her at the side of her mouth.'

'Thanks a million, kid,' he said. 'Now go hide again, OK?'

She scrambled back up the hay bales and he tugged at a strap coming off a metal ring at the side of the mouth. He led her out of the stall and headed for the door. Stepped with her into the yard. He walked her across the yard like he'd done it every day of his life.

Bobby Greer was waiting on the porch steps. The mare walked up to him and stopped. Bobby checked the same things Ellie had.

He nodded. 'Not bad,' he said.

Reacher said nothing.

'But you took longer than I expected.'

Reacher shrugged. 'I'm new to them. I always find it's better to go slow, the first time. Until they're familiar with me.'

Bobby nodded again. 'You can go now. I'll put her away.'

Reacher walked away to the bunkhouse. When he got to the upper storey, he found Carmen with a set of folded sheets.

'I got you these,' she said. 'From the linen closet in the bathroom. I didn't know if you would realise where they were.'

'Carmen, this is crazy,' he said. 'You should get out, right now. They're going to realise I'm a phoney. I'm not going to last a day. I might not even be here on Monday.'

'I know what I'm going to do,' she said. 'I'm going to take a beating, Monday night. Then I'm going to come find you, wherever you are. Then you'll *see*, and maybe you'll change your mind.'

Maybe it *would* change his mind. That was what she was counting on, and that was what he was afraid of. The difference between cold blood and hot blood.

'I have to go find Ellie,' she said. 'It's her bedtime.'

'She's in the barn. She showed me how with the horse.'

Carmen nodded. 'She's a good kid.'

'That's for sure,' he said. 'Saved my bacon.'

She handed the sheets to him. 'You want to come riding tomorrow?' she asked.

'I don't know how.'

'I'll teach you.' She went down the stairs.

He made up his bed, went back down and stepped outside. He heard the sound of footsteps. Squinted into the sunset and saw Ellie walking towards him, her hair lit from behind.

'I came to say good night,' she said.

He remembered being entertained in family quarters on a base somewhere, polite army kids saying a formal farewell. You shook their little hands and off they went. He smiled at her.

'OK, good night, Ellie,' he said. He put out his hand.

She looked at it. 'You're supposed to give me a kiss,' she said.

'Am I?'

'Of *course* you are.'

'OK,' he said. He started to bend down.

'No, pick me up,' she said, holding up her arms.

He paused a beat and then swung her in the air and kissed her cheek, gently. 'Good night,' he said again.

'Carry me,' she said. 'I'm tired.'

He carried her across the yard to the house. Carmen was waiting on the porch, watching them approach.

'I want Mr Reacher to come in and say good night,' Ellie said.

'Well, I don't know if he can.'

'I only work here,' Reacher said. 'I don't live here.'

'Nobody will *know*,' Ellie said. 'Come through the kitchen. There's only the maid there. She works here and she's allowed in the house.'

Carmen glanced at Reacher. He shrugged back. *What's the worst can happen?* He lowered Ellie to the ground. She took her mother's hand and they walked together to the kitchen door.

SUNSET, THE BOY WROTE, and noted the time. The two men crawled backwards from the gulch and stretched. *Off duty*, the boy wrote, and noted the time. Then they pulled the rocks off the tarp hiding their pick-up. Folded it and stowed it in the load bed, and climbed into the cab. Drove out the far side of the gulch and headed west towards the red horizon.

INSIDE THE KITCHEN the maid was loading a huge dishwasher. It had probably been the very latest thing around the time man first walked on the moon. She looked up and said nothing.

'This way,' Ellie whispered. She led them through a door into a hallway, up some wooden stairs, across a landing and right into a corridor. Her room was at the end of the corridor.

'We'll get washed,' Carmen said. 'Mr Reacher will wait here, OK?'

He sat down on the end of the narrow bed. Ellie turned and followed her mother out to the bathroom. The old air conditioner thumped and rattled patiently.

When Ellie and Carmen came back into the room, Ellie was in her pyjamas. She climbed onto the bed and curled up.

'OK, good night, kid,' he said. 'Sleep well.'

'Kiss me,' she said.

He bent down and kissed her forehead. It was warm and damp and smelt of soap.

'Thank you for being our friend,' she said.

He stood up and stepped towards the door.

'I'll see you tomorrow,' she said.

He went down the stairs and through the kitchen. The maid was gone. He stepped out into the night and caught gleams of white in the darkness to his right. A T-shirt. A face. A semicircle of forehead showing through the back of a ball cap. Bobby Greer, again.

'Bobby,' he said. 'Enjoy your ride?'

Bobby ignored the enquiry. 'I was waiting for you.'

'Why?'

'Just making sure you came back out again.'

'Why wouldn't I?'

'You tell me. Why would you go in there in the first place? All three of you, like a little family.'

Reacher shrugged. 'I kissed the kid good night,' he said. 'You got a problem with that?'

Bobby was quiet for a beat. 'Let me walk you back to the bunkhouse,' he said. 'I need to talk to you.'

He walked through the yard. Reacher kept pace.

'My brother had a problem,' Bobby said. 'I guess you know that.'

'I heard he cheated on his taxes,' Reacher said.

Bobby nodded in the dark. 'IRS snoops are everywhere.'

'Is that how they found him? Snooping?'

'Well, how else would they?' Bobby asked. He walked ahead a couple of paces. 'Anyway, Sloop went to jail,' he said.

Reacher nodded. 'Getting out Monday, I heard.'

'That's right. So he's not going to be too happy finding you here, kissing his kid, getting friendly with his wife.'

Reacher shrugged as he walked. 'I'm just here to work.'

'Right, as a wrangler. Not as a nursemaid.'

'I get time off, right?'

'But you need to be careful how you spend it.'

'A man can't choose his friends?'

'Sloop ain't going to be happy, he gets home and finds some outsider has chosen his wife and kid for his friends.'

Reacher stopped walking. Stood still in the dark. 'Thing is, Bobby, why would I give a rat's ass what makes your brother happy?'

Bobby stopped too. 'Because we're a family. Get that through your head. Or you won't work here long. You could get run out of here.'

Reacher smiled. 'Who you going to call? The sheriff? Guy like that could get a heart attack, just thinking about it.'

Bobby shook his head. 'West Texas, we look after things personally. It's a tradition.'

Reacher took a step closer. 'So you going to do it?' he said.

'Josh and Billy will do what they're told.'

'The little guys? The maid might be better. Or you, even.'

'Josh and Billy get in the ring with bulls that weigh a ton and a half. They ain't going to be too worried about you.'

Reacher started walking again. 'Whatever, Bobby. I only said good night to the kid. No reason to start World War Three over it. She's starved for company. So is her mother. What can I do about it?'

'You can get smart about it, is what,' Bobby said. 'She lies about everything. So whatever big story she's been telling you, don't go making a fool out of yourself, falling for it. You wouldn't be the first.'

'What does that mean?' Reacher said.

'Exactly what I said. Josh and Billy ran him off.'

Reacher said nothing. Bobby smiled at him.

'Don't believe her,' he said. 'There are things she doesn't tell you, and what she does tell you is mostly lies.'

'Why doesn't she have a key to the door?'

'She had a key. She lost it. It's never locked, anyway. Why the hell would it be locked? We're sixty miles from the nearest crossroads.'

'So why does she have to knock?'

'She doesn't have to knock. She could walk right in. She just puts on a big thing about how we exclude her. But it's all bullshit.'

Reacher said nothing.

'So you work if you want to,' Bobby said. 'But stay away from her and the kid. And I'm saying that for your sake, OK?' Then he turned in the dark and headed back to the house.

FOUR

Reacher went to bed, even though it was quite early. Sleep when you can, so you won't need to when you can't. That was his rule.

He heard Josh and Billy come back at two in the morning. He heard the pick-up engine growing nearer and louder, turning in at the gate. He heard it drive into the shed beneath him and the motor switch off. Then footsteps on the stairs, loud and clumsy. He tracked their sounds past him, over to the bathroom, back to their bunks. Then there was nothing but the wet rhythmic breathing of men who had worked hard all day and drunk hard all night.

It was already hot when he woke. He checked his watch. Ten past six, Saturday morning. He threw back the sheet and walked to the bathroom. Josh and Billy were still asleep.

He showered and dressed, then headed down the stairs and outside into the dawn.

THE WATCHERS ASSEMBLED piecemeal, like they had five times before. One of the men drove the pick-up to the boy's place, then to the second man's place, where they found the routine had changed.

'He just called me,' the second man explained. 'We got to go to some place on the Coyanosa Draw for new instructions, face to face.'

'Face to face with who?' the first man said. 'Not him, right?'

'No, some new people we're going to be working with.'

The boy said nothing. The first man just shrugged. 'OK with me.'

'Plus, we're going to get paid,' the second man said.

'Even better,' the first man said.

The second man squeezed onto the bench seat and closed his door and the pick-up turned and headed north.

REACHER WALKED to the barn. He ducked in the door and glanced around, rehearsing the work he might be expected to perform. The horses would need feeding, presumably. What did they eat? Hay, he guessed. There were bales of it all over the place. He found a separate corner room stacked with sacks of feed supplement. Big waxed-paper bags, from some specialist supplier in San Angelo.

He came out of the barn and walked up the track past the house, towards the road. Heard the front door open behind him and turned to see Bobby Greer stepping out on the porch. He was carrying a rifle. 'I was on my way to get you up,' he said. 'I need a driver.'

'Why?' Reacher asked. 'Where are you going?'

'Hunting,' Bobby said. 'In the pick-up. You drive while I shoot.'

'You shoot from a truck?'

'I'll show you,' Bobby said. He walked across to the motor barn. Stopped next to the newer pick-up. It had a roll bar built into the load bed. 'You drive,' he said. 'I'm here, leaning on the bar. Gives me a three-hundred-sixty-degree field of fire.'

'While we're moving?'

'That's the skill of it. It's fun. Sloop invented it. He was real good.'

'What are you hunting?'

'Armadillo,' Bobby said. 'Hunting's pretty good, south of here. Dillo chilli, can't beat it for lunch.'

Reacher said nothing.

'You never ate armadillo?' Bobby asked.

Reacher shook his head.

'Good eating,' Bobby said. 'Back when my granddaddy was a boy, depression times, it was about all the eating there was. Now the tree-huggers have got it protected. But if it's on our land, it's ours to shoot. That's the way I see it.'

'I don't think so,' Reacher said. 'I don't like hunting.'

'You work here, Reacher. You'll do what you're told.'

'We need to discuss some formalities, before I work here.'

'Like what?'

'Like wages.'

'Two hundred a week,' Bobby said. 'Bed thrown in. OK?'

Reacher shrugged. It was a long time since he'd worked for $200 a week. But then he wasn't there for the money. 'OK,' he said.

'And you'll do whatever Josh and Billy tell you to.'

'OK,' Reacher said again. 'But I won't take you hunting. Not now, not ever. Call it a matter of conscience.'

Bobby was quiet for a long moment. 'I'll find ways to keep you away from her, you know. Every day, I'll find something.'

'I'll be in the barn,' Reacher said, and walked away.

Ellie brought his breakfast to him there: scrambled eggs. She was concentrating on remembering a message. 'My mommy says, don't forget the riding lesson,' she recited. 'She wants you to meet her here in the barn after lunch.' Then she ran back to the house.

THE COYANOSA DRAW was sparsely populated. There were abandoned farmsteads, far from each other, far from anywhere. One had an old house baked grey by the sun. In front of it was an empty barn. It had no doors, just an open wall facing the house.

The Crown Victoria was waiting inside. The barn had an exterior staircase leading up to a hayloft, with a small platform outside the door at the top. The woman was on the platform, from where she could survey the approach road. She saw the watchers' pick-up two miles away. She waited until she was sure it was unaccompanied and then walked down the stairs. Signalled to the others.

They got out of the car. The pick-up pulled round the corner and they directed it into the barn. One of them gave a thumbs up to halt it. He stepped alongside the driver's window and his partner stepped to the passenger door.

The driver wound down his window. The intrigue of new instructions, the prospect of a big payday. On the passenger's side, the second man did the same thing. Then they both died, shot in the head with nine-millimetre bullets. The boy lived exactly one second longer, his notebook clutched in his hands. Then the small dark man leaned in and shot him twice in the chest.

REACHER DOZED a couple of hours before Carmen herself brought his armadillo lunch. She left without a word. He tried the meal. The meat was halfway between sweet and ordinary. It had been shredded, chopped and mixed with beans and chilli sauce. He had eaten worse, and he was hungry, which helped. He took his time, then he carried the dish back to the kitchen. Bobby was standing on the porch steps.

'Horses need more feed supplement,' he called. 'You'll go with Josh and Billy to pick it up. After siesta.'

Reacher nodded and walked on to the kitchen. Gave the used dish to the maid and thanked her for the meal. Then he walked to the barn and went inside and sat on a bale of straw to wait.

Carmen came in ten minutes later. She had changed into jeans and a sleeveless cotton shirt. She was carrying a straw hat and her handbag which she hung on a nail in the wall. Readied two horses in a quarter of the time he had taken to do one. She led his horse out of its stall. It was one of the geldings. He took the rein from her.

'Walk him out,' she said.

'Shouldn't we have leather pants? And riding gloves?'

'You kidding? We never wear that stuff here. It's way too hot.'

Her horse was the smaller mare. She wedged her hat on her head and put her handbag in a saddlebag. Then she followed him, leading her mare out into the yard. 'OK, like this,' she said. She stood on the mare's left and put her left foot in the stirrup. Gripped the horn with her left hand and jacked herself smoothly into the saddle.

He tried it and suddenly he was up.

'Put your right foot in,' she said.

He jammed his foot into the other stirrup.

'Now bunch the reins on the horn, in your left hand.'

That was easy. It was just a question of imitating the movies.

'OK, now just relax. And kick gently with your heels.'

He kicked once and the horse lurched into a walk.

'Good,' she said. 'I'll go in front and he'll follow.' She clicked her tongue and kicked her heels and her horse moved smoothly round his. She led him past the house, under the gate and across the road.

'How far are we going?' he called.

'We need to get over the rise,' she said. 'Down into the gulches.'

She slowed to let his horse move up alongside hers.

'Bobby told me the door's never locked,' he said.

'Sometimes it is, sometimes it isn't.'

'He told me you don't have to knock, either.'

'Since Sloop's been gone, if I don't knock, they run and grab a rifle. Then they go, "Oh sorry, but strangers prowling around the house make us nervous."'

'He also told me you brought some other guy down here, and he got Josh and Billy to run him off.'

She was quiet for a long moment. 'I met a man up in Pecos,' she said. 'About a year ago. We had an affair. At first just at his place up there. But he wanted more.'

'So you brought him here?'

'It was his idea. He thought he could get work, and be close to me. I thought it was crazy, but I went along with it. It actually worked for two or three weeks. Then Bobby caught us.'

'And what happened?'

'That was the end of it. My friend left. I saw him again, just once, back in Pecos. He was scared. Wouldn't talk to me.'

'Did Bobby tell Sloop?'

'He promised he wouldn't. We had a deal.'

'What kind of a deal?'

'The usual kind. If I'd do something for him, he'd keep quiet.'

'What kind of something?'

She paused. 'Something I really don't want to tell you about.'

They reached the top of a rise, a mile away from the red house, and moved down an incline to a dry gulch with a flat floor, all stone and sand. By the time Reacher's horse stepped into the gulch, Carmen was slipping out of the saddle. His horse stopped next to hers and he got off by doing the opposite of what had got him on.

She led both horses to the rim of the gulch and heaved a large stone over the free ends of both sets of reins. She lifted the flap of her saddlebag and took out her handbag. Zipped it open, slipped her hand in and came out with a handgun.

'Please show me how to use this,' she said.

He looked at the gun. It was a Lorcin L-22 automatic, with a two-and-a-half-inch barrel.

'Is it legal?'

She nodded. 'I did all the proper paperwork. Is it any good?'

'I guess,' he said. 'Where are the bullets?'

She took a small box out of her bag. It was packed with .22 shells. 'Show me how to load it,' she said.

He shook his head. 'Guns are dangerous, Carmen. You shouldn't keep one around Ellie. There might be an accident.'

'I want to learn to use it,' she said. 'For self-confidence.'

He shrugged. 'OK,' he said. 'Your life, your kid, your decision. But guns are serious business. So pay attention.'

He took the gun and laid it flat on his palm. 'Two warnings,' he said. 'This is a short barrel. Two and a half inches. It makes it an inaccurate weapon. If you use it, you need to get very close. *Touching* the target if you can. Try to use this thing across a room, you'll miss by miles.'

'OK,' she said.

'Second warning.' He dug a bullet out of the box and held it up. 'This thing is tiny. And slow. So it's not necessarily going to do a lot of damage. One shot isn't going to be enough. So you need to keep pulling the trigger until the gun is empty.'

'OK,' she said again.

'Now watch.' He clicked out the magazine and fed nine bullets into it. Clicked it back in and jacked the first shell into the breech. Took out the magazine again and refilled the empty spot at the bottom. Clicked it back in and cocked the gun and left the safety catch on. 'Cocked and locked,' he said. 'You do two things. Push the safety catch, and pull the trigger ten times.' He handed the gun to her. 'Try it,' he told her. 'The safety, and the trigger.'

She used her left hand to unlatch the safety, pointed it in her right, closed her eyes and pulled the trigger. The gun twisted down. A chip of rock and a spurt of dust kicked off the floor ten feet away. There was a metallic ricochet *whang* and a muted ring as the shell case ejected. The horses shuffled, then silence closed in again.

'Put the safety back on,' he said.

She clicked the catch. He undid his top button and slipped his shirt over his head. Walked fifteen feet and hung the shirt on the rim of the gulch, spreading it out to represent a man's torso. He walked back and stood behind her.

'Now shoot my shirt,' he said. 'You always aim for the body, because it's the biggest target and the most vulnerable.'

'I can't,' she said. 'You don't want holes in your shirt.'

'I figure there isn't much of a risk,' he said. 'Try it.'

She clicked the safety catch off. Pointed the gun, closed her eyes and fired. Reacher guessed she missed by twenty feet, high and wide.

'Keep your eyes open,' he said.

She kept her eyes open. Missed again, maybe six feet to the left.

'Let me try,' he said.

She passed him the gun. He closed one eye and sighted in.

'I'm aiming for where the pocket was,' he said. He fired a double-tap, two shots in quick succession. The first hit the shirt in the armpit opposite the torn pocket. The second hit centrally but low. He handed the gun back. 'Your turn again,' he said.

She fired three more, all misses. She lowered the gun, disappointed.

'So what have you learned?' he asked.

'I need to get close,' she said.

'Damn right,' he said. 'It's not entirely your fault. I missed by twelve inches, from fifteen feet. And I can shoot. I won competitions for pistol shooting in the army. Couple of years, I was the best.' He took the gun and reloaded it. He cocked it and locked it and laid it on the ground. 'Leave it there,' he said. 'Unless you're very sure.'

She stood still for a long time. Then she picked up the gun. Slipped it back into her bag. He retrieved his shirt and pulled it over his head. Neither bullet hole showed. One was under his arm, and the other below the waistband of his trousers. Then he tracked around the gulch and picked up all eight spent shell cases. It was an old habit, and good housekeeping. He jingled them together in his hand like small change and put them in his trouser pocket.

IT WAS LATE in the afternoon when they got back. Josh and Billy were leaning against the wall of the barn, in the shade. Their pick-up was ready for the trip to the feed supplier. It was parked in the yard.

'I'll put the horses away,' Carmen said.

They dismounted together in front of the barn door.

'You ready?' Billy called.

'He should have been ready a half-hour ago,' Josh said.

For that, Reacher made them wait. He walked to the bunkhouse, slowly. He used the bathroom. Rinsed dust off his face, splashed cold water over his shirt. Walked slowly back. The pick-up had turned to face the gate and the engine was running. Josh was sitting in the driver's seat. Billy was standing next to the passenger door. 'So let's go,' he called. He put Reacher in the middle seat. Josh slammed his door. Billy crowded in on the other side and Josh took off towards the gate. Paused at the road and then made a left, at which point Reacher knew the situation was a lot worse than he had guessed.

HE HAD SEEN the feed bags in the storeroom, plenty of them, maybe forty. Big bags, probably thirty pounds to a bag. Twelve hundred pounds of feed. How fast were four horses and a pony going to eat their way through that?

He had understood that fetching more feed was Bobby's way of getting him out of Carmen's life for a spell. But they weren't fetching feed. They had turned left. The feed supplier was in San Angelo. He had seen it forty times, once on each bag, printed in big clear letters. And San Angelo was northeast of Echo County. Not southwest. They should have turned right.

So, Bobby was planning to get him out of Carmen's life *permanently*. Josh and Billy had been told to get rid of him. And *Josh and Billy will do what they're told*, Bobby had said. Reacher smiled. They didn't know he'd seen the feed bags. They didn't know a left turn instead of a right would mean anything to him.

'How far is it?' he asked, innocently.

'Less than a couple hours,' Josh said. 'Hundred miles is all.'

So maybe they were headed to the bar they had mentioned yesterday. Maybe they had friends there.

'We coming straight back?' Reacher asked.

'We're going for a couple beers first,' Billy said.

'The feed store open late? On a Saturday?'

'Big order, they'll accommodate us,' Billy said.

Maybe it was a new supplier. Maybe they changed their source.

'I guess you use them a lot,' he said.

'All the years we've been here,' Josh said.

'Then we're going straight back?'

'Sure,' Billy said. 'You'll be back in time for your beauty sleep.'

'That's good,' Reacher said. 'Because that's the way I like it.'

Billy said nothing and stared idly out of his window. Josh just smiled and kept the speed at a steady sixty.

The road got rougher the further south they drove. The sun was low in the west. A sign on the shoulder said ECHO 5 MILES.

'I thought Echo was north,' Reacher said. 'Where Ellie's school is.'

'It's split,' Billy said. 'Half of it up there, half of it down here. Hundred sixty miles of nothing in between.'

'World's biggest town, end to end,' Josh said.

A cluster of small buildings came into view in the distance. There were tin advertisements on the shoulder, three miles out, announcing a gas station, a store and a bar, the Longhorn Lounge. It was the first establishment they came to. Ten or twelve pick-ups were parked nose-in to the building. Nearest the door was the sheriff's car.

Josh bumped across the parking lot and put the truck with the others. He turned the motor off. Put the keys in his pocket. Josh and Billy opened their doors together and swung out. Reacher slid out through the passenger door.

'OK,' Billy said. 'We're buying.'

There was an inside lobby with a payphone. Then there was a second door that led into the bar itself. Billy pushed it open.

A bar is a military cop's place of business. Maybe 90 per cent of low-grade trouble in the service happens in bars. So a military cop is all eyes on the way into a bar. First, he counts the exits. The Longhorn Lounge had three: a front door, a back door out beyond the rest rooms, and a private door from the office behind the bar.

Then the MP looks at the crowd. He looks for knots of trouble. Who falls silent and stares? Where are the challenges? Nowhere, in the Longhorn. There were maybe twenty-five people in the room, all men, all tanned, lean and dressed in denim, none paying any attention beyond casual glances and nods of easy familiarity towards Billy and Josh. The sheriff was nowhere to be seen. But there was an unoccupied stool at the bar with a fresh bottle in front of it.

Then the MP looks for weapons. There was an antique revolver above the bar, wired onto a wooden plaque with a message branded into it: WE DON'T CALL 911. There would be a few handguns in the place. The pool table worried him more. It sat in the middle of the room, covered in hard celluloid balls, four guys with four cues using it, maybe a dozen more cues in a rack on the nearest wall. A pool cue is a good bar-room weapon. Short enough to be handy, long enough to be useful, made of fine hardwood and nicely weighted with lead.

Beyond the pool table was an area with small tables and stools. Billy held up three fingers to the barman and got three cold bottles. He carried them towards the tables. Reacher stepped ahead and got there first. He wanted his choice of seats. Back to the wall. All three exits in view, if possible. He threaded his way in and sat down. Josh sat to his half-right, and Billy sat half-left. Pushed a bottle across the table. The sheriff came into the room from the direction of the rest rooms. He paused when he saw Reacher, then sat down at the bar.

Billy raised his bottle like a toast. 'Good luck,' he said.

You're going to need it, pal, Reacher thought. He took a long pull from his own bottle.

'I need to make a phone call,' Billy said. He went out to the lobby.

Reacher took another sip of his beer and counted the people in the room. There were twenty-three, excluding himself. Billy came back and spoke to the sheriff. The sheriff nodded. Drained his bottle and stood up. Glanced in Reacher's direction and then pushed out through the door. Billy threaded his way back to the table.

'Sheriff's leaving,' he said. 'He has urgent business elsewhere.'

'Did you make your call?' Josh asked, like it was rehearsed.

'Yes, I made my call,' Billy said. Then he sat down. 'Don't you want to know who I called?' he said, looking at Reacher.

'Why would I give a rat's ass who you called?' Reacher said.

'I called for the ambulance,' Billy said. 'Best to do it ahead of time. It comes all the way from Presidio. Can take hours to get here.'

'See, there was a guy we ran off,' Josh said. 'He was knocking boots with the Mexican woman. Bobby didn't think that was appropriate, what with Sloop being in prison, and all. So we got asked to take care of it. We brought him down here.'

'What's this other guy got to do with me?' Reacher asked.

'You're in the same category. Bobby says you're knocking boots with her too.'

'And you believe him?'

Billy nodded. 'Sure we do. She comes on to *him*. He told us that. So why should you be any different? And hey, she's a good-looking piece of ass. I'd go there myself, except she's Sloop's. You got to respect family, even with beaners. That's the rule around here.'

Reacher said nothing.

'Her other guy was a schoolteacher,' Billy said. 'Got way out of line. So we brought him down here, and we took him out back, and we got us a hog-butchering knife, and we got a couple of guys to hold him, and we pulled his pants down, and told him we were going to cut it off. He was crying and whimpering. Promising he'd get himself lost. Pleading with us not to cut. But we cut just a little anyway. Then we told him if we ever saw his face again, we'd take it all the way off. And you know what? We never saw his face again.'

'So it worked,' Josh said. 'Only problem was he nearly bled out, from the wound. We should have called ahead for the ambulance.

So this time we did call ahead. So you should be grateful.'

'You aim to cut me, it'll be you in the ambulance,' Reacher said.

'You think?'

Reacher looked at each of them in turn, openly and evenly. He felt confident. It was a long time since he'd lost a two-on-one bar fight. 'Your choice,' he said. 'Quit now, or go to the hospital.'

'Well, you know what?' Josh said, smiling. 'I think we'll stay with the programme. Because whatever the hell kind of a guy you think you are, we're the ones got a lot of friends in here. And you don't.'

It was clearly true. Some kind of subliminal vibe was quieting the room, making people restless and watchful. They were glancing over, then glancing at each other. Reacher could feel tension in the air. Maybe it was going to be a lot worse than two-on-one.

Billy smiled. 'We don't scare easy. Call it a professional thing.'

They get in the ring with bulls that weigh a ton and a half, Bobby had said. *They ain't going to be worried about you.* Reacher knew nothing about rodeos, except from TV or the movies. He guessed the riders sat on a fence near the pen, and jumped on as the bull was released into the ring. Then they had to stay on. If they didn't, they could get stomped. Or gored. So these guys had dumb courage. And strength. And resilience. They were accustomed to pain and injury. But they were also accustomed to some kind of pattern. A structured build-up. A measured countdown, before the action started. They were accustomed to waiting, counting off the seconds, tensing up, breathing deeply, getting ready for it.

'So let's do it,' he said. 'Right now, in the yard.' He came out from behind the table and stepped past Josh before he could react. Walked to the right of the pool table, heading for the rest-room exit. Knots of people blocked him, then parted to let him through. He heard Josh and Billy following. He felt them counting down, tensing up, getting ready. Maybe twenty paces to the exit, maybe thirty seconds to the yard. *Twenty-nine, twenty-eight.* He kept his steps even, building on the rhythm. *Twenty-seven, twenty-six.* Arms loose by his side. *Twenty-five, twenty-four.* He snatched the last pool cue from the rack and reversed it in his hands and scythed a complete 180-degree turn and hit Billy as hard as he could in the side of the head. There was a crunch and Billy went down. He swung at Josh. Josh's hand came up to block the blow and his forearm broke. He screamed and Reacher swung for the head, connecting hard. Josh went down head-to-toe with Billy, and Reacher stood over them both and swung again four more times, fast and hard. *Hit hard, hit early, get your retaliation in first.* While they're still waiting for the bell.

The other men in the bar had spun away from the action and now they were crowding back in again, slowly and warily. Reacher turned a menacing circle with the cue held ready. He bent and took the truck keys from Josh's pocket. Then he dropped the cue and barged his way through the crowd to the door. Nobody tried to stop him. Clearly friendship had its limits in Echo County. He made it back to the truck. Slid inside, fired it up and peeled away north.

IT WAS DARK when he turned in under the ranch gate. But every light in the Red House was burning. And there were two cars parked in the yard. One was the sheriff's. The other was a lime-green Lincoln.

The front door was standing open. Reacher stepped up, looked in and saw the sheriff, and Rusty Greer, and Bobby, and Carmen. She was wearing a dress. It was red and black. She looked numb. There was a man in a suit at the opposite end of the room. He was sleek and slightly overweight, not short, not tall. Maybe thirty years old, with light-coloured hair receding from a domed brow. He had a pale indoor face, split into a huge politician's smile.

Reacher paused on the porch and decided not to enter. But his weight put a creak into the boards and Bobby heard it. He glanced out into the night and did a perfect double take. Stood completely still for a second and then came hurrying through the door. 'What are you doing here?' he asked.

'I work here,' Reacher said. 'Remember?'

'Where are Josh and Billy?'

'They quit.'

Bobby's absence and the voices on the porch had pulled people to the door. Rusty Greer was first out, followed by the sheriff, looking puzzled, and the guy in the suit. Carmen stayed inside.

'Well, I'm Hack Walker,' the guy in the suit said, holding out his hand. 'I'm the DA in Pecos, and a friend of the family.'

'Sloop's oldest friend,' Rusty said, absently.

Reacher took the guy's hand. 'Jack Reacher,' he said. 'I work here.'

'You registered to vote here yet?' the guy asked. 'Because if so, I just want to point out I'm running for judge in November and I'd surely like to count on your support.'

'Hack's brought us the most delightful news,' Rusty said.

'Al Eugene showed up?' Reacher asked.

'No, not yet,' Rusty said. 'Something else entirely.'

Everybody started beaming. Reacher glanced beyond them at Carmen standing alone in the foyer. She wasn't beaming.

'You're getting Sloop out early,' he said. 'Tomorrow, I guess.'

'That's for sure,' Hack Walker said. 'They claimed they couldn't do administration on the weekend, but I changed their minds. They said it would be the first Sunday release in the history of the system.'

'Hack's going to drive us up there,' Rusty said. 'We're leaving soon. We're going to drive all night.'

'We're going to be waiting on the sidewalk,' Hack said. 'Right outside the prison gate, seven o'clock in the morning. Old Sloop's going to get a big welcome.'

'You all going?' Reacher asked.

'I'm not,' Carmen said. She had come out onto the porch. 'I have to stay and see to Ellie,' she said.

'Plenty of room in the car,' Hack said. 'Ellie can come too.'

Carmen shook her head. 'I don't want her to see her father walking out of a prison door.'

'Then I guess I'll stay too,' Bobby said. 'Sloop will understand.'

Carmen walked back into the house. Rusty and Hack Walker drifted after her. The sheriff and Bobby stayed on the porch.

'So why did they quit?' Bobby asked.

'Well, they didn't exactly quit,' Reacher said. 'I was trying to sugar the pill, for the family, was all. Truth is we were in a bar, and they picked a fight with some guy and lost.'

Bobby stared. 'Who was the guy?'

'Just some stranger, minding his own business.'

Bobby paused. 'Was it you?'

'Me?' Reacher said. 'Why would they pick a fight with me, Bobby? What possible reason would they have for that?'

Bobby turned and stalked into the house. Slammed the door loudly behind him. The sheriff stayed where he was.

'Bobby told me down here folks sort out their own differences,' Reacher said. 'He implied cops stay out of private disputes. He said it's some kind of a big old West Texas tradition.'

The sheriff was quiet for a moment. 'Well, you could put it that way,' he said. 'And I'm a very traditional guy.'

Reacher nodded. 'I'm very glad to hear it.'

The sheriff moved to his car and started the engine. Headed out down the driveway and accelerated into the distance.

REACHER WALKED to the horse barn and sat on a hay bale. After a time he heard feet on the boards of the porch, then on the steps, then the crunch of dust as they crossed the yard. He heard the Lincoln's doors open and shut, the engine start. He stepped to the door and saw Hack Walker silhouetted at the wheel, Rusty Greer beside him.

The big car drove out under the gate and down the road. He waited just inside the barn door, trying to guess who would come for him first. Carmen, probably, he thought, but it was Bobby who stepped out on the porch, maybe five minutes after his mother had left. He came down the steps and headed towards the bunkhouse. Reacher stepped out of the barn and cut him off.

'Horses need watering,' Bobby said. 'And their stalls cleaning.'

'You do it,' Reacher said.

'What? I'm not doing it.'

'Then I'll make you do it,' Reacher said. 'Things just changed for you, Bobby. Soon as you set Josh and Billy on me, you crossed a line. Put yourself in a whole different situation. One where you do exactly what I tell you.'

Bobby said nothing.

Reacher looked straight at him. 'I tell you *jump*, you don't even ask how high. You just start jumping. That clear? I own you now.'

Bobby stood still. Reacher swung his right hand, aiming a big slow roundhouse slap. Bobby ducked away from it, straight into Reacher's left, which pulled the ball cap off his head.

'So go look after the horses,' Reacher said. 'You can sleep in there. I see you again before breakfast, I'll break your legs.'

Bobby walked slowly towards the barn. Reacher dropped the ball cap in the dirt and strolled up to the house.

FIVE

Reacher found Carmen in the parlour. She was sitting alone at the table, her back perfectly straight and her gaze blank and level, focused on a spot on the wall where there was nothing to see.

'Twice over,' she said. 'I feel cheated, twice over. First it was a year, and then it was nothing. Then it was forty-eight hours, but really it was only twenty-four.'

'You can still get out,' he said.

'Now it's less than twenty-four,' she said. 'It's sixteen, maybe.'

'Sixteen hours, you could be anywhere,' he said.

'Ellie's fast asleep,' she said. 'I can't wake her up and bundle her in a car and run away and be chased by the cops for ever.'

Reacher said nothing.

'I'm going to try to face it,' she said. 'A fresh start. I'm planning to tell him, enough is enough. I'm planning to tell him, he lays a hand on me again, I'll divorce him. Whatever it takes. However long.' She scraped back her chair and stood up. 'Come and see Ellie,' she said. 'She's so beautiful when she's asleep.'

She took his hand. Led him out into the rear lobby and up the back stairs. Down the corridor to Ellie's door. She eased it open and manoeuvred him so he could see inside the room.

A nightlight showed the child sprawled on her back with her arms thrown up round her head. Her hair was tumbled over the pillow. Long dark eyelashes rested on her cheeks like fans.

'She's six,' Carmen whispered. 'She needs a bed of her own, in a place of her own. I can't make her live like a fugitive. Do you see?'

He shrugged. He didn't, really. At six, he had lived exactly like a fugitive. He had at every age, right from birth to yesterday. He had moved from one service base to another, all around the world, often with no notice. It hadn't done him any harm.

Or, maybe it had. 'It's your call, I guess,' he said.

She pulled him back into the corridor and eased Ellie's door shut. 'I'll show you where I hid the gun,' she said. 'You can tell me if you approve.'

She walked ahead of him down the corridor. She was wearing heels and her dress swayed with every step. Her hair hung down her back and merged with the black pattern on the red fabric of the dress. She turned left, then right, and stepped through an archway. There was a staircase, leading down.

'Where are we going?' he asked.

'Separate wing,' she said.

The staircase led to a ground-floor hallway, which led out of the main building to a master suite. It was as big as a small house. There was a dressing area, a bathroom, a sitting room and a bedroom.

'In here,' she said. She led him to the bedroom. 'You see what I mean? We're a long way from anywhere. Nobody hears anything. And I try to be quiet, anyway. If I scream, he hits me harder.'

He nodded and looked around. There was a kingsize bed close to the window, with side tables by the head, and a chest-high piece of furniture full of drawers opposite the foot.

She opened the drawer on the top right. 'I listened to your advice,' she said. 'This is too high for Ellie.'

He moved closer. It was her underwear drawer.

'You could have told me where it was,' he said. 'You didn't need to show me.'

She was quiet for a beat. 'He'll want sex, won't he?' she said.

Reacher made no reply.

'He's been locked up a year and a half,' she said. 'But I'm going to refuse. It's a woman's right, isn't it? To say no?'

'Of course it is,' he said.

'Even though the woman is married?'

'Most places,' he said.

'And it's also her right to say yes, isn't it?' she asked.

'Equally,' he said.

'I'd say yes to you.'

'I'm not asking.'

She paused. 'So is it OK for me to ask you?'

He looked straight at her. 'Depends on why, I guess.'

'Because I want to,' she said. 'I want to go to bed with you.'

'And?'

She shrugged. 'And I want to hurt Sloop a little, I guess.'

He said nothing.

'No strings attached,' she said. 'I'm not looking for it to change anything. About your decision, I mean. About Sloop.'

He nodded. 'It wouldn't change anything,' he said.

She looked away. 'So what's your answer?' she asked.

He watched her profile. Her face was blank. It was like all other possibilities were exhausted for her, and only instinct was left.

'No,' he said.

She was quiet for a long moment.

'Will you at least stay with me?' she asked.

REACHER WOKE UP on Sloop Greer's sofa with the Sunday dawn. He could hear the shower running. And he could smell coffee.

He got off the sofa and wandered through to the bedroom. There was a small coffee machine in one corner, with two mugs beside it. He filled a mug with coffee and wandered into the dressing area.

There were two closets. He opened one of them. There were rows of chinos and blue jeans and a rack of suits. He nudged open a jacket, looking for the label. It was a forty-four long. It would fit a guy about six feet two, maybe 200 pounds. So Sloop was not an especially big guy. Not a giant. But he was a foot taller and twice the weight of his wife. Not the world's fairest match-up.

There was a photograph frame face-down on a stack of shirts. He turned it over. A colour print showed three guys, maybe seventeen years old, maybe eighteen, leaning on the fender of an old-fashioned pick-up truck. They looked full of youthful energy and excitement. Their whole lives ahead of them. One was Hack Walker, a little slimmer, a little more muscular, a lot more hair. He guessed the other two were Al Eugene and Sloop Greer himself. Sloop looked like a younger version of Bobby.

He heard the shower shut off and put the photograph back and closed the slider. Moved back to the sitting room. A moment later the bathroom door opened and Carmen came out. She was wrapped in two white towels, one round her body, the other like a turban round her hair. 'Good morning,' she said.

'To you, too,' he said.

'It isn't, though, is it?' she said. 'It's a bad morning.'

'I guess,' he said.

'Use the shower if you want,' she said. 'I have to see to Ellie.'

'OK.' He stepped into the bathroom. It was huge and made out of some kind of reconstituted marble. It looked like a place he'd once stayed, in Vegas. He used the john and rinsed his mouth at the sink, then stripped off and stepped into the enormous glass shower stall. There was a shower head the size of a hubcap above him, and tall pipes in each corner with water jets pointing at him. He turned the faucet and a roaring deluge of warm water hit him from all sides. It was like standing under Niagara Falls. The side jets started pulsing hot and cold and he couldn't hear himself think. He washed as quickly as he could and then shut it all down.

He took a fresh towel from a stack and dried off. Wrapped the towel round him and stepped back into the dressing area. Carmen was buttoning her shirt. It was white, and she had white trousers on. Gold jewellery. Her skin looked dark against it and her hair was glossy and already curling in the heat.

'That was quick,' she said.

'Hell of a shower,' he said.

She slid her closet shut and twisted left and right to examine her reflection in the mirrored doors.

'You look good,' he said.

'Do I look Mexican enough? With the white clothes?'

He said nothing.

'No jeans today,' she said. 'I'm sick of trying to look like I was born a cowgirl in Amarillo.' She stretched tall and kissed him on the cheek. 'Thanks for staying,' she said. 'It helped me.'

He said nothing.

'Join us for breakfast,' she said. 'Twenty minutes.'

Then she walked out of the room, to wake her daughter.

He dressed and found a different way back into the house. The place was a warren. He came out through a living room he hadn't seen before and into the foyer with the rifles. He opened the front door and stepped out on the porch. It was already hot. He walked down to the barn and found Bobby asleep on a bed of straw.

'Rise and shine, little brother,' he called.

Bobby stirred and sat up, confused as to where he was, and why. Then he remembered, and went tense with resentment.

'Sleep well?' Reacher asked.

'They'll be back soon,' Bobby said. 'Then what do you think is going to happen?'

Reacher smiled. 'You mean, am I going to tell them I made you clean out the barn and sleep in the straw?'

'You couldn't tell them.'

'No, I guess I couldn't,' Reacher said. 'So are *you* going to?'

Bobby said nothing.

Reacher smiled again. 'No, I didn't think you would,' he said. 'So stay here until noon, then I'll let you in the house to get cleaned up.'

'What about breakfast?'

'Eat the horse food. Turns out there's bags of it, after all.'

He went to the parlour and the maid came in with a stack of plates. Four of them, with four sets of silverware and four paper napkins.

'I assume you're eating in here,' she said.

Reacher nodded. 'But Bobby isn't. He's staying in the barn.'

'Why?'

'I think a horse is sick.'

'It's pancakes,' the maid said. 'And that will have to do. They'll want a big lunch, so that's where my morning is going.'

'Pancakes are fine,' he said.

ELLIE ATE HER PANCAKES like she was starving. Reacher picked at his, watching Carmen. She ate nothing.

Afterwards, Ellie scrambled off her chair and ran out of the room like a miniature whirlwind.

'Will you talk to him?' Carmen asked.

'Sure,' he said.

'I think he needs to know it's not a secret any more.'

'I agree.'

Then she went off alone and Reacher set about killing time. He sat down on the swing seat. Then he did what most soldiers do when they're waiting for action. He went to sleep.

CARMEN WOKE HIM maybe an hour later. She touched him on the shoulder and he opened his eyes. She had changed clothes. Now she was in blue jeans and a checked shirt. She was wearing lizard-skin boots. A belt to match. Her hair was tied back and she had made up her face with pale powder and blue eye shadow.

'I don't want you to talk to him,' she said. 'Not yet.'

'Why not?'

'I thought it over again. It might set him off if he knows somebody else knows. I think it might be worse if we start out like that. It's better coming from me. At least at first.'

'Why did you change your clothes?'

'These are better,' she said. 'I don't want to provoke him.'

'Don't chicken out, Carmen,' he said. 'Stand and fight.'

'I will,' she said. 'Tonight. I'll tell him I'm not going to take it any more.' She went back into the house.

He settled back on the swing seat and tried to doze. But his internal clock was telling him the time was getting near. The way he remembered the maps of Texas, Abilene was probably less than seven hours from Echo County. Maybe nearer six. So assuming Sloop got out at seven, they could be home by one.

At twelve he saw Bobby come out of the horse barn. He crossed the yard and stepped up on the porch. Walked into the house. He came out again at a quarter to one, dressed in fresh jeans and a new T-shirt. Then Carmen and Ellie came out. Carmen was holding Ellie's hand and staggering slightly, like her knees were weak.

Reacher stood up and gestured that she should sit down. Ellie climbed up and sat next to her. Reacher stepped to the porch rail and watched the road.

He saw the dust cloud at the extremity of his vision. It grew until he could make out the lime-green Lincoln at its head. It came up the road, braked close to the gate and turned in sharply. Three figures were clearly visible inside. Hack Walker was at the wheel. Rusty Greer was in the back seat. And there was a large pale man in the front. He had short fair hair and a blue shirt. He was craning his head, looking around, smiling broadly. Sloop Greer, arriving home.

The Lincoln stopped next to the porch and the engine died. Three doors opened and all three people spilled out and Bobby and Ellie clattered down the porch steps towards them. Reacher moved back from the rail. Carmen stood up slowly and took his place there.

Sloop Greer's face and hands were white with prison pallor and he was overweight from the starchy food, but he was Bobby's brother. No doubt about that. He had the same hair, face, bones, posture. Bobby hugged him. Sloop hugged back and they staggered around and whooped and clapped each other on the back.

Sloop let Bobby go and squatted down and held his arms out to Ellie. She launched herself into his embrace. He whirled her up into the air, hugged her, kissed her cheek, set her down and looked up into the porch. He held out his hand, beckoning to his wife.

She took a deep breath and forced a smile and skipped down the steps. Took Sloop's hands and folded herself into his arms. They kissed, long enough so nobody would think they were brother and sister, but not so long that anybody would think there was real passion there. Bobby and his mother walked into the house and Reacher went down the steps into the yard. Hack Walker slid back into the Lincoln, fired it up and accelerated away.

Sloop was strolling across the yard, holding Ellie's hand in his right and Carmen's in his left. Carmen was saying nothing and Ellie was saying a lot. They all walked straight past Reacher, up the steps, three abreast. At the door Sloop turned to allow Ellie in ahead of him. He followed her across the threshold and then turned the other way to pull Carmen in after him.

REACHER SAW NOBODY except the maid for three hours. He stayed inside the bunkhouse and she brought him lunch. Then late in the afternoon he heard voices behind the horse barn and walked up there and found Sloop and Carmen and Ellie taking the air. It was still very hot. Sloop looked restless. He was sweating. Carmen looked nervous. Her face was slightly red. Maybe tension, maybe the heat. But it wasn't impossible she'd been slapped a couple of times.

'Ellie, come with me to see your pony,' she said.

'I saw him this morning, Mommy,' Ellie said.

Carmen held out her hand. 'But I didn't. So let's go see him again.'

They stepped behind Sloop and set off for the front of the barn. Carmen turned her head and mouthed, 'Talk to him,' as she walked. Sloop turned and watched them go. Turned back and looked at Reacher, like he was seeing him for the first time.

'Sloop Greer,' he said, and held out his hand.

Up close, he was an older, wiser version of Bobby. There was intelligence in his eyes. Not necessarily a pleasant sort of intelligence. It wasn't hard to imagine cruelty there. Reacher shook his hand. It was big-boned, but soft. A bully's hand, not a fighter's.

'Jack Reacher,' he said. 'How was prison?'

There was a split-second flash of surprise in the eyes. Then it was replaced by instant calm. Good self-control, Reacher thought.

'It was pretty awful,' Sloop said. 'You been in yourself?'

Quick, too. 'On the other side of the bars from you,' Reacher said.

'Bobby told me you were a cop. Now you're an itinerant worker.'

'I have to be. I didn't have a rich daddy.'

Sloop paused a beat. 'You were military, right? In the army?'

'Right, the army.'

'I never cared much for the military, myself.'

'So I gathered.'

'Yeah, how?'

'Well, I hear you opted out of paying for it.'

Another flash in the eyes, quickly gone. Not easy to rile, Reacher thought. But a spell in prison teaches anybody to keep things well below the surface.

'Shame you spoiled it by crying uncle and getting out early.'

'You think?'

Reacher nodded. 'If you can't do the time, don't do the crime.'

'You got out of the army. Maybe you couldn't do the time, either.'

Reacher smiled. Thanks for the opening, he thought. 'I had no choice,' he said. 'Fact is, they threw me out.'

'Yeah, why?'

'I broke the law, too.'

'Yeah, how?'

'Some scumbag of a colonel was beating up on his wife. Nice young woman. He did it in secret. So I couldn't prove it. But I wasn't about to let him get away with it. That wouldn't have been right. Because I don't like men who hit women. So one night, I caught him on his own. No witnesses. He's in a wheelchair now. Drinks through a straw. Wears a bib, because he drools all the time.'

Sloop was silent. Walk away now, Reacher thought, and you're confessing it. But Sloop stayed where he was, very still, staring into space, seeing nothing. Then he recovered. The eyes came back into focus. Not quickly, but not too slowly, either. A smart guy.

'Well, that makes me feel better,' he said. 'About withholding my taxes. They might have ended up in your pocket.'

'You don't approve?'

'No, I don't,' Sloop said.

'Of who?'

'Either of you,' Sloop said. 'You, or the other guy.'

Then he turned and walked away.

REACHER WENT BACK to the bunkhouse. The maid brought him dinner. Darkness fell. He lay down on his bed and sweated.

Then he heard a light tread on the bunkhouse stair. He sat up in time to see Carmen come up into the room.

'Did he hit you?' Reacher asked.

Her hand went up to her cheek. 'No,' she said.

'Did he?'

She looked away. 'Well, just once,' she said. 'Not hard.'

'I should go break his arms.'

'He called the sheriff. He wants you out of here.'

'It's OK,' Reacher said. 'I squared the sheriff away, before.'

She paused a beat. 'I've got to get back now. He thinks I'm with Ellie.' She started back down the stairs. 'You sure about the sheriff?'

'Don't worry,' he said. 'The sheriff won't do a thing.'

BUT THE SHERIFF did one thing. He passed the problem to the State Police. Ninety minutes later, a Texas Rangers cruiser turned in under the gate. Somebody directed it to the bunkhouse. Reacher heard it. He got off his bed and went down the stairs and when he got to the bottom he was lit up by the spotlight mounted in front of its windshield. The car doors opened and two Rangers got out.

They were not similar to the sheriff. They were young and fit and professional. Both were medium height, both halfway between lean and muscled. Both had military-style buzzcuts and immaculate uniforms. One was a sergeant, the other a trooper. The trooper was Hispanic. He was holding a shotgun.

'What?' Reacher called.

'Step to the hood of the car,' the sergeant called back.

Reacher kept his hands clear of his body and walked to the car.

'Assume the position,' the sergeant said.

Reacher put his palms on the fender and leaned down. The trooper covered him with the shotgun and the sergeant patted him down.

'OK, get in the car,' he said.

Reacher didn't move. 'What's this about?' he asked.

'A request from a property owner to remove a trespasser.'

'I'm not a trespasser. I work here.'

'Well, I guess they just terminated you. So now you're a trespasser. And we're going to remove you.'

'That's a State Police job?'

'Small community like this, we're on call to help the local guys, their days off.'

'OK, I'll leave,' Reacher said. 'I'll walk out to the road.'

'Then you'll be a vagrant on a county highway. That's against the law, too, around here, especially during the hours of darkness.'

'So where are we going?'

'You have to leave the county. We'll let you out in Pecos.'

'They owe me money. I never got paid.'

'So get in the car. We'll stop at the house.'

Reacher glanced left at the trooper, and the shotgun. Both of them looked businesslike. He glanced right, at the sergeant. He had his hand on the butt of his gun.

'There's a problem here,' he said. 'The daughter-in-law is getting smacked around by her husband.'

'She made a complaint?'

'She's scared to. The sheriff's a good old boy and she's a Hispanic woman from California.'

'Nothing we can do without a complaint.'

Reacher glanced at the trooper, who just shrugged.

'Like the man told you,' he said. 'Nothing we can do without we hear about it.'

'You're hearing about it now,' Reacher said. 'I'm telling you.'

The trooper shook his head. 'Needs to come from the victim.'

'Get in the car,' the sergeant said. He used his hand on the top of Reacher's head and folded him into the back seat. There was a heavy wire barrier in front of him. Either side, the door openers and window winders had been removed.

The sergeant and the trooper swung in together in the front and drove up to the house. All the Greers except Ellie were on the porch to see him go. All smiling, except Carmen. The sergeant stopped the car at the foot of the steps and buzzed his window down.

'This guy says you owe him wages,' he called.

'So tell him to sue us,' Bobby called back.

Reacher leaned forward to the metal grille. '¡Carmen!' he shouted. '¡Si hay un problema, llama directamente a estos hombres!'

The sergeant turned his head. 'What?'

'Nothing.'

The sergeant buzzed his window up again and pulled out towards the gate. 'What was that you called out to them?' he asked.

Reacher said nothing. The trooper answered for him.

'It was Spanish,' he said. 'For the woman. It meant, "Carmen, if there's trouble, call these guys direct." Terrible accent.'

They drove the same sixty miles he had covered the other way in the white Cadillac, back to the crossroads hamlet with Ellie's school, and kept going, heading for Pecos.

They never got there. The radio call came in an hour and thirty-five minutes into the ride. 'Blue Five, Blue Five,' it said.

The trooper unhooked the microphone and clicked the switch. 'Blue Five, copy, over,' he said.

'Required at the Red House Ranch immediately, sixty miles south of north Echo crossroads, domestic disturbance reported, over.'

'Copy, nature of incident, over?'

'Unclear at this time, believed violent, over.'

'Well, shit,' the sergeant said.

'Copy, on our way, out,' the trooper said. He replaced the microphone. Turned round. 'So she understood your Spanish. I guess your accent wasn't too far off, after all.'

Reacher said nothing. The sergeant turned his head. 'Look on the bright side, pal,' he said. 'Now we can do something about it.'

'I warned you,' Reacher said. 'And you should have damn well listened to me. So if she's hurt bad, it's on you. Pal.'

The sergeant pulled a turn across the whole of the road, shoulder to shoulder. Got it pointing south again and hustled.

They were back again two hours and thirty minutes after they left. First thing they saw was the sheriff's cruiser. The sergeant jammed to a stop behind it. 'Hell's he doing here?' he said. 'It's his day off.'

There was nobody in sight. The trooper opened his door. The sergeant shut down the motor and did the same.

'Let me out,' Reacher said.

'No dice, pal,' the sergeant said. 'You stay right there.'

They got out and went inside. Reacher waited. The car grew warm. The trooper came out after about twelve minutes. Walked back to the car, opened his door and leaned in for the microphone.

'Is she OK?' Reacher asked.

The guy nodded, sourly. 'She's fine,' he said. 'At least physically. But she's in a shitload of trouble.'

'Why?'

'Because the call wasn't about *him* attacking *her*. It was the other way around. She shot him. He's dead. So we just arrested her.'

SIX

Back-up arrived an hour later. It was an identical cruiser with another trooper driving and another sergeant riding alongside. They got out of their car and walked into the house. After twenty minutes, the Echo sheriff came out of the house and drove away.

Another hour later, an ambulance came. It was marked PRESIDIO FIRE DEPARTMENT. Maybe it was the same truck Billy had called the night before. It backed up to the porch steps. The crew got out and opened the rear doors. They took out a rolling gurney and the back-up sergeant met them on the steps and led them inside.

They came back out and lifted the gurney down the steps. Sloop Greer was just a large shape on it, wound into a white sheet. The medics slid the gurney inside the ambulance and closed the doors. Then the crew climbed back into their cab and headed north.

Five minutes later the cops came out with Carmen. She was dressed in the same jeans and shirt. Her hands were cuffed behind her back. Her head was down and her face was pale and her eyes were blank. The back-up cops held an elbow each. They brought her down the steps and walked her over to their cruiser. The trooper opened the rear door and the sergeant placed a hand on the top of her head and folded her inside. The trooper closed the door on her.

The back-up cops climbed into their cruiser and started it up. The first two slid into the front of Reacher's car and did the same. They waited for the back-up to ease ahead, then followed it out to the gate and accelerated north.

'Where are they taking her?' Reacher called.

'Pecos,' the sergeant said. 'County jail.'

'But this is Echo,' Reacher said. 'Not Pecos.'

'There are a hundred and fifty people in Echo County. You think they operate a separate jurisdiction just for them? With jails and all? And courthouses?'

'Well, that's going to be a real big problem,' Reacher said.

'Why?'

'Because Hack Walker is the Pecos DA. And he was Sloop Greer's buddy. So he'll be prosecuting the person who shot his friend.'

'Worried about a conflict of interest?'

'Aren't you?'

'Not really,' the sergeant said. 'We know Hack. He's not a fool. He sees some defence counsel about to nail him for an impropriety, he'll pass on it. He'll have to—what's the word— excuse himself?'

'Recuse,' Reacher said.

'Whatever. He'll give it to an assistant. And both the Pecos ADAs are women, actually. So a self-defence thing will get some sympathy.'

'It doesn't need sympathy,' Reacher said. 'It's plain as day.'

'And bear in mind Hack's running for judge in November,' the sergeant said. 'Lots of Mexican votes in Pecos County. He won't let anybody do anything that'll make him look bad in the newspaper. So she's lucky. A Mexican woman shoots a white man in Echo, gets tried for it by a woman ADA in Pecos, couldn't be better for her.'

'She's from California,' Reacher said. 'She's not Mexican.'

'But she looks Mexican,' the sergeant said. 'That's what's important to a guy who needs votes in Pecos County.'

The two State Police cruisers drove on in convoy. They passed the ambulance just short of the crossroads. Left it lumbering in their wake.

'The morgue's in Pecos, too,' the sergeant said. 'One of the oldest institutions in town, I guess. They needed it right from the get-go. Pecos was that kind of a place.'

'Carmen told me,' Reacher said. 'It was the real Wild West.'

'You going to stick around?'

'I guess so. I need to see she's OK. She told me there's a museum in town. Things to see. Somebody's grave.'

'Clay Allison's,' the sergeant said. 'Some old gunslinger.'

'Never killed a man who didn't need killing.'

The sergeant nodded in the mirror. 'That could be her position, right? She could call it the Clay Allison defence.'

'Why not? It was justifiable homicide, any way you cut it.'

The sergeant said nothing to that.

'Should be enough to make bail, at least,' Reacher said. 'She's got a kid back there. She needs bail, like tomorrow.'

'Tomorrow could be tough,' the sergeant said. 'There's a dead guy in the picture, after all. Who's her lawyer?'

'Hasn't got one.'

'She got money for one?'

'No.'

'Well, shit,' the sergeant said. 'How old is the kid?'

'Six. Why?'

'Having no lawyer is a big problem, is what. Kid's going to be seven and a half before Mom even gets a bail *hearing*.'

'She'll get a lawyer, right?'

'Constitution says so. But the question is, when? This is Texas.'

'You ask for a lawyer, you don't get one right away?'

'Not right away. You wait a long time. You get one when the indictment comes back. And that's how Hack Walker is going to avoid his little conflict problem, isn't it? He'll lock her up and forget about her. She's got no lawyer, who's to know? Could be Christmas before they get round to indicting her. By which time Hack will be a judge, most likely, not a prosecutor. No more conflict of interest. So don't spend your time at the museum. You want to help her, find her a lawyer.'

Nobody spoke the rest of the way into Pecos County. Eventually the sergeant slowed and let the back-up disappear ahead into the darkness. He pulled off onto the shoulder. 'We're back on patrol from here,' he said. 'Time to let you out.'

'Can't you drive me to the jail?'

'You're not going to jail. And we're not a taxicab company.'

'So where am I?'

The sergeant pointed straight ahead. 'Downtown Pecos,' he said. 'Couple miles, that way.'

'Where's the jail?'

'Crossroads before the railroad. In the courthouse basement.'

The sergeant opened his door and slid out. Opened Reacher's door. Reacher slid out and stood up.

'You take care, now,' the sergeant said. He climbed back into his seat and slammed his door. The car crunched its way back to the blacktop. Reacher watched its taillights disappear in the east. Then he set off walking north, towards the neon glow of Pecos.

He walked through one pool of light after another, along a strip of motels that got smarter and more expensive the further he moved away from the highway. Then there was a rodeo arena set back from the street. He walked in the road because the sidewalks had long tables set up on them, like outdoor market stalls. They were empty. But he could smell cantaloupe on the hot night air.

Beyond the market were a doughnut shop and a pizza parlour, both dark and closed. Sunday, the middle of the night, miles from anywhere. At the end of the strip was a crossroads, with a sign showing the museum was straight across. But before the turn was the courthouse. He ducked round to the back. No jail he had ever seen had an entrance on the street. There was a lit doorway in the back wall with two steps leading down from a parking area. The lot was fenced with razor wire and in one corner was a dusty Chevrolet. The jail door was steel and had NO ADMITTANCE stencilled across it. Above it was a small video camera angled down, with a red diode glowing above the lens.

He went down the steps and knocked on the door. Stepped back so the camera could pick him up. After a long moment, there was the click of a lock and a woman opened the door. She was dressed in a court bailiff's uniform. She was white, heavy, maybe fifty, with grey hair dyed the colour of sand. She had a wide belt loaded with a gun and a nightstick and a can of pepper spray. She looked on the ball.

'Yes?' she said.

'You got Carmen Greer in here?'

'Yes.'

'Can I see her?'

'No.'

'So when can I?'

'You a lawyer?'

'No.'

'Then Saturday,' she said. 'Visiting is Saturday, two to four.'

Almost a week.

'Can you write that down for me?' he said. He wanted to get inside. 'Maybe give me a list of what I'm allowed to bring her?'

The bailiff shrugged, turned and stepped inside. Reacher followed her into a lobby. Behind a high desk were cubbyholes. He saw Carmen's lizard-skin belt rolled in one of them. There was a small Ziplock bag with the fake ring in it.

The bailiff pulled a mimeographed sheet from a stack. Slid it across the top of the desk. 'And don't bring her anything that's not on the list, or we won't let you in.'

'Where's the DA's office?'

She pointed at the ceiling. 'Next floor. Go in the front.'

'When does it open?'

'About eight thirty.'

'You got lawyers in the neighbourhood?'

'Cheap lawyers or expensive lawyers?'

'Free lawyers.'

She smiled. 'Turn left at the crossroads. That's all it is, bondsmen and community lawyers.'

'Sure I can't see her? Even for a minute?'

'Not even.'

'When will you see her?'

'Every fifteen minutes. Suicide watch, though I don't think your friend is the type. She's a tough cookie.'

'Tell her Reacher was here. Tell her I'll stick around.'

The woman nodded. 'I'm sure she'll be thrilled,' she said.

REACHER WALKED almost all the way back to the highway, until the prices ducked under thirty bucks. Picked a place, woke the night clerk and bought the key to a room.

He slept until seven in the morning, showered and went to the doughnut shop. It was open and advertised Texas-sized doughnuts. He ate two with three cups of coffee. Then he went looking for clothes. Since he ended his brief flirtation with owning a house he had gone back to his preferred system of buying cheap items and junking them instead of laundering them.

He found a cheap store that sold a bit of everything. He found chinos, a khaki shirt, white underwear. The store had no fitting rooms. The clerk let him use the staff bathroom. He put on the new gear and transferred his stuff from pocket to pocket. He still had the eight shell cases from Carmen's Lorcin, rattling around like loose change. He weighed them in his hand and dropped them in his new trouser pocket.

He balled up the old clothes and stuffed them in the bathroom trash. Went back out to the till and paid thirty bucks in cash.

He waited on the sidewalk until eight o'clock, leaning against a wall under an awning to stay out of the sun. He figured the bailiffs would change shifts at eight. Sure enough, at five minutes past he saw the heavy woman drive out of the lot in the Chevrolet. She made a left and drove right past him. He crossed the street and walked down the side of the courthouse again. If the night shift won't help, maybe the day shift will.

But the day worker was just as bad. He was a man, a little younger, thinner, but otherwise the equivalent of his ópposite number. He confirmed only lawyers were allowed unrestricted access to prisoners. So Reacher came back up the steps and went looking for a lawyer.

He turned left at the crossroads and hit a strip that might have started out as anything but now was made up of low-rent operations serving the courthouse population: bail bondsmen and storefront legal missions, like the bailiff had said. The legal missions all had rows of desks facing the store windows with customer chairs in front of them and waiting areas inside the doors. Twenty past eight in the morning, they were all busy. All the clients were Hispanic. So were some of the lawyers, but overall they were a mixed bunch. Men, women, young, old, bright, defeated. The only thing they had in common was they all looked harassed to breaking point.

He chose the only establishment that had an empty chair in front of a lawyer. It was halfway down the street. The lawyer was a young white woman of maybe twenty-five with thick dark hair cut short. She had a good tan and was wearing a white sports bra instead of a shirt and there was a leather jacket over the back of her chair. She was on the phone, and on the point of tears.

He approached her desk and sat down. She kept on talking into the phone. She had dark eyes and white teeth. She was talking slow Spanish with an East Coast accent, haltingly enough that he could follow it. She was saying *Yes, we won but he won't pay. He just refuses.* Time to time she would stop and listen, then she would repeat herself. *We won, but he still won't pay.* Then she listened again. The question must have been *So what do we do now?* because she said *We go back to court, to enforce the judgment.* Then the question was obviously *How long does that take?* because she said *A year. Maybe two.* Reacher watched the woman's face. She was upset and embarrassed. Blinking back tears of bitter frustration. She said '*Llamaré de nuevo más tarde,*' and hung up. *I'll call again soon.*

Then she faced front and closed her eyes and breathed deeply through her nose, in and out, in and out. She opened her eyes and dropped a file into a drawer and focused across the desk at Reacher.

'Problem?' he asked her.

She shrugged and nodded all at the same time. 'Winning the case is only half the battle,' she said. 'Sometimes a lot less than half.'

'So what happened? Some guy won't pay up?' Reacher said.

She shrugged and nodded again. 'A rancher,' she said. 'Crashed his car into my client's truck. Injured my client and his wife and two of his children. He was on his way back from a party, drunk. They were on their way to market. It was harvest time and they couldn't work the fields and lost their whole crop.'

'Cantaloupe?'

'Bell peppers, actually. Rotted on the vine. We sued and won twenty thousand dollars. But the guy won't pay. He just refuses. He's waiting them out. He plans to starve them back to Mexico, and he will, because if we have to go back to court it'll take at least another year and they can't live another year on fresh air.'

'They didn't have insurance?'

'Premiums are too expensive. These people are barely scratching a living. All we could do was proceed directly against the rancher.'

'Tough break,' Reacher said.

'Unbelievable,' she said. 'The things these people go through, you just wouldn't believe it. This family I'm telling you about, the Border Patrol killed their eldest son.'

'They did?'

She nodded. 'Twelve years ago. They were illegals. They're walking north at night, and a patrol chases them in the dark with rifles and kills their eldest boy. They bury him and walk on.'

'Anything get done about it?'

'You kidding? They were illegals. They couldn't do anything. It happened all the time. And now they're settled and been through the immigration amnesty, we try to get them to trust the law, and then something like this happens. Anyway, how can I help you?'

'Not me,' Reacher said. 'A woman I know.'

'She needs a lawyer?'

'She shot her husband. He was abusing her.'

'When?'

'Last night. She's across the street, in jail.'

'Is he dead?'

Reacher nodded. 'As a doornail.'

Her shoulders sagged. She opened a drawer and took out a yellow pad. 'What's your name?' she asked.

'Reacher,' he said. 'What's your name?'

She wrote *Reacher* on the pad, first line.

'Alice,' she said. 'Alice Amanda Aaron.'

'You should go into private practice. You'd be first in the Yellow Pages.'

She smiled, just a little. 'One day, I will,' she said. 'This is a five-year bargain with my conscience.'

'Paying your dues?'

'Atoning,' she said. 'For my good fortune. For going to Harvard Law. For coming from a family where twenty thousand dollars is a month's common charge on the Park Avenue co-op instead of life or death during the winter in Texas.'

'Good for you, Alice,' he said.

'So tell me about your woman friend.'

'She's of Mexican heritage. Her husband was white. Her name is Carmen Greer and her husband was Sloop Greer. The abuse stopped for the last year and a half because he was in prison for tax evasion. He got out yesterday and started it up again and she shot him. Evidence and witnesses are going to be hard to find. The abuse was covert.'

'Injuries?' Alice asked, writing it all down.

'Fairly severe. But she always passed them off as accidental, to do with horses. Like she fell off them.'

'Why?'

Reacher shrugged. 'I don't know. Coercion, maybe.'

'But there's no doubt the abuse happened?'

'Not in my mind. And she needs bail. Today.'

'Bail?' Alice repeated, like it was a foreign word. 'Today? Forget it.'

'She's got a kid. A little girl called Ellie, six years old.'

'Doesn't help,' she said. 'Everybody's got kids. Only two ways to get bail in a case like this. First is we stage essentially the whole trial at the bail hearing. And we're not ready to do that. It'll be months before I can even *start* working on it. My calendar is full. And even when I *can* start, it'll take months to prepare, in these circumstances.'

'What circumstances?'

'Her word against a dead man's reputation. If we've got no eyewitnesses, we'll have to subpoena her medical records and find experts who can testify her injuries weren't caused by falling off horses. And clearly she's got no money, or you wouldn't be in here on her behalf, so we're going to have to find experts who'll appear for free. Which isn't impossible, but it can't be done in a hurry.'

'So what can be done in a hurry?'

'I can run over to the jail and say, "Hi, I'm your lawyer, I'll see you again in a year." That's about all can be done in a hurry.'

Reacher glanced around the room. It was teeming with people.

'Nobody else will be faster,' Alice said. 'I'm relatively new here. I've got less of a backlog.'

It seemed to be true. She had just two head-high stacks of files on her desk. The others all had three or four or five.

'You said there were two ways of getting bail.'

'Second way is we convince the DA not to oppose it. If we stand up and ask for bail and he stands up and says he has no objection, then all that matters is whether the judge thinks it's appropriate. And the judge will be influenced by the DA's position, probably.'

'Hack Walker was Sloop Greer's oldest buddy.'

Alice's shoulders sagged again. 'Great. He'll recuse himself, obviously. But his staff will go to bat for him. So forget bail.'

'But will you take the case?'

'Sure. That's what we do here. We take cases. So I'll call Hack's office, and I'll go see Carmen. But that's all I can do right now.'

Reacher shook his head. 'Not good enough, Alice,' he said. 'I want you to get to work right now. Make something happen.'

'I can't,' she said. 'Not for months. I told you that.'

'You interested in a deal?' he asked.

'A deal?'

'I could recover the twenty grand for your pepper growers. Today. And then you could start work for Carmen Greer. Today.'

'What are you, a debt collector?'

'No, but just suppose the next time you saw me I was walking back in here with a cheque for twenty grand in my pocket.'

'How would you do that?'

He shrugged. 'I'd just go ask for it. Who's the rancher?'

She glanced at the drawer. Shook her head. 'I can't tell you,' she said. 'I'm worried about the ethics.'

'I'm offering,' he said. 'You're not asking.'

She looked straight at him. 'I have to go to the bathroom,' she said. She stood up suddenly and walked away. She was wearing denim shorts and was taller than he had guessed. Short shorts, long legs. A fine tan. Walking, she looked pretty good from the back. She went through a door in the rear of the old store. He stood up, leaned over the desk and pulled open the drawer. Lifted the top file out. Shuffled through to a deposition. There was a name and address typed neatly in a box labelled DEFENDANT. He folded the paper and put it in his shirt pocket. Closed the file and dropped it back in the drawer. Shut the drawer and sat down. A moment later Alice Amanda Aaron came out through the rear door and walked back to the desk. She looked pretty good from the front, too.

'Any place around here I can borrow a car?' he asked her.

'Well, you can borrow mine, I guess,' she said. 'It's in the lot, behind the building.' She fiddled in her jacket pocket, behind her. Came out with a set of keys. 'It's a VW. There are maps in the glove box. You know, in case a person isn't familiar with the area.'

He took the keys and pushed back from the desk. 'Maybe I'll catch you later,' he said. He stood up and walked through the quiet crowd of people and out into the sun.

ALICE'S CAR was the only VW in the lot behind the building. It was a new-shape Beetle, bright yellow, New York plates, and there was more than a bunch of maps in the glove compartment. There was a handgun in there, too. It was a Heckler & Koch P7M10, four-inch barrel, ten .40 calibre shells.

Reacher racked the seat back and fired the engine up. He took the maps out of the glove box and spread them on the seat beside him. Took the folded paper from his shirt pocket and checked the maps for the rancher's address. It seemed to be somewhere northeast of town, maybe an hour away.

The VW had a manual transmission with a sharp clutch and he stalled twice before he got the hang of it. The map showed seven ways out of Pecos. He had come in on the southernmost, and it didn't have what he was looking for. The town's centre of gravity seemed to be lumped to the east of the crossroads, therefore east would be wrong. So he drove west away from the lawyers and found exactly what he wanted. Every town has a strip of auto dealers clustered together on one of the approaches, and Pecos was no different.

He cruised the strip looking for the right kind of place. There were two possibilities. Both had signs offering FOREIGN CAR SERVICE. Both of them offered FREE LOANERS. He chose the place further out of town. It had a used-car business in front. Behind the sales lot was a low shed with hydraulic hoists.

He drove the VW into the shed. Three mechanics drifted over. One looked like a foreman. Reacher asked him to adjust the VW's clutch so its action would be softer. The guy said it would cost forty bucks. Reacher agreed the price and asked for a loaner. The guy led him behind the shed and pointed to an ancient Chrysler LeBaron convertible. Reacher took Alice's gun with him, wrapped up in her maps. He placed it on the Chrysler's passenger seat. Then he asked the mechanic for a tow rope.

'What you want to tow?' the guy asked.

'Nothing,' Reacher said. 'I just want the rope, is all.'

The guy shrugged and walked away. Came back with a coil of rope. Reacher put it in the passenger footwell. Then he drove the LeBaron back into town and out again heading northeast.

He stopped in empty country, to unscrew the Chrysler's plates with a coin from his pocket. He stored them on the floor on the passenger's side, next to the rope. Then he drove on.

The rancher's name was listed on the legal paper as Lyndon J. Brewer. His address was just a route number, which Alice's map showed was a stretch of road that ran about forty miles before it disappeared into New Mexico. It was a dusty blacktop ribbon with a string of drooping power lines. The road was crossed by another and the resulting crossroads had a line of mailboxes laid out along a grey weathered plank. The mailboxes had people's names and ranch names on them together. BREWER was painted in black on a white box, and BIG HAT RANCH was painted right below it.

He found the entrance to Big Hat Ranch fifteen miles to the north. There was a fancy iron arch, painted white. He drove past it and stopped on the shoulder at the foot of the next power line pole. Got out of the car. There was a big transformer at the top of the pole where the line split off in a T and ran away at a right angle towards the ranch house. And, looping parallel all the way, about a foot lower down, the telephone line.

He took Alice's gun from under the maps on the passenger seat and the rope from the footwell. Tied one end of the rope into the trigger guard. Passed twenty feet of rope through his hands and swung the gun like a weight. Then he clamped the rope with his left hand and threw the gun with his right, aiming to slot it between the phone line and the electricity supply above it. The first time, he missed. The gun fell about a foot short. The second time it sailed through the gap and fell and snagged the rope over the wire. He lowered the gun. Untied it and tossed it back into the car and clamped the looped rope in both hands and pulled sharply. The phone line broke at the junction box and snaked to the ground.

He coiled the rope again and dropped it back in the footwell. Got in the car and backed up and turned in under the white-painted gate. Drove a mile down a driveway to a white-painted mansion. There were broad steps leading up to a double front door. He stopped the car, got out, went up the steps and rang the bell. Then he waited. He was about to use the bell again when the left-hand door opened. There was a maid standing there. She was dressed in a grey uniform and looked like she came from the Philippines.

'I'm here to see Lyndon Brewer,' Reacher said.

'Do you have an appointment?' the maid said.

'Yes, I do.'

'He didn't tell me.'

'He probably forgot,' Reacher said. 'I understand he's a bit of an asshole.'

Her face tensed. Not with shock. She was fighting a smile.

'Who shall I announce?'

'Rutherford B. Hayes,' Reacher said.

The maid paused and then smiled. 'He was the nineteenth President. The one after Ulysses S. Grant. Born 1822 in Ohio.'

'He's my ancestor,' Reacher said. 'Tell Mr Brewer I work for a bank in San Antonio and we just discovered stock in his grandfather's name worth a million dollars.'

The maid walked away and Reacher stepped through the door in time to see her climbing a wide staircase at the back of an entrance hall the size of a basketball court. The hall was hushed and cool, panelled in golden hardwood. The maid came back down the stairs, gliding, her hand just grazing the rail.

'He'll see you now. He's on the balcony, at the back of the house.'

There was an upstairs hall with the same dimensions and decor. French doors let out onto the rear balcony, which ran the width of the house. There was heavy wicker furniture arranged in a group. A man sat in a chair with a small table at his right hand. The table held a pitcher and a glass filled with what looked like lemonade. The man was a bull-necked guy of about sixty.

'Mr Hayes?' he called.

Reacher walked over and sat down without waiting for an invitation. 'You got children?' he asked.

'I have three sons,' Brewer replied.

'Any of them at home?'

'They're all away, working.'

'Your wife?'

'She's in Houston, visiting.'

'So it's just you and the maid today?'

'Why do you ask?' He was impatient and puzzled, but polite, like people are when you're about to give them a million dollars.

'I'm a banker,' Reacher said. 'I have to ask.'

'Tell me about the stock,' Brewer said.

'There is no stock. I lied about that.'

Brewer looked surprised. Then disappointed. Then irritated.

'So why are you here?' he asked.

'It's a technique we use. I'm really a loan officer. A person needs to borrow money, maybe he doesn't want his staff to know.'

'But I don't need to borrow money, Mr Hayes.'

'Really? We heard you had problems meeting your obligations.'

Brewer made the connection slowly. He put his hand down to the table and came back with a small silver bell. He shook it hard and it made a small tinkling sound. 'Maria!' he called.

The maid came soundlessly along the boards of the balcony.

'Call the police,' Brewer ordered. 'I want this man arrested.'

She ducked into the room directly behind Brewer's chair. It was a study. Reacher heard the sound of a phone being picked up, then rapid clicking as she tried to make it work.

'The phones are out,' she called.

'Go wait downstairs,' Reacher called back.

'What do you want?' Brewer asked.

'I want you to meet your legal obligation.'

Brewer started to stand up. Reacher put his arm out straight and shoved him back in his chair, hard enough to hurt.

'Sit still,' he said.

'Why are you doing this?'

'Because I'm a compassionate guy,' Reacher said. 'A family's in trouble. They're going to be worried all winter long. Disaster staring them in the face. Never knowing which day is going to bring everything crashing down around them. I don't like to see people living that way.'

'They don't like it, they should get back to Mexico, where they belong.'

Reacher glanced at him, surprised. 'I'm not talking about *them*,' he said. 'I'm talking about *you*. Your family.'

'My family?'

Reacher nodded. 'I stay mad at you, they'll all suffer. A car wreck here, a mugging there. You might fall down the stairs, break your leg. Or your wife might. The house might set on fire. Lots of accidents, one after the other. You'll never know when the next one is coming. It'll drive you crazy.'

'You couldn't get away with it.'

'I'm getting away with it right now. Give me that pitcher.'

Brewer hesitated. Then he picked it up and held it out. Reacher took it. It was fancy crystal and probably cost a thousand bucks. He tossed it over the balcony. There was a crash from the patio below.

'Oops,' he said.

'I'll have you arrested,' Brewer said. 'That's criminal damage.'

'Why? According to you, what the legal system says doesn't matter. Or does that only apply to you? Maybe you think you're special.'

Brewer said nothing. Reacher stood up and picked up his chair and threw it over the rail. It splintered on the stone below.

'Give me the cheque,' he said. 'You can afford it. You're rich.'

'It's a matter of principle,' Brewer said. 'They shouldn't be here.'

'And you should? Why? They were here first.'

'They lost. To us.'

'And now you're losing. To me.'

He bent down and picked up the silver bell from the table. It was probably an antique. Maybe two and a half inches in diameter. He held it between his thumb and fingers. Squeezed hard and crushed it out of shape. Transferred it into his palms and squashed the metal flat. Then he shoved it in Brewer's shirt pocket.

'Give me the cheque,' he said. 'Before I lose my temper.'

Brewer sighed. 'OK,' he said. He led the way into the study and over to the desk. Reacher stood behind him. He didn't want any revolvers appearing suddenly out of drawers.

'Make it out to cash,' he said.

Brewer wrote the cheque.

'It better not bounce,' Reacher said.

'It won't,' Brewer said.

'It does, you do, too. Off the patio.'

SEVEN

Reacher put the plates back on the LeBaron as soon as he was out of sight of the Brewer house. Then he drove back to Pecos and reclaimed Alice Aaron's VW from the mechanics. He paid them their forty bucks, but afterwards he wasn't sure they'd done anything to the car. The clutch felt as sharp as before.

He left it in the lot behind the building with the maps and the handgun in the glove box where he had found them. Entered the old store and found Alice at her desk. She was on the phone and there was a family in front of her. She had changed her clothes. Now she was wearing black linen trousers and a black jacket to match.

She saw him and put her hand over the phone and excused herself from her clients. He leaned down next to her.

'We've got problems,' she said. 'Hack Walker wants to see you.'

'Me?' he said. 'Why?'

'Better you hear it from him,' she said.

She turned back to the phone. He took the $20,000 cheque out of his pocket and smoothed it on the desktop. She saw it and stopped talking. He dropped her car keys on the desk and walked back out to the sidewalk. Turned right and headed for the courthouse.

THE PECOS COUNTY District Attorney's office occupied the whole of the courthouse's upper floor. There was an open area used as a secretarial pen, and beyond that were three offices, one for the DA and one for each of the assistants.

The secretarial pen had two desks, both occupied, the further one by a middle-aged woman who looked as if she belonged there, the nearer one by a young man who could have been an intern working his summer vacation from college. He looked up with a bright How-may-we-help-you? expression on his face.

'Hack Walker wants to see me,' Reacher said.

'Mr Reacher?' the kid asked.

Reacher nodded and the kid pointed to the corner office.

'He's expecting you,' he said.

Reacher threaded his way through to the corner office. The door had a plaque on it that read HENRY WALKER, DISTRICT ATTORNEY.

Reacher knocked once and went in without waiting for a reply.

The office had a mess of filing cabinets and a desk piled with paper and a computer and telephones. Walker was in his chair behind it, holding a framed photograph in both hands. He was staring at it. Serious distress on his face.

'What can I do for you?' Reacher asked.

Walker transferred his gaze from the photograph.

'Sit down,' he said. 'Please.'

There was a chair in front of the desk. Reacher turned it sideways to give himself some leg room. Walker propped the photograph on the desk so it was visible to both of them. It was the same shot Reacher had seen in Sloop Greer's closet. The three young men leaning on the old pick-up.

'Me and Sloop and Al Eugene,' Walker said. 'Now Al's a missing person and Sloop is dead.'

'No word on Eugene?'

Walker shook his head. 'Not a thing.'

'So what can I do for you?' Reacher asked again.

'I don't know, really,' Walker said. 'Maybe just listen awhile, maybe clarify some things for me.'

'What kind of things?'

Walker was quiet for a spell. 'I want to be a judge,' he said, 'because I could do some good. You familiar with how things work in Texas?'

'Not really.'

'Judges in Texas are elected. It's a weird state. A lot of rich people, but a lot of poor people too. The poor people need court-appointed lawyers, but there's no public defender system. The judges choose the poor people's lawyers for them, pick them from any law firm they want. They determine the fees, too. It's patronage, pure and simple. So who is the judge going to appoint? He's going to appoint somebody who contributed to his election campaign.'

'Not too good,' Reacher said.

'So I do two things,' Walker said. 'First, I aim to become a judge, so I can put things right. Second, right now, here in the DA's office we act out both sides. Every time, one of us assembles the prosecution case and another does the defence's work and tries to tear it down. We know nobody else will, and I couldn't sleep nights if we didn't.'

'Carmen Greer's defence is rock solid,' Reacher said.

'No, the Greer situation is a nightmare,' Walker said. 'For me personally, and as a candidate for a judgeship.'

'You have to recuse yourself.'

'Of course I'll recuse myself. But whatever happens, it's still my office. And that'll have repercussions for me.'

'You want to tell me what your problem is?'

'Don't you see? I'm looking at sending a Hispanic woman to death row. I do that, I can forget about the election. This county is heavily Hispanic. But I want to be a judge. And asking for the death penalty against a minority woman *now* will stop me dead.'

'So don't prosecute her. It wouldn't be justice, anyhow. Because it was self defence, pure and simple.'

'Let's talk it through,' Walker said. 'The spousal-abuse defence can work, but it has to be white-heat, spur-of-the-moment stuff. That's the law. There can't be premeditation. And Carmen premeditated like crazy. She bought the gun immediately she heard he was coming home. The paperwork comes through this office eventually, so I know that's true. She was ready and waiting to ambush him.'

Reacher said nothing.

'I know her,' Walker said. 'Obviously, I know her. Sloop was my friend, so I've known her as long as he did, near enough.'

'And?'

'I'm just going to take a few guesses, OK? And I don't want you to respond. Not a word. It might put you in a difficult position.'

'Difficult how?'

'You'll see, later. She probably told you she comes from a rich wine-growing family north of San Francisco, right?'

Reacher said nothing.

'She told you she met Sloop at UCLA, Sloop got her pregnant, they had to get married and her parents cut her off.'

Reacher said nothing.

'She told you Sloop hit her from the time she was pregnant. She said there were serious injuries that Sloop made her pass off as riding accidents.'

Reacher said nothing.

'She claimed it was her who tipped off the IRS, which made her all the more frantic about Sloop coming home.'

Reacher said nothing.

'OK,' Walker said. 'Now strictly speaking, anything she told you is hearsay and inadmissible in court. But in a situation like this, her lawyer will try to get the hearsay admitted, because it goes to her state of mind. And there *are* provisions that might allow it. So let's say you were allowed to testify. You'd paint a pretty horrible picture.'

'So where's the problem?'

'Problem is, if you testified, you'd be cross-examined too.'

'So?'

Walker looked down at the desk. 'Let me take a couple more guesses. Don't respond. And if I'm wrong, don't be offended. If I'm wrong, I apologise most sincerely in advance. OK?'

'OK.'

'My guess is the premeditation was extensive. My guess is she thought about it and then she tried to recruit you to do it for her.'

Reacher said nothing. Walker swallowed.

'Another guess,' he said. 'She offered you sex as a bribe.'

Reacher said nothing.

'You see?' Walker said. 'If I'm right, that stuff would come out too, under cross-examination. Evidence of thorough preparation.'

Reacher said nothing.

'It gets worse,' Walker said. 'Because if she's told you things, what matters is her *credibility*, right? Specifically, was she telling you the truth about the abuse? We'd test that by asking you questions we *do* know the answers to. We'd ask you innocent stuff first, like who she is and where she's from, and you'd tell us what she told you.'

'And?'

'And her credibility would fall apart.'

'Why?'

'Because I *know* this woman, and she makes things up. I've heard her stories, over and over. Did she in fact tell you she's from a rich wine-growing family?'

Reacher nodded. 'More or less. She said she's from a thousand acres in the Napa Valley. Isn't she?'

'She's from some barrio in South Central LA. Nobody knows anything about her parents. She probably doesn't, either.'

Reacher shrugged. 'Disguising a humble background isn't a crime.'

'She was never a student at UCLA. She was a stripper. She was a whore, Reacher. She serviced the UCLA fraternity parties. Sloop met her when she was performing. He fell for her. You know, *Let me take you away from all this*, sort of thing. She looked at Sloop and saw a meal ticket. She went to live with him. Came off the pill and lied about it and got pregnant. Whereupon Sloop did the decent thing.'

'Even if it *is* true, does it justify him hitting her?' Reacher said.

'Of course not,' Walker said. 'But he didn't hit her. I *knew* Sloop.

He was a lot of things, and to be truthful, not all of them good. He was lazy, a little casual in business. A little dishonest. But all his faults came from the feeling he was a Texan gentleman. I'm very aware of that, because I was a poor boy by comparison. It made him a little arrogant, but part of being a gentleman in Texas is you would *never, ever* hit a woman. Whoever the woman was.'

'What else would you say? You were his friend.'

Walker nodded. 'I take your point. But there's nothing else to go on. No evidence, no witnesses, nothing. We were close. I was with them a thousand times. I heard about the horseback-riding accidents as they happened. There weren't *that* many, and they seemed genuine. We'll ask for the medical records, of course, but don't hold out much hope they'll be ambiguous.'

'Abuse can be covert.'

'*That* covert? Sloop and Carmen saw friends every day. And before you told the story to Alice Aaron, nobody in Texas had heard the faintest whiff of a rumour about violence between them. So all we've got is her word. You're the only other person who ever heard it. But if you take the stand to back her up, then the *other* stuff you'll have to say will prove she's a liar. Like, *did* she say she'd tipped off the IRS?'

'Yes, she did. She said she called them. Some special unit.'

Walker shook his head. 'They caught him through bank records. It was an accidental by-product of an audit on somebody else. I know that because Sloop went straight to Al Eugene and Al came straight to me for advice. I saw the indictment. Carmen is a liar, Reacher.'

'So why are we talking?'

'Because I'm not an angry friend trying to protect my buddy's reputation. If her motive was something real cold, like money, she has to go down. But if her medical records are remotely plausible, I want to try to save her with the abuse thing.'

Reacher said nothing.

'OK, what I really mean is I want to try to save myself,' Walker said. 'Try to save my chances in the election. Or both things, OK? Her *and* me. Ellie, too.'

'So what would you want from me?'

'If we go down that road, I'd want you to lie on the stand,' Walker said. 'I'd want you to repeat what she told you about the beatings, and modify what she told you about everything else, in order to preserve her credibility.'

'I don't know,' Reacher said.

'I don't, either. But maybe it won't have to go all the way to trial. If the medical evidence is a little flexible, and we take a deposition from Carmen, and one from you, then maybe dropping the charges altogether would be justified.'

'You sure?'

Walker sighed. 'No, I'm not *sure*. I hate this whole thing. But Sloop's dead. Nothing's going to bring him back. It'll trash his memory. But it would save Carmen. And he loved her, Reacher. In a way nobody else could understand. The disapproval he brought down on himself was unbelievable. From his family, from polite society. He'd be happy to exchange his reputation for her life, I think.'

Reacher shrugged and stood up. 'Get back to me,' he said. Then he turned round and walked out of the room.

'So YES OR NO about Carmen and Sloop?' Alice said.

'She convinced me,' Reacher said. 'No doubt about it.'

They were on opposite sides of Alice's desk in the legal mission. It was the middle of the day, and the heat was so brutal it was enforcing a siesta on the whole town. The humidity was rising. The ancient air conditioner above the door was making no difference at all. Alice had changed into shorts again. She was leaning back in her chair, arms above her head, her back arched off the sticky vinyl. She was slick with sweat from head to foot. Over the tan it made her skin look oiled. Reacher's shirt was soaked.

Alice looked at him. 'You understand the exact legalities here?'

He nodded. 'If there *was* abuse, she's blown it by being so premeditated. If there *wasn't*, then it's murder one. And whatever, she has zero credibility because she lies and exaggerates. Ball game over, if Walker didn't want to be judge so bad.'

'Exactly,' Alice said.

'You happy about riding that kind of luck?'

'No,' Alice said. 'Not morally, not practically. Maybe Hack's got a love child somewhere, and it'll come out and he'll have to withdraw anyway. It's a long time until November. Counting on him to stay electable would be foolish. His tactical problem with Carmen could disappear at any time. So she needs a properly structured defence.'

Reacher smiled. 'You're even smarter than I figured.'

'You need to stay off the stand,' she said. 'Safer for her. Without you, the gun is the only thing that suggests premeditation. And we should be able to argue that *buying* the gun and *using* it weren't necessarily connected. Maybe she bought it for another reason.'

Reacher said nothing.

'They're testing it at the lab,' she said. 'Ballistics and fingerprints. Two sets of prints, they say. Hers, I guess, maybe his too. Maybe they struggled over it. Maybe the whole thing was an accident.'

Reacher shook his head. 'The second set must be mine. She asked me to teach her how to shoot. We went to the gulch and practised.'

'When?'

'Saturday. The day before he got home.'

'Christ, Reacher,' she said. 'What if they subpoena you?'

'Then I'll lie, I guess. It wouldn't be a totally radical concept.'

'What would you say about your prints on the gun?'

'I'd say I found it dumped somewhere. Innocently gave it back to her. Make it look like she had reconsidered after buying it.'

'You comfortable with saying stuff like that?'

'If the ends justify the means, I am. You?'

She nodded. 'I guess so.'

'So where do we start?'

'We back-pedal on the premeditation, then we prove the abuse through medical records. I've started the paperwork. We joined the DA's office for a common-cause subpoena. All Texas hospitals and all neighbouring states. Domestic violence, that's standard procedure, because people sometimes drive all over to hide it. The hospitals generally react fast, so we should get the records overnight. If the injuries *were* caused by violence, then the records will at least show they *could* have been. With careful jury selection, we'll get at least half and half don't-knows and not-guiltys. The not-guiltys will wear down the don't-knows within a couple of days. Especially if it's this hot.'

Reacher pulled the soaked fabric of his shirt off his skin. 'Can't stay this hot much longer, can it?'

'Hey, I'm talking about *next* summer,' Alice said.

He stared at her. 'You're kidding. What about Ellie?'

She shrugged. 'Just pray the medical records look good. If they do, we've got a shot at getting Hack to drop the charges altogether.'

'When are you going to go see her?'

'Later this afternoon. First I'm going to the bank to cash a twenty-thousand-dollar cheque. Then I'm going to put the money in a grocery bag and deliver it. You should come with me and be my bodyguard. Not every day I carry twenty thousand dollars around.'

'OK,' Reacher said.

THE BANK SHOWED no particular excitement about forking over twenty grand in mixed bills. The teller just counted the money three times and stacked it in a brown-paper grocery bag Alice provided for the purpose. Reacher carried it back to the parking lot for her.

The interior of the VW had heated up to the point where they couldn't get in right away. Alice started the air going and left the doors open until the blowers took thirty degrees off it. Then they slid inside. Alice drove.

'You ever felt heat like this before?' she asked.

'Maybe,' he said. 'Once or twice. Saudi Arabia, the Pacific.'

She asked him when he'd been there, and he responded with the expanded ten-minute version of his autobiography because he found he was enjoying her company. The first thirty-six years made a nicely linear tale of accomplishment and progress. The last few years were harder, as usual. The aimlessness, the drifting. He saw them as a triumph of disengagement, but he knew other people didn't. So as always he just told the story and let her think whatever she wanted.

She turned onto a farm track passing through a few acres of cultivated ground. There were rows of turned earth, an improvised irrigation system, and wooden frames to carry wires to support the bushes that no longer grew. Everything was dry and crisp and fallow.

There was a house a hundred yards beyond the last row of turned earth. It was small and low. There was a barn, with an irrigation pump venting through the roof, and a damaged three-quarter-ton truck. Alice parked next to it.

'They're called García,' she said. 'I'm sure they're home.'

TWENTY THOUSAND DOLLARS in a grocery bag had an effect like he'd never seen before. It was literally a gift of life. There were five Garcías, two generations, two in the older and three in the younger. The parents were maybe in their late forties and the offspring were a girl and two boys in their twenties. They all stood quietly together inside the doorway. Alice said a bright hello and walked straight past them and spilled the money on their kitchen table.

'He changed his mind,' she said, in Spanish.

The Garcías formed a semicircle round the table, silent, looking at the money. They didn't ask questions. Just accepted it had finally happened and then burst out with a long list of plans. First, they would get the telephone and electricity reconnected. Then they would pay back what they had borrowed. They would buy diesel for the irrigation pump. Then they would get their truck fixed and drive to town for seed and fertiliser.

Reacher hung back and looked around the room. It opened to a front parlour. The parlour had a yard-long encyclopedia set and a bunch of religious statuettes on a shelf. A single picture on the wall. The photograph of a boy, maybe fourteen, smiling shyly. The picture was in a black frame and had a dusty square of black fabric round it.

'My eldest son,' a voice said. 'That picture was made just before we left our village in Mexico.'

Reacher turned and found the mother standing behind him.

'He was killed, on the journey here,' she said.

Reacher nodded. 'I heard. The Border Patrol. I'm very sorry.'

'It was twelve years ago. His name was Raoul.'

'What happened?' Reacher asked.

'It was awful,' she said. 'They hunted us for three hours in the night. We were walking and running, they had a truck with bright lights. We got split up, in the dark. Raoul was with his sister. She was twelve. He sent her one way and walked the other way, into the lights. He knew it was worse if they captured girls. They didn't try to arrest him. Just shot him down and drove away. They came near where I was hiding. They were laughing. Like it was a sport.'

'I'm very sorry,' Reacher said again.

The woman shrugged. 'It was a bad time, a bad area. We found that out later. More than twenty people were killed on that route in a year. Some of the girls were carried away and never seen again.'

The woman gazed at the picture a moment longer, then she forced a smile and gestured that Reacher should rejoin the party in the kitchen. 'We have tequila,' she said. 'Saved especially for this day.'

There were shot glasses on the table, and the daughter was filling them from a bottle. The girl that Raoul had saved, all grown up.

The tequila was rough and Raoul's memory was everywhere, so they refused a second shot and left the Garcías alone with their celebrations. They headed back to Pecos.

'Did the Border Patrol ever get investigated?' he asked.

She nodded. 'Thoroughly, according to the record.'

'And?'

'And nothing. It was a whitewash. Nobody was even indicted.'

'But did it stop?'

'As suddenly as it started. So obviously they got the message.'

THEY MADE IT BACK to Pecos inside an hour and found Alice's desk covered in little handwritten notes. She read them through.

'I'm going to check in with Carmen at the jail,' she said. 'But the prints and ballistics are back from the lab. Hack Walker wants to see you about them.'

They walked to the door and braved the scorching sidewalk. They split up in front of the courthouse. Alice walked on towards the jailhouse entrance and Reacher went up the front steps and inside. Upstairs, the intern pointed silently to Hack Walker's door. Reacher went straight in and found Walker studying a technical report.

'She killed him,' he said. 'Everything matches.'

Reacher sat down in front of the desk.

'Your prints were on the gun, too,' Walker said. 'You're in the national fingerprint database. You know that?'

Reacher nodded. 'All military personnel are.'

'So maybe you found the gun discarded,' Walker said. 'Maybe you picked it up and put it away in a place of safety.'

'Maybe,' Reacher said.

'You a praying man?'

'No,' Reacher said.

'You should be. You should get on your knees and thank somebody. Maybe the State cops. Maybe Sloop for calling the sheriff.'

'Why?'

'They saved your life. You were in a squad car when this went down. If they'd left you in the bunkhouse, you'd be number-one suspect.'

'Why?'

'Your prints were on the gun,' Walker said again. '*And* on every one of the shell cases. *And* on the magazine. *And* on the ammunition box. You loaded that gun, Reacher. Probably test-fired it too, they think, then reloaded it ready for action. She bought it, so it was technically *her* possession, but it was effectively *your* weapon.'

Reacher said nothing.

'You knew where the bedroom was, didn't you? I talked to Bobby. Did you really think he'd just sit quiet in the barn? He probably watched you two going at it, through the window.'

'I didn't sleep with her,' Reacher said. 'I was on the sofa.'

Walker smiled. 'Think a jury would believe you? Or an ex-whore? I don't. We could easily prove some kind of a sexual jealousy motive. So you're a lucky man, Reacher.'

Reacher said nothing. Walker sighed. 'So *now* what have I got? The premeditation thing is going from bad to worse. Clearly she thought and thought, even to the extent of hooking up with some ex-army guy to give her weapons training. We got your record. You were a pistol-shooting champ two straight years. What am I going to do?'

'What you planned,' Reacher said. 'Wait for the medical reports.'

Walker went quiet. Then he nodded. 'We'll have them tomorrow. And you know what? I've hired a defence expert to look at them. Because I want somebody to persuade me there's a faint possibility Carmen's telling the truth, so I can let her go without looking crazy.'

'So relax,' Reacher said. 'It'll be over tomorrow.'

'I hope so,' Walker said. 'Al Eugene's office is sending over some financial stuff. Al did all that kind of work for Sloop. If there's no financial motive and the medical reports are good, maybe I *can* relax.'

'She had no money,' Reacher said. 'It was one of her problems.'

'Good,' Walker said. 'Because *her* problems solve *my* problems.'

'You should be more proactive,' Reacher said. 'With the election.'

'Yeah, how?'

'Do something popular.'

'Like what?'

'Like reopen something about the Border Patrol. People would like that. I just met a family whose son was murdered by them.'

Walker just shook his head. 'Ancient history.'

'Not to those families,' Reacher said. 'There were twenty-some homicides in a year. Most of the survivors live around here, probably. And most of them will be voters by now.'

'The Border Patrol was investigated,' Walker said. 'Before my time, but it was pretty damn thorough. I went through the files years ago.'

'You have the files?'

'Sure. Mostly happened down in Echo, and all that stuff comes here. It was clearly a bunch of rogue officers, and the investigation most likely served to warn them off. They probably quit. Border Patrol has a pretty good turnover of staff. The bad guys could be anywhere by now.'

'OK,' Reacher said. 'Your decision.'

He went out through the hot trapped air in the stairwell and stepped outside. It was hotter still on the sidewalk. He made it down to the mission with sweat running into his eyes. He pushed in through the door and found Alice sitting alone at her desk.

'You back already?' he said, surprised. 'Did you see her?'

She nodded.

'What did she say?'

'She doesn't want me to represent her,' Alice said.

'Why the hell not?'

'I don't know. She didn't say. She was fairly calm, fairly rational.'

'Did you try to persuade her?'

'Of course I did. To a point. But I wanted to get out of there before she lost it and started hollering. A witness hears her say it, I lose all standing. I plan to go back and try again later.'

'Did you tell her I sent you?'

'Sure I did. Made no difference.'

'Go back about seven, OK?' Reacher said. 'When the upstairs offices are empty and before the night shift woman comes on. She struck me as nosier than the day guy. He probably won't pay much attention. So you can press her some. Let her holler, if she wants.'

'OK,' she said. 'Seven o'clock it is. Where will I find you?'

'I'm in the last motel before the highway. Room eleven, name of Millard Fillmore.'

'Who is Millard Fillmore?'

'President, three before Abraham Lincoln. From New York.'

He left her and walked as far as the pizza parlour. He went in and ordered iced water and an anchovy pizza, heavy on the fish. He figured his body needed to replace salt.

AS HE ATE IT, a new description was being passed to the killing crew. The call was rerouted through Dallas and Las Vegas to a motel room a hundred miles from Pecos. The call was made by a man. It contained a detailed identification of a supplementary job in the Pecos area, a new target, a male, starting with his name and age, and accompanied by a run-down of his physical appearance and likely destinations within the next forty-eight hours.

The information was taken by the woman. She made no notes. She listened until the caller stopped talking and then she named the crew's price. Then she listened to the silence on the other end. Listened to the guy deciding whether to negotiate the cost. But he didn't. Just said OK and hung up.

REACHER PAID HIS BILL and walked back to his motel room. He took a shower, rinsed his clothes in the sink and arranged them on a chair to dry. Then he turned the room air to high and lay down on the bed to wait for Alice. Checked his watch. He figured if she got there any time after eight o'clock it would be a good sign, because if Carmen decided to get serious they would need to talk for at least an hour. He closed his eyes and tried to sleep.

EIGHT

At seven twenty he heard a tentative knock at his door. Rolled off the bed and wrapped a towel round his waist and opened up. Alice was standing there. She just shook her head. He stepped back into the room. She followed him inside.

She had changed back into the black trousers and jacket. The trousers had a high waistband, so high it almost met the bottom edge of the sports bra. There was an inch of tanned midriff showing.

'I asked her, was it me?' Alice said. 'Did she want someone different? Older? A man? Hispanic? She said she didn't want anyone at all.'

'That's crazy.'

'Yes, it is,' Alice said. 'I described her predicament. You know, in case she wasn't seeing it clearly. It made no difference.'

'Let me put my trousers on,' Reacher said.

He scooped them off the chair and ducked into the bathroom. He pulled them on, still wet, and zipped them up. Came back out.

'I tried everything,' Alice said. 'I said, "Show me your arm." She said, "What for?" I said, "I want to see how good your veins are. Because that's where the lethal injection will go." I told her she'd be strapped down on the gurney, I described the drugs she'd get. I told her about the people behind the glass, there to watch her die.'

'And?'

'It made no difference at all. Like talking to the wall.'

'How hard did you push?'

'I shouted a little. But she just repeated herself.'

'Did anybody hear her?'

'Not yet. But I'm worried. Logically her next move is to put it in writing. Then I can't even get in the door. Nor can anybody else.'

'So what do we do?'

'We have to ignore her completely and keep dealing with Walker. If we can get him to drop the charges, then we've set her free whether she wants us to or not.' She paused. 'You want dinner?'

He was full of pizza, but the inch of midriff was attractive.

'Sure,' he said. 'Where?'

She paused again. 'My place?' she said. 'It's difficult for me to eat out around here. I'm a vegetarian. So usually I cook for myself.'

He smiled. 'Sounds good to me.' He shrugged his damp shirt on. Found his shoes. Locked up the room and followed her to the car.

She drove a couple of miles west to a residential complex and parked. Inside her unit there was a living room with a kitchen area at the back. A staircase.

'I'm going to shower,' she said. 'Make yourself at home.'

She disappeared upstairs. He took a look around. There was a phone on a table with four speed dials programmed. Top slot was labelled *Work*. Second was *J Home*. Third was *J Work*. Fourth was *M & D*. On a bookshelf was a photograph in a silver frame, showing a couple in their mid-fifties. The woman looked like an older version of Alice. The Park Avenue parents, no doubt. Mom and Dad, M & D. He figured J was probably a boyfriend, but there was no photograph of him. Maybe his picture was upstairs, next to her bed.

She came back down within ten minutes. She was wearing shorts again with a T-shirt that said *Harvard Soccer*. The shorts were short and the T-shirt was tight. She had dispensed with the sports bra. That was clear. She was barefoot and looked altogether sensational.

'You played soccer?' he asked.

'My partner did,' she said.

He smiled at the warning. 'Does he still?'

'He's a she. Judith. I'm gay. Does that bother you?'

'Why would it?'

Alice shrugged. 'It bothers some people.'

'Not this one. What does Judith do?'

'She's a lawyer, too. She's in Mississippi right now.'

'Same reasons?'

Alice nodded. 'A five-year plan.'

'There's hope for the legal profession yet.'

'So it doesn't bother you?' she said. 'That it's just a meal with a new friend and then back to the motel on your own?'

'I never thought it would be anything else,' he lied.

HE WOKE EARLY in the morning and rinsed his clothes and put them on wet. They were dry by the time he reached the law offices.

Alice was already at her desk. A Mexican guy occupying one of her client chairs was talking quietly to her. The intern from Walker's office was waiting behind the Mexican's shoulder, holding a FedEx packet in his hand. Reacher took a place right behind him. Eventually Alice's client stood up and shuffled away.

The intern laid the FedEx packet on the desk. 'Carmen Greer's medical reports,' he said. 'These are the originals. Mr Walker took copies. He wants a conference at nine thirty.'

'We'll be there,' Alice said.

She pulled the packet towards her. The intern followed the Mexican out. Reacher sat down. Alice glanced at him, her fingers resting on the packet, a puzzled expression on her face. He shrugged. The packet was a lot thinner than he had expected, too.

She spilled the contents on the desk. There were four separate reports in individual green covers. Each cover was marked with Carmen's name and social security number and a patient reference. There were dates on all of them, ranging back more than six years. Reacher slid his chair round the desk and put it next to Alice's. She stacked the four reports in date order, the oldest at the top. She opened it so it was between them. 'OK,' she said. 'Let's see.'

The first report was about Ellie's birth. The whole thing was timed in hours and minutes. There was a lot of gynaecological stuff but no mention of facial bruising, or a split lip, or loosened teeth.

The second report, dated in the spring, fifteen months after child-birth, concerned two cracked ribs. An X-ray was attached. The attending physician had noted that the patient reported being thrown from a horse and landing against the top rail of a section of fencing.

'What do you think?' Alice asked.

'Could be something,' Reacher said.

The third report was dated six months later. It concerned severe bruising to Carmen's lower right leg. The same physician noted she reported falling from a horse while jumping and landing with her shin against the pole that constituted the obstacle the horse was attempting. X-rays had been aken. The bone was not fractured. Painkillers had been prescribed.

The fourth report was dated two and a half years later. It showed a broken collarbone. All the names in the file were new. It seemed like the whole ER staff had been replaced. There was a new name for the attending physician, and she made no comment about Carmen's claim to have fallen off her horse onto rocks. There were extensive notes about the injury. There was an X-ray film.

'This isn't enough, Alice,' Reacher said. 'We've got the collarbone, but she claimed he broke her arm. Also her jaw. She said she'd had three teeth reimplanted. Two possibilities. One, the hospital records system screwed up.'

Alice shook her head. 'Very unlikely.'

He nodded again. 'Agreed. So two, she *was* lying.'

Alice was quiet for a long moment. 'Exaggerating, maybe,' she said. 'You know, to lock you in. To make sure of your help.'

He checked his watch. It was twenty past nine. He leaned sideways and slipped the reports back into the FedEx packet. 'Let's go see what Hack thinks,' he said.

THERE WAS A VISITOR seated in Walker's office. He was a man of maybe seventy and he was mopping his brow with a large white handkerchief. Walker had his jacket off and was sitting absolutely still in his chair with his head in his hands. He had copies of the medical reports laid side by side on his desk and he was staring at them like they were written in a foreign language. He looked up blankly, then he made a vague gesture towards the stranger.

'This is Cowan Black,' he said. 'Professor of forensic medicine.'

Alice shook the guy's hand. 'Pleased to meet you,' she said. She introduced Reacher and they all shuffled their chairs into an approximate semicircle round the desk.

'The reports came in first thing,' Walker said. 'Everything on file from Texas, one hospital only. Nothing from Oklahoma, Arkansas, New Mexico or Louisiana. I photocopied everything and immediately sent the originals over to you. Dr Black has studied the copies. He wants to see the X-rays. Those, I couldn't copy.'

Reacher passed the FedEx packet to Black, who spilled the contents and extracted the three X-ray films. He held them up against the light and studied them, one by one. Then he slipped them back in their folders.

Walker sat forward. 'So, Dr Black, are you able to offer us a preliminary opinion?'

Black picked up the first folder. 'This is routine obstetrics.'

'Nothing untoward?'

'Nothing at all.'

'The others?'

Black switched files, to the damaged ribs. Pulled the X-ray film out again. He held it up and pointed here and there on it. 'There is stretching and tearing of the ligaments all over the place. This was a heavy diffuse blow with a broad, blunt instrument.'

'What kind of a blunt instrument?' Walker asked.

'Something long and hard and rounded, maybe five or six inches in diameter. Something exactly like a fencing rail.'

'It couldn't have been a kick?'

Black shook his head. 'No,' he said. 'A kick transfers a lot of energy through a tiny contact area. We would see the cracked bones, for sure, but we wouldn't see the ligament stretching at all.'

'What about a knee?'

'Blunt, but an essentially circular impact site. The ligament stretching would show a completely different pattern.'

Walker drummed his fingers on his desk. He was starting to sweat. 'Any way a person could have done it?' he asked.

Black shrugged. 'If he were some kind of contortionist, maybe. If he could hold his whole leg completely rigid and somehow jump up and hit her in the side with it. I would say it was impossible.'

'What about the bruised shin?' Walker asked.

Black opened the third file. 'Again, the shape of the bruise is what you'd get from the impact of a long hard rounded object,' he said. 'Like a fence rail again, or maybe a sewer pipe, striking against the front of the shin at an oblique angle.'

'Could he have hit her with a length of pipe?'

Black shrugged again. 'Theoretically, I suppose,' he said. 'If he was standing behind her, and somehow could reach over her, and he struck her almost but not quite parallel with her leg. He'd have to do it two-handed, because nobody can hold a six-inch diameter pipe one-handed. Probably he'd have to stand on a chair, and position her very carefully in front of it. It's not very likely, is it?'

'But is it possible?'

'No,' Black said. 'It isn't possible. I say that now, and I'd certainly have to say it under oath.'

Walker was quiet again. 'What about the collarbone?' he asked.

Black picked up the last report. 'These are very detailed notes,' he said. 'Clearly an excellent physician.'

'But what do they tell you?'

'It's a classic injury,' Black said. 'The collarbone is like a circuit breaker. A person falls, and they try to break their fall by throwing out their hand. Their body weight is turned into a severe impact that travels up through their rigid arm, through their rigid shoulder joint.

If it wasn't for the collarbone, that force would travel into the neck, and probably break it, causing paralysis. Or into the brain pan, causing unconsciousness, maybe coma. But evolution chooses the least of all evils. The collarbone snaps, dissipating the force. Inconvenient, painful, but not life-threatening. And generations of bicyclists and inline skaters and horseback riders have reason to be grateful for it.'

'Falling can't be the only way,' Walker said.

'It's the *main* way,' Black said. 'I've seen it happen other ways. A downward blow with a baseball bat might break the collarbone.'

'There's no evidence a baseball bat was involved any other time,' Walker said.

Nobody spoke.

'OK,' Walker said. 'Let me put it this way. I need evidence there was physical abuse against this woman. Is there any here?'

Black went quiet for a spell. Then he simply shook his head. 'No,' he said. 'Not within the bounds of reasonable likelihood. She was an unlucky horseback rider. That's all I see.'

'No reasonable doubt?' Walker said. 'Just a shred will do.'

'I'm afraid not. If I had been retained by Ms Aaron directly, I would tell her that her client's word is not to be trusted. And I say that reluctantly, with a long record of preferring to take the defence's side. A record I aim to continue, for as long as I'm spared. Which might not be much longer, if this damn heat keeps up.' He paused a second and looked around. 'For which reason I must take my leave of you now,' he said. He squared the reports together and slipped them back into the FedEx packet. Handed it to Reacher, who was nearest. Then he stood up and walked slowly out of the office.

Alice and Reacher said nothing. Just watched Walker at his desk. Walker dropped his head into his hands and closed his eyes.

'Go away,' he said. 'Just get the hell out of here and leave me alone.'

THE AIR IN THE STAIRWELL was hot, and it was worse still out on the sidewalk. Reacher swapped the FedEx packet into his left hand and caught Alice's arm with his right. Stopped her at the kerb.

'Is there a good jeweller in town?' he asked.

'I guess,' she said. 'Why?'

'I want you to sign out her personal property. You're still her lawyer, as far as anybody knows. We'll get her ring appraised. Then we'll find out if she's telling the truth about *anything*.'

'You still got doubts?'

'I'm from the army. First we check, then we double-check.'

'OK,' she said. 'If you want.'

They turned round and walked down the alley and she took possession of Carmen's lizard-skin belt and her ring by signing a form that specified both items as material evidence. Then they went looking for a jeweller. They found one ten minutes later.

'So how do we do this?' Alice asked.

'Make out it's an estate sale,' Reacher said. 'Maybe it belonged to your grandmother.'

The guy in the store was old and stooped. Alice produced the ring and told him she'd inherited it. Told him she was thinking of selling it, if the price was right.

The guy held it under a lamp and put a loupe in his eye. He turned the stone left and right. It flashed in the light. He picked up a slip of card that had circular holes punched through it. They started small and got bigger. He tried the stone in the holes until he found one that fitted. 'Two and a quarter carats,' he said. 'Cut is handsome. Colour is good, maybe *just* on the yellow side of truly excellent. Clarity isn't flawless, but not far off. How much do you want for it?'

'Whatever it's worth,' Alice said.

'I could give you twenty,' the guy said.

'Twenty what?'

'Thousand dollars,' the guy said.

'Twenty thousand dollars?'

The guy put up his hands, palms out, defensively. 'I know, I know,' he said. 'Someone probably told you it's worth more. And maybe it is, retail, some big fancy store, Dallas or somewhere. But this is Pecos, and you're selling, not buying.'

'I'll think about it,' Alice said.

'Twenty-five?' the guy said. 'That's about as high as I can go.'

THEY STOPPED on the sidewalk outside the store. Alice opened her bag and put the ring in a zippered compartment.

'Guy like that says twenty-five, it's got to be worth sixty,' Reacher said. 'My guess is he's not the Better Business Bureau's poster boy.'

'A lot more than thirty dollars, anyway,' Alice said. 'A fake? Cubic zirconium? She's playing us for fools.'

He nodded, vaguely. He knew she meant *playing you for a fool*.

They walked west through the heat, back to the mission.

'I want to try one last thing,' he said.

'Why?' she asked.

'Because I'm from the army,' he said. 'First we double-check, then we triple-check.'

She sighed. A little impatience there. 'What do you want to do?'

'There's an eyewitness we can talk to.'

'An *eyewitness*? Where?'

'In school, down in Echo.'

'The kid? She's six years old.'

'If it was happening, I'll bet she knows. She's sharp as a tack.'

Alice stood completely still for a second. Then she glanced in through the windows. The place was crowded with customers.

'It's not fair to *them*,' she said. 'I need to move on.'

'Just this one last thing.'

'I'll lend you the car again. You can go alone.'

He shook his head. 'I need your opinion. You're the lawyer. And I won't get in the schoolhouse without you.'

'I can't do it. It'll take all day.'

'How long would it have taken to get the money from the rancher?'

She was quiet for a moment. 'OK,' she said. 'A deal's a deal, I guess.'

'WHY, EXACTLY?' she asked.

They were in the yellow VW, heading south out of Pecos.

'Because I was an investigator,' he said.

'OK,' she said. 'Investigators investigate. That, I follow. But don't they *stop* investigating? I mean, ever? When they *know* already?'

'Investigators never know,' he said. 'They feel and they guess.'

'I thought they dealt in facts.'

'Eventually they do,' he said. 'But ninety-nine per cent of the time it's about what you *feel*. About people.'

'Weren't you ever wrong before?'

'Of course I was. But I don't think I'm wrong now. I know things about people, Alice.'

'So do I,' she said. 'Like, I know Carmen Greer suckered you.'

He said nothing more. Just watched her drive, and looked at the view ahead. He had the FedEx packet on his knees. He fanned himself with it. Balanced it on his fingers. Turned it over and over aimlessly. Stared down at the front and the back, the label, the meaningless little words all over it, EXTREMELY URGENT, sender, addressee, commodity description, dimensions in inches, twelve by nine, weight in pounds, two point six, payment, overnight. He shook his head and pitched it behind him, onto the back seat.

When they arrived at the crossroads, Alice parked and they went into the school. They were out again a minute later. Ellie Greer wasn't there, and she hadn't been there the day before, either.

'Understandable, I guess,' Alice said. 'Traumatic time for her.'

Reacher nodded. 'So let's go. It's only another hour south.'

'Great,' Alice said.

They got back in the VW and drove the next sixty miles without talking. Reacher recognised the landmarks. He saw the old oil field, on the distant horizon off to the left. Greer Three.

'It's coming up,' he said.

Alice slowed. The red-painted picket fence replaced the wire and the gate swam into view. Alice turned in under it. The small car bounced across the yard. She stopped it close to the porch steps and turned off the motor. The place was silent. But people were home, because all the cars were lined up in the vehicle barn.

They got out of the car. He led her up the porch steps and knocked on the door. It opened almost immediately. Rusty Greer was standing there. She was holding a .22 rifle.

'It's you,' she said. 'I thought it might be Bobby.'

'You lost him?' Reacher said.

Rusty shrugged. 'He went out. He isn't back yet.'

'All the cars are here.'

'Somebody picked him up,' Rusty said. 'I was upstairs. Didn't see them. Just heard them.'

'This is Carmen's lawyer,' Reacher said. 'We need to see Ellie.'

Rusty smiled. 'Ellie's not here.'

'Well, where is she?' Reacher asked. 'She's not in school.'

Rusty said nothing.

'Mrs Greer, we need to know where Ellie is,' Alice said.

Rusty smiled again. 'I don't know where she is, lawyer girl.'

'Why not?' Alice asked.

'Because Family Services took her, that's why not. They came for her this morning.'

'And you let them take her?' Reacher said.

'Why wouldn't I? I don't want her. Now that Sloop is gone.'

Reacher stared at her. 'But she's your granddaughter.'

'That's a fact I was never thrilled about,' Rusty said.

'Where did they take her?'

'An orphanage, I guess,' Rusty said. 'And then she'll get adopted, if anybody wants her. Which they probably won't. I understand half-breeds are very difficult to place. Decent folk generally don't want beaner trash.'

IT WAS THREE in the afternoon when they got back. There was the usual thicket of messages on Alice's desk, five of them from Hack Walker, each more urgent than the last.

'Shall we go?' Alice asked.

'Don't tell him about the diamond,' Reacher said.

'It's over now, don't you see?'

And it was. Reacher saw it right away in Walker's face. There was relaxation there. Finality. Closure. Some kind of peace. He was sitting behind his desk. His desk was covered with papers. They were arranged in two piles. One was taller than the other.

'What?' Reacher asked.

Walker ignored him and handed a single sheet to Alice. 'Waiver of her Miranda rights,' he said. 'She's declining legal representation, and she's declaring that it's entirely voluntary. And she adds that she refused *your* representation from the very start.'

'I doubted her competence,' Alice said.

'I'll give you the benefit of the doubt. But there's no doubt now. So you're here purely as a courtesy, OK? Both of you.'

Then Walker handed over the smaller pile of papers. Alice fanned them out and Reacher leaned to look at them. They were computer print-outs covered in figures and dates. They were bank records, five separate accounts. Two were current accounts, three were money-market deposits. They were titled *Greer Non-Discretionary Trust 1* to *5*. There was a composite total somewhere near $2 million.

'Al Eugene's people messengered them over,' Walker said. 'Now look at the bottom sheets.'

Alice riffled through. Reacher read over her shoulder. There was a lot of legal text. It added up to the formal minutes of a trust agreement. A notarised deed was attached. It stated that for the time being a single trustee was in absolute control of all Sloop Greer's funds. That single trustee was identified as Sloop Greer's legal wife, Carmen.

'She had two million bucks in the bank,' Walker said.

Reacher glanced at Alice.

She nodded. 'He's right,' she said.

'Now look at the last clause of the minutes,' Walker said.

Alice turned the page. The last clause concerned reversion. The trusts would return the funds to Sloop's control at a future date to be specified by him. Unless he first became irreversibly mentally incapacitated. Or died. Whereupon all existing balances would become Carmen's sole property, in the first instance as a matter of prior agreement, and in the second as a matter of inheritance.

'Is all of that clear?' Walker asked.

Reacher said nothing, but Alice nodded.

Then Walker passed her the taller pile. 'Now read this,' he said.

'What is it?' she asked.

'A transcript,' Walker said. 'Of her confession.'

There was silence.

'She confessed?' Alice said. 'When?'

'We videotaped it,' Walker said. 'Noon today. My assistant went to see her as soon as the financial stuff came in. We tried to find you first, but we couldn't. Then she told us she didn't want a lawyer anyway. So we had her sign the waiver. Then she spilled her guts. We brought her up here and videotaped the whole thing over again.'

Reacher was half listening, half reading. It wasn't pretty. Went all the way back to her LA days. She had been an illegitimate child. She had been a hooker. *Street stroller*, she called it. Some odd barrio expression, Reacher assumed. Then she came off the streets and started stripping. She had latched onto Sloop. *My meal ticket*, she called him. Then it became a story of impatience. She was bored witless in Texas. She wanted out, but she wanted money. Sloop's IRS trouble was a godsend. The trusts were tempting. She tried to have him killed in prison, which she knew from her peers was possible, but she found out that a federal minimum-security facility wasn't that sort of place. So she waited. As soon as she heard he was getting out, she bought the gun and went recruiting. She planned to leverage her marks with invented stories about domestic violence. Reacher had refused, so she did it herself. Having already fabricated the abuse claims, she intended to use them to get off with self-defence. But then she realised her hospital records would come up blank, so she was confessing and throwing herself on the mercy of the prosecutor. Her signature was scrawled on the bottom of every page.

'What about the election?' Reacher asked. The last hope.

Walker shrugged. 'Texas code says it's a capital crime. Murder for remuneration. But a guilty plea saves the taxpayer the cost of a trial. Justifies me asking for a life sentence instead. The way I see it, with a story like that she's going to look very bad, whoever you are. So if I back off the death penalty, I'll look magnanimous. Generous, even. The whites will fret a little, but the Mexicans will eat it up.'

'I've got her property,' Alice said. 'A belt and a ring.'

'Take them to storage. We'll be moving her, later.'

'Where?'

'The penitentiary. We can't keep her here any more.'

'No, I meant where's storage?'

'Same building as the morgue. Make sure you get a receipt.'

REACHER WALKED WITH HER over to the morgue. He felt like he was insulated inside some kind of sensory-deprivation suit. Alice was talking to him, but he was hearing nothing that she said. All he could hear was a small voice inside his head saying *You were completely wrong*. It was a voice he had heard before, but that didn't make it any easier to hear again, because he had built his whole career on hearing it fewer times than the next guy.

The morgue was a low industrial shed behind the street. Alice put the lizard-skin belt on the reception counter and dug in her handbag for the ring. She told the attendant they were for *Texas* v. *Carmen Greer*. He went away and came back with the evidence box.

'No, it's personal property,' she said. 'Not evidence. Sorry.'

The guy gave a Why-didn't-you-say-so? look and turned round.

'Wait,' Reacher called. 'Let me see that.'

The guy turned back and slid the box across the counter. It had no lid; it was really just a cardboard tray three inches deep. Somebody had written *Greer* on the front edge. The Lorcin was in a plastic bag. Two shell cases were in a separate bag. Two .22 bullets were in a bag each. One bag was marked *Intercranial 1*, the other *Intercranial 2*.

'Is the pathologist here?' Reacher asked.

'Sure,' the guy said. He pointed to a double door. 'In there.'

Reacher went through. He saw a glass door in the far corner. Behind it was an office, with a man in green scrubs at a desk. Reacher knocked. The man looked up. Mouthed, 'Come in.' Reacher went in.

'Help you?' the guy said.

'Only two bullets in Sloop Greer?' Reacher said.

'Who are you?'

'I'm with the perp's lawyer,' Reacher said. 'She's outside.'

'OK,' the guy said. 'What about the bullets?'

'How many were there?'

'Two,' the guy said. 'Hell of a time getting them out.'

'Can I see the body?'

'Why?'

'I'm worried about a miscarriage of justice.'

It's a line that usually works with pathologists. They figure there's going to be a trial, they'll be called on for evidence, the last thing they want is to be humiliated by the defence on cross-examination. So they prefer to get any doubts squared away beforehand.

'OK,' he said. 'It's in the freezer.'

He had another door at the back of his office which led to a dim corridor. At the end of the corridor was an insulated steel door.

The guy operated the handle and they went inside. There was a bank of twenty-seven stainless-steel drawers on the far wall, nine across, three high. Eight of them were occupied. They had tags slipped into little receptacles on the front, the sort of thing you see on filing cabinets. The air in the room was frosty. Reacher's breath clouded in front of him. The pathologist checked the tags and slid a drawer. It came out easily, on runners.

Sloop Greer was on his back and naked. His eyes were open, blank and staring. He had two bullet holes in his forehead, about three inches apart. They were neat holes, blue and ridged at the edges, like they had been carefully drilled.

Reacher closed his eyes. Then he smiled. A big, broad grin.

There was a knock at the open door. Reacher opened his eyes. Alice was standing there. 'What are you doing?' she called.

'What comes after quadruple-check?' he called back.

'Quintuple-check,' she said. 'Why?'

'And after that?'

'Sextuple,' she said. 'Why?'

'Because we're going to be doing a whole lot of checking now.'

'Why?'

'Because there's something wrong here, Alice. Come take a look.'

Alice walked slowly across the tile. 'What's wrong?' she asked.

'Tell me what you see,' Reacher said.

She dropped her eyes towards the corpse like it required a physical effort. 'Shot in the head,' she said. 'Twice.'

'How far apart are the holes?'

'Maybe three inches.'

'What else do you see?'

'Nothing,' she said.

He nodded. 'Exactly. Look closer. The holes are clean, right?'

She took a step nearer the drawer. Bent slightly from the waist. 'They look clean,' she said.

'That has implications,' he said. 'First thing out of a gun barrel is an explosion of hot gas. If the muzzle was tight against the forehead, the gas tears itself a big star-shaped hole. That's absent here. Next thing out of the barrel is flame. If it was a real close shot, two or three inches, we'd see burning of the skin. That's absent, too. Next thing out is soot. If it was a shot from six or eight inches, we'd see smudging on his forehead. That's not here, either. Next thing out is gunpowder particles. If it was a shot from a foot away, maybe a foot and a half, we'd see it. Tiny black dots. You see it?'

'No,' Alice said.

'Right. All we see is the bullet holes. Nothing else. No evidence at all to suggest they were from close range. Depends on the exact powder in the shells, but they look to me like shots from three or four feet away, absolute minimum.'

'Eight feet six inches,' the pathologist said. 'That's my estimate.'

Reacher glanced at him. 'You tested the powder?'

The guy shook his head. 'Crime scene diagrams. He was found near the bedside table, up near the head of the bed. We know she wasn't next to him or we'd have found all that close-range stuff you just mentioned. So the nearest she *could* have been was on the other side of the bed. Firing across it, diagonally, according to the trajectories. It was a kingsize bed, so my best guess is eight feet six inches.'

'You prepared to say so on the stand?' Reacher asked.

'Sure. And that's only the minimum. Could have been more.'

'But what does it mean?' Alice asked.

'Means Carmen didn't do it,' Reacher said.

'Why not?'

'How big is a man's forehead? Five inches across and two high? No way she could have hit a target that small from eight feet plus.'

'How do you know?'

'Because I saw her shoot, the day before. She was hopeless. She couldn't have hit the side of a barn from eight feet plus.'

'She could have got lucky.'

'Sure, once. But not twice. Twice means they were aimed shots. And they're close together, horizontally. He'd have started falling after the first one. Which means it was a double-tap. *Bang bang*, like that, no hesitation. That's skilful shooting.'

'She could have been faking,' Alice said. 'She lied about everything else. Maybe she was an expert shot, but claimed not to be.'

'She wasn't faking,' Reacher said. 'All my life I've seen people shoot. Either you can or you can't. And if you can, it shows. You can't hide it.'

NINE

'It's a can of worms,' Hack Walker said. 'You know what I mean? Best not to open it. Things could get out of hand real quick.'

They were back in Walker's office.

'You understand?' Walker asked. 'It makes things worse again.'

'You think?' Alice said.

Walker nodded. 'Let's say Reacher is right, which is a stretch, frankly, because all he's got is a highly subjective opinion based on an impression she chose to give him that she couldn't shoot. But let's say he's right, for the sake of argument. What does that give us?'

'What?'

'A conspiracy, is what. We know she tried to rope Reacher in. Now you've got her roping somebody else in. She tells them where and when, they show up, get the gun, do the deed. If it happened that way, she's instigated a conspiracy to commit murder for remuneration. Hired a killer, cold-blooded as hell. In comparison, a solo shot looks almost benign. We leave it exactly the way we got it, along with the guilty plea, I'm happy asking for a life sentence. But we start talking conspiracy, we're back on track for death row. Plus, she already said she did it herself. Which I think is true. But if it isn't, then her confession was a calculated lie, designed to cover her ass, because she knew a conspiracy would look worse. And we'd have to react to that. We couldn't let that go. It would make us look like fools.'

Alice said nothing. Reacher just shrugged.

'So leave it alone,' Walker said. 'That's my suggestion. If it would help her, I'd look at it. But it won't.'

'You happy to leave it alone,' Alice asked. 'As a prosecutor? Somebody could be getting clean away with something.'

Walker shook his head. 'If it happened the way Reacher thinks. *If.* If is a very big word. I got to say I think it's highly unlikely, and I'm a real enthusiastic prosecutor.'

Reacher said nothing. Alice nodded again. 'OK,' she said. 'I'm not her lawyer anyway.'

She stood up slowly and tapped Reacher on the shoulder. Gave him a What-can-we-do? look and headed for the door. He stood up and followed her.

ALICE AND REACHER walked to the bus depot. It was fifty yards from the courthouse. There was a tiny office hut papered on the outside with schedules. There was a woman in it, sitting on a high stool, reading a magazine.

'So where will you head?' Alice asked.

'First bus out,' he said. 'That's my rule.'

They read the schedules. Next departure was to Topeka, Kansas. It was due in from Phoenix, Arizona, in half an hour.

He tapped on the glass and the woman sold him a one-way ticket.

'Good luck, Alice,' he said. 'Four and a half years from now, I'll look for you in the Yellow Pages.'

She smiled. 'Take care, Reacher,' she said.

THE BUS ROLLED IN. It was a Greyhound, heat shimmering visibly from its air conditioner grilles. The door opened and three people got off. Reacher got on. The driver took his ticket.

'Two minutes, OK?' the guy said. 'I need a comfort stop.'

Reacher shuffled down the aisle and found a double seat empty. It was on the left, which would face the evening sun all the way after they turned north at Abilene. But the windows were tinted and the air was cold, so he figured he'd be OK. He sat down. Stretched out. The eight spent shells in his pocket were uncomfortable against his thigh. He took them out and held them in his palm.

Abilene, he thought.

The driver climbed back in and slid into his seat and the door wheezed shut behind him.

'Wait,' Reacher called. He shuffled forward again, all the way down the aisle. 'I changed my mind,' he said. 'I'm getting off.'

The driver looked blank, but he operated the mechanism and the door wheezed open. Reacher stepped down into the heat and walked away. He heard the bus leave behind him.

He walked to the law office. Alice was at her desk, talking to a woman with a baby. She looked up, surprised.

'Bus didn't come?' she asked.

'I need to ask you a legal question,' he said.

'Is it quick?'

He nodded. 'Civilian law, if some guy tells an attorney about a crime, how far can the cops press the attorney for the details?'

'It would be privileged information,' Alice said. 'Between lawyer and client. The cops couldn't press at all.'

'Can I use your phone?'

She shrugged. 'Sure,' she said. 'Squeeze in.'

He took a spare chair and put it next to hers, behind the desk.

'Got phone books for Abilene?' he asked.

'Bottom drawer,' she said. 'All of Texas.'

She turned back to the woman with the baby and restarted their discussion. He opened the drawer and found the right book. There was an information page near the front, with the emergency services laid out in big letters. He dialled the State Police, Abilene office. A woman answered and asked how she could help.

'I have information,' he said. 'About a crime.'

The woman put him on hold. Thirty seconds later the call was picked up elsewhere. Sounded like a squad room. Phones were ringing in the background and there was faint people noise all around.

'Sergeant Rodriguez,' a voice said.

'I have information about a crime,' Reacher said again.

'Your name, sir?'

'Chester Arthur,' Reacher said. 'I'm a lawyer in Pecos County.'

'OK, Mr Arthur, go ahead.'

'You guys found an abandoned automobile south of Abilene on Friday. A Mercedes Benz belonging to a lawyer called Al Eugene. He's currently listed as a missing person. I have a client says Eugene was abducted from his car and killed near the scene.'

'What's your client's name, sir?'

'Can't tell you that,' Reacher said. 'Privileged information. And the fact is I'm not sure I even believe him. I need you to check his story from your end. If he's making sense, then maybe I can persuade him to come forward.'

'What is he telling you?'

'He says Eugene was flagged down and put in another car. He was driven north to a concealed location on the left-hand side of the road, and then he was shot and his body was hidden.'

Alice had stopped her conversation and was staring at him.

'We already searched the area.'

'What kind of a radius?' Reacher asked.

'Immediate surroundings.'

'No, my guy says a mile or two north. You need to look under vegetation, in the cracks in the rock, pumping houses, anything there is. Some spot near where a vehicle could have pulled off the road.'

'A mile or two north of the abandoned car? On the left?'

'He's pretty sure,' Reacher said.

'You got a phone number?'

'I'll call you back,' Reacher said. 'An hour from now.' He hung up.

The woman with the baby was gone. Alice was still staring at him. 'What?' she said.

'We should have focused on Eugene before.'

'Why?'

'Because what's the one solid fact we've got here?'

'What?'

'Carmen didn't shoot Sloop, that's what.'

'That's an opinion, not a fact.'

'No, it's a fact, Alice. Believe me, I *know* these things.'

She shrugged. 'OK, so?'

'So somebody else shot him. Why? We know Eugene is missing, we know Sloop is dead. They were connected, lawyer and client. So let's assume Eugene is dead, too. For the sake of argument. They were working together on a deal that sprung Sloop from jail. Some kind of a big deal, because that isn't easy. It must have involved heavy-duty information. Big trouble for somebody. Suppose that somebody took them *both* out, for revenge, or to stop the flow of information?'

'Where did you get this idea?'

'Think about it, Alice. Anybody who shoots that well is a professional. Professionals plan ahead, at least a few days. And if Carmen had hired a professional a few days ahead, why would she trawl around Texas looking for guys like me hitching rides? And why would she allow Sloop to be killed in her own bedroom, where she would be the number-one suspect? With her own gun?'

'So what do you think happened?'

'I think some hit team took Eugene out on Friday and covered their ass by hiding the body so it won't be found until the trail is completely cold. Then they took Sloop out on Sunday and covered their ass by making it look like Carmen did it.'

'But she was with him. Wouldn't she have *said*?'

'Maybe she was with Ellie at the time. Maybe she walked back into the bedroom and found it done. Or maybe she was in the shower.'

'Then she'd have heard the shots.'

'Not with that shower. It's like Niagara Falls. And a .22 is quiet.'

'How do you know where they'll find Eugene's body? Assuming you're right?'

'I thought about how I would do it. They obviously had a vehicle of their own, out there in the middle of nowhere. Maybe they staged a breakdown. Flagged him down, forced him into their vehicle, drove him away. But they wouldn't want to keep him in there long. Too risky. Two or three minutes maximum, I figure, which is a mile or two from a standing start.'

'Why north? Why on the left side?'

'I'd have driven way north first. Turned back and scouted the near-side shoulder. Picked my place and measured a couple of miles back, turned round again and set up and waited for him.'

'Conceivable,' she said. 'But the Sloop thing? That's impossible. They went down to that house? In Echo, in the middle of nowhere? Hid out and crept in? While she was in the shower?'

'I could have done it,' he said. 'And I'm assuming they're as good as me. Maybe they're better than me.'

'But she *confessed* to it,' Alice said. 'Why would she do that? If it was really nothing at all to do with her?'

'We'll figure that out later. First, we wait an hour.'

He left Alice with work to do and decided he'd finally take a look at the Wild West museum. When he got there, it was closed. Too late in the day. But he could see an alley leading to an open area at the back. Behind the buildings was Clay Allison's grave. The headstone was handsome. ROBERT CLAY ALLISON 1840–1887. HE NEVER KILLED A MAN THAT DID NOT NEED KILLING. Reacher had no middle name. It was Jack Reacher, plain and simple. Born 1960, not dead yet. He wondered what his headstone would look like. Probably wouldn't have one. There was nobody to arrange it.

Reacher walked back to Alice's office. She was still at her desk. A Mexican couple were in her client chairs. She pointed vaguely at his chair, which was still placed next to hers. He sat down. Picked up the phone and dialled the Abilene number. He gave his name as Chester Arthur and asked for Sergeant Rodriguez.

He was on hold a whole minute. Then Rodriguez picked up.

'We need your client's name, Mr Arthur,' Rodriguez said.

'What did your people find?' Reacher asked.

'Exactly what you said, sir. Mile and a half north, on the left, in a deep limestone crevasse. Shot once through the right eye.'

'Was it a .22?'

'No way. Nine-millimetre, at least. Most of his head is gone.'

'My guy's not the doer,' Reacher said. 'I'll talk to him and maybe he'll call you.' Then he hung up before Rodriguez could start arguing. Alice was staring at him again.

'Which President was Chester Arthur?' Alice asked.

'After Garfield, before Grover Cleveland. From Vermont.'

'So they found Eugene,' she said. 'So now what?'

'Now we go warn Hack Walker.'

'*Warn* him?'

Reacher nodded. 'Think about it, Alice. Maybe what we've got here is two out of two, but it's more likely to be two out of three. They were a threesome, Hack and Al and Sloop. Carmen said they all worked together on the deal. She said Hack brokered it with the feds. Hack knew what they knew, for sure. So he could be next.'

Alice turned to her clients. 'Sorry, got to go,' she said.

HACK WALKER was packing up for the day. It was after six and his office windows were growing dim with dusk. They told him Eugene was dead and watched the colour drain out of his face. His skin contracted and puckered under a mask of sweat. He clawed his way round his desk and dumped himself down in his chair. He said nothing for a long moment. Then he nodded slowly.

'I guess I always knew,' he said. 'But I was, you know, hoping.'

Alice went straight into Reacher's two-for-three theory. The deal, the dangerous knowledge. The warning. Walker's colour came back, slowly. He stayed quiet, thinking hard. Then he shook his head.

'Can't be right,' he said. 'Because the deal was really nothing at all. Sloop caved in and undertook to pay the taxes and the penalties. He got desperate, couldn't stand the jail time. Al contacted the IRS, made the offer, they didn't bat an eye. It's routine. The federal prosecutor needed to sign off on it, which is where I came in. I hustled it through, is all, a little faster than it might have gone without me. It was a routine IRS matter. And believe me, nobody gets killed over a routine IRS matter.' He shook his head again. Then he opened his eyes wide and went very still. 'I want you to leave now,' he said.

Alice nodded. 'We're very sorry for your loss. We know that you were friends.'

But Walker just looked confused, like that wasn't what he was worrying about.

'What?' Reacher said.

'We shouldn't talk any more, is what,' Walker said.

'Why not?'

'Because we're going around in a circle, and we're finishing up in a place where we don't want to be.'

'We are?'

'Think about it, guys. Nobody gets killed over a routine IRS matter. Or do they? Sloop and Al were fixing to take the trust money away from Carmen and give most of it to the government. Now Sloop and Al are dead. Her motive is getting better all the time. We keep talking like this, I've *got* to think conspiracy. Two deaths, not one. No choice, I've got to. And I don't want to do that.'

'There was no conspiracy,' Reacher said. 'If she'd already hired people, why did she pick me up?'

Walker shrugged. 'To confuse the issue? Distance herself?'

'Is she *that* smart?'

'I think she is.'

'So prove it. Show us she hired somebody. You've got her bank records. Show us the payment.'

'The payment?'

'You think these people work for free?'

Walker made a face. Took keys from his pocket and unlocked a drawer in his desk. Lifted out the pile of financial information. *Greer Non-Discretionary Trust 1* to *5*. He went through them, page by page. Then he squared them together again and reversed them on the desk. His face was blank.

Alice picked them up. Leafed through, scanning the debit column. There were plenty of debits. But they were all small and random.

'Add up the last month,' Reacher said.

She scanned back. 'Nine hundred, round figures,' she said.

Reacher nodded. 'Nine hundred bucks doesn't buy you somebody who can operate the way we've seen. We need to go talk to her.'

'We can't,' Walker said. 'She's on the road, headed for the penitentiary.'

'She didn't do it,' Reacher said.

'So why did she confess?'

Reacher closed his eyes. Sat still for a moment. 'She was forced to,' he said. 'Somebody got to her.'

'Who?'

Reacher opened his eyes. 'I don't know,' he said. 'But we can find out. Get the bailiff's log from downstairs. See who came to visit her.'

Walker picked up the phone and dialled an internal number. Asked for the visitor's log to be brought up. Three minutes later the bailiff came in. It was the day guy. He was carrying a book.

Walker took it from him and opened it up. Scanned through it and reversed it on the desk. Used his finger to point. Carmen Greer was logged in during the early hours of Monday morning. She was logged out two hours ago, into the custody of the Texas Department of Correction. In between Alice had visited her twice, on Monday afternoon and at seven the same evening. She had received one other visitor, twice. At nine o'clock on Monday morning and again on Tuesday at noon, the same Assistant District Attorney had gone down to see her.

'Preliminary interview, and then the confession,' Walker said.

There were no other entries.

Reacher looked at the log again. The first ADA interview had lasted two minutes. Clearly Carmen had refused to say a word. The second interview had lasted twelve minutes. After that she had been escorted upstairs for the videotape.

'Nobody else?' he asked.

'There were phone calls,' the bailiff said.

'When?'

'All day Monday, and Tuesday morning.'

'Who was calling her?'

'Her lawyer.'

'Her *lawyer*?' Alice said.

The guy nodded. 'It was a big pain in the ass,' he said. 'I had to keep bringing her in and out to the phone.'

'Who was the lawyer?' Alice asked.

'We're not allowed to ask, ma'am. It's a confidentiality thing.'

'Man or woman?'

'It was a man.'

'Hispanic?'

'I don't think so. He sounded like a regular guy. His voice was a little muffled. I think it was a bad phone line.'

'Same guy every time?'

'I think so.'

There was silence in the office. Walker nodded vaguely and the bailiff took it for a dismissal. They heard him walk out.

'She didn't tell us she was represented,' Walker said. 'She told us she didn't *want* representation.'

'She told me the same thing,' Alice said.

'We need to know who this person was,' Reacher said. 'We need to get the phone company to trace the calls.'

Walker shook his head. 'Can't do it. Legal discussions are privileged.'

Reacher stared at him. 'You really think it was a *lawyer*?'

'Don't you?'

'Of course not. It was some guy, threatening her, forcing her to lie. Think about it, Walker. First time your ADA saw her, she wouldn't say a word. Twenty-seven hours later, she's confessing. Only thing that happened in between was a bunch of calls from this guy.'

'But what kind of threat could make her say that?'

'Call Family Services,' Reacher said. 'Right now.'

Hack Walker just stared at him.

'You asked what kind of a threat could make her confess to something she didn't do,' Reacher said. 'Don't you see? They must have got her kid.'

Walker unlocked another drawer and lifted out a heavy black binder. Opened it up and thumbed through and grabbed his phone and dialled a number. Some kind of an evening emergency contact. It was picked up and he asked the question, using Ellie's full name, Mary Ellen Greer. There was a long pause. Then an answer. Walker put the phone down, very slowly. 'They never heard of her,' he said.

Silence. Walker closed his eyes, and then opened them again.

'OK,' he said. 'Resources are going to be a problem. State Police, of course. And the FBI, because this is a kidnap. But we've got to move immediately. Speed is paramount. They could be taking her anywhere. So I want you two to go down to Echo, right now, get the full story from Rusty. Descriptions and everything.'

'Rusty won't talk to us,' Reacher said. 'She's too hostile. What about the Echo sheriff?'

'That guy is useless. He's probably drunk right now. You'll have to do it.' Walker opened another drawer and took two chromium stars from a box. Tossed them onto the desk. 'Raise your right hands,' he said. 'Repeat after me.' He mumbled his way through some kind of oath. Reacher and Alice repeated it back, as far as they could catch it. Walker nodded. 'Now you're sheriff's deputies,' he said. 'Rusty will *have* to talk to you.'

Reacher just stared at him.

'What?' Walker said.

'You can still do that here? Deputise people?'

'Sure I can,' Walker said. 'Just like the Wild West. Now get going, OK? I've got a million calls to make.'

Reacher took his chromium star and stood up, an accredited law-enforcement official again for the first time in four and a quarter years. Alice stood up alongside him.

'Meet back here directly,' Walker said. 'And good luck.'

Eight minutes later they were in the yellow VW again, heading south towards the Red House for the second time that day.

THE WOMAN TOOK THE CALL. She didn't need to talk, just listened, because it was a one-sided message. When it was over, she hung up the phone. 'It's tonight,' she said.

'What is?' the tall man asked.

'The supplementary job,' she said. 'The Pecos thing. Seems like the situation up there is unravelling slightly. They found Eugene's body already. So we move tonight, before things get any worse.'

'Who's the target?' the tall man asked.

'His name's Jack Reacher. A drifter, ex-military. I've got a description. There's a girl lawyer in the picture. She'll need attention, too.'

'We do them simultaneous with this baby-sitting gig?'

The woman shrugged. 'Like we always said, we keep the baby-sitting going as long as possible, but we reserve the right to terminate when necessary.'

The men looked at each other. Ellie watched them from the bed.

REACHER WAS NOT good company on the ride south. He didn't talk at all for the first hour and a half. Dark had fallen and he kept the VW's dome light on and studied the maps from the glove compartment. In particular he concentrated on a large-scale topographical sheet that showed the southern part of Echo County.

'I don't understand why she lied about the diamond,' he said.

Alice shrugged. She was pushing the little car as fast as it was willing to go. 'She lied about everything,' she said.

'The ring was different,' he said.

'Different how?'

'A different sort of lie. The only thing I can't explain to myself.'

'The *only* thing?'

'I can see this whole situation in my mind. From every angle. Except for the ring. The ring screws it up.'

'You want to explain that?'

'No point,' he said. 'Until I figure it out.' He opened the glove compartment and took out the Heckler & Koch. Checked the load. It still held its full complement of ten shells. He jacked the first round into the chamber. Then he cocked the pistol and locked it. Eased up off the passenger seat and slipped it into his pocket.

'You think we're going to need that?' she asked.

'Sooner or later,' he said.

'You know what's going on, don't you?' she asked.

'Aside from the diamond ring.'

'Tell me,' she said.

'Did you ever ride a horse?'

'No,' she said. 'I'm a city girl.'

'You ever ride a bike?'

'In New York City?'

'Inline skating?'

'A little, back when it was cool.'

'You ever fall?'

'Once, pretty badly.'

He nodded. 'That meal you made for me. You weighed out the ingredients?'

'You have to.'

'So you've got scales in your kitchen?'

'Sure,' she said.

'The scales of justice,' he said.

'Reacher, what the hell are you talking about?'

He glanced to his left. The red picket fence was racing backwards through the edge of her headlight beams.

'We're here,' he said. 'I'll tell you later.'

She turned in under the gate and bumped across the yard.

'Face it towards the motor barn,' he said. 'And leave the headlights on. I want to take a look at that old pick-up truck.'

'OK,' she said. She coasted a yard or two and hauled on the steering wheel until the headlight beams washed into the right-hand end of the barn. They lit up half of the new pick-up, half of the Jeep Cherokee, and all of the old pick-up between them.

They got out of the car. The night air felt damp. It was cloudy and there were insects floating everywhere. They walked over for a better look at the abandoned truck. It was a Chevrolet, maybe twenty years old, but still a recognisable ancestor of the newer truck alongside it. It had bulbous fenders and dulled paint and a roll bar built into the load bed. It probably hadn't been started in a decade. The springs sagged and the tyres were flat and the rubber was perished.

'I think it's the truck in the photo,' Reacher said. 'The one in Walker's office? Him and Sloop and Eugene leaning on the fender?'

'Trucks all look the same to me,' Alice said. She ducked back into the VW and killed the lights. Then he led her to the main entrance. He knocked. Waited. Bobby Greer opened the door.

'So you came home,' Reacher said.

Bobby scowled. 'My buddies took me out,' he said. 'To help with the grieving process.'

Reacher opened his palm to show off the chromium star. 'Police,' he said. 'Hack Walker deputised us. We need to see your mother.'

He led Alice past Bobby through the hall and into the parlour. Rusty Greer was sitting at the table.

'We're here on official business, Mrs Greer,' Reacher said. He showed her the badge in his palm. 'We need some answers.'

'I've done nothing wrong,' Rusty said.

Reacher shook his head. 'As a matter of fact, you've done everything wrong.'

'Like what?'

'Like, my grandmother would have died before she let her grandchildren get taken away. Literally. Over her dead body, she'd have said, and she'd have damn well meant every word.'

'It was for the child's own good,' Rusty said. 'And I had no choice. They had papers.'

'You given grandchildren away before?'

'No.'

'So how do you know they were the *right* papers?'

'They looked right,' Rusty said. 'All full of big words, aforementioned, hereinafter, the State of Texas.'

'They were fakes,' Reacher said. 'It was a kidnap, Mrs Greer. They took your granddaughter to threaten your daughter-in-law with. We need descriptions. How many were there?'

'Two people. A man and a woman.'

'White?'

'Yes.'

'What did they look like?'

Rusty shrugged. 'Ordinary,' she said. 'Normal. Like social workers. From a city. They had a big car.'

'Hair? Eyes? Clothes?'

'Fair hair, I think. Both of them. Cheap suits. The woman wore a skirt. Blue eyes, I think. The man was tall.'

'What about their car?'

'I don't know about cars. It was a big sedan.'

'Colour?'

'Grey or blue, maybe. Not dark.'

'You got any humble pie in the kitchen?'

'Why?'

'Because I should cram it down your throat until it chokes you. Those are the ones who killed Al Eugene.'

'Killed? Al is dead?' She went pale and said, 'What about—?' Then she stopped. She couldn't add the word Ellie.

'Not yet,' Reacher said. 'That's my guess. And my hope. Ought to be *your* hope, too, because if they hurt her, I'm going to come back here and break your spine.'

'WHAT NOW?' Alice asked.

'Back to Pecos,' Reacher said.

She drove out to the gate and turned north into the darkness. 'Why do you think it was the same people as killed Eugene?'

'It's a deployment issue,' he said. 'I can't see anybody using a separate hit team and kidnap team. Not down here in the middle of nowhere. So I think it's one team. Either a hit team moonlighting on the kidnap, or a kidnap team moonlighting on the hits. Probably the former, because the way they did Eugene was pretty expert.'

'All they did was shoot him. Anybody could do that.'

'No, they couldn't. They shot him through the eye. It's a tiny target. And in a situation like that, it's a snap shot. You raise the gun, you fire. *One, two*. No rational reason to pick such a tiny target. It's a kind of exuberance. Not exactly showing off, as such. More like just celebrating your own skill and precision.'

'And now they've got the kid,' Alice said.

'And they're uneasy about it, because they're moonlighting. They're used to each other alone, accustomed to normal procedures. Having a kid around makes them worried about being static and visible.'

'They'll look like a family. A man, a woman, a little girl.'

'I think there's more than two of them.'

'Why?'

'Because if it was me, I'd want three. In the service, we used three. Basically a driver, a shooter and a back-watcher.'

'Why are they holding Ellie?' she said. 'I mean, *still* holding her? They already coerced the confession. So what's still to gain?'

'You're the lawyer,' he said. 'You have to figure that one out. When does it become set in stone? You know, irrevocable?'

'Never, really. A confession can be retracted any time. But in practice, I guess if she answered *nolo contendere* to the grand jury indictment, that would be regarded as a milestone.'

'And how soon could that happen?'

'Tomorrow, easily. Grand jury sits more or less permanently. It would take ten minutes. So maybe tomorrow they'll let her go.'

'Maybe they won't. They'll be worried she could make the ID.'

'So what do we do?'

'We try to figure out where she is.' He opened the glove compartment and took out the maps again. Found a large-scale plan of Pecos County and spread it on his knee. Clicked on the dome light.

'But they could be anywhere,' Alice said. 'I mean, there must be a million hide-outs. Abandoned farmsteads, ruined buildings.'

'No, I think they're using motels,' Reacher said.

'Why?'

'Because appearances are important to them. Part of their technique. They suckered Al Eugene and they looked plausible to Rusty Greer. So they need running water and showers.'

'There are hundreds of motels here,' she said.

He nodded. 'And they're moving around, almost certainly. A different place every day. Basic security.'

'So how do we find the right one?'

He held the map where it caught the light.

'We find it in our heads. Figure out what *we'd* do. That should be the same as what *they'd* do.'

'So are we going to start now?'

'No, we're going back to your office. I don't like frontal assaults. Not against people this good, not with a kid in the crossfire.'

'So what do we do?'

'Divide and rule. Lure two of them out. Maybe capture a tongue.'

'A tongue? What's that?'

'An enemy prisoner who'll talk.'

'How do we do that?'

'We decoy them. They're already aware we know about them. So they'll come for us, try a little damage control.'

'They *know* we know? But how?'

'Somebody just told them.'

'Who?'

Reacher didn't reply. Just stared down at the map.

TEN

Alice parked in the lot behind the law offices. She had a key to the rear door. There were a lot of shadows, and Reacher was very vigilant as they walked. But they made it inside OK.

'Call Walker and give him an update,' Reacher said.

He made her sit back to back with him at somebody else's desk in the centre of the room, so he could watch the front entrance while she watched the rear. He rested the pistol in his lap. Then he dialled Sergeant Rodriguez's number in Abilene. Rodriguez was still on duty, and he sounded unhappy about it.

'We checked with the Bar Association,' he said. 'There are no lawyers licensed in Texas called Chester Arthur.'

'I'm from Vermont,' Reacher said. 'I'm volunteering down here, *pro bono*.'

'Like hell you are.'

'I'll deal,' Reacher said. 'Names, in exchange for conversation.'

'With who?'

'With you, maybe. How long have you been a Ranger?'

'Seventeen years.'

'How much do you know about the Border Patrol?'

'Enough, I guess.'

'You prepared to give me a straight yes–no answer?'

'What's the question?'

'You recall the Border Patrol investigation twelve years ago?'

'Maybe.'

'Was it a whitewash?'

Rodriguez paused, and then he answered, with a single word.

'I'll call you back,' Reacher said. He hung up, then turned and spoke over his shoulder to Alice. 'You get Walker?' he asked.

'He's up to speed,' she said. 'He wants us to wait for him here, for when he's through with the FBI.'

Reacher shook his head. 'Can't wait here. We'll go to him.'

She paused. 'Why was the lie about the ring different?'

'Because everything else is hearsay. But I found out for myself the ring wasn't a fake. Feels very different.'

'I don't see how it's important.'

'It's important because I've got a whole big theory going and the lie about the ring screws it up like crazy.'

'What's the big theory?'

'Something Ben Franklin once wrote,' Reacher said.

'What are you, a walking encyclopedia?'

'I remember stuff I read, is all. And I remember something Bobby Greer said, too, about armadillos.'

She just looked at him. 'You're crazy,' she said.

He nodded. 'It's only a theory. It needs to be tested.
'

THEY WALKED THROUGH THE HEAT to the courthouse building. There was a breeze, blowing in from the south. It felt damp and urgent. Walker was on his own in his office, looking very tired. His desk was a mess of phone books and paper.

'Well, it's started,' he said. 'FBI and State Police, roadblocks, helicopters, more than a hundred and fifty people on the ground. But there's a storm coming in, which ain't going to help.'

'You need us any more?' Reacher asked.

Walker shook his head. 'We should leave it to the professionals now. I'm going home, grab a couple hours' rest.'

Reacher looked around the office. The door, the floor, the windows, the desk, the filing cabinets.

'I guess we'll do the same thing,' he said. 'We'll go to Alice's place. Call us if you need us. Or if you get any news, OK?'

Walker nodded. 'I will,' he said. 'I promise.'

'WE'LL GO AS FBI AGAIN,' the woman said.

'All of us?' the driver asked. 'What about the kid?'

The woman paused. If she had to split the team two and one, she wanted the tall guy with her, not the driver.

'You stay with the kid,' she said.

'Abort horizon?' the driver asked.

It was their standard operating procedure. Whenever the team was split, the woman set an abort horizon. Which meant that you waited until the time had passed, and then, if the team wasn't together again, you got the hell out, every man for himself.

'Four hours, OK?' the woman said. 'Done and dusted.'

They did the same things they had done for Al Eugene, only faster because the Crown Vic was parked in the motel's lot, not hidden in a dusty lay-by. They pulled the wheel covers off and threw them in the trunk. They attached the communications antennas to the rear window and the trunk lid. They zipped blue jackets over their shirts. They loaded up with spare ammunition. They squared the souvenir ball-caps on their heads. They checked the loads in their nine-millimetre pistols and jammed the guns in their pockets. The tall fair man slipped into the driver's seat. The woman paused outside the motel-room door. 'Four hours,' she said again. 'Done and dusted.'

The driver nodded and closed the door behind her. Glanced over at the kid in the bed. *Done and dusted* meant *Leave nothing at all behind, especially live witnesses.*

REACHER TOOK the Heckler & Koch and the FedEx packet out of the VW and carried them into Alice's house, straight through the living room and into the kitchen area. 'Where're the scales?' he asked.

She pushed past him and opened a cupboard. Used two hands and lifted the big kitchen scales onto the countertop. There was a chromium bowl resting in a cradle above the dial. He opened cupboards until he found a cellophane-wrapped packet of chopped nuts. Put the packet in the bowl. The pointer read two pounds. He looked at the label on the packet and saw *2lb*.

'Good enough,' he said.

He put the nuts back in the cupboard and tried the FedEx packet. It weighed one pound and one ounce.

'OK, let's go,' he said. 'You got a screwdriver?'

'Under the sink.'

He bent down and found a toolbox in the cupboard. He opened it and selected a medium-sized screwdriver.

She locked up and followed him out to the VW.

'OK, back to the courthouse,' he said. 'Something I want there.'

She drove. Parked in the lot behind the building. They walked round and tried the street door. It was locked.

'I'm going to kick it in,' he said.

'There's probably an alarm.'

'There's definitely an alarm. I'm going to set it off.'

'Then the cops will come.'

'They won't come right away. We've got three minutes, maybe.'

He took two paces back, launched forward and smashed the flat of his sole above the handle. The wood splintered and sagged open a half-inch. He kicked again and the door crashed back. A blue light outside started flashing and an electric bell started ringing.

'Get the car,' he said. 'Get it started and wait for me in the alley.'

He ran up the stairs and kicked in the outer office door. Jinked through the secretarial pen and kicked in Walker's door. He went straight for the filing cabinets. The lights were off and the office was dark and he had to peer close to read the labels. The filing system was arranged partly in date order and partly by the alphabet. He found a cabinet marked *B* and jammed the tip of the screwdriver into the keyhole and hammered it in with the heel of his hand. Turned it and broke the lock. Pulled the drawer.

The files all had tiny labels encased in plastic tabs. The labels were all typed with words starting with B. But the contents of the files were way too recent. Nothing more than four years old. He stepped sideways and skipped the next *B* drawer and went to the next but one. The bell was ringing loud and the glare of the blue strobe pulsed in through the windows.

He broke the lock and slid the drawer. He had been in the building two minutes and thirty seconds. He could hear a siren under the noise of the bell. He checked the dates on the tabs and found what he was looking for three-quarters of the way back through the drawer. It was a two-inch-thick collection of paperwork in a heavy paper sling. He lifted the whole thing out and tucked it under his arm. Left the drawer open. Ran through the pen and down the stairs. Ducked round into the alley and straight into the VW.

'Go,' he said.

'Where?' Alice asked.

'South,' he said. 'To the Red House.'

'Why? What's there?'

'Everything,' he said.

She took off fast and fifty yards later Reacher saw red lights pulsing behind them. The Pecos Police Department, arriving a minute too late. He smiled and turned his head in time to catch a glimpse of a big sedan nosing left two hundred yards ahead of them into the road that led to Alice's place. It flashed through the yellow wash of a streetlight and disappeared. It looked like a police-spec Crown Victoria, plain steel wheels and VHF antennas on the back.

'Fast as you can,' he said to Alice. Then he laid the captured paperwork on his knees and clicked on the dome light so he could read it.

The B was for Border Patrol, and the file summarised the crimes committed by it twelve years ago and the measures taken in response. It made for unpleasant reading.

There was a map in the file. Most of the ambushes had taken place inside a pear-shaped pocket of territory with the southerly bulge sitting mostly inside the Echo County line.

Border Patrol brass launched a full-scale investigation one August, eleven months after the first rumours surfaced. There was one more attack at the end of that month, then nothing. Denied an ongoing forensic basis for examination, the investigation got nowhere. There were preventive measures enforced, like strict accounting of ammunition. But no conclusions were reached. It was a thorough job, and to their credit the brass kept hard at it, but a retrospective investigation into a closed paramilitary world, where the only witnesses denied ever having been near the border in the first place, was hopeless. The matter wound down. Time passed. The homicides had stopped, the survivors were building new lives, the immigration amnesties had insulated the outrage. The tempo of investigation slowed to a halt. The files were sealed four years later.

'So?' Alice said.

Reacher closed the file. Pitched it behind him into the rear seat.

'She didn't lie about the ring,' he said.

'She said it was a fake worth thirty bucks.'

'And she thought that was the truth. Because some jeweller in Pecos laughed at her and *told* her it was a fake worth thirty bucks. And she believed him. But he was trying to rip her off, was all, trying to buy it for thirty bucks and sell it again for sixty thousand. Exact same thing happened to some of these immigrants in the file. Their first experience of America.'

'The *jeweller* lied?'

He nodded. 'I should have figured it before, because it's obvious. Probably the exact same guy we went to. I figured he didn't look like the Better Business Bureau's poster boy.'

'He didn't try to rip *us* off.'

'No, Alice, he didn't. Because you're a sharp-looking white lawyer and I'm a big tough-looking white guy. She was a small Mexican

131

woman, all alone and desperate and scared. He saw an opportunity with her that he didn't see with us.'

Alice was quiet for a second. 'So what does it mean?'

Reacher clicked off the dome light. 'It means all our ducks are in a neat little row. And it means you should drive faster, because right now we're maybe twenty minutes ahead of the bad guys, and I want to keep it that way as long as I can.'

She blew through the sleeping crossroads hamlet and made the remaining sixty miles in forty minutes, which Reacher figured was pretty good for a four-cylinder import. She turned in under the gate and stopped at the porch steps. It was close to two in the morning.

'Leave it running,' Reacher said.

He led her up to the door. Hammered hard on it and got no reply. Tried the handle. It was unlocked. *Why would it be locked? We're sixty miles from the nearest crossroads.* He swung it open and they stepped straight into the hall.

'Hold your arms out,' he said.

He unloaded all six .22 hunting rifles out of the rack on the wall and laid them in her arms. She staggered under the weight.

'Go put them in the car,' he said.

There was the sound of footsteps, and Bobby Greer came out of the parlour door, rubbing sleep out of his eyes.

'Hell you think you're doing?' he said.

'I'm commandeering your weapons,' Reacher said. 'On behalf of the Echo County sheriff. I'm a deputy, remember? I want the others.'

'There aren't any others.'

'Yes, there are, Bobby. No self-respecting redneck like you would be satisfied with a bunch of .22 popguns. Where's the heavy metal?'

Bobby paused. Then he shrugged. 'OK,' he said.

He padded across the foyer and pushed open a door that led into a small, dark space. He flicked on a light and Reacher saw another gun rack filled with four 30-30 Winchesters.

'Ammunition?' Reacher asked.

Bobby opened a drawer in the gun rack's pedestal. Took out a cardboard box of Winchester cartridges.

'I've got some special loads, too,' he said. Took out another box. 'I made them myself. More power.'

Reacher nodded. 'Take them all out to the car, OK?' He took the four rifles out of the rack and followed Bobby out of the house.

Alice was sitting in the car. The six .22s were on the seat behind her. Bobby leaned in and placed the ammunition next to them. Reacher stacked the Winchesters upright behind the passenger seat. Then he turned back to Bobby.

'I'm going to borrow your Jeep,' he said.

Bobby shrugged. 'Keys are in it,' he said.

'You and your mother stay in the house now,' Reacher said. 'Anybody seen out and about will be considered hostile, OK?'

Bobby nodded. Turned and walked back inside the house. Reacher leaned into the VW to talk to Alice.

'Why do we need ten rifles?' she said.

'We don't. I don't want to give them to the bad guys, is all.'

'They're coming here?'

'They're about ten minutes behind us.'

'So what do we do?'

'We're all going out in the desert.'

'Is there going to be shooting?'

'Probably.'

'Is that smart? You said yourself, they're good shots.'

'With handguns. Best way to defend against handguns is hide a long way off and shoot back with the biggest rifle you can find.'

She shook her head. 'I can't be a part of this, Reacher. It's not right. And I've never even held a rifle.'

'You don't have to shoot,' he said. 'But you have to identify exactly who comes for us. I'm relying on you. It's vital.'

'How will I see? It's dark out there.'

'We'll fix that.'

'This is not right,' she said again. 'The police should handle this. Or the FBI. You can't just shoot at people.'

The air was heavy with storm. The breeze was blowing again and he could smell pressure and voltage building in the sky.

'Rules of engagement, Alice,' he said. 'I'll wait for an overtly hostile act before I do anything. Just like the US army. OK?'

'We'll be killed.'

'You'll be hiding far away.'

'Then *you'll* be killed. You said it yourself, they're good at this.'

'They're good at walking up to somebody and shooting them in the head. What they're like out in the open is anybody's guess.'

'You're crazy.'

'Seven minutes,' he said.

She glanced back at the road from the north. Then she shook her head, shoved the gearstick into first and held her foot on the clutch.

He squeezed her shoulder. 'Follow me close, OK?' he said.

He ran down to the motor barn and got into the Greer family's Cherokee. Started the engine and switched on the headlights. Reversed into the yard and headed down the dirt track into open country. Checked the mirror and saw the VW right behind him. Looked ahead again and saw the first raindrop hit his windshield. It was as big as a silver dollar.

THEY DROVE IN CONVOY for five miles through the dark. Cloud cover was low and thick but the rain not more than occasional splattering drops. Reacher held steady around forty miles an hour and followed the track through the brush. The Jeep was bouncing and jarring. The VW was struggling to keep pace. Its headlights were swinging and jumping in his mirrors.

Five miles from the house the ground rose slowly and shaded into mesa. Rocky outcrops channelled them southeast; stands of mesquite funnelled them tighter. Soon there was nothing more than a pair of deep ruts worn through the hardpan. Ledges and sinkholes and dense patches of thorny brush meant they had no choice but to follow them.

Then the track ran across a miniature limestone mesa. The stone was a raised pan as big as a football field, and roughly oval in shape. Reacher swung the Jeep in a circle and used the headlights to check the perimeter. All round the edges the ground fell away a couple of feet into rocky soil. Stunted bushes crowded anywhere they could find to put their roots. He liked what he saw.

He drove to the far end of the rock table and stopped where the track bumped down off it and disappeared onwards. Alice pulled the VW alongside him. He jumped out of the Jeep and ducked down to her window. Alice buzzed the window down.

'Turn it round and back it up to the edge,' he said. 'All the way back. Block the track.'

She manoeuvred the car and ran it back until it was centred in the mouth of the track and the rear wheels were tight against the drop. She left the front facing north, the way they had come. He nosed the Jeep next to her and opened the tailgate.

'Kill the motor and the lights,' he called. 'Get the rifles.'

She passed him the Winchesters, one at a time. He laid them sideways in the Jeep's load space. She passed him the .22s, and he pitched them into the brush. She passed him the two boxes of ammunition. He laid them alongside the rifles. Ducked round to the driver's door and switched the engine off. Silence fell. He listened hard and scanned the northern horizon. Infrequent raindrops hit his shoulders. That was all. Nothing else. Blackness and silence everywhere.

He came back to the tailgate and opened the ammunition boxes. He took one of Bobby's out. *I made them myself*, Bobby had said. *More power*. So Bobby had probably tamped a whole lot of extra powder into each one. And maybe he had used hotter powder than normal. Which would give him the muzzle flash from hell. Reacher smiled and took more of the shells out of the box. Muzzle flash was exactly what he was looking for.

He loaded the first Winchester with a single sample of Bobby's hand-loads. The second he filled with seven of them. The third he loaded alternately until it was full with four stock and three hand-loads. The fourth rifle he filled entirely with factory ammo. He laid the guns left to right in sequence across the Jeep's load space and closed the tailgate on them. He stepped round to the driver's seat and Alice climbed in beside him.

'Where are we going now?' she asked.

He started the engine and backed away from the parked VW.

'Think of this mesa like a clock face,' he said. 'We came in at the six o'clock position. Your car is parked at the twelve. You're going to be hiding on the rim at the eight. Your job is to fire a rifle, one shot, and then scoot down to the seven.'

'You said I wouldn't have to shoot.'

'I changed the plan,' he said.

'But I told you, I can't fire a rifle.'

'Yes, you can. You just pull the trigger. It's easy. Don't worry about aiming or anything. All I want is the sound and the flash.'

She shook her head. 'Great,' she said.

He pulled the Jeep close to the edge of the limestone table and stopped. Opened the tailgate and took out the first rifle. Checked his bearings and ran to the fractured rock lip and laid the gun on the ground with the barrel pointing at the emptiness twenty feet in front of the distant VW. He racked the lever.

'It's ready to fire,' he said. 'And this is the eight o'clock spot. Stay down below the lip, fire the gun, and then move to the seven. Crouch low all the way. And then watch, real careful. They might fire in your direction, but I guarantee they'll miss, OK?'

'Are you sure?'

'Superman couldn't hit anything with a handgun in the dark at this distance.'

'They might get lucky.'

'No, Alice, tonight they're not going to get lucky. Believe me.'

'But how will I know when to fire?'

'You'll know.'

'Great,' she said again.

He climbed back into the Jeep and hustled it across the mesa to the four o'clock position. Spun the wheel and reversed the car and backed it straight off the rock. It bumped down two feet and came to a shuddering stop in the undergrowth. He killed the engine and the lights. Took the fourth rifle and propped it upright against the passenger door. Carried the second and third with him, climbed back onto the ledge and ran to the two o'clock spot. Laid the third rifle on the lip of the rock and ran to the parked VW. Ducked inside and unscrewed the dome light. Eased the driver's door back to three inches from closed and left it. Measured twenty feet clockwise and laid the second rifle on the ground, on the rim of the ledge, somewhere between the twelve and the one. About twelve seventeen, to be pedantic, he thought. Then he crawled back and lay face-down on the ground, tight up against the VW. He settled down to wait. Eight minutes, perhaps, he thought. Maybe nine.

IT WAS ELEVEN MINUTES. He saw a flash in the north and at first thought it was lightning, but then it happened again and he saw it was headlight beams bouncing across rough terrain and catching the low grey cloud overhead. A vehicle was heading his way; he knew it would, because the landscape gave it no other choice but to stay on the track. He could feel pressure and electricity in the sky above. The raindrops were falling harder and a little faster. It felt like a fuse was burning and the storm was set to explode. Not yet, he thought. Please, give me five minutes more.

Thirty seconds later he could hear an engine. Eight cylinders. The sound rose and fell as the wheels gripped the dirt and then bounced and lost traction. Load-carrying suspension, he thought. Bobby's pick-up, probably. The one he used to hunt armadillo.

Then the truck burst into sight. It bounced up onto the mesa travelling fast. It accelerated on the flatter terrain. Seventy yards away. Fifty. It came straight at him until the bouncing headlights washed over the stationary VW directly ahead of it. The yellow paint above Reacher's shoulder glowed impossibly bright. Then the truck jammed to a panic stop. All four wheels locked and the truck slewed slightly left and came to rest facing eleven o'clock, maybe thirty yards in front of him. The far edge of the headlight beams washed over him. He forced himself tighter under the VW.

Nothing happened for a second. Then the pick-up driver killed his lights and total darkness came back. No sound at all beyond the truck engine idling.

Now, Alice, Reacher thought.

Nothing happened.

Shoot, Alice, he thought. Just pull the damn trigger.

Nothing happened.

He closed his eyes, paused another whole endless second and braced himself to launch outwards anyway. Opened his eyes and took a breath and started moving.

Then Alice fired. There was a monstrous muzzle flash to his right and the buzzing whine of a supersonic bullet high in the air and a split second later a barking crash clapped across the landscape. He rolled out from under the VW, reached in through the driver's door and flicked the headlights on. Jumped backwards and kept rolling and came up into a low crouch six feet away to see the pick-up caught perfectly in the cone of light. Three people in it. A driver in the cab. Two figures crouching in the load bed, holding the roll bar one-handed. All three with their heads turned abruptly on their shoulders, rigid and frozen and staring back at the spot Alice had fired from.

They were immobile a split second longer, then they reacted. The driver flicked his lights back on. The pick-up and the VW glared at each other like it was a contest. Reacher was dazzled by the light but he saw the figures in the load bed were wearing caps and blue jackets. One figure was smaller than the other. A woman, he thought. And suddenly he knew she was the shooter. Small hands, neat fingers. Carmen's Lorcin automatic could have been built for her.

They both had handguns. They leaned on the pick-up's roof and started shooting at the VW's lights. Their caps said FBI on the front. He froze. What the hell? Then he relaxed. Fake apparel, fake ID, a tricked-up Crown Vic. They just went to Alice's place in it. And that's how they stopped Al Eugene on Friday. He heard the dull thumps of nine-millimetre pistols firing fast. He saw the VW's windshield explode, then the VW's lights were gone and he could see nothing behind the dazzle of the pick-up's lights. He sensed the pistols turning back to where they had fixed Alice's firing position. He saw tiny oblique muzzle flashes and heard bullets whining away from him.

He crawled to the rim of the mesa and tracked fifteen feet left. Found the Winchester he had placed at twelve seventeen, full of Bobby Greer's hand-loads. He fired without aiming. A tremendous flame leapt out of the muzzle. He racked the lever and hustled right, towards the VW. Fired again. Two huge flashes, moving counter-clockwise. From the pick-up it would look like a person traversing right to left. A smart shooter would fire ahead of the last flash and hope to hit the moving target. Deflection shooting. They went for it. He heard bullets whining off the rock near the car.

But by then he was on the move in the opposite direction, clock-wise again. He dropped the rifle and bent low and ran for the next one. It was there at two o'clock, the third Winchester. He aimed into the blackness eight feet behind the pick-up's headlights and four feet above. Fired. He heard the woman's voice shout a command and the pick-up's headlights died. He fired at the same spot with the next shell, which was a hand-load. The gout of flame spat out and lit up the mesa and he jinked five feet right. Tracked the frozen visual target in his mind and fired the second factory bullet. He heard a sharp scream. Danced one pace to his right and fired the next hand-load. The muzzle flash showed him a body falling head first out of the pick-up bed. One down. It was the man. Reacher aimed again slightly left of the place the man had fallen from. Racked the lever. It moved a quarter-inch and jammed.

Then two things happened. First the pick-up moved. It lurched forward and peeled away in a tight circle and headed north, the way it had come. Then a handgun started firing close to the VW. The woman was out of the truck, firing fast. A hail of bullets. They were missing him by three or four feet. The truck raced away. Its lights flicked on again. It thumped down off the rock table and hurtled back towards the red house. Its noise faded to nothing. He realised the rain had changed. The heavy drops had stopped and in their place was an insistent patter of drizzle. It grew perceptibly harder and harder within seconds like he was standing in a shower stall and an unseen hand was opening the faucet wider and wider.

He laid the rifle in the dust, which was already wet, turning to mud. He moved left, tracking back towards the hidden Jeep, maybe forty yards away. The rain hissed and roared on the mesquite bushes all round him. The good news was it took making noise out of the equation. He wouldn't have backed himself to move as quietly as the woman could. A frame six feet five in height and 250 pounds in weight was good for a lot of things, but not for silent progress through desert vegetation at night. The bad news was visibility was soon going to be zero. They could bump into each other.

He made it back to the Jeep at the four o'clock position. Found the fourth rifle propped against its door, full of factory shells. He aimed across the mesa towards the eleven. Pulled the trigger. Fired four more spaced shots, at the twelve, the one, the two, the three. He slid the gun under the Jeep and waded west through the brush until he was forty feet from the edge of the rock. Pulled Alice's Heckler & Koch out of his pocket, knocked the safety off and waited for lightning to strike. Five more minutes, he guessed. He worked south through the undergrowth, back towards the VW. The rain was building relentlessly. The noise was astonishing.

He was opposite the two o'clock position and thirty feet from the ledge when the lightning started. He fell to a crouch and stared straight ahead. Saw nothing. Turned and scanned left. Saw the woman seventy feet away, crouched in the lee of the ledge. She was looking straight at him. Her gun was rigid in her hand and her arm was fully extended from the shoulder. He saw the muzzle flash as she fired at him, a tiny dull spark overwhelmed by the storm.

She missed him. The lightning died and plunged the world back into absolute darkness. Reacher fired once at the remembered target and listened hard. Nothing. Probably a miss.

The next lightning flash was nearer. He scanned left. The woman had moved closer. She was sixty feet away from him, still tight against the mesa. She fired at him and missed by four feet. He fired back. Probably a miss. Eight left.

He tracked his gun hand left to right along the theoretical direction she must be moving. Waited for the lightning. It came sooner than he expected. He squinted ahead. The woman was gone. He jerked left and saw a smudge of blue backtracking away in the opposite direction. He fired instinctively just ahead of it and the lightning died and darkness and noise and chaos collapsed around him.

THE STORM DRIFTED north and east and pushed the leading edge of rain ahead of it. It reached the motel building and built steadily and quickly from a whisper to a patter to a hard drumming on the metal roof. The loud noise woke Ellie from a troubled sleep. She opened her eyes and saw the small dark man with hair on his arms. He was sitting very still in a chair near the bed, watching her.

'Hi, kid,' he said.

Ellie said nothing.

'Can't sleep?'

Ellie looked up at the ceiling. 'Raining,' she said. 'It's noisy.'

The man nodded, and checked his watch. Ellie pulled the sheet over her head.

HE JUMPED OUT of his crouch and ran as hard as he could, back and left, curving round in a circle. He crashed through the brush, hurdling mesquite, splashing through puddles, sliding through the mud. He needed to outflank her before the next lightning bolt.

He ran in a big looping curve, then slowed and skidded and eased in close to the limestone ledge maybe twenty feet north of where he had first seen her. She had moved south, and then back, so now she would be on her way south again. She ought to be thirty feet ahead by now. Right in front of him. He walked after her, fast and easy. Kept loose, trying to second-guess the rhythm of the lightning, staying ready to hit the wet earth.

The flash lit up the whole landscape. Reacher dropped to a crouch and stared. She wasn't there. She was nowhere in front of him. He dropped full length into the mud and lay still. Maybe she had gone for the Jeep. Too far, surely. So he crawled south on his knees and elbows. Ten feet, twenty, twenty-five. And then he smelt perfume.

It was somehow intensified by the rain. *Was* it perfume? Or was it something from nature, like a night flower suddenly blooming in the storm? No, it was a woman's perfume. He stopped moving and lay still. Held his breath. Waited for the lightning.

There was a split-second tearing sound in the sky and a gigantic thunderclap crashed and a bolt of lightning fired absolutely simultaneously. The desert lit up brighter than day. The woman was three feet in front of him. She was slumped face-down on the ground. Her legs were bent at the knees and her arms were folded under her. Her gun had fallen next to her shoulder. It was half submerged in the mud. He used the last of the lightning flash to scrabble for it and hurl it away. Then the light died and he used the afterimage retained in his eyes to find her neck.

There was no pulse. She was already very cold.

Deflection shooting. His third bullet, instinctively placed just ahead of her as she scrambled away from him. She had jumped straight into its path. His left arm started shaking. He told himself it was because he was holding it an an unnatural angle. Then he started laughing. It built quickly, like the rain. He had been stalking a woman he had already shot dead.

The next flash was sheet lightning again, vague and diffuse and flickering. He rolled the body over. Tore open her jacket and shirt. He had hit her in the left armpit. It was through-and-through, exiting in the opposite wall of her chest. Probably got her heart, both lungs and her spine. A .40 bullet was not a subtle thing.

She was medium-sized. Blonde hair, soaked and full of mud where it spilled out under the FBI cap. He pushed the cap up so he could see her face. It was slightly familiar. He had seen her before. Where? The diner. The Coke floats. Friday, school quitting time, a Crown Victoria, three passengers. He had pegged them as a sales team. Wrong again.

He put Alice's gun back in his pocket and walked back to the Jeep. It was so dark and he had so much rain in his eyes that he thumped right into it before he knew he was there. He tracked round it with a hand and found the driver's door.

He put the headlights on bright and started the wipers beating fast. He selected four-wheel drive and slid around for a while before the front tyres caught and dragged the car up the slope. Then he hooked a wide curve across to the seven o'clock position. He hit the horn twice and Alice walked out of the mesquite into the headlight beams, soaked to the skin. She ran round to the passenger door.

'What happened?'

He drove off again, zigzagging the Jeep to fan the headlight beams back and forth across the mesa. Thirty feet in front of the wrecked VW, he found the first guy's body. He dipped the lights so they would shine on it, and jumped out. The guy was dead. He had taken the Winchester's bullet in the stomach. He was tall and heavily built. Reacher scanned back to the scene in the diner. By the till. The woman, two men. One big and fair, one small and dark. Then he walked back to the Jeep and slid inside.

'Two dead,' he said. 'That's what happened. But the driver escaped. Did you ID him?'

'They came to kill us, didn't they?'

'That was the plan. Did you ID the driver?'

She said nothing.

'It's very important, Alice,' he said. 'For Ellie's sake. We don't have a tongue. That part didn't work out. They're both dead.'

She shook her head. 'I'm sorry. I was running. The lights were only on a second or two.'

'I've seen these people before,' he said. 'On Friday, up at the crossroads. Must have been after they got Eugene. They must have been scouting the area. Three of them. A woman, a big guy, a small dark guy. I can account for the woman and the big guy. So was it the small dark guy driving tonight?'

'I didn't really see.'

'Gut feeling?' Reacher said. 'First impression? You must have got a glimpse. Or seen a silhouette.'

'Didn't you?'

He nodded. 'He was facing away from me, looking down to where you fired from. There was a lot of glare. Then I was shooting, and then he took off. But I don't think he was small.'

She nodded, too. 'Gut feeling, he wasn't small. Or dark. It was just a blur, but I'd say he was big enough. Maybe fair-haired.'

'Makes sense,' Reacher said. 'They left one of the team behind to guard Ellie.'

'So who was driving?'

'Their client. The guy who hired them. That's my guess. Because they were short-handed, and because they needed local knowledge.'

'He got away.'

Reacher smiled. 'He can run, but he can't hide.'

ELEVEN

They went to take a look at the wrecked VW. It was beyond help. Alice didn't seem too concerned about it. She just shrugged and turned away. Reacher took the maps from the glove compartment, turned the Jeep round and headed back to the Red House. The rain was easing back to drizzle.

Reacher swerved round the motor barn and saw pale lights flickering behind some of the windows in the house. 'Candles,' he said.

'Power must be out,' Alice said. 'Lightning must have hit the lines.'

He turned the car so the headlights washed deep into the barn. Bobby's pick-up was in its place, but it was wet and streaked with mud. Water was dripping out of the load bed.

Reacher stared into the mirror. Then he turned his head and watched the road from the north. 'Somebody's coming,' he said. There was a faint glow of headlights behind them, many miles distant. 'Let's go say howdy to the Greers.'

He led her up the porch steps and pushed open the door. The hallway had candles burning. He ushered Alice into the parlour. More candles were burning, and a Coleman lantern was standing on a credenza against the end wall, hissing softly.

Bobby and his mother were sitting together at the table. Rusty was fully dressed, in jeans and a shirt.

'Why are you up?' Reacher asked. 'It's three in the morning.'

Neither of them answered.

'Your truck was out tonight,' Reacher said.

'But we weren't,' Bobby said. 'We stayed in, like you told us to.'

Reacher heard a car drive up to the porch. The engine died. The *clunk* of a door closing. Feet on the porch steps. The house door opening, footsteps crossing the hall. Then the parlour door opened. Hack Walker stepped into the room.

'Good,' Reacher said. 'We don't have much time.'

'Did you rob my office?' Walker replied.

Reacher nodded. 'I was curious.'

'About what?'

'About details,' Reacher said. 'I'm a details guy.'

'You didn't need to break in. I'd have shown you the files.'

'You weren't there.'

'Whatever, you shouldn't have broken in. You're in trouble for it. You can understand that, right? Big trouble.'

Reacher smiled. 'Sit down, Hack,' he said.

Walker paused a second. Then he sat down next to Rusty Greer. 'You got something for me?' he asked.

Reacher sat opposite. Laid his hands palm-down on the wood.

'I was a cop of sorts for thirteen years,' he said.

'So?'

'Carmen had no money with her. I *know* that. Two million in the bank, and she travels three hundred miles with a single dollar in her purse? Sleeps in the car, doesn't eat? Leapfrogs from one Mobil station to the next, just to keep going? That didn't tie up for me.'

'She was play-acting. That's who she is.'

'If Carmen had two million in the bank but travelled with a single dollar just in case she bumped into a guy as suspicious as me, then she is the best-prepared con artist in the history of the world.'

'So what are you saying?'

'I'm saying it didn't tie up for me. So it got me thinking about the money. And then something else didn't tie up. The collarbone.'

'What about it?'

Reacher turned to face Alice. 'When you fell off your inline skates, did you break your collarbone?'

'No,' Alice said.

'Any injuries at all?'

'I tore up my hand. A lot of road rash.'

'You put your hand out to break your fall?'

'Reflex,' she said. 'It's impossible not to.'

Reacher nodded. Turned back to Walker. 'I rode with Carmen on Saturday,' he said. 'My first time ever. The thing I really remember is how *high* I was. It's scary up there. So the thing is, if Carmen fell off, from that height, onto rocky dirt, hard enough to bust her collarbone, how is it that she didn't get road rash, too? On her hand?'

'Maybe she did.'

'The hospital didn't write it up.'

'Maybe they forgot.'

'It was a very detailed report. New staff, working hard. I noticed that, and Cowan Black did, too. He said they were very thorough. They wouldn't have neglected lacerations to the palm.'

'She must have worn riding gloves.'

Reacher shook his head. 'She told me nobody wears gloves down here. Too hot. And she definitely wouldn't have said that if gloves had once saved her from serious road rash. She'd have been a big fan of gloves, in that case.'

'So?'

'So I started to wonder if the collarbone thing *could* have been from Sloop hitting her. Only she also claimed he had broken her arm and her jaw and knocked her teeth loose, and there was no mention of all that stuff, so I stopped wondering. Especially when I found out the ring was real.'

'A son of mine would never hit a woman,' Rusty said.

Reacher turned to her. 'We'll get to what Sloop did and didn't do real soon. But right now, keep quiet, OK? Hack and I have business.'

'What business?' Walker said.

'This business,' Reacher said, and propped Alice's gun on the tabletop, the butt resting on the wood and the muzzle pointing straight at Walker's chest.

'What the hell are you doing?' Walker said.

'I figured out the thing with the diamond,' he said. 'Then everything else fell neatly into place. Especially with you giving us the badges and sending us down here to speak with Rusty.'

'What are you talking about?'

'You knew Carmen pretty well. You knew what she must have told me. Which was the truth. So you just reversed everything. Like she told me she was from Napa, and you said, *Hey, I bet she told you she's from Napa, but she isn't, you know*. Like she told me she'd called the IRS, and you said, *Hey, I bet she told you she called the IRS, but she didn't, really*. It was like *you* knew the real truth and were reluctantly exposing commonplace lies she had told before. But it was *you* who was lying. It was very, very effective. Like a conjuring trick. And you dressed it all up behind pretending you wanted to save her.'

'I *did* want to save her. I *am* saving her.'

'Bullshit, Hack. Your only aim was to coerce a confession out of her for something she didn't do. Your hired guns kidnapped Ellie so you could force Carmen to confess. I was your only problem. I recruited Alice. We were in your face from Monday morning onward. So you misled us. You let us down slowly and regretfully, point by point. It was beautifully done.'

'You're crazy,' Walker said.

'No, I'm not. You were even smart enough to reveal a cynical reason for *wanting* to save her. About wanting to be a judge, so I wouldn't think you were too good to be true. That was a great touch, Hack. But all the time you were talking to her on the phone, muffling your voice to get past the desk clerk, telling him you were her lawyer, telling *her* if she ever spoke to a *real* lawyer, you'd hurt Ellie. Which is why she refused to speak with Alice. Then you wrote out a bunch of phoney financial statements on your computer. And you drafted the phoney trust deeds. And the phoney Family Services papers. Then as soon as you heard your people had picked up the kid you got back on the phone and coached Carmen through the phoney confession, feeding back to *her* all the lies you'd told *me*. Then you sent your assistant downstairs to listen to them.'

'This is nonsense.'

Reacher shrugged. 'So let's prove it. Let's call the FBI and ask them how the hunt for Ellie is going.'

'Phones are out,' Bobby said. 'Electrical storm.'

Reacher nodded. 'OK, no problem.'

He kept the gun pointed at Walker's chest and turned to face Rusty. 'Tell me what the FBI agents asked you,' he said.

Rusty looked blank. 'What FBI agents?'

'No FBI agents came here tonight?'

She just shook her head. Reacher nodded.

'*You* were play-acting, Hack,' he said. 'You told us you'd called the FBI and the State Police, and there were roadblocks and helicopters and more than a hundred and fifty people on the ground. But you didn't call anybody. Because if you had, the *first* thing they would have done is come down here. They'd have talked to Rusty. They'd have brought sketch artists and crime-scene technicians. This is the scene of the crime, after all. And Rusty is the only witness.'

'There *were* FBI people here,' Bobby said. 'I saw them in the yard.'

Reacher shook his head. 'There were people wearing FBI hats,' he said. 'Two of them. But they aren't wearing those hats any more.'

Walker said nothing.

'Big mistake, Hack,' Reacher said. 'Giving us those stupid badges and sending us down here. You knew Rusty was the vital witness. You also knew she wouldn't cooperate with me. So it was an inexplicable decision for a DA to take, to send us down here. I couldn't believe it. Then I saw why. You wanted to know where we were, at all times. So you could send your people after us.'

'What people?'

'The hired guns, Hack. The people in the FBI hats. The people you sent to kill Al Eugene. The people you sent to kill Sloop. They were very professional. Al Eugene was no problem. Could have been anybody, out there in the middle of nowhere. But Sloop was harder. He was just home from prison, wasn't going any place for a spell. So it had to be done right here, which was risky. They made you agree to cover their asses by framing Carmen. Then you made *them* agree to help you do it by moonlighting as the kidnap team.'

'This is ridiculous,' Walker said.

'You knew Carmen had bought a gun,' Reacher said. 'You told me, the paperwork comes through your office. And you knew *why* she bought it. You knew all about Sloop and what he did to her. You knew their bedroom was a torture chamber. So she wants to hide a gun in there, where does she put it? Three choices, really. Top shelf of her closet, her bedside table, or her underwear drawer. Common sense. Same for any woman in any bedroom. I know it, and your people knew it. They probably watched through the window until she went to shower, they slipped some gloves on, a minute later they're in the room, they cover Sloop with their own guns until they find Carmen's, and they shoot him with it. They're outside again thirty seconds later. A quick sprint back to where they left their car on the road, and they're gone. This house is a warren. But you know it well. You're a friend of the family. You assured them they could be in and out without being seen. Probably drew them a floor plan.'

Walker closed his eyes. Said nothing. He looked old and pale.

'But you made mistakes, Hack,' Reacher said. 'The financial reports were clumsy. Lots of money, hardly any expenditure. How likely is that? What is she, a miser, too? And the medical reports—'

Walker opened his eyes, defiant. 'The medical reports,' he repeated. 'You saw them. They *prove* she was lying.'

Reacher nodded. 'Leaving them in the FedEx packet was neat. They looked like they were hot off the truck. But you should have torn the label off. Because FedEx charges by weight. And I weighed the packet on Alice's kitchen scales. One pound, one ounce. The label said two pounds and nine ounces. So either FedEx ripped off the hospital by padding the charge, or you took out about sixty per cent of the contents and trashed them. And you know what? I vote for you checking the contents before you sent them over to us. Anything about the beatings went in the trash. All you left were the genuine accidents. But the road rash thing passed you by, so you left the collarbone in by mistake. Or maybe you felt you *had* to leave it in, because you know she's got a healed knot clearly visible and you figured I'd have noticed it.'

Walker said nothing. Reacher smiled.

'But you were mostly pretty good,' he said. 'When I made the link to Eugene, you kept on track. You were shocked. You went all grey and sweaty. Not because you were upset about Al. But because he'd been found so soon. You hadn't planned on that. Still, you thought for ten seconds and came up with the IRS motive. But you were so busy thinking, you forgot to be scared enough. About the two-for-three possibility. It was a plausible threat. You should have been much more worried. Anybody else would have been.'

Walker said nothing.

'And you got Sloop out on a Sunday,' Reacher said. 'Not easy. But you didn't do it for him. You did it so he could be killed on a Sunday, so Carmen could be framed on a Sunday and spend the maximum time in jail before visitors could get near her the next Saturday. To give yourself five clear days to work on her.'

Walker said nothing. Bobby was leaning forward, staring at him. '*You* sent people to kill my brother?' he breathed.

'Why would I?' Walker said. 'What possible motive could I have?'

'You wanted to be a judge,' Reacher said. 'Not because you wanted to do good. It was because you wanted the trappings. You were greedy for money and power. And it was right there in front of you. But first you had to get elected. And what sort of a thing stops a person getting elected?'

Walker just shrugged.

'Scandal,' Reacher said. 'Old secrets, coming back at you from the past. Sloop and Al and you were a threesome, way back when. Did all kinds of stuff together. So there's Sloop, in prison. He can't stand it in there. So he thinks, how do I get out? Not by repaying my debts. By figuring, my old pal Hack is running for judge. Big prize, all that money and power. What's he prepared to do to get it? So he calls you up and says he could start some rumours about some old activities if you don't broker his way out of there. You figure Sloop wouldn't incriminate *himself* by talking about something you all did together, so at first you relax. Then you realise there's a large gap between the sort of *facts* that would convict you and the sort of *rumours* that would wreck your chances in the election. So you take some of your campaign donations and arrange to pay off the IRS with it. Now Sloop's happy. But you're not. Sloop's threatened you once. What about the next time he wants something? And Al's involved, because he's Sloop's lawyer. So it's all fresh in Al's mind too. Your chances of making judge are suddenly vulnerable.'

Walker said nothing.

'You know what Ben Franklin once wrote?' Reacher said. 'Three may keep a secret, if two of them are dead.'

'What was the secret?' Alice whispered.

'Three boys in rural Texas,' Reacher said. 'Growing up together, playing ball, having fun. They get a little older, they turn their attention to what their dads are doing. The guns, the rifles, the hunting. Maybe they start with armadillos. They shouldn't, really, because they're protected. By the tree-huggers. But the attitude is, they're on my land, they're mine to hunt. Bobby said that to me. But armadillos are slow. Too easy. The three boys are growing up. They're three young men now. High-school seniors. They want a little more excitement. So they go looking for coyotes, maybe. Worthier opponents. They hunt at night. They use a truck. They range far and wide. And soon they find bigger game. Soon they find a *real* thrill.'

'What?'

'Mexicans,' Reacher said. 'Maybe they started with a girl. Maybe they didn't mean to kill her. But they did anyway. Maybe they *had* to. Couple of days, they're nervous. They hold their breath. But there's no comeback. Nobody cares. So hey, this is suddenly *fun*. It becomes a sport. They take that old pick-up, one of them driving, two of them in the load bed. Bobby said Sloop invented that technique. Said he was real good at it. I expect he was. I expect they all were. They got plenty of practice. They did it twenty-five times in a year.'

'That was the Border Patrol,' Bobby said.

'No, it wasn't. The report wasn't a whitewash. It didn't read like one, and the inside word is it was kosher. Sergeant Rodriguez told me that. And people like Sergeant Rodriguez *know* things like that, believe me. The investigation got nowhere because it was looking in the wrong place. It wasn't a bunch of rogue officers. It was three local boys called Sloop Greer and Al Eugene and Hack Walker.'

Silence in the room.

'The attacks were mostly in Echo County,' Reacher said. 'That struck me as odd. Why would the Border Patrol come so far north? Truth is, they didn't. Three Echo boys went a little ways south.'

Silence.

'The attacks stopped in late August,' Reacher said. 'Why was that? Not because the investigation scared them off. They didn't *know* about the investigation. It was because college opens early September. They went off to be freshmen. The next summer it was too dangerous or they'd grown out of it. The whole thing faded into history, until twelve years later Sloop was sitting in a cell somewhere and dragged it all up because he was so desperate to get out.'

Everybody was staring straight at Walker. His eyes were closed tight and he was deathly pale.

'No,' he said. 'It wasn't like that. I was just going to take Ellie. Just temporarily. I hired some local people to do it. They watched her for a week. I went up to the jail and told Sloop, don't mess with me. But he didn't care. He said, go ahead and take Ellie. He didn't want her.

He was all conflicted. He married Carmen to punish himself for what we did, I think. That's why he hit her. She was a permanent reminder. Ellie too. So taking her wasn't a threat to Sloop.'

'So then you hired some more people.'

'It was a long time ago, Reacher. We were kids at the time. We all agreed we would never even mention it again. We promised each other. Never, *ever*. It was the unmentionable thing. Like it had never happened. Like it was just a bad dream.'

'Are you armed?' Reacher asked Walker.

Walker nodded. 'Pistol, in my pocket.'

'Get it for me, Mrs Greer,' Reacher said.

Rusty went for Walker's pocket. She came out with a Colt Detective Special.

'Where's Ellie, Hack?' Reacher asked.

'I don't know,' Walker said. 'They use motels. I don't know which one. They wouldn't tell me. They said it's safer that way.'

'How do you contact them?'

'A Dallas number. It must be rerouted.'

'Phones are out,' Bobby said.

Reacher raised Alice's gun. Held it straight out across the table. The muzzle came to rest two feet from Walker's face.

'Watch the trigger finger, Hack,' he said.

He tightened his finger until the skin shone white in the candle-light. The trigger moved back a sixteenth of an inch, then an eighth.

'You want to die, Hack?'

Walker nodded. 'Yes, please,' he whispered.

'Tell me first,' Reacher said. 'Make it right. Where is she?'

'I don't *know*,' Walker said.

Reacher sighed and slackened his finger and lowered the gun back to the tabletop. Nobody moved, until Rusty's hand came up with the revolver in it. She brought it level with Hack Walker's forehead, the muzzle no more than two inches from his skin.

'You killed my boy,' she whispered.

Walker nodded, very slightly. 'I'm sorry,' he whispered back.

'No, Rusty,' Reacher said.

'Mom,' Bobby called.

The Colt's hammer clicked back.

'*No*,' Alice shouted.

The hammer tripped. The gun fired. There was colossal noise and flame. Then Rusty fired again. The second bullet followed the first straight through Walker's head and he went down. Rusty kept the gun rock-steady in the air above him and fired into space. The third shot splintered the wall, the fourth hit the Coleman lantern and shattered its glass, and the fifth hit its kerosene reservoir and exploded it over a ten-foot square of wall. It blew sideways and ignited with a bright flash and the sixth shot hit the exact centre of the flames. She kept on pumping the trigger even after the gun was empty.

The kerosene set the wall on fire immediately. The dry old wood burned fiercely. Blue flames crept upwards and sideways and the faded red paint bubbled and peeled ahead of them. Tongues of flame found the vertical seams between the boards and raced up them. Within seconds the wall was burning along its full height. Then the fire started creeping sideways very fast, coming round behind everybody in the room.

'Out,' Reacher shouted.

Alice was already on her feet and Bobby was staring at the fire. Reacher pulled Rusty out of her chair and straight-armed her out of the room. Alice had the front door open. She ran down the steps to the yard and Reacher pushed Rusty after her. He ducked back inside the hall. It was filling with smoke. Bobby was coughing near the parlour door. The parlour was already an inferno. Reacher grabbed Bobby by the wrist. Twisted his arm and grabbed the back of his belt and ran him out into the darkness. Hustled him down the steps and shoved him towards the centre of the yard.

'It's burning down,' Bobby screamed. 'All of it.'

The windows were alive with yellow light. Flames were dancing behind them. There were loud cracking sounds from inside as timbers yielded and moved. The soaked roof was already steaming gently.

Reacher grabbed Alice's hand and ran straight for the Jeep. 'You drive,' he called. 'North, OK?'

He pushed her towards the driver's door and ran round the hood. She pulled her seat forward and he racked his back. Unfolded the maps. To his left the Red House was burning fiercely. Both floors now. The maid ran out of the kitchen door, wrapped in a bathrobe.

Alice slammed the selector into drive and the car took off. She slewed past Walker's Lincoln. Made the right under the gate without pausing. Accelerated hard. He riffled through the maps on his knees and found the large-scale sheet showing Pecos County in its entirety. Then he reached up and clicked the dome light on.

'Faster,' he said. 'I've got a real bad feeling about this.'

THE FOUR HOURS were long gone, but the driver waited anyway. He looked over at the bed. Looked at the sleeping child in it. He felt a certain reluctance. How could he not? He wasn't a monster. He would do what he had to do, but he wasn't going to *enjoy* it.

He walked over and opened the door and hung the DO NOT DISTURB tag on the outside handle. Closed the door and locked it from the inside. He slipped the chain on and started into the room.

ALICE DROVE AS FAST as she dared. Reacher held the map high, where it caught the light from the roof console. He stared hard at it and checked the scale and held his finger and thumb apart like a little compass and traced a circle.

'You done any tourist stuff around here?' he asked.

'Some, I guess. I went to the McDonald Observatory.'

He checked the map. 'That's eighty miles,' he said. 'Too far.'

'For what?'

'For them to have been today. I think they'll have been a half-hour from Pecos by road, max. Twenty-five miles, thirty tops.'

'Why?'

'To be close to Walker. He might have planned on smuggling Carmen out, if necessary. Or maybe bringing Ellie in to see her. Whatever it took to convince her that the threat was real. So I think they'll have holed up somewhere nearby.'

'And near a tourist attraction?'

'Definitely,' he said. 'That's key.'

She gripped the wheel and drove. Dropped her eyes to the speedo.

'Oh God,' she whispered.

'What?'

'We're out of gas. It's right on empty. The warning light is on.'

He was quiet for a second. 'Keep going,' he said. 'We'll be OK.'

She drove on. He kept his eyes on the windshield.

'Reacher, we're out of gas,' Alice said.

'Don't worry about it.'

She drove on. The car rocked hard. The headlights bounced ahead of them. The tyres whined on the streaming blacktop. She glanced down again.

'It's right on *empty*, Reacher,' she said. '*Below* empty'

'Don't worry,' he said again.

'Why not?'

Another mile.

'That's why not,' he said suddenly.

The right edge of the headlight beam washed over the ragged gravel shoulder and lit up a steel-blue Ford Crown Victoria. It had four VHF antennas on the back and no wheel covers.

'We'll use that,' he said. 'It should have most of a tank.'

She pulled in behind it. 'This is theirs? Why is it here?'

'Walker left it here.'

'How did you know?'

'It's pretty obvious. They came down from Pecos in two cars, this and the Lincoln. They dumped the Lincoln here and used the Ford the rest of the way. Then Walker ran away from the mesa, put the pick-up back in the barn, drove the Ford back up here, retrieved his Lincoln and came back down in it for our benefit. To make us think it was his first visit, if we happened to be still alive and looking.'

'What about the keys?'

'They'll be in it. Walker wasn't in the right frame of mind to worry about Hertz losing a rental car.'

Alice jumped out and checked. Gave a thumbs up. The keys were in it. Reacher followed her with the maps. They got into the Crown Vic and he racked his seat back and she pulled hers forward. She fired it up and they were on the road again within thirty seconds, already doing sixty miles an hour.

'Go faster. Nobody will stop you. We look just like a squad car.'

She accelerated to seventy-five, then eighty. He found the dome light and clicked it on and returned to the maps.

'What's at Balmorhea Recreation Area?' he asked. It was southwest of Pecos, only thirty miles out. The right sort of distance.

'It's a desert oasis,' she said. 'Like a huge lake, very clear. You can swim and scuba dive there.'

But not the right sort of place. 'I don't think so,' he said.

He checked the map again. 'What about Fort Stockton?' he asked.

'It's just a town,' she said. 'No different from Pecos, really. But *Old* Fort Stockton is worth seeing, I guess.'

He looked at the map. Old Fort Stockton was marked as a historic ruin, north of the town itself. Nearer Pecos. He measured the distance. Maybe forty-five miles. Possible.

'What is it exactly?' he asked.

'An old military fort,' she said. 'The Buffalo Soldiers were there. Confederates had torn the place down. The Buffaloes rebuilt it. Eighteen sixty-seven, I think.'

He checked again. The ruins were southeast of Pecos, accessible from Route 285, which looked like a decent road. Probably a fast road. Probably a *typical* road. He closed his eyes. Alice raced on. The Crown Vic was quiet. It was warm and comfortable. He wanted to go to sleep. He was very tired.

'I like the Old Fort Stockton area,' he said.

'You think they were there?'

He was quiet again, another whole mile.

'Not *there*,' he said. 'But nearby. Think about it, from their point of view.'

'I can't,' she said. 'I'm not like them.'

'So pretend,' he said. 'What were they?'

'I don't know.'

'They were professionals. Quiet and unobtrusive. Like chameleons. Good at camouflage. Good at not being noticed. Put yourself in their shoes, Alice. Who are they? I thought they were a sales team. Rusty Greer thought they were social workers. Apparently Al Eugene thought they were FBI agents. So your strength is you look normal and ordinary. You're white, you look middle class, and you've got this Crown Victoria, which when it's not all tricked up with radio antennas looks like an ordinary family sedan.'

'OK.'

'But now you've got a kid with you. So now you're a normal, ordinary, respectable, plausible middle-class family.'

'But there were three of them.'

He kept his eyes closed. 'One of the men was an uncle,' he said. 'You're a middle-class family, on vacation. Not a Disneyland type of family. You're not in shorts and T-shirts. You look quiet, a little earnest, a little studious. You're obviously from out of state, so you're travelling. Where to? Ask yourself the questions they must have asked themselves. Where will you blend in? Where would an earnest, studious, middle-class family go, with their six-year-old daughter? Where's a proper, enlightening, educational place to take her? Even though she's way too young and doesn't care? Even though people laugh behind your back at how politically correct you are?'

'Old Fort Stockton,' Alice said.

'Exactly. You show the kid the glorious history of the African-American soldiers, even though you'd have a heart attack if she grew up and wanted to date one. But you're driving a Ford, not a BMW or a Cadillac. You're *sensible*. Not rich. Careful about your expenditure.

You resent overpaying. Motels, as much as cars. So you drive in from the north and you stay at a place far enough out to be reasonable. Not the dumps in the middle of nowhere. But on the fringes of the Fort Stockton tourist area. Where the value is good.'

He opened his eyes. 'That's where you would stay, Alice,' he said. 'It is?'

He nodded. 'A place where they get plenty of earnest, not-rich middle-class families on vacation. A place where you won't stand out in anybody's memory for a second. And a place where you're only thirty, thirty-five minutes from Pecos by a fast road.'

HE DECIDED TO TAKE a shower first. An excusable delay. He had time. The room was locked. The child was asleep. He stripped off his clothes, stepped into the bathroom and set the water running. Pushed the shower curtain aside and stepped into the torrent.

He stood in the warm water and let the water sluice over his body. Then he washed his hands and forearms thoroughly and carefully, like he was a surgeon preparing for a procedure.

'HOW FAR NOW?' Alice asked.

'Twenty-five miles,' Reacher said. 'We need a plan.'

'For taking this guy?' she said. 'I wouldn't have a clue.'

'No, for later. For getting Carmen back.'

'Habeas corpus,' she said. 'We'll go to a federal judge and enter an emergency motion. Tell the whole story. But we'll need testimony. So you'll have to keep this one alive. If that's not too much to ask.'

HE STOOD THERE in the warm stream of water. He had a new thought. He would need money. The others weren't coming back. The killing crew was history. He knew that. He was unemployed again. And he was unhappy about that. He wasn't good at going out and creating things for himself. Teamwork had suited him just fine. Now he was back on his own. He had some money stashed under his mattress at home, but it wasn't a lot. He'd need more.

So maybe he should take the kid with him back to LA. Sell her there. He knew people who facilitated adoptions, or other stuff he wouldn't want to enquire too closely about. She was what? Six? And white? Worth a lot of money to somebody, especially with all that fair hair. The Crown Vic was gone, but he could steal a car out of the motel parking lot. Keep the kid in the trunk. No problem.

TWELVE

She woke up because of the noise of the shower.

The man was in the shower.

There were no lights on in the room, but the drapes weren't drawn and a yellow glow was coming in from outside.

Her clothes were folded on the table by the window. She put them on. Sat down on the floor to buckle her shoes. Then she stood up and crept past the bathroom door, very quietly. She crept down the hallway, past the closet, all the way to the door. She stood still and looked at the door. She could see a handle, a lever thing, and a chain thing. She thought hard. The lever was probably a lock. She didn't know what the chain thing was for. She imagined the door opening. It would get a little way and the chain would stop it.

She had to get the chain thing off. It might slide along. She stretched up and slid it all the way sideways until the end fell into the hole. She reached up with both hands. The end of the chain was a little circle. She pushed it up and picked at it at the same time and it came out. It rattled down and swung and hit the door frame with a noise that sounded very loud. She held her breath and listened.

The shower was still running.

She tried the lever. She put her thumb on one side and her finger on the other and turned it. It wouldn't move. She used both hands and tried harder. Suddenly it clicked back all the way. *A big click*.

She stood still and listened. *The shower had stopped*.

She froze. Stood still, blank with panic.

ALICE KEPT HER FOOT DOWN and passed the Fort Stockton city limit doing ninety. There was a sign: PECOS 48 MILES. Reacher leaned forward, moving his head rapidly side to side, scanning both shoulders of the road. Low buildings flashed past. Some of them were motels.

It was about guessing and feeling now, about living in a zone where he was blanking out everything except the tiny murmurs from his subconscious mind. And they were saying: Not that one. No. No.

HE TURNED THE WATER OFF, rattled the curtain back and stepped out of the tub. Wrapped a towel round his waist and walked out of the bathroom. Light spilled out with him. He stopped dead. Stared at the empty bed. He took an involuntary step towards it. But there was just the rumpled sheet. He checked the window. It was closed and locked from the inside. Then he ran to the door. The chain was off. The lock was clicked back.

He opened the door. The DO NOT DISTURB tag was lying on the concrete walk, a foot from the doorway. She'd got out.

He fixed the door so it wouldn't lock behind him and ran out into the night, barefoot, wearing just his towel. He ran ten paces into the parking lot and stood still. He spun a complete circle. Where the hell did she go? A kid that age, she'd have just run for it. As fast as she could. Probably towards the road. He whirled round. Back towards the door. He'd need his clothes. Couldn't chase her in a towel.

THE LOW CLUMPS of buildings petered out. There was just desert.

'Turn around,' he said.

She hit the brakes and pulled a violent turn, shoulder to shoulder across the road. Straightened and headed back south.

'Slower now,' he said. 'Now we're looking at this with their eyes.'

The first motel they came back to had two one-storey wings of six rooms each.

'No,' Reacher said. 'We don't stop at the first place we see. We'd more likely go for the second place.'

The second place was 400 yards south. A possibility. The office was face-on to the highway but the cabins ran away into the distance behind it, which made the lot U-shaped. And concealed.

'Drive through,' he said.

She swung into the lot and nosed down the row. It was eight cabins long. Three cars were parked. She swung round the far end and up the other side. Eight more cabins. Another three cars.

'Well?' she asked.

He shook his head. 'No,' he said. 'Occupancy ratio is wrong. Sixteen cabins, six cars. I'd need to see eight cars, at least.'

'Why?'

'They didn't want a place that's practically empty. Too likely to be remembered. They were looking for somewhere around two-thirds full, which would be ten or eleven cars for sixteen cabins. They've got two rooms but right now no car at all, so that would be eight or nine cars for sixteen cabins.'

She shrugged. Eased back to the road and continued south.

HE GOT A COUPLE of paces towards the door and stopped dead. There was a yellow light off to one side of the lot, casting a low glow over the soaked blacktop. It showed him his footsteps. They were a line of curious fluid imprints blotted into the dampness.

But he couldn't see *her* footprints.

There was just one set of tracks, and they were his. No doubt about it. She hadn't come out. He smiled. She was hiding in the room.

He ran the final eight steps and ducked back inside. Closed the door gently and fastened the chain and clicked the lock.

'Come on out,' he called softly.

There was no response, but he hadn't really expected one.

'I'm coming to get you,' he called.

He started by the window, where there was an upholstered chair across the corner of the room. But she wasn't there. He got on his knees and looked under the beds. Not there, either. The closet. He slid the doors and checked. Nothing there. He ran his eyes over the room again. Nothing doing. She wasn't in the bathroom, because he had *been* in the bathroom.

Unless . . .

Unless she had been under the bed or in the closet and then had ducked into the bathroom while he was outside. He stepped over and opened the bathroom door. Pulled back the shower curtain in one dramatic sweeping move.

'There you are,' he said.

She was pressed up into the corner of the tub, wearing a T-shirt and shorts and shoes. The back of her right hand was jammed in her mouth. Her eyes were wide open. They were dark and huge.

'I changed my mind,' he said. 'I was going to take you with me.'

THE THIRD MOTEL had a painted sign. No neon. Just a board, carefully lettered in a script so fancy Reacher wasn't sure what it said. *Something Canyon*, maybe, with old-fashioned spelling, *Cañon*, like Spanish. The letters were shadowed in gold.

'I like this,' he said. 'Very tasteful.'

'Go in?' Alice asked.

'You bet.'

There was a little entrance road through twenty yards of garden. The plantings were sad and scorched by the heat, but they were an *attempt* at something.

'I like this,' he said again.

It was the same shape as the last place. An office first, with a U-shaped parking lot snaking round two back-to-back rows of cabins set at ninety degrees to the road. Alice drove the complete circle. Ten cabins to a row, twenty in total, twelve cars parked neatly next to twelve doors. Three Chevrolets, three Hondas, two Toyotas, two Buicks, an old Saab and an Audi.

'Two-thirds minus two,' Reacher said.

'Is this the place?' Alice asked. She stopped next to the office.

He said nothing. Just opened the door and slid out. The heat was coming back. It was full of the smell of soaked earth. He could hear drains running and gutters dripping. The office was dark and the door was locked. There was a neat brass button for the night bell. He leaned his thumb on it.

A light came on at the back of the office and a man stepped out. Reacher took the Echo County deputy's star out of his pocket and clicked it flat against the glass. The man walked to the door and undid the lock. Reacher stepped inside and walked past him. The fliers in the rack covered all the tourist attractions within a hundred miles. Old Fort Stockton featured prominently. All worthy stuff. Nothing about rodeos or gun shows or real estate. He waved to Alice. Gestured her in after him. 'This is the place,' he said.

'Is it?'

He nodded. 'Looks right to me.'

'You cops?' the office guy asked, looking out at the car.

'I need to see your register,' Reacher said. 'For tonight's guests.'

The office guy hesitated like there were procedures involved. Reacher pulled the Heckler & Koch from his pocket.

'Right now,' he said. 'We don't have time to mess about.'

The guy ducked round the counter and reversed a big leather ledger.

'What names?' Alice asked.

'No idea,' he said. 'Just look at the cars.'

There were five columns to a page. Date, name, home address, vehicle make, date of departure. There were twenty lines, for twenty cabins. Sixteen were occupied. Eleven cabins had a vehicle make entered directly against them. Four cabins were marked in two pairs of two, each sharing a vehicle.

'Families,' the night clerk said. 'Or large parties.'

'Did you check them in?' Reacher asked.

The guy shook his head. 'I'm the night man,' he said.

Reacher ran the gun muzzle down the fourth column. Three

Chevrolets, three Hondas, two Toyotas, two Buicks, one Saab, one Audi. And one Ford. He touched the muzzle to the word *Ford*.

'That's the Crown Vic,' he said. 'That's them.'

'You think?' Alice said.

'I know. I can feel it.'

They had taken two rooms, not adjacent, but in the same wing. Rooms five and eight.

'OK,' he said again. 'I'm going to take a look.'

He pointed to Alice. 'You call the State Police and start doing your thing with the federal judge, OK?'

'You need a key?' the night clerk asked.

'No,' Reacher said. 'I don't need a key.'

Then he walked out into the damp warmth of the night.

THE RIGHT-HAND ROW of cabins started with number one. There was a concrete walkway leading past each door. He moved quickly and quietly along it. There was nothing to see except doors. They came at regular intervals. No windows. The windows would be at the back.

Cabin number five had a DO NOT DISTURB tag lying on the concrete a foot from the doorway. He stepped over it. If you've got a stolen kid, you keep her in the room furthest from the office. He walked on and stopped outside number eight. Put his ear to the crack of the door and listened. Heard nothing. He walked silently on to the end of the row. Walked round the bend of the U. The two cabin blocks were parallel, facing each other across a thirty-foot-wide rectangle of garden. It was desert horticulture, with low spiky plants growing out of raked gravel, rocks and boulders carefully placed.

He passed by ten's window, then nine's, then crouched low and eased against the wall. Crawled forward and positioned himself directly under eight's windowsill. He raised his head, slowly and carefully. Looked into the room.

Nothing doing. The room was empty, completely undisturbed. It might never have been occupied. He stood up. Ran past seven and six, straight to five's window. Looked in.

And saw a small dark man wearing a towel dragging Ellie out of the bathroom. Bright light was spilling out behind him. He had both her wrists caught in one hand above her head. She was kicking and bucking violently in his grip. Reacher stared in for maybe a quarter of a second, long enough to sense the layout of the room and see a black nine-millimetre handgun with a silencer lying on the credenza.

Then he bent down and picked up a rock from the garden. He heaved it straight through the window. The screen disintegrated and glass shattered and he followed it headfirst into the room with the window frame caught round his shoulders like a wreath of victory.

The small dark man froze for a split second and then let Ellie go and scrabbled towards the credenza. Reacher batted away the splintered frame and got there first and caught him by the throat with his right hand and jammed him back against the wall and followed up with a left to the gut and let him fall and kicked him once in the head. Saw his eyes roll up into his skull. Then he turned to Ellie. 'You OK?' he asked.

She thought about it and nodded. She was very composed. No tears, no screaming.

He smiled, picked up the phone and dialled zero. The night guy answered. Reacher told him to send Alice to room five. Then he walked over and unlatched the chain and unlocked the door.

Alice stepped inside a minute later. Ellie looked at her.

'This is Alice,' Reacher said. 'She's helping your mom.'

'Where is my mom?'

'She'll be with you soon,' Alice said.

Then she looked down at the small dark guy. He was inert on the floor, pressed up against the wall, arms and legs tangled.

'Is he alive?' she whispered.

Reacher nodded. 'Concussed, is all. I think. I hope.'

'State Police is responding,' she whispered. 'And I called my boss at home. Got him out of bed. He's setting up a chambers meeting with a judge, first thing. But he says we'll need a straightforward confession from this guy if we want to avoid a big delay.'

Reacher nodded. 'We'll get one.'

He bent down and twisted the small dark man's towel round his neck and used it to drag him into the bathroom.

Twenty minutes later he came out and found two State cops standing in the room. A sergeant and a trooper. He nodded to them and picked up the driver's clothes. Tossed them into the bathroom.

'So?' the sergeant said.

'He's offering a full and voluntary confession,' Reacher said.

The cops glanced at each other and went into the bathroom.

'I have to get back,' Alice said. 'I have to prepare the writ. Lot of work involved, with habeas corpus.'

'Take the Crown Vic,' Reacher said. 'I'll wait here with Ellie.'

The cops brought the driver out of the bathroom. He was dressed and his hands were cuffed behind him. He was bent over and white with pain and already talking fast. The cops hustled him straight out to their cruiser and the room door swung shut behind them.

Reacher asked Alice to send the night clerk down with a master key and she walked away towards the office. He turned to Ellie.

'Tired?' he said.

'Yes,' she said.

'Your mom will come soon,' he said. 'We'll wait for her right here. But let's change rooms, shall we? This one's got a broken window.'

She giggled. 'You broke it. With that rock.'

'Let's try room eight,' he said. 'It's nice and clean.'

She took his hand and they walked out together and along the concrete walkway to number eight. The clerk met them with a pass key and Ellie got straight into the bed nearest the window. Reacher lay down on the other and watched her until she was sound asleep. Then he wrapped his arm under his head and tried to doze.

LESS THAN TWO HOURS LATER the new day dawned. Reacher opened his eyes after a short uneasy rest. Ellie was shaking his shoulder.

'I'm hungry,' she said.

'Me too,' he said back. 'What would you like?'

'Ice cream,' she said.

'OK,' he said. 'But eggs first. Maybe bacon. You're a kid. You need good nutrition.'

He fumbled the phone book out of the bedside drawer and found a diner listed that was maybe a mile nearer Fort Stockton. He called them and bribed them with the promise of a twenty-dollar tip to drive breakfast out to the motel. He sent Ellie into the bathroom to get washed up. By the time she came out, the food had arrived. Scrambled eggs, bacon, toast, jam, cola for her, coffee for him. And a huge plastic dish of ice cream with chocolate sauce.

He ate the food and drank the coffee and felt some energy coming back. Saw the same effect in Ellie. Then they dragged chairs out to the concrete walk and set them side by side and sat down to wait.

They waited more than four hours.

A few minutes after eleven Reacher was standing a couple of paces into the lot and he saw the Crown Vic in the distance.

'Hey, kid,' he called. 'Check this out.'

She stood next to him and shaded her eyes with her hand. The big car slowed and turned in and drove up right next to them. Alice was in the driver's seat. Carmen was next to her. She looked pale and washed out but she was smiling and her eyes were wide with joy. She had the door open before the car stopped moving and she came out and skipped round the hood. Ellie ran to her and jumped into her arms. They staggered around together in the sunlight. There was shrieking and crying and laughter all at the same time. He squatted next to the car. Alice buzzed her window down.

'Everything squared away?' he asked her.

'For us,' she said. 'Cops have a lot of paperwork ahead.'

'Anything about me?'

'They were asking about last night. I said I did it all.'

'Why?'

She smiled. 'Because I'm a lawyer. I called it self-defence and they bought it without hesitating. It was my car out there, and my gun. They'd have given you a much harder time.'

'So we're all home free?'

'Especially Carmen.'

He looked up. Carmen had Ellie on her hip, with her face buried in her neck. She was walking aimless random circles with her. Then she raised her head and squinted against the sun and smiled with such abandoned joy that Reacher found himself smiling along with her.

'She got plans?' he asked.

'Moving up to Pecos,' Alice said. 'We'll sort through Sloop's affairs. There's probably some cash somewhere. She's talking about moving into a place like mine. Maybe working part-time. Maybe even looking at law school.'

Now Ellie was leading her by the hand round the parking lot, talking a mile a minute. They looked perfect together. Ellie was hopping with energy and Carmen looked serene and radiant and very beautiful. Reacher stood up and leaned against the car.

'You want lunch?'

'Here?'

'I've got a thing going with a diner.'

'Tuna salad will do it for me.'

He went inside and used the phone. Ordered three sandwiches. Came out and found Ellie and Carmen looking for him.

'I'm going to a new school soon,' Ellie said.

'You'll do great,' he said. 'You're smart as a whip.'

Then Carmen let go of her daughter's hand and stepped near him, a little shy and silent and awkward for a second. Then she smiled wide and put her arms round his chest and hugged him hard. 'Thanks,' was all she said.

He hugged her back. 'I'm sorry it took so long.'

'Did my clue help?'

'Clue?' he said.

'I left a clue for you. In the confession.'

He said nothing. She unwound herself from his embrace and took his arm and led him to where Ellie wouldn't hear her.

'He made me say I was a whore. But I pretended to be nervous and I got the words wrong. I said street stroller.'

He nodded. 'I remember.'

'But it's really streetwalker, isn't it? To be correct? That was the clue. You were supposed to think, it's not *stroller*, it's *walker*. Get it? *It's Walker*. Meaning it's Hack Walker doing all of this.'

He went very quiet. 'I missed that,' he said.

'So how did you know?'

'I guess I took the long way round.'

She just smiled again. Laced her arm into his and walked him back to the car, where Ellie was laughing with Alice.

'You going to be OK?' he asked her.

She nodded. 'But I feel very guilty. People died.'

He shrugged. 'Like Clay Allison said.'

'Thanks,' she said again.

'*No hay de qué, señora.*'

'*Señorita,*' she said.

CARMEN AND ELLIE AND ALICE drifted inside to get washed up for lunch. He watched the door close behind them and just walked away. It seemed the natural thing to do. He didn't want anybody to try to keep him there. He jogged to the road and turned south. Walked a whole hot mile before he got a ride from a farm truck. He got out at the next interchange and waited until an eighteen-wheeler slowed and stopped next to him. He walked round the massive hood and looked up at the window. The window came down.

The driver leaned out. 'Los Angeles?' he called.

'Anywhere,' Reacher called back.

LEE CHILD

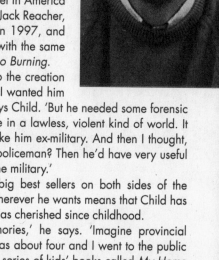

When faced with redundancy after two decades of employment with Granada Television in Manchester, Lee Child turned misfortune to his advantage by deciding to fulfil a long-held ambition of writing a best-selling novel. Set in America and featuring ex-military policeman Jack Reacher, *Killing Floor* made a huge impact in 1997, and has been followed by more novels with the same main character, the latest being *Echo Burning*.

Lee Child put a lot of thought into the creation of Jack Reacher and his character. 'I wanted him to be a complete loner, a drifter,' says Child. 'But he needed some forensic skills, and he needed to be at home in a lawless, violent kind of world. It was pretty obvious that I had to make him ex-military. And then I thought, Well, why not make him a military policeman? Then he'd have very useful contacts and insider knowledge of the military.'

The Reacher novels have been big best sellers on both sides of the Atlantic, and the freedom to work wherever he wants means that Child has realised another ambition—one he has cherished since childhood.

'It was one of my earliest memories,' he says. 'Imagine provincial England at the end of the fifties. I was about four and I went to the public library with my mother. There was a series of kids' books called *My Home in . . .* and the only one our library had was *My Home in America*. There were twelve pages, each with a big colour illustration of a home. There was a prairie farmhouse, a California bungalow, a New England colonial— and my favourite—a Manhattan apartment with a little boy sitting by the window, looking down at the city below. Right away, I knew I wanted to be that boy.'

The dream of an American lifestyle lingered in Lee Child's mind, and in the summer of 1998 he finally made it a reality, moving to the northern part of New York State with his American wife and daughter. 'Writing has brought me a lot of rewards,' he says. 'But this is the best of all of them.'

FORCE 12

James Thayer

Controlled by a state-of-the-art computer, *Victory is the most highly automated yacht ever built. A powerful weather-prediction system and sophisticated sail and rudder controls make her the fastest boat in the world—virtually unsinkable and almost certainly unbeatable.*

Or so her creator, billionaire Rex Wyman, believes.

Now, in some of the roughest seas on earth, her systems are about to malfunction.

 # *Prologue*

The raft flipped over, and his brother had drowned, and Jess McKay's memories were still merciless, even after all the years. Every day since, every hour since, McKay had returned in his mind to that river, trying to nudge his memory, hoping it would play out some other way, some less shameful way, but his brother always remained dead, and Jess always remained a coward.

Mount Index, in the Cascade Range in Washington State, is a noble granite peak, rugged in all its aspects except that it is slender by local standards. Each spring Mount Index issues its prodigious snow melt to the Skykomish River, which swells and rolls as it drops quickly through the wilderness towards Puget Sound.

That day, those years ago, Jess McKay crouched on a rounded boulder, speaking loudly over the rush of water. 'Where'd you get the oars?'

'These are paddles, not oars.' His older brother Matt didn't look up from the inflatable raft, where he was working with a length of clothes line to secure his backpack to one of the raft's D-rings. 'They've been in Uncle Dan's garage for years, hanging on the wall.'

'He knows we're up here? He gave them to you?'

'Not exactly. I drove over to his house and borrowed them when he was away at work. He won't mind.'

Jess asked, 'How many times you going to run the river?'

'The company told me to come back when I had some white-water rafting experience, so I'm going to load up on experience.' Matt tossed Jess a life jacket, also borrowed from his uncle's garage. 'A dozen times, I figure.'

Matt McKay was a senior at Everett High School, and had applied for a summer job at Cascade Adventures, a company that took customers on guided raft journeys in western Washington.

'Did you tell Mom and Dad we were coming up here?' Jess asked as he tried to figure out how to fit into the life jacket.

'What do you think?'

'Me neither.' Jess wrestled the jacket around himself, then connected the clasps.

Matt looked up from the raft and asked, 'You kissed her yet?'

Jess could feel colour flash across his face. 'I don't know who you're talking about.' He was a dreadful liar.

'Don't give me that.' Matt laughed. 'The blonde in the ponytail you escort from second to third period every day.'

Jess ignored him, staring at the water coursing round the boulder. He was a freshman in high school, same school as his big brother. Matt and his football buddies owned the place, while Jess bumbled along, aimless and overwhelmed. Matt—who liked to tease him, but never in front of friends, and never meanly—had confided that he, too, had felt like a moron and a klutz his freshman year. It scarcely seemed possible. Matt was golden. Everything he did, he did easily. Big and strong, charming, with a quick smile full of perfect teeth, blond hair and grey-green eyes, Matt was everything Jess was not, except the colouring and teeth.

Matt called jubilantly, 'She's ready for launch.' He pushed the raft the few feet across river stones to the water. 'You're in front.'

Matt had been unable to find a second life jacket, but Uncle Dan's garage had yielded a water skier's life ring, too big for Matt even though he cinched it tightly.

The raft, which Matt had bought at a pawnshop, was made of urethane tubes, with a plywood deck. It was seven feet long and weighed just fifty pounds. The raft was Day-Glo orange, and some prior owner had painted red and yellow licks of fire on the bow, like on a hot rod. It had been patched at the waterline.

Jess stepped over stones to the raft, climbed over a tube and sat on a low wooden seat, gripping his paddle tightly. Matt pushed the raft from shore out into the current and, with a gleeful whoop, he leapt into the stern. His knees bumped Jess's back as he settled in.

The acceleration was startling. Their spot on the bank seemed to flee behind them as the raft was pulled to the centre of the river and then propelled downstream. The brothers dug their paddles into the water several times, but there was nothing for them to do, as the river had taken over.

The banks sped by, and granite boulders the size of automobiles appeared to have been tossed willy-nilly on the shores and into the river. When the forest on the south bank opened, sunlight swept across the river, and the boulders, studded with numberless flecks of mica, glittered. The river was a raw wilderness, primitive and fierce, without a trace of humankind's notice or influence, as it had been since the night of time.

'Hey, Matt, what . . .?' Jess pointed ahead, where the water appeared to end, as if it had a brim.

'Hang on,' his brother yelled.

The raft sank over a fall no more than two feet high, but Jess yelled involuntarily as their craft plunged into the whirl of water below the drop. The raft rebounded then lunged ahead, settled, then dipped over a smaller fall, Matt laughing crazily. A moment later they entered an idly circling whirlpool tucked behind an outcropping.

'That's as much fun as you are going to have in your entire life, baby brother,' Matt exulted. He swept the blade through the water, and the raft glided from behind its protective boulder and back into the current. The river was shallow here, with stones just under the surface, and the raft began to buck. Matt whooped and pulled at the water with his paddle.

The valley narrowed, leaving only a strip of sky overhead, and the water quickened. Jess cocked his head. A bass rumble like a locomotive came from downstream, and their little craft was rushing towards it. Above the canyon an osprey slipped through the sky, impartial, the undersides of its wings ghostly white.

The river stalled and smoothed behind the sheltering arm of a monolith that jutted out into the stream and blocked the sky. The raft slowed, and neared the vertical bulwark of granite. The roar from the west was unceasing. Jess leaned over the tube to dip his hand into the river. The water was so cold it seemed to bite him.

The vortex of water behind the stone mass moved slowly, and the raft curled round, seeming to wheel on an axis. Then suddenly it gained a will of its own as it accelerated and spun out from behind the crag into a narrow chute of water.

Matt yelled, 'Hey, what's . . .?'

The raft shot through the channel, towers of stone close on both sides, and then bounced against a slab of rock. Jess's paddle caught in a crevice and was yanked from his hands. He tried to grab it, but found only the rough canyon wall. For several heartbeats the river remained solid and blue, but at a downward angle and the speed ever increasing. Then the canyon bed fell away and the rush of water plunged down in a foaming tumult.

The valley below flashed in front of him, and then Jess tumbled down, the raft pulling away. He yelled, but it was chopped off when water enveloped him, turning him in ragged somersaults. He was lost in a crashing spume, and falling and falling.

His arm smashed into an unseen boulder as he rolled in a universe of frothing white water, without bearings and without air and without his brother. He scraped on stones on the river bottom. Skin on his back peeled away. He forced his eyes to open, but all he could see was the blind white of the turbulence. He kicked frantically, trying to push himself to the surface, but the water rolled him over and over. When his lungs worked involuntarily, his windpipe filled with water. He had the vague impression he was drowning.

Then the river released him, and the ferment fell away, and he gagged and coughed and found that he could breathe again. He shook his head like a dog, clearing his eyes. The raft was well downstream, disappearing behind a turn. His knees found a surface, and he scrambled up a grade of rounded stones, climbing out of the river. He bent over, gasping for breath. Then he remembered his brother. He turned back to the river, calling out, 'Matt!'

His brother was right in front of him, an arm's reach away, moving with the current, an open wound on his forehead. His flotation ring had been stripped from him and was bobbing along in the current behind him.

Matt lifted a hand towards his brother and cried out, 'Jess, help! Help!' Then he disappeared beneath the surface, as if invisible arms had dragged him under.

Breathing in huge gulps, Jess stepped along the stony shore, trying to keep up with the current that held his brother, seeing only the churning white surface. And then Matt was there again, his mouth open and his eyes white all around, water breaking over him, thirty feet out into the river. His eyes locked on Jess. 'Please . . . Jess . . . help . . .' and down he went again, covered by the furious flow.

Jess stumbled along the bank, dodging boulders and river debris, waving his arms as he tried to keep his balance. The rapids gave way to a short expanse of calmer water, still moving, but without the whiter violence.

Matt emerged again. He screamed, 'Jess . . . Jess . . . help me!' An arm flailed uselessly against the water. Something was wrong with Matt's other arm. It trailed behind him in the water. He drifted downstream towards another loud and boiling cataract.

Then began the fifteen seconds that forever branded Jess McKay.

Jess stood on the river bank, his hands out to his brother, reaching out to him. Jess cried out Matt's name. But Jess did not enter the water. He was riveted by fear. His legs would not move.

All he had to do was step off the bank and swim to his brother. His life jacket would keep him afloat, would surely keep both of them above the surface. *Just that, just that small thing, go, and go now, jump back into the current, and reclaim your brother*.

'Jess . . .' Weaker now, just Matt's chin above water.

Those wretched seconds unfolded and when Matt's head disappeared again it was for good, and the time given Jess to make his choice was gone and would never return.

Water swept endlessly by.

 *Chapter one*

Snow was absorbing blood from his leg, and the red colour expanded in a circle that looked like a bull's eye, and the pilot knew he did not have long. Huge snowflakes flew past him, so thick he could see little beyond his boots, and his boots were being covered by snow, so he supposed he would soon see nothing but white. The mountain was claiming him. In a few moments he would cease being a human, and would become a topographic feature, another small wrinkle on the side of McKinley.

At least, that's where he thought he was, Mount McKinley. His F-16 Viper had quit on him, just flamed out. Then the plane began to roll like it was on a spit, so he pulled the lever and out he went, into the blast of air, gratified when his chute opened. Snow had softened the impact and he had landed in fine shape. The chute dragged him along as if he were a plough, but he managed to release it.

The pilot's name was Peter Bradley, and he had until about an hour ago been participating in an air force combat exercise. He was posted to the 18th Fighter Squadron, flying from Eielson Air Force Base southeast of Fairbanks, Alaska. He had taken the Arctic survival course at the Cool School at Eielson, and they had made him plenty cold and hungry, but not like this, out here, alone and with a broken leg. At the Cool School he had learned about the lethargy and disorientation that accompany freezing to death. He wondered how long his mind had left.

God, he would like to see his wife again. He could fly a Viper but Karen was the brains in the family. He laughed weakly, his breath rolling away behind him in a streaming cloud. He was wearing a sage-green flight suit and a winter-weight flight jacket, and he might as well have been wrapped in rice paper for all the good the jacket was doing. A Snickers bar was in a pocket on the left sleeve, held in place by a Velcro flap. A Snickers would be good right now.

He had landed just fine, he brought up the memory again. Had released his parachute from the harness after a short slide along the snow, then had taken four steps, and he must have been on a snow bridge because then the snow under his boots had suddenly given way. He fell awhile, then smacked the ground and started to slide, his leg catching on some rock and snapping, and finally he stopped where he was now, and hadn't been able to move an inch since.

Bradley's head came up. He abruptly felt as if he were not alone. Peculiar because he surely was. He looked right and left into the blur of snow. He asked aloud, 'Is someone there?'

No one, of course. Not on the mountain in November. He had met his wife, Karen, at the commissary at Fairchild Air Force Base, near Spokane, where the air force had sent him for survival school— not that anything he learned there was doing any good now, the numbness up to his thighs and a Snickers bar he couldn't reach because his hands wouldn't work. Karen managed the commissary and he was standing at the magazine rack looking at bra ads in a *Cosmopolitan*—for the first time in his life, he swore to her later. She passed behind him as he was studying the ads and she laughed, and they were married six weeks later.

He wondered where he was, why everything was white. He had bailed out in daylight, so the sun was up there, but obscured and indifferent. He was above the tree line, and the Arctic wind was almost noiseless, a muted sigh. He sat on the snow, bleeding.

His wife. He could smell her perfume, right there on the mountain. He looked left again. 'Karen?' Joy suffused him, and a giddiness, and he could see clearly, if only for a few feet. The dead white of the storm took on a soft rose hue. This was hardly like dying, up here on this mountain, just an easy letting go.

Still, his wife, down in Fairbanks. He wished he could see her one more time. It seemed such a small thing, seeing Karen, but she was far away. He recalled their honeymoon. They had gone somewhere warm but he couldn't remember where, would never remember now. His memories were going. Cold was all around. He was dying.

'Bingo.'

A word. Out there in front of him. God's voice, surely. Bradley had hoped for something more majestic, some nice quote from the Old Testament, but *bingo* was fine. Who was an air force lieutenant to second-guess the Lord?

'You're alive, looks like. That's a good start, Lieutenant Bradley.'

The snow resolved itself into a man, standing in front of Bradley, then bent over him. Big red parka with an American flag sewn on the sleeve. His gloves had fur on the back so he could wipe his brow. He carried a mountain axe. 'Are you in pain?' he asked.

Bradley could only whisper. 'Not any more.'

The man removed a pack from his back. 'We're going to fix you up. No worries now.' His climbing harness was affixed to a rope that disappeared behind him. 'Broken leg,' the man said.

Following the rope, a second fellow emerged from the storm, and then a third, all wearing red parkas. The first man spoke quickly into a radio, then said to his team, 'The bag and a heated IV.'

The others didn't say anything. They moved in silent and swift choreography. A hypothermia kit was opened, and an olive-drab patient-treatment bag resembling a large sleeping-bag was unrolled. Handle straps were sewn along it at intervals that matched the patient's shoulders and knees. A ruff of artificial fur rimmed the head opening. The lead rescuer checked Bradley's pulse and a few other things the pilot couldn't follow.

Then the rescuers placed an inflatable splint round the fractured leg, and Peter Bradley was stuffed into the bag, none too gently. The lead rescuer activated several three-pound chemical heating pouches, wrapped them in cloth from the backpack to ensure they didn't burn the pilot, then slipped them into the patient treatment bag. The first rescuer gently wiped the snow from Bradley's face, as kind an act as the pilot had ever experienced.

A stretcher made of thin plastic was unrolled and tucked under the pilot. Bradley's mind flickered like a candle. He and his new bride had honeymooned in Mexico. That was it. Cactus and desert and the high sun. Bradley moved his mouth, but couldn't force out any words.

The first rescuer leaned closer, and the pilot tried again. 'Is my wife Karen with you?'

The rescuer bent still lower. 'Your wife? She's down in Fairbanks. She'll be getting a phone call any minute telling her that we've found you and that you're alive.'

Karen was standing over to the left, in her blue parka with the hood, wearing the perfume he had purchased for her in Mexico. Let his rescuers think otherwise.

'What's your name?' the pilot asked.

'Jess McKay. Captain, 212th Rescue Squadron.'

'Nobody hired us to chat,' the second rescuer growled. 'The helicopter is waiting downhill, and my TV dinner is still in the oven. Probably burned to black.'

'PJ humour,' McKay said. 'It takes some getting used to.'

The rope snaking after him, the third pararescue jumper climbed thirty paces uphill to anchor the others. McKay and the second PJ gripped the stretcher and they started down the mountain.

'We've got you now,' McKay said. 'You'll be OK.'

'No, I'm dead,' the pilot replied. 'I'm quite sure. Dead.'

'Not out here in the cold.' McKay grinned under his mask. 'That's not the way we work. We don't consider a man dead until he is warm and dead.'

'TIME TO THE NEXT TACK, please?' Gwen Weld asked.

A deep voice came from many speakers, filling the room but directionless, like the voice of God. 'Two minutes, twelve seconds.'

'Thank you.'

The machine did not respond. She had demanded that the 'You are welcome' and—worse—the 'No problem' lines of code be removed because she could think of nothing as worthless as social grace from a pack of silicon chips.

Then she loudly cleared her throat—'Ahhemmm'—followed by three quick clicks of her tongue, then a soft purr.

'Pardon?' the Voice asked after half a beat.

176

She smiled at the small victory. She despised the Voice.

'Please repeat the instruction or enquiry, Ms Weld.'

Embarrassed for herself, she said, 'Strike that.' Teasing a computer. How low could she go?

She had been toying with the Voice to distract herself, to dilute her fear. Her hand on the computer mouse was still trembling, even though she had been in this dreadful room on the sailboat *Victory* ninety minutes and she should have calmed by now. The room was without a single window, lit by rude fluorescent lights and by monitors that glowed with anaemic techno hues. Its hatches fore and aft were heavy steel, with wheel locks on them like those in an old submarine, a curious throwback to earlier times.

The room was called the chart room by the boat's owner in a bit of irony because there was not a nautical chart, tide table, or current chart in it. Rather, almost every vertical surface was covered with flat-panel monitors. Secured to the table so they wouldn't slide off when the boat was heeled over were two more monitors, three laptop computers, and microphones. An old mariner might have searched for a bit of brass or bevelled glass, something to connect this room to the history of sailing, but there were none. No sextants or compass or barometer, nothing that spoke of the sea. The room was entirely clinical, more a laboratory than a chart room.

Gwen Weld had designed this room. At least, as team leader she had assembled the software systems that were running behind every surface. In the mock-up at WorldQuest's Boise offices she hadn't suffered this fear when she had tested the systems hour after hour. Out here, though, on the rolling, pitching boat, the room pressed in on her, and she was breathing swiftly and perspiring. That she had put together this tight room did nothing to allay her fright. And she was disgusted with herself. Was Rex Wyman's power over her such that she would nail herself inside this floating coffin?

Gwen had once owned a Cal 29, and knew how to sail. And in crafting the systems for this boat, she had become even more of a student of the sea. What she learned had unsettled her, had made open water seem an enemy. The sea offers illusion as truth, and hides peril behind a façade of benevolence and familiarity.

A mile out from Cannon Beach, *Victory* sliced through this precarious sea, Gwen Weld in the narrow room below deck. The bow bit cleanly, throwing little water. The wind was southerly, and the boat was on a broad reach, its massive boom swung out over the port rail.

Shrouds and stays were perfectly taut, and the running rigging was arrayed so that the sails fully engaged the quartering wind. The mainsail and jib were filled with air, billowing and majestic. *Victory*'s mast rose 193 feet above the deck, and the mast and sails formed an aerodynamic wedge that precisely worked the wind. The vessel was muscular yet sleek, and it coursed powerfully through the following sea, bowing and plunging into the swells. Fog hid the sun, and the low sky was dazzling. Nothing was visible ahead but a wash of white. *Victory* seemed to be bounding into the radiant unknown.

And there was much to know just outside *Victory*'s small disk of sea. Dead ahead—300 yards and closing—stood House Rock, an indomitable granite obelisk that has been indifferent to an eternity of Pacific storms. House Rock jutted up from the ocean floor half a mile from the shoreline. The base of the grey rock was wet from ocean spray and shiny as oilskin. The tapered cap of the granite column towered forty feet above the moving sea, waiting, infinitely patient amid the restless water.

Victory came on, its sails bent to their work. Ahead the haze took on a peculiar shade, a suggestion of fixity. Then more colour and a new angularity. House Rock formed out of the haze. The boat rushed forward and the rock was now fully visible, a giant slab with waves crashing against its barnacled base and sending spume skywards in great drafts. *Victory* closed on House Rock.

Forty yards from the rock—little more than a length of the boat—*Victory* swung abruptly to starboard, heeling over to bury the port rail as it turned into the wind. Gwen Weld sank with her chair. She had touched nothing in her room but the coffee cup. The main and jib were taken in almost instantly, bringing them to perfect trim on the new course.

Within seconds, *Victory*'s certain doom had been transformed into another giddy leap over ocean swells, off in another direction, House Rock receding swiftly, then blinking out as the haze closed in again. From the east came the thunder of breakers dashing against the Oregon coast's harsh cliffs. The boat came about again, the prow swinging across the compass points into the wind, the mainsail and jib losing air, the boom—the size of a telephone pole—racing across the deck like a scythe. The boat's new course would take it into the shore cliffs within moments.

A hundred generations of seafarers would have recognised *Victory* for what she was, with her sails set to the wind in a manner known to the ages, but a closer look would have left those ancient sailors baffled. Stainless-steel winches for the sheets were powered from below deck and were without cranks, and several were accompanied by secondary power winches that handled messenger lines. The mainsail could be furled within the mainmast. The jib rolled around a mechanical jib stay, and its spread of sail could be reduced automatically. Hundreds of tension sensors the size and colour of Band-Aids dappled the sails. The old sailors would also wonder at the materials: the carbon-fibre of the mast, the sixty-five tons of aluminium in the hull, the Kevlar cordage, the Dacron and Mylar of the sails, the sixty miles of fibre-optic cable below decks. And those bygone mariners would be clueless regarding the antennas, radar domes, gimballed satellite dishes and cameras.

But nothing about *Victory* would so puzzle—and also alarm—the sailors as the cockpit, which contained built-in benches and nothing more. No spoked wheel, nothing to control the rudder. No binnacle and its instruments. The cockpit was barren.

Then those old sailors would suspect that *Victory* was a ghost ship. No crew worked the deck. No skipper, no helmsman, no navigator, no line handlers. *Victory*'s size—155 feet with a thirty-foot beam—demanded a crew of twenty on deck, yet there was no one.

And *Victory* would have been a ghost ship, were not Gwen Weld in its belly, sipping coffee. She, a computer engineer, was *Victory*'s entire crew. Gwen had laboured on this venture for two years, but now that she was on board there was little to do, so she stared at a monitor that displayed a view from a camera atop the mainmast. She could change the view to one of a dozen other exterior cameras, or she could change to many interior views of *Victory*, including watching her own back and head from a camera mounted behind her. Rex was weird with all his cameras. He had them in his houses, too.

She sipped her coffee. Gwen had never suffered motion sickness, was immune to it, it seemed. She wasn't immune from fear, though, and that was the hell of it, down here in this box.

From the speakers: 'How's it going, Gwen?'

This wasn't the Voice. This was *Victory*'s owner, Rex Wyman. She didn't like his voice coming from all directions—as if he were inside her head—so she entered several keystrokes so that his words would come from the speaker on the table a few feet away.

She faced the speaker. 'You know as well as I do that everything is fine, Rex. You have it all in front of you, just like I do.'

'You're still upset about the article in *People*, sounds like,' Wyman said. He might be in Boise or New York City or Jakarta. She had no way of knowing unless he told her.

'The article doesn't bother me at all.'

'Not at all?' he asked.

'It suggests that my position as vice-president for systems integration at WorldQuest is due to my relationship with you. Why would that bother me?' She hoped her tones were sufficiently dry.

'Nice picture of you, though,' Wyman said.

He was teasing her. She usually tossed it back, and they would end up laughing. She was too fearful—in this boat, headed at breakneck speed for the rocky shore—to joust with him.

'We were going to keep it quiet, Rex. That was part of our deal.'

'I didn't know a reporter was going to be at the party, honey. Give me a second, Gwen.' Wyman covered the microphone to give someone an instruction, probably Roger Hall, who spent his life at Wyman's elbow, electronic memo pad at the ready.

Gwen Weld's hair was as dark as a crow's wing, and she wrapped a loose strand of it round a finger, waiting for Rex. She usually wore it to her shoulder, but today it was in a ponytail, which gave her a girlish look she tried to avoid, particularly at the office.

Her features were slightly magnified, filling the oval of her face. Her eyes were startlingly blue. Gas blue, her mother had once called them. Her mother had green eyes, and claimed she had no idea where Gwen's blue eyes came from. From my father, Gwen had wanted to shout, but when Gwen was a child, her mother had made it clear that to even mention him would hurt her deeply, so whether her father had blue eyes had been a mystery.

Her chin carried a delicate notch. Her nose was a touch large, with a modest bump on the ridge. As she had gained some of age's perspective, she had begun to think of her nose as masterful, as an indication of character. On her ears were small diamonds that picked up the colour of her eyes. She was wearing deck shoes, jeans and a Gore-Tex jacket decorated with a WorldQuest emblem.

'I'm back.' Wyman's voice came from the speaker. 'You are half a minute from *Victory*'s coming tack.'

'I thought you were going to be on board today,' she said, staring at the speaker as if she might somehow see Wyman's expression.

'Well, let me be frank,' he said. The phrase was one of Wyman's favourites. 'I cannot be seen to be putting too much time or effort into *Victory*. Gwen, you know how important the boat's success is to me—what is riding on *Victory*—but I can't let my competitors know.'

'They know you've spent fifty million dollars on this boat.'

'The whole world also knows that fifty million dollars is pocket change to me. But I only have as much time as anybody else. If I take a couple days off to go on a sea trial, my competitors are going to seize on it. They'll start to dig around. I don't want that.'

Wyman had ordered up *Victory* from Royal Huisman Shipyards like anyone else would buy a set of car tyres. At least, that's what Wyman wanted the world to think. Gwen Weld knew better. She knew the stakes represented by *Victory*.

'This has been a huge success, Gwen,' said Rex Wyman. 'My crews on *Pelican* and in Boise agree.'

Pelican was the sailboat's mothership, stationed six miles off the coast, a converted oil-rig service vessel, 150 feet in length, with a helicopter pad on the stern. On *Pelican* was a room identical to *Victory*'s command centre, with the same monitors displaying the same information regarding *Victory*. Another room—same monitors, same displays—was at WorldQuest headquarters in Boise. While Gwen Weld was alone on *Victory*, dozens of engineers and sailboat designers and professional skippers were monitoring its progress. Sail trials had been performed earlier in the month with a live crew on board. This was the first test of the combined systems.

Rex Wyman had a talent for generating favourable publicity. Nothing required *Victory* to be without a crew on this day of the systems trial, except for Wyman's notion of what made for the better story. The press would send this sensational news around the world: the most expensive sailing yacht in history had sailed a hazardous course in a strong wind and blinding fog, with no one on board except the senior vice-president for research.

'Where are you, Rex?' she finally had to ask.

'On a runway at Charles de Gaulle. We're fifth from take-off.'

As *Victory* flew southwest towards the shore, the distance between the keel and the ocean floor closed quickly. When the wind tore a hole in the fog, the coastline was suddenly visible. The boat was on a course for the shallows and the high brown cliffs.

'You mentioned we might meet at your place Friday,' she said.

'Which place did I say?' he asked.

Wyman loved to do that, offer a reminder that he was now a citizen of the world, with five homes on three continents.

'In Sun Valley,' she said. 'Toby is going to be there visiting his parents. Maybe we could all get together.'

'Toby hung up on me last time we talked,' Wyman said. Toby Odell and Wyman had founded WorldQuest.

'He's been doing that for twenty years, you told me so yourself.'

'Yeah, well maybe,' Wyman said from France. 'Here you go, looks like. Only three feet between the boat and the bottom of the ocean. Any other boat is seconds from grounding.'

She could see it herself. On one of the monitors there was a three-dimensional graphic of the ocean floor with the boat superimposed over it. The graphic slid across the screen as *Victory* moved towards certain grounding.

'Helms alee,' intoned the Voice. Software and mechanical and hydraulic systems did their work. Gwen's chair sank under her as *Victory* came about to its new heading, west by southwest to the open sea, escaping the treacherous shore.

'We did it!' She could hear elation in Rex's voice. '*Victory* is everything I said it would be, Gwen. Are you believing me now?'

'I've always believed you,' she said simply.

'*Pelican* will pick you up in an hour, and take *Victory* in tow.'

'About this weekend . . .'

'Meet me in Ketchum,' he replied. 'Friday evening. Roger will make sure a car picks you up.'

'I'll be there.'

'Got to go,' Wyman said. 'Love you.' He cut the connection.

With sails grand in the wind and her prow splitting the sea, *Victory* sped towards a rendezvous with the tender.

Her voice full of melancholy, Gwen answered to nobody, 'Love you, too.'

Chapter two

The Harbor Yacht Club was on San Francisco Bay. The two-storey Mediterranean stucco clubhouse had a red tile roof, vast windows that looked out onto the bay, and a first-storey deck that was lined with spectators, many with drinks in their hands. Wisteria covered the east side of the building, some of its tendrils lacing round the deck's wrought-iron banisters. The caterer's white tents were on the lawn between the clubhouse and the docks, and waiters carrying trays passed among the guests.

A large Mitsubishi Diamond Vision screen had been set up on the yacht club's patio, behind a podium. On the screen in vivid greens and blues was the WorldQuest logo. Folding chairs ranged out in front. Two bars on the patio were well attended, the bartenders working quickly. Inside the clubhouse was a buffet, and a steady stream of guests walked out onto the patio with plates in their hands.

Guests also crowded the yacht club's docks. They leaned forward to peer at *Victory*, their hands behind their backs as if at an art gallery, knowing they shouldn't touch the object of the admiration. Guards were stationed on the pier, fore, mid and aft of the boat, acting like tour guides. Sipping their martinis and Scotch, guests nodded knowingly at design features. A few stared at the puzzling items topside, the curious rigging, peculiar antennas and some equipment hidden in a mount forward of the wheel.

The crowd gathered round the podium. Guests emerged from the clubhouse to join them. From the dock Gwen couldn't see what was going on; it looked like a procession from the building to the podium. Then Gwen heard Rex Wyman's amplified voice.

'Thank you, Mayor. It is always a delight to visit the Harbor Yacht Club, which has made my team and me feel so welcome.'

'Hello, Gwen,' a voice came from Gwen's right.

She turned to see a shy grin under a baseball cap. Toby Odell was wearing slacks for once, but he looked uncomfortable in them, with his fists jammed low in the pockets. He was lost in an enormous mustard-coloured sweater. He nodded at her, encouraging her to remember his name, as if there were a chance she or anyone would forget, but this hopeful nodding and hesitant grin were an old habit back from a time when he was invisible.

She smiled at him. 'I didn't think the twentieth richest man in the country could sneak up on people, Toby, but here you are.'

He laughed. 'I'm down to twenty-first. Another Walton was found.'

Toby Odell had once told Gwen that he had celebrated World-Quest's massively successful initial public offering by purchasing a Rolex wristwatch, and had worn it for two days. The first day he thought it elegant; the second day he thought it silly. So he replaced it with a Timex Ironman, and now he never wore jewellery or anything else the slightest bit pricey.

Rex Wyman's words drifted over the docks. 'The gentleman's sport of sailboat racing is going to be changed for ever.'

Gwen said, 'My Lord, Toby, have you shaved your head, up under that baseball cap?' She let him pluck the cap from his head.

He said, 'It's the new thing at my office with all the coders. Bald head with a tattoo on top. I shaved my head, but haven't found the courage for the tattoo yet. I've been to a tanning parlour to get this nice bronze look.'

Wyman intoned, 'No longer will the Sydney–Hobart and the Fastnet Race be the premier weather challenges for the blue-water sail racer. In their place, I present to you the Pacific Winter Challenge.'

With a flourish, Wyman raised his hand in the direction of the Mitsubishi screen, where the WorldQuest logo disappeared and was replaced with a map of the Pacific Ocean, from California west to the coast of Japan and north to the Bering Sea.

Wyman continued, 'Those sailors who accept the challenge will depart from San Francisco Bay—the bridge will serve as the starting line—and sail across the Pacific to Tokyo.'

'Some renowned racers have accepted Rex's challenge,' Odell said. 'See that woman over there? The tall woman with black hair? Her name is Genevieve DeLong. She gets more press in France than the country's President. She's a national heroine for winning the BOC Challenge. When she sails with a crew, they're all world-class. And her boats—her financing has always been a mystery and I think it's probably the French government—are always state of the art.'

'Who else should I know about here?'

'Duncan Davis. He set the Los Angeles to Honolulu Transpac monohull record at a little over seven days.'

Odell's fingers were slender and long, pianist's fingers. Since he had left WorldQuest—taking forty per cent of the stock with him—he had purchased controlling interest in fifteen small companies based in Silicon Valley or North Carolina's Research Triangle or in the Seattle area. Some business writers said he was doing nothing more than gambling with his money, but Odell lived his life being underestimated, and while a few of the companies had come to nothing, others had soared.

'The Challenge will be sailed along the shortest distance between the two cities,' Wyman declared over the speaker, 'the five-thousand-two-hundred-mile rhumb line between San Francisco and Tokyo via Alaska's Aleutian Islands, the same course a plane takes.'

The Mitsubishi screen displayed the route, a red arch, with one end touching the point that represented San Francisco and the other touching Tokyo, the arch sweeping up high on the map then soaring south again as it crossed the vast expanse of blue. With the Pacific Ocean flattened on the screen, the route appeared to trend too far north, only to have to return south towards Japan, a vast half-circle.

A flat map is an illusion, and does not account for the curvature of the earth. Sailing due west from San Francisco to Tokyo—the two cities are within two degrees of being on the same latitude—would add 200 miles to the journey, as compared with sailing north in a great arc on the rhumb line.

Wyman's voice fluttered in the wind. 'But there will be one detour: the boats will veer off the rhumb line to sail north through the Aleutians to round the Pribilof Islands, well into the Bering Sea, the expanse of wild water between Alaska and Siberia.'

Rex Wyman had met Tobin Odell at the Ratskeller Tavern in Moscow, Idaho, when they were both juniors at the University of Idaho. Wyman's father was a wheat farmer in Idaho, and Wyman was studying agronomics. Toby Odell was majoring in mathematics, and was raised in Sun Valley. The Ratskeller only had one pinball machine, and Wyman was waiting for Odell, a stranger to him, to finish with the Super Tic-Tac-Toe. Sensing a brother in pinball, Odell, concentrating on the ball, said he was the only guy in history from Sun Valley who preferred pinball to skiing. They began taking turns at the Super Tic-Tac-Toe, talking all the while. Each discovered a fascinating fact about the other: Wyman was dissatisfied with his Kaypro's operating system, and was trying to rewrite the code, and Odell had purchased a bag of parts from a Radio Shack, and was building his own computer. Their friendship began that night.

They were soon spending their time driving Wyman's old Honda Accord to the Radio Shack, studying the inch-thick Sparkman Electronics catalogue, and welding and soldering and splicing. Odell moved into Wyman's dorm room. With sockets and wiring and transistors and microchips everywhere—on every shelf, strung over the beds' headboards, filling the closets—the room became the computer, and they lived inside it.

In their sophomore year, the university had opened a school of computer science, but Wyman and Odell had quickly determined they already knew more than was being taught at any of the classes. They came to understand that building computers was like building model planes; they were never more than the sum of their parts and that some guy in Japan was probably building a better one at that very moment. So Wyman and Odell turned to programming.

They stopped sitting side-by-side and sharing one computer as soon as they moved out of the University of Idaho dormitory, but in the early years, in WorldQuest Corporation's strip-mall office, they worked together with the same single-mindedness. They often completed each other's sentences. They napped at their desks. They ordered take-out Chinese, sometimes three times a day. The first product was modest: a time-entry system for accountants and lawyers. Soon there were twenty-five employees, and then fifty.

They were adapting the computer language TALENT, used on industry and government mainframe computers, for desktop computers, which were just becoming available. Wyman and Odell named their product *Quest* and licensed it to a new Japanese computer corporation, Nova, which was locked into the Quest operating system, and began offering WorldQuest applications as part of their software packages. The Nova computer was a success, capturing twenty per cent of world personal computer sales by 1990.

Wyman and Odell took WorldQuest public in 1990. They celebrated becoming billionaires by purchasing the Super Tic-Tac-Toe pinball machine from the Ratskeller, and moving it to their office.

Wyman found he had a gift for selling the product. His youth and energy dazzled. His wide smile, his ability to listen intently, and his skill at imparting his vision to companies considering WorldQuest products left deep impressions. To corporate chiefs around the world, Rex Wyman represented the future.

While Wyman blossomed, Toby Odell proved to be photophobic, turning away from the light, preferring the shadow. Wyman began taking lunch with this or that CEO, but Odell still hovered over his keyboard for twenty-hour stretches. Wyman flew to Geneva and Sydney for conferences, but Odell still ordered take-out Chinese. In 1993, Wyman purchased a block of Odell's stock, giving him controlling interest in WorldQuest. He became president of the board of directors and chief executive officer, positions that had been shared by them. On the day Wyman assumed all the titles, Odell left the company. He still owned a sizable portion of it and he benefited when the WorldQuest stock price rose. Other than that, he no longer had anything to do with the corporation. For years, the nature of Wyman and Odell's split had been the source of much speculation in the media.

'I read a *People* magazine article about you, Toby,' Gwen Weld said. 'It said you are bitter about leaving WorldQuest.'

He laughed sharply.

'I've read a lot of accounts of the break-up,' she said cautiously. 'The story seems to change, sort of evolves.'

'That's Rex's doing. He wants the world to think he outsmarted me. It adds a ruthless element to his character, and completes the picture of him as business wizard instead of just a software geek.'

'But the truth is, what?'

'I tired of it, so I let him buy me out.'

'Would Rex tell me the same story?'

'Unless he has started to lie to you, like he has to everybody else.' He suddenly held up a hand. 'I misspoke, Gwen. I'm . . . I'm under a bit of stress. Rex has sort of dared me to do something and I should dismiss it out of hand, but I just can't.'

'What would Rex do?' Gwen asked.

Toby Odell veiled his eyes and half turned away. 'He has asked me to crew *Victory* with him on the challenge. I don't know if I . . .' His voice softened to nothing and was lost in Wyman's voice coming over the loudspeakers.

'The Pacific Winter Challenge's true test of our sailing abilities is found in the race's middle name,' Wyman said. 'Winter. Those sailors who accept the challenge will find themselves in some of the world's most dangerous waters during the most dangerous season.' As Wyman ended the yacht club audience applauded.

Odell said under his breath, 'Rex thinks I'm afraid of the race.'

She asked, 'Are you afraid, Toby?'

'Of the sea? No.' He looked at her. 'I've got bigger things to be afraid of than the sea.'

The Westview High School marching band crashed their cymbals and rolled their snare drums as the yacht club's commodore stepped up to the podium. He introduced the Mayor of San Francisco, who bounded up to the platform.

Out on the dock, Odell said, changing the subject, 'In the past six years, Rex Wyman has gone through eleven girlfriends. That means each lasts a little more than six months.'

'Toby, it's my guess you've got better things to think about.'

Odell placed his empty glass on a passing waiter's tray. 'You are only into month three. In month six, you'll be out the door.'

'Toby, do I look like I need a nanny?'

'I'm trying to do you a favour. I met every one of those eleven girl-friends. I didn't say a word of caution to any of them. I figured they knew what they were getting into and they deserved it. But I'm meddling with you because I like you, Gwen.'

'And it's sweet of you, Toby.' She reached over to pat his arm. 'Now, butt out.'

Gwen Weld had been born on Manhattan's Upper East Side, in a fifteen-room apartment that overlooked Central Park, in the pantry, just off the kitchen. Her mother, Mary Weld, was the house-cleaner. Mary had feared being fired when her pregnancy had begun to show, so she hadn't dared take a day off as her term approached. Jobs were scarce for a heavily pregnant, unmarried girl with a thick County Cork accent and no papers at all. The baby came early. Mary gave birth lying on the floor in the little room filled with jars of olives and caviar and bottles of wine.

When Gwen was growing up, the great puzzle of her life was whether her mother had left Ireland for New York because she was pregnant, or whether Mary was simply a drop in the latest wave of Irish to flee their homeland looking for a better life. Mary Weld provided her daughter with love and meals and once in a while new clothes for school—at least they were new to Gwen—but nowhere to call home because the two of them changed apartments every few months. And Mary provided no history. They were Irish, Mary could hardly hide that, and she had let slip she was from County Cork. Other than that, nothing.

When Gwen came to an age where she realised many children had fathers, she asked her mother about her father. Gwen was six years old, and she could not now recall the form of her question, but Mary's response was the most vivid memory of her childhood. Her eyes wild, Mary turned to Gwen, gripped her arms with a desperate force, and said, 'You are never to ask about him. Do you understand me now, Gwen? Never, never again.' With that, Mary Weld drew a curtain over her past, one she would never lift.

Then there was the moment when the answer came to Gwen. She was in her junior year at New York University, and was studying in a cubicle, and the thought came from nowhere and swarmed over her: her mother was hiding. The leaving of Ireland when she was pregnant, the constant changing of addresses in the Bronx, the endless series of menial jobs, the refusal to ever try for US citizenship, never travelling. Gwen then understood that her mother was living her life without leaving a paper trail. She never applied for credit cards, never purchased anything through the mail, never applied for a driver's licence, never did anything where she had to identify herself. The reason Mary Weld never tried to better herself, her daughter in that instant understood, was that to do so—to try for college or better-paying jobs—would require her to prove who she was. For reasons unknown to Gwen, her mother could never do this.

Gwen sat there in her cubicle, her head in her hands, lost in pity for her mother, memories of their hard life washing over her. She resolved to demand an explanation.

There was never to be an explanation, not from Mary Weld, at least. Mary came home from work one day that very week, sat down on the tattered sofa near the window, and died. An aneurysm, her life blinking out in an instant, her crossword puzzle and pen falling onto her lap.

Gwen had dug through her mother's meagre possessions and found an essay, written—judging from the careful penmanship— when her mother was twelve or thirteen years old. The essay was titled 'The Sea and Ireland'. Under the title was the name Mary Strickland. Gwen had never before seen the name. The words 'Belgooly Parish School' were under the name.

Gwen travelled to Ireland the summer after her mother died, to County Cork, carrying a photograph of her mother as a teenager, a snapshot her mom had brought to America years ago. She found herself in the hamlet of Belgooly, south of the city of Cork and within two miles of the Atlantic Ocean. She found a Strickland in the phone book, and came to a whitewashed cottage that had geranium-filled flower boxes below the windows. She walked up the stone path to the house and rang the bell.

The door opened and her mother stood there, staring out at her.

At least, it could have been her mother, with the dark hair, the large, pale blue eyes, the sharp chin, and the slender, willowy figure.

'Yes?' The woman's voice was the ghost of a whisper. She may have just seen some of herself in Gwen. 'May I help you?'

Without a word, Gwen held up the photograph of her mother.

The woman at the door leaned forward, intent on the photo. After a few seconds, she said, 'Oh my. Oh, my lost Mary.'

She stepped onto the porch and gathered Gwen into her arms, and the woman began to weep quietly. Then, without releasing Gwen, the woman turned her towards the door and escorted her inside.

That afternoon, over a pot of tea, the woman, Colleen Strickland Mallory, told Gwen that when Mary Strickland was eighteen years old, Mary had fallen in with a John Hannon, 'a fellow I never saw when he wasn't acting the maggot. He'd been in jail for thievery. Couldn't hold a job. But charming. Oh, my, he was charming.'

'So this John Hannon is my father?' Gwen could barely say it.

'Was your father,' Colleen corrected her. 'John Hannon is dead, and has been for twenty years.'

Gwen's hand flew to her mouth.

Her aunt nodded sagely. 'Mary was wild for John Hannon. And our mam and dad and me never understood it, because John was so mean.' She shook her head. 'He'd slap her and everything. It was terrible. She'd come home crying and trying to hide her bruised face.'

When Colleen lifted her cup and saucer, they rattled together, her hands shaking. 'One March night, John Hannon was found dead on the side of Western Road, not far from the greyhound track. He had been stabbed a couple of times in his throat. After that night Mary was never seen again in Ireland.'

The snare drums sounded again, a long roll, followed by the trumpets ringing out with a call to the gate.

Toby Odell nodded towards the clubhouse patio doors. 'Here he comes. The big entrance.'

On cue from the mayor, Rex Wyman came through the doors and smiled at the crowd, his teeth flashing like mirrors. His face was tanned and smooth. His seal-brown hair was carefully combed, and didn't give an inch in the breeze, as if it were lacquered in place. Though Wyman stood just a fraction over six feet, he seemed outsized, larger than life, like a statue in the park.

Odell looked at Gwen. 'You've got some iron to you, some courage and strength. I can tell, just from the little I know you, standing up to Rex like you do. I don't know if I've got that iron, and now this invitation to crew *Victory* with Rex. I don't know . . .' His voice trailed off.

'I inherited a bit of iron from my mother, maybe.' She smiled to herself.

Those years ago, Gwen was first astonished and horrified that her mother had killed someone but her opinion quickly turned around. John Hannon had learned a hard lesson about messing with Strickland women.

Odell said, 'Maybe you inherited iron from your father, too?'

Gwen replied with a venom she couldn't contain, 'He is dead and in hell, and the world is a better place because of it.'

Wyman was holding up the bottle of champagne with which he would in a moment christen *Victory*.

Odell stared at Gwen out of the corner of his eyes. A small grin was on his face.

LONNIE GARVIN had put in a twelve-hour day, but he was still working swiftly. He was angry and his teeth were clamped together. He was on the deck of his crabber, *Hornet*, and had spent the day working on seven-bys: crab pots that are seven feet high, seven feet deep, and a yard wide, twice the size of a refrigerator. Two hundred of them were on deck, and each weighed 750 pounds empty.

He knew better than to allow emotions to eat at him, but there they were, a corrosive concoction of impotence and frustration and rage. His life's work was draining away, and he was helpless.

There was a time when Garvin could sit in his wheelhouse, studying the charts and reports, laying out his strategy for the season, chatting with his skipper buddies on the radio, enjoying his coffee. No more. Now he couldn't afford the hands to repair the crab pots or the boat. Moving crab pots around *Hornet*'s deck was easier in a rough sea because the deck hand could time his shove with the roll of the boat, and so push downhill. But *Hornet* was in port, and every inch Garvin shoved a pot across his deck hurt to his bones. He was fuming that it had come to this.

He surveyed his boat, every beloved bolt and scupper. *Hornet* was all steel, a stiff-ribbed vessel with a square bottom, square stern, and a hard chine, all of which allowed it to spring upright on keel after every roll. The bow was rounded and it flared up from the bulwarks, designed specifically for the Bering Sea.

The pilothouse was forward, riding high above the deck. In the superstructure below the pilothouse were the galley and mess, crew quarters and storerooms. And then further below were fuel wing tanks on each side of the engine room, four double-bottom crab tanks, a centreline deep tank and a compartment for the steering gear. On deck behind the wheelhouse were two cranes and two drums. Everything first rate. Garvin had even picked out the black walnut trim for the pilothouse and crew staterooms.

At a distance, *Hornet* was still majestic, with its royal blue hull and white superstructure, and its radar tower high above the wheelhouse.

It was a broad-shouldered, nose-down bull of a boat. It meant business, even a landlubber knew that just from glancing at it. But up close, a careful eye could detect *Hornet*'s distress. Rust stains marred the hull below the scuppers. Sealant around the pilothouse windows had shrunk and cracked. Paint on the deck railings was chipped, exposing steel. A hundred other things above deck needed attention, and even more below deck.

The boat was like a herd of dairy cows. It never relented in its demand for more work from him. He couldn't afford to hire help, and couldn't take it to a boat yard. He'd been doing it all himself. He was tired. God, but he was tired.

The cellphone chirruped. Garvin lifted it off the capstan.

'Yeah?' he said, too dispirited to be civil.

He listened, his eyes narrowing with thought, then closing with resignation. 'All right, Booney,' he said. 'I owe you one.'

The world-weariness falling away, Lonnie Garvin quickly closed two deck hatches, then climbed the ladder to the wheelhouse. He cranked over the starboard engine, a Caterpillar as big as a pick-up truck. The port engine was down. It had been overheating, sending steam off its pipes. So he could use only one of *Hornet*'s engines.

With the starboard engine rumbling, Garvin scanned the gauges. He had less than 200 gallons of diesel on board, about a hundred in each of the tanks. He was always careful about keeping them evenly filled, transferring fuel from one to the other when needed. Same with the catch. Crabs were distributed evenly into starboard and port tanks. Otherwise the boat was out of balance.

Garvin raced out of the wheelhouse and back down the ladder, sliding down, not using the rungs. He ran along the rail to the forward mooring line, freed it and threw it onto the wharf. Then to the aft line, tossing it off, too. Breathing hard now, Garvin returned to the wheelhouse. He would otherwise never contemplate—not for a crazed instant—taking *Hornet* to sea without at least two deck hands. But the sheriff was coming and Garvin had to escape.

Last off-season, Jacobson Electric in Seattle had installed a water-cooled Volvo Penta generator on *Hornet*. The bill came to $25,000. Garvin had scraped up the deposit and pledged *Hornet* as security. He had made the first two payments, but none since. Jacobson Electric held off as long as they could, but finally had turned the account over to their lawyers, a bloodthirsty Seattle firm.

In their own defence, these lawyers would argue that vigour is required when the collateral can be moved around, which is to say, hidden. Unlike a mortgaged home, a boat can easily be concealed, particularly in Alaska, where even today not all the shoreline is charted. Maritime law compensates for the portability of the security by allowing creditors to act quickly. Unknown to Lonnie Garvin, Jacobson Electric had filed a complaint that very morning in the federal court for the district of Anchorage, and had obtained a warrant for *Hornet*'s arrest.

The US Marshall's office in Anchorage has its own jet, which had landed at Dutch Harbor a few minutes earlier. A while back, Garvin had asked a freight forwarder, who had an office near the runway, to keep his eye out for the sheriff's plane and to give a call if it landed. Maybe this was a false alarm, but probably not, not with Garvin's creditors working at his door with a battering ram.

Moored at the pier forward of Hornet was Max Freeman's sixty-five-foot trawler, *Pacific Crest*. Garvin hadn't seen Freeman all day and he hoped he was in a bar or in his Unalaska apartment, because Freeman wouldn't at all like what Garvin was about to do.

With the engine revving just above idle, Garvin engaged the running gear. The starboard propeller kicked up white water. *Hornet* shuddered, then rumbled forward, just an inch, then a little more. *Hornet*'s manoeuvrability was hampered by the dead port engine and by the lack of deck hands to nudge the boat away from the pier. The wheel hard to starboard, Garvin willed *Hornet* to defy the laws ·of physics and to miss *Pacific Crest*.

Hornet could not oblige. Its prow bumped *Pacific Crest*'s stern, brushing it more than ramming it, and Garvin heard wood shatter. He couldn't see below *Hornet*'s high prow, couldn't see the damage he had just inflicted on Freeman's boat. Maybe it was just the safety rail. Still, Max Freeman was going to go purple when he saw what Garvin had just done to his trawler.

Garvin would call him on the cellphone in a few minutes. Freeman would understand, if it was only his safety rail, two hours' labour and a hundred dollars, compared with Garvin losing his entire vessel.

The big Cat rumbling, *Hornet* glided forward, pushing *Pacific Crest*, which resisted because it was tied fore and aft to the dock. More wood gave way with a sharp crack. Max Freeman was going to have a heart attack. Garvin glanced over his shoulder, through the wheelhouse's port windows towards the dock and the road.

A car turned into the boat yard. It would be the sheriff, fresh from the airport. The sun flashed on the windshield, hiding the occupants. Then the reflection slipped away as the car came to a stop. Garvin could see the driver. A marshall, sure enough, wearing the service's silly hat. Probably a deputy marshall, told by the court to go to Dutch Harbor and seize Lonnie Garvin's boat.

Sitting next to the deputy was Will Slewberg, the custodian appointed by the court to care for *Hornet* once the deputy made the arrest. He was despised universally along the docks, viewed as a vulture. Slewberg was first out of the car, a wiry little man with a flapping coat, beginning to run across the gravel lot towards *Hornet* before the deputy was even out of the car.

Garvin tapped the accelerator bar again. Something else cracked on *Pacific Crest*'s stern. *Hornet*'s bow slipped further to sea, straining against *Pacific Crest*'s stern, sliding along it to starboard. Freeman's boat listed to starboard as *Hornet* pushed it.

Now the deputy was following Slewberg across the lot towards the pier, closing in on *Hornet*. If they got on board *Hornet*, Garvin might never set foot on his boat again.

And here the marshall came, out onto the dock, raising an arm to signal Garvin. *Hornet*'s prow was still snagged on the trawler, still prodding it and scraping its stern. The deputy and Slewberg were fifty yards away, pumping their arms, Slewberg waving some document at Garvin up in the wheelhouse, maybe the complaint.

The boat suddenly lurched forward, free of *Pacific Crest*, which settled back on its keel. Garvin punched the throttle. The gap between ship and pier widened an inch at a time. One hand on the wheel, Garvin peered through a window down over the safety rail seeing the wooden pier, then a growing expanse of water between hull and pier. He exhaled hugely.

The deputy and Will Slewberg ran onto the wharf and right up to its edge. From high overhead, Garvin saw the deputy smile, a small thing meant for him and not for Slewberg.

Garvin understood the smile. Marshalls hated making vessel arrests, putting hard-working fishermen out of business. The deputy might have precisely timed his arrival in the car, slacking off on the accelerator a bit to let *Hornet* get under way, Garvin wouldn't have been surprised. The custodian, though, was vibrating with anger.

So *Hornet* was away, leaving the harbour behind, cruising towards the headland then out to sea. Garvin rationed himself a grin. He deserved it, and he didn't know when he would be able to smile

Chapter three

Several days after Rex Wyman's announcement at the yacht club, Gwen followed the billionaire back onto the dock. She had long legs, but even so had to break into a trot several times to keep up. Rex's aide Roger Hall was behind her, churning his small legs. Hall owned a master's degree in economics from Vanderbilt, but he had the soul of a valet. Hall was always with Rex, or just outside the door, or at the end of a shout, and Gwen had almost ceased seeing him.

Wyman called over his shoulder, 'They've done it. I knew they would, if they just had enough money poured on them.'

Wyman had met Gwen in Sun Valley for their romantic weekend alone—Gwen called them *Weekends Alone Plus Roger Hall*—but almost immediately Wyman had received an urgent message from his robotics engineers aboard *Victory*. Gwen's hopes for the weekend had vanished when Wyman's Gulfstream took off with them both aboard, bound for the west coast. A car had met them at San Francisco International.

Wyman slowed on the dock, allowing her to catch up. 'You've been the computer systems manager on the project, Gwen.'

'Sure.' She worked at controlling the anger in her voice.

'Still, you've got no idea of the effort that has gone into the boat.'

By effort, Wyman usually meant money.

He continued, 'I hired Oregon Automation, the research firm near Beaverton. They specialise in industrial robots. I subsidised an entire division, thirty engineers and technicians, working on *Victory*'s robotics systems. The cost of this research, you've got no idea.'

Yes, she did. He wasn't picking up on her foul mood.

Night was thick along the waterfront. The moon was hidden behind low, bruise-black clouds. Metal fixtures along the dock cast low cones of yellow light, guiding the way. Soft light came through curtains covering portholes in some of the boats.

'They told me it couldn't be done.' He laughed, a rude sound that smacked against the hull of an old bull-nose Chris Craft they were passing. 'But I goaded them and Oregon Automation's director of research went for it.'

Gwen reached for his arm, trying to pull him to a stop. 'Rex, I need to talk with you.' She had been abiding her anger, and trying to place it in the context of a great man on the great mission, to reduce the affront to her caused by the instantly changed plans.

He resisted for an instant, intent on getting to *Victory*. His face was pinched with disapproval, then it softened slowly. He turned to her, but not before one last gaze down the dock, into the night, where *Victory* lay. 'I'm terribly sorry, Gwen,' he said in his dulcet voice.

'You could have been a mortician, you sound so sincere.' She despised little scenes and she was determined not to create one.

'I need you to trust me on this, Gwen.' He moved closer to her, putting a hand on her arm. Roger Hall immediately stepped back, out of hearing range. 'WorldQuest has suffered some reverses.'

Gwen knew that WorldQuest's stock price had fallen by half in the prior twelve months, a downward slide that baffled shareholders who had once thought Rex Wyman infallible. Gwen's stock in WorldQuest was worth $6 million. A year ago it had been worth twice that. 'It's only paper,' Wyman had assured her.

'Rex, I don't want to talk about your damned business.'

'Then what?' He grimaced as he said it. 'Sorry, I know what you mean. I do this to you sometimes, just go off and change the plans.'

'I'd been looking forward to our time together in Idaho for a month.'

'Yeah, I know.' He sounded like a penitent.

'After each long day working on *Victory*'s systems, I'd look at the calendar again and say, one less day until Rex and I can be together.'

He looked at her, holding her with his eyes, his expression entirely earnest, his face seeking understanding and forgiveness. She felt the stirrings that had first attracted her to him.

Her voice firmed. 'I'm always the expendable appointment,' she said. 'You get a call—it could be from anyone, a senator or a prime minister or Bill Gates or the King of Prussia—and off you go.'

He reached for her hands and held them in both of his. 'I need to ask that you put up with this craziness until the race is under way. It begins in one week. Let's get *Victory* under way.'

'And after that?'

'Things change.'

'A weekend alone will mean a weekend alone?'

'I promise, yes.'

She nodded, accepting the promise because she believed him, sort of, and because she had no other choice.

They began again towards *Victory*, Roger Hall following.

Wyman held her hand as they walked. 'I've rolled the dice with *Victory*, Gwen. Its integrated system is going to make or break me.'

'The high-end sailboat market isn't big, Rex.' She was teasing.

'Nobody'll buy the system for a sailboat. It's the big universities, the prisons, the military bases. Those'll be my customers.'

'Don't forget the sewage plants.' It was an attempt to make him laugh. As usual, though, his earnestness was hard to dislodge.

'There's been a couple of things gone sour. It's more than the stock. Ever heard of the trans-Caucasian pipeline?'

'An oil venture?'

'Natural gas. I invested two hundred million dollars in the project with a Russian company named Mid Asia Transport. Solid people with connections all the way up to the Kremlin.'

'What happened?'

'I'm not sure,' Wyman said. 'I've sent some people to check, but . . .' He shrugged. 'It's gone, I think. The corruption over there was beyond my understanding.'

Two hundred million dollars. Wyman might have been speaking a foreign language, so incomprehensible were these figures.

Gwen recalled the day she became a millionaire, a day that combined a vesting in that year's WorldQuest stock options and a run-up in WorldQuest price on the NASDAQ. She was sitting in her cubicle when a whoop went up in the room as the ticker price was flashed on a monitor. She wasn't the only WorldQuest employee who had joined the millionaire ranks that day.

She had sworn that once her assets hit that magic number, she would splurge on a month-long trip to Australia and New Zealand—she had not taken a holiday in three years—and spend some money. That week, she sat opposite the travel agent, pen in hand, cheque book in front of her, and she could not get her pen to fill in the figure on the cheque. Mortified, she had offered vast apologies to the travel agent and then fled. A year earlier, at the half-million-dollar mark, she had run from a Jaguar showroom, leaving the salesman seconds from closing a deal on an XJ saloon.

Gwen had never—not once in her life—paused at a store window, seen a coat or dress she liked, and gone inside to buy it. She had never—not once—purchased something on impulse. She lived in a one-room apartment in an area of Boise known for modest apartments and take-out pizza joints. She shopped at Costco.

Only when she began dating Rex Wyman did she loosen up a little, a very little. Rex couldn't be seen with a rag on his arm. A few dresses and jewellery, but only after ferocious shopping and price comparisons. She started going to a hair salon, an expense she thought the equivalent of tossing money down a storm drain, but Rex had insisted, politely but pointedly.

She had often wondered how wealth affected her and Rex's relationship. Money meant nothing to Rex because he had so much of it, and it meant nothing to her because she was constitutionally incapable of spending any of it. Maybe their disregard for money was one of the reasons they were attracted to each other.

Gwen remembered her great lesson about money. Her mother had kept a ceramic pot of coins on the kitchen counter, wherever they lived. She used it for subway money. One day when she was thirteen, Gwen helped herself to two quarters. She wanted to go over to Mike's Candy and Soda store during lunch with her school friends. She still remembered the taste of the Sugar Babies she had purchased with the money. That night at supper, her mom asked Gwen to pick any day next week, Monday through Friday. Puzzled, Gwen picked Tuesday. 'All right,' her mother had said. 'Tuesday morning, I'm going to get out of bed at three thirty and walk across the bridge into Manhattan, then up to the east side. It'll take me four hours to walk to work. With the two quarters that are missing from the change pot, I would have taken the subway like every other morning.' And her mom had done just that; she arose at three thirty and went off to work, her daughter awake and weeping in her room. Gwen had never stolen anything since. And she had never had another Sugar Baby since, either.

Gwen and Wyman came to a checkpoint on the dock, where a security agent shone a flashlight in their faces before letting them by.

A man wearing a navy-blue woollen coat approached them. He was grinning widely, triumph written on his face.

Victory rose above them, its mast and shrouds and stays filling the night sky, its blade-sharp prow descending from the nose into the black water. Massive and silent, every edge refined, every square inch the subject of dozens of meetings, *Victory* reminded Gwen of a shark. Same predatory lines. She had never told Rex, as he would have laughed, but the boat gave her the creeps.

She couldn't place the origin of the disturbing sensation. Sitting there dockside, placid and bobbing, *Victory* aroused wariness and a touch of revulsion, and she didn't know why. Something about the boat, in its sweeping hull and its mast and lines. She couldn't name it, couldn't tell which aspect of the vessel was sending forth this impression. But *Victory* had an aura of controlled menace about it, some elemental and threatening power.

'Hi, Gwen,' the man in the blue coat said. 'Ready for the show?'

The three of them boarded *Victory* across a gangplank. The man was Ramish Advani, Oregon Automation's chief of robotics. He wore his blue-black hair in a Beatles haircut. Gwen knew his delicate face masked a ferocious intelligence. Once, when she was visiting OA's labs, she had found him sitting in his office, staring at a blank wall. She had knocked lightly on the open door. He didn't look away from the wall. When she finally touched his arm, he jumped. 'Are you in a trance, Ramish?' He had replied he was playing chess. 'Where're your chess pieces and your board?' He had smiled. 'I don't need them.' 'And your opponent?' Gwen had asked. He had replied, 'I don't need an opponent either.'

Advani led them forward under shrouds and along the port rail, passing the mast. Attached to the deck forward of the mast was a mechanical protuberance never before seen at sea.

'Meet the OA 1542.' Advani beamed. 'Installed, up and running, and at your service.'

Wyman stared at the thing. 'It's magnificent.'

'It's frightening,' Gwen said.

Advani said, 'There'll be no crew working the spinnaker. It will be handled by this modular telerobot task-execution system.'

'That's a mouthful for a robotic arm, isn't it?' Wyman asked.

Advani said, 'We call it *Stretch*.'

The mechanism consisted of five tubes attached to each other with enclosed joints, the lowest tubes of the arm having the widest girth. The arm branched three feet off the deck, a second arm extended from the larger one. The arm components were entirely enclosed in lightweight titanium and plastic, and the main branch was twenty feet long. The smaller branch was half that. The system had not been affixed to the deck during the sea trials or the party to announce the race because it hadn't been ready yet.

The engineer continued, 'You can see that *Stretch* is mobile, starboard to port, travelling on enclosed wheels on a embedded rail, much like a welding robot in an auto plant. The system is designed to operate in gale force winds and seas.'

'And the hands?' Wyman asked.

'We engineers call them end effectors,' Advani replied. '*Stretch* has two, one on each branch. The spinnaker pole you see there at the tip of the main arm is collapsible, like Nelson's telescope. The effector anchors the spinnaker pole, so we don't need to attach the pole to the mast by a bracket, as in other sailboats. The smaller effector handles the guy and the reaching hook, just as a crewman's hands would.'

'Ramish, does it work?' Wyman said.

Advani said, 'It would be foolish to raise the spinnaker while *Victory* is tied to a dock. Your boat would be ripped from its moorings.' He pulled an egg from his pocket. He held it up on three fingers, balancing it there so Wyman could study it. Then the engineer tossed the egg into the air towards the bow. It soared up, arced out and began its descent, surely to splatter onto *Victory*'s deck or perhaps plunge into the water.

Until that instant, the robotic arm had been entirely inert. Gwen had thought the ungainly thing was just resting there, waiting for someone to turn on a switch. But OA 1542, also known as *Stretch*, leapt into life. The upper extender, which held the collapsible pole, inclined to port, and the lower branch shot forward, its extender opening. The machine was almost silent, just a slight purr.

Stretch caught the egg, plucked it from the air on its descent. Just as quietly, the arm pivoted, travelled a few feet towards Advani and held the egg out to him. When the engineer took the egg from the mechanical hand, *Stretch* returned to its neutral station and posture. Ten seconds had elapsed since Gwen first saw the egg.

'Your question, Rex, was whether *Stretch* works?' Advani asked.

Wyman said, 'I said it was impossible, that you couldn't produce a robot that would handle a spinnaker on a jibe, but I was wrong.'

'We made a wager,' Advani said. 'You remember?'

Wyman dug into a pocket and brought out a set of keys on a foam bobber that would keep the keys from sinking were they to drop into the water. He held them up. 'You win.'

He was about to hand them over, but Gwen caught his hand.

Her voice stern, she said, 'Wait a minute. I'll bet you hard-boiled that egg, Ramish.'

Grinning like a fiend, Advani held his hand out over the port rail and crushed the egg. The white and the yolk dribbled from his fingers into the water below. Then he wiped his hand.

She released Wyman's hand and he handed over the key. Advani gripped it like a life ring. They congratulated Advani, then Gwen took Wyman's arm as they left *Victory*, walking back along the dock.

'That was cool, Rex. Wagering that big boat and handing over the keys.'

'I reward success,' he said, his voice oddly low. He waited a beat, then added, 'And I punish failure.'

'WHAT WAS THAT, a baseball?' Toby Odell asked, staring at the screen.

'Too small to be a baseball,' Brady Lane replied. 'Something smaller. And did you see that robot shoot out after it? It'd make shortstop on any pro team.'

Odell and his employee Brady Lane were studying a flat-screen monitor. The infrared camera was on the mast of a boat moored across the dock from *Victory*.

'I'll be damned. The robot caught an egg.' Odell laughed, pointing at the screen. 'The engineer just squished it between his fingers.'

'Awesome,' Brady Lane said. He was twenty-two years old, and wore five rings in one ear and two in the other. Odell had never seen him without a navy-blue woollen watch cap, summer or winter. Lane was as restless as a whippet, and the only time he sat still was in front of a computer keyboard and monitor, when a calm would descend upon him. He had served five months in prison for hacking into Bank America's main server and fiddling with some files, 'about four thousand files, Your Honour,' he had candidly told the judge. Toby Odell had hired him two days after he walked out of federal prison at Lompoc, California.

Odell and Lane and five others were arranged around the office of Wayward Souls, Inc., as they called themselves. They had no official name, nothing on the door of the office in San Francisco's China Basin, near the new baseball park. The room was on the first floor of a warehouse. Desks were planks laid on trestles. A skateboard rack was near the door. Computers more than six months old—and thus outdated—were stacked haphazardly in the room's corners. Wiring was duct-taped to the ceiling. There was no receptionist and few telephones. A bunk bed was in a corner, with no blankets, just two mattresses. As in a casino, no clocks were on the wall. The employees rarely cared what time it was.

The office was a shambles by design. Toby Odell's employees were in their early twenties; most were college drop-outs. They were hardcore hackers who had jumped at Odell's offer to be paid for their obsession. Odell owned eighteen companies—media, software, entertainment—but this one, Wayward Souls, Inc, was where he spent most of his time.

Odell modestly called himself a code guy. More accurately, he had become an inveterate hacker. Hacking offered a sense of being at the forefront of computing, where he once was. It offered adventure and danger, and the Wayward Souls, with their pranks and energy and laughter, made Odell feel that he was still at the cutting edge, just as he had been when he and Rex Wyman had sat in their tiny room, sharing a computer, working on their new operating system.

Odell and Lane watched the monitor. 'See that pod, right on *Victory*'s nose? There's another pod like that atop the mast.'

'What are they?' Lane asked. 'Radar?'

'They are modified terrain-mapping devices, using laser range finders,' said Odell. 'Each range finder uses three laser beams, and three sets of spinning and nodding mirrors to scan the beams over the ocean's waves. The lasers measure each wave in four ways: length, height, period and speed.'

'So what does the computer do with it?' Lane asked.

'It generates elevation maps that determine *Victory*'s location amid the moving waves and rollers. The range finders are assisted by hundreds of sensors in *Victory*'s hull that detect the presence of water at any given millisecond, so that the computer knows when a wave is passing along the hull. New wave maps are generated ten times a second, so *Victory* is certain of the location and direction and speed and height of all waves within that vicinity.'

'Wouldn't a human being be better at that? A lookout, or the guy at the wheel?'

Odell shook his head. 'In a cross sea, where waves are coming at different directions from different storms, no human can perceive all that is going on. And in the dark, waves can't be seen by a human. *Victory*'s system works equally well, day or night.'

'So *Victory*'s steering system makes continuing adjustments according to the waves it is encountering?'

Odell nodded. 'Adjustments to rudder and sails. The computer is both the boatswain and the coxswain.'

'Pure coolness.' Brady Lane leaned back in his chair. 'But what's the point? Why is Wyman putting so much effort and money into this boat?'

'You ever played poker, Brady?'

'Some.'

'If you stick with your current five cards, you know what your hand is. But, say, if you ask for two new cards, you face thousands of potential outcomes. If you ask for three new cards, you face thousands more. This is a called a combinatorial explosion.'

'So?'

'A decision-making process—a simple yes or no—repeated many times quickly can expand to an immense array. *Victory* is designed to show it can handle a vast combinatorial explosion. This wave-mapping system does it, as do the meteorological processing and navigation functions on the ship. Some say only human wisdom can be relied on to make choices at this level.'

Brady asked, 'So Wyman thinks his system can handle such a combinatorial explosion—so much data—that it amounts to wisdom? Artificial intelligence, then?'

'He claims that sail racing in heavy weather is the ultimate test.'

'So what if *Victory* passes the test?'

'There's huge worldwide markets for such a system, everything from cars and tanks that drive themselves to prisons that run themselves,' Odell replied. 'Rex is betting the farm on *Victory*. Rather, he's betting his company, WorldQuest.'

Lane looked at him. 'So you're really going on the Challenge?'

Odell glanced around the office, then he looked back at the monitor, which showed *Victory.* His words were a bit too loud, as if he were trying to convince himself. 'I wouldn't miss it.'

JESS MCKAY SAT at the card table that served as a desk, his laptop in front of him, connected to a printer on the table. The gooseneck lamp was low over his work so it wouldn't wake his roommate, Santiago Ramirez, who had fallen asleep on a couch.

Ramirez was a competitive weightlifter and held the Alaska record for the clean-and-jerk. When he wasn't on duty, he was almost always at the gym. Ramirez was huge—six feet four and at least 230 pounds, and he could move his mass with surprising speed. His brown hair was cut close to his scalp. His hands were big and blunt. Ramirez had a brawler's presence.

McKay and Ramirez were pararescue jumpers with the Alaska Air National Guards' 212th Rescue Squadron (RQS), based at Anchorage's Kulis Air National Guard Base. The 212th's peacetime mission is performing search and rescue during the air force training exercises that occur in Alaska. The PJs also rescue civilians—hunters, hikers, campers, climbers—who usually have overestimated their abilities and underestimated the Alaskan wilderness.

The apartment McKay and Ramirez shared had the appearance of a dorm room, with most of the furniture included in the rent, and every piece of it sprung or faded or nicked. A brick-and-board bookshelf was against one wall. The television set belonged to Ramirez, but hadn't been hooked to the cable because neither he nor McKay had the time or inclination to watch television.

McKay had printed out twenty letters this evening, each with the same addressee—John McKay—but with different addresses. The letter contained only twelve sentences, but he had spent a month drafting it. It had to be perfect, had to inveigle a reply.

The Internet had helped in his search. How many John McKays could there be in the world? Plenty, it turned out. He had sent emails to all the John McKays for whom he could find email addresses. That hadn't panned out. Now he was reduced to communicating the old-fashioned way, sending letters. He was working on the John McKays in Southern California. He did his address searching and letter printing late at night, when Sandy Ramirez was asleep. A couple of times Sandy had woken and groggily asked what he was doing, and Jess had always replied he was surfing the Internet.

McKay looked again at the computer screen, at the California site listing John McKays. He typed in another address on his form letter.

Ramirez spoke from the couch. 'Have you found your father yet?'

McKay pivoted in the chair. 'Damn it, Sandy, have you been reading my files?'

'We're partners. It's part of the deal.'

'Sandy, this is my private affair and none of your business.'

'Sure, I understand,' he said, yawning. 'So when is the last time you saw him?'

McKay closed his eyes a moment. 'Six years ago.'

'What happened?'

After a moment, McKay replied, 'My mom died, of pancreatic cancer. Real sudden. And then my dad disappeared.'

'What do you mean?'

McKay tried a shrug. 'He just vanished.'

'People don't just disappear for no reason.'

'My dad did. Maybe he had a reason. Maybe not. I don't know. He and I never really got along, not when I was in high school, and not later, either.'

'Why?'

Jess studied his screen. He could feel his friend staring at him. 'It was about my older brother, Matt.'

'You have an older brother?' Ramirez said. 'I never knew that.'

'He's dead,' McKay replied in a diminished tone. 'He drowned when he was a senior in high school in a river near our home.'

Ramirez was silent for a moment. Then he asked. 'So what does that have to do with you and your dad not getting along?'

McKay carefully weighed his words. 'I was in the same raft as my brother. We fell off in the rapids.'

Ramirez rose from the sofa to step into the kitchen. He returned with a box of Wheat Thins. He opened them and dug out a handful. After a moment chewing, he asked, 'You made it to shore and Matt didn't, that what happened?'

'Yeah. My father never got over it. He hung around until Mom died, then he left.'

'You mean, he just packed a bag and went out the door?'

McKay said, 'We were both at my mother's funeral that day. I went over to my uncle's home after the graveside service, and when I got home, Dad was gone.'

'No forwarding address? No note? Nothing?'

McKay shook his head.

'Why did he run off like that?'

'He was never the same after Matt died.' McKay's voice was the ghost of a whisper. 'He never forgave me.'

'What's to forgive? I don't get it? Wasn't it the luck of the draw? You made it to shore and your brother Matt didn't.'

'Yeah.' McKay turned back to his computer. 'The luck of the draw, must've been.'

'So what's the point of trying to find your father again, writing all those letters?'

'I just want him to know I'm still around and would like to see him, is all.'

Ramirez lay back down and closed his eyes. 'Jess, if your dad walked away like that, he's not going to answer a letter.'

'Maybe not,' McKay said, his hands on the keyboard. 'But I don't know what else to do. I'd like to see him again, just to talk.'

Ramirez was quickly asleep again, the box of Wheat Thins beside him on the sofa. McKay wiped away teardrops that had fallen onto his keyboard, then began again with his letters.

Rex Wyman's Pacific Winter Challenge war room was in the marina district in San Francisco, not far from *Victory,* moored at the Harbor Yacht Club's dock. The war room looked nothing like a windowless and dark weapons room aboard an aircraft carrier, but rather was open and cheery, with windows and bright lights. Wyman made sure the five vases in the room had fresh arrangements weekly. Computer monitors were everywhere. In a nod to RAF Second World War plotting rooms, an enormous map of the North Pacific Ocean covered one wall, ready to have the progress of each boat marked. A rolling ladder was near the map.

Gwen Weld was running simulations, surrounded by three computer monitors. It was nine o'clock in the morning, and Gwen had been at this station for four hours. The Pacific Winter Challenge began the following day.

Gwen lifted a copy of that morning's newspaper, which was filled with news of the impending race and all its festivities. People expected hyperbole from Rex Wyman, and he had obliged, saying the Pacific Winter Challenge 'was the biggest thing to hit San Francisco since the earthquake'. The race had the scent of a heavyweight prize fight, with San Francisco's hotels packed, the ballrooms booked, the limousine services busy. Wyman was convinced that nothing worthwhile was ever accomplished without a balloon launch, and he was determined to have the world's first million-balloon release as the race started. He had arranged that each balloon could be redeemed at a 7-Eleven for a Slurpy.

Wyman had contracted with Waterford Crystal to design and construct the Challenge's trophy, and it was to be the largest crystal sculpture ever produced, weighing more than a ton. A crowd exceeding half a million people was expected along the San Francisco and Marin County shores. Two hundred thousand coffee mugs, each with the WorldQuest logo, were to be distributed.

Wyman had told Gwen that he was creating a great thirst in his competitors, particularly the Americans. Twelve American boats had entered the race and Wyman was delighted. There were also boats from France, England, Italy, Australia and New Zealand.

Gwen's computer sounded, an alert that she had new email. It was from an address she didn't recognise, and it said, 'If you are the skipper of *Victory*, may I chat with you a moment?' It gave a private address for real-time chat. It was signed, 'Captain Jess McKay, 212th Rescue Squadron, AFNG, Anchorage, Alaska.'

She entered the address, then typed, '*Victory* doesn't have a skipper. It has an owner. I am the systems manager. May I help you? Gwen Weld.' She punched the keyboard to send it.

A new window opened, and a few seconds later came the reply. 'A boat needs a skipper, someone in charge. Are you that person?'

She typed, '*Victory* will be making its own decisions. Why do you ask, and, if I may be impertinent, who are you?'

'My team will be asked to rescue your sorry carcasses when the time comes, and I'm not looking forward to it. This message is sent in an unofficial capacity.'

'*Victory* is the safest boat ever built. I'm not worried.'

'Have you ever been in the Bering Sea?' Captain McKay wrote. 'Do you have any conception of what the Bering Sea is like?'

She replied, 'We have more information on the Bering Sea than you can possibly imagine.'

'I'm talking about you,' appeared on her screen. 'You, not your gimmicky boat. Do you know what you are getting yourself into?'

She hesitated over the keyboard. 'We have run endless computer simulations and *Victory* has proven herself during sea trials. The boat was designed for the Bering Sea.'

'What about all the other sailors you are luring into this idiocy? If you lead your pack of fools up into these waters in the dead of winter, you will have much on your conscience. Goodbye.'

She quickly typed, 'Don't hang up on me on that pious note. You don't know anything about *Victory* or Rex Wyman. How dare you be so condescending?'

After a moment came, 'My apologies. I don't tolerate fools well.'

'Rex Wyman is not a fool.'

The reply from Alaska appeared on her screen: 'I wasn't talking about Rex Wyman.'

Chapter four

Nineteen ocean racers approached the start, with the breeze flowing into the bay through the Golden Gate. The starting line was between the committee boat and a buoy, on an approximate line between Coit Tower and the east tip of Alcatraz Island. A gun sounded, alerting skippers to a new flag being run up on the committee boat, a flag indicating one minute to the start. The boats rushed towards the starting line, their masts lined up like soldiers.

Rex Wyman was in *Victory*'s cockpit, his hands on the safety rail. 'The only thing I couldn't control was the weather, but I got a break.'

Gwen stood near the companionway. The wind was light but steady off the port bow, and it blew her hair back over her shoulders.

Wyman asked, 'How many seconds until the start?'

The Voice replied, 'Thirty-one seconds.' Speakers were mounted near the companionway and along the sides of the cockpit.

Waves were only a foot high. Softened by high clouds, the sun was a flat silver disk sending forth watery light. Nineteen masts sliced through the air on the same course. The boats jockeyed expertly, positioning themselves for the starting line.

Toby Odell was sitting in the cockpit, a cup of tea in his hands. He was the only person aboard wearing a life jacket. 'You could walk from San Francisco to Sausalito on all the boats, Rex.'

Wyman's publicity campaign had worked. Thousands of pleasure boats filled the bay. The coastguard and harbour police prowled the starting lanes, keeping the spectator boats back, giving the racing boats an open seaway towards the Golden Gate. The shore was packed with spectators. Dozens of helicopters and planes were overhead.

'Time to start?' Wyman asked.

'Twelve seconds,' came from *Victory*.

The boats cut through the water, closing in on the starting line, as evenly spaced as teeth on a comb. The crews' jackets and trousers were distinctive colours—blue on the French boat, green on the Australian, red and black on Duncan Davis's boat—lending the procession a martial air.

Wyman turned to Gwen and grinned. 'Here we go. The start.' His gaze slipped past her to the camera mounted above the companionway. It was a tiny thing, its lens the size of a quarter.

She chided, 'You're not supposed to look at the camera, Rex.'

'It's hard not to, with so many of them.'

Toby Odell asked, 'Hit count, Boat?'

'Ninety-two and a half million hits on the main and mirror sites,' *Victory* replied.

Wyman had hoped for a hundred million hits on the WorldQuest web site, where it was possible for Internet users to choose between six cameras on *Victory*'s deck, and another six below deck. Gwen would have privacy only in the head and on her bunk. The cameras provided streaming video in real time, broadcast over satellites. Millions of voyeurs would be along for the ride.

Victory said, 'Ten seconds to the start. Nine . . . eight . . .'

The racing lane narrowed ahead as spectator boats crept forward. Helicopters vied for space above the armada. A wall of green and blue balloons began their ascent from the San Francisco side.

The Voice said, 'Three . . . two . . . one . . . start.'

The gun fired on the committee boat just as all nineteen sailboats crossed the line. *Victory* surged forward. The audience on the shore and on the spectator boats cheered, and boat horns blared.

'By God, we're under way,' Wyman said, bracing his hands on the safety rail. 'After all the work.'

Gwen stepped to his side to give him a congratulatory hug, but he half turned, 'Roger, get Sid Paler on the line, will you?'

Gwen's breath caught in her throat. Sid Paler was a WorldQuest vice-president of marketing. She grimaced, and quickly turned away from the rail so Rex wouldn't see her expression. She walked along the safety rail towards the bow.

Maybe it was silly, but despite *Victory*'s serious purpose and the rigours of the race, the notion of a getaway had taken hold in Gwen's mind. Two of them on a boat. Well, with just a few others. Out in the Pacific, the sea and the wind. Maybe to compensate for her increasing fear of the race, she had generated a lush fantasy about their romantic weeks at sea. But Rex's order to Roger Hall shattered her illusion. She tossed her getaway hopes overboard.

Victory and the other racers swept along, passing hundreds of spectator boats. Off *Victory*'s port rail was *Lion Rampant*, Duncan Davis's boat. Duncan Davis had been unable to lower his binoculars, pointed at *Victory*'s cockpit, as if he simply could not credit the evidence of his own eyes: *Victory* had no wheel.

There indeed was a wheel, and it was stored in a locker below the cockpit, and could be raised hydraulically should the automatic rudder system fail. Wyman's shipyard had simply refused to build the boat without a means of mechanically steering from the cockpit.

Now all nineteen boats were headed on a bead for the Golden Gate. The bridge was closed for the morning, and pedestrians filled the bridge deck.

Gwen moved further along the rail. On board *Victory*, in addition to herself and Wyman, and Toby Odell and Roger Hall, there were two professional sail racers hired for the Challenge. She approached one of them at the port rail.

'I feel foolish, standing here,' Jeff Chapman said. 'Nothing to do.'

She smiled at him. 'The first time Rex tells you to make coffee for him, tell him to drop dead. He tries that with everybody.'

Chapman's cheeks and forehead were red and creased, a seagoing face. His sandy hair was short. His blue eyes were full of life. He had sailed across three oceans, and had placed second at the Barcelona Olympics in an Olympic 470. Chapman suffered from an unfortunate reverse correlation between his love of sailing and his possession of money, so he had spent most of his sailing career crewing. Skippers knew they were lucky when Chapman signed on with them.

Gwen stepped round Chapman and came to the second professional sailor hired for the Challenge, Ed Lash, known in racing circles as Fast Eddie. Indeed he was fast, finishing first in the Victoria–Maui race, and first in a Transpac, from Los Angeles to Honolulu.

Lash said, 'I'm not sure I'll add the Challenge to my résumé. Me, lounging around on deck while a computer runs the boat.'

'Rex says this'll be as big as Lindbergh's flight,' she replied. 'You'll go down in history.'

Fast Eddie was a small-boned man, slight in every direction, with tightly wound muscles and a strong, corded neck. His Adam's apple and chin were prominent. His wild black hair may never have seen a comb. He shaved once a week and so usually was wearing dark stubble. Once, when he was a teenager, he forgot to duck, and a boom cracked into his face, flattening his nose. It had been badly reset and now always pointed off in another direction.

Gwen counted the crew on Duncan Davis's nearby boat. Eighteen of them, enough for round-the-clock sailing in hard weather. There were six people on *Victory*. Wyman had said it would be enough.

The boats moved with precision, as if on a parade ground. The race lane narrowed, the boats squeezing together for the dash past the fort and under the Golden Gate. Balloons filled the sky. Evidence of festivities were in all directions—on both shores, on the bridge overhead—but Gwen detected, she was not sure how, that the racers had already left the fun and celebration behind. The boats nosed ahead, then slipped back, then came ahead again, already fighting for every inch of air and knot of speed.

Then the racers slipped under the Golden Gate Bridge, and suddenly the entire expanse of ocean was theirs.

THE BOATS RACED northwest, the California coast slipping away off the starboard quarter. The wind was from the southwest, and the seas were light. *Victory* rose and fell with the modest rollers, a gentle, soporific motion. Gwen had spent an hour below in the control room, doing little but staring at screens, but then had made tea in the microwave and had emerged through the companionway to the cockpit to find Rex Wyman holding a knife.

'This is my big reward.' He held up the pocket knife and a two-foot wooden stick.

She laughed. 'What are the world's citizens, who are watching you this minute on the Internet, going to think when their computer hero spends his first hours at sea whittling?'

He grinned. 'My father was in the navy for a while, and when I was a kid he showed me how to whittle a chain from a branch. You carve each link so that they are connected.'

'You are going to whittle a chain?' She laughed again. 'I'm dumbfounded. Are you trying to earn a merit badge?'

'I've been focused on this piece of wood for months. Working those eighteen-hour days, I told myself I could start carving it the moment my work on the project was done and *Victory* took over.' Wyman dug the knife into the stick. 'Plus, I'm going to drive my competitors crazy.'

The sailboats were arrayed on both sides of *Victory*, though they had fallen back in the last hour. The nearest was Genevieve DeLong's *Remember the Bastille*.

'Driving them crazy?' she prompted him.

Wyman said with glee, 'The race of the century is just under way, and the entire world knows the skipper of *Victory* is whittling a stick.'

The breeze was unseasonably warm, and the cockpit was comfortable. Gwen wore a sweater and heavy khaki trousers with pockets along the thighs. Toby Odell was also in the cockpit, bent over his laptop.

Wyman said, 'Duncan Davis and Genevieve DeLong and the others are all endlessly adjusting their trim, making tiny changes to sail and rudder, trying to get every last ounce of push from the wind.'

Gwen looked southwest. Even at this distance, about half a mile, she could see Genevieve DeLong's black hair as she ducked under *Remember the Bastille*'s boom.

'It's exhausting work, even in these easy seas,' Wyman said. 'And they'll hear on their radios that I'm sitting in *Victory*'s cockpit, whittling a piece of wood, chatting with a beautiful woman. It'll just kill them.' He laughed.

The sun was hidden by high clouds, and the sea was lit by uncertain grey light. Wind stirred up a few whitecaps. Haze hid the receding coast. To the north, a band of purple clouds was releasing its burden of rain, visible as a wafting curtain below the clouds.

Wyman asked, '*Victory*, what is the distance to the rain cloud ahead?'

'Four point three miles,' the ship said.

Wyman couldn't help himself. 'Toby, is that cool or what?'

Odell grinned. 'It's pretty cool, I have to admit.'

Wyman announced, 'I think *Victory* needs just a touch more publicity.' With that, he turned to Gwen, wrapped his arms round her, and kissed her long and hard on her lips, with her sputtering a bit for lack of breath.

When he finally released her, she said, 'What was that about?'

He smiled widely. 'Thanks to our cameras, that big smooch was just seen by the entire planet, and tomorrow morning every tabloid in the world will have a grainy photo and a big headline, something like LOVE NEST AFLOAT or HEADED NORTH IN A SEA OF LOVE or THE BILLIONAIRE AND HIS BABE.'

She frowned. 'So much for sailing professionalism.'

Jeff Chapman emerged through the companionway, a video camera in his hand. He braced himself against the safety rail on the windward side and began taking videos of the other boats.

'Do you remember the first time I kissed you?' Wyman asked.

The question startled Gwen. 'Sure,' she replied. 'Who could forget that, as awkward a kiss as I've ever received?' She leaned towards him so their shoulders touched. To hell with the Internet voyeurs.

He laughed brightly. 'I thought I was smooth.'

'You were,' she said. 'It was the paperwork that was awkward. After our third date we were sitting in front of a fireplace in your Boise home, and you said, "I'd like to kiss you, and if you are so inclined, would you sign this?" And you pulled out a document from a table drawer.'

He waved her comment away. 'It was a simple sexual harassment disclaimer. My lawyers insisted.'

She laughed. 'It sure killed the mood.'

Wyman stopped whittling. 'I knew you a long time before you knew me.'

'Not likely,' she said. 'The entire world knew of you before you laid eyes on me.'

'I mean, I was walking into our Boise building two years ago with Bruce Arnold, and he nudged me and said, "There's the woman you should meet."'

'I didn't know that.' Arnold was WorldQuest's general counsel.

'Arnold said you were the one person in the company smarter than he was, and that included me.'

'Two years ago? What took you so long?'

'I watched you for a while.'

She stopped smiling. 'What do you mean, you watched me?'

'I made a few enquiries. I'm your employer. I'm entitled to enquire. I promoted you, didn't I?'

Gwen knew that Ted Landers, vice-president and chief of WorldQuest's security division, had dug around in her past when she and Rex Wyman had begun dating.

'Wait a minute.' Her voice was suddenly crabbed. 'What's the sequence of events? You decided you wanted to date me, so you snooped around, then you promoted me?'

'Well, the sequence isn't really relevant.'

She stood up, glaring at him, the deck rolling under her. 'Vice-presidents are in your same office building, on the same floor. Was that it? Give me the job so you could hop into my office now and chat me up, and get me to go out with you?'

'I promoted you because you were qualified,' Wyman protested, waving the stick for emphasis. 'You've been working hard, and you're dead tired, and it's making you say crazy things.'

Gwen Weld was prickly about her hard-won accomplishments. She was a widely respected computer engineer, and here Rex Wyman suggested she was given a job so he could date her. She was furious. She turned to stomp down the companionway to leave him and his idiot whittling.

And then *Victory* hiccuped. Or something.

Without warning, the boat turned hard to starboard, its bow abruptly swinging east in a flying jibe. The boom rushed in from the starboard side, sweeping across the deck with the speed and force of a locomotive, dumping the air from one side of the sail and then immediately filling the sail on the other side.

The massive boom caught Jeff Chapman full in the chest, blowing him out over the side of the ship, his feet catching in the safety rail so that he cartwheeled out and down into the water.

Rex Wyman yelled, an unintelligible, strangled sound. Then *Victory* jibed back, and the boom raced again from one side to the other, the sail stiffening under its load of wind. The boat was on its north-by-northwest course again. Ten seconds had elapsed.

Behind *Victory*, *Remember the Bastille* turned towards Chapman. A crewman was already preparing a sling to lift him on board. By the race's rules, the minutes spent rescuing another boat's crew would be deducted from *Remember the Bastille*'s finishing time.

Wyman didn't look aft, not once, as if Jeff Chapman had never been on his boat. Wyman demanded, '*Victory*, explain your jibe.'

The Voice came from all around. 'Please restate your question.'

'The jibe,' screamed Wyman. '*Victory*, why in hell did you just jibe, and then jibe again back to the original course?'

The disembodied voice said politely, 'My last jibe was two hours, forty-seven minutes ago.'

Gwen stepped away from the companionway and put an arm on Wyman to calm him. Toby Odell laid his laptop aside and went to the stern to watch Chapman's rescue. Roger Hall and Fast Eddie Lash came up through the companionway and joined Odell at the aft rail, pointing and speculating. *Remember the Bastille* had dumped its wind and was slowing quickly, Chapman bobbing off its starboard quarter. Genevieve DeLong herself threw the sling towards him. FRENCH HEROINE RESCUES DROWNING YANK, the headlines in *Le Monde* would surely read tomorrow.

Wyman's face bunched and coloured and he sagged towards Gwen. She pushed him back towards the bench. He blindly reached out to the rail to lower himself.

Gwen sat next to him and put a hand on his knee. 'I'll figure it out, Rex. A glitch, is all.' Then she left him in the cockpit to go below, wondering where she would begin.

THE STREET WAS STRANGE to Jess McKay, as he'd never before visited Anacortes, in Washington State. He drove in a rented Mercury, the wipers working, squinting at street signs. At intersections, the channel could be seen to the north, the little ferry returning to Anacortes from Guemes Island.

Anacortes was one of the oldest towns on the west coast, so some of the homes in the north section were a hundred years old with Victorian touches to the trim. These large homes with fish-scale siding, friezes, parapets and widow's walks alternated with smaller, plain homes built a generation or two later.

McKay drove slowly. No one was out walking this Saturday morning. The rain was too heavy. He had never been more nervous. He was gripping the steering wheel so hard his knuckles were white.

Jess McKay had received a letter from his uncle Dan yesterday. The letter was vague and sort of an apology. Uncle Dan wanted to do right by Jess. The letter contained an address. Jess had boarded an Alaska Airlines red-eye from Anchorage to Seattle, and had rented a car and driven north along Interstate 5 to Anacortes.

Soggy brown leaves littered the street. The windshield wipers beat a steady tattoo. Jess slowed the car, narrowing his eyes at an address on a door, then at another. This was it.

The car pulled to the kerb. He stared at the house through raindrops on the car's side window. It was a house as a face, with a window on each side of a door. The house was light blue with white trim. A wrought-iron rail surrounded a concrete porch. At the south corner was a hydrangea bush, its blossoms turned brown. A driveway to the side of the house went to a garage in the back yard.

Matt's death had devastated the McKay family. Jess's mother hid her grief and shock behind a steady countenance. His father's anguish was evident in his every word and every gesture. John McKay would live his life without another happy day. His golden son was gone and nothing would ever be the same.

As the months wore on after Matt's death, Jess turned inwards. He lost weight and lost interest in school. At some point his father began to suspect there was more to the drowning than he had been told. He used his wiles on Jess, who was desperate for reassurance and affection and normalcy. Suddenly Jess found his dad willing to be in the same room as him, willing to talk about a few things. A couple of times they played catch with a baseball, like they had before the tragedy. Hammered by guilt for months, with no one to unburden himself to, Jess responded.

Over the course of a week, Jess let his dad know that on that terrible day he had seen Matt in trouble, that Matt had cried out and reached for him, but Jess was too far away to help. Then, while Jess and his father were playing catch in the front yard, Jess allowed that he was pretty close to Matt that day, that he might've been able to help Matt, if he'd been quicker and a little braver. Jess might've saved him, he finally admitted.

That was all John McKay needed to know. One son failed to save the other. Without a word, John McKay dropped his mitt and ball onto the grass and turned towards the house. From that moment, his surviving son was dead to him.

John McKay scarcely recognised his son, except to step round him in the kitchen. A week might pass without a word between them. Years passed in this poisoned household. Then in his sophomore year at the University of Washington, Jess came home for Christmas, and his father was 'away on business', his mother had tearfully said. Later, his mother fell quickly to cancer. A real-estate agent sold the Everett house within a week of his mother's funeral. Jess hadn't seen his father since.

Rain beat on the car's roof. McKay had to work to release his grip on the steering wheel. He pulled a piece of paper from his pocket and read his own handwriting. Just three sentences. He read them over and over, making sure he had memorised them.

Then he opened the door and climbed out of the car. Wind and rain bit into him. He stepped up to the porch. He stood there a moment, his finger paused at the doorbell. He hoped he'd be able to get his three sentences out without breaking down. He rang the doorbell, then squared his shoulders. A moment passed, Jess not breathing. Then something caught his eye, a movement to his right. He turned his head. A shape was behind the window, partly hidden by daylight's reflection. Jess leaned towards it.

It was his father. He stared without expression at his son.

'Dad,' was all Jess could say, not loud enough to be heard through the window.

Then John McKay stepped back into the room, away from the window and into the shadows. Jess rang the bell again, and waited again. His hands were trembling, and not from the cold.

Then a car backed down the driveway, alongside the house, moving quickly. It was a Honda Accord. Jess bent down to peer through the window as it passed. His father was behind the wheel. The car backed onto the street, then took off the way Jess had come.

Jess stood on the porch a moment, his gaze down the street where his father's car had disappeared. He took a long, ragged breath, then he stepped down from the porch and crossed the walkway towards his car. He dug into his jeans pocket for the slip of paper where he had written the three sentences. He balled up the paper and tossed it onto his father's lawn.

Lonnie Garvin pulled back on *Hornet*'s throttle to reduce freezing spray blowing in over the bow. His windshield wiper cranked back and forth. Skies were leaden and dusk was quickly approaching, though it was only three in the afternoon. Quartz vapour lights were already switched on, flooding the crab deck with unnatural white light. Fifteen-foot waves split against *Hornet*'s bow. The crew was setting gear, the crabber term for baiting and launching crab pots.

Hornet had been making ice all day, wind-blown spray freezing to the boat. Garvin pressed the PA button. 'I'm going to slow her down. Get your bats. We're getting heavy.'

His words boomed out over the work deck. Then he used the intercom to summon the engineer. Garvin watched in the closed-circuit television monitor as the crew grabbed baseball bats and began knocking ice off the railings and gear and superstructure. The more ice on board, the lower the boat sat in the water, and the more top-heavy it became, making its maximum righting angle—the greatest angle of heel from which the boat could recover—less and less.

When the engineer, Lars Anders, arrived, Garvin said, 'Take the wheel. I'm going out.'

Anders was a lumbering bear of a man, over six feet six. His fiefdom, the engine room, had a six-foot ceiling, so he worked bent over. Anders was a fourth-generation fisherman who could identify and fix every errant ping from a diesel engine and every unwanted hiss in a refrigeration system. Anders was partial to flannel shirts. An anarchist's beard hid his face. He wrapped his meaty hands on the wheel spokes. He had to stoop to peer out of the spinnaker window, a motor-driven circular glass segment that spun quickly, throwing off spray before it could turn to ice.

Garvin put his coat's hood over his head, inserted his hands into insulated gloves, grabbed his own baseball bat, then opened the hatch and sidled along the narrow walkway to the front of the wheelhouse. Sleet pelted his coat. Ice cracked under his boots. He hammered at icicles hanging from the wheelhouse overhang.

Then he cleared ice from the rungs that led up to the wheelhouse roof. He climbed up, the boat rolling into the wind, then away from it. Ice had formed all around the life-raft canister, which resembled a fifty-five-gallon Pepsi can. Garvin hacked ice from the steel bands that held the canister together. Otherwise, the canister might not automatically open, as it was designed to do when it hit water. Spray froze onto Garvin's moustache.

He climbed back down, then stepped into the wheelhouse to lay the bat aside. 'I'm going down to the crab deck. You OK at the wheel for a minute, Lars?'

Anders replied in his subwoofer voice, 'All engineers can steer a boat. Not all skippers can tune an engine.'

Garvin had heard it before. 'Then add some speed and keep *Victory* up against the tide line.'

He went through the hatch again, this time down the steps to the work deck. The crew had finished with their bats and now Ben Drum, who was known around the docks as 'Bang The', was working the crane, lifting a 300-pound crab pot from the stack and manoeuvring it across the rolling deck.

'How you doing, Bang The?' Garvin called above the wind.

'Never been better,' Drum replied, not taking his eyes off the swinging pot. He had a mangy week-old beard, brown in some spots and grey in others. He had shallow eyes and he was missing his lower front teeth. 'We're launching one every five minutes, so we're right on target.' When he was on deck, away from the alcohol in town, Bang The Drum was all business.

Lonnie nodded his appreciation. Except for the rookie, Nick Summers, his crew knew crabbing, or else they wouldn't be working for Garvin. His visits to the deck were for morale, not so much for issuing orders. His crew had been already tired when they arrived at the crab grounds. And now, launching the pots, they were working in constant cold, subject to battering machinery noise, and working encased in heavy foul-weather gear. Garvin checked for anybody with the Aleutian stare, someone who was losing his senses under the work. It happened all the time out here.

He crossed the pitching deck, littered with chunks of ice, and stepped around a stack of buoys to the launcher. An open aqueduct was built into the deck, side to side. Female and undersized crabs were tossed into the chute and washed overboard.

'How they going?' Garvin asked.

'Smooth as crap through a goose,' Ollie Nordquist said. Nordquist guided the pot onto the hydraulic launcher, then released the derrick cable. He had a bulbous red nose and a scraggly moustache. Between crab seasons he worked on a halibut long-liner off Petersburg, then fished for black cod and herring and halibut on a boat based in Ketchikan, then went 750 miles north to another herring season in Norton Sound, then travelled to Sitka for one more halibut season.

Nordquist didn't have a high-school diploma, but he often cleared $120,000 a year courtesy of the Bering Sea and his own year-round, backbreaking work. Garvin had agreed to a ten per cent share for each crewman, except the rookie, who would receive seven per cent.

Suddenly Nordquist yelled, 'A peeler! Get down!'

Garvin hurried round the launcher and pushed the rookie down, so that they were below the rail, protected by the gunwale. A frothing, freezing two-storey wave came over the rail at the starboard quarter, and for five seconds everyone and everything on the crab deck was underwater. Then the water flowed over the port rail and drained through the scuppers.

'You OK?' Garvin asked the rookie as they rose.

'I've been warmer in my life,' Nick Summers said, wiping water from his face. 'A few cold spots here and there, but no complaints.' Sea foam had pasted Summers's dark hair against his skull. His new beard, begun the day they had left port, was meagre.

'What's cold?' Garvin asked the rookie.

'Ah, it's nothing.'

The kid was a gamer. Garvin liked that about him.

But Garvin pressed him. 'Where? Your hands?'

'Nah. My left foot. There's been some water sloshing around inside my boot for a while.' He gestured with his free hand. 'It's nothing.'

Garvin barked, 'Come with me.' He led the young man forward through a hatch, then into the small galley. 'Take your boot off,' Garvin ordered. 'Let me see your foot.'

Summers pulled off his boot and shook it. Water splashed around inside. 'A leak. It's nothing I can't fix. I'll tuck things in better.'

Garvin said, 'Take a look at your foot, Nick.'

The boy removed his sodden woollen sock. Two of his toes were blue, almost purple.

'Can you feel anything in those toes?'

'They're a little numb, sure. But the blood'll return.'

Garvin opened a locker, where he pulled out a large plastic basin. At the sink, he filled the basin with warm water. Then he placed it on the deck. 'Put your foot into here. Your toes are only blue, not black. They'll get their colour back.'

Summers dipped into the basin.

'What about my work out there on deck?'

Garvin shoved his hands back into his gloves. 'Nick, you sit here with your foot in this bowl until I tell you otherwise.'

'OK, Skipper.'

'You're studying marine biology at University of Washington?'

Nick Summers looked up from his toes. 'I'm majoring in it.'

'Have you been on their big research vessel?'

'The *Thomas Thompson*. Yeah, I've been out on it.'

'Which boat is more fun? The *Thomas Thompson*, with all the professors and fellow students and petri dishes, or my boat *Hornet*?'

Summers laughed. 'This boat, for sure.'

Garvin grinned and said, 'Damn straight,' and left him there to return to the crab deck.

 ## *Chapter five*

'So you can't find it?' Gwen Weld had been in the boat's control room fourteen hours. She was speaking with *Victory*'s chief software architect, Rick Gagliardi, who was in Boise, and who was staring at screens containing the same content as Gwen's.

In Gwen's ear came, 'You sure you and the boss weren't imagining it, maybe a little too much wine at lunch?'

'Ask Jeff Chapman if we were imagining it. He is in a San Francisco hospital with a broken arm. He wasn't imagining the jibe that pitched him into the water.'

She could almost see Gagliardi grimace in frustration. Rex Wyman had lit into Gagliardi, firing him three times in the course of a fifteen-minute tirade, and then rehiring him just before ending the link. Eighty programmers and engineers were working with Gagliardi, trying to find the bug.

From Boise came, 'What I'm saying is that we can't find any trace of code that sent *Victory* into the jibe or any evidence in the recorders that the jibe ever happened.'

'Me neither,' she said. 'This may be a one-time event.' Gwen fiddled with her headset, which she had been wearing so long that the sides of her head were sore. 'Well, I'm going to go to my bunk and sleep ten hours. I'm exhausted.'

'Drink more coffee,' Gagliardi said into her ears. 'I need your help. My ass is on the line here.'

'So is mine,' she said.

'I've never before heard Rex yell like that. I thought he was going to drop over dead, he was so worked up. He was incoherent.'

'He's under a lot of pressure.'

'Yeah.' Gagliardi could put a lot of sarcasm into one word, but must have thought it insufficient because he added, 'Having billions of dollars can be a challenge.'

Gwen said she would return to her station in five minutes to continue working with Gagliardi, then she slipped the set off her head. The floor shifted as *Victory* adjusted to the wind. She gripped the table to help herself stand, then she reached for her empty cup. She had drunk so much coffee her fingers were trembling.

She moved forward through the hatch along the gangway, through a watertight hatch into *Victory*'s small living area, a combined salon and galley. The boat had a tiny crew, and so, unlike conditions aboard other racers, each of *Victory*'s crewpersons had a small cabin, rather than a bunk. But despite the few people on board and *Victory*'s grand dimensions—155-foot length overall with a thirty-foot draught—below decks was cramped.

As a safety measure, *Victory* had two watertight hatches, dividing the vessel into three compartments, each of which could be sealed off if the hull or deck were broached. The hatches slid side-to-side, and could be controlled hydraulically through the computer systems, or manually with a spoked wheel. She had seen the hatches tested. They could move quickly, sealing off an area before water flooded it. *Victory* would still float with two of the three compartments filled with sea water.

Forward of the living area were the small crew cabins. Wyman had made sure that his was no larger than anyone else's. Each cabin held a narrow berth, a small dresser and a hanging locker. Rex had installed a crystal single-stem vase in Gwen's room, attached to the dresser. He had put a rose into it when she wasn't looking.

She stepped over the base of a hatch into the living area. A curved settee was in front of a dining table. A bookcase and magazine rack and a few other pieces of utilitarian furniture filled the area. On the aft side was the interview area, set up with stage lights and two cameras. Painted on the bulkhead behind the stool for the interviewee was the WorldQuest logo.

To the starboard side was the galley. Nobody on board was a particularly good cook, so the freezers were stocked with frozen food. 'Frozen gourmet food,' Wyman had assured them. The cupboards were latched so they wouldn't fly open when the boat heeled over, as were the doors on the microwave, and on the oven, dishwasher and trash compactor. Most of the furniture was bolted to the deck. In the salon alone, five cameras provided views to Internet viewers. No spot in the living area or galley was off-camera. Thousands of people—maybe hundreds of thousands—might be watching Gwen help herself to more coffee.

The deck tilted under her, and she grabbed for the refrigerator and was reminded of the axiom, *Three points for the boat, one for yourself.* Moving her hand from one railing to another, she returned aft, through the hatch towards her computer room, her coffee remaining in the cup.

Surrounded by monitors, she lowered herself to her chair and sighed heavily. She had no clue where to search next for the bug that had afflicted *Victory*. A jibe that couldn't be explained and of which there was no record? Where did she look for that? On her screen was a string of code titled 'DW Nav AATR 42287'. Maybe it was here.

But also on her screen was a box containing the words, 'Do you know the location of all *Victory*'s fire extinguishers?—Jess McKay, 212th Rescue Squadron.'

She thought an extinguisher might be under the galley sink. There might be others? She entered, 'Of course I do. Why are you contacting me again, Captain?'

'My friend Sandy likes your green sweater.'

'Answer my question: why are you contacting me again?'

'Sailboats are like spouses,' appeared on Gwen's screen. 'Everything works better if you love your boat. Do you?'

'I don't love inanimate objects. I love people, and very few of those. You want to chat, is that it, Captain? Nobody for your Rescue Squad to rescue up in Alaska?'

'My guess is that you don't love *Victory* because it isn't really a boat,' McKay wrote. '*Victory* is more a surfboard than a boat.'

'*Victory* is the most expensive racing yacht ever built. Calling it a surfboard indicates you don't know much about . . .' She backspaced over the last six words, then went on, 'indicates you possess a vast well of unknowing.' Did that make sense? It was snappy, at least. She hit the enter key.

McKay's words appeared on the screen. 'I do *Victory* too much honour by calling it a surfboard. In fact, it is a media centre.'

'Don't you have to go to your swim lessons or something?' She sent it, then laughed. She was enjoying this, being testy to a complete stranger. She bent closer to the screen, waiting for his reply.

It came: 'You'll get backache, leaning over a keyboard like that.'

Gwen abruptly sat upright and glanced at the camera in the corner, one of two in the small room. It gave the captain an advantage, being able to examine her when she couldn't do the same to him. She didn't like it.

Nothing from Alaska appeared on the screen for a moment, then Captain McKay wrote, 'Your web biography makes you sound sensible. And in that big green sweater with your hair pulled back, you even look sensible. How did Wyman sucker you into this?'

Gwen fired off, 'You appear fond of pop psychology. Let me diagnose you, Captain. You spend time chatting with strangers like me on the web because you are up there in Alaska and you are lonely. No real friends. No family, just alone. So you use boat safety as a façade to pester me. Am I right?'

She waited for a response. None came.

She asked, 'Is that right? You've got no support system. No real friends. No mom or dad to complain to.'

Again she waited. Still, nothing came back. She exhaled slowly, scowled at herself, then wrote, 'I didn't mean to touch a nerve, Captain. I'm sorry if I did.'

Minutes passed and no reply came. She closed the box on her monitor and turned back to the code, looking for the bug, but for a long while her eyes wouldn't focus on the letters.

BEING AT SEA is like being in prison. Little privacy is to be found and the sailor can't walk away. A society that works well on land may become prickly at sea. Irritations mount. Slights are magnified. The skipper determines the shipboard atmosphere. He can soothe or he can aggravate. Sometimes he is aware of his effect on the crew, and sometimes he is not.

Rex Wyman put the binoculars to his eyes. 'Finally, the Frenchwoman's boat is hull down.'

'You never say her name,' Toby Odell said. 'Why?'

'She is pompous and arrogant, and I don't like her.' He glanced at Gwen. 'I offer enough pomposity and arrogance for any occasion.'

Odell laughed. *Victory* was on the high seas, having just crossed the forty-fifth latitude, halfway between the Equator and the North Pole. The wind had backed astern and a spinnaker was out, the robotic arm working smoothly, the merry wind pushing the boat along. The sun was setting on the western rim of the sea, sending forth a bronzed light that coloured the clouds overhead and the boat's hull.

Gwen was wearing a blue fleece-lined offshore jacket and matching waterproof trousers. The wind had a bite to it and her hands were in her jacket pockets. Framed by the blue and green spinnaker, Fast Eddie Lash wiped the forepeak rail with a cloth. Odell stepped towards the companionway, but the boat shifted and he caught a foot on the deck and had to grab the rail. Roger Hall was in the galley preparing dinner.

When Wyman moved forward to speak to Lash, Odell asked Gwen with a grin, 'Have you seen the gossip press?'

'Spare me whatever you are going to report,' Gwen replied.

'No way,' he said gleefully. 'With all the cameras below, the press has figured out that you and Rex have separate cabins on this boat. They are speculating that the romance has ended.'

'The truth is that I just need some space to myself.'

'Gwen, the truth, even if you can't bring yourself to see it, is that you are beginning to suspect Rex isn't the one for you.'

She was testy. 'Toby, you are talking about something you know nothing about, and you have no business knowing anything about.'

Wyman joined them and said, 'There's more to this boat than even you know about, Toby.'

'Such as?'

'*Victory* can go fast or it can go comfortable. To maximise speed, we've been running without stabilisers.' He raised his voice a little. '*Victory*, deploy stabilisers.'

The speakers responded. 'Deploy stabilisers.'

Gwen heard a faint hydraulic whine from the direction of the bow, and within seconds the deck, which had been rolling and pitching modestly in the light seas, became almost perfectly stable.

'What's the point?' Odell asked.

Wyman pointed. 'The top of the mast is almost two hundred feet above the deck. If you have to go up there in a bosun's chair, you'll be glad *Victory* can steady herself like this.'

Odell lifted his head to gaze at the masthead. It might've been the wind playing with his jacket, but Gwen thought Odell shuddered. Wyman opened a topside locker and brought out a handful of fabric and cable and clips. He held it up. It was a bosun's chair.

'Nobody should put to sea without knowing how to climb the

224

mast.' He turned and called, 'Eddie, rig the halyard, will you?'

Wyman held the bosun's chair next to Odell's midsection. 'Let's see if this fits, Toby.'

'Me? I'm not going up there, for God's sake.' He looked skywards again. The masthead was tiny and distant, more a part of the sky than of the boat.

'Don't worry about it, Toby. The winch does all the work. You won't even break a sweat.'

His eyes on Gwen, Odell asked, 'Have you been up there?'

She looked at Wyman. 'Once, when *Victory* was at the dock.'

'Come on,' Wyman insisted. 'Put some adventure into your life.'

Odell spread his hands to encompass *Victory*'s deck, and tried a laugh. 'This isn't adventure?'

'It's always the same,' Wyman said. 'I've always had to drag you along behind me. Make the decision, and drag Toby along.'

'What do you mean, drag me along?' Odell's tone was that of the school yard.

Gwen tried to end the argument. 'There's no need for anybody to go up the mast, Rex. Unless some repair is required, it's foolish to go up there.'

Wyman held up the bosun's chair, dangling it in front of his ex-partner. 'It'll make a man of you, something I've been trying to do for years.' Wyman laughed at his own joke.

After a long moment, Odell muttered, 'Well, what the hell.'

Gwen clucked her tongue, then moved aft towards the cockpit. She didn't want to be any part of it. Wyman and Odell had worked together in their tight little symbiotic, glorious and poisonous relationship for years. Who was she to monitor it?

Under her feet, *Victory*'s deck was as steady as a table. From the cockpit she watched Toby fitted into the bosun's chair. He gripped the line like a child holds the pole of a merry-go-round pony, fiercely and with concentration. The line ran from the chair up to the masthead, then back down to a stainless-steel windlass near the port rail. Ed Lash knelt next to the windlass, disapproval on his face.

When Wyman said something to the ubiquitous ears of the boat, Odell was lifted off the deck and slowly pulled skywards. His legs dangled beneath the chair. His face whitened and his eyes were clamped shut. Midway up, his eyes opened and he extended his feet to touch the mast. Pulled by the line, he began walking up the mast in a rather accomplished fashion.

Then Wyman said something else to the boat. *Victory*'s stabilisers and rudder immediately returned to their race setting. The boat slid into a roller and began to rise. At the same time, *Victory* turned fifteen degrees to port. The effect was to jerk Odell out and away from the mast, and swing him in a wide arc aft towards the mainsail.

Odell cried out. His legs frantically churned the air, seeking purchase that wasn't there, and then he slapped against the sail. As the boat crested the roller and the deck and mast tilted forward, Odell skidded along the sail towards the mast, the bosun's chair still rising. He smacked into the mast.

Wyman laughed, then cupped his mouth to call up, 'Take it easy up there, Toby. I've got a lot of money invested in this equipment.'

Gwen stared at Wyman, and so did Eddie Lash. The line slowed its pace as it neared the masthead. When he was at the top, Odell didn't tap the top of the masthead in triumph. He sat there, immobile, his legs swaying under him like ropes.

Wyman ordered the boat to stabilise itself. The winch reversed, and Odell slid down the mast, his head bent forward, hiding his eyes. When his feet touched the deck, he jumped, startled.

His eyes opened and his expression instantly transformed to indignation and anger.

'So how was it up there, Toby?' Wyman asked.

Odell gave him a corrosive look, but said nothing. He struggled out of the bosun's chair, then threw it onto the deck. He walked aft towards the cockpit, passing Gwen. His face was purpled with anger. He didn't look at her and disappeared below deck.

Gwen approached Wyman, who was stowing the bosun's chair in a locker. 'Was that really necessary, Rex? Frightening Toby like that, and humiliating him?'

He waved away her comment, not looking up from the locker. 'We've been doing that to each other for twenty years. One day he gets it. The next day I get it. It's how we work together.'

She turned away and left him there, returning to the control room, wondering about Odell, and about Rex Wyman.

IN MANY MAPS of the Pacific Ocean, the compass rose is placed in the Bering Sea. When heading north to the Bering Sea, sailors often say they are travelling into the compass rose. Early cartographers would write *Hic sunt dracones*, here lie dragons, on their maps here.

The Bering Sea is a triangle, 940 miles north to south at its longest, and 1,100 east to west at its base. The sea's north apex connects to the Arctic Ocean, where the continents are only fifty-three miles apart. The base is an arc consisting of the Alaska Peninsula in the east, the Aleutian Islands in the south and the Commander Islands to the west.

The Bering Sea's combination of geography, hydrology and climate make it one of the most dangerous bodies of water on the planet. Arctic winds flow from Siberia and Alaska. Twelve-thousand-foot mountain ranges on both continents channel and quicken the winds as they spill onto the Bering Sea. Gusts, called williwaw winds, shoot down from the mountain passes at speeds of up to 150 miles an hour, flattening anything in front of them. Williwaw winds carry ice and grit, and are erratic, screaming along one moment, then abruptly still the next.

In the northern and eastern parts of the Bering Sea, the mean annual air temperature is minus fourteen degrees Fahrenheit, and in the south it is thirty-nine degrees. Many Alaska towns on the Gulf of Alaska and the Bering Sea routinely report wind-chill factors of minus fifty degrees.

Only two civilian professions regularly broach the Bering Sea, shippers—most often Russian—and commercial fishermen. On average, thirty commercial fishermen die in Alaskan waters each year. Some drown, some freeze to death.

In winter, when the crabbers are out, the Bering Sea's water temperature is thirty-eight degrees. Cold water takes heat from a human body twenty-five times faster than does cold air. A person who falls into the Bering Sea begins to shiver violently within seconds, and within a few minutes his thinking becomes groggy and confused. After ten minutes in the water, sensation in the hands and feet is lost, then in the arms and legs. At this point, he is almost incapable of doing anything to help himself, such as crawling into a life raft or grabbing a line. Skin turns blue. The pulse weakens. When the body temperature falls below ninety degrees, shivering abruptly stops. When it falls a few degrees further, the person can no longer tread water, as the limbs simply won't obey. After twenty-five minutes in the Bering Sea, the heart seizes up due to the cold water flowing through it, and then everything else shuts down. A person wearing a life jacket will live half an hour longer, owing to the jacket's insulation. Someone in a survival suit may live several hours. If the person can climb into an inflatable, canopied life raft, he can survive for days.

The Bering Sea is not without charm. The stars appear in a vast sweep, more stars than night, as if painted across the sky with a thick brush. The sky often erupts in a luminescence, the aurora borealis, when the night sky shimmers with iridescent green and blue curtains and bars and patches that flicker and flutter and wave, then vanish in a bolt of brilliant white light, only to reappear seconds later.

Victory and the other competitors in the Pacific Winter Challenge were headed north to the Bering Sea, to this vast basin of chaotic and bitter and unforgiving wind and water.

'THE FRENCHWOMAN is better than I thought,' Rex Wyman said, binoculars at his eyes as he scanned the sea, even though he knew Genevieve DeLong and her boat were hidden by the horizon to the south. Wyman was leaning against the rail just forward of the cockpit. 'And so is Duncan Davis, damn him.'

'Maybe *Victory*'s efficiencies aren't the huge advantage you thought they would be,' Gwen suggested, touching upon heresy.

She was leaning against the Main Overboard Module in the cockpit. Next to it was an EPIRB, the emergency position-indicating radio beacon, fitted with a flotation collar, kept in the cockpit to be thrown into the sea should someone fall overboard. Nobody had thought of it when the boom had knocked Chapman over the rail.

Wyman shook his head, dismissing the notion. 'Every hour that passes, I gain a few yards, inexorably. This isn't a sprint, it's a marathon.' He raised his voice. '*Victory*, position of French boat.'

From the speakers came, 'Eight point two miles directly astern.'

Wyman then asked the other racers, ticking them off, listening to *Victory* give their positions.

Gwen was now wearing four layers, and her hood was up. Her gloves were waterproof, with cuffs reaching halfway up her forearms. Her cheeks were pink. She moved towards the hatch, but stepped aside for Roger Hall, who scrambled up into the cockpit to pass a note to Rex Wyman. When he read it, his face twisted into a ferocious scowl.

Wyman's voice rose. 'What's causing it?'

'Don't know,' Hall replied. 'Selling, of course. But we can't find out who or what is behind it.'

Gwen left them there and went below, stowing her coat and gloves in a foul-weather gear locker near her control room. She stopped at the coffeepot in the galley, then moved forward through the hatch to the cabins. She tapped on Toby Odell's door. He had been little seen since his ride up the bosun's chair. He missed that night's dinner and was still in his cabin at breakfast. He claimed he had a touch of seasickness.

She knocked again. She heard his voice, but couldn't make out his words, so she pushed open the door. 'Want some coffee, Toby?'

He was sitting on his bunk, a laptop next to him, plugged into a jack on the bulkhead. He smiled widely. 'I'm still off my feed. If I drink coffee, I'll be running to the head.'

She sat next to him. 'I thought you were faking seasickness and that you were down here sulking and pouting.'

He laughed. 'What would I be sulking about?'

'Being swung around the mast on the bosun's chair. Rex was being childish and cruel.'

Odell laughed again. 'And that's why you love him so.'

'He's just received some bad news, delivered in a note from Roger. I hope it's nothing to do with this boat, the only thing that separates us from the cold water.'

Odell entered a few keystrokes. 'I'm sure it's this: today WorldQuest stock was off eighteen points, fully a fourth of its market value. This follows yesterday, when it lost twelve points.'

Odell was wearing bifocals for his computer work. He wore an anti-seasickness patch behind his ear. Odell was slender, and his green woollen sweater hung loosely about him. His bald head had begun to lose its tanning-parlour bronze.

'That's not the first time I've been banged around,' Odell said, smiling. 'And I've banged him around some, too.'

'What do you mean?'

'It's how we work. It's always been that way. Every so often, we just have to nail each other.'

'Give me an example.' Gwen rested her chin on her palm.

'My junior year at Idaho, Rex set me up with a blind date. I hadn't had many dates, being sort of a dork.'

'You aren't a dork, Toby,' she said automatically.

'Anyway, Rex told me this girl—I still remember her name, Cassandra, if you can imagine—had just broken up with a football player, and was brokenhearted, and wanted to go out with someone with brains for a change. He showed me her picture in the yearbook. Wow. Blonde, big eyes. Really a beauty.'

'Rex was setting you up?'

'On the day of my big date with Cassandra, I did some really odd things for me, like change my shirt and trim my beard.'

'So what happened?'

'I showed up right on time and knocked on her door, my heart thumping. Cassandra, this great beauty, opened the door, took one look at me, and screamed like she had just seen Dracula, and slammed the door in my face.'

Gwen stopped smiling.

But Odell laughed. 'It took me all of three minutes to figure out that Rex had set me up. Turned out Cassandra was dating Rex and Cassandra was always good for a joke, and so they set me up.'

'That wasn't just a little prank. It was malicious.'

'Well, then I'm malicious, too, because I gave it right back to him.'

'How?'

'Did Rex ever tell you he was arrested and spent the night in jail during his senior year at Idaho?'

She leaned closer to him. 'He never told me about that.'

'Cops pulled him over late at night as he was on his way to get a pizza. They found a small bag of white substance in the trunk. He was cuffed and taken down to the station.'

'What happened?'

'Turned out the bag contained baking soda.'

'You?'

'I'd put the bag of baking soda in his trunk, and I made a call from a payphone. A tip to the police from a concerned citizen anxious to rid the neighbourhood of drug dealers. Rex was released the next day, after the police had run a test on the white powder.'

She shook her head. 'Your prank wasn't even clever. I'm surprised.'

Odell opened his hands. 'I was a kid.' He looked at her knowingly. 'I'm a lot more clever now, Gwen.'

She decided to play along. 'What do you mean?'

He smile slyly. 'Ever heard of the Swan Tower in Kuala Lumpur?'

'Tallest building in the world, hundred and twenty or so storeys.'

'Through interrelated holding companies, hidden in a way much easier to do in Malaysia, Rex owns sixty per cent of the Swan Tower.'

'So what did you do?'

'The Swan Tower was built on a piece of ground that has misaligned karmic influences.'

'What?' She laughed. 'Karmic influences?'

He said, 'You laugh because you didn't have four hundred million dollars tied up in a building that a grizzly old guy in a white robe said was unlucky.'

'What grizzly old guy?' she asked.

'A feng shui master who intoned that the building would poison the spirit of anybody who entered it, that all the doors to the building were devils' gates.'

'So he scared away tenants?'

'The Swan Tower maxed out at thirty per cent occupancy. Floor after floor of it sits empty. Rex and his other investors held off the bankers for a year, but now they've taken it. He lost his entire investment, four hundred million.'

She stared at him. 'What was your part in it?

'I gave a hundred thousand dollars to the feng shui master's favourite charity, which was, as it turned out, himself.'

She stood up from the bunk. 'You ever going to tell him?'

A chuckle. 'Some day, and we'll have a good laugh together. Just like we laugh about Cassandra, now that some time has passed.'

Gwen gripped the door latch. 'You and Rex have a weird relationship, Toby.' Their relationship was more than weird. It was dark, darker than she had known before.

'Yeah, weird, all right.' Odell clicked the keyboard. 'But it worked, didn't it? He and I created a business—created an industry—out of absolutely nothing. Friction produces innovation, is my theory.'

She left Toby in his cabin and stepped through the hatch into the salon. Rex Wyman and Roger Hall were entering it from aft. Wyman was in front. Just as he was stepping through, the heavy steel hatch swept across the opening, side-to-side, gliding with startling speed to seal off the compartment. The steel plate would have caught him, had not Roger Hall lunged forward and tackled him, knocking him onto the deck.

The door shut loudly, a metallic slam of finality. Roger Hall scrambled to his knees and Wyman pushed himself up to sitting, staring at the watertight hatch.

Gwen asked, '*Victory*, why was the number one hatch closed?'

The boat replied, 'The number one hatch is open.'

She tried again. '*Victory*, give the status of the aft watertight hatch.'

'The number one hatch is open.'

Gwen moved to the hatch and slowly cranked it open. Hall helped Wyman to his feet. He was unsteady, swaying with the boat's roll and staring at the hatch. His face was blanched with fear.

VICTORY HAD SAILED through Unimak Pass, between Akutan Island and Unimak Island in the Aleutians. The boat was now in the Bering Sea, bearing northwest towards the Pribilofs. The waves were twenty feet high and were coming at the boat off the port quarter, one after another, endlessly.

Victory soared up a wave, then fell down its windward side, and when the prow lanced one of these walls of water, green foam tumbled across the foredeck, bubbling and splashing and hiding the deck, then falling away to the sides again as the boat rose. The wind was westerly at fifteen knots, and it whistled in the rigging. The sky was a vast leaden bowl overhead.

The boat was 2,500 miles into the race. The nearest competitor, Genevieve DeLong in *Remember the Bastille*, was twenty miles behind *Victory*. Rex Wyman was chagrined that *Victory* had gained only twenty miles on its nearest rival, and he was still apprehensive about the bugs that had caused the mystery jibe and the dangerous hatch closure. The Boise office was still searching for the glitch.

Wyman had also hired an outside consultant to look for the problem, a company called Vi-Block, Inc. Wyman had come to believe that Gwen and the Boise office weren't going to find the bug, and this realisation had added to his foul mood.

But Gwen's confidence in *Victory* had risen as the boat had gained the northern latitudes and the weather had begun to deteriorate. The manual helm had not been raised. No one had tailed the sheets that controlled the headsail. No one had needed to secure the control lines. *Victory* was doing all the work, and doing it expertly, beyond the ability of the finest sailors in the world, who had fallen well behind in their boats. And her confidence had grown in more than just the boat's handling of itself. The sea will find any weak point in a boat's complex system, and will patiently work away at it. But the sea had found no chink in *Victory*. The vessel was taking these rough seas with equanimity.

Spray flew up along the rail and was blown downwind across the cockpit, wetting Gwen's face. She was entirely warm in her clothes and yellow dry suit, but even so those few drops of water across her cheeks made her shiver.

Eddie Lash came through the cockpit hatch, smiling at her. He was wearing a dry suit identical to hers.

'You're up early,' she said.

'Rex says the boat can check all its own systems, but I'm going to look around anyway, like I do every day.' The wind flattened the hood against the side of his face. 'Check the pins in the turnbuckles and the bolts securing the fore stay, that sort of thing.'

He moved forward along the rail, keeping one hand on the safety rail. With little to do, Lash spend his time checking and rechecking the rigging and searching for chafing.

Gwen passed through the hatch and went below, then hung her wet clothes into a heated and dehumidified gear locker. She moved forward along the gangway to the salon. She no longer had to think with each of her lopsided steps, but *Victory* was bounding more now that it was in the Bering Sea, the deck endlessly tilting up and down so that moving around below deck had become a chore.

She entered the salon. Wyman was on a stool, under bright lights. He was wearing a microphone and was smiling into a camera, answering questions. His smile faltered for an instant. 'No, I don't have any concerns about WorldQuest stock.'

Gwen entered her control room, where all the monitors were glowing and dozens of tiny green and amber lights were always on. The place had become a refuge for her, even though cameras broadcast her every move to the Internet. Odell seldom entered the room. The professional sailor, Fast Eddie Lash wanted nothing to do with the computers there. Roger Hall did most of the cooking, and wasn't interested in the computer systems. Wyman mostly stayed away.

She put on her headset and reached for her keyboard to contact Rick Gagliardi in Boise when a new message appeared on her screen: 'A storm is coming. Are you prepared? —Jess McKay, 212th RQS.'

She replied, 'It's already stormy here. But we are aware of the new weather system coming our way.'

McKay sent from Anchorage, 'A low-pressure system is going to make your boat much less comfortable. The northwest winds might quickly change to southwest, and seas will begin to run across your northwest wave pattern.'

'Yes, that's a possibility we have accommodated. *Victory* knows everything about the storm. We are prepared.' She sounded officious, she knew. Gwen didn't want to talk about the weather with Captain McKay. 'Are you watching me right now, Captain?' she asked.

After a few seconds, 'I'm one of probably fifty thousand people watching you on the Internet.'

'Yes, but you have me at a disadvantage,' she wrote.

'How do you figure?'

'You know what I look like. I don't know what you look like.'

'I have a digital photo, and I'm uploading it right now.'

The email arrived with the attached picture. She opened it. There on her screen, was a photo of Jess McKay, dressed in a jumpsuit, gloves and boots, with a helmet over his head, darkly tinted goggles, and a balaclava that hid the rest of his face.

'I just received your photo, Captain. The lack of sun in the Alaska winter hasn't diminished your sense of humour, apparently.' Gwen wanted to ask her friend if Sandy was a man or a woman. Instead, 'Is Sandy a PJ?'

'A PJ on adrenaline.'

'Do you live with him in a barracks?' she asked.

'In an apartment. Have you and Rex Wyman had a falling out?'

'Why do you ask?'

'You are fishing around, asking questions about me, trying to determine if I'm single.'

She laughed. 'The truth is, it's either ask you questions, or return to work on some code problems we have here.'

'The problem that sent one of your crewmen over the rail?'

'That never happened, is our official position on the subject.' She thought for a moment before continuing. 'I wrote something last time we were in contact that made you disconnect. I'm sorry if I said something wrong.'

It took a full moment before McKay replied, 'It was nothing.'

'Something about friends and family? Are you having problems?'

'Nothing that hasn't been resolved.'

'One day when she was a young woman, my mother stuck a knife into a fellow's throat and killed him, and spent the rest of her life in hiding. How's that for family problems?' My Lord. Gwen couldn't believe she had just written that to a stranger.

'Your mom sounds like a lot of fun,' came from Anchorage. 'She ought to meet my father.'

'May I call you something other than Captain?'

'If I'm lucky, in two years you can call me Major. My name is Jess.'

She wrote, 'Let's talk about your girlfriend.' What in the world made her ask that?

'I am currently between girlfriends. And why are you asking about girlfriends? I'm here to lecture you about fire extinguishers.'

'Did the last girlfriend ditch you? Maybe because you wouldn't open up to her?'

What kind of question was that, she asked herself. She was flirting with this guy. She was too old to flirt.

'I've got the race on TV here,' McKay wrote. 'A couple more boats are approaching Unimak Pass.'

'Maybe those girlfriends dumped you because you are inept at changing the subject of a conversation.'

Jess McKay asked, 'Are you lonely?'

'My boyfriend is on board. How can I be lonely?' It sounded hollow, even as she wrote it.

'So, you are lonely,' McKay wrote back. 'It happens: the more crowded things get, the more isolated the sailor becomes. The sailor turns inward.'

'I guess there's a little truth to that.' More than a little, she thought.

'There are three kinds of skippers: the autocrat, the democrat, and the laissez-faire,' came up on her screen. 'It's my guess that Rex Wyman belongs in the first group.'

'Rex orders how things are to be done, usually in fine detail. He determines what each of us is to do, and he doesn't consult with us regarding our tasks. So I suppose he is an autocrat. Or maybe the boat is the autocrat, as it makes most of the decisions.'

Rex had begun to wear on the crew. He was angry and worried over the bug or the virus in *Victory*'s system. He was bickering with Eddie Lash over the smallest of matters. And Rex often yelled at his factotum, the hapless Roger Hall. Toby Odell mostly sat in front of his laptop, either in the salon or in his cabin. Whenever Gwen passed behind him and glanced at the screen, it appeared he was playing solitaire. But Toby was quick with the keyboard, and was obsessively private, and probably he was doing something else on his computer—running his businesses—and making sure no one knew of it, flicking over to solitaire when anyone approached.

'I'm going to ask you a personal question, Jess, and I want you to answer it, and not give me some dodge like you usually do.'

'Go ahead,' appeared on her screen.

'Have you ever loved anyone? And remember, you are duty bound by our new friendship to answer my question.' She didn't know this guy, knew almost nothing about him. But talking to this stranger—kidding him, flirting with him—was liberating. This was as much fun as she was going to have aboard *Victory*, she decided.

'I'm not sure if I've ever loved anybody,' McKay wrote.

So she asked, 'Do you love your father?'

A long moment passed, and there was no reply.

'Jess, don't hang up on me. I can count on my fingers the number of times I've ever talked about love with anyone.'

'I've got to go,' appeared on her screen. 'My partner Sandy is yelling at me to hurry about something. Goodbye.'

She leaned back in her chair and grinned at herself. This little exchange of messages had left her giddy. She felt as if she had been passing notes to the boy sitting in the desk behind her in a junior high school class. Then she caught herself fantasising about the time after the finish of the Pacific Winter Challenge, when she would find herself in Japan. She could return to Boise via Anchorage. Maybe take this Captain McKay to dinner. She laughed, tapping her keyboard affectionately.

Then her room went black. She caught her breath and gripped the table edge to orientate herself. The overhead lights were off. The desk lights were off. The monitors were out. Even the little green and amber and red computer power lights were dark.

Gwen tried to rise in her chair, tried to move towards the door, but *Victory* lurched, then plunged, then slammed into a wave broadside. The boat was suddenly adrift.

She tried again to get out of the chair. But *Victory* was now crosswise to the sea, waves hitting the boat square on the hull, and rolling it. Gwen lost her footing, tumbled out of the chair, cracked her head against the corner of her monitor, then fell to the deck.

She lay there, pain coursing from her head down her neck, in a cabin so dark she could only suspect she was conscious.

MCKAY PUSHED HIS WAY into his apartment, Ramirez at his heels. They had just returned from a spruce forest at the edge of Lake Iliamna, answering the call of an emergency beacon. It turned out to be a false alarm. And now McKay and Ramirez were back in Anchorage. They were operating on four hours' sleep in the last twenty-four.

McKay hung up his gear and was asleep within fifteen seconds of hitting the pillow.

When he was sure McKay was asleep, Sandy Ramirez turned on the computer monitor, and brought up Gwen Weld's chat link.

Ramirez typed: 'Gwen: On your way back from Tokyo after the race, why don't you stop in Anchorage? —Jess.'

Ramirez grinned to himself as he pressed the SEND button.

Chapter six

Storms are created when warm air and cold air masses collide. Masses of cold and warm air that collide create areas of high pressure with clockwise winds. Low pressure forms at the edge where the bodies of air have pushed into each other. Then anticlockwise winds are stirred as warm air advances on the east side and cold air begins moving on the west side. A warm and a cold front are thus formed. Clouds quickly build as the low pressure area becomes stronger. As barometric pressure decreases, winds begin in earnest, clouds grow thicker and rain begins to fall first only lightly, then in wind-driven sheets. When all this happens quickly, meteorologists call it a *weather bomb*, defined as when the barometric pressure drops one millibar an hour for twenty-four hours.

The Aleutian Low is one of the world's major pressure systems, and it was about to set off a weather bomb in the Bering Sea, the barometer falling towards an astonishing 28.17. Four boats had already quit the race. As the remaining Pacific Winter Challenge racers entered the Bering Sea, this twisting frontal system was already dangerous, but it was about to be joined by an unusual secondary depression, more intense than the first. Secondary depressions form more quickly than the original depression, and are less predictable, and they pull the wind into a fury and raise massive waves, and they can close down the Bering Sea and the Alaskan coast. The coming storm would be called a *no memory* wind by Tlingit elders on the Alaskan coast, because no Tlingit alive had a memory of one like it.

For this storm, the National Weather Service early knew a gale was coming, then with the plunging glass began to suspect it would be worse than a standard Bering Sea winter storm. Then the Service detected a secondary depression, and knew a weather bomb was imminent. It issued warnings.

The storm warnings came in time to clear the Bering Sea of its commercial fishermen, and Dutch Harbor and Kodiak quickly filled with the muscular crab boats. Now safe, many skippers huddled around VHF radio receivers on the bridges of their moored boats and at fish broker offices, hoping no maydays were heard.

At three in the afternoon the day the storm rose, the main depression was tracking southeast at thirty-five knots. The secondary depression was moving south at thirty knots. Both depressions were expected to deepen progressively, and, as they did so, they would merge, causing unrelenting violence over much of the Bering Sea. The forecast was updated at five o'clock that afternoon, when it was predicted that both fronts had gained five knots an hour.

Some of this was known aboard *Victory*. But not all of it.

GWEN WELD sat on her bunk. Toby Odell sat next to her, gently pushing a plastic bag containing ice cubes against her forehead.

'This bruise is already purpling, Gwen,' he said.

'Where's Rex?' She grimaced at the pressure of the bag.

'In the control room.'

'I'd better go help.'

'Help with what? We are all OK, except for your bump.'

The lights had been out for only sixty seconds. Abruptly without rudder control, *Victory* had listed fifty degrees in a trough of a wave, but had righted itself. When the power returned, the rudder began to work again and the boat returned to its northwest course. Eddie Lash had gone to the engine room to check the generators. He could find nothing wrong with them. Wyman had demanded that the boat report, but the Voice had said it had no record of a generator failure, and no record of a power interruption.

Gwen rose unsteadily from her berth. Odell's eyes reflected his concern and he made a feeble attempt to pull her back, but she gripped both edges of the hatch, which one moment was above her and the next below her as the boat rolled, and pulled herself through into the gangway, then stepped aft through the watertight hatch.

The cross seas Captain McKay had predicted now surrounded *Victory*. Rather than the heave and drop that Gwen had become accustomed to during the prior days, *Victory* was now doing three things at once: pitching, that is, plunging fore and aft like a seesaw; yawing, which is turning side to side, like someone shaking his head; and rolling on a fore–aft axis. The accumulation of these forces made *Victory* act like a state fairground ride with a name like *Octopus* or *Whirl-A-Way*.

Gwen widened her stance, took short steps, and kept both hands on bolted-down fixtures. The deck under her feet bucked and lurched. The bulkhead spun. The salon didn't have hand rails where she needed them, so she had to drop to her knees and crawl aft, the galley's counters and the chairs above her. Her head throbbed, sending bolts of pain down her neck and into her shoulders. Who would have thought a computer monitor could deliver such a blow, the computer rising up to strike back at its master? She smiled, despite herself, despite the lurching deck, despite the pain.

Gripping the hatch rim, Gwen pulled herself up and entered the control room. Rex Wyman was in her chair, wearing her headset. He wasn't shouting, but he was close. 'I want you to escort Gagliardi from his desk. Don't let him take anything from his office other than photos of his family. Don't let him take any computer disks. You got that?' It appeared that Gagliardi, *Victory*'s chief software architect, was being fired again, perhaps for good this time.

Wyman ripped the headset off his head and threw it on the table. 'Whatever is wrong with *Victory*'s code—those lines of bad programming—didn't spring from the ground like Topsy,' Wyman said.

She tried to console him. 'Weird lapses are inevitable in any new boat, Rex.'

'Not like this, not something so critical that it can bring down the entire system.'

He exhaled loudly, then closed his eyes. Gwen thought Wyman looked caged, like a bobcat just put into a small pen. Energy, rage and frustration were coursing through him and had no outlet.

His eyes opened. 'Have you checked on Roger?'

'I will in a minute.'

'Give him a pill. Give him a dozen, I don't care.'

Gwen left Wyman there, and fought her way out of the bounding room. She lunged forward to grip the dining table, then slid along it, the deck under her feet rolling. She made it to the watertight hatch, and the boat dropped and she fell through the hatch like jumping off a dock. She found her feet when the boat's prow swung back up. She passed Toby Odell's door. Inside, Odell was on his bunk, this time truly seasick. She banged on Roger Hall's door. She didn't wait for him to answer.

She found him in his berth, cowering in a corner, his eyes closed, his arms crossed in front, hugging himself. His spectacles were on the bunk next to him.

Gwen had never much liked Roger Hall, the utter sycophant, the pure company man. She had chatted with him only a few times, always awkwardly. She didn't know if he was married, didn't know where he was raised, didn't know what he did before he latched onto Rex Wyman, nothing.

The berth sank under him and he moaned, then the hull received a blow from a wave that bounced them both into the air for an instant, and threw Hall's glasses onto the deck. Gwen bent to retrieve them. They slid away, then back towards her, and she plucked them up.

Hall's eyes were still locked shut, and he made small sounds, a pathetic bleating. His face was white-green, the colour of a fish belly.

Gwen sat next to him. She put a hand on his shoulder. 'Roger? How are you doing?' He had already taken a Valium. He took them all the time, Rex had said. The pill hadn't helped.

The cabin fell ten feet, then lifted and spun, shoving her into Roger Hall. He flinched at the contact, then he leaned slightly into her, hesitantly. She put an arm around his shoulder, hugging him and said, 'I'm scared, too. Everybody is. But we are OK, Roger. The boat is doing just what it's supposed to do.'

He was limp against her. His voice was soft, little more than breath. 'I have to get off this boat,' he said. 'I have to get off.'

'We'll all get off. We are fine, Roger.'

Hall was panting with fear. 'We have to convince Rex to turn *Victory* around, to head to some harbour.'

'Maybe I can talk to him, Roger.'

His round eyes were locked on hers. 'Gwen, listen to me. Rex is going to kill us all. I'm sure of it.'

'That's silly, Roger.'

'You and me, Gwen. Let's go to Rex and demand he get us into a harbour. He'd listen to both of us. And I'm sure Eddie Lash has seen enough of this craziness. And Toby, too.'

The little cabin rose, then rotated and sank, dropping them and pushing them against the bunk like a giant hand.

She said, 'I'll talk to him, Roger, see what he has to say. Now calm down, will you?' She held Roger Hall tightly, as if he were a child.

He was trembling. 'What if Rex orders us to continue the race? I can't do it, Gwen. I'm scared to death.'

She squeezed him, then released him and stood up, her stance wide on the moving deck. 'Roger, I'll go talk to Rex. And sure this is a miserable ride, but we're dry and we're warm and we're all OK.' She smiled at him. 'OK?'

He curled up in his berth. 'Yeah, Gwen,' he said without a trace of conviction. 'Thanks. We're OK.'

Things weren't OK. Oregon Automation's robotic arm was exceedingly clever, and it had been brilliantly designed. Rex had admitted to Gwen that spinnakers wouldn't be used much during the race, but said the media 'will eat the damn thing up'. *Victory* had been designed and manufactured by a legendary shipyard. But the robotic arm had been made and installed by landlubbers.

A single cubic yard of ocean water weighs almost 1,500 pounds. At that moment, as Gwen was leaving Roger's cabin, a thirty-foot wall of water swept across the deck, crashed into the robotic arm and ripped it from the deck, sweeping it over the lee rail into the sea where it disappeared in an instant. When the arm broke loose, it tore open the deck. Water poured into the boat.

Gwen heard the metallic tearing as the robotic arm was blasted away, and, startled, she looked forward along the gangway just as the frothing jade-green sea rushed in through the hole five feet forward of Hall's cabin. The water dumped in, tons of it, and it swept aft as the boat rose on a wave, and it washed Gwen off her feet and tumbled her along the gangway in a freezing torrent as if she were in a miner's sluice.

AT LAST, Fast Eddie Lash had something to do, and he was fast. He had been in the engine room and had heard the shriek of the mounting bolts pulled from the deck. He raced up through the engine room hatch, his sea legs negotiating the rocking deck. Wyman emerged from the control room as Lash ran into the salon, his shoes splashing in sea water that shifted side to side as the boat rolled.

Toby Odell pushed open his cabin door and waded into the salon, the water washing against his legs. Gwen was on her feet when Eddie Lash reached her. She was soaked and shivering. She said loudly, 'Help me get Roger out of his cabin.'

She and Lash moved against the current coming down the gangway. She pulled open Hall's door. He was still on the bunk, his eyes shut. She and Lash pulled him to his feet and into the gangway.

She guided Hall into the salon, settling him onto the lounger while Lash ran upstream towards the sail locker. The boat slid sideways, then rolled to port. Lash held an arm against a bulkhead as he opened a locker. He pulled out a spare storm jib, a small triangle of nylon laminated between two layers of polyester, then he entered the tool room and came out with a nylon tool bag. He hurried back down the gangway into the salon.

'Tell the hatch to close itself,' he ordered.

'*Victory*, close the forward hatch,' Wyman called.

As the boat nose-dived down another wave, the massive door slid across the opening, sealing off the forward area.

The Voice said, unnecessarily, 'The forward hatch is closed.'

'Rex, get into heavy gear and bring up the helm,' Lash said. 'We're going topside.'

Wyman said, 'The boat's steering just fine, Eddie.'

'I don't want to chance the power going out again. If the rudder isn't working, we'll be in trouble out there on the bow.'

Wyman was unused to taking orders, but Lash had sailed into a dozen storms. Wyman said aloud, '*Victory*, raise the helm.'

The Voice said, 'The helm is raised.'

'Gwen,' Lash said, 'you and Toby get into storm suits, too. I want both of you at the helm.'

Wyman said, 'The helm has power assist.'

'If the power goes out, there'll only be cable between the helm and rudder. It'll take two people on the wheel.'

Lash led them aft, then opened a locker to pull out heavy-weather gear. The clothing was bulky and Gwen had to wrestle it on, bracing herself in the gangway as the boat yawed and pitched.

'Check the bilge, Rex.' Lash refused to speak to the boat.

'*Victory*, report the status of the bilge.'

The boat replied, 'The bilge is receiving water at the rate of two hundred gallons a minute. The pumps are working, and the bilge now has an average of six inches of water.'

Gwen was soon encased in orange gear. This was heavier clothing than the yellow bib overalls she had worn topside before the boat entered the Bering Sea. Insulation in the orange gear was thick throughout. She pulled up the hood and lifted the flap over her mouth. The orange was vibrant, and she and the others resembled road flares. She buckled herself into a safety harness, then she helped Odell with his harness.

Lash pushed opened the cockpit hatch. Icy air blasted through the opening. In an infantryman's crouch to keep his centre of gravity low, Lash climbed out, and the other three followed.

The view from the cockpit was disorientating, because where Gwen might expect to see a horizon there was instead a slope of water rushing towards the boat. The oncoming wave shouldered aside the sky, and when it reached *Victory* it lifted the boat as if it were balsa.

Gwen fastened her safety harness to a bolt. The wheel was eight feet across and made of stainless steel. Gwen gripped it tightly, feeling it move under her hands.

Wyman and Lash walked forward along the rail, Lash carrying the bundled sail. The tool bag was over Wyman's shoulder. Bent over, they moved slowly, from one grip to the next. Spray shot up as the hull pounded the water, and the water was instantly turned to ice pellets, which were blown across the deck.

The sky was framed by shifting wave tops. The daylight was tinged with dark green, a sickly colour Gwen had never seen before. Noise was inescapable and frightening. The Arctic wind piped through the rigging, but the worst of it was the full-throated roar of unseen waves breaking in the distance.

Odell leaned towards her and spoke into her ear. 'You'll look back on this and claim you were having fun.'

She tried a smile at him, but it faltered. The wheel moved under her hands.

Wyman and Lash had reached the bow. They were going to rig a stopgap patch, tying down the sail over the hole in the deck, securing it to the deck fittings. It wouldn't keep the gangway completely dry, but the patch would prevent the tons of sea water from flowing into the boat.

The wheel turned, then turned back, making constant adjustments to the course to keep *Victory* quartered to the oncoming waves. Gwen's view of Wyman and Lash was abruptly obscured by spray, then the boat cleared a wave and the spray dropped away, and there they were, bent over their work, their orange heavy-weather gear a bright contrast to the murky green sea.

The storm sail flapped as Wyman and Lash tried to spread it out over the ragged opening in the deck, trying to dodge the wind. Lash brought something out of his tool bag. Wyman and Lash wrestled with the sail, keeping it and themselves low over the deck. The boat rolled and yawed. Spray caught them as if coming from a fire hose.

Gwen could see that both Wyman and Lash had connected their safety harnesses to the boat. They spread out two corners of the sail, the third corner flapping wildly. Wyman held down the sail on the port side, the windward side, while Lash unbuckled his safety harness to crawl to the starboard side of the deck. *Victory* slid down a wave and her prow caught the next wave, and frothing green sea water sped across the deck, splashing against the two men and threatening to carry away their patch. They pulled it back over the hole.

As Lash was about to reattach the clip of his safety harness, wind caught the underside of the sail being used as a patch and ripped it from Wyman's hands. The sail flew across the deck and caught Lash across his body just as he was about to click his harness into place.

Propelled by the furious wind, the sail wrapped round Eddie Lash, then carried him across the deck, spun him over the rail and dropped him into the Bering Sea.

'THE TWO Fs are working against you,' Jess McKay sent from Anchorage. 'Fear and fatigue. It's a dangerous combination.'

Gwen's hands were on her keyboard. 'I just saw a man die. I'm afraid. Really afraid.'

'He's not dead yet. We are looking for him. You threw the floating EPIRB into the water within seconds after Lash went overboard. There's a chance we'll get to him.'

'He wasn't in a survival suit, just heavy-weather gear,' she wrote. 'Why aren't you looking for him, Jess? You, yourself?'

'Another crew was sent. I might get the next call. I don't know yet. Is the deck patched?'

'Rex came back in, got another storm sail, and he and Toby Odell went forward to put the sail over the opening while I was at the wheel. We aren't taking on water any more, other than maybe a gallon a minute that works its way under the patch. Rex is going to try to epoxy a piece of wood onto the hole from the gangway inside, and that'll stop the slow leak.'

'Gwen, your boat is like a bottle. A bottle can ride out any storm if its top is sealed and it doesn't hit rocks.'

'Believe me, I feel like I'm in a bottle,' she wrote.

'Take down our base VHF radio frequency. If all your fancy communication gear fails, you'll be able to get hold of me through it.'

She jotted down the frequency on a pad of paper.

Then McKay asked, 'How are you doing?'

'The crew is not doing well.'

'No, I mean you. How are you holding up?'

She hesitated. She was unused to such questions. When had Rex Wyman ever asked her how she was doing, and meant it? Not some casual greeting at the end of the day, but looked her in the eyes and asked her, wanting to know?

'I'm not doing well,' she typed. 'Not at all.'

'What's wrong, other than being on a boat in the Bering Sea in the middle of winter?'

'Well, it's that, mostly. This room is bucking like a rodeo horse, the whole ship is, and I'm exhausted, fighting it. I haven't been able to sleep because my bunk goes up and down and left and right. I'm so tired I'm having trouble thinking.'

'Is water everywhere below?' McKay asked.

'No moving water. It's all been drained. But the deck is wet. Everything is wet down here.'

She squeezed her eyes closed. The room rocketed upwards. Then a cross wave smashed into the starboard quarter and it sent the room sideways.

She wrote, 'I'm not dealing with Eddie's loss too well. I started weeping when I saw his empty place at the galley table. I'm really having trouble, Jess.'

'Does *Victory* know about the big new low-pressure system—the secondary front—coming down from the Arctic that is going to merge with the one you are already facing? Have you heard the Weather Service Bureau warnings and the coastguard alerts?'

'I'm not aware of them. I think the computer system knows of them, though.'

'So you are saying that nobody on the boat knows what is coming, but your computer might know? That's crazy. It really is.'

'Yeah, I suppose it is,' she typed.

'There's only one boat left in the race—the Frenchwoman. There's no race left, except between her boat and yours.'

She typed, 'Everyone else has sobered up and quit.'

'Why don't you tell Rex Wyman to turn *Victory* around? The minute you turn back, and head southeast, *Victory* will no longer be ramming those waves, and you'll be able to run before the sea, going in its direction. It'll make a huge difference.'

'Me, telling Rex to abandon the race? You don't understand the dynamic of our relationship.'

'I don't understand the dynamic of any relationship, believe me. But the crew is being derelict in their duty if they aren't candid with the skipper.'

She searched for something to say to Jess McKay, desperate to keep in contact with him. 'I'm glad you contacted me, Jess.'

McKay wrote, 'On my screen this morning, I found a message from you, saying you would think about it. Think about what?'

'Your invitation. Honest to God, it means a lot to me, sitting here in this watery hell. It gives me something to focus on, something fun, something solid. I said I would think about it but I guess I was just being coy.'

'What invitation?' appeared on her screen.

'What invitation? To visit Anchorage on my way back from Tokyo after the race. Don't tell me you don't remember.'

A moment passed before a reply appeared. 'Oh, *that* invitation. It slipped my mind for a second. Sorry.'

'So, am I invited?'

Seconds elapsed, then came, 'I would love to have you visit me in Anchorage. Gwen.'

'Really?'

'Really.'

She grinned, then typed, 'I'll think about it.'

'So you've called a meeting.' Wyman smiled narrowly. 'I thought only the skipper could do that. This has the troubling scent of a mutiny.' He laughed, sort of.

Gwen Weld sighed heavily. 'Rex, I haven't spoken with Toby or Roger about this, us getting together and talking. We aren't ganging up on you. I just want to give you my thinking, and see what everybody has to say about it.'

They had gathered in the galley. Hall sat unsteadily on the chair. His fear had ground away whatever personality he once had. Toby Odell's bald head gleamed from the overhead light. His face was wan, and the bags under his eyes resembled black oysters. He had always been thin, but now he appeared little more than a sack full of bones. He was cheery, though, even now. His expectant eyes clicked back and forth between Rex Wyman and Gwen.

Gwen's voice was level. 'There's a secondary weather system about to descend on us, Rex.'

He shook his head. 'The wind has topped out. This is the worst of it and we are doing just fine.'

The boat rose and fell and rolled and righted, and then was punched sideways. They were all holding the table's edges, and they swayed as the direction of gravity seemed to shift randomly.

'I've got better information than this boat has, Rex,' Gwen said. 'I'm in contact with a member of the 212th Rescue Squadron in Anchorage. He mentioned this incoming depression, a system that is going to merge with the main weather system, and make things much, much rougher out here. Everybody in Alaska knows about it.'

Wyman stared at her.

'After he signed off, I spent some time with Boise. *Victory* has not received, or it has received and dumped, all information regarding this secondary depression.'

'Of course *Victory* knows about it.' Wyman had shifted his gaze from Gwen to a bulkhead. His face—normally so animated—was blank. 'We get the information before the Weather Bureau does.'

'What I'm saying, Rex, is that a fifty-year storm is heading our way, and your boat doesn't know a damned thing about it.'

'Well, we know about it now.'

Gwen glanced at Hall, who was blinking rapidly, as if in a dust storm. Odell followed the discussion, his head going back and forth.

She said, 'We need to turn around, Rex. The race is over. The minute we turn around, this boat will be safer and more comfortable. We'll be following the sea.'

'What do you mean, the race is over?' He rallied. 'Genevieve DeLong is on our trail as we speak. And she'll never quit.'

Gwen said loudly, '*Victory*, give the maritime weather forecast at our current location for the next twenty-four hours.'

The system pitched its voice above the wail of wind and water. 'Northwest winds forty-five to fifty knots, subsiding to twenty to twenty-five knots within the next ten to twelve hours. One point five inches of precipitation within the next twenty-four hours. Less than half an inch in the subsequent twenty-four hours.'

'See?' Wyman said. 'The storm is subsiding.'

She pointed at a speaker, one of the twenty in the salon. 'Rex, *Victory* is either lying to you or it is ignorant.'

He said loudly, '*Victory*, connect me with George Croft at the Anchorage office of the National Weather Service.'

From the speakers came, 'This is George Croft.'

'George, this is Rex Wyman aboard *Victory*.'

'Yes, sir. I haven't heard from you in a while.'

'Will you tell me the forecast for the next twenty-four hours for the Bering Sea between the Pribilofs and Unimak Island.'

'You're kidding. You don't know that?'

'Just humour me, will you, George?'

'We are expecting a secondary depression to deepen winds in your area. Winds will hit seventy knots. Seas running southeast will be fifty feet, maybe higher. Cross seas will be pronounced.'

'Are you sure?' Wyman asked.

George Croft in Anchorage yelled into his phone, 'What the hell do you think I'm being paid for? I'm as sure about this gale as I'm sure you are a lunatic, being out there. You've got a weather bomb coming right at you, Wyman . . .'

'Thank you,' Wyman said calmly. '*Victory*, cut the connection.'

He rubbed his eyes, then must have remembered that the world was watching on the Internet, so he quickly dropped his hand.

Wyman said, 'Maybe *Victory* knows more about the incoming weather than the weather service does.'

'No,' she shouted. 'It's the same thing as the boom that swept Jeff Chapman off the deck and the watertight hatch that almost split you in half and our power blackouts. *Victory* is faulty, terribly and dangerously faulty, and this is another symptom.'

'There's a different way to look at all this, Gwen,' Wyman said. '*Victory* is taming the most dangerous sea on earth. With every mile, it proves again our software's worth. People on land see the video, and they wonder how in the world an automated boat can handle it. If WorldQuest can create such a boat, it can do anything.'

Gwen studied Wyman. There was somehow a separation between what she had been telling Wyman and what Wyman was hearing, as if she were speaking Japanese. 'Rex . . .'

'The worse the weather, the more we succeed. Do you understand?'

She exhaled slowly. 'No, I don't.'

'So, no,' he declared. 'We don't turn back. Our destination is Japan.'

Roger Hall had given no indication that anything said at the galley table had registered on him. He had sat there, vacant and trembling, gutted by his fear. But he must have heard Rex Wyman just then, and must have fully understood him.

Hall leapt up from his chair and screamed, 'I want off this boat,' and he slammed a fist into Wyman's nose, which cracked like kindling. Wyman fell sideways out of his chair to the deck.

NO NATION has learned the capricious nature of the sea better than the French. They learned in episodes of giddy joy and utter despair. In AD 793 the pitiless sea brought the Vikings to France, where they extorted six tons of silver and gold bullion from the citizens of Paris. A more generous sea carried William the Conqueror from Normandy to England in 1066, allowing him to overrun England. But then in

1805 the sea delivered the French fleet to Admiral Nelson off Cape Trafalgar, where the French were destroyed quickly. Then a charitable sea delivered Allied rescuers to Normandy in 1944. So, hope or heartbreak from the sea. One day riches, the next day calamity.

One minute the French boat *Remember the Bastille* was on coastguard radar screens, and the next minute it was not. Not one word was received by radio from Genevieve DeLong or her crew. No mayday, no EPIRB signal, nothing. The French heroine, her crew of twenty-one and her boat simply vanished. The signal of an emergency rescue beacon cannot penetrate an upside-down carbon-fibre hull, so there was speculation that her boat capsized, then went down, which could have taken all of ninety seconds.

Coastguard planes flew over *Remember the Bastille*'s last reported position, but they found not a trace: no hull, no oil slick, no debris, no life rafts, nothing. The indifferent sea had swallowed the French boat, and so the sea shattered French hearts once again.

HIS CELLPHONE woke him, and Lonnie Garvin took five seconds to remember where he was. He knew well enough he was in the skipper's berth behind *Hornet*'s wheelhouse, but he was fuzzy on precisely where his boat was moored. He had been dodging from place to place, keeping ahead of his creditors.

A hundred-foot trawler should be easy to spot anywhere. How can a huge vessel be hidden? the creditors demanded of the sheriff. But Garvin had many friends in Alaskan ports, on the boats and in the chandleries and fish brokerages and fuel terminals, even in the government buildings. Not many people were going to call the sheriff to inform him of *Hornet*'s location so the boat could be seized.

Garvin sat up on the bunk and reached for the chirping phone. The boat rocked idly on Seal Bay's protected waters. Alaska has perhaps fifteen Seal Bays. This one was on the lee side of Unalaska Island, three sea miles from Dutch Harbor. He looked at the clock. It was five in the morning. Who would be calling him at five?

He opened the phone and put it to his ear and said 'Hello.'

He heard, 'Thank you, thank you, sweetie. That was a close call, but you made it.' Garvin's wife laughed. Her name was Allison. The luckiest day of his life was the day he met her, and he told her so often, and believed it fervently still, even after all the years.

'What was a close call?' he asked.

'I had maxed out everything, Lonnie. I didn't have one cent of credit left on our cards, and we had six dollars in our bank account. But you did it. You must be my big hero.'

He smiled. He had felt guilty, out on his boat in Alaska, while his wife juggled off dunning calls in Seattle. He said, 'I haven't been your hero lately.'

'Twenty thousand dollars makes you my hero. How'd you do it?'

'Sweetie, I don't have a clue what you are talking about.'

'Come on, Lonnie,' she said gaily. 'I went to the bank yesterday to see about our credit line. The teller gave me a statement of our account. It showed we have twenty thousand dollars in it.'

'Twenty thousand?' Garvin asked. 'The bank has made a mistake. That's not our money. We need to tell them that right away.'

'Well, it's too late,' she said, a touch of defiance in her voice. 'Last night I wrote cheques to Visa and American Express and the oil companies and the phone company, and mailed them. I even Fed Exed the cheque to the mortgage company.'

'Oh, man.' Garvin could put much fatigue into two words.

'You didn't put twenty thousand into our account? You sure?'

He laughed tiredly. 'I would've remembered, you can bet.'

'So what should I do?'

'Go up and tell the bank that the money can't possibly be ours, and they'll straighten it out.'

'What about the cheques I wrote?' Allison's voice was dark with disappointment.

'We'll deal with the card companies and the others when they call, I suppose.'

'Meaning, I'll have to deal with them, down here in Seattle. Lonnie, you have no idea how much I hate this.'

'I know, and I'm trying to work it out,' he said. 'I'll call tonight.'

He said goodbye, but hadn't put the phone down before it rang again. One of his crewmen, probably. 'Yeah?' Garvin braced himself for bad news.

'Mr Garvin?' The phone crackled with static. 'This is Rex Wyman aboard *Victory*.'

Rex Wyman? The idiot billionaire out on the Bering Sea? What were the chances of Rex Wyman calling him. None.

Garvin said, 'Bang The, I'm going to be pissed if you are fall-down drunk and calling me from some Dutch Harbor tavern.'

'My crew wishes we were in some Dutch Harbor tavern right now, Mr Garvin, but we're not.'

Garvin looked at the cellphone as if it might be broken. The voice didn't sound like it belonged to Bang The Drum. He returned the phone to his ear, then said, 'I don't often get calls from the Rex Wymans of the world. And maybe this isn't one of them, either.'

'Do you have a television set that can tune to CNN? I'm on that channel live right now, from *Victory*'s control room. I'll turn to the camera and wave to you, or give you some signal. That'll prove I am who I say I am.'

'I don't have a TV here.' Then he couldn't resist adding, 'Boats don't need TVs. They need sailors.'

'You may be right, and that's why I'm calling tonight.'

'What do you have in mind?' Maybe this *was* Rex Wyman.

'I want you to bring *Hornet* from Dutch Harbor and towards our position in the event I need a tow.'

'Are you in trouble now?' Garvin asked quickly. The unwritten code of the sea is that a sailor must give assistance to anyone who is in peril. Garvin fully subscribed to the code.

'Some of my crew believes we are, and I calmed them down by promising to get a boat out here to give assistance if we need it.'

'Why don't you call the coastguard or somebody?'

'They won't dispatch rescuers unless rescuing is needed, and rescue isn't needed at this time.'

Garvin said, 'Well, I'm not leaving port in this dirty weather, if that's what you have in mind, Mr Wyman.'

'I had my people do some investigating. I like to know about folks I do business with. Let me run some numbers for you. Your home mortgage is with American Surety, who filed a foreclosure six weeks ago. You are about to lose your home.'

Garvin flushed with anger. 'You've got no right to know that.'

'You owe thirty-two thousand dollars on assorted credit cards. You owe businesses in Dutch Harbor twenty-two thousand, and businesses in Kodiak thirty-five thousand, and businesses in Anacortes fifty-two thousand. Twelve suppliers have filed liens against your boat. Have you checked your bank account lately?'

Understanding straightened Garvin's back. 'The twenty thousand?'

'That's what I pay to people who listen closely to me. That money's yours just for listening to my proposal. You can say no after you hear me out, and that twenty thousand will still be yours.'

'You have my attention,' Garvin said by way of understatement.

'Your reputation as a heavy-weather sailor is widely known.

Hornet was built for these seas. I want you and your crew to immediately set sail for our predicted position, and I want you to have cable long and tough enough to tow us.'

'You are out in a deadly sea, Mr Wyman. Only a fool would head in your direction.'

'Where there is risk, there is reward,' Wyman said.

Garvin hesitated before asking, 'What sort of reward?'

Wyman spoke for two more minutes, Garvin listening intently. When Garvin closed the cellphone, he dressed quickly, then sprinted down to the crew quarters to wake his engineer.

Two HOURS LATER *Hornet* pulled into the cannery dock in Dutch Harbor. Bang The Drum was on the dock, ready to catch the line Garvin threw down. Ollie Nordquist and the rookie Nick Summers were also there. Nordquist and Summers had been patiently waiting for Garvin to make some arrangement for fuel and provisions that would allow *Hornet* to return to the crab grounds, and Garvin had telephoned earlier in the morning, telling them to meet him. They had brought their duffle bags, which they had placed in black plastic garbage bags against the rain that was sweeping the dock, propelled by a freezing westerly wind.

Also at the dock was Milt Robinson, the manager of the Unalaska Branch of the Alaska First Bank. Rain dappled his spectacles. His small moustache was neatly trimmed. He held a briefcase, and was wearing a wide grin and a hooded parka. It was seven in the morning. The sun had not yet risen.

After guiding *Hornet* into the slip and seeing it secured, Garvin jumped over the rail onto the dock. The engineer, Lars Anders, remained on board. Milt Robinson led the others to his van. Allard Machinery on Nanchuck Road in Unalaska was their first stop. Fritz Allard was just opening the shop doors as Garvin arrived.

Garvin said, 'I need some wire rope, Fritz. Three thousand feet of one-inch ought to do it. I need it right now.'

Allard's smile faltered and his expression became one of embarrassed sympathy. He said quietly, 'Lonnie, you know I can't let you have some wire rope. I'm already carrying about forty-five hundred dollars for you, and I just can't go higher.'

Garvin nodded at the banker, Milt Robinson, who asked, 'How much for the cable?'

'Well, it's three dollars a foot.'

Allard opened the briefcase to remove a paper-bound stack of bills. 'I'll pay for it right now.'

The shop owner looked at Garvin. 'Your parents die or something, Lonnie? You finally come into your inheritance?'

'I'm in a real hurry, Fritz,' Garvin said, out of earshot of his crew. 'My deal depends on me leaving port in the next two hours.'

Allard smiled. 'I'm happy to see you back in business, Lonnie.'

The next stop was the Unalaska Lucky Store, where each person in *Hornet*'s crew manoeuvred two shopping carts up and down the aisles, filling them with provisions. When the total was rung up, Milt Robinson handed cash to the clerk.

Garvin and his crew and the banker made three more stops in Unalaska before returning to Dutch Harbor.

As soon as the crew and the banker climbed on board *Hornet*, it pulled away from the dock. As the boat crossed the harbour towards the Texaco depot, Garvin gathered everyone in the wheelhouse.

He turned to his crew. 'I've sort of let you men think that we've been provisioning *Hornet* to return to the crab beds when the weather breaks. That's not my plan. I'm taking *Hornet* out today, just as soon as we are fuelled.'

They stared at him. The banker smiled slightly.

Then Bang The Drum said, 'Yeah, right, skipper. And I'm swearing off Jim Beam for ever.'

Lars Anders turned from the wheel. 'That's crazy, Lonnie. Don't kid us about crap like that. It puts stupid ideas in these weak heads and it might chase out something useful from their brains.'

The crew laughed.

'I had an interesting phone call early this morning,' Garvin said. 'From the billionaire Rex Wyman.'

'The goof out in the Bering Sea?' Drum asked.

Garvin told his crew that Wyman had offered to charter *Hornet* to escort *Victory* during the storm, and to tow the sailboat if necessary. He didn't mention the financial part of the deal.

Then Garvin said, 'I can't ask you to go out with me. And if you decline to crew *Hornet* on this charter, I'll still be hiring you for the crab lines when I return.'

Nick Summers eyed Drum and Nordquist, looking for a clue as to how he should be reacting, but the experienced hands let little be known from their expressions.

The skipper continued, 'Wyman is prepared to make it worth your while to go out with me. He'll pay ten thousand dollars now, and another ten thousand when we return to port, to each of you.'

Hornet drew abreast of the Texaco dock.

'Twenty thousand dollars.' Drum savoured the words, letting them play around in his teeth. 'Count me in.'

'I never thought I'd see twenty thousand dollars in my whole life,' Nick Summers said. 'I'm in, too.'

'Me, too.' Nordquist rubbed two fingers together.

Lars Anders was busy at the wheel, manoeuvring *Hornet* nearer the fuel dock. But he said angrily, 'Damn it, Lonnie. These three guys are too foolish to know what they're doing, but you know better. You know this boat shouldn't leave this harbour.'

Garvin said, more to himself, 'You may be right, Lars. But I'm going to lose *Hornet* if I don't go out, plain and simple.'

The banker once again opened his briefcase. He handed a wrapped stack of bills first to Bang The Drum, then to Ollie Nordquist, then to Nick Summers.

When the boat arrived at the Texaco dock, the crew left the wheel-house to help moor *Hornet*. Milt Robinson also left, as the fuel distributor was his final transaction on behalf of Rex Wyman this day.

Anders, the back of his neck red with anger, shifted to reverse and the boat gently bumped the fuel dock. He pushed the gear controls to neutral.

'It's a risk, I know,' Garvin said. 'I'm not asking you to go.'

Anders shut down the engines. He stared out of the window, refusing to look at his skipper. 'I quit *Hornet*. Right now. I had trust in your judgment and that's why I loved being on this boat. No longer. This is too crazy.' Anders's words were choppy. He was on the verge of bawling. 'It . . . it says something about you, Lonnie, that you would take this fool's money and leave port in this wind. I'm done with you and this boat.'

He turned from the wheel and brushed by Garvin, headed below for his gear. Garvin closed his eyes a moment, cursing himself. A crab boat couldn't afford to lose an engineer like Lars Anders. And Anders was his closest Alaska friend.

Garvin looked around at his wheelhouse, at the mahogany panels, at his swivel chair behind the spoked wheel. God, he loved this boat. The prospect of losing *Hornet* had worked on him like a disease for a year. And now there was a chance to save his boat. What was there to even think about?

He left the wheelhouse to join his crew below, wrestling with the diesel hose. 'Our deal depends on us getting out there fast,' he told Drum and Nordquist and Summers, urging them on.

A few minutes after fuelling began, Lars Anders jumped from *Hornet*'s deck to the dock, and without a word to anybody started for shore, his duffle bag over his shoulder.

Commercial fishermen know that they should never hurry, because hurrying leads to errors, that the sea is unforgiving of mistakes. But Lonnie Garvin and his crew were in a hurry, filling the big double-bottom diesel tanks below *Hornet*'s deck, and they did indeed make a mistake just then. It was a slight thing, of little note in almost any other circumstance, and something easily remedied. But a mistake, still. The Bering Sea would soon exploit it.

 *Chapter seven*

McKay poured himself a bowl of cereal. It was three in the morning. He and Ramirez had just coptered a high-capacity water pump out to a crabber who got caught out. The boat's crew had installed it and now the crabber would make port in good shape.

He sat in the chair in front of the computer, wondering how he would ever be able to gain his feet again. God, he was tired. He blinked several times before he could make out the words on the screen. They read, 'Come on, Jess. Get home. I need you.'

When McKay lifted his hands to the keyboard, his arms felt weighted. He typed, slowly, 'I'm here. You there, Gwen?'

Within several seconds appeared her reply, 'You are back, thank God. We've had some crazy things happen here. Have you been watching on the Internet?'

'I've been busy.'

'The whole world watched Roger Hall slug Rex Wyman. He flattened his nose, and I don't mean metaphorically.'

McKay used his mouse to bring up a bookmarked web site. 'I've got you on my screen now.'

A few seconds later, McKay watched Gwen Weld turn to the camera to wave. Her face was drawn, with dark lines under her eyes. She turned back to her monitor, then the boat must have rolled to port, because she was pushed back in her chair. She struggled to return her hands to the keyboard.

On McKay's screen came, 'Rex flipped out. He grabbed Roger by his collar and lifted him from the chair, and marched him to his cabin. None of the cabins lock from the outside, but Rex rigged a line to the hatch handle so the door won't open.'

'So Roger Hall is locked in his cabin?' McKay asked. 'That's about as unsafe a thing as I can imagine on a boat.'

'Rex is under a lot of pressure,' appeared on McKay's screen. 'He's been watching his empire shrink. "Collapse" might be a better word. There's a panic going on in the stock. And Rex sits at the galley table ranting about a conspiracy to ruin him.'

McKay asked, 'Who is the villain in Wyman's conspiracy?'

'The boat. Rex has begun to hate *Victory*. Each glitch in the system receives massive publicity.'

As intrigued as Jess was with Gwen Weld, and as much as he wanted to help, sleep pulled at him, and his head seemed filled with wool.

'So look at my shipmates,' appeared on McKay's screen. 'Rex rants about mutiny. Roger Hall is so terrified he is catatonic, and now Toby Odell has something really wrong with him.'

'What?' That's all McKay's numbed brain could think of.

'At first I thought he was seasick, but it's more than that. I went into his cabin to ask him what was wrong. His shaving kit was open, and he was counting out some pills, and when the boat yawed, everything spilled out of his kit. I scrambled around, helping him gather his stuff. He had a lot of pill bottles in his kit.'

McKay wrote, 'What kind of medicines?'

'One was for Lanalt, a morphine-based painkiller.'

'Never heard of it.'

'It's most often used for cancer patients. Terminal cancer patients. And now Toby's bald head makes sense. I think he lost his hair due to chemotherapy or radiation therapy.'

McKay stared at the screen, trying to concentrate on it. Sleep swept across him like a wave. He felt himself shutting down.

A long moment passed. Then up on McKay's screen came, 'Jess, you still with me?' A few more seconds elapsed. 'You've fallen asleep, haven't you? There on dry land. God, I wish I was with you, sitting next to you, or lying next to you. Good night, Jess.'

McKay was indeed asleep, there in his chair. He wouldn't read her last message until morning.

In *VICTORY*'S GALLEY, Gwen dabbed at Wyman's face with a damp towel. Blood was caked on his cheeks and jaw. His nose was off-kilter, skewed to the left.

Toby Odell was also at the table. His face was haggard. The sound of water and wind filled the space, a constant shriek that overwhelmed anything less than a yell.

At the top of her voice, Gwen said, 'Rex, now is not a good time, I know, but I've got to tell you that I'm leaving WorldQuest.'

He moved his head to look at her. 'You are quitting?'

'I quit. Right now. I'll do what I can for *Victory* in the control room, but when—and if—I ever get off this boat, I'm through with it, and with WorldQuest.'

'And with me?' he asked, his tone entirely level.

'We should talk about that later, in private.'

'I've never hidden anything from Toby. You can talk now.'

Odell had been listening, despite his closed eyes. He laughed. 'And I never hide anything from Rex. Almost nothing, that is.'

She said loudly, 'I need to get away from you, Rex. I'm sorry. I don't know how else to say it. I just . . .'

The Voice interrupted her, 'Rudder control has been lost.'

Wyman recoiled, his eyes wide. Using the table for a handhold, he struggled upright. He moved aft, staggering as the deck dropped from under him and tilted forward. He scrambled uphill towards the control room.

Gwen followed him slowly, walking with her feet wide apart. When she reached the control room, Wyman was sitting in her chair, shouting into a microphone. The boat rolled to starboard and kept on rolling. Surely the mast was in the water. Gwen glanced at a monitor that showed the view from the masthead. She could see only bubbles. The boat began to right itself.

'What do you mean we have a server crash?' Wyman yelled.

Wyman glanced at Gwen. He punched a button so that the voice of Rick Gagliardi, *Victory*'s chief software designer, was broadcast over speakers in the control room. Wyman had rehired him a day ago.

Gagliardi said, '*Victory*'s server has been hit with an enormous volume of data.'

'What kind of data?' Wyman barked.

'Millions and millions of digital packets,' Gagliardi replied.

Gwen fought her way to a bolted-down chair next to Wyman.

Wyman demanded, 'What sort of packets?'

'They are brief pings, asking for information, or diagnostic messages. They are anonymous and coming all at once, from everywhere. They overloaded the server and put it out of action.'

'That's impossible.' Wyman's expression was of chagrined wrath. 'No computer or network can overload our server.'

The boat rolled and this time stayed on its side until a second wave rolled it further. Gwen had to hang onto the chair arms. The keel was in the air for a few seconds and the masthead well under the churning sea. Then *Victory* ponderously rose again.

Gagliardi said, 'It isn't one computer doing it. This is an attempt by a black-hat hacker to shut down our operation by overloading it. The hacker planted zombies on other computers. These are otherwise benign, innocent third-party computers, at least three hundred zombie computers, we've determined.'

'What are you doing about it?'

Gagliardi replied, 'We are redirecting our server's traffic to another server. It's taking some time.'

'Are *Victory*'s cameras working?'

'No. We can't get images here, anyway. We've got you on old-fashioned VHF. This isn't over our satellite network.'

'Who did this? Who is the black hat?'

'We're working on that, too. Your on-board computer still controls some functions, including the helm. You'd better raise the helm, Rex. And then you'd better go topside.'

'Topside?' Wyman asked in a low tone.

'You are going to lose *Victory* unless you get some rudder control,' Gagliardi said over the speakers. 'It'll founder and sink.'

Gwen saw fear in Wyman's eyes, and it seemed entirely foreign on his masterful face. He moved past her, out of the control room.

Before she knew what she was saying, Gwen called, 'I'll go topside with you, Rex.'

BROACHING IS WHEN a boat turns so that it is lying along the trough of the wave, which can then hit the boat full force stem to stern. And this is what happened to *Victory* at that moment.

An incoming wave lifted *Victory* effortlessly, as if the boat were a piece of driftwood. As *Victory* tipped further and further to starboard on the massive slope of marbled water, the crest of the wave broke overhead. Tons of turbulent white and green water fell on the boat from above. *Victory* trembled and rolled, and kept on rolling as the torrent turned the boat as if it were on a spit.

Below decks, Gwen was preparing herself for another mast-in-the water roll, where the boat would lie over in the water, then come back up. She had experienced this manoeuvre dozens of times in the past hour, hundreds in the last day. This time, though, the boat didn't stop. It kept on rolling. The cabin spun and Gwen was thrown onto her back, then rolled along the hull. Then she fell off the hull, fell five feet, and landed on the ceiling as the boat was upside-down. She skittered along the ceiling, then fell again, landing on the deck in a heap. She lay there, unable to gather the will to rise.

Victory was made to slice through the water. All the boat's technological marvels were directed at attaining maximum speed. *Victory* was not made to roll through 360 degrees. Many things happened during that roll, all of them bad.

In the galley, pans and pots flew out of their lockers and whipped around the cabin. Two glass serving bowls shattered against a bulkhead. The stove jumped its gimbals and tumbled through the air. Sliding cartons of milk and a pot roast pushed open the refrigerator door, and suddenly all the refrigerator's contents were being tossed around the galley. Drawers popped open and cutlery shot across the cabin. Back pressure punched through the pipes servicing the head and sewage was blown out of the toilet.

Odell had been sitting at the galley table, gripping its edge, but when the deck was above him on the boat's roll, he fell heavily, landing on the ceiling. A bread knife creased his chin and a fork punctured the skin of his forehead. A cutting board jumped its mount, was propelled through the air and clipped his temple. Senseless, he skidded around the cabin like a rag doll.

Gear lockers swung open. Coats and boots and bib overalls were whirled out into the cabin, many wrapping around Rex Wyman. He slid along the bulkhead, trying to cast the gear away.

Wyman cried out, '*Victory*, raise the helm.'

He bounced against the deck as the boat rolled upright. He tried to rise, but fell back, and lay there for a few seconds, gasping. Then he levered himself up to his knees. He crawled aft towards the hatch, grabbed heavy-weather gear and tried to get his legs into a pair of insulated overalls.

Not everything bad that was occurring during the roll was happening in the living quarters. In the engine room, batteries broke lose and ricocheted around the room. One smashed the electric starter, disabling the port engine, then bounced and rammed the desalinator.

Water will find a way through any weakness in the deck or joinery. All boats require pumping during a gale. Sea water leaked through the deck, and seeped into the cabin. Bilge pumps are not designed to be turned upside-down. Foul bilge water found its way through the rolling deck, and it began to rain bilge water in the salon as *Victory* was upside-down.

'*Victory*, is the helm up?' Wyman yelled. His forehead was turning purple. He had landed on his head during the roll.

The Voice was silent. That irritably calm, vaguely malevolent, omniscient voice no longer came from the walls.

Wyman said to Gwen over the noise of the storm, 'Gagliardi said they were dumping functions off into another server. We'll get the systems back online here in a minute.'

Gwen crawled forward towards Toby Odell, still on the floor in the galley. Odell was on his back, sliding back and forth on the rocking deck. He was trying to sit up but didn't have the strength. Gwen grabbed his arm. 'Toby, you OK?'

'No, I'm not.'

Gwen helped Toby to his feet, then guided him to his cabin, where she helped him into his berth, then pulled a blanket over him.

'You're really ill, aren't you, Toby? I saw all your pills.'

'I'm fine in the short run.' He coughed raggedly. 'I feel pretty good, day to day. It's the long run that has me worried. Of course, the long run should have us all worried.' He laughed gently.

Kneeling next to his berth, she looked at him with affection. Toby Odell was always ready with a word of praise or a funny one-line bit of self-deprecation. He was that likable, forgettable fellow found in every classroom as a child and every neighbourhood as an adult, except for one thing; he had hooked up with Wyman.

'Is it cancer, Toby?' she asked.

He nodded. 'Liver cancer.'

'Is it treatable?'

'Liver cancer isn't one of those cancers where there's much success treating. But I've taken charge of the disease, Gwen.'

The sea was loud, just outside the hull. 'What do you mean?'

'It's not going to kill me. I'm going to kill it.'

His words were so final that she shivered.

'I've seen the future,' he added. 'It's as plain as your face in front of me. I'm not leaving this boat alive.'

'That's foolish talk.' She gripped his arm under the blanket. 'I'm going to leave you here and check out the control room. I'll be back. I want to talk to you about this.'

He smiled knowingly, something of his old smile.

Leaving him in his cabin, Gwen moved aft into the salon, pushing through debris and several inches of water. Rex was below, in the engine room, using cranks to manually raise the helm. She fought her way into the control room. No water had made it into that room, and the bolts holding down her equipment had held. Some of her monitors were on, others were black. The boat's stand-alone computer system supported some functions, but not many.

Just as she picked up the VHF handset, Rex Wyman appeared in the hatch. He had donned the insulated overalls and the coat and was now working on the zippers and the Velcro. 'What are you doing?' he demanded.

'I'm sending a mayday.'

He stared at her. 'Put the radio down. Nobody calls a mayday except me.'

'We are taking on water, Rex. You can see for yourself. Our bilge pumps are out. We need rescue.'

He pointed at her like a prosecutor. 'Put the damned radio down.' Gwen caught her breath, afraid of him and afraid of *Victory*.

Suddenly her dark monitors lit up, and almost as quickly *Victory* began responding to its rudder. The boat turned towards the wind. Wyman glanced around the control room. It had sprung to life, filled with reassuring light from the monitors.

Wyman demanded, '*Victory*, report on the heading and speed.'

'Bearing north by northwest, ground speed of four knots.'

Wyman's face transformed. One moment he had the look of a killer, the next his expression was of a gleeful child opening a gift.

'*Victory*, report on the jib.'

'Forward hydraulic pumps two and three are inoperable. Forward hydraulic pump one is operating, but the system is not receiving jib wind-resistance data.'

Wyman looked at a monitor. 'Show camera four POV on monitor one.' The scene on the monitor switched from the masthead camera to one mounted amidships. The image showed that the jib had been torn away during the roll.

'There's no jib-resistance data because there's no jib.' Wyman laughed. 'Hell, who needs a jib? *Victory*, report on the engine systems.'

'Main engine one and main engine two are presently inoperable. Generator one is inoperable. Generator two is functioning.'

Again Wyman laughed. 'We can get along on one generator. *Victory*, what other systems are inoperable?'

'The desalinator, the galley stove, number two VHF radio . . .'

'You're back online, looks like from here,' Rick Gagliardi's words interrupted the Voice.

'We're in good shape here, Rick.' Wyman sounded like he had just won the Pacific Winter Challenge. 'What'd you do in Boise?'

'Set up a mirror server.'

'Are *Victory*'s cameras feeding the Internet?'

'I'm looking at you right now on my screen,' Gagliardi replied.

'How many times have I fired you this week, Rick?'

'Three, I think. Maybe four. I get confused.'

'I'm giving you a free pass, just like in Monopoly. Next time I fire you, take it out of your pocket, and you can stay at your desk.'

And only then did Gwen remember Roger Hall, alone in his cabin. She pushed herself out of her chair and went to his cabin. She leaned heavily against his door as she knocked. 'Roger, can I come in?' she called.

Nothing came from the cabin. She called again. Still nothing. Scowling, she fumbled with Rex's jury-rigged lock on the door, untying amateurish knots. She pushed open the door.

Roger Hall was on the deck below his bunk. He was belly-down, and splayed out in an unnatural position. His head was twisted so that he was looking over his shoulder at the ceiling, too far over his shoulder. His eyes were open.

Gwen dropped to her knees. She pressed her fingers on his neck at the jugular vein. There was no pulse.

When *Victory* rolled, Roger Hall had been bounced off the ceiling and then off the deck. His neck had been broken.

TWO OF *HORNET*'S CREW, Bang The Drum and the kid, Nick Summers, were out on deck, cracking off built-up ice with baseball bats. The third crewman, Ollie Nordquist, was in the galley, rigging a storm shutter out of Lexan sheeting, installing it over a suspect porthole. In the wheelhouse, Lonnie Garvin turned the helm slightly with each new wave, repositioning the trawler to take the wave at an angle of about thirty degrees.

Hornet's windshield wipers beat back and forth. Garvin had never seen seas like this, a mountain range of water, one roaring peak after another. His boat would struggle up one embankment of water, totter at the foaming top, and then surf down the other side. And then the boat would do it again, and again. Holding onto the wheel, Garvin felt as if he were alternating push-ups with chin-ups.

Hornet was acting sluggishly and seemed out of trim. He looked at the television screen that showed the crab deck. Ice was building up on the plastic tarps that covered the pots, but the crew would soon get to them with their bats. Garvin was comforted by the glow of his instruments. He patted the wood console in front of him. Truth be told, he loved this boat. Not like he loved his wife and his kids, but still his bond of affection for *Hornet* was as strong as any emotion he had ever known.

The Bering Sea was a peculiar olive green, with angry swirls of white and grey. The cross seas added a touch of anarchy, with errant waves smashing against the boat from unexpected angles at irregular intervals. Garvin's hands on the spokes were white with his effort to hold onto the wheel. The night sky was so low that racing black clouds seemed to brush the wave tips.

The hatch opened, and Nick Summers stepped over the rim into the wheelhouse. He was carrying a dented baseball bat. 'Ollie and I are done, stem to stern. *Hornet* is clear of ice.'

Ollie Nordquist followed Summers into the pilothouse. Both men were wearing safety harnesses over their clothing. Nordquist carried a crowbar in his hand.

Garvin grinned at Summers. 'In this storm, knocking ice off our boat is going to be like painting the Golden Gate Bridge.' He waited a beat. 'The minute you are done, you begin again.'

Summers laughed.

'Go below, get some coffee. Then I'll need you topside again.' The men clattered down the companionway to the galley.

Once again, standing at the wheel, Garvin checked off his mental list. Had he done everything? Had he missed something?

The survival suits were in their bags in an easily accessed locker. Each suit had a personal EPIRB. The life jackets were new, and each had a strobe. He had used Wyman's money to purchase a man-overboard pole. Also he had purchased a new six-man throw-overboard life raft that was inflated with carbon dioxide and had self-erecting canopies, a ballast system, a conical sea anchor, a dry-cell light system and an on-board EPIRB.

In a wave trough, Garvin again noticed the boat's sluggishness. Then it came to him. The trawler wasn't righting, not completely. In these miserable seas it was critical that the vessel retain the ability to return upright.

He looked at his fuel gauges, dimly lit in green. Garvin had purposely not taken on a full load of fuel. He wasn't going out for a month of crabbing. He'd be out for a couple of days, max. He had more than enough diesel on board.

The trouble was, most of the diesel had been put into the starboard tanks. Garvin hadn't taken the time to balance his fuel load while loading it in Dutch Harbor. He scowled. If he deliberately hadn't balanced the load while fuelling, he should have started doing so immediately on departing the harbour. He had simply forgotten, with the rough seas disguising the boat's imbalance.

Garvin threw the switch for the fuel-transfer pump. Within thirty minutes, the boat should be balanced. He glanced at the fuel gauge for the port tank. It wasn't filling. The pump indicator light was glowing green, but no diesel was being transferred. He quickly switched off the pump before it overheated.

Garvin bit down on his lower lip. There could be only one explanation: the bitterly cold sea had frozen his fuel transfer lines. He should have balanced the fuel load while still in Dutch Harbor. He had made a mistake, a big one.

He picked up an intercom handset. 'Ollie and Bang The, get up here in a hurry.'

ONCE AGAIN WYMAN was in the control room, Gwen Weld's area. He owned the entire boat, but she wished he'd stay away from her territory. He was tapping the table anxiously, waiting for the call to come in. The monitors indicated wind speed had increased three knots over the past hour. Gwen's head was down on her arms at the table next to a computer monitor. She no longer cared if Wyman viewed her as the diligent sailor. She needed sleep, and she needed to get off this hell boat.

When Gwen had told Wyman of Roger Hall's death, Wyman had shaken his head, but had said nothing at all. And how had she responded to this callousness? She had had no energy left for any anger or indignation. She only noticed that Wyman's hair was dirty, one of those little observations that come unbidden, don't fit anywhere, and aren't soon forgotten. Wyman loved a mirror, and was obsessed with his hair, and here it was greasy and matted. She was thinking only right enough to know she wasn't thinking right. She wanted to sleep. Anything for some sleep. Roger Hall's body was wrapped in a sail and lying in his berth. At least he was asleep.

'Rex, you there?' came from the control room's speakers.

'What do you have, Ted?'

'We first ran a course of digital forensics, but didn't come up with anything,' Ted Landers, Wyman's security chief, said. 'So we started investigating the old-fashioned way, using informants in the hacker world. We have dozens of them, as you know. Hackers are highly intelligent, but they don't have wisdom. They almost always brag.'

Wyman said into the microphone, 'Come on, Ted. Lay it out.'

'You don't know how thorough the virus is, Rex.'

The boat's motion pulled Gwen back in her chair, making her sit upright. Up the boat went, higher and higher. She gripped the arms of her chair with the little strength she had left.

Landers's voice came again, '*Victory*'s roll, its three-sixty? *Victory*'s server was programmed by the virus to cut out the rudder just before a rogue wave hit.'

Landers paused a few seconds, perhaps to let his news sink in.

He was rewarded when Wyman asked, 'What do you mean?'

'It was no accident your boat rolled. I've been told by my people that it's a miraculous piece of software design, using your system to spot the big wave, then cutting out the rudder.'

Wyman glanced at Gwen and his eyes narrowed. He switched off the speakers and lifted a handset so she couldn't hear Ted Landers.

Wyman said, 'Cut to the chase, Ted. Who is the hacker? Who has been trying to ruin me?' He listened, the handset to his ear. His face suddenly knotted with fury at Landers's words.

This time all systems failed. *Victory* shut down completely. Lights throughout the boat instantly went off and all the monitors in Gwen's control room went to black.

Wyman yelled in rage. Gwen could do nothing but grip the arms of her chair. The control room was as dark as a cave. The boat quickly fell off the wind. And this time there was no idle moment of wallowing in a trough before the big wave hit. It roared over *Victory*, enveloping it and rolling it with ease, an errant toy in the vast universe of storm-driven water. Within seconds, the boat was upside-down—turning turtle, the cute sailing phrase entirely at odds with the frightening event—and its bulbous keel was in the air, and then the boat continued to roll, pushed by the massive wave.

During this roll, this second 360 degrees, Gwen, hanging on desperately to her chair, heard new noises: loud popping, like gunfire, and then a grinding squeal, a sound high above the rush of wind and water. It was a mechanical sound, metal being twisted by an irresistible force.

As the mammoth wave rolled the boat, Gwen hung from her chair, but the boat kept turning, and her fingers slipped, and she fell, plummeted into utter darkness. She didn't remember landing.

WEAK LIGHT brought her round. She blinked several times, trying to chase the fuzziness from her brain. She was lying on the control-room deck. The back of her head throbbed. She touched it gently. It was damp. She brought away blood on her fingers. The pain filled her head. She tried to sit up.

None of the monitors was operating, nor were any of the overhead lights. Light came only from side emergency lamps, small frosted glass bulbs behind metal grids. She didn't know how long she had been unconscious, maybe only a few seconds.

'USAFNG fourteen to *Victory*. Can you hear me?'

The voice came from the table, wispy words filled with static. She braced a foot against the bulkhead, then levered herself onto her chair, using the boat's roll for momentum. The boat staggered under a wave and she was punched back into the chair.

'Gwen, can you lift up the handset?'

The words came from a handheld VHF radio. She pressed the SEND button, but a new bolt of pain came from the back of her head. She couldn't find the energy to say anything.

'Gwen, are you in your control room? Can you hear me?' It was Jess McKay's voice.

She pressed the button. 'We've rolled again.' She groaned. 'This is a nice little radio, reaching you all the way in Anchorage.' What was she saying?

'You are being patched through. Listen to me, Gwen. We saw your roll on our screens, and as the mast hit the water, your video signal blacked out. We think *Victory* has lost its mast, lost its rigging.'

'I . . . couldn't care less.'

'Yes, you do. Are you with me, Gwen? Are you injured?'

She pressed the button. 'I'm with you.'

'We are coming to get you, but you and Wyman and Odell need to do something right now. Your mast and boom are probably hanging by the rigging, across your deck or off the boat in the water. They are going to punch holes in your hull or deck unless you cut them free. Do you understand me?'

Rex Wyman appeared in the hatchway. He was drenched. He said, 'A porthole blew out. We stuffed a cushion into it.'

From the radio came, 'Gwen, you are in a survival storm now.'

'Who is that?' Wyman asked, duck-walking to a seat.

'A pararescue jumper,' she said. 'They are on their way. He says the boom and mast are down,' Gwen said.

'Yeah, I know. Through the porthole, I could see some cable hanging from the deck.'

She managed to press the VHF button. 'Maybe we should get into a life raft and wait for you, instead of going out on deck and fooling with the rigging.'

From the radio came, 'The last thing—the very last thing—you want to do is to get into a life raft. We will be far less able to spot you—even with your beacons—in a life raft. *Victory* will float even if it's half filled with water. Stay with it.'

A cross wave collided with *Victory* and Gwen was thrown against the table. The handset fell and dangled on its cord.

'Do you have tools on board?' McKay asked over the radio.

Wyman snatched the handset and shouted into the microphone, 'What do you think? Of course we have tools.'

'Get bolt cutters, if you have them, and hacksaws. Then get out on deck and cut away the rigging. You'll need as much help topside as possible. The boom and mast are heavy.'

'Yes, you are right, of course,' Wyman said. 'We'll go out.'

'Is your deck heating system working?'

'No. We're running on emergency power, on the batteries.'

'Then you'll need to go out on deck right now. The spray is probably freezing over your hatches. Within a few moments you'll have solid ice over them and you'll be sealed inside like a tomb.'

After a beat, Wyman said, 'Yes, of course.' He didn't like to be told his business. He handed Gwen the VHF and left.

'Gwen, are you there?' McKay asked.

She pressed the button. 'I'm here, sort of.'

'The most important tool you have now is yourself.' The wavy VHF reception couldn't hide the urgency in his voice. 'If you are not committed to surviving, you won't.'

She replied, 'That wine we'll have together, Jess? When I get off this boat, I'll buy.'

She put the handset into its mount, then followed Wyman from the control room towards the gear lockers.

GWEN TURNED the hatch handle and pulled. The hatch remained stuck in its frame. Wyman stepped up to it with Odell right behind. All three were wearing heavy-weather gear. Wyman braced a foot against the bulkhead next to the hatch, and he and Gwen pulled on it. It opened with the loud crack of ice breaking.

Gwen gathered her hammer and hacksaw and pulled herself through the hatch, Wyman and Odell following her, both carrying tools. Arctic wind cut through Gwen and she was suddenly so cold she looked down at herself, instinctively thinking she may have entirely forgotten to dress. She was wearing five insulated layers. She pushed against the wind towards the cockpit's scuppers, then secured her safety harness. She hammered the ice from a scupper so water in the cockpit could drain, then unhitched her harness to move to the next scupper.

Waves rose on both sides of the boat, sheer inclines of foaming water. A wave closed on the boat like a predator and lifted it with sickening swiftness. Gwen's legs buckled with the upward acceleration and she fell onto the ice-shrouded deck, losing her hammer. She slid towards the edge of the boat, towards the bottomless sea— but caught herself on a safety-rail stanchion, one leg hanging off the edge. She kicked her leg, found purchase, and pushed herself back onto the deck. The hammer was gone.

Gwen could see Wyman and Odell, bent over the fallen mast, cutting the rigging, their harnesses attached to stanchions. She moved in an infantryman's crawl, one handhold to the next, to join them. The boom was missing, torn from the mast as the mast fell. The stays and sheets were now a jumbled mess, strung out all over the hull.

She began running her hacksaw back and forth across a cable. Wyman was bear-hugging the long handles of a bolt cutter, trying to generate enough pressure to sever another cable. Odell worked with a hacksaw. The lower three feet of the mast still rose from the deck, but ended in a twisted metal stub.

Odell was finally successful with his cable, and he crawled over the fallen mast to Gwen's side of the boat. Wyman severed another cable just as the boat was soaring up another wave. He moved along the deck towards Gwen and shouted into her ear, 'One more and it's free. Stand back.'

She unhooked the safety clip and crawled aft. Toby Odell was behind her. When they reached the cockpit, both secured their harnesses to hull bolts. Gwen was shivering violently and clamped her jaw closed to prevent her teeth clattering. Ice covered Odell's hood and mask. She could only see his eyes. They seemed merry.

Just as Rex Wyman came into the cockpit, Odell yelled over the wind, 'Had enough, Rex?'

Wyman stared at him and Gwen turned to look at them.

Odell laughed harshly. 'Want me to swing *Victory*'s boom again or shut off the power or suddenly close the hatch?'

She stepped closer to Odell, trying to catch all his words.

'Want me to crash *Victory*'s main server again?' Odell bellowed.

Wyman's face opened with understanding. He stared at Odell.

'Or have you had enough?' Odell demanded.

Wyman's face re-formed around hostile eyes. 'Ted Landers just told me about the Wayward Souls. I didn't believe it. I told him it couldn't be you.'

Odell laughed again. 'You didn't think I had forgotten Cassandra, did you? Or any of the other crap you pulled?'

Gwen wanted desperately to go below, but the name Cassandra caught her up. It took her a second. Then she recalled Toby Odell's humiliating story of the blind date.

'And I haven't forgotten that you cut me out of your company.' Odell laughed, a fluty hysterical sound. 'And I've forgiven none of it, and—'

Wyman stabbed the bolt cutters at Odell's chest. Odell staggered back, slipped on ice, then collapsed to the deck.

'Rex,' Gwen cried out. 'Don't.'

Wyman raised the bolt cutters, ready to chop down at Odell, but Gwen lunged at him. The boat yawed. Her feet slipped and instead of blocking a blow, she tumbled into Wyman's legs. He planted a foot against her shoulder and roughly pushed her away. She slid across the cockpit. Gagging, Odell tried to rise, but fell back against the rail.

Wyman dropped the bolt cutters, snatched the front of Odell's suit and lifted him towards the top rail. He held him there and shouted over the storm. 'Have I had enough, Toby?'

Gwen called out, but spray lashed into her face and her words were washed away.

Wyman savagely shoved Odell over the rail. Odell spun into the sea. His safety line was still attached to the boat. He was hauled along in his harness like a fish lure, skipping along the wave crests, then completely submerged, then reappearing. Wyman grabbed the shears. Gwen crawled towards him, shouting words she couldn't hear and couldn't understand.

A wave crested across the deck, immersing it in foaming water, toppling Wyman and slapping Gwen against the port rail. Wyman rose unsteadily, wiping an arm across his eyes. He glared down at his ex-partner. Then he placed the bolt-cutter's jaws on Odell's safety line. Odell stared up at Wyman.

'Have I had enough, Toby?' Wyman raged. 'You figure it out.'

Wyman squeezed the bolt cutters and the safety line snapped into two. Odell sped aft, one arm in the air as if waving, and Gwen saw that peculiar expression in his eyes, that same ironic, condescending look he always wore. She desperately reached for the cockpit's life ring to throw to him, but it was iced over and stuck to the boat. Same with the floating EPIRB.

Quickly, Odell became an insignificant dark speck in the tumult all around. Then a comber broke over him and he disappeared.

'Yes, Toby.' Wyman screamed at the sea. 'I've had enough.'

Chapter eight

McKay and Ramirez were strapped into jump seats in the Pave Hawk helicopter. Captain Ross Macklin was at the controls. Lieutenant Joe Junius was the copilot, and Second Lieutenant Lance Urban was the engineer. Also on board were two other PJs. The PJs were in full gear—heavily insulated dry suits, tanks and masks. The copter crew and the PJs were all wearing headsets.

The Pave Hawk helicopter's primary military mission is exfiltration, infiltration and resupply of special tactics forces, and combat search and rescue. This was a peacetime search and rescue, but, looking out the helicopter's windows at the storm below, the crew and the PJs suspected it would be more like wartime, with the elements as the mortal enemy.

The pilot, Ross Macklin, said, 'A thousand feet is usually the best altitude for spotting things on the sea, but I can't get down that low because it'd be in the spray. We can't see a thing from up here, and we won't be able to see a thing down there.'

'Do we have the call yet?' McKay asked.

'I'm still waiting on it. Our destination is something of a guess right now.'

A Hercules search-and-rescue plane was far ahead of the helicopter, zeroing in on *Victory*'s emergency beacon, and would soon try to make visual contact with the sailboat. *Victory*'s EPIRB had led the Hercules to a general area, but spotting a boat in these seas would be chancy. Once the crew had found it, they would circle the boat, monitoring *Victory*'s condition until the helicopter arrived.

The Pave Hawk was flying into headwinds. Ross Macklin strained against his safety belts, leaning forward to peer out of the sleet-blown window. 'I can't see a damned thing,' he said.

Ramirez said, 'How about giving us only the good news, Ross.'

REX WYMAN had been sending *Victory*'s GPS readings over the radio to Lonnie Garvin. *Hornet* was travelling north against the seas. Garvin was at the helm, his eyes straining through the sleety window. His target, *Victory*, was close, maybe within sighting distance, but sleet falling in thick folds obscured everything beyond his boat.

The engines had drawn down the starboard tanks some, and the boat wasn't so imbalanced, but he was still worried. A TV screen on his console showed a closed-circuit view of his engine room. Bang The Drum was below, trying to thaw several feet of pipe, which would allow the transfer of fuel. He was using two space heaters but reported that he might as soon be spitting at the pipes for all the effect he was having. Ollie Nordquist was on the crab deck, scraping off ice—some of it sheets two feet thick—with the deck crane's hydraulically powered arm. Nick Summers was batting away ice built up around the hatches on the superstructure.

The VHF radio crackled into life. 'Garvin, here's our latest position.' It was Rex Wyman's voice, sounding breathless and strained.

Garvin lifted the overhead microphone. 'We're right on you, according to our GPS reading. I can't see you yet, though.'

Wyman radioed, 'I'm ready to go topside to receive a line.'

'Let me find you first,' Garvin replied. Then *Hornet* and *Victory* crested waves at the same moment, and suddenly the huge crippled sailboat was right in front of Garvin. 'Wyman, get out on deck, and go forward to your samson post, and we'll get the line to you.'

Garvin worked his boat upwind, so *Victory* would be in its lee. Then he pulled back the throttles and pressed an intercom button. 'Ollie, you and Nick move aft. Get ready with the line.'

Hornet was now so close that Garvin could see the mess on *Victory*'s deck, the low, jagged stump of the mast, and rigging littering the deck and hanging over the sides. He could see Wyman moving forward on the deck. The billionaire was half crawling, half walking, keeping both hands on the boat. A comber broke over *Victory*'s deck, and for an instant Garvin thought Wyman might have been swept away, but the water receded, and Wyman was still making his way forward.

Ollie Nordquist was carrying a handheld radio, a little Motorola, another item purchased with Wyman's money back in Dutch Harbor. The radio's twin was on the pilothouse console.

Over the radio came Nordquist's voice, 'We're on the aft rail, behind the pots. We're hitched up, but we're plenty wet.'

Garvin acknowledged the message. *Victory* was within a hundred yards. The glittering sailboat had strutted out of San Francisco harbour, and on its way north it had dominated the sea as if sailing were child's play. Now, stripped of its mast and boom, its rigging tangled on the deck, *Victory* looked pitiable.

The crab boat careened down a wave, nearer to the sailboat. As *Hornet* fell, Garvin could feel the breaker drag down the aft end. He knew Ollie and Nick wouldn't be able to last long out there. Garvin needed to corral *Victory* on the first pass.

Lifted by a massive roller, *Victory* suddenly appeared, startlingly close to *Hornet*. The two boats bobbed together, less than fifty yards separating them, the air between them opaque with spray. Then they fell off the same wave, down towards a trough.

In those few seconds of relative calm, Garvin punched *Hornet* into reverse, backing the trawler towards *Victory*. A new wave lifted them both and they rose in harmony. Then down they went again.

'Back farther,' came over the Motorola. Nick Summers's voice. He would be handling the radio while Ollie Nordquist had the coiled end of the line in his hands. 'Give us a dozen feet, skipper.'

Garvin tapped back on the throttles.

'Give us a couple more,' Summers called. 'Almost there.'

Garvin nudged back the throttles. He waited five seconds, ten seconds, the next wave rising off his starboard side.

'He's got our line,' yelled Summers. 'He's bent down now, tying it to his samson post.'

'Tell him to hurry the hell up,' Garvin said to himself.

For those moments, *Hornet* was broached to the incoming sea, a hazardous position Garvin would never otherwise put his boat into. And he was in an unbalanced boat. The trawler rolled to starboard, to the side where his fuel lay, but lumbering and hesitating and lifted by the next wave, *Hornet* slowly righted itself. Garvin breathed in through his teeth. God, he hated being afraid out here, because that meant he had committed a grave error. He didn't believe in bad luck, not out on the water. A sailor who says he had bad luck is confessing that he wasn't prepared or didn't have skill.

'Lonnie, we've got it secured.' This time it was Ollie Nordquist hollering into the radio. 'We're coming back in.'

Garvin slowly pushed the throttles forward and spun the wheel. The trawler turned towards the next wave, riding up its front side, then cresting the wave and sliding down the back side. The line connecting the two boats sank into the wave and grew taut. At that same instant, a cross wave lunged at *Victory*, staggering the sailboat.

Victory's hull and its samson post had been engineered to rigorous standards. But not to Bering Sea standards, not to force 12 wind and sea standards. The trawler had been so engineered, and so had the cable connecting the two vessels, so if anything were to give way, it must be the sailboat.

When *Hornet* sped down the wave, and when, at the same time, the cross wave smacked against *Victory*'s hull, the sailboat's prow—the front four feet of the hull—was wrenched from the boat. Suddenly, where there had been sparkling chrome and lovely lines there were now twisted metal shanks and ragged fibreglass splinters framing a gaping hole.

Victory was open to the sea.

GWEN WELD was in *Victory*'s salon, clinging to the table. She had thought that the storm's noise was as loud as anything could be, that nothing in the universe could be louder.

Except this. Her head snapped towards the new sound, a grinding tear coming from the bow. A geyser of water shot through the forward companionway. Gwen had no time to react as it soared into the salon. A scythe of water cut her legs from under her and swept her aft. The water released her as the boat rolled, and she found herself beached near the table. But water continued to gush through the forward hatch with the force of a broken main.

Gwen could now tell the bow of the boat was lower in the water. Lying there shivering violently, she knew *Victory* was sinking.

The boat rolled, and the chilled water—only four degrees Fahrenheit from ice—swamped her again. Now there was two feet of water in the salon. Gwen crawled like an amphibian downhill to the hatch separating the berths, sail lockers and tool room from the salon. As the boat pitched forward on a cross wave, she willed her hands to work and she cranked the hatch wheel.

The steel hatch moved slowly. Gwen repositioned herself so she could put her back into the work, a new swell of water lifting her off the deck. She was floating *inside* a boat. The idea troubled her, but only vaguely. Her mind was incapable of anything more.

Except knowing she had to yank. This much she understood. She savagely pulled on the hatch wheel again and again. The hatch slid, pinching the incoming stream. She heaved again and the edge of the door slid into the frame, choking off the sea water.

She climbed unsteadily up the deck looking for somewhere dry. The water inside the boat sloshed back and forth, carrying cushions and clothing and wood spoons and paper and bottles.

A rush of cold air whipped into her. She looked up towards the cockpit hatch that had just opened and closed. Rex Wyman stood in the companionway, water pouring off his heavy weather gear.

Gwen was now inside the boat with all that frigid and tossing sea water, and with a murderer.

Hornet HAD UNDERGONE a stability test shortly after it was launched. This test set the boat's baseline stability, showing how far the trawler could heel over and then right itself. At the end of the testing, the naval engineer issued a stability letter, which set forth the best manner to trim *Hornet*—to balance the boat—in various weather conditions, including storms where ice built up on the deck and superstructure. *Hornet*'s danger point was a generous forty degrees.

Lonnie Garvin knew more about trimming his own boat than any naval architect ever would. Still, all his hard-won knowledge and all his skipper's instincts were suddenly for naught when Ollie Nordquist opened the hatch to the cockpit and yelled over the bellow of the storm, 'Lonnie, the deck's not clearing!'

Garvin looked at his work-deck monitor. The deck between the crab-pot stack and the superstructure was underwater.

And only then was Garvin struck—fully struck—with the foolishness of his mission to rescue *Victory* and to save his own boat and crabbing career with Rex Wyman's money. The boat was so low in the sea that water wasn't draining off the work deck. It meant that *Hornet* was being claimed by the sea.

He shouted, 'Can you get any ice off the deck, Ollie?'

'The boat is making ice faster than we can get rid of it.'

Summers pushed into the wheelhouse. Water slid off his coat.

Garvin said, 'All, right, let's . . .'

He didn't have time to complete the sentence. A three-storey breaking wave caught *Hornet*, and tons of water hammered the trawler's deck. The crab pots—secure in any other sea on any other day—broke their chains. The torrent of water swept the tarp-wrapped stack to the starboard rail as easily as if the stack were on rollers.

Already out of trim to starboard due to an imbalanced fuel load, and already low in the water under the weight of ice, *Hornet* now listed mortally. The boat's maximum righting angle—the angle at which it could roll and then recover—had been surpassed. Heeled to leeward, the crab pots against the starboard rail, *Hornet* was doomed.

And Garvin knew it immediately. Still hanging on to the wheel, as if it could do anything now, he shouted, 'Get into survival suits.'

Nick Summers said, 'But don't you think . . .'

'Do as I tell you, Nick. We're going into the water.'

Garvin grabbed his VHF handset, then reached up to switch to the emergency channel.

'Mayday,' Garvin said into the microphone. 'Mayday. This is the crab trawler *Hornet*. Do you read me? Mayday.'

A voice returned on the radio immediately. 'This is the United States Coast Guard Com-Sta Kodiak. We read you, *Hornet*. Give me your coordinates.'

Garvin looked at his GPS. 'Latitude fifty-six degrees thirty-two minutes north, longitude one hundred sixty-seven degrees twenty-two minutes west.'

After a moment, the Guardsman asked, 'Is this the *Victory*?'

'No, hell no. It's *Hornet*, a crab trawler.'

'The Air Force National Guard has an operation going right in your area—right now. What are you doing out there?'

'I'm losing my boat, is what I'm doing,' Garvin shouted. 'Can we get to business?'

'Describe *Hornet*.'

'A hundred feet long. Superstructure forward. The superstructure is white. Large crab deck aft. Large pot crane on the deck.'

From the radio came, 'What colour is the bottom of the hull?'

A moment passed before Garvin understood what the dreadful question implied. Then he said, 'It's blue.' He added weakly, 'Royal blue.' God, he loved that colour and he loved this boat.

'I'll pass it on to the search and rescue team. Are you in survival suits?'

Garvin barked, 'I don't need to be walked through abandoning a boat, Admiral. I know damn well what to do.' He was about to throw the handset down—he would never need it or ever see it again, same with the rest of his boat—but Garvin was polite to his soul, always had been, and so he put the handset back to his mouth. 'Sorry, Coast Guard. I'm under a bit of stress out here.'

'I fully understand, *Hornet*. Rescuers are on the way.'

With *Hornet* lower in the water and leaning more and more, its superstructure was now more exposed to the breaking waves. An enormous tumbling breaker smashed the wheelhouse and punched out a so-called storm-proof window. The water shot through the opening and churned the contents of the wheelhouse—human and equipment—as if in a mixer. Garvin pushed himself to his feet. He yelled, 'Get into your suits! Now! Do it!'

The water drained away. Garvin tore open the long vinyl bag and pulled out the suit. He glanced around at this beloved place. His electronics were scattered about the wet deck. Charts were everywhere, some rolled in tubes, some loose. Radios hung from the ceiling, swaying back and forth on wires. Each time *Hornet* listed, it didn't quite make it as far upright as the prior time.

A survival suit is donned by lying on the deck. Garvin and his crew wiggled into their suits. The suits were orange, and whistles hung from the front. Along sleeves and across chests were strips of reflective tapes. Boots, gloves and hoods were built into the suit.

Ollie Nordquist said, 'You owe me a beer when we get back to port, Lonnie.'

In his survival suit, Garvin crawled across the deck to Nick Summers, checking the kid's suit. 'All right. Let's go.'

Then the numbers hit Lonnie Garvin. There were only three people in the pilothouse.

'Where's Bang The?' he yelled. 'Ah, hell.' He grabbed Nick

Summers by the shoulders and turned him towards the hatch. 'You two get out on deck and throw the life raft canister overboard, but make sure it's secured to the hull first. Then into the water you go. Bang The and I'll be there in a minute.'

Garvin waited until Summers had opened the hatch and stepped out onto the heaving gangway. Then he shouted into Nordquist's ear. 'There's a knife in the life raft. If the boat goes down before I'm there, make damned sure to cut that line between the raft and the boat.'

Nordquist nodded, the movement almost lost in the bulk of his survival suit.

'But don't cut the raft's sea anchor line by mistake.'

Nordquist looked morosely at his skipper. 'I hadn't thought about that, but I will.' Then he went through the hatch.

Hornet lurched to starboard a few more degrees. Garvin scrambled down the companionway towards the galley and crew quarters. An ominous draught rose from below. Air was being displaced below decks. He glanced into the galley, then stepped down into the engine room. 'Bang The, you there?' he called.

The boat answered, not Bang The Drum, and did so by dousing the lights. Garvin was now in a black catacomb. The companionway steps no longer went straight down, they travelled at an angle as the boat leaned. Garvin gripped the rail with both hands and felt his way sideways down towards the engine room. The bulky survival suit made him clumsy, and the thick gloves made it hard to feel his way along. When the boat listed a few more degrees, *Hornet* groaned—a fearsome, throaty sound—as weight was shifted throughout the boat and welds and metal plates were tested.

'Bang The, where are you?' Garvin shouted.

The skipper could see nothing in front of him, only black on black. The air coming at him smelt of fish and fuel and bilge. He manoeuvred lower on the steps, then came to flowing water. He jumped down into it, onto the sloping engine-room deck. He could see nothing, but the sound of water coming into the engine room told him all he needed to know: *Hornet* had four or five minutes left on the surface. Sea water was up to his chest and rising. He pushed forward into the room.

'Drum, you here?'

Garvin moved his arms back and forth, groping in the black water. The boat's moan increased in pitch. Waves against the hull created a steady roar.

'Ah, hell. Drum, where are you?'

In the blackness, Bang The Drum floated into Garvin, startling him. Drum was floating face-up, his feet dragging on the deck below.

With one hand, Garvin felt his way forward, and with the other hand he pulled Drum towards the companionway. He tried dragging Drum up the steps towards the galley, but didn't have the strength.

'Come on, damn you.' Then the skipper added, 'I'm afraid for both of us, Bang The. Really afraid. We've got to get out of here.'

Garvin gulped a lungful of air, then ducked under the water, going down to his knees. He floated Drum across his shoulders. Then the skipper stood up, his legs shaking inside the survival suit. He climbed up, one step after another, out of the water to the tilted galley deck.

'You'd better be alive after all this, Bang The,' he said.

Carrying Drum like a stevedore, Garvin negotiated more steps, up towards the pilothouse, and the boat was now heeled over so much that he had to lean against the partition and slide on his shoulder and hip, slipping Drum along with him. In the pilothouse Garvin tried to slide Drum off his shoulders, but they both fell to the steep deck. Drum's forehead was bloody. A two-inch gash was still spilling blood. Garvin pulled out another survival suit and started cramming Drum into it.

When Drum groaned, Garvin said, 'At least you're alive.'

Garvin zipped up Drum's suit, then tightened the fittings around his wrists and face. The trawler lurched and Drum began sliding along the inclined deck. The skipper grabbed Drum's survival suit at the shoulders and slid him towards the hatch. Garvin yanked open the hatch. *Hornet* was sinking stern first. Only the superstructure and the forward hull were now above water. The skipper couldn't see the life raft. He was in a canyon of water, water in every direction except straight up.

He didn't have time for one last look at *Hornet*. Didn't have time for a goodbye. His trawler was sinking beneath his feet.

Garvin balanced Drum on the rail, sat on the rail himself, then dragged Drum over the side. They fell into the bounding sea.

GWEN PRESSED HERSELF against the bulkhead in *Victory*'s control room, staring at Wyman, deathly afraid of him, wanting away from him. But the boat's stern was almost out of the sea, lifted by the waterlogged front end. The control room was the only place still habitable.

So she was finally alone with Wyman, and had his complete attention, something she had fervently desired for months, and had she the strength, she might have thought it funny.

'It was Toby all along,' he said. 'Toby did it all, one thing after another to ruin me. I never saw it coming.'

Wyman was in her chair, talking to a black monitor screen, not to her. His elbows were on the table and his head was in his hands. He might have been weeping, she couldn't tell. She had just seen her boyfriend—a man she had been subtly inveigling to make a commitment to her—kill someone, just out and out murder Toby Odell.

The past few days had physically transformed Rex Wyman. His boyish good looks and his gloss of urbanity had been stripped away from him and replaced with axe-hewn features. His cheekbones were newly blunt and his jaw bonier. He had not been able to shave, or to eat much, and his cheeks were sunken and shadowed.

He glared at her and shouted over the rush of the storm. 'Toby was the first of the hackers, did you know that? He might have invented hacking. He started that crap back when we were in college.'

'Rex, listen to me. We are being locked down here. We have to go topside. We can talk about this later.'

He might not have heard her. 'One of Toby's new businesses was called the Wayward Souls, I just found out from Ted Landers. A bunch of twenty-year-old hackers. At Toby's direction, much of what they did was aimed at WorldQuest and at *Victory* and at me. Toby spent millions and millions of dollars on his sabotage.'

Wyman tugged hard at one of his ears, an odd, muscular motion, as if he were trying to pull apart his face. 'Landers caught one of Odell's hackers, a kid named Brady Lane, who had been bragging online about his hacking accomplishments. Ted Landers questioned him and within a few hours Lane was telling everything.'

She looked over his shoulder, measuring an escape. It was hopeless. In the tiny control room, he entirely blocked the way to the hatch. He looked demented, his hair matted and tangled and his eyes glowing as if from within.

'Toby controlled it all, from the timing of the boom's swing that vaulted Chapman off the boat, to the power outage, and *Victory*'s ignorance of the incoming storm.'

The boat rocked and Wyman slammed into the table. He didn't seem to care.

'And the downward pressure on WorldQuest stock, that was

mostly Toby.' Wyman's hands went to his head and he pressed his temples with his fingers. 'Over the years Toby had sold much of his WorldQuest stock to dummy corporations, all controlled by him. Toby directed a massive sell-off of WorldQuest stock over the past year, so it lost almost ninety per cent of its value, all Toby's work.'

She closed her eyes.

He said, 'And some other stuff, like ruining my investment in a building in Malaysia. And a Caucasus pipeline investment. He made me lose that, too. Toby cost me billions and billions of dollars.'

Wyman abruptly seemed reasonable. 'He was the code guy and I was the business guy. After WorldQuest got going, I could hire a hundred, a thousand code guys. I forced him out and he kicked and screamed the entire time. But we kept it quiet, because a rancorous breakup always turns a stock down.'

Wyman lifted the radio and called *Hornet* again. There was no answer. He threw down the handset. His face screwed up and he shook his head. 'But Toby and I patched it up. We became friends again after a couple of years. Now I know it was just a ruse on his part. He was just lying in wait, setting his traps.'

Gwen pushed herself upright, her stance wide against the roll of the boat. She was going to try to get out of the boat.

Wyman said, 'I've got to admire the guy, really. He set out to ruin me and he has.'

Then he turned to her and saw that she was trying to get past him. He lifted himself out of the chair and viciously shoved her against the bulkhead. The back of her head hit it and she slid down to the deck.

'Don't worry about it, Gwen.' He returned to his chair without offering her a glance. 'I'll figure it out. I always do.'

LONNIE GARVIN KICKED his legs, trying to swim away from *Hornet*, which had rolled onto its side. A comber burst over the hull, rolling the boat more, and it slid lower in the water. Garvin churned the water with one hand and kicked his legs, tugging Drum along. The waves kept trying to pull Drum away from him, but Garvin held him close. The sea had outsmarted him at every turn, but it wasn't going to do this one last thing, to drown Ben Drum without Garvin having a say in it.

The trawler slid further under, and now the pilothouse was no longer visible. Only the stem remained, that lovely prow that had anchored Garvin's view of the sea when he was in the pilothouse gazing out of the windows. Then it, too, went down, slipping below the surface, until the boat disappeared. Garvin stared at the sea where *Hornet* had been, thinking that the unfettered wave that rushed over the spot was a poor memorial for his beloved trawler.

'I'm right here in the sea, aren't I?' Bang The Drum said, his first words since Garvin had carried him out of the engine room.

'We're in a fix, Bang The.'

'That you, Lonnie?' Drum tried to turn his head to look over his shoulder. Sea water had washed blood from the gash in Drum's head, which had been cut to the bone.

Garvin said, 'You've got a bad cut on your forehead, Bang The.'

'I can't feel it.' Drum spit saltwater from his mouth. 'I suppose we're going to die out here, Lonnie. Is that what's happening?'

'Maybe,' Garvin replied into his ear. 'But you and I'll take a lot of killing, and we're still breathing. That's the main thing. If we can keep breathing, we won't die.'

'You always made a lot of sense,' Drum said. 'That's why I've always favoured crewing for you.' Drum brought a hand out of the water. 'What's that?'

Garvin couldn't see anything but spray and a glimpse of wave behind it. 'It's nothing, Bang The.'

'I thought I saw something.'

A mammoth wave lifted Garvin and Drum, and they soared towards the black clouds overhead. Garvin peered into the blind white of the spray.

'There it is again,' Drum said.

Garvin wiped his face with a hand. Then he might have seen a flash of orange, a slight smudge in the white spray.

'It's the life raft,' Garvin hollered jubilantly.

Garvin searched under the water for the whistle, fumbling in his thick gloves. He brought it up to his mouth and blew. The shrill note was swallowed by the peal of the storm.

The raft was gone. Then water swallowed Garvin and Drum, a vast tumult of churning green and white foam. When they emerged from the surf, the raft was right in front of them, thirty or forty yards away. Ollie Nordquist was leaning over the inflatable tube at the hatch, using a paddle, trying to get closer, paddling furiously.

Nordquist passed the paddle to Nick Summers, whose head came into view in the hatch. Summers worked the water with strong strokes, Nordquist holding his legs from behind.

Garvin could make out Summers's face now, the eyes above the flap. The kid was usually eager but a bit vacant. Garvin had never seen such fierce determination on the boy's face as he fiercely dug the sea with his paddle. Nordquist was behind Summers. Garvin could see the grin on Nordquist's face.

Then the raft was close enough for Summers to extend his paddle. Garvin gripped it and was pulled to the tube. Nordquist and Summers grabbed Drum and hauled him up and through the hatch. Then they pulled Garvin up and in. Nordquist sealed the flap over the hatch. Nick Summers collapsed, breathing in huge gulps. Everybody was grinning, even Drum, though his smile looked slightly addled.

Garvin roughly patted Nick Summers on the shoulder. 'See what you would've missed, had you stayed in college this quarter?'

'WE'RE AT THREE THOUSAND feet,' Ross Macklin said over the intercom. 'Looks like snow down there.'

McKay leaned forward to peer out of the hatch. The surface of the Bering Sea was hidden by a layer of wind-driven spray.

'The boat is below us somewhere,' Macklin said. 'The Hercules can't get a better fix on it . . . Hey, I've got a signal.'

The PJs in the helicopter's bay had been listening to Macklin and the copilot communicate with the Hercules high above them and with the Kodiak Coast Guard station. Macklin was putting the radio feed through the intercom. The chatter helped keep McKay's mind off the rough ride. McKay hadn't heard the new signal. He pressed his ear cup more tightly against his head. He heard only static.

'It's scratchy,' Macklin said. 'I'm going to cut out the squelch.'

The static abruptly faded and McKay heard Gwen Weld's voice, 'Mayday. This is the sailing boat *Victory*.'

Macklin said, '*Victory*, we are somewhere overhead, but we can't make you out on the surface. Do you copy me?'

'Yes, I can hear you. We're sinking. I've been injured. I can't . . .'

Macklin said, 'I'm going to use a radio direction finder on the copter. I want you to count to ten twice and keep your radio button pressed down. You copy?'

'Yes. I can do that.' She began a count.

To all sides of the helicopter, the horizon was close, and was a narrow strip of ochre green and sulphurous yellow, a menacing haze.

Above were the smudged black clouds, so low they appeared to touch the helicopter's rotor.

'Keep counting, *Victory*,' Macklin ordered.

McKay could hear Gwen Weld count. He looked out of the window again. She was somewhere below, maybe within a mile or two.

'The needle just jumped through one-eighty,' the copilot said. '*Victory* is right below us.'

'Mark the coordinates,' replied the pilot. 'Get a floating EPIRB ready. I'm taking it down slowly, real slowly. You PJs get ready.'

Macklin was grappling with the controls, and the wind was tossing the Pave Hawk in all directions. 'My altimeter is jinking around because of the waves,' the pilot said. 'Get the door open. I need visuals from you guys back there.'

McKay braced himself next to the door, then attached a safety harness to a bolt. He and Ramirez slid open the door. The blast of frigid air was like a body blow. McKay was enclosed in a heavily insulated state-of-the-art immersion suit, as warm as a human body can be in such conditions, and still he was cold.

'I've just turned on the midnight sun,' Macklin said. This was a powerful spotlight. 'That help?'

McKay said into the helmet intercom, 'It just turns the foam yellow. I can't see a thing. Get lower.'

'Yeah, I'll get lower,' Macklin said, 'but you know what happens when rotors hit water.'

The main rotor was spinning at 8,000 rotations per minute. If the blades bit into a wave, they would shatter like icicles.

Secured by his safety line, Ramirez readied the hydraulic winch alongside the copter's door, securing a basket to it. Frozen spray whipped into the cabin. The copter bucked in the violent wind.

'Wave crests visible now,' Ramirez called into the intercom. Then he added, 'Jess, will you look at that? We'll be earning our pay cheques in a few minutes.'

Across that patch of sea visible to the PJs rolled white-topped parapets of waves, the troughs far below the crests.

McKay worked with the belaying line. The two other PJs would remain in the copter in reserve, and would be handling the lines and winch. They gathered at the hatch, fastening their safety lines.

'You see the boat?' Macklin called.

'No, nothing but water.'

'There it is,' called the flight engineer.

After a moment, *Victory* came into view below McKay.

'That's it?' Ramirez asked. 'Looks like an iceberg.'

Victory was not recognisable as a boat. The aft half of the vessel was above water, inclined so that the stern was six or eight feet into the air. Ice completely covered the vessel above water. The cockpit and features on the deck were visible only in a vague white outline.

Ramirez said, 'The cockpit hatch is sealed shut, Jess. You got a heavier tool? Your knife isn't going to pack it.'

One of the PJs passed McKay a ball-pein hammer from the copter's tool kit. McKay fit it into his harness.

The Pave Hawk was capable of allowing four PJs to lower themselves by ropes at the same time, but here only one would descend first. Macklin didn't want four of them dangling under the copter, perhaps smashing into each other in the wind.

McKay set his belay, and Ramirez double-checked it. Then McKay stepped off the ledge, and down into the storm he went.

GWEN WELD PUSHED herself off the deck. The back of her head pulsed with pain. The control room rolled under her feet, but the boat wasn't swaying as it had been. The storm still pummelled the boat, yet *Victory* was lethargic, no longer responding fully to the punishing waves. The vessel was low in the water, its bow submerged.

Rex Wyman was still in her chair, his fingers on a useless keyboard. He stared at a monitor's black screen, studying his dark reflection. He shook his head several times, a quick movement, like a tic. He was blinking repeatedly.

Gwen was unsteady on her feet, and was bruised from Rex ramming her into the bulkhead. She took a step towards him, towards the hatch out to the lockers.

'We'll be OK,' he said tonelessly. 'The watertight hatches are closed. We aren't taking on any more water. We'll float.'

'I'm getting out,' she said dully. 'We're being iced in.'

He started to rise from his chair, started to hold up a hand to stop her again. But she was faster. She lifted a keyboard from the table and used it to hit him, a solid blow to the side of his head. He slid back down into the chair and leaned forward, groaning.

She squeezed by the chair, then moved out of the control room to the aft hatch. It was closed, and she knew the forward hatch was also closed. From a locker she pulled out a bag containing a survival suit. She had never put one on. She rolled it out and instinctively knew that she had get down on the deck to put it on. She sat down, putting her feet into the suit. She struggled with it, tugging and pulling, wiggling into it.

She forced herself to concentrate. She wanted to lie back on the deck and take a nap, maybe for ever. And she knew, from somewhere in a far corner of her mind, that she had to fight sleep, fight the overwhelming urge to simply lie down and close her eyes.

She glanced aft, watching for Wyman. She fitted her hands into the gloves, then zipped up all round. She stood up, the deck moving under her. The survival suit was bulky. She shuffled aft to the hatch out to the cockpit. The narrow corridor was dimly lit by backup batteries.

'Gwen, we're OK,' came from behind her.

Wyman was on his feet, staggering against a locker, his hand at his temple. He bent over as if trying to catch his breath.

'We're floating.' His words were more a groan. 'We'll be OK.'

But they weren't OK. Dead and in a watery grave, Toby Odell was not done with his ex-partner. At that moment, another bit of deadly mischief was under way.

Gwen heard a mechanical sound, a low grinding. She looked forward beyond Wyman to the watertight hatch. It was opening slowly. Several feet of sea water were in the salon behind the hatch. And further forward, the first watertight hatch was also opening. The emergency electrical system was powering the doors as they opened, another bit of brilliance from the Wayward Souls.

Wyman gazed stupidly at the hatches, his hand still pressed onto his head. Sea water was bubbling through the forward hatch, beginning to fill the salon.

Gwen turned to the cockpit hatch, the only way out of *Victory* now. She worked the handle, then yanked on it. The hatch was sealed shut with built-up ice.

Gwen looked at Wyman, then at the hatch again. She and the billionaire were sealed inside *Victory*, and the boat, a hole in its prow, was settling lower and lower into the sea.

IN THE SPRAY-FILLED AIR, McKay couldn't see the surface of the water until he was almost into it. Ice particles pummelled him at buckshot velocity. He belayed down, the Pave Hawk keeping him fifty yards from *Victory*. He wanted to board *Victory* on his own terms, not the Bering Sea's terms, a comber slamming him into the hull.

He spoke into his helmet microphone. 'I'm twenty feet above the wave crests. Get me closer to the boat, Ross.'

McKay swung side to side as the wind played with him. Below, *Victory* resembled a shelf of ice, something broken off an iceberg, a growler, fishermen call them.

'Get closer, Ross. I can't see the cockpit hatch. It's under ice.'

With the seas heaving and falling, McKay didn't want to drop directly onto the boat. He was aiming for the water alongside *Victory*. Nor did he want to hit the water too far from the boat, because large objects drift at a greater speed then small ones. *Victory* might move away from him.

McKay lowered himself several more feet, until breaking waves were ten feet or so under him. A scuba regulator was hanging in front of his mouth. The wind was so strong that he had to position his diving fins so they would catch less air and pull him out of line.

McKay stared at the water, timing his release. *Victory* was no longer riding the waves, but was anchored by its own weight, no longer lively in the sea. He turned his head to grab the regulator mouthpiece in his jaw. Then the boat was directly under him, and then he swung away from it, and then he released the belay and the fast rope and fell into the water.

When McKay surfaced, *Victory* was thirty yards away. He kicked towards it. He was above the boat, then he was below it. *Victory* was a moving target.

A comber punched him forward, and then on the next wave he skidded down some of the incline, and then he could touch *Victory*'s hull. He swam forward, and came to the point where *Victory*'s deck entered the water. He glanced overhead at the Pave Hawk. A flickering window in the spray allowed him to see Sandy Ramirez push himself out of the helicopter.

McKay kicked his legs, swimming onto the sailboat's deck. Then he scrambled up towards the stern, his feet slipping and his hands unable to find a hold that wasn't ice. He kept low, almost a crawl, and he came to the cockpit. Then he pulled the hammer from his belt. He could see the outlines of the hatch in the ice.

He hammered frantically, chipping away at the sheet of ice covering the entryway. He looked forward. The sea was almost to the cockpit. Then he hammered angrily, ice slivers flying. He spat out his mouthpiece so he could draw more air, which was raw in his throat. His arm burning, McKay cried out in frustration, maybe Gwen's name, maybe just a primitive call. He hammered and he hammered more, and his arms were weakening.

Sandy Ramirez appeared next to McKay. He was carrying a tool, not a crowbar but something similar, with a flange at one end.

Ramirez motioned McKay to one side and then he lit into the ice with the bar. Shards of it flew away. Quickly some of the hatch was exposed, then more. Now the hatch handle was above the ice. McKay turned it, then kicked it savagely.

The hatch cover flew open, falling inwards. Gwen was just inside the hatch, only her wide eyes visible under the survival suit. McKay reached down for her, but a wave shot across the cockpit, dumping water down through the hatch, and blowing her back into the boat.

Ramirez screamed above the storm, 'Jess, don't you go into that boat, damn you.'

Ramirez moved to block his partner, but he was big and McKay was quick. McKay fell through the opening into the boat.

Under the water, inside a boat in the rocking sea, McKay was disorientated, unable to tell which way was to the surface. He kicked once, guessing, but then a hand grabbed his arm, pulling him up. He came to the surface next to Gwen. The boat's interior was dark. He shoved his mouthpiece back in.

Above him, Ramirez leaned through the hatch. Something bumped McKay. He turned his head to see Rex Wyman next to him. Four feet of air space remained below deck.

His face twisted with horror, Wyman kicked the water and reached for Ramirez's hand. Ramirez slapped it aside, grabbed the woman and lifted her up through the hatch.

Water poured through the opening, now steadily, not a wave but rather the mass of the sea.

'Get ready,' McKay shouted at Wyman.

McKay positioned Wyman, trying to hoist him up, but McKay's legs couldn't find anything to brace himself on. More water came through the hatch, a steady and increasing stream.

Back down came Ramirez's arm. Wyman reached for it.

Ramirez swatted aside Wyman's arm and grabbed Jess McKay by his survival suit's hood. Ramirez dug his fingers into a space between McKay's hair and the fabric. He yanked mightily, lifting McKay. Then when McKay's head was out of the cockpit, Ramirez hooked McKay's arm and pulled him up and through.

Wyman's arm appeared in the hatchway. He might have been

screaming, but the sound was overwhelmed by the storm. White water poured into the hatch, sending him back down into the boat.

Ramirez threw McKay out of the cockpit into the Bering Sea, seized Gwen Weld by an arm, then stepped over the rail and walked into the sea, dragging her behind him. *Victory*'s stern disappeared beneath the surface and the boat was gone.

 *Epilogue*

Jess McKay sat awkwardly on the chair, not knowing what to do with his legs, which he crossed and uncrossed, or with his eyes, which watched her for a while, until she opened her eyes to watch him, and then he would look away.

Behind her bed was a headwall with outlets for oxygen, nitrous oxide and medical air. A blood-pressure gauge was on the wall, and an IV stand and bag were near her shoulder, the tube running to her right arm. A tray of untouched food was on a rolling table, as were a bottle of wine and two glasses McKay had sneaked in. The room at Alaska Regional Hospital had a big plate-glass window looking out onto DeBarr Road in Anchorage.

'This isn't where I was hoping to have our glass of wine together,' Gwen said.

'How long have you slept?' McKay asked.

'Twelve hours, and I'm still tired.' She continued to stare at him. 'You look better without the helmet and goggles and face mask you were wearing in the photo you emailed me. You're a blond, Jess.' She grinned at him.

'I was blonder when I was a kid.' What a moronic thing to say.

'And you are real.' She reached out with her hand and touched his ear, then moved her fingers along his jaw, hesitating, letting her hand rest on his cheek a moment. 'So many times when we were emailing each other, I had the idea that you didn't exist, that my email conversations with you were generated by the boat somehow, to trick me. But you are really you.' She let her hand fall away.

McKay pulled a corkscrew from his pocket and clumsily fitted it to the bottle's cork. 'Most things I drink have pop-tops.' McKay turned the corkscrew, then said quietly, 'You are staring at me.'

'Yes.'

He cleared his throat. 'I'll pour you some wine.'

McKay half filled a glass, then passed it to her. His own glass was to his mouth before he realised she was waiting for a toast. He smiled, then clinked her glass.

'Here's to dry land,' he said, raising his glass.

She still stared at him, and then she smiled, and to Jess it was a knowing smile, but he didn't know what she was knowing. She raised her head and wet her lips with the wine. On the pillow her black hair framed her face. Her right forearm was bruised from one of her rolls across the boat's deck, one of many contusions, but other than those she was all right, the doctor had told McKay.

Gwen said, 'Are your eyes blue or grey or green? I can't tell.'

'It says green on my driver's licence, but it depends on the light.'

'Smells like a hospital in here.' He wondered what she was doing, inventorying him.

Sandy Ramirez walked into the room. He was grinning, and he went over to the bed to plant a kiss on Gwen Weld's forehead. 'I'm the other guy, behind the other set of goggles,' he said.

McKay introduced Ramirez, who found a chair and spun it round so he could lean forward on the seat back.

'Good news regarding *Hornet*'s crew,' Ramirez said. 'Another team picked them up. They've all been checked out and they're fine.'

'Why was *Hornet* out there?' McKay asked. 'You'd think a crab skipper would know better.'

'Money. I spoke with *Hornet*'s skipper, Lonnie Garvin. Wyman offered Garvin half a million dollars to attempt the rescue of *Victory*, and another half a million if Garvin were successful.'

McKay asked, 'How is Garvin going to get his money for the rescue attempt, now that Rex Wyman is dead?'

'Wyman paid up front. Garvin had half a million in his bank before he left Dutch Harbor. And *Hornet* had an all-risk policy on it, so Garvin will be reimbursed the cost of his boat. He doesn't know whether to kick himself for risking himself and his crew, or to celebrate because he's got no financial worries.'

'I'd mostly celebrate surviving, if I were him,' Gwen said. 'Same thing I'm celebrating, lying here in a hospital bed.'

Ramirez asked, 'So what are you two planning?'

McKay felt the blood rise in his face. 'We are planning to drink these glasses of wine. Why don't you join us?'

'You two aren't planning anything?' Ramirez asked, pouring wine into a hospital glass.

McKay said, 'Gwen has a flight back south to Boise. If time allows, we're going to have dinner somewhere before she goes. You aren't invited.'

'I just thought of something.' Gwen's voice was soft. 'Except for the last few days aboard *Victory*, this is the first time in six years that I haven't looked at WorldQuest's stock price every thirty minutes, to see how the company was doing. It's wonderful lying here, not thinking about that.'

'It's up nine dollars today,' McKay said, then frowned at himself for bringing it up.

Ramirez laughed. 'You are ruining this nice romantic hospital mood, Jess.'

McKay glanced at Gwen. 'Yesterday Microsoft offered to purchase two of WorldQuest's four divisions. Big news all around the world. WorldQuest's board will probably accept the deal, the analysts say. The other divisions will be folded.'

Ramirez threw back the wine and then placed his glass on the table. He lifted himself from the chair. 'I'm due at the gym.' Ramirez blew Gwen a kiss.

He left them alone in the hospital room. When Jess looked again at Gwen, her eyes were half closed. 'I'm still tired, Jess.'

He nodded, holding his wine.

Her eyes opened, and again they gazed at him. Her eyes were intense and candid, and bright with emotion and very blue. He looked away, and when he could look back, those eyes were still on him. She reached for his hand and brought it to her side, and she held it. Her eyes closed again.

They held hands, and just before sleep she said, 'I don't have a flight back south, Jess.'

JAMES THAYER

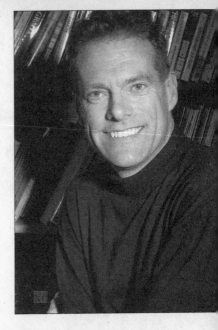

Reading *Force 12*, one imagines that James Thayer must be a hands-on sailor with experience of the terror of being on very rough seas. 'I've sailed,' he once told an interviewer, 'but sailing is one of those things that I like reading about more than I like doing. My home is my office, I have a beautiful view of Puget Sound, and I see sailing all the time. I'm just not sure I want to do it.'

To help him capture the full sense of what it's like to fight for survival in fifty-foot waves and gale-force winds, Thayer read Sebastian Junger's *The Perfect Storm*, plus numerous books, magazines and a wealth of on-line information about nautical matters. He also researched the computer technology at the heart of his story.

Next on the list were crab-fishing—for a crab fisherman is key to the plot of *Force 12*—and air-sea rescue, because one of the heroes in the story is a PJ, a pararescue jumper. The US Air Force's pararescue jumpers, Thayer learned, are a truly elite team only a few hundred strong, whose chief function is to rescue downed pilots from behind enemy lines. But they are trained to carry out rescue operations anywhere in any conditions—from mountaintop rescues to operating in a hurricane at sea.

Last but not least, to round off his plot Thayer drew on his experience of maritime law. He was a practising lawyer in Seattle for years before he became a full-time writer, and handled many legal cases involving Alaskan commercial fishermen who, like his character Lonnie Garvin in *Force 12*, are 'tough, smart, brave people who have the most dangerous job on earth'.

Thayer is at work on his twelfth novel, which will be about an architect's attempt to build the world's largest building in Hong Kong harbour. Sounds like more research is on the cards? 'Hey,' Thayer responds. 'I like to learn something new.'

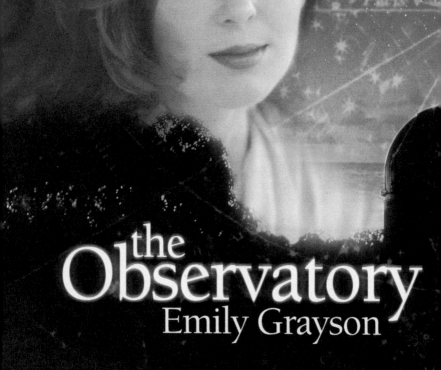

the Observatory

Emily Grayson

Harper and Liz are twins, but they have always been as different as fire and ice. While a glittering marriage and an artistic career long ago beckoned Harper away from her home town, Liz continues to work there as a librarian. Seemingly destined to live in the shadow of her beautiful, talented sister, she has resigned herself to a life alone.

Now, in a time of grief, comes a chance for the sisters to be reconciled . . . a chance for Liz to find happiness. But will the future be eclipsed by the past?

Chapter One

Even though my sister and I are twins, throughout our lives no one ever had trouble telling us apart. We weren't identical in any way. It wasn't just the lengths of our hair, or the clothes we wore, although that was part of it. Over the years she let her dark red hair grow long and wild, while I kept mine cut bluntly just above the shoulders. She preferred flowing fabrics, and beads at the throat and wrist, while I usually wore a single antique silver necklace that my mother gave me before she died.

But there was something else about us that people saw: the way that Harper had become the kind of woman who men instantaneously responded to. Unlike Harper, though, I was often overlooked by men. I'd had relationships occasionally, but I never got the sense that any man would feel about me the way most men felt about my sister. I pretended that it didn't really matter, but it did. It would come at me in the middle of the night, when I'd wake up from a dream in which I'd been lying in the arms of some unknown man. The dream would fall away, and I'd be left lying in my bed for the rest of the night, awake and alone.

Then one afternoon, in the middle of a cold, terrible winter, I met a man named David Fields. He looked at me for a long time, and for the next few months never stopped looking. For a while there, he made me feel, I think, the way men made Harper feel.

Not that I ever knew exactly what my sister felt about anything. As girls, she and I were never close; now we were fully grown and understood that we didn't need to force a relationship any more. One day I realised that I couldn't remember the last time I'd talked to Harper, and that I didn't miss her at all.

And then, suddenly, she was back.

Harper returned to my life the day after New Year's Day. It was snowing, and I'd just come home from the Water Mill, a local bar where I'd been with my friends from the Longwood Falls Library, where I was head librarian. Those of us who didn't have spouses or kids at home had gathered together to be away from our silent, wintry houses for just a while longer. Now I was in my bedroom, getting changed into an old pink nightgown, the news of the world droning dully in the background, when my doorbell rang.

The sound was startling. I slipped on a robe and headed downstairs. Through the yellow and green panes of stained glass on the front door, I could make out my elderly aunt Leatrice standing on the porch. I opened the door and saw that she was crying. She hurried through the doorway, putting her arms around me, snow in her hair.

'Aunt Leatrice,' I said, alarmed. 'What is it?'

My beloved aunt—my late mother's sister, a small, birdlike woman of seventy who lived several streets away—stepped back and regarded me. 'Oh, Liz,' she said, her voice choked and unfamiliar, 'something has happened.'

She pulled away, shaking her head, and I followed her into the den. My aunt sat in one of the green wing chairs that faced the fire, and I perched nervously on the edge of the other. I was afraid she was going to say that something had happened to Harper. I took a breath and steeled myself for the news.

Instead, what my aunt said was, 'It's Doe.'

Doe: my niece. My sister's daughter. Eight years old.

'There was a sledding accident,' my aunt went on. 'It happened this morning, in Stone Point. She was going down a hill. Something happened, a chunk of ice in the path, and the sled caught, and there was a tree, and she was killed.'

'Oh my God,' I heard myself say.

My aunt began crying again. I helped her out of her damp coat, poured her some brandy, and built a small, clumsy fire in the hearth. The fire popped and whistled while my aunt drank and continued to sob. Eventually, the fire died down and my aunt, too tired to keep crying, fell asleep in the chair, snoring a little in the way that elderly people often do. I covered her with a rug, then I poked at the ashes in the fireplace, shut off the lights and went upstairs to bed.

The fact was, I didn't know Doe. I'd seen her once, a week after she was born, at a party her mother threw at the Stone Point house. Stone Point is a wealthy town on Long Island Sound. All the houses there are huge and look out over the water and have names; my sister's house is called The Eaves. Stone Point is an old town with a history; a famous yacht race takes place there every August, and once, back in the 1960s, a beautiful Olympic swimmer named Maggie Thorpe dived into the water off the Point and was never seen again. My sister's town is a place of glamour and genteel drama, and the one time I'd visited there for her baby's welcoming party, I'd left feeling more inadequate than ever.

That day, the rooms on the ground floor of Harper's house had been crowded with guests drinking champagne from long flutes and nibbling smoked salmon canapés. Everyone was talking and laughing and arguing loudly about topics I knew nothing about, such as ice fishing and the restorative mud baths of Italy. Extravagant baby gifts were presented: a stuffed bear as big as a refrigerator, a child-sized Fiat with a real engine and leather seats.

At one point, my sister's newborn Domenica—who'd been nicknamed Doe—was produced from a room upstairs, held aloft by a nurse. I remember staring into the eyes of that little baby who had a sprig of red hair that was the same colour as Harper's and mine. Something caught in my throat in that moment, but after the applause and the exclamations, the nurse and baby vanished again, and the guests were free to resume their drinking.

I considered retrieving my gift—a simple baby doll in a red-checked outfit—and sending something more extravagant later. But in the end I left it there, and later I received a cordial but impersonal thankyou note from my sister and her husband, Carlo Brico, a much older Italian businessman and art collector. I didn't know Carlo, and hadn't even been invited to their wedding, which was described in the paper as 'intimate' and had taken place in Venice. When, a year after Doe's birth, an invitation arrived for a party in honour of Harper's second child, a boy named Nick, I declined.

My aunt Leatrice, however, was involved in all their lives, and she kept me aware of the children's progress over the years: how Doe loved horses and ballet class and ice cream, and was as idiosyncratic as her mother; how Nick was the serious one, quiet and intelligent like Carlo but sometimes moody and unresponsive.

It was Aunt Leatrice—not me—who had somehow stayed in my sister's good graces, and who got to know the children, and loved them deeply. All of which made me wonder now, as I rested my head back against the pillow on my bed and closed my eyes, why exactly I was crying.

WHEN THE SUN came up I felt so heavy-hearted that it was difficult to get out of bed and start my day. Once upon a time I'd lived in this room with Harper, though we'd barely spent any time in it together except to sleep. Now the place bore no resemblance to that girlhood room. The striped rose wallpaper was gone, and so were the twin beds. When I moved back into the house after my parents' deaths, I completely redecorated with a big brass bed and blond wood furniture.

The house had long ago been rid of traces of my sister, except for one. Inside the pantry off the kitchen were the old pencil markings on the door that my mother had drawn to measure our heights over time. Always, we were head to head, Harper and I, twin sisters who were nothing alike in the ways that matter.

Longwood Falls, where we lived from the day we were born, is a small town in upstate New York, the sort of place where everyone knows everyone's business. 'Liz Mallory is so quiet,' they would say. 'So responsible and courteous.' Then they would add, 'But, now, her *sister*, she's a real original. Not to mention a wildcat.'

And it was true. Harper was wild, but she was also accomplished. She did everything before anyone else had thought of doing it. She dressed with her own self-invented style and elegance. She created collages out of scraps of material, machine parts and discarded household items—things it would never have occurred to me could be used in that way. She was an artist and a rebel, and she was infuriating and formidable. But wherever she went, people knew she was there.

Harper never confided in me, never asked whether I wanted to come and join her and her pack of friends who seemed more sophisticated than my slightly shy, hesitant crowd. She would ride in Warren Jett's vintage convertible, drinking from a bottle of tequila, her head thrown back, hair blowing.

By the time high school ended, it was clear what our futures would be: everyone knew that Harper was headed for New York City, where she was going to attend art school and become a famous painter, while I was certain to stay right here and have a more average, uneventful life.

Which isn't to say that I was a complete wallflower. I became involved with a few men over the years. A couple of them had already dated Harper and been dumped by her; I was an afterthought. And even when I went out with someone she hadn't already been involved with, he always wanted to know all about her. So, in a sort of defensive stance, I never allowed myself to get too close to any man, because I feared he'd be disappointed by what he found. And I never really experienced pleasure.

Pleasure was for Harper. And she did experience a great deal of pleasure. She went from white-hot prodigy in the 1980s to a figure of lasting prominence, and I heard about her goings-on from my proud but bewildered parents, and from reading about her in the tabloids. Or else I would see an announcement of one of her art shows in the *New York Times*. 'Harper Mallory: Recent Works' it would say, though I was never invited to the openings.

She was rich and famous, and I had a modest life on a small scale. My job at the Longwood Falls Library gave me a great deal of responsibility, and I took pride in what I did. But sometimes, as I walked through all that wooded silence, I just wanted to scream. Where was *my* chance at something wonderful? Where was *my* big career, *my* beautiful children? Where was *my* life?

After my parents died within a year of each other—my mother first, following a long struggle with cancer, then my grieving father of an unexpected heart attack—I moved back into the white frame house where I'd grown up. Harper didn't care; one of her paintings, those large canvases with the haunted faces of men and women, would have fetched as big a price as the house would have. We saw each other briefly at our parents' funerals; after the reception and some awkward moments of forced conversation, she was gone in the shiny black Town Car that had brought her.

That was over a decade earlier. Now my sister and I were thirty-six. Three years ago, Harper's marriage ended, and Carlo, a distracted, older man without much time to give his children, had moved back to Milan, remarried and had a baby with his new wife. Time passed; Nick turned seven, and Doe turned eight. It was said by my aunt that Doe was Harper's favourite, because she reminded her of herself.

THE ROADS WERE BAD throughout the entire six-hour trip to the funeral the next day. The wipers whooshed as they kept the front window clear of slushy rain. Aunt Leatrice sat beside me, but neither of us could bear to talk very much.

When we arrived in Stone Point, the pretty church was crowded. I looked around for Harper, but had no time to find her, for the service started soon after I arrived, and my aunt and I had to quickly find seats at the back.

Suddenly, a man stood up and gestured for me and Aunt Leatrice to take his place. We didn't exchange words; I only took in the fact that he was a handsome man, freshly shaven, who looked a little uncomfortable in a suit. His name, though I didn't know it at the time, was David Fields. He was the man I would soon fall in love with, but, of course, I didn't know this either. It's strange the way you can come upon someone and have no idea that this person who means nothing to you will some day mean everything.

I helped Aunt Leatrice sit down and then I squeezed in beside her, nodding thanks to the man who had given us his seat, and then turning away from him. When the coffin was carried in—tiny and simple, made of a polished rosewood that was almost the colour of Doe's hair—the entire congregation seemed to slump down and cry in unison. Their tears continued throughout the psalm recited by the minister, and during the eulogy given by Caitlin, Doe's best friend.

Caitlin, who at the age of eight was blonde and flushed with nervousness, stood up in front of everyone, clutching a doll to her chest. 'See this doll?' said Caitlin into the microphone, her voice a trembling whisper. 'Doe gave it to me.'

I looked at the doll. It was faded and old, and wore a tattered red-checked outfit. A chill travelled through me as I realised this was the doll that I had given my niece when she was born.

'She said it was for being her best friend,' Caitlin continued. 'It was *her* doll since she was born, but she wanted me to have it.' She paused, looking sidelong towards the coffin. 'I'll always keep this doll, Doe,' she said. 'And I promise to take care of her for ever.'

I leaned back. If I, who hadn't known my niece at all, was feeling this distraught, I couldn't even imagine what my sister must be going through. At the end of the service, when everyone stood up, I still couldn't find Harper. I figured I'd soon see her back at the house, where the reception was to be held.

As I was about to leave, though, something caught my eye. It was the back of a woman's head, the red hair carelessly hacked off as short as a boy's, as though it had been done in a great hurry, with blunt shears. Something about the slope of the shoulders and the long neck looked familiar. Just then, the woman turned her head and met my gaze.

It was my sister. This utterly changed person who stood facing me in the cold winter church was practically a stranger to me, a stranger with a bad haircut and eyes that appeared as lifeless and frozen as the trees along the road that I'd been travelling for hours.

They say that even when twins live separate lives, if something terrible happens to one, the other can't help but be changed, too. Harper had experienced something unbearable, and I suddenly had a glimpse of the extent of it. She seemed to have disappeared from the world and been replaced by someone strange and different. And the thing was, I felt strange and different, too. It was as though she and I were locked together now, and the intensity of it made me feel panicky, overwhelmed. Though she let herself be stiffly embraced, and politely accepted the inadequate words of sorrow that I had to offer, I knew enough to be frightened.

AT THE RECEPTION, guests stood in clusters and talked in low voices. Harper was nearby and they didn't want to say anything that would possibly upset her any further. But whenever I glanced at my sister from across her huge living room, I saw that she was beyond the reach of their voices.

She sat on the long white couch, a fragile, drunken woman with shorn-off hair. In her hand was a glass of bourbon, refilled many times by a butler who didn't dare dissuade her each time she demanded a refill. If anyone came near her, she turned away. When I glanced over again, I saw that she had put the glass down on the coffee table and was leaving the room.

As I watched her go, I felt the pressure of a hand on my shoulder, and I looked up to see my sister's ex-husband, Carlo. His dark hair was raked back off his large, handsome face, and he wore a dark, double-breasted suit that must have cost millions of lire. Carlo had been travelling with his new wife and infant son in the Pyrenees when Doe was killed, and he'd arrived from Europe this morning, just in time for her funeral. He was a remote man who, since the divorce, had seen Nick and Doe just once a year, but it was clear that he was terribly broken by the death.

'Carlo,' I said, standing and lightly taking the hand of my former brother-in-law, whom I'd met only a couple of times. 'I don't know what to say,' I began lamely. 'I'm very sorry.'

He waved away my words. 'I almost feel that I have no right here at The Eaves,' he said in a halting voice, heavy with accent. 'Harper, she hates me. Our divorce was not pleasant, to say the least.' He gave a small, bitter laugh. 'And now my Doe is gone and Harper will not speak to me.' He paused, shaking his head, wiping his eyes with a linen handkerchief. 'She has closed herself up completely.'

'I can see that,' I said.

'It is not good for her,' he said. 'She must talk to people, she must cry with them, or else she will not be able to cope.'

Suddenly, Carlo's eyes brightened briefly. 'Perhaps,' he said, 'she will talk to you.'

'Me? I doubt it,' I told him. 'She's never had too much to say to me before. I can't imagine why she'd suddenly start now.'

'You are her closest blood relative,' Carlo said. 'I know she is difficult. Everyone who has ever met her knows that,' he said. 'But please, if you would at least try, I'd be very grateful, Liz.'

I looked at Carlo. In a day or two he would be flying back on a private jet to his new family in Milan. I couldn't understand how he could leave so quickly, but there were plenty of things about the geometry of other people's lives that I didn't understand. Without really knowing why, I nodded and told Carlo I would try to talk to Harper, but that he shouldn't expect much.

Walking up the wide marble staircase that my sister had recently ascended, I felt like the stand-in for a movie star, following in her path. What would I say to Harper? We'd already had our brief moment together in the church. To try to take it any further would be awkward, I knew, but still I continued up the stairs, because I'd told Carlo I would do this.

There were many rooms along the lushly carpeted first-floor hallway; through open doors I could see antique clocks and mirrors and, in one room, a small bronze Degas statue of a dancing girl. I noticed that a door was shut, and this one I immediately knew to be Harper's. I knocked hard, and there was no reply, so I turned the knob and entered the room. It was unlit, but the natural light from the windows threw a bluish spill over everything.

My sister was lying there on her back, fully dressed with her eyes closed. I stood right beside her and said her name.

After a moment, she opened her eyes and said, 'Go away, Liz.' Then she closed her eyes again.

'I don't want to go away,' I told her. 'Aunt Leatrice and I drove all the way here. And it wasn't for the hors d'oeuvres,' I tried.

'Well, if it was for the conversation,' she said, 'you'll have to excuse me if I don't rise to the occasion. I'm not exactly in the mood to meet my social obligations.' Her voice was growing rawer and angrier by the word. 'Thank you for coming all this way, Liz. Thank Aunt Leatrice. Thank anybody downstairs who's drinking my liquor and eating my food and talking about the latest opening and trying to meet the right gallery owner and already moving on with their lives. They can all get along quite well without me.' She paused, and then she added, 'And they will.'

Her words were strange, disturbing, and seemed to hint of hurting herself. 'What do you mean?' I asked nervously.

She opened her eyes again and gave me a questioning look. Then she understood. 'I don't mean *that*,' she said, and her voice softened. 'Not that I haven't thought about it, believe me. But I couldn't do that to Nick. I have to find a way to survive.'

She waited a moment, then said, 'I have a house on an island off the Florida coast. It's very remote. Sometimes I go there to work. But now, I think I should go there and just . . . completely disappear for a while.'

'Are you sure it's a good idea to be all alone?' I asked.

'No,' she said tightly. 'I'm not. But do you have a better suggestion?'

I shook my head. Harper was right; I couldn't begin to comprehend the magnitude of her grief. I was quiet, just looking at her, taking in her shorn hair, her face, blotchy from so much crying and drinking, and her words, which were starting to make sense to me. My twin sister, who had always surrounded herself with so much activity, had reached a point at which she was desperate for silence.

'Well,' I tried, 'if you ever need anything—'

'Oh, Liz,' she said, and now her voice was barely a whisper. 'It's too late. You and I have never been friends; we've never even liked each other.' She paused. 'I can say that, can't I?'

'Yes,' I said softly. 'You can.'

It was true, of course. I walked over to the windows then; I'm not sure why. I stood looking out over the snowy road and the thicket of woods slipping into late-afternoon half-light.

Suddenly, I was surprised to see a figure moving along the road. I realised that it was a child walking. And then, with a start, I realised that it was my nephew, Nick. *Nick*. He had been forgotten by almost everyone in the middle of all the drama. He was heading away from home, going down the road towards who knew where.

I felt suddenly afraid for him. 'There's Nick,' I said. 'Walking in the snow.'

Harper glanced out of the windows. 'So he is,' she said, seeming uninterested.

'Should he be out there all by himself?' I asked. 'I don't think a car could see him easily today. And besides, it's freezing.'

Harper waved her hand vaguely. 'He'll be all right. He'll come in when he's ready,' she said. 'He always does.'

I looked at her sharply, realising that in her state she could only think of her own loss, and very little else. 'And what if he doesn't come in?' I persisted. 'And what about while you're in Florida on that island. What about then?'

'Sanibel Island,' she said. 'Jeannette, the cook, will attend to Nick. She does an excellent job. Besides,' she added, 'I wouldn't be much use to him here. He'd see me lying in bed and crying all day; it would frighten him.'

But I couldn't tolerate the idea of my nephew being left in the care of the cook, however kindly and maternal she was. 'Harper,' I said firmly, 'that won't do. He needs more than that.' The strength of my own voice surprised me.

Apparently, it surprised Harper, too. She arched an eyebrow at me. 'Why, Liz,' she said, 'I've never heard you speak with such . . . conviction.'

I felt my face grow warm. 'I'm going downstairs now,' I said.

'Fine,' said Harper.

I turned and looked at her again. She had sunk back against the cushions, her eyes closing. 'Do you need anything?' I asked softly.

'Yes,' she said. 'Tell the butler to bring me a double bourbon.'

'All right,' I said, though I had no intention of doing so.

THE SNOW WAS FIERCE by the time I stepped outside. The leather boots I'd worn today were lined with fleece, but their tread wasn't substantial, and I slipped in the thick, deep snow that was mixed through with ice. But still I kept crunching along the slippery road, heading in the direction of my nephew. I called his name a few times, but either he didn't hear me or he chose not to.

Where was Nick going? I wondered as the snow flew into my mouth and I felt my eyelashes become speckled with ice. The road turned to the right and went up steeply. Still I followed him until finally we were both at the top of a hill.

Nick was facing away from me and peering downwards. He was a small boy in a grey coat that was way too big for him. He wasn't wearing mittens or a hat, and his hair was practically white with snow. He was seven years old, but in some ways he resembled a tiny old man.

'Nick?' I said again, coming forward and touching him on the shoulder. He flinched and turned quickly; apparently he hadn't known I was following him. He stared at me, startled and suspicious. 'It's your aunt Liz,' I said.

He studied me a moment, surprised. Then, apparently seeing my resemblance to his mother, he quickly nodded.

'Let me take you inside,' I said.

He shook his head and moved slightly away. Instinctively, I trailed after him, looking in the direction he was looking. I understood that this was the place where Nick's sister had been killed.

I followed his gaze down the steep hill. The snow that had fallen in the last two days had covered over any traces of the accident. Now this was just a plain white hill with trees on either side, the kind of hill sledded down by children everywhere. The kind that Harper and I used to sled down in Longwood Falls. I would sit upright on my sled, clutching the steering mechanism and trying to keep it from going too fast, while Harper would lie flat on her stomach, eyes closed for the entire ride.

Now my eyes burned from tears for the little girl I hadn't known. I looked down at my nephew, Nick, in his oversized coat, and I felt an enormous rush of tenderness.

'It's not your fault,' I said after a moment, and I'm not sure why I thought to say this. 'The accident, I mean.'

He looked at me, shocked, and at first I thought he was offended that I would think he had been having such ideas. But then his expression changed slightly, and I knew that I'd been right about him.

'It *is* my fault!' he said with sudden passion. 'It was my idea to go sledding; she wanted to make snow angels instead. I told her snow angels were dumb and boring.'

'You couldn't have known,' I insisted. 'No one can ever know. It's mysterious, the way these things happen. You have to believe me: you aren't responsible.'

No one had thought to say such a thing to him; no one had even realised he might feel guilty, that he might harbour this feeling silently for a long time.

'Did my mom send you out here to get me?' he asked, and I shook my head no.

'No one sent me,' I said. 'I wanted to come.'

'Go away,' he said. 'I don't want you here. Just go away.' His voice was the dictator's pout of an angry child, but there was also such an unimaginable sadness beneath it that I would have let him speak to me that way as long as he needed. I stood for a few moments while he continued to tell me that I should just go back to wherever it was that I had come from.

Finally he was done. We stood and regarded each other, and then, in a deadpan voice, I said, 'I don't know, maybe I'm crazy, but I'm beginning to get the feeling that you don't want me here.'

Nick looked puzzled, then he said, 'Are you trying to be funny?'

I nodded. 'Trying. But not succeeding, I guess.'

'No,' he agreed. 'Not succeeding at all.' He seemed to take some satisfaction from my failure at humour.

I exhaled hard and said again, 'Come on, let's go in,' and this time Nick agreed.

So we walked back to the house together, and though he still wore a dark, brooding expression, some unspoken thing was taking place between us, an odd relationship was forming in silence and freezing weather between a little boy and a grown woman who didn't know each other.

Once inside, I sat with Nick at the kitchen table while the serving staff efficiently worked, preparing triangular sandwiches with the crusts removed and arranging them on silver trays. Nick wolfed down six little cheese triangles without much trouble, and chased them with a tall glass of milk and a wedge of chocolate cake roughly the size of a shoe.

'When was the last time you ate?' I asked, and he just shrugged. I marvelled at the appetite of this boy, something I hadn't had the chance to witness before.

I knew almost nothing about children. A long time ago, when I'd been in a relationship with a lawyer in my town named Jeff Hardesty, I'd briefly imagined marrying him and having children. I had always expected love to be clear, vivid, the *it* I'd always heard about. Whatever I'd had with Jeff wasn't *it*, at least not for me, not at that point in my life. Jeff and I disentangled from each other, and after a while he moved north to Buffalo, and that was that. Slowly my twenties slipped into my thirties. Occasionally there were other men, but no *it*.

All around me, I saw other people fall in love and have children. I went to wedding showers and then baby showers. Did I imagine that such things would happen to me? In truth, I'd just foolishly imagined that a person's life 'fell into place'. And then I'd sat back and watched as Harper's life fell into place, not mine.

I glanced over at Nick now, and he put down his cake fork. His face was speckled with crumbs, and there was a white slash of milk above his upper lip. There was an intensity to his eyes, and then he said, 'It should have been me.'

I stared at him, knowing what he meant but not wanting to believe it. 'What should have been you?' I asked.

'On the hill,' he said. 'My mom wished it was me. Doe was her favourite.'

'No one would wish something like that,' I said. But actually I had no idea of what went on in my sister's mind. 'She loves you, Nick,' I continued. 'I mean, come on, she's your mother.'

'Doe was her *daughter*,' he said. 'They were exactly alike; that's what everyone said. They looked alike, the same red hair, and people said she was wilful, just like my mom.'

'Do you think so?' I asked.

'I don't know,' said Nick, shrugging. 'What's *wilful* mean?'

In that moment I was reminded that he was just a little boy sitting at a table drinking milk and eating a piece of cake. An ordinary little boy whose feet barely brushed the floor and who I had missed out on getting to know.

I imagined Nick wandering outside for ever, just trudging along that road for so long that he became lost or forgotten. I felt an urgency as I looked at him.

Back in Longwood Falls, my job waited at the red-brick library. They would be expecting me there on Monday morning. The door-man would say hello to me as I came in, and so would the young woman who worked at the checkout desk. I felt safe in that building, surrounded by books—objects that comforted me almost in the way that people were meant to comfort one another.

But I wasn't going to go back yet. I wanted to help my nephew, Nick, to keep him company while his mother disappeared to recuperate on Sanibel Island. Even if he didn't want my help, I would take care of him in a way that no one else would. I knew it was the right thing to do. For the first time ever, it was Harper's turn to retreat from the world, and my turn to enter it.

 Chapter Two

Soon we were on our own, Nick and I. Harper had tried to insist that I didn't need to stay, but she didn't have the heart for a fight. She seemed barely alive, barely responsive. As she was heading out of the front door for the car to take her to the airport, she commented that for once she was able to pack light. For the first time, she explained, she wouldn't be taking her art supplies with her.

'I don't have it in me any more,' she said. 'It's over.'

'You can't know that,' I answered.

'Yes I can,' she said, and the sudden strength of her voice silenced me. 'I've locked up the studio for ever,' she went on. 'I can't imagine painting again. I mean, who the hell cares?'

'I do,' I tried.

'I don't,' she said, and swept into the waiting car.

I watched Nick, on the steps, as he sat looking at her car slowly disappear down the drive. Earlier, I'd driven Aunt Leatrice to the railway station. It's just you and me now, I thought as I gazed down at the fragile, unmoving figure of a seven-year-old boy. It's just you and me and this great big house.

Nick and I were going to have to get to know each other now. The first thing I learned about him was not to ask questions. His favourite reply was a shrug, and usually I accepted these non-responses and just moved on. I learned to let Nick lead me where he wanted to go, which turned out to be playing round after round of Monopoly and Clue. When that became boring, we sometimes strapped on cross-country skis and headed out into the endless expanse of snow. My sister's property extended for miles, and every day Nick and I ventured someplace new. At night, we sat on scatter cushions in front of the fire in the living room, and I read to him.

Nick liked to close his eyes and hear the words said aloud. Sometimes, as I read to him, I wished that he would lean his head against my shoulder, but he never did. I wished he would let me offer him the comfort I knew he needed, but not once did the opportunity arise.

Every night, his mother called from Florida and Nick supplied her with the highlights of his day. Then he would hand the phone over to me, and in her painfully flat voice my sister would supply me with the highlights of *her* day—telling me whether she managed to get out of bed before noon, or not.

I tried not to seem too worried, and I reminded her that grief wasn't something you could rush, and to take as long as she needed. And I meant it; the director of the Longwood Falls Library had been surprised when I had asked for a leave of absence, and he was understandably concerned by the word *indefinite*, but what could he say? Like all family emergencies, this one was unpredictable.

One day, on a walk together, Nick wordlessly led me down a path into the woods behind the house. I'd finally abandoned the inadequate boots I'd brought with me. Now I was wearing my sister's. Harper had insisted I take anything of hers that I liked, since we wore the same size. After a while, I saw a clearing on the path ahead, and in the centre of it a simple frame building. I'd seen it before and assumed that it housed Jeannette and the butler, Tom.

'What is this place?' I asked Nick.

'My mom's studio,' he said as we approached. 'She does all her painting here.'

So this was the studio that I'd heard so much about over the years. The door was locked with a bulky padlock, so Nick and I looked through the cold, leaded-glass windowpanes.

I'd seen pictures of the studio's interior before in a design magazine, but even those elegant photographs hadn't done the place justice: an airy, white room with bleached wooden floors, cathedral ceilings, and an abundance of sun that bathed the place in the kind of perfect, lemon-coloured light any artist would covet.

Against one wall was a long, paint-spattered table covered with a smorgasbord of art supplies. There were implements of various types, from long industrial rollers to Japanese brushes made up of a few hairs bound together on a slender stick of bamboo. There were stretched canvases, still pristine and untouched, and large, dented silver cans of turpentine and linseed oil. There was a bed in a corner of the room, neatly made, and a kitchenette where meals could be prepared. I thought that an artist working in this studio would never want to leave.

But Harper had. She had walked away and vowed never to return. Looking in through the studio windows, I suddenly felt that this was the saddest place on earth. I was about to turn away, but something caught my eye.

It was a large canvas, propped up on an easel by the far wall. It was mostly abstract, and though I could barely see it, I could tell that it was a half-finished painting of a child with flame-coloured hair and sly, half-closed eyes. I shielded my eyes with my hand and stood looking hard at this painting of Doe, half-finished, that would never be completed.

'So do you like my mom's studio?' Nick asked.

I turned from the window. 'Yes,' I answered, and I understood that he didn't yet know about his mother's decision.

'I could show you something else,' he volunteered. 'Do you want to see the Point?'

I was cold and would have liked to go inside, but the offer from Nick was so uncharacteristically forthcoming that I quickly answered, 'All right.'

Stone Point had been named for a long, smooth piece of land that jutted out into the Sound. Nick and I trudged through the snow towards the Point. By the time we arrived at our destination afternoon had dropped away, turning to dusk.

As we walked out onto the narrow stretch of land I saw that there was a man standing at the tip. He had a telescope tipped up towards the heavens and was tightening the screws, and then peering into it, swinging it lightly to the left and then the right, as though searching for something in particular. When he heard us coming, he turned round, and I found myself facing a man who seemed familiar. He appeared to be studying me, too. After a moment, it came to me: he was the man at the funeral who had given me his seat.

He was close to forty, tall and lean, wearing a worn leather flying jacket. His face was handsome, and his hair was wavy and dark brown. 'Have we met?' he asked.

'No, but I think we saw each other at the church the other day,' I said. 'You gave my aunt and me a place to sit.' He nodded, remembering, and seemed about to introduce himself, but all of a sudden Nick stepped forward.

'Mr Fields,' he said. He reached out to shake hands with the man, as he'd most likely been taught. But the man ignored his hand and gave him a hug instead.

'Hey, Nick,' he said softly, pulling back to take a look at my nephew. 'I've been thinking about you. Did you get my letter?'

'Yes,' said Nick, seeming both pleased and deeply embarrassed at the attention. 'Thanks a lot.' He looked over at the telescope. 'What are you doing?' he asked.

'Trying out my latest toy,' said the man. His voice was soft and hesitant, but rough-edged, too. 'Want to have a look?'

'Sure,' said Nick, and the man lowered the telescope and helped Nick get a good view of something through the eyepiece. As Nick stared up at the heavens, the man casually turned to me.

'I'm David Fields,' he said. 'Nick's teacher at the Craighead School.'

'Liz Mallory,' I said, and I extended my gloved hand. He shook it with a gloved hand of his own, soft brown leather that had been broken in over the years. 'I'm his aunt.'

'I figured it was something like that,' he said. 'You're staying with the family?' he asked, and I nodded.

'I'm staying with Nick,' I amended. 'His mother went away.'

'Oh?' He sounded surprised.

'She has a house on an island off Florida,' I said, and David nodded. 'She said she needed to be completely alone.'

'I can understand that,' he said. We stood quietly for a moment, and then he told me in a low voice that he'd been concerned about how Nick was going to get along during the school holidays.

'He's doing pretty well,' I said. 'We've been spending all our time together, playing games, walking around.'

'I'm glad to hear that,' said David. 'I worry.'

We couldn't say too much about Nick's situation because he was standing right there, but it was clear that both of us genuinely cared about this uncommunicative little boy.

I liked David Fields right away, yet I felt uneasy in his presence. I knew that I didn't look very attractive all bundled up in my winter coat and thick woollen hat. For some reason, I wanted to look good for this man; I wanted him to like me. This was a sensation I hadn't experienced in a long time.

'Would you like a look through the telescope?' David asked me, and I nodded.

'What were you looking at up there?' I asked.

'Saturn,' he said.

When David adjusted the telescope for me, I looked through it and saw that one of the stars that had looked ordinary before was now miraculously changed into a planet, complete with a set of hazy rings.

'Look at that,' I said quietly. 'It's just like in all the pictures I've ever seen. It's beautiful.'

'Yes,' said David. 'It really is.' He paused. 'A few years ago you couldn't have seen those rings even if you'd looked through this telescope,' he said.

'Why not?' I asked.

'Because the earth was passing through what's known as the "ring plane" of Saturn, and the edges of the rings were facing us, edge on, so they would have been invisible.'

'Well, I'm glad to see them now,' I said, staring at the shimmering rings and the muted colours that swam within the sphere of the planet itself. I stood back from the telescope, letting Saturn return to an ordinary pinpoint. Suddenly, as I watched the sky, something shot across it, leaving a diagonal scratch of light in its wake.

'What was that?' I asked, startled. 'A shooting star?'

He nodded. 'Yes,' he said. 'Just burning itself out as it goes; that's what they do. Bits of ice turning to fire.'

'Where is it?' Nick asked, searching the sky.

'Gone,' David answered. 'That's the thing about shooting stars. But you can always keep looking for another one.'

Nick did. While he was staring up at the heavens, I asked David how long he'd been watching the sky.

'Practically always,' he said with a shrug. 'When I was a boy I used to come out here to the Point and look at things for hours. I didn't have a telescope then, only a pair of good binoculars.'

'So what were you looking for?' I asked lightly. 'UFOs?'

'No,' he said, but he didn't elaborate.

'Is it a secret?' I asked, and when he didn't reply, I said, 'I know. A mystery woman.'

It was an innocent, silly joke, but suddenly David's mood changed completely. He straightened up, turning slightly away from me. 'No,' he said. 'It wasn't a mystery woman.' His voice was suddenly cold. Then he glanced at his watch and said, 'Well, I should get back. Excuse me, Nick.'

Nick moved away from the telescope and we watched as David quickly packed it up. I wanted to ask what it was I'd said to offend him, but I couldn't find the voice. We stood awkwardly in the wind for a moment more as Nick's teacher tucked the telescope under his arm, and then we headed off in different directions.

FOR THE REST of the evening I felt agitated and upset. After dinner, Nick enticed me into a game of Monopoly, and though I played for a while, I finally cried off. I went upstairs to my bedroom, which was located in a wing used only for guests.

The room that Harper had given me was pretty, with deep, forest-green carpeting and a delicate wallpaper pattern of climbing vines. There was a full-length antique oval mirror on a cherrywood stand, and as I undressed for bed I stood for a moment in front of it, critically peering at my reflection. At the age of thirty-six, my body was still taut and hadn't been stretched by childbirth. I looked much the way I had when I was twenty-six, or even sixteen: slender, long legs, full breasts. I knew that I was pretty in a muted, understated way, but suddenly I worried that my solitude was visible, was written in bold face all over me. I quickly pulled on my nightgown and stepped into bed, not wanting to dwell on this depressing possibility.

But the morning brought a surprise. I was sitting in the sunroom and having breakfast when the butler, Tom, tall and pokerfaced, came in, holding a cordless telephone.

'Ms Mallory, there's a telephone call for you,' he said.

I assumed that the call was from someone at the library; but instead, a man's voice was on the line, familiar in its hesitance and slightly rough edges. 'I'm really sorry I was rude yesterday,' he said, instead of the usual 'hello'.

'Excuse me?' I said.

'At the Point,' he said. There was a pause. 'This is David Fields,' he went on. 'Nick's teacher.'

'Oh. Hello,' I said, feeling myself become suffused with awkwardness and excitement. 'You weren't rude,' I lied.

'Yes, I was. I obsessed about it all last night. I want a chance to explain.'

'There's no need,' I said.

'It would make me feel better. How about tomorrow night. Are you by any chance free for dinner?'

I wanted to laugh. Of course, I had no plans; all I did here in Stone

Point was spend time with Nick. But David Fields couldn't possibly know that. We were absolute strangers to each other, and he was graciously extending himself to me.

The next night David picked me up at seven in his slightly battered car. I was relieved that he wasn't driving one of the very expensive cars that could be seen all around Stone Point. He was a teacher who drove a car that needed a few repairs. This made me feel more at ease. I was wearing a long-sleeved, black woollen dress of Harper's. It was the kind of dress that could have been worn to dinner at a four-star restaurant or at an informal coffee shop; I wasn't sure what kind of date this would be.

David Fields got out of his car and stood at the door of Harper's house in the flying jacket he'd worn when we'd met, but now it was unzipped, revealing a grey turtleneck sweater beneath.

'Shall we?' he asked, not coming in any further than the front hall, with its shining marble tiles.

I said yes, and slipped on my coat. Nick quickly came down to say hi before we left. Jeannette had promised to play Clue with him that evening after she was done in the kitchen, so he would be well occupied. He seemed excited to see his teacher in his home, the way any child would.

We drove in relative silence to Scotto's, the Italian restaurant in town where David had made reservations. The moment we walked in, I knew this was the kind of place I would have chosen. It was unpretentious, small and pretty; I couldn't imagine that Harper would have ever wanted to eat here. Her tastes sent her to restaurants where the food was carefully arranged on the plate into little sculptures that looked almost too artistic to eat. But Scotto's had soothing, basic Italian food: deep bowls of handmade ribbon pasta that gave off the fragrances of butter and garlic. All around us, people were laughing, and candlelight lent the entire room warmth. It was the perfect antidote to the winter night.

David and I were led to a booth in the back of the room. The table linen was slightly thin in a couple of spots, but the basket of bread was crusty and delicious, and David ordered a bottle of red wine, which brought an extra bit of heat to my face and relaxed me a little. I was nervous, I realised, in a way that I hadn't been in years. It was as though I somehow knew that this night was important.

David took a sip of his wine and then put the glass down. 'What happened the other day,' he finally said in a soft, halting voice, 'I'm sorry about it. I realise that I got very weird all of a sudden, and I don't know what you must have thought.' He looked at me inquisitively. 'Maybe you'll tell me,' he said.

'I thought that I'd become too personal,' I said. 'That I was asking you too much about yourself.'

David frowned slightly. 'Oh no,' he said. 'That wasn't it. I like it when people ask questions. It shows that they're listening. I'm a teacher, remember.' He shook his head. 'But when you asked what I was looking for through those binoculars when I was a boy, and you made that joke about the "mystery woman", I just closed right up.' He took another swallow of wine; this was difficult for him. 'What I was looking for, actually,' he went on, '*was* kind of a mystery woman. My mother.'

'Your mother?' I asked, puzzled. 'What do you mean?'

'She drowned when I was six years old,' said David. 'She'd been swimming and she disappeared. I was completely crushed and my father was a wreck. And because I was an only child, I had no one. Right after she died, I started spending the day looking through the binoculars. I guess I kept thinking that I'd be the one to find her. There were all these rescue boats circling the area, and helicopters, too. They didn't turn up a thing,' he said, shaking his head. 'She's still out there somewhere.'

The entire time he was speaking, I sat absolutely still. His eyes had a sorrowful quality about them, and his voice was filled with a kind of limitless pain, as though he was still that boy whose mother had been taken from him for ever.

Something occurred to me. 'Your mother,' I said. 'Was she that Olympic swimmer, Maggie Thorpe?'

David nodded. 'Her married name was Fields, my father's name,' he said. 'But everyone still remembered her from the Olympics, when she was known as Maggie Thorpe. So they called her that in all the articles and the obituaries.'

'It happened in the sixties?' I asked.

'Nineteen sixty-five,' said David. 'August.'

'What was she like?' I asked. 'Or is that too personal?'

'No, not at all,' he said. 'When I'm prepared for it, I like talking about it.' He took a moment to answer. 'She was a terrific mother. She taught me to swim when I was practically a baby. She'd hold me in her arms, and I would feel the water all around us, but it felt as warm as a bath, because she was there.'

We ate as we talked, but though I recall that the food was delicious, I don't remember eating; I was much too involved with listening to David.

'My mother's disappearance had one good effect on me,' he said. 'Day after day I'd look out over the water for her. But one day I got bored and I turned the binoculars to the sky. And there I found something that would wind up being a huge part of my life. The stars.' He broke off a piece of bread. 'Did you know that I live in an observatory?' he said.

'Is this a joke?' I asked, but he shook his head no.

'I rent a cottage on an estate here in town,' David said. 'A huge estate called Red Briar. The owner, an old guy named Boyd, is this total astronomy nut. A long time ago, he built his own observatory in the grounds of the estate, but then he got bored with it and let it fall into disrepair. When I moved in, he paid me to restore the place, and now it's basically mine to use as much as I like. I actually live on the ground floor. Right above me is the telescope. My roof is a giant dome.'

I shook my head, amazed. 'I can't even picture it,' I said.

'Oh, you will,' he said quietly. 'It's a wonderful place.' Then his posture shifted slightly and he looked down at his hands. 'But other than giving me my love of the stars,' he said, 'my mother's drowning did mostly destructive things to me. It made me very suspicious of people. I always expected them to leave me. And I guess, in a way, it became a self-fulfilling prophecy.'

'When you say "people",' I said, 'do you mean "women"?'

He nodded, slightly embarrassed, and pushed a hand through the hair that had fallen in his face.

'There was one woman in particular,' he said. 'It was a couple of years ago, and I'm over it now, but I still think about it sometimes.' He looked down at his plate, poking at a piece of pasta in the shape of a butterfly. 'I thought she was great,' he said. 'And apparently she thought a lot of me, too. We saw each other all the time. It was obsessive. And then, suddenly . . .' He shrugged. 'She was done with me. Decided I wasn't right for her. I started having dreams about my mother, which I hadn't done in years. I guess I felt as though I was being abandoned all over again.'

'And I guess you were,' I said.

He looked at me, our eyes meeting, neither of us turning away. I watched his eyes, his lips, the broad shoulders beneath his sweater, and I felt a surprising wave of feeling cross my body.

'I like talking to you, Liz,' he said, and he continued to look steadily at me.

'You seem surprised by that,' I said.

'Well, I don't even know you,' he said. 'I've been talking your ear off during dinner, and you haven't told me anything about yourself.'

'That's all right,' I said. 'It's not a particularly interesting story.'

'No. I want to hear,' he said. 'I told my story during the appetiser and main course. So you tell yours during dessert and coffee.'

What was there to tell? I wondered. I hadn't been abandoned by a man, and I hadn't had a trauma at an early age, as he had. I told him about how I had loved my parents, and how, after they were gone, I'd made the decision to stay on in the house where I had grown up.

'That's pretty unusual, isn't it?' he asked. 'Being so faithful to what you know. Liking it so much that you want it to continue for ever. I guess we have that in common; we've both stayed in the town where we grew up.'

I looked away slightly, knowing that it wasn't so much a question of *liking* what my life in Longwood Falls had held as it was of being fearful of trying something new.

'It's more complicated than that,' I said uneasily, and then I told him about my sister, and how I'd always known I could never compete with her. 'Basically I decided it was less painful to settle for a small, unexceptional life, instead of trying for something bigger, flashier. Something like what she has.'

'Are those the only options for a life?' David asked. 'Small and unexceptional versus big and flashy? How about a happy life?'

'I'm not sure what happiness would mean,' I said carefully. 'That is, I have a general understanding of it, but when it comes to what it would feel like—real, uninterrupted happiness—I guess I draw a total blank.'

'Me, too,' he admitted.

We were eating dessert now, densely layered Italian cake flavoured with espresso. I ate slowly, savouring the bitter and the sweet, as well as the fact that I was talking about my life to a man who was listening carefully, as though savouring each word I spoke.

What I remember most from that first evening was how we watched each other, each of us studying the other. I also remember all the talking we did. We talked and talked. Not as though we had known each other for ever, but rather as though we were two people who hadn't known each other until now, and felt the need to make up for lost time.

It was anyone's guess where this was headed. I was here in Stone Point in order to take care of my sister's son, and I would leave when Harper was strong enough to return. Three hundred miles away was my own house, and my own cold bed neatly spread with the pale blue coverlet I'd knitted. But across the table was a man with dark eyes and long, beautiful hands. A man whose mother had dived into the dark water many years ago and never returned.

I saw, as we sat together, that the restaurant had largely emptied and waiters were quietly clearing tables. Dreamy, late-night music—Sinatra from many decades ago—played on an old juke-box. 'Where did you go?' David asked as our plates were cleared.

'Nowhere,' I said, and realised that I had been momentarily day-dreaming. 'I'm right here.'

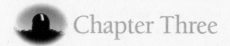 Chapter Three

The morning that the school holidays ended, I got up early to join Nick for breakfast. I found him sitting at the far end of the long dining-room table by himself, reading the back of a cereal box.

'Do you mind?' I asked, pointing to a chair beside him, and Nick shook his head. 'What are you reading?'

Nick shrugged.

'May I?' I reached for the cereal box and turned it round so I could see the back. It was covered with brightly coloured drawings—riddles, I realised. I read one to myself, then, covering the answer, turned the box so Nick could see it.

'Have you done this one yet?' I asked him.

He spooned some cereal and shook his head.

'OK,' I said. 'Guess what this is.'

Nick placed the spoon in the bowl and leaned forward, studying the riddle with an impressive level of concentration. The drawing appeared to be a letter C with short lines sticking straight away from it like porcupine quills.

'Give up?' I asked.

He looked up at me.

'A centipede doing sit-ups,' I read aloud.

At first, nothing. Then, slowly—slowly—a smile formed on Nick's face, almost as if it were emerging despite his best efforts to contain it. This was the first time I'd ever seen Nick smile—the first time I'd ever seen him show real pleasure. Usually what he showed while playing a board game was *appreciation*—a mature understanding of the intricacies of the game and not a boyish response.

It was beginning to occur to me that Nick approached everything with this same determination and seriousness of purpose. It was, I thought now as I looked at Nick sitting next to me at the table, dressed for school, a manner that fitted a boy in a navy blazer and matching tie over a pale blue shirt. His hair was damp, his parting perfect. It struck me as odd and sad that my sister, the free spirit, would raise a boy who looked as if he should be addressed as 'Master', and I had to wonder: Was Nick so serious because of what had happened to his sister, or was this the way he always was?

'Listen, Nick,' I said. 'How do you get to school? Bus?'

He shook his head. 'No. Tom takes me. The butler.'

'Well,' I said, 'what would you say if *I* drove you every day? In my slightly dusty car that needs an oil change.'

He looked up, thinking I might be making a joke. Then he said, 'Really?' I nodded, but still he looked doubtful.

'I'd like to,' I said, 'if you'd like me to.'

He said, 'All right,' but I noticed that he had to glance around first, as though we were breaking some unwritten law.

I can't say it didn't occur to me that I might see David when I dropped Nick off. Since that evening at Scotto's, we'd got together once more, this time over dinner at a seafood restaurant with hanging nets. It all went as effortlessly as the first time. Later, after he'd driven me home, and we were standing together on the gravel drive, he leaned forward and lightly grazed my cheek with his lips. He paused for a moment, as if he wanted to say something, but then seemed to think better of it. He shoved his hands in his pockets, turned away, and headed back to his car. I watched him go, bewildered and excited and wondering when I would see him again.

Now, as I turned my car through the tall iron gates of Craighead School, I couldn't help straining to see over the heads of children chasing one another up the front steps. I don't know what I expected—Mr Fields, the second-grade teacher, on duty at the front door, I guess. I felt Nick watching me.

I smiled quickly. 'I'll see you at three,' I said, but he didn't move. He kept studying me with the same intensity he'd brought to that riddle on the back of the cereal box.

'Thank you for the ride, Aunt Liz,' he finally said, and then he grabbed his oversized backpack and was gone.

I DIDN'T WANT to go back to The Eaves. The idea of being in that cavernous house without Nick seemed unpleasant. Compared to those empty, endless hallways, even the overpriced shops on Horseshoe Lane in Stone Point seemed welcoming. But after I'd made my way from one end of the expensive shopping district to the other before lunch, I couldn't help wondering how I would pass my time the next day, and the day after that.

Just before three o'clock, I drove back to the school to pick up Nick. I pulled my car into the line of vehicles idling in the long drive-way. Some mothers had got out of their cars to wait together and chat; they were all tall, wealthy-looking women, their hair fashionably styled and streaked. They were like Harper—like Harper used to be, anyway—sexually desirable, restless women with energy and entitlement. As I watched them, I couldn't help thinking of David, the handsome, unmarried second-grade teacher.

I knew it was absurd to feel jealous; there was nothing to base this feeling on except a vague stirring of possessiveness. I could imagine one of these women borrowing David as she might a handyman or gardener—someone good-looking and strong to occupy a few lonely hours. But I couldn't imagine any of them appreciating the man I alone had discovered over dinner—the modest, wounded, and gently handsome David.

And then there he was, knocking on the passenger window, jarring me from my thoughts about him.

'Sorry I scared you,' he said when I'd rolled down the window. 'I've been trying to get your attention, but you seemed lost in thought.'

'How did you know I was here?' I asked.

'Nick told me,' said David. 'He'll be out in a minute, but I wanted to talk to you first.'

He briefly looked towards the group of women I'd been watching. Then he leaned closer, through the open window. 'I've really been having a nice time with you,' he said, his voice lower now.

'Me, too,' I told him. I found myself glancing back at the other women, and saw that in fact they *were* looking at us.

'Are you busy Friday night?' David asked. 'I was thinking maybe you could come over to my cottage at Red Briar. Around eight? I'll fix some dinner, and we could head up to the observatory. If you're interested, that is.'

'I am,' I said quietly.

'Well, that's great,' said David. One of the women, I noticed then, had broken away from the others and was walking our way. In a loud voice, David quickly began to improvise. 'And I think he's doing fine,' he said. 'He's a great kid. I don't think you have to worry.' Then he turned round and swiftly headed back to the school, his tie flapping up over his shoulder like a wing.

THE REST OF THE WEEK passed effortlessly, dreamily, and I had no trouble finding something to occupy my days. I drove Nick to school, I returned to Horseshoe Lane a couple of times and actually bought myself an expensive blouse to wear to dinner on Friday.

I also explored the Stone Point Library, a big, imposing building on the water, introduced myself to the elderly head librarian there, and picked up some pointers on correcting cataloguing problems back in Longwood Falls.

But it was the promise of Friday night that illuminated the entire week for me. If it turned out the way I thought it might, then it would be one of those times that forever divide a life, paring it cleanly into a before and after.

This hope was an unfair burden to place on any occasion, but I was no longer a young girl living under the illusion of immortality, a life stretching endlessly ahead, full of infinite possibility. Life wasn't something to be squandered. There was a chance at love, perhaps a last chance, and it waited inside an observatory in the middle of winter. David and I both wanted answers, and we hoped we could get them in whatever time remained, before Harper came home and the clock struck midnight and my ball gown turned back into rags.

On Friday evening I dressed in the outfit I'd spent the week piecing together, but as I appraised myself in the mirror, I saw that something was missing. Then I knew what it was. I headed for my sister's dressing room. There I confronted Harper's collection of silk scarves, each hanging on its own brass hook. I plucked a gold scarf free and quickly knotted it, tucking one end behind my hair, letting the other drop easily. I turned towards the full-length mirror. *Ready or not*, I thought, and then I corrected myself. *Ready.*

DAVID'S COTTAGE WAS LOCATED on an estate five miles away. There were several buildings behind the mansion, but it was easy to tell which was David's: his was the one with the round roof.

As I got out of my car and walked up to the door of the cottage, I could see him through the window, slicing something on a cutting board in the kitchen, his shoulders moving with the rhythm of the strokes. I stopped and watched him for a moment, maybe to steal a secret glimpse of David, or maybe just to prolong the moment before I crossed that threshold. Then, I knocked.

After a moment, the door opened. David, holding a bottle of red wine by its neck and a Swiss army knife with its corkscrew open, smiled at me. He stepped outside, brushed my cheek with the lightest kiss, and then looked up.

'Good,' he said, nodding to himself.

I followed his gaze. The sky was clear; many stars were out.

'Possibly very good,' David went on. 'We'll see.' And he held his arm out, indicating that I should precede him inside, and took my coat.

The cottage was really only one big circular room. The kitchen occupied half of the front section, and a low beige couch and wooden coffee table the other half. There were striking landscape photographs on the walls and an Oriental rug with a complex design on the floor. The place was strange and beautiful and snug; it seemed utterly private and away from the rest of the world.

'It's wonderful,' I said with genuine feeling, and David seemed pleased.

But then I noticed in the middle of the room a huge structure that ran from floor to ceiling. It was made of concrete blocks, fitted together, and followed the curve of the outer wall.

Slowly I walked round it, David following behind.

'This,' he explained, 'is the base of the telescope.' As I walked round it, I passed from the front part of the cottage to the back, which was occupied by a neatly made bed with a Mexican blanket across it, and a handsome old schoolteacher's desk strewn with papers. 'It goes down another ten feet or so,' David said. 'Right into bedrock.'

'I'm impressed,' I said.

'Telescopes are really sensitive,' he said. 'They'll pick up the tiniest vibration.' He slapped the concrete with his hand, and it made a fleshy, echoless sound. 'But this won't budge,' he said.

'It's sort of like living in a lighthouse,' I told him, running one of my hands along the concrete. The surface was pebbly and cool.

'More than you know,' he said. He held up the bottle of wine. 'Want some wine?' he asked. I nodded, and he gripped the Swiss Army corkscrew, eased it in, and began twisting. 'In a lighthouse,' he said, 'you're at land's end, looking out across the water. Up in the observatory, it's the same thing, except you're at the ends of the earth, and the sea you're looking across is space. The universe.' He pulled the cork free. Then he turned to the counter and quickly poured two glasses of wine. 'Up there,' he said, 'it's easy to forget about everything else.' He handed me a glass and picked up one for himself. 'You're all alone. It's just you. You and . . . whatever.'

I raised my glass. 'To "whatever", then,' I said.

We toasted lightly. Then I noticed that something about me seemed to have caught his eye.

'That scarf,' he said. 'It's really nice.' He reached out and gently lifted the end of it that hung down from my neck. It figured. The one thing that he had singled out for a compliment was my sister's contribution to the ensemble. It had to be an accessory of hers that I'd added, at a moment's notice, that provided the magic touch.

I might have allowed David's careless compliment to ruin the evening. But when he lifted the end of the scarf off my neck, his fingers brushed the skin there, and I felt a charge, an almost electrical kind of response. I held perfectly still while David ran the gold silk between two fingers. I don't think I even breathed until he let the scarf slip away.

'So when does the show begin?' I asked nervously, breaking the silence. 'The star show, I mean.'

'Whenever you like,' he said softly. 'We could go up now.'

This last statement seemed to be more of a question. I nodded hesitantly. David took my wineglass and placed it on the counter, then held up my coat. 'Here,' he said. 'You'll need this.'

I slipped into it. 'What about you?' I asked.

'I'll be fine,' he said, pointing to his soft, royal-blue fisherman's sweater.

He offered me his hand. 'This way,' he said, and began to lead me round the circular wall. He opened a door in the outer wall, then led me up a metal spiral staircase, into darkness. When we reached the landing, David suggested we wait a moment for my eyes to adjust.

Slowly, I began to see that something was looming over us, and in a moment I could make out what it was: the silhouette of the telescope against the night sky. And then I could see the outline of the opening in the dome. David led me several paces over, then one step up. Then he released my hand, turned me by the shoulders so that I was facing him, and reached behind me. 'Here,' he said.

I turned. Very dimly I could distinguish the shape of two seats, side by side, like a porch swing.

'The observer's chair,' he said.

I sat down. The seat was cushioned and comfortable.

David sat beside me and said, 'Ready?'

'Ready,' I said, though I wasn't sure for what.

David leaned forward and gripped something round resting between us. It was a steering wheel of sorts and, as he rotated it to the left, an amazing thing happened: we rose.

Without meaning to, I let out a light whoop. 'Sorry,' I said, raising my hand to my lips.

'Don't be. Let it out. Why not?' David said.

The seat appeared to be on some sort of gear and pulley system; by turning the wheel, he made it advance along a set of tracks that took us both back and up. 'This is an exact replica of the observatory at Harvard, only smaller,' David said. 'The original dates from the eighteen forties.' He let go of the wheel and turned to me. 'Would you like to drive?' he asked.

And so I did. I held the wheel and worked it to the left until we came to a jarring stop at the top, which made me whoop again, and by then we were both laughing so hard I turned the wheel back over to him. He worked it to the right and we began our descent.

Halfway down, David stopped. 'Now here's the good part,' he said, reaching out in the darkness for the end of the telescope. He leaned forward and pressed into the eyepiece. He lowered the seat further, but didn't remove his eye from the telescope. 'There it is.' David pulled away from the eyepiece. 'Now I want you to see this,' he told me. 'But don't touch anything or you'll knock it out of whack. Just gently, here, lean forward, like this—'

I did as he said. It was as though he'd told a child he had a surprise, and to close her eyes, and suddenly: Open them!

'Do you see it?' he asked me with quiet excitement.

'Oh,' was all I could say.

It was Saturn—the same Saturn we'd seen together the first day we'd met, out on Stone Point. But now, under the much greater magnification of this massive telescope, the planet leapt to life: the swirls of grey and gold on the surface, the silver rings, and somehow the whole miraculous sight suspended in the dark.

'It's just the most beautiful thing,' I said.

'I wanted you to see that,' said David. His voice was a whisper now. 'To see what you were missing last time.'

I turned from the eyepiece. His face was close to mine. Was he seeing the desire in my eyes that I was seeing in his? I turned my face upwards, under his, and the last thing I remember seeing as I closed my eyes was his dark silhouette moving into place over me, obscuring the sky, eclipsing the heavens.

His hands were inside my coat, as if trying to find warmth. And I reached beneath his sweater, touched him along his chest, feeling the smooth planes of muscle. I wanted us to stay suspended in this place, in this soft, swaying chair under the stars themselves. As I pulled him closer, David was with me entirely. I'd never felt that with anyone before, and I doubted I'd ever feel it with anyone else. It was like one of those comets that only comes around once in a lifetime, so you'd better know exactly where and when to look.

Later, we lay on Old Man Boyd's observer's chair, silent except for our gradually slowing breathing. David's chin rested against my shoulder. Then I felt him lift his head and gaze at me in the dark.

'OK,' he said. 'You can open your eyes.'

WE WERE SCARED; we'd have been crazy not to be. What was happening to us was so sudden, so complete. We shakily descended the observatory's circular metal staircase. I sat in a chair wearing David's oversized bathrobe, while he cooked chicken and whisked a mustard dressing for the salad that he'd been preparing when I'd arrived, and then we went to bed. This time we proceeded with each other more slowly. We lingered under the bright zigzags of the Mexican blanket, beginning to learn the touch of a new partner.

Later, we lay and talked softly. At one point, David said that we ought to give his cottage a name.

'It's only fair,' he said. 'All the houses around here have names; why not mine?' And so we ironically christened his cottage Stardust, laughing as we did, sharing another giddy moment together.

Outside the window I could see a midwinter sky packed full of stars. Just as David had said, it was easy to imagine that we were totally on our own out here. He'd been talking then about the observatory upstairs, but it was true downstairs as well.

'I see what you mean,' I said at one point, 'about this being the end of the world.'

He had one arm thrown back behind his head, exposing the thatch of hair under it. 'Not "end of the world", Liz,' he said. '"Ends of the earth".'

I ran a finger along David's chest. 'Well, you know what I mean,' I said.

He took a long time to respond, and when he did he didn't look at me. 'Maybe you were right the first time,' he said. 'That's what it can be like, when you feel things for somebody and it doesn't work out.'

'I guess I wouldn't know about that,' I said softly. I thought of Jeff Hardesty, back in Longwood Falls, all those years ago. We'd ended the relationship and he'd moved away. I hadn't broken his heart and he hadn't broken mine.

At last David turned towards me and said, 'I hope you never find out.' Then we said nothing more about it.

Late that night I left David's house and went back to The Eaves. When I looked into Nick's room, I saw that he was still fast asleep, his mouth open, his face flushed. I walked to his bed and impulsively kissed his forehead, and I wished I could tell this little boy, 'I'm in love with your teacher.' What David and I had was too raw, too fragile to be spoken about.

I understood that part of what had brought us together so breathlessly was that we were running out of time. Under other circumstances, we might have been able to get to know each other slowly over weeks, months. But the fact was, we didn't have the luxury of time; soon my sister would be home and I was supposed to head back to Longwood Falls.

When I was with David, I experienced everything in a way I never had before. Which was why, when David and I lay in bed again the next time, and he propped himself up on his elbow and said, 'Listen, Liz, we have to talk,' I froze in place, my stomach tightening. We'd been lovers for a matter of days, and now I was hearing the words that, this early in a relationship, can mean only one thing: *This isn't working.* And in that moment, my world fell away.

But what David said was, 'I'm going to Hawaii next weekend to see the observatories there. They're some of the biggest in the world. This is a trip I've been planning for a long time. Obviously it's not the ideal moment, but it's very important to me.'

'OK,' I heard myself say, still not sure where this conversation was going.

'Anyway,' he said, 'the point is that I've got airline mileage that I've been saving up for something important, and I was thinking, this is it. If you wanted to go with me, it might be a chance for us to get away together.'

My relief was palpable. 'I thought you were getting ready to tell me we shouldn't see each other any more,' I said.

'No, no,' he said. 'It's the opposite.'

I waited a moment. Then I said, 'I'll go with you. I mean, assuming that Harper says it's OK. Jeannette's there, and Nick will be in good hands, and it's only for a few days, but I'll have to ask.'

David sank back on his pillow, smiling with sleepy contentment. 'I hope she says yes,' he said. Then he turned to me, and in a quiet voice he said, 'I love you, Liz.'

I waited, letting the words shimmer for an extra moment. 'I love you, too,' I told him, my voice suddenly hoarse.

'Are you scared?' he asked.

I nodded. 'You?'

'Yes,' he said. 'Very.'

We barely knew each other, and had spent only two nights together, yet it seemed that we'd already come a great distance. We wanted to focus solely on each other in a way we couldn't here in Stone Point. For a few days, forget about Nick. Forget about Harper. Forget about everybody and everything but us.

THE NEXT DAY, I called Harper while Nick was out of the house and asked her permission. I had anticipated some surprise on her part that I'd got involved with someone, perhaps even mild shock that it was Mr Fields, her son's teacher. What I got instead was silence, a discomfort that was impossible to miss. And I realised that I'd been insensitive. Here was Harper, overwhelmed by grief, barely able to get through the day, and here was her sister, asking for permission to go to Hawaii with a lover.

'That's great, Liz,' she finally said softly. 'Yes, by all means, go.'

'Are you sure? You don't think it's weird?'

'Weird how?' she asked after a long moment.

'Well, because he's Nick's teacher,' I said.

Another pause, then: 'I'm happy for you, Liz. Really.'

That evening, I told Nick I was thinking of going away for a few days. He and I were playing Clue on the living-room rug. As I talked to Nick, he started fidgeting with a game-piece.

'I'll be going to Hawaii,' I told him. 'With Mr Fields.'

Now Nick looked up. 'My teacher?'

'That's right. You know I've been spending time with him.'

'Can I come?' he asked.

'No, I don't think that's possible,' I said.

Nick turned away sharply, throwing down the game-piece and not saying anything. The intensity of his reaction surprised me, and for a moment I didn't know how to respond.

'Well, I just won't go to Hawaii then,' I said. 'I'm so sorry, Nick. I had no idea it would upset you that much if I went away for a few days. But no, you're right, I'll definitely—'

'It's not that. It's not Hawaii.'

His voice was thin. His back was to me. I could see his shoulders hunching, his neck straining with the effort not to burst into tears.

'All right, then,' I said, after a moment. 'What is it?'

'You're going away for good soon, aren't you?' he asked.

'You mean back to Longwood Falls?' He nodded his head. 'Well, I'm supposed to, when your mom is strong enough to come home,' I stammered.

I reached out to touch his shoulder, but he jerked away. 'Nick, listen to me.'

'No!' he said, and he put his hands over his ears. I got down on my knees and tried to look him in the eyes. But Nick only stared through me as if I'd already left, one more ghost in a life already overcrowded with them.

'All right then, don't listen,' I said, 'but I'm going to keep talking anyway, because I think you ought to hear this. When I go back to Longwood Falls, we'll talk on the phone, and I'll drive down to visit you. And you can even come up to stay with me, in the house where your mom and I grew up. I promise you, we'll always be friends, no matter what happens. I promise.'

Something crossed his face then—a look of surrender—and the tears came at last. He put his hands down and collapsed against me. I'd never seen Nick cry before. I held him and talked to him for a long time, until the sobbing stopped.

Finally he was quiet, and then he fell asleep in my arms. I must have fallen asleep, too, for the next thing I remember, he was shaking me awake, saying, 'Aunt Liz, I want you to go.'

'What?' I said, coming fully out of sleep, recalling the first day we'd met, out on the hill, and how he'd said the same thing then.

'I want you to go to Hawaii, and bring me back a piece of a volcano, OK? My friends will be so jealous.'

I knew that his desire for me to go on this trip had very little to do with volcanic rock. Though only seven years old, Nick saw how much I really wanted to be alone with David. 'It's only for a few days,' Nick added. 'I'll be fine. Go, Aunt Liz. *Go*.'

 Chapter Four

From the aeroplane heading into the Hawaiian Islands, I could see the sun slanting light on an amazing expanse of turquoise water. David and I held hands as the plane touched down at the airport. Local women festooned us with garlands made of fragrant pink frangipani flowers when we arrived. As we walked across the tarmac, the heat was strong, and I felt overdressed. We'd taken off in the middle of winter, and seemingly landed in the middle of summer.

At our hotel in Hilo, a bellboy showed us to our suite, which had a balcony that overlooked the white sand of the beach. We stood out there for a little while, feeling the breeze ripple across us and watching the swimmers play in the water below.

David took me by the shoulder and turned me towards him. 'So here we are, Liz,' he said quietly.

'It feels so strange,' I said. I looked at him. 'Are you growing a beard?' I asked, and he reached up to the stubble on his chin.

'I forgot to shave before we left,' he admitted.

'I like it,' I said, running my hand along the roughness of his face.

He came forward and we kissed, and then we went inside, letting our clothing drop into soft piles and looking at each other with shyness. After a few moments David went into the bathroom and I heard the sound of water running as he filled the oversized marble whirlpool bath We settled into the scented water and began to kiss, to touch each other in the warm slide of the bath. His new beard was slightly harsh against my face, a contrast to the softness of his hands and the gentle heat of the water.

After a while we left the bath and moved to the bed. The sheets were soft white linen, and later we lay entwined in them, in each other, not wanting to move. Eventually, David got up and brought us a can of pineapple juice from the minibar, flipping open the pop-top. We passed it back and forth, drinking thirstily, and though I'd never particularly liked pineapple juice before, it tasted sweet and cool now, and I knew that he'd chosen it as a symbol of our trip, our entry into this exotic land where spiky pineapples improbably grew on trees, where the beach sand was as fine as flour, and where our time belonged only to us.

THE NEXT MORNING we set out for the observatories. I was walking out of our hotel room in a pair of shorts and a T-shirt when David called to me.

'Here,' he said. 'You'll need this.'

He was handing me my coat. I started to reach for it, then stopped, figuring it was some sort of joke.

'Trust me,' he said.

I nodded, accepted the coat, and we were off. I leaned back in the front seat of our rented four-wheel-drive vehicle and minutes later we were outside Hilo and the gentle vegetation abruptly ended, replaced by cactuses.

In the distance rose Mauna Loa, which David had explained to me was an active volcano. I could see steam venting from it. To the other side of the road rose its nearly identical twin, Mauna Kea, a dormant volcano and our destination for the day. They were like Harper and me, I thought to myself. Twins who were entirely different.

Every few minutes, the landscape changed. For a while, it was the ashen, uninterrupted black of volcanic residue. Then we turned, and the road rose, and we were surrounded by rolling green hills. Then the view vanished as we drove upwards through clouds, and when we came out of the clouds, the hillside was covered with twiglike shrubs and the occasional bush. Finally we stopped at what appeared to be a chalet. We climbed out of the car, and to my surprise the air was bracing, even cold.

'I see what you mean,' I said, grabbing my coat from the back seat. David only smiled.

'So where are the telescopes?' I asked.

David pointed past me. I turned; the mountain rose behind me.

'There's more?' I said.

'Yes,' he said. 'This is where we can acclimatise ourselves. We're already at nine thousand feet, and the summit's nearly fourteen thousand.' He turned towards the chalet. 'And this is where the astronomers stay. Hold on a minute.' Before I could say another word, David had trotted off. A tall, grey-haired man was leaving the chalet for the parking lot, and David walked right up to him, said something, and shook his hand. I got back into the car as the men fell into conversation, eyeing the sky together.

After a few minutes David climbed back into the car. As he steered us onto the winding gravel road to begin the final stretch up the mountain, he was smiling to himself.

'Do you know who that was?' he finally said, and then he mentioned some name I'd never heard of, and he explained that this was a very important astronomer, a hero of sorts to him. As David described for me what this astronomer had accomplished, it occurred to me that I'd never before seen him so excited, so animated, so alive—and it troubled me in a way. I knew that David had a side to him that I couldn't reach. The last time we'd been together in his cottage, we'd made love lying beneath the Mexican blanket, and then sat up and talked for a while. Suddenly he'd eased himself out of bed, as if his mind were elsewhere. 'Where are you going?' I'd asked him gently, although I already knew the answer.

'The observatory.'

He'd said it matter-of-factly, but the word now came to mean more to me than that circular room over our heads. I understood that it was his refuge, the place where he could lose himself in a way he couldn't even with me. He pulled on a sweater and a pair of trousers and work boots, and walked up the steel staircase. A minute later I heard the rattle of chains as the ancient pulleys of the observer's chair churned away. I lay staring out of the window for a while, seeing the same sky that David was seeing, yet knowing I wasn't.

Now we were a long way from that place we jokingly called Stardust. The Hawaiian landscape was changing yet again. There was no vegetation here near the top of the mountain, only great grey boulders and slabs, as barren as Mars. And still we climbed. My breath came shorter, and a dull ache began hammering somewhere at the back of my neck. I watched the road. The grey of the rocks was replaced by white—smooth, unbroken, as blinding as the sun.

'Snow,' I said. 'In Hawaii.'

And then we rounded one last bend, and suddenly the top of the mountain came into view, and with it the domes of the observatories, one after another, whiter even than the snow. We cruised past a couple, then finally David stopped the car on a ledge. I climbed out, pulled the belt of my coat tight, and walked to the lip.

It was hard to tell where the snow ended and the clouds began; where the clouds broke and the ocean poked through. This blur of sky and earth and water stretched for ever in every direction, as if there were no directions any more, as if we'd left the points of the compass behind us. And maybe we had. It was just us now—the sun, too, settling into a reddish haze at the horizon to one side of us, and nightfall rushing up on us from the other side.

It was us in the gathering darkness. Nothing but us.

David was standing with his hand on his hips, mouth slightly open, head tipped back.

'Tell me something,' I said. 'Tell me what you see.'

He took a breath, then said, 'Where to begin? Remember the first time we went out to dinner, how I said I used to go to the Point as a kid and look at the sky with my binoculars?'

'I remember.'

'Well, as I kept looking, I kept learning more and more about the planets and stars and galaxies. I started bringing star charts, then investing in better equipment. The more I'd find, the more I couldn't wait to get back there and try something even more difficult.

'But the thing is,' he went on, 'the time comes when you begin to realise that the more you look, the less you know. Sure, you understand how far apart everything is. And then it's too much, and you can't make sense of it. What's the difference between a billion years or ten billion years? Between a trillion miles or a hundred trillion miles?'

He stopped, considering whether to go on.

'But it's not just how big everything is, or how old. It's what happens out there.' He laughed, but it was a bitter kind of laugh. 'I'm sorry to say this, Liz, but the universe is not a happy place. It's full of unspeakable violence. You know those TV documentaries about animals in the wilderness, and everything looks so peaceful out there on the African veld? But then you get closer, and you see the way animals are always hunting one another and killing one another, and how they have to do that in order to survive.

'Well, the universe is a lot like that, only a million times worse,' he went on. 'It's ruthless. Full of things devouring one another, burning up and exploding and crashing into one another and then disappearing for ever. Galaxies come to life, and a few billion years later the stars start to blink out, one by one. And once there was this beautiful spiral of light, with who knows how many stars with who knows how many planets, and then it's gone. Now you see it, now you don't.'

'Fire and ice,' I said, thinking of the meteor we'd seen together that first night at the Point.

'And how do you make sense of that?' he said. 'Why do you even try? But you do try.' He stopped. His head was up, staring down the heavens themselves. 'That's the hard part.'

'To keep looking,' I said.

He nodded. For once, I knew exactly what to say. I just didn't know if I dared to say it. But I knew this, too: if I didn't say it, David and I would never have a chance.

'You can stop looking now,' I said softly.

For a moment, David didn't respond. Then he said, 'I know. That's what terrifies me the most.'

As we stood there, I had to use the back of my hand to wipe the tears from my face, and then from his. Still, we didn't move. It was as if neither of us wanted to leave the mountain just yet. We stood there a few minutes longer, not just leaning into each other in the absolute darkness of the end of the world, but leaning into each other in the absolute darkness of the end of the world together.

ON OUR FINAL AFTERNOON in Hawaii, after we'd gone for one last dip in the ocean, David announced he had an errand he needed to run alone. When he returned to our room a short while later he asked me to close my eyes and hold out my hand. I felt something light and square descend there, and when I opened my eyes I found that he'd presented me with a tiny box. It was wrapped in tissue paper the same shade as the sea outside our window, and it was small enough to hold a piece of jewellery—a ring, maybe.

'Oh,' I said.

'Open it.'

As I turned the box over and slipped a fingernail under the tape, I noticed that my hands were trembling slightly. The two halves of the turquoise tissue paper parted easily and fell to the carpet. I turned the box over, lifted the lid and saw a glimmer of gold. I reached inside and pinched my fingers around—

'A key?'

'To Stardust,' David said, slightly embarrassed. 'So that after you go back to Longwood Falls, and you want to come to stay, you can just let yourself in.' He paused. 'Look, Liz, it wouldn't be fair to ask you to give up your life in Longwood Falls. And I can't leave my students. But I'm hoping you'll start to think of the observatory as a kind of second home. A place you can come to whenever you want.'

'Are you sure?' I asked.

'Yes,' he said. 'Completely. I just know that I want us to be together as much as possible, in whatever way we can.' He stopped and gave me an odd look. 'Are *you* sure?'

It was strange. Although I'd been involved with a few different men over the years, there had never been anyone I really wanted to come home to. But with David, I could imagine letting myself into that place where I felt so comfortable, where I knew he waited. Now I came forward and kissed him, my fingers closing over the golden key.

THE FOLLOWING AFTERNOON, after a disorientating night of air travel, I was back at my sister's house. My arms were heavy with gifts for Nick: three different kinds of macadamia nuts, a make-your-own-volcano kit, and, of course, one rock. The taxi from the airport had dropped a sleepy, stumbling David off at the observatory, then took me on to The Eaves, but when I walked in the front door, I was met with a surprise.

Harper was standing there.

For a second I just stared, as though she was a mirage caused by extreme jet lag.

'What are you doing here?' I asked.

'Aren't you going to say hello?' my sister asked me, and in a shaky voice I dutifully said hello, put down my bags, then came forward and kissed her.

'I thought I would surprise you,' Harper said. 'I was getting kind of antsy down there on the island, and I missed Nick so much, and I just thought to myself: It's time. So yesterday I decided I'd arrange for my return to coincide with yours. And here I am.'

There she was. She looked rested now; I could see that right away. Her hair was growing back, stylish again, her skin was tanned, and she no longer wore the intensely shell-shocked look she'd worn the day of the funeral. She was, if nothing else, intact.

Before I had a chance to say anything to her, though, Nick bounded down the stairs to see me. He looked different too. It was almost as though in my short time away he'd changed in some physical way. Then I realised that if he looked different it wasn't because I had been gone. It was because his mother was back.

The three of us went and sat in the living room, and as Nick opened his presents, Harper turned to me and quietly said, 'Thank you, Liz. You took good care of Nick.'

'I loved it,' I said. 'He's a wonderful boy. We've really got to know each other.'

'Well,' she said, 'you've still got to be pretty tired of being a baby sitter. Now that I'm back, you're relieved of your duties. You can go back to your own life.' I didn't say anything. 'I thought you'd be glad,' she said. But when I looked at her with a complicated expression on my face, Harper said, 'Oh.' Then she nodded her head slightly. 'It's David. Of course. I should have realised.'

And she was right; it was David. I hadn't expected Harper back so soon, and her presence here left me free to go. Yet suddenly that option seemed far from desirable, and even before I knew what I was saying, I'd said it, and I'd meant it:

'Actually—actually, I'm not going back.'

LATER THAT AFTERNOON, I stopped by the observatory to tell David what I wanted to do. He blinked several times, absorbing the news, then kissed me hard and lifted me high in the air. I made him swear that if he had any reservations about my staying on he had to tell me right now, but he promised that he had none.

'Are you kidding?' he said. 'This is what I was hoping you'd do.'

'You should have said something,' I said.

'You could have said something, too,' David answered, and I laughed lightly.

'Well,' I said, 'now I have.'

'OK,' he said. 'Now it's my turn to say something.' He leaned into me and whispered. 'Let's go to bed.'

I laughed again. 'I have to get back to The Eaves for dinner,' I said.

'Dinner's not for a couple of hours.'

I glanced at the bed and imagined slipping under that Mexican blanket with David. 'Well, maybe I could stay for a little while,' I said.

AS WE LAY TOGETHER on David's bed and the last streaks of twilight left the sky outside the window and neither of us made a move to turn on a light, it was possible to imagine that many days might end like this for years to come. In our short time together David and I had already fallen into a rhythm as if we'd been doing this all our lives. One week we were following our predictable individual paths through the emptiness of space; the next, we'd fallen into each other's orbits, there to follow the graceful tug and pull of our mutual attraction.

'Better be careful,' David said to me, when I tried out for him this astronomical interpretation of our lives. 'We don't want to collide, or anything.'

'Oh, I don't know. I've got no complaints about the collision we just had.'

He smiled. 'I mean the crash-and-burn kind.'

'So do I.'

I had learned to look at the heavens the way David did—to see in the stars the same unforgiving character that a man who'd lost his mother as a little boy might find there. But couldn't he learn to see what I saw above, too: light, beauty, hope?

'David,' I said, 'aren't there any double planets or stars out there that don't crash and burn? Is that what you tell your students the heavens are all about—doom and gloom?'

A full moon was just rising above the trees outside the window. David studied me closely in the bluish light that lay across our bed. Finally he got up on his knees, unlatched the window and leaned out. I got up on my knees and joined him, elbows on the ledge, craning out into the cold evening air. 'There we go,' he said. 'See Orion?'

I followed his gaze. 'The three stars in a row right there?' I said.

'Now look a little above, to the left. Those two bright stars?'

'I see them.'

'Liz Mallory, I give you Castor and Pollux,' he said. 'Sons of Leda. Twins, actually. Oh.'

'What's the matter?'

'Nothing. I just realised, you know, *twins*. Like you and Harper.'

'Well, that's all right,' I said. I brought my head back through the window into the cottage. 'No crashing and burning there,' I said. 'Not any more.'

THE FOLLOWING AFTERNOON I picked Nick up at school. This time I was early, and I got out of the car. I paced the sidewalk, straining for a glimpse of David's classroom through the windows of the school across the lawn.

At the far end of the first floor, some sort of presentation seemed to be in progress. Through the tall, arched windows I could see a little girl holding a giant hand-painted picture of the sun over her head while boys and girls holding pictures of planets circled around her. And there at the head of the classroom, choreographing the dance of the solar system, was David, nodding his head and waving his arms in some grand explanation, and an odd thing happened then. It wasn't the kids in his classroom who I imagined him teaching at that moment; it was our own child, the boy or girl we might have together. The child I suddenly couldn't wait to meet, the child I suddenly couldn't bear to be without.

I stood as if in a trance, watching the planets make their revolution, watching life go on and on, bringing love with it, and sadness, and children, and entire unexpected lives. It wasn't until David dismissed his students and they pulled off their costumes and began to stream from the classroom, that I finally stopped looking.

Afterwards, I drove Nick home to The Eaves. I was heading up the front steps, planning just to gather up my belongings to take over to David's, when I caught sight of Harper coming up the path from the woods. She was wearing an old sweatshirt streaked with smears of yellow and blue, and suddenly I realised what she'd been doing.

'Harper, you've been painting,' I said, walking back down the steps.

She shrugged, seeming self-conscious, as though she'd been caught doing something illicit. 'Not really,' she said. 'Just mixing some colours. Experimenting a little.' She lowered her eyes.

'Well, I'd love to see the studio some time,' I said. 'When you're ready. I confess Nick and I looked through the window once while you were gone. It looked beautiful.'

Harper looked back up at me, considering. Then she gestured with her head and said, 'OK. Come on.'

It was clear that she wasn't yet comfortable returning to her work. She was on fragile ground here—or on no ground, as if she were on a tightrope. I understood it was my responsibility not to say or do anything, as she was taking these first, tentative steps, that might make her look down.

The padlock on the studio was gone now, and the door swung open easily. My sister stepped aside, and I entered before her.

'It's a wonderful place,' I said quietly.

'Yes,' said Harper, as if, even after all these years, she were as much in awe of this safe haven she'd created for herself in the middle of the woods as a visitor might be. 'It really is.'

'You used to tell Mom and Dad that you were going to have a real studio some day. Is this the way you pictured it?'

Harper paused, thinking about this, and then she nodded. 'Yes,' she said. 'I think it is.' After a moment she added, 'But the rest of my life isn't. I'm not sure *what* I pictured.'

We sat down on the bed in the corner of the room and our knees brushed against each other. 'To answer your question from before,' she said, 'I *have* been painting a little. I started during my last few days on Sanibel Island. I've had an idea about a painting. A series of paintings, actually—' She stopped herself. 'I don't really want to talk about it, though. It's too new, too raw.' She looked down and smiled slightly, to herself. 'Do you know what Nick's made me promise I'll do tonight when you're gone? Play Clue with him. God, I can't remember the last time I played Clue.'

'No, you never were big on board games, were you?' I said.

'I never had the patience for them. They bored me to tears.'

'But you'll play Clue for Nick's sake,' I said.

'Yes,' she said. 'It's what mothers do. I'm finding that out, finally. It's the little things that children care about. The big stuff—the fact that you've given them a trust fund, or a beautiful home on the water—they barely notice.'

'Yes,' I said. 'That's true.'

Then there was a long pause, and I saw that Harper seemed to be struggling to say something. She reached out and took my hands, as if it were the most natural gesture in the world between the two of us. 'Being with David,' she finally said, 'it seems to have done something for you. You seem much more open. Less guarded. I feel like I can really talk to you for the first time.' She paused uneasily. 'Or maybe it's me that's changed.'

'Harper—' I said.

'No, let me finish.' She was looking down at our joined hands. 'You'd think with the two of us being twins it would be easy to talk like this. But sometimes I think we had it harder than regular sisters.'

'In a way, we did,' I said.

She released my hands then. She let go and raised her arms, spreading them wide, as if to take in the estate and all of Stone Point. 'Can you believe this life I've fallen into?' She shook her head. 'It's not what we knew in Longwood Falls, is it?'

'No, it's not.'

'It creeps up on you, like an addiction. It's like: Here's a little something that will make your life a little easier, and here's a little something else. And, of course, you want your life to be easier, so you say yes to everything, but then one day you're not the person you ever wanted to be.' She took a breath. 'Anyway, I just want to say that Nick thinks you're a terrific aunt. And I'm glad you're going to be living so nearby.'

'It'll be good to be here,' I said. 'There, I mean.' I waved vaguely. 'Wherever.'

My sister abruptly stood up from the bed. 'I've got to get out of these clothes,' she said suddenly. 'I must look like a walking Jackson Pollock painting.'

As Harper walked towards the bathroom to wash and change, I asked her if I could take a look around.

'Why not?' she said, shrugging, and then she went into the bathroom, shutting the door behind her. I was tempted to leave then, to let myself out and not risk spoiling the fragile moment. It had been glorious to watch my sister start to come back, to extend herself to me in a way she never had. And then it occurred to me that I had done exactly the same thing, with David.

I stood up and began to walk around the studio, really looking hard at the old canvases that leaned against walls, appreciating for the first time the detail of my sister's brushwork, and her use of hybrid tones that I'd never seen before. I walked over to a large wooden storage rack where she kept some of her finished paintings, and carefully I lifted one out from its slot. It was a beautiful, if melancholy, painting of Nick and Doe when they were small. They sat leaning together, exhausted, as if at the end of a very long day. After a moment I slipped the painting back in and took out the next one, which was a painting of Carlo, dressed in a pale linen summer suit, looking every bit as commanding and wealthy and elegant as he did in real life. My sister had a way of capturing the truth about people, a talent I could only admire.

I slipped the painting of Carlo back in its slot, and pulled out the next painting, lifting it swiftly. I stood holding it in both hands, and it took me only a moment to understand what I was looking at.

It was a painting of David, and in it he lay naked on a bed, sprawled with unmistakable ease across a Mexican blanket decorated with colourful zigzags.

Chapter Five

'Clean at last,' called Harper from the bathroom.

I kept looking at the painting, not taking my eyes off it. David's body was fully visible: the long legs, the tapering of hair on the torso, the musculature, the entire beautiful body that I had touched and held and which I had begun to feel belonged to me. David's eyes looked out from the depths of the canvas, telling me something that I suppose I should have always known.

Harper walked back into the room tugging a comb through her hair. Her mouth was moving, making words, but I couldn't hear what she was saying. Instead, I just kept looking at that mouth, imagining it on David's. I imagined Harper putting down her paint-brush and joining David in his bed, our bed, the bed I now held in my hand.

I shoved the painting back in its slot.

'All set, Liz?' But I just stood there, not knowing where to look: not at Harper, not at the paintings, not at anything.

'Liz?'

Had he taken Harper upstairs to the observatory, too? Was that what I'd been for David, what I'd always been throughout my life, a poor substitute for my sister?

'Liz, are you all right?' Harper's voice was strained with worry now. 'What's going on?'

Or worse, were they still lovers? Suddenly, anything was possible. I had to find out. I had to know everything.

I lifted the painting again and turned it round so she could see it. And in that split second, looking at Harper's face, I had my answer. For her eyes had widened and her mouth had gone slack, and she had the unmistakable look of someone who has been caught.

'It's true, then,' I began. 'You and David were lovers.'

She eased the painting from my hand and slowly returned it to where it had come from. 'Yes,' she said after a moment. 'We were.'

'Are you still?'

She shook her head vehemently. 'Of course not. It ended two years ago.' She waited a beat. 'I wouldn't do that to you, Liz.'

This comment enraged me. 'You wouldn't do that,' I said, 'but instead you *would* keep this fact from me, as though it's completely irrelevant?'

'Let me explain—'

'You'd let me think that I was the one he wanted,' I interrupted, 'when all along he was thinking about you: the more dynamic twin, the more exciting one.'

'Oh, I don't think so,' she said.

'Come on, Harper,' I went on. 'They always get obsessed with you. I've seen it happen throughout our lives. Don't tell me you don't know what I'm talking about.'

'I see. That's what this is really about, isn't it?' she said. 'Look, I probably shouldn't have kept it from you, but if this is just one more chance for you to feel sorry for yourself—'

'So why *didn't* you tell me?' I cut her off. 'On the phone when I called you to ask about going to Hawaii? What about five minutes ago, when we were sitting on that bed over there and you were saying how you'd never been able to talk to me like this before?'

'Because it's *over*,' she said. 'There's nothing to tell.'

'Nothing to tell? You call having had an affair with the man your sister is seriously involved with "nothing to tell"? My God, this life of yours really has done something to you.'

'I'll tell you what it hasn't done,' she said, her voice suddenly hard and cruel. 'It hasn't made me meek and self-pitying.'

I thought of how she'd had so much in her life: wealth, fame, children, lovers. She'd even briefly had David. Suddenly I stepped forward and did something I still can't quite believe I did: slapped her.

Harper cried out and put her own hand to her face. There was a shocked silence as we both took in what I'd just done. Then she lowered her hand.

'At least,' she said, 'when I feel sorry for myself and go off somewhere and collapse, I've got a damn good reason.'

I turned away. 'That's not fair,' I said.

'Since when is life fair?' said Harper. 'If it was fair, I'd still have my daughter.' I could hear her breathe heavily, gathering herself. 'I'll tell you what happened, if you want to know.'

I didn't answer. She went on. 'We were lovers years ago. We met jogging on the beach, and one thing led to another. My marriage had failed. I was lonely, and so was he. It wasn't love. It was a physical thing.'

'This is supposed to make me feel better?' I asked.

'I'm trying to get you to see that this isn't about *you*. I was on the rebound from Carlo,' she went on in a quieter voice. 'I was in no position to be involved with anyone, and I broke it off. I handled it badly. He was angry. Begged me to change my mind, but I wouldn't.' She shrugged. 'Occasionally, after that, we'd run into each other in town, but we didn't speak. It wasn't until Nick was in his class that we had any contact with each other. And that's the whole story.'

Here it was, all over again, the story of our lives—the beautiful sister gets everything she wants, and the lesser sister gets whatever's left, and nothing Harper could say could change that.

'I have to go,' I said.

'Liz, please.'

'Do you have something new to tell me?' I asked.

She shook her head.

'Then goodbye, Harper,' I said, and I walked out of her studio. She knew where I was going, and she didn't try to follow.

DAVID CAME TO THE DOOR, his face breaking into a smile at my arrival. I stood looking past him and across the room, feeling a surprising sense of indifference towards this place that I had loved. He saw something in my face and said to me, 'Liz, what is it?'

I looked at him. 'I know about you and Harper,' I said. He didn't reply but just stood there, shaken and unblinking. 'Were you planning on keeping it from me for ever?' I asked.

David appeared shocked. He ran a hand through his tangle of hair and in a quiet voice he said, 'No. No, I wasn't.'

'You should have told me right away,' I said.

'Why?' asked David.

'It was your responsibility.'

'Who says?' he asked. 'Why was it my responsibility to make myself look really pathetic in your eyes—to be just another jerk who got dumped by your sister?' He took a breath and stepped closer to me. 'She used me, Liz. I didn't tell you at first because I was *embarrassed*. I just wanted the whole thing to be buried for ever.'

'Well, it's been dug up,' I said. Something occurred to me then. 'She was the woman who abandoned you, wasn't she?' I asked.

'Yes,' he said. 'She was.'

David paced around the cottage nervously. 'I dreaded telling you. I knew you'd be upset. You'd assume Harper was the real thing for me, and you were the consolation prize.'

'That's exactly right,' I said. 'I think you got involved with me because I was the next best thing to her.'

'It's not a contest!' he said, and he was shouting now. 'Can't you get that through your head? This isn't about you and your sister; it's about you and me!'

I looked away from him and around the small living room. I'd imagined growing older with David here. I saw us upstairs in the observatory, our future son or daughter sitting in David's lap as we went for a ride in the chair. Then the image began to fade, to disappear before it had had a chance to become real.

'I'm going home,' I said to him.

'I'll come by tomorrow,' David said. 'We can get past this.'

'I mean *home*,' I said. 'I'm going home to Longwood Falls.'

David stared at me. 'You can do better than that, Liz.'

'Apparently not.' I turned to go.

'I suppose I should have expected this,' he said.

I stopped.

'I've spent my whole life being extremely cautious, holding myself back.' There was a sharp edge to David's voice that hadn't been there a moment before. He was rapidly becoming as angry as I was. 'People *leave*; it's just what they do. You can tell yourself that you've found the exception, the one who's there for the long run, but you're only kidding yourself. I convinced myself that you would never do this to me.' David shook his head. 'But you're no different from any of them.' He took a sharp inward breath and added, 'You're no better than your sister. In some ways, maybe you're even worse. A decent, thoughtful person who runs a library, takes good care of her nephew. Claims she wants a bigger life, something she can call her own. So then she's actually about to get that life, and what does she do? She lets it be destroyed by something that happened a long time ago.'

I looked at David, not even trying to argue with what he was saying. The fact was, I'd always wonder whether he still quietly longed for Harper. I'd always feel like I was the one he settled for. The idea of 'getting past this'—of staying in Stone Point, of trying to establish a relationship with my sister and nephew while building a life with David—suddenly seemed absurd.

'I'm sorry,' I whispered, barely able to find a voice.

He studied me for a moment. 'Me, too,' he said.

These were the last words David spoke to me before I left. I knew that they were likely to be the last words he would ever speak to me. The idea of never seeing him again, never hearing his voice, or waking up against him, our bodies slowly breaking the surface of sleep like two drowsy swimmers, left me breathless, stunned.

Now I silently said goodbye. David and I stood and looked at each other, and there was no way to undo this, to come gratefully into each other's arms as we'd done so many other nights in this cottage.

Without another word I walked out, heading back to my car. Then something made me turn and look back. In one of the windows David suddenly appeared for a moment, and our eyes met, and then he stepped out of the frame for the very last time.

I NEEDED TO GO BACK to Harper's house briefly to gather my belongings. I'd hoped to do it swiftly and quietly, not wanting to make a scene. But as I stood in the guest room packing, there was a knock on my door. I opened it, expecting that it was Harper.

But it was Nick. He was ready for bed, wearing his pyjamas and a pair of furry slippers in the shape of reindeer. His hair was still damp from his bath. It broke my heart to see him, to know what my unexpected departure was likely to do to him.

'Aunt Liz,' he said. 'I know it's late, but do you want to play something with me?'

I shook my head no. 'I'm so sorry, honey,' I said quietly, and the phrase encompassed all that I felt for Nick in this moment.

'Are you getting ready to go to Mr Fields's place?' he asked.

I shook my head and sighed heavily. Then I came forward, taking his hands in mine. 'I'm leaving for real,' I told him. 'I'm going back to Longwood Falls.'

He stared at me. 'Longwood Falls?' he said. 'When you came back from Hawaii, you said you were going to stay here in Stone Point. That you'd still pick me up at school sometimes, and that we'd always do stuff.'

'We can still do stuff,' I said carefully, and my throat thickened; I didn't want to start to cry right now. There had been enough pain in this house to last a lifetime. 'You'll come and visit me,' I said. 'We'll arrange it as often as we can.'

'But you said—'

'Well, I changed my mind,' I said. 'As it turns out, I have to go back there after all.'

'For ever?' he asked, and the words were chilling. *Was* this for ever? Most likely, I knew, it was. People's lives didn't keep offering an unlimited series of new possibilities.

'Yes,' I said, nodding. 'Probably for ever.'

Nick looked away from me, shifting his gaze towards the wall of windows and the Sound invisibly beyond. 'I can't believe it,' he said, his voice cracking.

'No, no, Nick, you'll be OK,' I said gently. 'You've got your mom back.'

Nick turned back to me now, and something wild and fearful had entered his eyes. 'You promised,' he said, his voice rising up. 'You *promised*.' And with that he turned and ran from the room. I heard the heavy front door of the house slam behind him.

By the time I made my way outside he had gone off into the dark. I was worried, for he was wearing only pyjamas and slippers, and there was still snow on the ground. 'Nick, wait!' I shouted, but there was no answer.

I turned back inside the house and ran upstairs to Harper's room. I told her what had happened, the words coming out all at once.

'What have you done?' Harper said, her eyes narrowed.

'I'm sorry,' I tried. 'It just happened, and—'

'I don't want to hear it,' she said. She shrugged into her coat. 'If anything happens to him . . .' she said, letting her voice trail off. She'd already lost one child; now her second one was out there in the night. My sister pressed two call buttons on the house intercom, gathering Tom and Jeannette together. She handed out flashlights and soon we were all off searching for Nick.

I headed down the path to Harper's studio, thinking that perhaps Nick was hiding out there. But the place was completely dark. And then I realised where I'd find him.

As I came to the top of the hill where his sister had died, I stopped a moment and swept my flashlight across the open field. It took me only a moment to locate a tiny figure standing in the distance, just as I'd found him that first day.

'Nick!' I called, and he started to run.

'Go away,' he said, just as he'd said that first day, but I caught up wtih him. He slipped and fell to one knee, and I slipped after him, and together we tumbled to the snow and dirt. 'Get away from me!' he yelled, trying to stand up. I wrapped him in my arms, smothering him like a fire with a blanket. 'I hate you!' he yelled. 'Let me go! Mommy! Mommy!'

And then a hand was on my shoulder, a firm, adult grip, pulling me back. I looked up to find Tom, the butler, standing over us.

'That's enough now,' Tom said, and Nick grew still.

And then Harper caught up with us, kneeling down and gathering her son tightly in her arms, wrapping him up in them as though she would never let go. I stayed sitting on the damp, cold earth, trying to catch my breath while the two of them leaned into each other, crying and sobbing together.

'I miss Doe,' I heard Nick say. 'Oh, Mommy, I miss her so much.'

'So do I,' Harper said.

'I can't believe it,' he said. 'I'll never see her again. Never!'

'I can't believe it either,' said Harper.

'Oh, Mommy.'

'Nick, sweetie, oh, my Nick.'

'She was laughing so much. Remember how she laughed sometimes, and it sounded almost like a scream? When she went down the hill she was just laughing and laughing like that.'

'I know.'

'It's not fair.'

'No. No, it's not. Not fair at all.'

'I'm worried that I'll forget her, Mommy.'

'Oh, no, Nick, we won't forget her. Not ever.'

I'd caught my breath now. I stood up and backed away, until I couldn't hear what they were saying any more, until I couldn't even tell whether they were talking or just rocking each other in the moonlight, taking comfort and giving it back in whatever way they could.

Tom and Jeannette had closed around them. I was standing outside their circle now, watching from several paces behind. How different Harper seemed from the woman who had lain in her bed the day of Doe's funeral, unconcerned that Nick was outside alone in a snowstorm. One thing was certain: Harper had come back to life. It was strange the way bad things sometimes brought good, almost in afterthought.

And good things brought bad. I had let myself fall in love for the first time ever, and look what had happened. But I couldn't think about David any more tonight. I was tired, and it was late, and I had a very long drive ahead of me. I was thirty-six years old, and for the briefest of moments I'd let myself be opened like the aperture of one of David's telescopes, finally letting in light.

 Chapter Six

So I did what I knew how to do best: I fled. I drove long into the night, stopping at 2.00am for coffee and a slice of cold pie at one of those roadside rest stops. By the time I pulled into the driveway of my house, the sky was still black. I looked out of the window; there was my house, an inanimate object waiting in the dark. I hadn't been inside in a very long time. I walked up the steps and opened the front door, immediately reaching for the light switch on the wall. The front hall brightened, revealing my home exactly the way I'd left it, though somehow sadder, smaller.

So here I was, back in Longwood Falls. I went upstairs to my bedroom, took off my clothes and bunched them up into a ball, which I tossed onto a chair. Then I climbed into bed without a nightgown, wanting to feel the punitively cold sheets against my skin. I lay in the darkness for a while, telling myself that I was home again, but knowing that it wasn't really true.

AS THE WEEKS PASSED, I found myself slowly returning to my old routine, and tried hard to convince myself that I was the same person I'd been when I'd lived here before. But I couldn't fool myself into thinking that was so, and in fact I couldn't fool any of my friends at the library. I'd gone to Stone Point quietly lonely and passive, but I'd returned with an air of heartbreak that couldn't be disguised.

Then, one Saturday afternoon in late March, a library trainee came into my office and told me that a man was here to see me. 'He didn't give his name,' the trainee said. I stood quickly, my throat suddenly going dry. If it was David out there, what would I say to him? I smoothed down my blouse and quickly raked a hand through my hair, then walked out of my office.

But there, standing by the circulation desk, was a man who bore no resemblance to David Fields. It was Jeff Hardesty, the lawyer with whom I'd been involved years earlier. He looked older now, and his blond hair had thinned, but he was essentially the same, a pleasant if ordinary-looking man in a grey business suit.

When Jeff saw me, he smiled and kissed my cheek. He told me that he had just moved back to Longwood Falls, where he was going to be joining the town's oldest law firm. The Victorian house he had bought was six blocks away from mine. 'Would you have a drink with me later, Liz?' he asked.

I paused, considering, but realised I wasn't quite up to it. 'I'm kind of busy, Jeff,' I told him, and he said that it was all right, he'd be back. I turned away uneasily. In some way I still felt I belonged to David, even though we hadn't seen each other for many weeks. I was still lost in a kind of sadness, a melancholy meditation on what I'd given up, and it threatened to take me over completely.

Even Aunt Leatrice saw how unhappy I was. When I first came back to Longwood Falls, she was, of course, very pleased to have me back, but she admitted to being puzzled by why I'd left Stone Point on such obviously bad terms with Harper.

'You're sisters, you two,' she said when I came and visited her for tea one afternoon. 'I don't understand what's happening. Please tell me.'

I shook my head, declining to offer an explanation.

'Well,' she said, 'both of you are being extremely mysterious.'

From the pocket of her sweater she slowly withdrew a folded piece of Harper's personal stationery. 'I received this yesterday,' said Aunt Leatrice, handing it to me.

So here was the reason that I'd been invited to tea this afternoon. I opened the note warily and began to read:

Dear Aunt Leatrice,

I was so glad to hear from you last week and have that good talk. I understand how you feel about the situation with Liz, and I respect your point of view, but I also want to ask that you trust me in terms of how I am handling things. The grief that I've experienced this year has made me able to see things as never before. And this is what I see:

That I wasn't a terrific sister. I know that siblings often have problems, but I think they were particularly extreme in our case.

That I wasn't a terrific mother. Before Liz arrived and took over, I never understood what Nick needed. And now I do. He and I are close in a way that we never were before. Our lives have a terrible, shared emptiness in them since Doe died. But they also seem to have an emptiness—a surprising one—since Liz left.

I don't really want to go into details about the rift between Liz and me. Let's just say that I withheld information from her, so she's withholding herself from me.

Well, I guess I'll sign off now, Aunt Leatrice. I am working on a new series of paintings, and I'd love for you to see them sometime.
Love, Harper

PS Nick would like to add a few words.

At the bottom of the letter were several sentences in Nick's large handwriting. I smiled at Nick's words and handed the letter back to my aunt, who sat watching me expectantly. I'd written to Nick several times, but he'd never responded. Seeing his simple printing now made me long to be with him, to return to my role as his aunt and his friend, even though he wanted nothing to do with me.

'Liz, I want you to listen to me,' said Aunt Leatrice. She blotted her lips with a napkin. 'It's never easy being someone's sister,' she said. 'Your own mother and I—we had a hard time of it.'

'You did?' I said. It was the first I'd ever heard of this.

'Oh, yes, your mother could be quite difficult,' she said. 'There was always a certain competition between us. An antagonism. I'm not sure how it started, but I think it worked both ways.'

I was very surprised to hear all this. In my memories, my mother was easy-going, gentle, extremely fair. I'd never taken her for someone who would give her own sister a hard time. 'You were so close as adults,' I said. 'How did you get to that point?'

My aunt shrugged. 'I don't know exactly,' she said. 'I guess we were just able to let go of all the hurt and anger that had built up over the decades. All I know is that one day it was gone, and she and I were friends. We stayed that way until the day she died.'

But I couldn't let go of the fact that Harper had betrayed me. I guess I was more stubborn than the other women in the family. 'Harper and I can't be friends,' I said to my aunt.

She looked at me sternly, and then after a moment she sighed. 'I'm very sorry to hear you say that, Liz,' she said. Then she stood up extremely slowly, clutching the edge of the table to balance herself. 'I need to take a rest now,' she said, ending our visit. I helped Aunt Leatrice upstairs to her bedroom, then I left her house, heading out into the fading afternoon.

I went home, tossing my keys lightly on the hall table and heading into the kitchen. The light on the answering machine was blinking, and I went to play back the messages. I was barely listening, when suddenly the kitchen was filled with David's voice. My breath caught.

'Hi, Liz,' he said quietly, hesitantly. 'Look, I recently came across the roll of film we took in Hawaii. I guess I forgot all about it, and so I brought it in to the drugstore and today the pictures came back.' He paused. 'God, you look so pretty in them,' he said. He fell silent again, and then he said, 'I think it's crazy that we're not speaking. There's a lot that I want to say. You didn't give me the chance the night you left. So please,' he said, 'give me a call when you get home.' He paused, and then he added, 'I miss you.' There was a click as David hung up his phone.

I felt light-headed, and carefully sat down at the table. I considered calling him, but then I remembered the painting in Harper's studio, and how badly I'd felt David had treated me. I was aware that I'd treated him badly, too, but I didn't know how else to behave, and so I didn't call him.

Two days later David called again, but I forced myself not to pick up. He called again one more time after that, and still I didn't take the call. And then he never called again.

I was agitated constantly as the weeks passed and could barely sleep. Whenever I did sleep I dreamed of David: his brown hair falling in his eyes, the flying jacket he'd worn in the winter cold.

One evening after work, I locked the library door for the night and walked up three flights to the newspaper archives. I switched on one of the timer lights and searched among the bound copies of the *Longwood Falls Ledger* until I located the volume that included issues from August 1965. I went through each issue from that month until I came upon what I'd been searching for.

There it was, a large obituary, the headline reading, MAGGIE THORPE, OLYMPIC SWIMMER, AGED 36. David's mother had been exactly my age when she drowned. The photograph caught my eye and I felt myself involuntarily take in a hard breath.

It was a picture of the swimmer with her son, David, aged six. In the photograph, David was a small boy with a buzz cut. He had thin legs but a long, straight torso and arms that were beginning to show the first hint of the definition that was to come. He was smiling shyly, the same smile he still wore now, nearly thirty-five years later. He looked so breathtakingly young, so untouched by the world. It wouldn't be long after this picture was snapped that his world would collapse into itself and he would pick up a pair of binoculars and endlessly search the horizon.

How could people just *disappear*? I wondered. It wasn't only through death that you lost them, as Harper had lost Doe for ever, but also through love, and through unforgiveness. As I sat in the still-ness of the library, a tear dropped down onto the aged newsprint, followed a moment later by another. I dried the pages of newspaper lightly with the back of my hand, and just then the timed light clicked off, leaving me to silently say goodbye in darkness to the van-ishing image of that lost little boy.

I sat on the cool tiles of the floor, hugging my knees and crying silently for a long time. I must have fallen asleep there, because the next thing I knew, a very sweet old doorman who'd worked at the library since I was a little girl was gently shaking me awake. I looked up, shocked, at the man in the green uniform.

'Good morning, Miss Mallory,' he said to me with a slight trace of worry in his voice.

'Oh, good morning, George,' I said, trying to sound nonchalant. I stood up and stretched, as though it was a perfectly ordinary thing for the head librarian to be discovered fast asleep and fully dressed in her library first thing in the morning.

I went out of the front door, stepping into the daylight. But I kept thinking of David's face, imagining him at six years of age and then imagining him now, as a grown man. I knew suddenly and defini-tively that I had to be with him again. I had to say I was sorry for my part in all this—my abruptness when I left, my refusal to listen to what he had to say, my feelings of inferiority to Harper that had coloured everything in my life.

So I got back into my car, and I drove bleary-eyed all the way to Stone Point without stopping. I'm certain I exceeded the speed limit; all I knew was that I had to see him now. As I drove, I felt pleasure coming back to me the way it had when David and I had first fallen in love. *I was going back to him.*

I arrived in Stone Point in the late afternoon and drove my car slowly up the path of Red Briar, straight to Stardust. The trees were in bloom, and everything looked fertile and gorgeous. If David would have me back, I'd soon be living here, as we'd planned, walk-ing along this path with him under the arching trees.

As I approached the observatory, I noticed that David's car wasn't there. He was out; this was disappointing, but I would wait. I parked and walked up to the cottage, deciding to peer though the windows. But the blinds were closed in the middle of the afternoon. I quickly walked to the front door and knocked. There was no answer, and then I remembered something.

I reached into my pocket for my key ring. Nestled among my house and car and library keys was the gold key that David had given me. I inserted it into the lock, turned the knob, and the door gently swung open. I walked inside, and stood in the middle of his living room, feeling a shock that I almost can't begin to describe.

All his things were gone. The entire room was empty, the floor covered with a light layer of dust. I'm not sure how long I stood there, staring. But the next thing I knew I heard a man's voice behind me.

'David?' I said instinctively, quickly turning round.

Before me stood an elderly stranger. He hoisted a pair of hedge clippers over one shoulder. 'Can I help you, miss?' he asked.

'What happened to David?' I said in a controlled but frantic voice. 'David Fields?'

'Well,' said the man, scratching his chin with an earth-dusted hand. 'I'm just the gardener, but if you're talking about the gentleman who lived here in the cottage, he's moved away. Can't say where exactly. Mr Boyd said something about Europe, I think, and told me I could use the cottage for storage of my gardening equipment, at least for a while. Mr Boyd said he might rent the place to someone else—a young couple up from Texas. Newlyweds. This'll be their honeymoon cottage, I guess.'

I sank down to the floor, sitting there for a moment in a daze.

'Are you all right, miss?' the gardener asked, but I couldn't speak. I shook my head, stood up slowly, and hurried out of the cottage.

MONTHS WENT BY, and I never told anyone that I had gone back to Stone Point that day. As I continued to live inside my sorrow and resignation that David was gone for good, I felt a kind of restlessness stir in me. Summer had turned to fall, and there was once again a snap in the air, which reminded me that it was only a little while before I'd feel my aloneness with an intensity that always came on in Longwood Falls when the weather grew cold and people retreated to their separate homes.

I thought I might shrivel up and disappear if I was alone again for another winter. And so I did something I'd never imagined I would do: I finally let Jeff Hardesty take me to dinner.

He'd stopped at the library several times since he first moved back, and we'd had short, pleasant enough chats. In Buffalo he'd briefly been married to another lawyer, and their subsequent divorce was straightforward and amicable. When he asked me about my own life,

I was vague, talking about work first and then, when pressed, giving him a short, abridged version of my time in Stone Point, and the story of David.

Now, one day in late November, nine months since I'd seen David, Jeff dropped into the library on his lunch break. David was off seeing the world, perhaps already in love with another woman, while I was still here, in the place where I'd always been. I couldn't spend the rest of my life thinking only of the man I'd once loved and lost. So I agreed to have dinner with the man I'd once been involved with but hadn't loved.

At the end of that evening, Jeff asked if he could see me again. I gazed at this unexciting but decent man who stood there in a slightly creased, dark brown suit and tie. At the end of my first date with David, my entire body had been awakened, snapped to attention as if through some hidden source of electricity. But now I just felt pleasantly tired. I told Jeff sure, it would be fine to get together again soon.

I went out with him again, and then again after that. On Saturday nights we'd have dinner at a local restaurant and then go to a movie, or occasionally we'd have dinner at my house, and then watch a video. Sometimes, Jeff would fall asleep on the couch, and I would cover him with a blanket and let him spend the night there.

One night, after he'd been asleep for a while and I'd gone upstairs to bed, I woke up to hear someone saying my name. I looked up in the dim room and saw Jeff standing by my bed. 'Can I join you?' he whispered in the darkness. 'It's been so long.'

I looked at him. Jeff was devoted to me, and would never hurt me the way David had. So he wasn't exciting, so he didn't have the passion and sadness and depth that David had; what good had those qualities done me, anyway?

I nodded, not saying a word, and Jeff slipped into the bed beside me, as he used to do. He was a good man, I reminded myself as he gently looped his arms around me and began to kiss my face, my neck, my hair. Did it matter that he cared about me more than I did about him? I told myself that we could manage, that it was rare for affections to be equal, the way they had seemed for a while between David and me. For me, happiness was an elusive thing. I knew that, having found it once before in my life, I wasn't likely to find it again. And so I put my arms around him and we sank deeper into the bed.

As THE WEEKS PASSED, Jeff and I once again became known in Longwood Falls as a couple. My friends said they were very happy for me, and they loved the story of our reunion. But even though my feelings about Jeff could never go past a certain point, I told myself that the illusion of contentedness might some day magically transform into the real thing.

One night, after Jeff and I had just finished a quiet supper and were settling down for an old Katharine Hepburn movie we'd rented, I happened to notice that the moon looked particularly luminous and that it was pouring its reflected light into the window of my living room. It was a full moon, and the shadows and crevices and etching of imperfections could be seen even from this great distance. The moon was amazing, I thought. If David were here right now we would have stood and stared at it together for a long time.

'Look at that moon,' I told Jeff, and he turned and looked.

'What about it?' he asked, slightly puzzled.

'Well, isn't it beautiful?' I asked.

He took a moment. 'Looks like a moon to me, Liz,' he said, shrugging. Then he said, 'Is there something here that I'm missing? I mean, is it some sort of special moon?'

I shook my head. 'No,' I finally said in a very quiet voice. 'It's not special. Forget it.'

He turned away from the window, back to the television. 'Come on,' he said. 'Enough about the moon. The movie's starting.'

Then we sat back and watched our movie, his hand in mine.

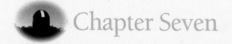 Chapter Seven

When Jeff and I had been together for six months, he decided we should celebrate the anniversary by having drinks at the Water Mill. I didn't particularly feel like celebrating, but it seemed important to him, so we sat at a rickety table in the back of the bar that night and toasted each other with glasses of champagne.

'To a great half-year,' Jeff said as we held up our glasses. Then he added, 'I'm so glad to have you back.'

Our glasses lightly chimed together, and the sound seemed to me like a bell that signified the beginning of the rest of my life. I put down my glass without taking the requisite sip. My hand shook, and some of the champagne sloshed over the rim. I realised that I felt like bursting into tears.

'Are you OK, Liz?' Jeff asked, and when I didn't answer he leaned forward, taking my hand. I knew, at that moment, that I couldn't continue seeing him; it wasn't fair. So I told him, speaking slowly and carefully and apologising over and over again.

After his initial astonishment, he said, 'I thought we had something good here?' He put down his own glass.

'We did, Jeff,' I said. 'But do you really think "good" is enough? This is what we went through last time, isn't it? Except last time, you agreed with me. But now you don't seem to.'

'I don't know what's enough,' he said in a hard voice. 'I just know that we'd found something nice, and this time it was a relief. Neither of us is getting any younger, in case you hadn't noticed.'

I tried to tell him I was sorry again, and to make him see that what he felt for me he would certainly feel for someone else. But he said he didn't want to talk about it any more, and he reached into his wallet, extracted some notes, and left them on the table. Then he turned and left me sitting in the back of the bar with a full glass of champagne fizzing and settling in front of me.

For a long time, I felt terrible about Jeff. When we passed each other in town we nodded hello but didn't stop to speak. One day, I saw him in the window of a restaurant with a woman with long dark hair and a pretty smile. They were sharing a big plate of fried zucchini and laughing; I hoped they were happy.

My thoughts turned inevitably back to David. It seemed to me as though Stone Point, and everyone associated with the place, was part of a dream I'd once had a long time ago. Had I really lived at The Eaves, and fallen in love beneath the dome of an observatory? I had, but none of it had any relevance to my life in Longwood Falls.

Then one Saturday afternoon in September, a clear, vivid autumn day, I came home from the grocery store to find a chauffeur-driven car in my drive. Just then the back door opened and Harper stepped out. I was so startled that my groceries almost slipped from my arms.

It had been eighteen months since I had seen her, and the change in her appearance was startling. Her hair was longer, and her face looked full, flushed, livelier than it had. She wore a cornflower-blue dress, a blazer, and a simple strand of onyx beads.

'Harper,' I said, trying to keep calm, 'what are you doing here?'

355

'I came to bring you an invitation,' she said. She reached into a pocket of her blazer and pulled out an envelope. As I unfolded the piece of stationery inside, I could see her maroon monogram embossed on the cream-coloured notepaper.

PLEASE COME TO AN OPENING
OF AN EXHIBIT OF
HARPER MALLORY'S RECENT WORKS.
SUNDAY, SEPTEMBER 18, 4.00PM,
AT THE PAINTER'S STUDIO AT THE EAVES,
STONE POINT, NEW YORK.

'But that's tomorrow,' I said, confused. 'I can't possibly just leave everything and—'

'Please,' said my sister. 'Please try. I really want you there, Liz. I can't tell you how much,' said Harper.

I didn't respond. We stood there for a moment, and finally Harper said, 'I've been in the car for hours. And so has my driver. Are you at least going to offer us something cold to drink?'

I nodded. The driver said he didn't need a drink, and that he'd prefer to stay in the car. Then I opened the front door of my house, letting Harper inside, and for the first time in many years she entered the place where we'd grown up together.

She stood for a while looking around in a kind of wonder. 'All this time,' she said, 'I've remembered the house as being so ordinary. But it's nice here, Liz, it really is. You really put your heart into it,' she added softly.

When the groceries were put away, Harper and I went and sat on the sun porch, and I poured her a mug of fresh cider. She settled herself in, taking a few long sips and leaning back against the cushioned chair before beginning to speak.

'You know, there are some things about what happened that you don't understand,' she finally said. I waited for her to go on, not knowing what she was getting at. 'I never got a chance to tell you why I broke things off with David,' she continued.

'You told me you were on the rebound from your marriage.'

'I was,' she said. 'But that wasn't all. I also stopped seeing him . . . because he was wonderful.'

I looked at her. 'That doesn't make any sense.'

'Not to you, maybe,' she said. 'But to me it does. The thing is, I felt

356

that I didn't deserve someone like David. Someone kind and thoughtful. Someone who actually listens. As we kept seeing each other, I started to find out how special he was, and it scared me.'

'Why?' I asked, not comprehending.

'I have a bad track record with men,' said Harper. 'As you may have noticed.' She looked on the verge of tears, and I didn't understand the reason for her sudden display of emotion. 'You're the good one, Liz, not me,' she said. 'The entire time we were growing up, I always had to hear from everyone we knew about how thoughtful and responsible you were. You were the *good* twin. Which made me, by default, the bad one.' She took a breath, then said, 'So I guess I never felt that I deserved a good man.'

I was stunned. 'I had no idea that you ever gave me a second thought, Harper,' I said quietly.

'Oh, you were always on my mind, Liz,' she said. 'I knew I'd never be able to stop comparing us.'

'I thought that was my job,' I said.

'It worked both ways,' she replied. 'In high school, you were so smart and focused and responsible. I knew I couldn't live up to that, and I didn't want to try. Mom and Dad were clearly disappointed that I was so different.'

'They weren't disappointed in you,' I said. 'They were disappointed in me! They were proud of you, Harper; I know that for a fact.' But in that moment I saw that neither of us knew the truth, because there wasn't one singular truth; there were many.

She put down her mug of cider. 'And *I* know for a fact,' she said, 'that David wasn't happy with me when we were involved.'

'Come on,' I said. 'When you left him he was just devastated.'

But Harper shook her head. 'I think, if he were to really face what happened, he'd see that he was relieved when I broke up with him. Oh, he was devastated all right that he'd been *left*. Because of his mother, he would have felt devastated being left by *any* woman.' She shook her head. 'He and I were totally wrong for each other, and he knew it. He's a simpler person than I am; he doesn't require much to get him through life.' She smiled ruefully. 'Me, I'm high maintenance.'

I couldn't help but nod in agreement. We sat in silence for a while; it was taking me quite some time to absorb everything she'd just said. But shocked as I was by what she'd told me about the breakup, I knew it didn't matter any more. All of this was in the past.

What did matter, I thought, was whether she and I could move beyond what had happened and stay in each other's lives. I realised, as I sat with her, that I was beginning to feel a sensation of contentment, the kind that comes when you're with someone you've known for ever.

'About that art show of yours,' I said quietly. 'I'm not sure I have anything to wear.'

'You'll really come?' she asked, and I nodded. I would drive back to Stone Point with her that evening.

As I went upstairs to pack, Harper wandered around, looking through the rooms that had made up her past. After a moment I heard her exclaim, 'Oh my God, Liz,' she called. 'Look at this.'

I came downstairs and went to the pantry, where she was standing and pointing to the inside of the door. There on the wall, faint but still visible, were the pencil marks our mother had made to measure our heights over the years.

Harper grabbed a pencil. 'Stand here,' she instructed me, and I stood obediently with my head touching the door, and she made a new mark, then handed the pencil to me and stood where I'd been standing. I wrote a tiny line by the top of her head, and added the date. As always, the lines were at the same level. Then, in a moment of quiet intensity, we both stood back to look at the pantry door, marvelling at how we'd grown.

LATER, SITTING TOGETHER in the back seat of her car for six hours, my sister and I talked about everything we'd never really got round to talking about over the course of our lives. When we arrived in Stone Point, night had fallen. Tom and Jeannette welcomed me back into The Eaves. The household wasn't as formal and reserved as it had once been. Instead, it seemed to be a place that was finally showing signs of being a home.

'Can I go upstairs and find Nick?' I asked, and Harper said of course. I walked faster and faster, practically breaking into a run as I headed towards his room. The door was open and he was sitting in the lower bunk of his bunk bed, reading a book. I approached him carefully. 'Hi, Nick,' I said.

He looked up, shocked to see me, and then he quickly sprang to his feet. 'Aunt *Liz*?' he said, and in that moment I was shocked, too. He was so much longer and lankier now, and his face had taken on a real maturity. On his wall were taped some posters of racing cars and basketball players, replacing the jungle scenes that used to be there.

And then I noticed, on the top of the table next to his bed, a small object: the piece of volcanic rock that he'd begged me to bring back from Hawaii.

'What are you doing here?' Nick asked, remembering that he was angry with me.

'Your mother brought me,' I said. 'To come and see her art show.'

'Oh, so you're not staying?' he said.

'No. I have a life up in Longwood Falls,' I replied. 'A job. A house. I know it's easy to forget that.' I paused, and then I added, 'Back when I was staying here, I almost forgot it myself.'

He regarded me for a long moment. 'You left me, Aunt Liz,' he said. 'I thought we were friends.'

'We are,' I said. 'And we always will be. I'm very sorry I let you down, Nick, that I left in such a hurry.' I saw his expression shift slightly. 'It's like with Doe,' I added softly. 'First she was here, and then she wasn't. I did that, too, and I wasn't fair to you.'

He looked away from me because he knew he appeared upset, and he was embarrassed. 'I guess not,' he said.

'Nick, I didn't think it through at the time, and I'm very ashamed of myself,' I said. 'Can't we be the way we were? Can't we play endless games of Monopoly and Clue?'

'I don't play those games any more, Aunt Liz,' he said in a scornful voice. 'I'm into chess now.'

'Well, did you know I'm a whiz at chess?' I tried. 'A grand master.'

He looked at me sceptically. 'You are not,' he said.

'I guess you'll have to find out for yourself,' I told him, and at this point he broke into the slightest of smiles. 'Oh, come here, Nick,' I said, and I moved towards him and gathered him to me. Despite himself, he came willingly, as if relieved to be forced not to be mad at me any more.

THE NEXT AFTERNOON, Harper and I headed to the studio shortly before four o'clock, when the other guests for the art show were to arrive. 'Come on in,' Harper said, opening the door. 'I wanted you to be the first to see it.'

The beautiful white room was filled with paintings different from any of Harper's previous work. They weren't tormented or dream-like, and their subjects weren't people. These were pictures of various animals and objects and places, and they were all exquisite.

At first, I didn't understand the significance of the work, but simply admired it as I walked around. There was a painting of a horse, its neck dipped down to graze in a field, and another painting of an ice-cream stand at twilight, a neon cone illuminating the sky. There was a picture of a child's ballerina costume hanging in a closet. Then I came upon a painting of an old doll with a tattered red-checked dress. I realised, with a start, that it was a picture of the doll I'd given Doe when she was just born.

I understood now that Harper's art show was a celebration of Doe. Not a maudlin tribute to a child who had died, but one that was filled with the things that had once excited and engaged that child, and filled her with life.

'Oh, Harper,' I said. 'You've really done it.'

Then I embraced her, and both of us began to cry. We cried for Doe, who had graced Harper's life for eight short years, and who had then left her for ever.

'I still have that dream,' she said. 'The unbearable one in which you see the person who's died—in this case, Doe—and she tells you, "Mommy, I didn't die after all," and you start kissing her and hugging her and you're ecstatic.' Harper took a breath. 'And then you wake up,' she said. 'And you find out it was only a dream. She isn't alive after all, and she never will be.'

She shook her head sadly. 'But it's not just dreams,' she said. 'It's daydreams, too. I think about what Doe would have been like as she got older. I picture her at seventeen, with long red hair, sprawled out across her bed endlessly talking on the telephone to her friends. And I picture taking her to college, helping her set up her room.' She paused. 'I even picture her getting married, can you believe it?' She wiped at her eyes as she spoke, but the tears kept coming. 'I like to think she would have met someone who would have cherished her,' she said.

'Oh, she would have, Harper,' I said.

After she finished talking, Harper and I cried and cried. It felt very good to cry like that with her, and I remembered that my sister's former husband, Carlo, had wanted me to make sure that Harper would have someone she could talk with, someone she could cry with. Well, she had someone now, I thought as I held her in the middle of the studio, not wanting to let go.

Afterwards, we sat together on the floor of that room for quite a while, drinking glasses of white wine that Harper poured for us, and eating slivers of cheese. I glanced at my watch a few times, for it was after four thirty, and no one else had arrived.

'When are the other people coming?' I asked her. 'Didn't the invitation say four o'clock?'

Harper smiled. 'I have a confession. There are no other people. I only invited one person. You.' She paused. 'I really wanted to see you, and I knew Nick did, too, even though he wouldn't admit it. And I wanted you to see my work. It was the only way to get you here.' Suddenly she stood up. 'Actually, there's one more painting I want you to see, not part of this series.'

'It's nothing that will upset me, is it?' I asked.

Harper smiled slightly. 'No,' she said.

I followed her to an easel facing the far wall. In one swift motion Harper turned the easel round on its delicate legs.

Facing me was a picture of a woman. She looked intelligent, sexually knowing, filled with secrets. Her hair was red, and she held herself with a certain kind of powerful grace. 'You made a self-portrait,' I said. 'It's wonderful.'

But Harper shook her head. 'No,' she said quietly. 'This is a portrait of you. It's the way you looked after you met David.'

I stared at the painting. Had I really seemed so self-possessed after I met David? I supposed that I had, but still it was shocking to see hard evidence of this. For the picture showed something very simple and ordinary, yet extraordinary, too: a woman in love.

I felt my legs suddenly give way, and I sank down to the floor of the studio as though the breath had been knocked out of me. Harper immediately came and sat beside me.

'I didn't know it would affect you like this,' she said. 'I thought you were totally over David.'

I looked away from her, embarrassed. 'That couldn't be further from the truth,' I said. 'But it's so pathetic, isn't it? Here I am, thirty-eight years old and still in love with a man who lives somewhere in Europe.'

'Liz,' said Harper in a soft voice, 'he's back.'

I stared at her. 'Don't make jokes,' I said.

'It's not a joke,' she said. 'He was on a sabbatical. I think he put his furniture in storage, so the cottage could be rented. He came back a few weeks ago, for the start of school.'

My heart was thudding. Harper slid closer to me on the floor and took my hands in hers. 'Listen to me,' she said quietly. 'You can go back to him. It's not too late.'

'No,' I said. 'It is.'

'It never is,' said Harper.

'I'm sure he's got over me. What we had was amazing, but it was also extremely brief.'

'David,' said Harper, 'takes a long time to get over things. Haven't you noticed?'

THAT NIGHT, after the sky had grown dark, and Harper and Nick had sat down in the living room to play chess, I slipped out of the house and borrowed one of Harper's cars. I drove nervously over the local roads until I came to Red Briar. I could see the top of the observatory's dome poking up above a stand of trees, like the forehead of a giant. There it was: Stardust. And this time, the lights were on.

I drove up to the building, parked Harper's car beside it, and got out. I was apprehensive and shaky. I didn't have a clue as to what I would even say.

Something made me turn then; it wasn't a sound, but was more a sensation of David's presence. He was up on the hill just past the observatory, facing away from me as he had been the first time we'd met, standing there with his telescope. As I walked up the hill, he heard me and turned. Then he just stood and stared, no expression crossing his face.

'Are you looking at Saturn?' I heard myself ask.

David shook his head. 'No,' he said after a moment, and he didn't offer anything more.

I stood several feet away from him, but even from that distance I could see that he looked a bit older, handsome but weary.

'What are you doing here, Liz?' he asked, but his tone of voice made it clear that he wasn't all that interested in the answer.

'I'm not sure,' I said.

He fiddled with the screws on his telescope, and peered through the eyepiece at an object far away.

'Is it a star you're looking at?' I asked.

'Actually,' he said, 'I'm just killing time.'

'Oh?'

'There's going to be a meteor shower in a little while,' he said flatly. 'I won't need the telescope for that.'

'A meteor shower? What are meteor showers, exactly?' I asked.

I saw his face reflexively adopt a teacher's expression. 'Once or twice a year,' he began, 'if we regularly cross the orbit of a comet, we'll be hit by this big crowd of meteoroids. Since all the meteors are going along in the same orbit, they'll seem to be coming from the same location in the sky. It's called the "radiant".'

'I like that word,' I said. '"Radiant". It sounds hopeful.'

'Things in the sky,' he said curtly, 'aren't hopeful or unhopeful. They just *are*.' He paused. 'That's what I like about them, I guess.' He returned to the telescope now, as if his brief, halfhearted interest in me was already faltering.

'You can't even look at me, can you?' I said quietly.

So he did. Hard. He stood and gazed at me defiantly, his arms folded across his chest. 'Here. I'm looking at you. But why should I?' he asked. 'I begged you to talk things through with me. I left messages, but you never called back. You acted like what we'd had together didn't matter at all.' He stopped talking for a moment, and then, in a quieter voice, he added, 'I didn't know you could be so cruel.'

I waited a second, then I said, 'But you did know. It's what you've always seen up there in your observatory: the way everything in the universe just moves along on its own path, not caring about the destruction it's leaving behind.' I took a breath. 'You were drawn to it because of what happened to you when you were six. I mean, things happen up there that can't be undone. Terrible things.' I came closer to him, so close that I could see a small pulse fluttering unevenly in his temple. 'But there's a difference between what goes on up there and what goes on down *here*, on earth.' I swallowed, feeling my throat tighten. 'People can be cruel,' I said, 'and they can make big mistakes.'

'Yes, they can,' he said.

'But it's what happens next that counts,' I said. He kept looking at me, his expression unchanged. 'I'm asking you to forgive me,' I told him. 'Please, David.'

'So why did it take you so long to say this?' he asked.

'I drove all the way back here last year to say it,' I said. 'I came to the cottage, and it was empty. The gardener told me you were gone. I can't tell you what it did to me. I fell apart.'

He looked at me, his expression perceptibly softening for the first time as I watched.

'I couldn't stay here, after what had happened with you,' he said. 'I had a sabbatical coming, so I went away for a year. I guess the gardener didn't know I'd be back.' He shrugged. 'I went to Padua,

363

where Galileo lived. And I went to England, to Greenwich and Stonehenge. I just went from place to place, taking pictures, taking notes, sleeping in these little hotels, travelling around on this self-guided astronomy tour, but I had a terrible time. I was so lonely, you have no idea.'

And at that moment, something happened. A streak filled the night sky, flaring brightly before vanishing.

'Did you—' he said.

'Yes, yes, I saw it,' I said. The meteor shower was beginning, and we both leaned our heads back and simply looked up, waiting for whatever was next. In a moment we were rewarded with another arc of light, impossibly graceful, heartbreakingly brief.

'Look at that,' I said quietly. 'And it's just fire and ice.'

High above us, frozen chunks of rock were burning up as they hurtled through space and time. *Fire*, I thought, remembering how we'd held each other in his bed. Then I thought, *ice*, recalling how we'd both, in our own way, betrayed the other. Love was never one thing or another, yet I hadn't known this before, and now I did.

'Yes,' David said. 'But it's beautiful while it lasts.'

He turned away from the sky to look at me. This time, he looked and looked. Then he stepped forward so we were touching, and I leaned my head against his chest. All I'd wanted for so long was to be with David again, to be held by him and to hold him. What I'd wanted had seemed simple, and yet it had taken me such a long time. But here it was, at last: a man and a woman in the middle of their lives, standing together under a sky filled with light.

EMILY GRAYSON

Anyone who reads *The Observatory* is likely to be struck by the rather uncommon abode that David Fields calls home. After all, not many of us live within rounded walls and have a high-powered telescope in the attic. One might assume that the author lives in similarly exotic surroundings, but in Emily Grayson's own words, 'My home is painfully usual—an apartment in Manhattan. But astronomy is indeed a special interest,' she notes. 'In fact I once visited the observatory on a dormant volcano in Hawaii and right away I knew it would make an evocative setting for a scene in a novel.'

Another aspect of the book that is quite remote from Emily Grayson's personal experience is the sibling rivalry at the centre of it. 'I do have a sister, and though our relationship is nothing like the one between Harper and Liz, I've always been interested in the connections between sisters in both life and fiction.'

The New-York-born writer got started on her career early. 'I can't remember a time in my life when I wasn't writing; as a little girl I was always working on stories, novels, poems, plays, etc, and I was thrilled when I realised I could turn this hobby into a profession.' Indeed, she throws herself into each project with the focus and commitment of a person pursuing a beloved pastime. 'I tend to write at the speed of light,' she reveals. 'My books are short and intense, and I work on them in a whirlwind, rising early and staying at the computer as long as I can tolerate.'

It should come as no surprise that a writer who lists among her favourite authors Jane Austen, Maeve Binchy, Rosamunde Pilcher and E.M. Forster ('Quite an eclectic bunch, I know!'), might some day choose to set a book in the British Isles. And indeed the love story she is currently working on, *The Rose and the Stag*, is set on British soil during the Second World War.

Emily Grayson fiercely guards her privacy. She likes to keep a clear division between her private life and her career as an author and so declines to be photographed or reveal any further details about her identity.

THE FALLS
IAN RANKIN

In 1836, children playing on an Edinburgh hillside found seventeen small coffins, each holding a wooden doll.

More than a century later, Detective Inspector Rebus of the Lothian and Borders Police discovers a similar artefact close to the home of a missing student.

So begins his toughest case yet, an investigation that will take him to the dark heart of the city, past and present . . .

Chapter One

'You think I killed her, don't you?'

He sat well forward on the sofa, head slumped in towards his chest. His hair was lank, long-fringed. Both knees worked like pistons, the heels of his grubby trainers never meeting the floor.

'You on anything, David?' Rebus asked.

The young man looked up. His eyes were bloodshot, his lean, angular face unshaved. His name was David Costello. Not Dave or Davy: David, he'd made that clear. The media had varied its descriptions of him. He was 'the boyfriend', 'the tragic boyfriend', 'the missing student's boyfriend'. He was 'David Costello, 22' or 'fellow student David Costello'. He 'shared a flat with Ms Balfour' or was 'a frequent visitor' to the 'disappearance riddle flat'.

Nor was the flat just a flat. It was 'the flat in Edinburgh's fashionable New Town', the 'quarter-million flat owned by Ms Balfour's parents'. John and Jacqueline Balfour were 'the numbed family'. Their daughter was 'Philippa, 20, a student of art history at the University of Edinburgh'. She was 'pretty', 'vivacious', 'carefree'.

And now she was missing.

Detective Inspector John Rebus shifted position, from in front of the marble fireplace to slightly to one side of it.

'The doctor gave me some pills,' Costello said finally.

'Did you take them?' Rebus asked.

The young man shook his head slowly, eyes still on Rebus.

'Don't blame you,' Rebus said, sliding his hands into his pockets. 'Knock you out for a few hours, but they don't change anything.'

It was two days since Philippa—known to friends and family as 'Flip'—had gone missing. Two days wasn't long, but her disappearance was out of character. Friends had called the flat at around seven in the evening to confirm that Flip would be meeting up with them within the hour at one of those small, trendy bars on the South Side.

Seven, seven fifteen, she probably left the flat. Tina, Trist, Camille and Albie were already on their second round of drinks. Rebus had consulted the files to confirm those names. Trist was short for Tristram and Albie was Albert. Trist was with Tina; Albie was with Camille. Flip should have been with David, but David, she explained on the phone, wouldn't be joining them. 'Another bust-up,' she said, not sounding too concerned.

A steep hill separated her flat from Princes Street. Another climb from there would take her to the Old Town, the South Side. No way she'd be walking. But records from her home telephone and mobile had failed to find a match for any taxi firm in the city. So if she'd taken one, she'd hailed it on the street. If she'd got as far as hailing one.

'I didn't kill her, you know,' David Costello said.

'Nobody's saying you did.'

'No? But the search warrant . . .' Costello began.

'It's standard, any case of this kind,' Rebus explained. It was, too: suspicious disappearance, you checked all the places the person might be. You searched the boyfriend's flat. Because nine times out of ten, it's someone the victim knows: spouse, lover, son or daughter.

Flip Balfour's parents had appeared on TV, pleading with her to make contact. Police were at the family home, intercepting calls in case any ransom demand should arrive. Police were wandering through David Costello's flat on the Canongate, hoping to turn up something. And police were here, in Flip Balfour's flat, 'baby-sitting' David Costello—stopping the media from getting too close. This was what the young man had been told, and it was partly true.

Flip's flat had been searched the previous day. Costello had keys. The phone call to Costello's own flat had come at 10.00pm: Trist, asking if he'd heard from Flip because she hadn't turned up.

'She's not with you, is she?'

'I'm the last person she'd come to,' Costello had complained.

'Heard you'd fallen out. What is it this time?' Trist's voice had been slurred, ever-so-slightly amused. Costello hadn't answered him. He'd cut the call and tried Flip's mobile, got her answering service, left a message asking her to phone him. Police had listened to the recording, trying to read falseness into each word or phrase. Trist had phoned Costello again at midnight. The group had been to Flip's flat: no one home. They waited until Costello himself arrived at the flat, unlocking it with his key. No sign of Flip inside.

In their minds, she was already a Missing Person, what police called a MisPer, but they'd waited till next morning before calling Flip's family home in East Lothian. Mrs Balfour had dialled 999 immediately. After receiving what she felt was short shrift from the police switchboard, she'd called her husband at his London office. John Balfour was the senior partner in a private bank, and if the Chief Constable of Lothian and Borders Police wasn't a client, someone certainly was: within an hour, officers were on the case—orders from the Big House, meaning Force HQ in Fettes Avenue.

David Costello had unlocked the flat for the two CID men. Within, they found no signs of a disturbance, no clues as to Philippa Balfour's whereabouts, fate, or state of mind. It was a tidy flat. The drawing room was large, with twin windows rising from floor level. There were two bedrooms, one turned into a study. There was a lot of David Costello's stuff in the bedroom. Someone had piled his clothes on a chair, then placed some books and CDs on top, crowning the structure with a washbag.

When asked, Costello could only assume it was Flip's work. His words: 'We'd had a falling-out. This was probably her way of dealing with it.' Yes, they'd had arguments before, but no, she'd never piled up all his stuff, not that he could remember.

John Balfour had flown up to Scotland by private jet and was at the New Town flat almost before the police. 'Well?' had been his first question. Costello himself offered an answer: 'I'm sorry.'

Much had been read into those words by CID officers, discussing the case in private. An argument with your girlfriend turns nasty; next you know, she's dead; you hide the body but, confronted by her father, innate breeding takes over and you blurt out a semi-confession. *I'm sorry.*

So many ways to read those two short words. Sorry we argued; sorry you've been troubled; sorry this has happened; sorry I didn't look after her; sorry for what I've done . . .

And now David Costello's parents were in town, too. They'd taken two rooms at the Caledonian, one of the best hotels. They lived on the outskirts of Dublin. The father, Thomas, was described as 'independently wealthy', while the mother, Theresa, was an interior designer.

There'd been some discussion back at St Leonard's as to why they'd need two rooms, and even more discussion about what St Leonard's was doing in a New Town case. The nearest cop shop to the flat was Gayfield Square, but additional officers had been drafted in from Leith, St Leonard's and Torphichen.

'Do you want anything?' Rebus said now. 'Tea? Coffee?'

Costello shook his head.

'Mind if I . . .?'

Costello looked at him, seeming not to understand. Then realisation dawned. 'Go ahead,' he said, gesturing to the kitchen.

'Thanks,' Rebus said. He closed the door after him and stood for a moment in the hallway, glad to be out of the stifling drawing room. There were sounds coming from the study. Rebus stuck his head round the door. 'I'm putting the kettle on.'

'Good idea. Tea please.' Detective Constable Siobhan Clarke didn't take her eyes from the computer screen.

'Anything?'

'Nothing yet. Letters to friends, some of her essays. I've got about a thousand emails to go through.'

Rebus left her and went into the kitchen, filled the kettle and searched for mugs and tea bags.

'When can I go home?'

Rebus turned to where Costello was now standing in the hall.

'Might be better if you didn't,' Rebus told him. 'Reporters and cameras . . . they'll keep on at you, phoning day and night.'

'I can't stay here,' Costello said, running his hands through his hair. 'Flip should be here. It's almost too much. I keep remembering that the last time we were here together, we were having a row.'

'What was it about?'

Costello laughed hollowly. 'I can't even remember.'

'You argue a lot?' Rebus tried to make the question sound casual.

Costello just stood there, staring into space, head shaking slowly. Rebus turned away, separated two Darjeeling tea bags and dropped them into the mugs. Was Costello unravelling? The betting at St Leonard's that David Costello had something to hide was even money; you could get two-to-one at Torphichen, while Gayfield had him odds-on favourite.

'Your parents said you could move into their hotel,' Rebus said.

'They've booked two rooms, so one's probably going spare.'

Costello didn't take the bait. He turned away, put his head round the study door. 'Have you found what you're looking for?' he asked.

'It could take some time, David,' Siobhan said.

'You won't find any answers in there.' When she didn't answer, he straightened a little and said, 'Some sort of expert, are you?'

'It's something that has to be done,' she said quietly.

He seemed about to add something, but thought better of it, and stalked back towards the drawing room instead. Rebus took a cup of tea through to Clarke. 'What did you think?' he asked.

She considered for a moment. 'Seems genuine enough.'

'Maybe you're just a sucker for a pretty face.'

She snorted and said, 'Maybe. So what's *your* thinking?'

'Press conference tomorrow,' Rebus reminded her. 'Reckon we can persuade Mr Costello to make a public appeal?'

REBUS HEADED HOME and started to fill a bath. He felt like a long soak, and squeezed some washing-up liquid under the hot tap.

Philippa Balfour's bathroom had boasted over a dozen different balms, lotions and oils. Rebus did his own stock-take: razor, shaving cream, toothpaste and toothbrush, plus a bar of soap. When he closed the cabinet, he met the gaze of his reflection. Grey-faced, hair streaked grey, too. Jowly, even when he stuck out his chin. Tried smiling, saw teeth which had missed their last two appointments. His dentist was threatening to strike him from his list.

'Get in line, pal,' Rebus muttered, turning away from the mirror before undressing.

THE RETIREMENT PARTY for Detective Chief Superintendent 'Farmer' Watson had commenced at six. The Police Club on Leith Walk had been decked out with streamers, balloons and a huge banner which read: FROM UNDER ARREST TO A WELL-DESERVED REST. Someone had dumped a bale of straw on the dance floor, completing the farmyard scene with an inflatable pig and sheep.

The bar was doing roaring business when Rebus arrived. He'd passed a trio of departing Big House brass on his way in. Checked his watch: six forty. They'd given the retiring DCS forty minutes of their valuable time.

Rebus had missed the presentation at St Leonard's. But he'd heard about the speech made by Assistant Chief Constable Colin Carswell.

'What can I get you, John?' the Farmer said, leaving his table to join Rebus at the bar.

'Maybe a small whisky, sir.'

'Half-bottle of malt over here when you've a minute!' the Farmer roared at the barman. The Farmer's eyes narrowed as he focused on Rebus. 'Did you see those buggers from the Big House?'

'Passed them as I came in.'

'Orange juices all round, then a quick handshake before home.'

Rebus smiled, told the barman to make it an Ardbeg.

'A bloody double, mind,' the Farmer ordered.

'Been enjoying a drink yourself, sir?' Rebus asked.

The Farmer blew out his cheeks. 'Few old pals came to see me off.' He nodded in the direction of the table. Rebus looked. He saw a posse of faces he knew from the Lothian and Borders Divisional HQs. Macari, Allder, Shug Davidson, Ellen Wylie. Bill Pryde was in conversation with Bobby Hogan. George 'Hi-Ho' Silvers was finding that DCs Phyllida Hawes and Siobhan Clarke weren't about to fall for his chat-up lines. And Grant Hood was standing next to a couple of Crime Squad officers called Claverhouse and Ormiston, trying not to look as though he was sucking up to them.

'If anyone knew about this,' Rebus said, 'the bad guys would have a field day. Who's left to mind the store?'

The Farmer laughed. 'It's a skeleton crew at St Leonard's, all right.'

'Good turnout. Wonder if I'd get as many at mine.'

'More, I'd bet.' The Farmer leaned close. 'The brass would all be there for a start, just to make sure they weren't dreaming.'

It was Rebus's turn to smile. He lifted his glass, toasted his boss. They both savoured their drinks, then suddenly the Farmer's arms went into the air, the smile broadening into a grin. 'Here she is, here she is. Just when I thought I was being stood up.'

His embrace almost swamped DCI Gill Templer. The Farmer planted a kiss on her cheek. 'You're not the floor show by any chance?' he asked. Then he mimed a slap to his forehead. 'Sexist language—are you going to report me?'

'I'll let it go this time,' Gill said, 'in exchange for a drink.'

'My shout,' Rebus said. 'What'll you have?'

'Long vodka.'

Bobby Hogan was yelling for the Farmer to go settle an argument.

'Duty calls,' the Farmer said by way of an apology, before heading unsteadily across the floor.

'His party piece?' Gill guessed.

Rebus shrugged. The Farmer's speciality was naming all the books of the Bible. His record was just under a minute.

'Long vodka,' Rebus told the barman. He raised his whisky glass. 'And a couple more of these.' He saw Gill's look. 'One's for the Farmer,' he explained.

'Of course.' She was smiling, but the smile didn't reach her eyes. She watched the barman filling the glasses. 'How's the Balfour case?'

Rebus looked at her. 'Is this my new Chief Super asking?'

'John . . .'

Funny how that single word could say so much. Rebus wasn't sure he caught all the nuances, but he caught enough: *John, don't push this. John, I know there's a history between us, but that's long-dead.*

Gill Templer had worked her arse off to get where she was now, but she was also under the microscope—plenty of people would want her to fail, including some she probably counted as friends.

Rebus paid for the drinks. A cheer went up as the Farmer's recitation finished.

THE KARAOKE STARTED at nine. Personnel at the party changed as some headed off, either to prepare for the night shift or because their pager had news for them. Others arrived, having been home to change out of work clothes. Rebus went outside and felt the sweat cooling on his back.

The streets were deserted, pavements glistening from an earlier downpour, street light reflected in them. Rebus took a left at the Tron Kirk and headed down the Canongate. A patrol car was parked opposite David Costello's flat, two bodies inside: one awake, the other asleep. They were detective constables from Gayfield serving on the thankless night shift. Rebus was just another passer-by to the one who was awake. He had a newspaper folded in front of him, angled towards what light there was. When Rebus thumped the roof of the patrol car, the paper flew, landing on the head of the sleeper, who jerked awake and clawed at the smothering sheets.

As the passenger-side window was wound down, Rebus leaned on the sill. 'Your one o'clock alarm call, gentlemen.'

The passenger's name was Pat Connolly, and he'd spent his first few years in CID waging a campaign against the nickname 'Paddy'. His colleague was Tommy Daniels, who seemed at ease—as he did in all things—with his own nickname of 'Distant'. Tommy to Tom-Tom to

Distant Drums to Distant was the logic behind the name, but it also said much about the young man's character. Having been so rudely awakened, upon seeing and recognising Rebus all he'd done was roll his eyes.

'Could've fetched us a coffee,' Connolly was complaining.

'Could have,' Rebus agreed. 'Or maybe a dictionary.' He glanced towards the newspaper crossword. Less than a quarter of the grid had been filled in. 'Quiet night?'

'Apart from foreigners asking directions,' Connolly said. Rebus smiled and looked down the street. This was the heart of tourist Edinburgh. A hotel up by the traffic lights, a knitwear shop across the road, John Knox's house. At one time, the Old Town had been all there was of Edinburgh: a narrow spine running from the Castle to Holyrood. Then, as the place became ever more crowded and insanitary, the New Town had been built, its Georgian elegance a calculated snub to the Old Town and those who couldn't afford to move.

'Is he home?' he said now.

'Would we be here if he wasn't?' Connolly's eyes were on his partner, who was pouring tomato soup from a Thermos. Distant sniffed the liquid hesitantly, then took a quick gulp.

'Mind if I ask you a question?' Rebus had crouched down, felt his knees crack with the effort.

'Fire away,' Connolly said.

'What do you do if you need a pee?'

Connolly smiled. 'If Distant's asleep, I just use his Thermos.'

The mouthful of soup almost exploded from Distant's nostrils. Rebus straightened up, feeling the blood pound in his ears: weather warning, force-ten hangover on its way.

'You going in?' Connolly asked.

Rebus looked at the tenement. 'Thinking about it.'

'Just come from the Farmer's leaving do?'

Rebus turned towards the car. 'What's your point?'

'Well, you've had a drink, haven't you? Might not be the best time for a house call . . . sir.'

'You're probably right . . . Paddy,' Rebus said, making for the door.

'REMEMBER WHAT YOU asked me?'

Rebus had accepted a black coffee from David Costello. Middle of the night, but Costello hadn't been asleep. Black T-shirt, black jeans, bare feet. He'd made an off-licence run at some point: the bag was on the floor, the half-bottle of Bell's sitting not far from it, only a couple of measures down. Not a drinker then, Rebus surmised. It was a non-drinker's idea of how you handled a crisis—you drank whisky, but had to buy some first, and no point lashing out on a whole bottle.

The living room was small, the flat itself reached from a turreted stairwell, its stone steps worn concave. Costello was seated on a red futon; Rebus had chosen one of two straight-backed wooden chairs. Bookshelves lined the walls.

Costello ran his hand through his hair, didn't say anything.

'You asked if I thought you did it,' Rebus said, answering his own question. '"You think I killed her, don't you?" is how you phrased it.'

Costello nodded. 'It's so obvious, isn't it? We'd fallen out. I accept that you have to regard me as a suspect.'

'David, right now you're the *only* suspect.'

'You really think something's happened to her?'

'What do you think?'

Costello shook his head. 'I've done nothing but rack my brains since this all started.'

They sat in silence for a few moments.

'What are you doing here?' Costello asked suddenly.

'It's on my way home.' Rebus scanned the room. 'The search party didn't make a mess, then?'

'Could have been worse.'

Rebus took a sip of coffee. 'You wouldn't have left the body here though, would you?' Costello looked at him. 'Sorry, I'm being . . . I mean, it's just theoretical. I'm not trying to say anything. But the forensics, they weren't looking for a body. They deal in things you and me can't even see. Flecks of blood, fibres, a single hair.' Rebus shook his head slowly. 'Juries eat that stuff up.' He put down the mug, reached into a pocket for his cigarette packet. 'Mind if I . . .?

Costello hesitated. 'Actually, I'll take one, if that's all right.'

'Be my guest.' Rebus took one out of the packet, lit it, then tossed both packet and lighter to the younger man. 'How did you and Flip meet?' he asked.

'Dinner party. We clicked straight away. Next morning, after break-fast, we took a walk through Warriston Cemetery. That was when I first felt that I loved her . . . I mean, that it wasn't just going to be a one-night stand.'

'You like films?' Rebus said. He was noticing that one bookshelf seemed to be all books about movies.

Costello nodded. 'I'd like to try writing a script some day.'

'Good for you.' Turning from the bookshelves, Rebus's foot brushed something: a metal toy soldier, no more than an inch high. He stooped to pick it up. The musket had been snapped off, the head twisted over to one side. He placed it on a shelf before sitting down again. 'You didn't go to the hotel?' he asked after a pause.

'No.'

'Did your parents cancel the other room then?' he asked.

'They sleep in separate rooms, Inspector.' Costello looked up. 'Not a crime, is it?'

'I'm not best placed to judge. My wife left me more years ago than I can remember.'

'I'll bet you *do* remember.'

Rebus smiled. 'Guilty.'

Costello rested his head against the futon, stifled a yawn.

Rebus finished his coffee. 'Maybe she'll turn up. People do things sometimes, don't they? Take a notion to head for the hills.'

Costello shook his head. 'She knew they were waiting for her in the bar. She wouldn't have forgotten that.'

'No? Say she'd just met someone else . . . an impulse thing.'

'Someone else?'

'It's possible, isn't it?'

Costello's eyes darkened. 'I don't know. It was one of the things I thought about—whether she'd met someone. But she'd have told me. That's the way Flip is: she can't keep anything to herself.' He stifled another yawn. 'I should get some sleep.'

'What time's the press conference?'

'Early afternoon. To catch the main news bulletins.'

Rebus nodded. 'Don't be nervous out there, just be yourself.'

Costello stubbed out his cigarette. 'Who else could I be?' He made to hand the packet and lighter back to Rebus.

'Keep them. Never know when you might feel the need.' He got to his feet. Costello stood up too, now, and he was smiling, though without much humour.

'You never did answer that question, did you?' he said.

'I'm keeping an open mind, Mr Costello.'

As Rebus made for the door, Costello called out to him. He was wiping the cigarette packet with a handkerchief. He did the same with the lighter, then tossed both items towards Rebus. They fell at his feet.

'I think your need's probably greater than mine.'

Rebus stooped to pick them up. 'Why the handkerchief?'

'Can't be too careful,' Costello said. 'Evidence can turn up in the strangest places.'

Rebus straightened. All the years he'd been on the force, he'd never seen a suspect do anything like that. It had meant Costello was expecting to be set up. Or, perhaps, that was what it was intended to look like. It had shown Rebus a side of the young man that was cool and calculating, capable of thinking ahead . . .

 **Chapter Two**

It was one of those cool, crepuscular days that could have belonged to any of at least three Scottish seasons, a sky like slate roofing and a wind that Rebus's father would have called 'snell'.

Rebus drew up outside a converted police box at the corner of the Meadows, and ordered, as he did most mornings on his way to work, a milky coffee. Then he added 'double-shot'. He didn't need to—the woman behind the counter knew the order by heart.

At St Leonard's, Rebus stayed in his car, enjoying a last cigarette with his drink. The station's back door opened and Siobhan Clarke stepped out. She saw his car and smiled at the inevitability of the scene. As she came forward, Rebus lowered the window.

'The condemned man ate a hearty breakfast,' she said.

'And a good morning to you too.'

'Boss wants to see you.'

'He sent the right sniffer dog.'

Siobhan didn't say anything as Rebus got out of the car. They were halfway across the car park before he heard the words: 'It's not a "he" any more.' He stopped in his tracks.

'I'd forgotten,' he admitted, and as she opened the door for him, he had the sudden image of a gamekeeper opening a trap.

THE FARMER'S PHOTOS had gone and there were some Good Luck cards on top of the filing cabinet, but otherwise the room was just as before, down to the potted cactus on the windowsill. Gill Templer looked uncomfortable in the Farmer's chair, his daily bulk having moulded it in ways that would never fit her slimmer proportions.

'Sit down, John.' Then, when he was halfway onto the seat, 'And tell me what last night was all about.'

'Last night?'

'You decided to visit Ms Balfour's boyfriend. How wise was that?'

'It was on the way home. I stopped to talk to Connolly and Daniels. Costello's light was on; I thought I'd make sure he was all right.'

'The caring copper.' She paused. 'That's presumably why Mr Costello felt it necessary to mention your visit to his solicitor?'

'I don't know why he did that.' Rebus shifted on his chair.

'His lawyer's talking about "harassment". We might have to pull the surveillance.' Her eyes were fixed on him. 'How much did you have to drink last night, John?'

'More than I should have.'

Gill raised an eyebrow. 'I want you to see a doctor. Your drinking, your diet, your general health . . . I want you to take a medical, and whatever the doctor says, I want you to abide by it.'

Rebus snorted, drained his coffee, then held up the beaker. 'Half-fat milk.'

She almost smiled. 'It's a start, I suppose.'

'Look, Gill . . .' He got up, tipped the beaker into the waste bin. 'My drinking doesn't interfere with my work.'

'It did last night.'

He shook his head, but her face had hardened. 'On you go, John. I'll make that appointment for you.'

He turned, pulled open the door. He was halfway out when she called, smiling, 'Going to wish me well in the new job?'

Rebus tried for a sneer but couldn't quite manage one. Gill held her smile until he'd slammed shut the door.

THE MAIN INCIDENT ROOM for the Philippa Balfour inquiry was based at Gayfield Square—much closer to her flat—so Rebus drove straight over.

With Gill Templer promoted, they were down a DCI at St Leonard's. Detective Inspector Bill Pryde wanted the job, and was trying to stamp his authority on the Balfour case. Rebus, newly arrived at the Gayfield Square incident room, could only stand and marvel. Pryde had smartened himself up—the suit looked brand new, the shirt laundered, the tie expensive. Pryde had been put in charge of assignments, which meant putting teams out on the street for the daily drudgery of doorsteppings and interviews. Neighbours were being questioned—sometimes for the second or third time—as were friends, students and university staff. Flights and ferry crossings were being checked, the official photograph faxed to train operators, bus companies and neighbouring police forces. It would be someone's job to collate information on fresh corpses throughout Scotland, while another team would focus on hospital admissions . . . It all took time and effort, the public face of the inquiry, and behind the scenes other questions would be asked of the missing person's immediate family and friends.

At last, Pryde finished giving instructions to the group of officers around him. He caught sight of Rebus and gave a huge wink, rubbing his hand over his forehead as he approached.

'Got to be careful,' Rebus said. 'Power corrupts, and all that.'

'Forgive me,' Pryde said, dropping his voice, 'but I'm getting a real buzz.'

'That's because you can do it, Bill. It's just taken the Big House twenty years to recognise the fact.'

Pryde nodded. 'We're done with baby-sitting the boyfriend,' he said. 'Orders from the new boss.'

'I heard. Well, it won't do any harm to the operation budget,' Rebus commented. 'So is there work for me today, Bill?'

Pryde flicked through the sheets of paper on his clipboard. 'Neighbours?' he suggested.

Rebus nodded. 'Neighbours it is,' he said.

REBUS WAS ASSIGNED the flats either side of Philippa Balfour's.

His partner for the day, DC Phyllida Hawes, followed him up the steps of the first tenement. Actually, Rebus wasn't sure you could call them 'tenements', not down in the New Town, with its Georgian architecture, its art galleries and antique emporia. There were one or two flats per landing, some with brass nameplates, but others went so low as to boast just a piece of card or paper. The landings themselves were bright and cared for: welcome mats and tubs of flowers.

The first stairwell went like clockwork: two flats with nobody home, cards dropped through both letterboxes; fifteen minutes in each of the other flats—'just a few back-up questions . . . see if you've thought of anything to add . . .' The householders had shaken their heads, had professed themselves still shocked.

There was a main door to a flat at ground level, a much grander affair, with a marble entrance hall, Doric columns either side. The occupier was renting it long term, worked in 'the financial sector'. Rebus saw a pattern emerging: graphic designer; training consultant; events organiser . . . and now the financial sector.

'Does no one have real jobs any more?' he asked Hawes. They were back on the street, Rebus enjoying a cigarette. 'When I was younger, there was always something rakish about the New Town. Caftans and wacky baccy, parties and ne'er-do-wells.'

'Not much space left for them these days,' Hawes agreed. 'Where do you live?'

'Marchmont,' he told her. 'You?'

'Livingston. It was all I could afford at the time.'

'Bought mine years back, two wages coming in . . .'

She looked at him. 'No need to apologise.'

'Prices weren't as crazy back then, that's all I meant.' He was trying not to sound defensive. It was that meeting with Gill, and the way his visit to Costello had KO'd the surveillance . . . Maybe it was time to talk to someone about the drinking . . . He flicked the stub of his cigarette onto the roadway.

'Next call,' he said now, 'if we're offered tea, we take it.'

Hawes nodded.

Two more no-one-homes, and then, on the first landing, the door was opened by a face Rebus recognised but couldn't place.

'It's about Philippa Balfour's disappearance,' Hawes was explaining. 'I believe two of my colleagues spoke to you earlier. This is just by way of a follow-up.'

'Yes, of course.' The door opened a little wider. The man looked at Rebus and smiled. 'You're having trouble placing me, but I remember you.' The smile widened. 'You always remember the virgins.'

As they were shown down the hall, the man introduced himself as Donald Devlin, and Rebus knew him. The first autopsy he had ever attended as a CID officer, Devlin had done the cutting. He'd been Professor of Forensic Medicine at the university, and the city's chief pathologist at the time. Sandy Gates had been his assistant. Now, Gates was Professor of Forensic Medicine, with Dr Curt as his 'junior'. On the walls of the hallway were framed photos of Devlin receiving various prizes and awards.

'The name's not coming to me,' Devlin said, gesturing for the two officers to precede him into a cluttered drawing room.

'DI Rebus.'

'It would have been Detective Constable back then?' Devlin guessed.

Rebus nodded.

'Moving out, sir?' Hawes asked, looking around her at the profusion of storage boxes and black bin-liners.

Devlin chuckled. He was a short, portly man, probably in his mid-seventies. His grey cardigan had lost most of its shape and half its buttons, and his charcoal trousers were held up with braces. His face was puffy and red-veined, his eyes small blue dots behind a pair of metal-framed spectacles.

'In a manner of speaking, I suppose,' he said. 'Let's just say that if the Grim Reaper is the *ne plus ultra* of removers, then I'm acting as his unpaid assistant.'

Rebus recalled that Devlin had always spoken like this, never settling for six words where a dozen would do.

'You're moving into a home?' Hawes guessed.

The old man chuckled again. 'Not quite ready for the heave-ho yet, alas. No, all I'm doing is dispensing with a few unwanted items, making it easier for those family members who'll wish to pick over the carcass of my estate after I've shuffled off.'

Hawes had reached into a box for a leather-bound book. 'You're binning all of it?'

'By no means,' Devlin tutted. 'The volume in your hand, for example, an early edition of Donaldson's anatomical sketches, I intend to offer to the College of Surgeons.'

Rebus was staring at a framed news report on the wall: a murder conviction dated 1957. 'Your first case?' he guessed.

'Actually, yes. A young bride bludgeoned to death by her husband. They were in the city on honeymoon.'

'Must cheer the place up,' Hawes commented.

'My wife thought it macabre too,' Devlin admitted. 'After she died, I put it back up.'

'Well,' Hawes said, dropping the book back into its box and looking in vain for somewhere to sit, 'sooner we're finished, the sooner you can get back to your clearout.'

'A pragmatist: good to see.' Devlin smiled. 'Better to take our tête-à-tête into the dining room, I think.'

Rebus nodded and made to follow, his gaze drifting to an invitation on the mantelpiece. It was from the Royal College of Surgeons, a dinner at Surgeons' Hall. 'Black tie and decorations' it said along the bottom. The only decorations *he* had were in a box in his hall cupboard. They went up every Christmas.

The dining room was dominated by a long wooden table, six un-upholstered, straight-backed chairs, and a dark-stained sideboard spread with a dusty array of glassware and silver.

On the table lay a half-finished jigsaw: central Edinburgh photographed from above. 'Any and all help,' Devlin said, waving a hand expansively over the puzzle, 'will be most gratefully received.'

'Looks like a lot of pieces,' Rebus said.

'Just the two thousand.'

Hawes was looking at her notes. 'At the first interview, you said you'd been home that evening.'

'That's right.'

'And you didn't see Philippa Balfour?'

'Your information is correct thus far.'

Rebus, deciding against the chairs, leaned back, putting his weight on the windowsill, and folded his arms. 'You were in all evening, and didn't hear or see anything untoward?'

'Nothing.'

'Have you ever had a falling-out with Ms Balfour?' Hawes asked.

'What is there to fall out about?'

'Nothing now,' Hawes stated coldly, irritated by his answers.

Devlin gave her a look and turned towards Rebus. 'I see you're interested in the table, Inspector.'

Rebus had been running his fingers along the grain of the wood.

'It's nineteenth-century,' Devlin went on, 'crafted by a fellow anatomist.' He glanced towards Hawes, then back to Rebus. 'There *was* something I remembered . . . probably nothing important.'

'Yes, sir?'

'A man standing outside.'

'When was this?' Rebus asked.

'A couple of days before she vanished, and the day before that, too.' Devlin shrugged, all too aware of the effect his words were having. Hawes had reddened; she was dying to scream out something like *When were you going to tell us?*

Rebus kept his voice level. 'Did you get a good look at him?'

Another shrug. 'In his twenties, short dark hair . . . neat.'

'Her boyfriend maybe?'

'Oh no, I know David.'

'You do?' Rebus asked, casually scanning the jigsaw.

'Yes. We met a few times in the stairwell. Nice chap . . .'

'How was he dressed, the man you saw?' Hawes asked.

Devlin relished the glare that accompanied her words. 'Jacket and trousers,' he said, glancing down at his cardigan. 'I can't be more specific, never having been a follower of fashion.'

'Do you think,' Rebus asked, 'that if you thought about it, maybe you could come up with a fuller description?'

'I rather doubt it, but of course if you think it important . . .'

'Early days, sir. You know yourself, we can't rule anything out.'

'Of course, of course.' Rebus was treating Devlin as a fellow professional . . . and it was working.

'We might even try to put together a Photofit,' Rebus went on. 'That way, if it turns out to be a neighbour or someone anyone knows, we can eliminate him straight away.'

'Seems reasonable,' Devlin agreed.

'Thanks again, sir,' Rebus said, as Devlin showed them out.

As the two detectives made their way up to the next landing, Hawes muttered, 'Bloody men!'

'Sorry?'

'Do you suppose for one second,' she went on, 'that if it had been two female officers down there, he'd have said anything?'

'I think that would depend how he was handled.'

Hawes glared at him, seeking levity that wasn't there.

'Part of our job,' Rebus went on, 'is pretending we like everyone, pretending we're interested in everything they have to say.'

'He just—'

'Got on your nerves? Mine too. Bit pompous, but that's just his way. You can't let it show. You're right: I'm not sure he'd have told us anything. He'd dismissed it as irrelevant. But then he opened up, just to put *you* in your place.' Rebus smiled. 'Good work. It's not often I get to play "good cop" around here.'

'It wasn't just that he got on my nerves,' Hawes conceded. 'He gave me the creeps. That newspaper clipping . . .'

'The one on the wall?'

She nodded. '*That* gave me the creeps.'

'He's a pathologist. They've thicker skins than most of us.'

She thought about this, and allowed herself a little smile. 'As I was getting up to leave, I couldn't help noticing a piece of jigsaw on the floor under the table . . .'

'Where it still sits?' Rebus guessed, smiling too now. 'With that kind of eye for detail, we'll make a detective of you yet . . .'

He pressed the next door-buzzer, and it was back to work.

THE FIRST MAJOR news conference took place at the Big House, with a live feed to the inquiry room at Gayfield Square, where officers were sitting two and three to a desk. The conversation was muted. Rebus stood at the back of the room. A bit too far from the TV, but he wasn't about to move. Bill Pryde stood next to him, clearly exhausted and just as clearly trying not to show it.

On the TV, the crowd was settling. The police video cam swung round as a door opened and a file of bodies trooped into the room, quieting the hubbub. Rebus could hear the sudden whirr of camera motors. Flashes of illumination. Ellen Wylie first, the new liaison officer, then Gill Templer, followed by David Costello and John Balfour.

The group sat at a long table in front of an array of microphones. The camera zoomed in on Costello's face then panned back a little to take in his upper body, but it was Ellen Wylie's voice that came over the loudspeaker, preceded by a nervous clearing of the throat.

'Good afternoon, ladies and gentlemen, and thank you for joining us. I'll just go over the format before we get started . . .'

Siobhan Clarke was over to Rebus's left, sitting on a desk alongside Grant Hood. Hood was staring at the floor. Maybe he was concentrating on Wylie's voice: Rebus remembered that the pair of them had worked closely together on the Grieve case a few months before. Siobhan was watching the screen, but her gaze kept wandering.

She wanted that job, Rebus thought to himself. And now she was hurting. Press Liaison would have been a step up for Siobhan, especially on a high-profile case. He willed her to turn his way, so he could offer something—a smile or shrug, or just a nod of understanding. But her eyes were back on the screen again. Wylie had finished her spiel, and it was Gill Templer's turn. She was summarising and updating the details of the case, an old hand at news conferences.

The camera, however, showed no interest in the two CID officers. It was there to concentrate on David Costello, and—to a far lesser extent—Philippa Balfour's father. The two men sat next to one another, and the camera moved slowly between them.

The younger man hadn't shaved, and looked to be in the same clothes as the previous night. His eyes flitted between cameras, never sure where he should be looking. His voice was dry and thin. 'We don't know what happened to Flip, and we desperately want to know. All of us, her friends, her family . . .' He glanced towards John Balfour. 'All those who know and love her, we need to know. Flip, if you're watching this, please get in touch with one of us. Just so we know you're . . . you've not come to any harm. We're worried sick.' His eyes were shining with the onset of tears. He stopped for a second, bowed his head, then drew himself straight again. John Balfour put his hand out to squeeze the younger man's shoulder, then Balfour himself started speaking, his voice booming.

'If anyone's holding my daughter, please get in touch. I'd like to talk with you, whoever you are, whyever you've done what you've done. And if anyone knows Flip's whereabouts, there'll be a number on screen at the end of this broadcast. I just need to know Flip's alive and well. To people watching this at home, please take a second to study Flip's photograph.' A further clicking of cameras as he held up the photo. 'Her name's Philippa Balfour and she's just twenty. If you've seen her, please get in touch. Thank you.'

The reporters were ready with their questions, but David Costello was already on his feet and making for the exit.

It was Wylie's voice again: '. . . not appropriate at this time . . . I'd like to thank you for your continuing support . . .' But the questions battered against her. Meantime the video cam was back on John Balfour. He looked quite composed, a handsome man in his mid-forties, hands clasped on the table in front of him, unblinking as the flashguns threw his shadow onto the wall behind.

'No, I really don't . . .'

'Mr Costello!' the journalists were yelling. 'Could we just ask . . .?'

'DS Wylie,' another voice barked, 'can you tell us something about possible motives for the abduction?'

'We don't have any motives yet.' Wylie was sounding flustered.

'But you accept that it *is* an abduction?'

'I don't . . . no, that's not what I meant.'

'Then what *did* you mean, DS Wylie?'

'I just . . . I didn't say anything about . . .'

And then Ellen Wylie's voice was replaced by Gill Templer's. The voice of authority. 'Steve,' she said, 'you know only too well that we can't speculate on details like that. If you want to make up lies just to sell a few more papers, that's your concern, but it's hardly respectful to Philippa Balfour's family and friends.'

Further questions were handled by Gill, who insisted on some calm beforehand. Although Rebus couldn't see her, he imagined Ellen Wylie would be shrinking visibly. Then Balfour interrupted to say that he'd like to respond to a couple of the points raised. He did so calmly, and then the conference started to break up.

'A cool customer,' Pryde said, before moving off to regroup his troops. It was time to get back to the real work again.

Grant Hood approached. 'Remind me,' he said. 'Which station was giving the longest odds on the boyfriend?'

'Torphichen,' Rebus told him.

'Then that's where my money's going.' He looked to Rebus for a reaction, but didn't get one. 'Come on, sir,' he went on, 'it was written all over his face!' Hood shook his head and moved past Rebus.

The tape of Costello's performance would go to the psychologists. They'd be looking for a glimmer of something, a short burst of illumination. Rebus wasn't sure they'd find it.

Siobhan was standing in front of him. 'Interesting, wasn't it?'

'Singularly interesting,' he agreed.

She smiled. 'You caught that too?'

He nodded. 'Costello kept saying "we", while her father used "I".'

'As if Flip's mother didn't matter.'

Rebus was thoughtful. 'It might just mean that Mr Balfour has an inflated sense of his own importance.' He paused. 'Wouldn't that be a first in a merchant banker? How's the computer stuff going?'

She smiled—'computer stuff' just about summed up Rebus's knowledge of hard disks and the like. 'I got past her password, so I can check her most recent emails . . . soon as I get back to my desk. Although there's no way of telling what's been deleted.'

They'd moved out of the office and into the corridor. 'I'm heading back to St Leonard's. Need a lift?' he said.

She shook her head. 'Got my car with me.'

'Fair enough.' He chuckled. 'Won't it be funny if Miss Balfour traipses back from an unannounced shopping spree?'

'It would be a relief,' Siobhan said solemnly. 'But I don't think that's going to happen, do you?'

'No,' Rebus said quietly.

BACK AT HIS DESK, he went through the files again, concentrating on family background. John Balfour was the third generation of a banking family. He had taken over the business in the 1980s and opened a London office, concentrating his efforts there. The family relocated north in the late eighties after the death of John's father. Their home, Junipers, was a baronial mansion in sixteen acres of countryside between Gullane and Haddington. The Edinburgh office, still in its original premises in Charlotte Square, was run by an old university friend of John Balfour's called Ranald Marr.

When Balfour was interviewed, the emphasis had been on the possibility of a kidnapping for profit. But as yet, all they'd had were a few crank notes. Another possibility was a deal gone sour: revenge the motive. Balfour was adamant that he had no enemies. But he'd denied the team access to his bank's client base.

'These people trust me. Without trust, the bank's finished.'

'Sir, with respect, your daughter's well-being might depend—'

'I'm aware of that!'

After which the interview had never lost its edge of antagonism.

The bottom line: Balfour's was conservatively estimated to be worth around £130 million, with John Balfour's personal wealth comprising maybe five per cent of the whole. Six and a half million reasons for a professional abduction. But wouldn't a professional have made contact by now?

Jacqueline Balfour had been born Jacqueline Gil-Martin, her father a diplomat and landowner. The family estate was 900 acres of Perthshire, which Jacqueline had been running when she'd met John Balfour, on a trip to her father's bank in Edinburgh. They'd married a year later, and Philippa had been born two years after that.

None of which, in all probability, was pertinent to the inquiry. All the same, it was what Rebus enjoyed about the job: constructing a web of relationships, peering into other people's lives . . .

He turned to the notes on David Costello. Dublin-born and educated. The father, Thomas Costello, didn't seem to have turned a day's work in his life, his needs supplied by a trust fund set up by his father, a land developer. David's mother, Theresa, was something else again. She had gone to art school but dropped out and got a job instead, window-dressing in a department store. From there she moved to interior design—for shops at first, and then for wealthy individuals. Which was how she met Thomas Costello. By the time they married, both her parents were dead. Theresa had built up her one-woman company until it had a turnover in the low millions. She was fifty-one now, and showing no signs of slacking, while her husband remained the man-about-town. Clippings from the Irish news showed him at racing events, garden parties and the like. In none of the photos did he appear with Theresa. Separate rooms in their Edinburgh hotel . . . As their son said, it was hardly a crime.

David had been late going to university, having taken a year out to travel the world. He was now in the third year of his MA degree in

389

English Language and Literature. Rebus remembered the books in his living room: Milton, Wordsworth, Hardy . . .

'Enjoying the view?'

Rebus opened his eyes. 'Deep in thought, Siobhan.'

'You weren't dropping off, then?'

Rebus glared at her. 'Far from it.'

She handed him a sheet of paper. 'Tell me what you think it means.'

Subj: Hellbank
Date: 5/9
From: Quizmaster@PaganOmerta.com
To: Flipside1223@HXRmail.com
Did you survive Hellbank? Time running out. Stricture awaits your call.

Rebus looked up at her. 'Going to give me a clue?'

She took back the sheet of paper. 'It's an email print-out. Philippa had a couple of dozen messages waiting for her, dating back to the day she went missing. All of them except this one are addressed to her other name.'

'Her other name?'

'ISPs'—she paused—'Internet service providers will usually allow you a range of log-on names, as many as five or six. Flipside 1223 is a sort of alias. Her other emails all went to Flip-dot-Balfour.'

'So what does it mean?'

Siobhan expelled air. 'That's what I'm wondering. There's not a single *saved* message from her or to her in the name of Flipside 1223. So either she's been erasing them as she goes, or else this got to her by mistake.' Siobhan looked thoughtful. 'I'd like to track down whoever sent this, but the only way I can think of is to reply.'

'Let whoever it is know that Philippa's gone missing?'

Siobhan lowered her voice. 'I was thinking more along the lines of *her* replying.'

'Run it past DCS Templer when she gets in,' he cautioned.

THAT EVENING, Gill Templer hosted a celebratory gathering at the Palm Court in the Balmoral Hotel. A bottle of champagne sat in an ice bucket. Bowls of nibbles had been brought to the table.

'Remember to leave space for supper,' Gill told her guests. A table in Hadrian's had been booked for eight thirty. It had just gone half past seven, and the last arrival was coming through the door.

Slipping off her coat, Siobhan apologised. A waiter was already pouring champagne into her glass. 'Cheers,' she said, sitting down and lifting the glass. 'And congratulations.'

Gill Templer lifted her own glass and allowed herself a smile. 'I think I deserve it,' she said, to enthusiastic agreement.

Siobhan already knew two of the guests. Both Harriet Brough and Diana Metcalf were fiscals depute, and Siobhan had worked with them on several prosecutions.

'And this is Siobhan Clarke,' Gill was telling the last member of the party. 'A detective constable in my station. Siobhan, this is Jean Burchill. Jean works at the museum.'

'Oh? Which one?'

'The Museum of Scotland,' Burchill replied. 'Have you ever been?'

'I had a meal in The Tower once,' Siobhan said.

'Not quite the same thing.' Burchill's voice trailed off.

'No, what I meant was . . .' Siobhan tried to find a diplomatic way of putting it. 'I had a meal there just after it opened. The guy I was with . . . well, bad experience. It put me off going back.'

'Understood,' Harriet Brough said, as though every mishap in life could be explained by reference to the opposite sex.

'Well,' Gill said, 'it's women only tonight, so we can all relax.'

'Unless we hit a nightclub later,' Diana Metcalf said, eyes glinting.

Gill caught Siobhan's eye. 'Did you send that email?' she asked.

Jean Burchill tutted. 'No shoptalk, please.'

The fiscals agreed noisily, but Siobhan nodded anyway, to let Gill know the message had gone out. Whether anyone would be fooled by it was another matter. It was why she'd been late getting here, she'd been trying to work out what words to use.

'I saw the press conference on TV tonight,' Diana Metcalf said.

Jean Burchill groaned. 'What did I just say?'

Metcalf turned to her. 'This isn't shop, Jean.' Everyone's talking about it.' Then she turned to Gill. 'I don't think it was the boyfriend, do you?'

Gill just shrugged.

'See?' Jean Burchill said. 'Gill doesn't want to talk about it.'

'More likely the father,' Harriet Brough said. 'My brother was at school with him. A very cold fish.' She spoke with confidence and authority. 'Where was the mother?'

'Couldn't face it,' Gill answered. 'We did ask her.'

'She couldn't have made a worse job than those two,' Brough

stated, picking cashews out of the bowl next to her.

Gill looked suddenly tired. Siobhan decided on a change of subject and asked Jean Burchill what she did at the museum.

'I'm a senior curator,' Burchill explained. 'My main specialism is eighteenth- and nineteenth-century—'

'Her main specialism,' Harriet Brough interrupted, 'is death.'

Burchill smiled. 'It's true I put together exhibits on belief and—'

'What's truer,' Brough cut in, 'is that she puts together old coffins and pictures of dead babies. Gives me the collywobbles.'

Burchill smiled again. She was, Siobhan decided, very pretty. Small and slender, with straight brown hair in a pageboy cut. She wore no make-up, nor did she need any. She was all muted, pastel shades: jacket and trousers which had probably been called 'taupe' in the shop; grey sweater beneath the jacket. Late forties, like Brough and Metcalf. It struck Siobhan that *she* was the youngest person here by probably fifteen years.

'Jean and I were at school together,' Gill explained. 'Then we lost touch and bumped into one another just four or five years back.'

Burchill smiled at the memory.

'More champagne, ladies?' the waiter said, lifting the bottle from its ice bucket.

'About bloody time,' Harriet Brough snapped.

BETWEEN DESSERT AND COFFEE, Siobhan headed to the loo. Walking back along the corridor to the brasserie, she met Gill.

'Great minds,' Gill said with a smile.

'It was a lovely meal, Gill. Are you sure I can't . . . ?'

Gill touched her arm. 'My treat. It's not every day I have something to celebrate.' The smile melted from her lips. 'You think your email will work?' Siobhan shrugged, and Gill nodded, accepting the assessment. 'What did you reckon to the press conference?'

'The usual jungle—and it seemed as if you threw Ellen Wylie in there without a map.'

'Careful, Siobhan.' Gill's voice had lost all its warmth. As she spoke, her eyes surveyed the hallway. 'Ellen Wylie's been bending my ear for months. She wanted liaison, and as soon as I could, I gave it to her. I wanted to see if she was as good as she thinks she is.' Now her eyes met Siobhan's. 'She fell short.'

'How did that feel?'

Gill held up a finger. 'Don't push this, Siobhan.' She forced a smile.

'We'll talk later,' she added, sliding past Siobhan and pushing open the door to the loos. Then she paused. 'Ellen's no longer liaison officer. I *was* thinking of asking you . . .' The door closed behind her.

'Don't do me any favours,' Siobhan said, but to the closed door.

 **Chapter Three**

When Rebus arrived at St Leonard's, news was coming in of another search, this time of the lockup on Calton Road where David Costello garaged his MG sports car. The forensic unit had found nothing of apparent consequence. They already knew Flip Balfour's prints would be all over the car. The garage itself was clean.

Distant Daniels was playing errand boy, transferring paperwork between Gayfield and St Leonard's. 'A student with an MG,' he commented, shaking his head.

'Never mind the car,' Rebus told him. 'That lockup probably cost more than your flat.'

'You could be right.' The smile they shared was sour.

'DI Rebus?' Rebus turned towards the voice. 'My office.'

And it *was* her office. Already, Gill was making it her own. The Farmer's chair had gone, replaced by a more utilitarian model; a bunch of flowers sat on a filing cabinet.

Gill held a piece of paper out, so that Rebus had to get out of the visitor's chair to reach it. 'A place called Falls,' she said. 'Do you know it?' He shook his head slowly. 'Me neither,' she confided.

Rebus was busy reading the note. It was a telephone message. A doll had been found in Falls. 'A doll?' he said.

She nodded.' I want you to go take a look.'

Rebus burst out laughing. 'You're having me on.' But when he looked up, her face was blank.

'The doll was in a coffin, John.' She sounded tired all of a sudden.

'A kids' prank,' he said.

'Maybe.'

He checked the note again. 'It says here Falls is East Lothian. Let Haddington or somewhere take it.'

'I want *you* to take it. You see, Falls isn't just in East Lothian, John. It's where the Balfours live.'

HE DROVE OUT of Edinburgh along the A1. Traffic was light, the sun low and bright. East Lothian to him meant golf links and rocky beaches, flat farming land and commuter towns, fiercely protective of their own identities. Towns such as Haddington, Gullane and North Berwick—reserved, prosperous enclaves, their small shops supported by local communities that looked askance at the retail-park culture of the nearby capital.

Falls wasn't quite what he'd been expecting. At its centre was a short stretch of main road with houses either side. Nice detached houses with well-tended gardens, and a row of cottages that fronted the narrow pavement. One of them had a wooden sign outside with the word *Pottery* painted on it. Towards the end of the village was a 1930s council estate, grey semis with broken fences, tricycles lying outside. On the patch of grass that separated this estate from the main road, two kids were kicking a ball back and forth.

Then, as suddenly as he'd entered the village, he was out into countryside again. As he pulled over by the verge, a tractor he'd overtaken earlier came past him, turned into a half-ploughed field. The driver came to a juddering halt, eased himself from the cab, and started tinkering with the machinery at the back of his tractor.

Rebus got out of his car. 'Morning,' he said.

'Morning.'

'I'm a police officer. Do you know where I'd find Beverly Dodds?'

'See the cottage with the Pottery sign? That's her.' The man's voice was neutral. He still hadn't so much as glanced in Rebus's direction, concentrating instead on the blades of his plough. 'To do with that bloody doll, is it?'

'Yes.'

'Piece of bloody nonsense, going to you lot about that.'

'You don't think it has anything to do with Ms Balfour's disappearance?'

'Course it hasn't. Kids from Meadowside, that's all it is.'

'You're probably right. Meadowside's that patch of houses, is it?' Rebus nodded back towards the village.

The farm hand nodded agreement. 'Like I said, waste of time. Still, it's yours to waste, I suppose . . . and my taxes paying for it.'

'Do you know the family?'

The farm hand nodded again. 'They own this land.'

Rebus looked around, realising for the first time that there wasn't a single dwelling in sight. 'Where is their place, by the way?'

For the first time, the man locked eyes with Rebus. 'The track the other end of town,' he said. 'About a mile up that way, big gates, you can't miss them. The falls are up there too, about halfway.'

'Falls?'

'The waterfall. You'll want to see it, won't you?'

'Wouldn't want to waste your tax money on sightseeing,' Rebus said with a smile.

'It's not sightseeing though, is it? It's the scene of the bloody crime. Don't they tell you anything back in Edinburgh?'

A NARROW LANE wound uphill out of the village. It opened out a little eventually, and at that point Rebus pulled his Saab up onto the verge. He locked his car and climbed over a stile into a field where cows were grazing. He did his best to avoid the cow pats as he walked towards a line of nearby trees, following the route of the stream to the waterfall. This was where, the previous morning, Beverly Dodds had found a tiny coffin and, within it, a doll.

When he reached the waterfall he laughed out loud. The water dropped a full four feet.

'Not exactly Niagara, are you?' Rebus doubted anyone had seen whoever placed the doll here, always supposing it hadn't been washed down from above. Not that there *was* much above, just hills where you could walk for days without seeing another human soul.

He crouched down, rested a hand in the water. It was cold and clear. He scooped some up, watched it trickle through his fingers.

'I wouldn't drink any,' a voice called. He looked up into the light, saw a woman emerging from the line of trees. She wore a long muslin dress over her thin frame. With the sun behind her, the outline of her figure was discernible beneath the cloth. As she came forward, she ran a hand through long, curly blonde hair, taking it out of her eyes. 'The farmers,' she explained. 'All the chemicals they use run off the soil and into the streams. Organophosphates and who knows what.'

'I never touch the stuff,' Rebus said, drying his hand on his sleeve as he stood up. 'Are you Ms Dodds?'

'Everyone calls me Bev.' She stuck out a skeletal hand. Like chicken bones, Rebus thought, making sure not to squeeze too hard.

'DI Rebus,' he said. 'How did you know I was here?'

'I saw your car from my window. When you drove up the lane, I just knew instinctively.' She bounced on her toes, pleased to have been proved right. She reminded Rebus of a teenager, but her face told a different story: laughter lines around the eyes; the skin of the cheek-bones sagging. She had to be in her early fifties.

'Where exactly did you find this doll?'

She pointed towards the fall of water. 'Right at the foot, sitting on the bank. It was completely dry.'

'Why do you say that?'

'I know you'll have been wondering if it floated downstream.'

Rebus didn't let on that he'd been thinking exactly this, but she seemed to sense it anyway and bounced on her toes again.

'I don't suppose you brought it with you?' he asked.

She shook her head. 'It's down in the cottage.' She glanced round at his Saab. 'Think you can get your car turned?'

He nodded.

'Well, take your time,' she said, moving away. 'I'll head back and make some tea. See you at Wheel Cottage, Inspector.'

WHEEL, SHE EXPLAINED, warming the teapot, was for her potter's wheel. 'It began as therapy,' she went on. 'After my divorce.' She paused for a moment. 'But I found out I was actually quite good at it. I think that surprised quite a number of my old friends.' The way she said these last two words made Rebus think that these friends had no place in her new life. 'So maybe "wheel" stands for the wheel of life too,' she added, lifting the tray and leading him into what she called her 'parlour'.

It was a small, low-ceilinged room with bright patterns everywhere. There were several examples of what he took to be Beverly Dodds's work: glazed blue earthenware shaped into dishes and vases. He made sure she noticed him noticing them.

'Mostly early stuff,' she said, trying for a dismissive tone.

'They're very good,' he told her. She poured the tea and handed him a robust cup and saucer of the same blue colouring. He looked around the room but couldn't see any sign of a coffin or doll.

'In my workshop,' she said, seeming to read his mind again. 'I can fetch it, if you like.'

'Please,' he said. So she got up and left the room. Rebus looked around again. There was just the one small bookcase: arts and crafts mostly, and a couple of volumes on 'Wicca'. Rebus picked one up, started to flip through it.

'White magic,' the voice behind him said. 'The power of Nature.'

Rebus put the book back and turned towards her.

'Here we are,' she said. She was carrying the coffin as though part of some solemn procession. Rebus lifted it gently from her, as he felt was expected, and at the same time a thought hurtled through his brain: *She's unhinged . . . this is all her doing!* But his attention was diverted to the coffin itself. It was made of a dark wood, aged oak maybe, and held together with black nails, akin to carpet tacks. The whole thing was about eight inches long. It wasn't the work of a professional carpenter, even Rebus could tell that.

And then she lifted off the lid, her eyes wide and unblinking, fixed on his. 'It was nailed shut,' she explained. 'I prised it open.'

Inside, the small wooden doll lay, arms by its sides, its face blank, dressed in scraps of muslin. It had been carved with little artistry.

'The cloth's quite new and clean,' she was whispering.

He nodded. Clearly the coffin hadn't been outdoors long.

'I've seen some strange things, Bev . . .' Rebus said, his voice trailing off. 'Nothing else at the scene? Nothing unusual?'

She shook her head slowly. 'I walk up that way every week. This,' touching the coffin, 'was the only thing out of place.'

'Is there anyone in the village who's keen on woodwork?'

'Nearest joiner is Haddington. But who, in their right mind, would do something like *this*?'

Rebus smiled. 'I bet you've thought about it though.'

'I've thought of little else, Inspector. Normally I'd shrug something like this off, but with what's happened to the Balfour girl . . .'

'We don't know anything's happened,' Rebus felt bound to say.

'Surely it's connected though?'

'Doesn't mean it's not a crank.' He kept his eyes on hers as he spoke. 'In my experience, every village has its resident oddball.'

'Are you saying that I—' She broke off at the sound of a car drawing up outside. 'Oh,' she said, 'that'll be the reporter.'

Rebus followed her to the window. A young man was emerging from the driver's side of a red Ford Focus. In the passenger seat, a photographer was fixing a lens onto his camera.

'They were here before,' Bev was explaining. 'When the Balfour girl first went missing. Left me a card, and when this happened . . .'

'That wasn't the cleverest move, Ms Dodds,' Rebus said, trying to keep his anger in check as he followed her to the front door.

Hand on the door handle, she half turned towards him. 'At least *they* didn't accuse me of being a crank, Inspector.'

He wanted to say, *but they will*, but the damage was done.

The reporter's name was Steve Holly, and he worked for the Edinburgh office of a Glasgow tabloid. He was young, early twenties, short and a bit overweight. He had a notebook and pen in one hand, and shook Rebus's with the other.

'Don't think we've met,' he said, in a way that made Rebus suspect his name was not unknown to the reporter. 'This is Tony, my glamorous assistant.' The photographer was hefting a camera bag over one shoulder. 'What we thought, Bev, is if we take you to the waterfall, have you picking the coffin up off the ground. Then we could do a nice portrait of you in your studio.'

Bev stroked her neck, enjoying the thought. 'Yes, of course.'

Holly stared up at the sky. 'We'd better get a move on, eh?'

'Perfect just now,' the photographer explained to Bev. 'Won't stay that way for long.'

Bev looked up too, nodding agreement, one artist to another. Rebus had to admit: Holly was good.

Rebus said, 'I've got to get back to Edinburgh now. Any chance I can have your number, Mr Holly?'

'Should have my card somewhere.' The reporter began searching his pockets, produced a wallet and from it a business card.

'Thanks,' Rebus said. 'And if I could have a quick word . . . ?'

As he led Holly a few steps away, he saw that Bev was standing close beside the photographer, asking him if her clothes were suitable. Rebus turned his back on them, the better to mask what he was about to say. 'Have you seen this doll thing?' Holly was asking. Rebus nodded. Holly wrinkled his nose. 'Reckon we're wasting our time?' His tone was matey, inviting the truth.

'Almost certainly,' Rebus said, not believing it, and knowing that once Holly saw the bizarre carving he wouldn't believe it either. 'But a day out of the city . . .' Rebus went on, forcing levity into his tone.

'Surprised they sent a DI,' Holly remarked.

'We have to treat each lead seriously.'

'Sure, I understand that. I'd still have sent a DC or DS, tops.'

'Like I say—' But Holly was turning away from him, ready to get back to work. Rebus gripped his arm. 'You know that if this *does* turn out to be evidence, we would want it kept quiet?'

Holly nodded perfunctorily and tried for an American accent. 'Get your people to speak to my people.' He turned back to Bev and the photographer. 'Here, Bev, that what you're wearing? I just thought maybe you'd be comfier in a shorter skirt . . .'

REBUS DROVE BACK up the lane, wondering what else he might find. A half-mile further along, a wide driveway ended abruptly in a set of tall wrought-iron gates. He pulled over and got out of the car. The gates were padlocked shut. Beyond them he could see the driveway curve through a forest, the trees blocking any view of a house. There were no signs, but he knew this had to be Junipers.

Rebus left his car, walked a hundred yards beside a high wall until it tapered down, then hoisted himself over it and into the trees.

He made directly for the driveway and walked a full five minutes before the house, an elongated two-storey Gothic confection with turrets either end, came into view. Rebus supposed there'd be security of some kind—maybe a police officer manning the phone—but if so it was low-key. The house looked onto a spread of manicured lawn, flowerbeds either side. He couldn't imagine anyone actually being happy in such a dour setting. The house almost seemed to have a frown on it, a warning against gaiety and ill manners. He caught sight of a face at an upstairs window, but as soon as he saw it, it vanished again. A minute later the front door was hauled open and a woman appeared, holding a cordless phone.

'Mrs Balfour,' said Rebus as he walked towards her. 'I'm a police officer.'

A WPC came to the door, but she was ordered by Jacqueline Balfour to 'just go away'.

'Is there something you've come to tell me?' Jacqueline Balfour asked Rebus.

'No news,' he said quietly. Then, seeing all hope drain from her: 'There might be a lead down in the village.'

'What sort of lead?'

Suddenly he wished he'd never started. 'I can't really say just now.'

Mrs Balfour lead him into the drawing room.

'Did Philippa collect dolls?' Rebus asked.

'Dolls?' She was turning the cordless phone in her hand.

'It's just that someone found one, down by the waterfall.'

She shook her head. 'No dolls,' she said, as if feeling that somehow there should have been dolls in Philippa's life, and that their absence reflected badly on her as a mother.

'It's probably nothing,' Rebus said. 'Is Mr Balfour at home?'

'He'll be back later. He's in Edinburgh.' She stared at the phone. 'No one's going to call, are they? Everyone's been told to keep the line clear. In case *they* phone. But they won't, I know they won't.'

'You don't think she's been kidnapped, Mrs Balfour?'

She shook her head and stared at him, her eyes red-veined from crying, and shadowed underneath from lack of sleep. 'She's dead.' It came out almost in a whisper. 'You think so too, don't you?'

'It's far too early to be thinking that. I've known Missing Persons turn up weeks or months later.'

'Weeks or months? I can't bear the thought. I'd rather know . . . one way or the other.'

'When was the last time you saw her?'

'About ten days ago. We went shopping in Edinburgh.'

'Did she come to the house often?'

Jacqueline Balfour shook her head. 'He poisoned her.'

'Sorry?'

'David Costello. He poisoned her memories, made her think she could remember things, things that never happened. That last time we met . . . Flip kept asking about her childhood. She said it had been miserable for her, that we hadn't wanted her. Utter rubbish.'

'And David Costello put these ideas in her head?'

She took a deep breath and released it. 'That's my belief.'

Rebus was thoughtful. 'Why would he do something like that?'

'Because of who he is.' She left the statement hanging in the air. The ringing of the phone was a sudden cacophony.

'Hello?' she said into the handpiece. Then her face relaxed a little. 'Hello, darling, what time will you be home . . . ?'

Rebus waited till the call was finished. He was thinking of the press conference, the way John Balfour had said 'I' rather than 'we', as if his wife had no feelings, no existence . . .

'That was John,' she said.

Rebus nodded. 'He's in London a lot, isn't he? Do you see much of his business partner?'

She looked at him again. 'Ranald? He and his wife are probably our best friends. Why do you ask?'

Rebus made show of scratching his head. 'I don't know. Just making conversation, I suppose.'

'Well don't. John's always warning me not to give anything away, you never know who's fishing for some info on the bank.'

'We're not competitors here, Mrs Balfour.'

She bowed her head a little. 'Of course not. I apologise.'

'No need for apologies,' Rebus said, getting to his feet. 'This is your home, your rules. Wouldn't you say?'

'Well, when you put it like that . . .' She seemed to brighten a little. All the same, Rebus reckoned that whenever Jacqueline Balfour's husband was at home, it was *his* rules they played by . . .

BACK IN HIS Arden Street flat, Rebus took a can of beer from the fridge and settled into his chair by the living-room window. The kitchen was more of a mess than usual: some of the hall stuff was in there while rewiring went on. After that, he had a painter booked to slap on some magnolia, freshen the place up. The Property Centre had valued it at between £125,000 and £140,000. There was no mortgage outstanding. It was cash in the bank.

'You could retire on that,' Siobhan had told him. Well, maybe. He could certainly slip some money to Sammy, his daughter. Sammy was another reason for selling, or so he told himself. After her accident, she was finally out of the wheelchair but still used a pair of sticks. Two flights of tenement stairs were beyond her . . . not that she'd been a regular visitor even before the hit-and-run.

The students next door were playing something semi-raucous. It sounded like bad Hawkwind from twenty years before, which probably meant it was by some fashionable new band. He looked through his own collection, came up with a tape Siobhan had made of a band from New Zealand called The Mutton Birds. The second song was 'The Falls'.

He sat down again. There was a bottle on the floor: Talisker, a clean, honed taste. Glass beside it, so he poured, toasted the reflection in the window, leaned back and closed his eyes. The music was about loss and redemption. Places changing and people with them, dreams shifting ever further beyond reach. Perhaps it was time for a change . . .

ON HER WAY into work next morning, Siobhan thought of nothing but Quizmaster. Her first message—*Problem. Need to talk to you. Flipside*—seemed not to have worked. Today, she decided, she was going to end the pretence. She would email him as herself, and explain Flip's disappearance, asking him to get in touch.

St Leonard's was quiet when she arrived. The CID suite had a musty smell: too many bodies each day spending too long cooped up there. She opened a couple of windows, and sat down at her desk. When she checked, there were no messages on Flip's computer. She decided to keep the line open while she composed her new email. But after only a couple of lines, a message told her she had post. It was from Quizmaster, a simple *Good morning*. She hit REPLY and asked, *How did you know I was here?*

The response was immediate. *That's something Flipside wouldn't have to ask. Who are you?*

Siobhan typed quickly, *I'm a police officer, based in Edinburgh. We're investigating Philippa Balfour's disappearance.*

Who?

Flipside, she typed.

She never told me her real name. That's one of the rules.

OK, Siobhan typed, *can you tell me about Hellbank?*

You'd have to play the game. Give me a name to call you.

My name's Siobhan Clarke. I'm a detective constable with Lothian and Borders Police.

I get the feeling that's your real name, Siobhan. You've broken one of the first rules. But to answer your question, Hellbank is one level of the game. Stricture is the next level.

What sort of game? Could she have got into trouble?

Later.

Siobhan stared at the word angrily. *I need your cooperation*, she typed.

Then learn patience. I could shut down right now and you'd never find me. Do you accept that?

Yes. Siobhan was about ready to punch the screen.

And that was it. He'd gone offline. All she could do was wait. Or was it? The rest of the shift was drifting in. A couple of people said hello, but she wasn't listening. She'd had another idea. She reached for the phone book and a copy of Yellow Pages, drew her notebook towards her and picked up a pen.

SHE TRIED COMPUTER retailers first, until finally someone directed her towards a games shop on Leith Walk. 'It's D and D but they might be able to help,' the assistant told her. 'It's called Gandalf's.'

'D and D?'

'Sword and sorcery, dungeons and dragons,' he said.

Gandalf's was squeezed unpromisingly between a tattoo parlour and a chip shop. When she opened the door, she set off a set of wind chimes hanging just inside. Gandalf's had obviously been a second-hand bookshop once—the shelves now held an assortment of board games and playing pieces that looked like unpainted toy soldiers. A door at the back of the shop creaked open and a man appeared. He had a grey beard and ponytail, and a distended stomach clad in a Grateful Dead T-shirt.

'You look official,' he said glumly.

'CID,' Siobhan said, showing him her warrant card.

'Rent's only eight weeks late,' he grumbled. As he shuffled around the shop, she saw that he was wearing leather open-toed sandals. Like their owner, they had a good few miles on them.

'I don't think you can help me,' Siobhan admitted, looking around. 'I'm interested in something slightly more high-tech.'

He bristled at this. 'What do you mean?'

'Role-playing by computer.'

'Interactive?' She nodded and he shuffled past her to the door and locked it. She went on the defensive, but he merely shuffled past her again on his way to the far door. 'Down here,' he said, and Siobhan, feeling a bit like Alice at the mouth of the tunnel, eventually followed.

Down four or five steps, she came into a dank windowless room, only partially lit. There were boxes piled high—more games and accessories, she guessed, but on a table in one corner sat what looked like a state-of-the-art computer, its large screen as thin as a laptop's.

He sat down at the computer and started work. 'There are lots of games on the Net,' he was saying. 'You join a group of people to fight either against the program or against other teams. There are leagues.' He tapped the screen. 'See? This is a game called Doom.'

Her eyes ran down the league table. 'Does each player know who his teammate is, or who's on the opposing team?'

He stroked his beard. 'At most, they'd have a *nom de guerre*.'

Siobhan thought of Philippa, with her secret email name. 'And people can have lots of names, right?'

'Oh yes,' he said. 'You can amass dozens of names. This is the *virtual* world. People are free to invent virtual lives for themselves.'

'A case I'm working on, there's a game involved. It's got levels called Hellbank and Stricture. Someone called Quizmaster seems to be in charge.'

He was stroking his beard again. 'I don't know it,' he said at last. 'But it sounds like SIRPS: Simple Role-Play Scenario. Quizmaster sets tasks or questions, could be one player or dozens. How serious is the case?'

'A young woman's gone missing. She was playing the game.'

He rested his hands on his stomach. 'I'll ask around,' he said. 'See if we can track down Quizmaster for you.'

'Even if I had an idea what the game involved . . .'

He nodded, and Siobhan remembered her dialogue with Quizmaster. She'd asked about Hellbank. And his reply?

You'd have to play the game . . .

SHE KNEW THAT requisitioning a laptop would take time. She knew, also, that she could use Philippa Balfour's computer. But she didn't want to, for all sorts of reasons. Then she had a brainwave and got on her mobile. 'Grant? It's Siobhan. I need a favour . . .'

DC Grant Hood was only too happy to leave the office, make a trip home, returning with the laptop. Siobhan explained that she would need to use it for emails.

'It's up and ready,' Grant told her. He had always been keen to lend his high-tech kit to anyone who asked. He didn't use it himself; maybe he never got past the owner's manuals.

'I'll need your email address and pass name.'

'That means you can access *my* emails,' he said, sounding defensive.

'Don't worry. I'll save them for you . . . and I promise not to peek.'

'Then there's the matter of my fee,' Grant said.

She looked at him. 'Your fee?'

'Yet to be discussed.' His face broke into a grin.

She folded her arms. 'So what is it?'

'I don't know,' he told her. 'I'll have to think . . .'

Transaction complete, she headed back to her desk. She already had a connector that would link her mobile phone to the laptop, so getting online took her only a few minutes. Once there, she sent a note to Quizmaster, automatically giving him Grant's email address.

Maybe I want to play the game. Over to you. Siobhan.

Having sent the message, she left the line open. It would cost her a small fortune when her next mobile bill appeared, but she pushed that thought aside. For now, the game was the only lead she had.

REBUS WAS AT GAYFIELD SQUARE, and nothing was happening. Which was to say, the place was a flurry of activity, but all the sound and fury couldn't hide a creeping sense of desperation. Assistant Chief Constable Carswell had put in an appearance and made it plain that what they needed was 'a swift conclusion'. Both Templer and Pryde had used the phrase a little later, which was how Rebus knew.

'DI Rebus?' One of the uniforms was standing in front of him. 'Boss says she'd like a word.'

When he walked in, she told him to close the door. The place was cramped and smelt of sweat. Space being at a premium, Gill was sharing this space with two other detectives, working shifts.

'How did you get on in Falls?' she asked.

'I came to a swift conclusion.'

She glared at him. 'Which was?'

'That it'll make a good story for the tabloids.'

Gill nodded. 'I saw something in the evening paper last night.'

'The woman who found the doll—or says she did—has been talking.'

'"Or says she did"?'

He just shrugged.

'You think she might be behind it?'

Rebus slipped his hands into his pockets. 'Who knows?'

'Someone thinks they might. A friend of mine called Jean Burchill. She's a curator at the museum. I think you should talk to her.'

'And she knows something about this doll?'

'She might do. According to Jean, this is far from the first.'

REBUS ADMITTED that he'd never been inside the new Museum of Scotland before. 'The old museum, I used to take my daughter there when she was a kid.'

Jean Burchill tutted. 'But this is quite another thing, Inspector. It's all about who we are, our history and culture.'

'No stuffed animals and totem poles?'

She smiled. 'Not that I can think of.' Despite her age, she reminded him of a schoolgirl: that mixture of the shy and the knowing, the prim and the curious. They took a lift to the fourth floor and when the doors opened they walked out into a narrow corridor filled with images of death. 'The section on beliefs,' she said, her voice barely audible. 'Witchcraft and grave robbers and burials.' Near a black coach sat a large iron coffin. Rebus couldn't help reaching out to touch it.

'It's a mortsafe,' she said, then, seeing his lack of comprehension: 'The families of the deceased would lock the coffin inside a mortsafe for the first six months to deter the resurrectionists.'

'Meaning body snatchers?' Now, this was a piece of history he knew. 'Like Burke and Hare? Digging up corpses and selling them to the university?'

She peered at him like a teacher with a stubborn pupil. 'Burke and Hare didn't dig up anything. That's the whole point of their story: they killed people, then sold the bodies to the anatomists.'

'Right,' Rebus said.

They stopped at the furthest glass case. 'Here we are,' Burchill said. 'The Arthur's Seat coffins.'

Rebus looked. There were eight coffins in all. They were five or six inches long, well made, with nails studded into their lids. Inside the coffins were little wooden dolls, some wearing clothes.

'At one time they were all dressed. But the cloth perished.' She pointed to a photograph in the case. 'In 1836 children playing on Arthur's Seat found the concealed mouth of a cave. Inside were seventeen little coffins, of which only these eight survive.'

Rebus was staring at the photograph, trying to place where on the massive slopes of the hill it might be. Were he a betting man, he'd see short odds on a connection between these objects and the one found in Falls. Whoever had made and placed the coffin by the waterfall knew about the museum exhibit and had, for some reason, decided to copy it. Rebus looked around at the various sombre displays of mortality. 'You put this lot together?'

She nodded.

'Must make for a popular topic at parties.'

'You'd be surprised,' she said quietly. 'When it comes down to it, aren't we all curious about the things we fear?'

DOWNSTAIRS IN THE OLD MUSEUM, they sat on a bench carved to resemble a whale's rib cage.

Rebus said, 'The display upstairs said something about the dolls connecting to Burke and Hare?'

She nodded. 'A mock burial for the victims. We think they may have sold as many as seventeen bodies for dissection. It was a horrible crime. You see, a dissected body cannot rise up again on the day of the Last Judgment.'

'Not without its guts spilling out,' Rebus agreed.

She ignored him. 'Burke and Hare were arrested and tried. Hare testified against his friend, and only William Burke went to the gallows. Guess what happened to his body afterwards?'

That was an easy one. 'Dissection?' Rebus guessed.

She nodded. 'His body was taken to Old College, and used by an anatomy class. This was in January 1829.'

'And the coffins date from the early 1830s?'

She nodded again. 'They interest me because they are such a mystery,' she continued. 'In a museum, we live by rules of identification and classification. Dates and provenance may be uncertain, but we almost always know what we're dealing with: a casket, a key, the remains of a Roman burial site.'

'But with the coffins, you can't be sure what they mean.'

She smiled. 'Exactly. That makes them frustrating for a curator.'

'I know the feeling,' he said. 'It's like me with a case. If it can't be solved, it nips my head.'

'Something else,' she said. 'There've been other dolls, other places.'

'What?'

'Best thing is if I send you what I've got . . .'

REBUS SPENT the rest of that Friday waiting for his shift to end. Photos of David Costello's MG soft top had been placed on one of the walls, joining the haphazard jigsaw there. The car hadn't been washed of late. If it had been, the forensic boffins would have been asking David Costello why. More photos of Philippa's friends and acquaintances had been gathered and shown to Professor Devlin, who did not recognise any of them as the man he had seen outside his flat before Philippa's disappearance. A couple of prints of the boyfriend had been slipped in, which had caused Devlin to complain about 'tactics beneath contempt'.

Five days since that Sunday night. The more Rebus stared at the jigsaw on the wall, the less he saw. You tried not to care, tried to maintain objectivity, just as the training seminars told you to, but it was hard. Which was why, at day's end, he went home, showered and changed, and sat in his chair for an hour with a glass of Laphroaig and the Rolling Stones for company.

The next day, Saturday, he went to the football with Siobhan. The ground was full, as only happened with local derbies and when Glasgow came to town. Today it was Rangers. Siobhan had a season ticket. Rebus was in the seat next to her, thanks to another season-ticket-holder friend who couldn't make it.

'Nice guy?' Rebus asked her.

'Nice *family* guy.' She laughed. 'When are you going to stop trying to marry me off?'

'I was only asking,' he said with a grin. He'd noticed that TV cameras were covering the game. They would concentrate on the players. But it was the fans who really interested Rebus. He wondered what stories they could tell, what lives they'd led. Siobhan, on the other hand, brought the same concentration to the game as she did to police work, yelling out advice to the Hibs players, arguing each refereeing decision with fans nearby.

'Anything happening your end of the case?' Rebus asked her.

'Day off, John.' Her eyes never left the pitch.

'I know, I was just asking . . .'

'We can have a drink after,' Siobhan said.

'Try and stop me,' Rebus told her.

After the match they and a few thousand others went to find a drink. Siobhan's usual pub was heaving. Rebus took one look and suggested somewhere quieter.

She followed him as he cut through Lorne Street and came out on Leith Walk, where weary shoppers were struggling home. The pub he had in mind was an anonymous affair with bevelled windows and an oxblood carpet pocked with cigarette burns and blackened gum.

'You sure know how to treat a lady,' Siobhan complained.

'And would the lady like a Bacardi Breezer?'

'Pint of lager,' Siobhan said defiantly. Rebus ordered himself a pint of Eighty with a malt on the side. As they took their seats, Siobhan told him he seemed to know every bad pub in the city.

'Thanks,' he said without a trace of irony. 'So,' he lifted his glass, 'what's the news on Philippa Balfour's computer?'

'There's a game she was playing. I don't know much about it. It's run by someone called Quizmaster. I've made contact with him. And I'm waiting for him to get back to me.'

'Any other way we can track him down?'

'Not that I know of.'

'What about the game?'

'I don't know the first thing about it,' she admitted, attacking her drink. 'Gill's beginning to think it's a dead end.' Siobhan's face changed. 'She offered me the liaison post, you know.'

'I thought she might. Are you going to take it?' He watched her shake her head. 'Because of what happened to Ellen Wylie?'

'Not really.'

'Then why?'

She shrugged. 'Not ready for it, maybe.'

'You're ready,' he stated. 'Who's doing the job meantime?'

'Gill, I think.' She paused. 'We're going to find Flip's body, aren't we?'

'Maybe.'

She looked at him. 'You think she's still alive?'

'No,' he said bleakly, 'I don't.'

THAT NIGHT HE HIT a few more bars, sticking close to home at first, then hailing a taxi and asking to be taken to the Oxford Bar.

He'd asked Siobhan what her own plans were.

'A hot bath and a good book,' she'd told him. She'd been lying. He knew this because Grant Hood had told half the station he was taking her on a date, his reward for lending her his laptop. Not that Rebus had said anything to her: if she didn't want him to know, that was fair enough.

He asked Harry the barman for the phone book.

'It's over there,' Harry answered, obliging as ever.

Rebus flipped through but couldn't find the number he wanted. Then he remembered she'd given him her business card. He found it in his pocket. A home number had been added in pencil. He stepped outdoors and fired up his mobile . . . The phone was ringing. Saturday night, she was probably . . .

'Hello?'

'Ms Burchill? It's John Rebus here. Sorry to call you on a Saturday night.'

'That's all right. Is something the matter?'

'No, no . . . I just wondered if maybe we could meet. It was all very mysterious, what you said about there being other dolls.'

She laughed. 'You want to meet *now*?'

'Well, I was thinking maybe tomorrow. I know it's the day of rest, but we could maybe mix business with pleasure.' He winced. He hadn't thought through what he was going to say.

'And how could we do that?' she asked, sounding amused.

'Lunch?' he suggested.

'Where?'

Where indeed. He couldn't remember the last time he'd taken someone to lunch. He wanted somewhere impressive, somewhere . . .

'I'm guessing,' she said, 'that you like a fry-up on a Sunday.' It was almost as if she could feel his discomfort and wanted to help.

'Am I so transparent?'

'Quite the opposite. You're a flesh-and-blood Scottish male. I, on the other hand, like something simple, fresh and wholesome.'

Rebus laughed. 'The word "incompatible" springs to mind.'

'Maybe not. Where do you live?'

'Marchmont.'

'Then we'll go to Fenwick's,' she stated. 'It's perfect.'

'Great,' he said. 'Half twelve?'

'I look forward to it. Good night, Inspector.'

'I hope you're not going to call me Inspector all through lunch.'

In the silence that followed, he thought he could hear her smiling.

'See you tomorrow, John.'

He went back inside the pub and made for the bar.

'Same again, Harry,' he said, bouncing on his toes.

'You'll wait your turn like everyone else,' Harry growled at him. It didn't matter to Rebus, didn't bother him at all.

HE WAS TEN MINUTES EARLY. She walked in only five minutes later, so she was early too.

'Nice place,' he told her.

'Isn't it?' She was wearing a black two-piece over a grey silk blouse. A blood-red brooch sparkled just above her left breast.

'Do you live nearby?' he asked.

'Not exactly—Portobello.'

'But that's miles away! You should have said.'

'Why? I like this place. Now, what shall we have?'

He thought about a starter and a main course, but she seemed to know that really he wanted the fry-up, so that was what he ordered. She went for soup and duck. They decided to order coffee and wine at the same time.

'Very brunchy,' she said. 'Very Sunday somehow.'

He couldn't help but agree. They talked about Gill Templer to start with, finding common ground. Jean's questions were canny and probing.

'Gill can be a bit driven, wouldn't you say?'

'She does what she has to.'

'The pair of you had a fling a while back, didn't you?'

His eyes widened. 'She told you that?'

'No.' Jean paused, flattened her napkin against her lap. 'But I guessed it from the way she used to speak about you.'

'Used to?'

She smiled. 'It *was* a long time ago, wasn't it?'

'Prehistoric,' he was forced to agree. 'What about you?'

'I hope I'm not prehistoric.'

He smiled. 'I meant, tell me something about yourself.'

'I was born in Elgin, parents both teachers. Went to Glasgow University. Doctorate from Durham University, then postdoctoral studies in the USA. I got a job as a curator in Vancouver, then came back here when the opportunity arose. The old museum for twelve years, and now the new one.' She shrugged. 'That's about it.'

'You never married?'

She looked down. 'For a while, yes, in Canada. He died young.'

'I'm sorry.'

'You've got a daughter, haven't you?' she said suddenly, keen to change the subject.

'Samantha. She's . . . in her twenties now.'

Jean laughed. 'You don't know how old exactly, though?'

He tried a smile. 'It's not that. I was going to say that she's disabled. Probably not something you want to know.'

'Oh.' She was silent for a moment, then she said, 'But it's important to you, or it wouldn't have been the first thing you thought of.'

'True.' He didn't want to go into the whole story, and it seemed she wasn't going to ask him. 'How's the soup?'

'It's good.'

They sat in silence for a minute or two, then she asked him about police work. Usually Rebus felt awkward talking about the job, afraid his voice would betray his passion for it. He wasn't sure people were really interested in the suicides and autopsies, the petty grudges and black moods that led people to the cells. He might be dubious about methods and eventual outcomes, but he still got a thrill from the work itself. Someone like Jean Burchill, he felt, could peer beneath the surface and would realise that his enjoyment of the job was essentially cowardly. He concentrated on other people's lives and problems to stop him examining his own failings.

'You were going to tell me about other dolls,' he said eventually.

'After we've eaten,' she said firmly.

But after they'd eaten, she asked for the bill. They went halves on it, and found themselves outside, the afternoon sun doing its best to remove the chill from the day.

'Let's walk,' she said, sliding her arm through his.

'Where to?'

'The Meadows?' she suggested. So that was where they went.

The sun had brought people out to the tree-lined playing field. Frisbees were being thrown, while joggers and cyclists sped past.

'So where exactly is it you live?' she asked.

'Arden Street. Just off Warrender Park Road.'

'Not far then.'

He smiled, trying for eye contact. 'Are you angling for an invitation?'

'To be honest, yes.'

'The place is a tip.'

'I'd be disappointed if it were anything else. But my bladder says it'll settle for what's available . . .'

HE WAS DESPERATELY tidying the living room when he heard the toilet flush. He looked around and shook his head. The rewiring had come to a halt, with boards still up and cable straggling everywhere. It was like picking up a duster after a bomb strike—futile. So instead he went back into the kitchen and spooned coffee into two mugs.

She was standing in the doorway, watching him.

'Thank God I have an excuse for all the mess,' he said.

'I had my place rewired a few years back,' she commiserated.

'Sugar?' He handed her the mug.

She studied its milky surface. 'I don't even take milk.'

'Sorry.' He tried taking the mug from her, but she resisted.

'This'll be fine,' she said. Then she laughed. 'Some detective. You just watched me drink two cups of coffee in the restaurant.'

'And never noticed,' Rebus agreed, nodding.

'Is there space to sit down in the living room? Now that we've got to know one another a little, it's time to show you the dolls.'

He cleared an area of the dining table. She placed her shoulder bag on the floor and pulled out a folder.

'Thing is,' she said, 'I know this may sound barmy to some people, so I'm hoping you'll keep an open mind. Maybe that's why I wanted to know you a bit better . . .' She handed over the folder and he pulled out a sheaf of press cuttings. 'I came across the first one when someone wrote a letter to the museum, a couple of years back.' He held up the letter and she nodded. 'A Mrs Anderson in Perth. She'd heard the story of the Arthur's Seat coffins and wanted me to know that something similar had happened near Huntingtower.'

The clipping attached to the letter was from the *Courier*: MYSTERIOUS FIND NEAR LOCAL HOTEL. A coffin-shaped wooden box with a scrap of cloth nearby, found beneath some leaves in a copse when a dog had been out for its daily walk. The owner had taken the box to the hotel, thinking maybe it was some sort of toy. But no explanation had been found. The year was 1995.

'No doll?'

Jean shook her head. 'Could be some animal ran off with it.'

'Could be,' Rebus agreed. He turned to the second cutting. It was dated 1982 and was from a Glasgow evening paper: CHURCH CONDEMNS SICK JOKE FIND.

'It was Mrs Anderson herself told me about this one,' Jean explained. 'A churchyard, next to one of the gravestones. A little wooden coffin, this time with a doll inside.'

Rebus looked at the photo printed in the paper. 'It looks cruder, balsa wood or something.'

She nodded. 'I thought it was quite a coincidence. Ever since, I've been on the lookout for more examples.'

He separated the two final cuttings. 'And finding them, I see.'

'I tour the country, giving talks on behalf of the museum. Each time, I ask if anyone's heard of such a thing. I've struck lucky twice so far: 1977 in Nairn, 1972 in Dunfermline.'

Two more mystery finds. In Nairn, the coffin had been found on the beach; in Dunfermline, in the town's glen. One with a doll in it, one without.

'What do you make of it?' he asked.

'Shouldn't that be *my* question? Could there be a link with what you found in Falls?'

'I don't know.' He looked up at her. 'Why don't we find out?'

SUNDAY TRAFFIC slowed them down, though most of the cars were heading back into the city after a day in the country.

'Do you think there could be more?' he asked.

'It's possible. But the local history groups, they pick up on oddities like that, and people know I'm interested.' She rested her head against the passenger-side window. 'I think I'd have heard.'

In Falls there were cars parked either side of the main road, making for a bottleneck. Rebus didn't think he'd find a space, so turned into the lane and parked there. They walked down to Bev Dodds's cottage. She greeted them at the front door.

While tea was being made, Jean asked if she could see some of the pottery. An extension at the back of the cottage housed both the kitchen and a studio. Jean praised the various bowls and plates, but Rebus could tell she didn't like them.

'Ms Burchill works at the museum,' he said. 'She's a curator.'

'What a wonderful job. Whenever I'm in town, I try to visit.'

'Have you heard of the Arthur's Seat coffins?' Rebus asked.

'Steve told me about them,' Dodds said. Rebus presumed she meant Steve Holly, the reporter.

'Ms Burchill has an interest in them,' Rebus said. 'She'd like to see the doll you found.'

'Of course.' She slid open a drawer and brought out the coffin.

Jean handled it with care. 'It's quite well made,' she said. 'More like the Arthur's Seat coffins than those others.'

'Others?' Bev Dodds asked.

'Is it a copy of one of them?' Rebus asked, ignoring this.

'Not an exact copy, no,' Jean said. 'Different nails, and constructed slightly differently, too.'

'Has anyone shown interest in the museum's coffins recently? Maybe a researcher or someone?' Rebus said.

Jean shook her head. 'There was a doctoral student last year . . . but she went back to Toronto.'

'Is there some connection here?' Bev Dodds asked, wide-eyed. 'Something between the museum and the abduction?'

'We don't know that anyone's been abducted,' Rebus cautioned.

'All the same . . .'

'Ms Dodds . . . Bev . . .' Rebus fixed her with his eyes. 'It's important that this conversation stays confidential.'

When she nodded understanding, Rebus knew that within minutes of them leaving, she'd be on the phone to Steve Holly. He left his tea unfinished. 'We'd better be off.'

Jean took the hint, and placed her own cup on the draining board. 'That was lovely, thanks.'

'You're welcome.'

As they walked back up the lane, two cars passed them. Day-trippers, Rebus guessed, on their way to the waterfall. And afterwards, maybe they'd stop by the pottery, asking to see the famous coffin. They'd probably buy something, too . . .

'What are you thinking?' Jean asked, getting into the car.

'Nothing,' Rebus lied. Much later that night, he found himself thinking about Bev Dodds and the books of Wicca in her living room—only she didn't call it that, called it her 'parlour' instead, and a Stones song popped into his head: 'Spider and the Fly', B-side to 'Satisfaction'. He saw Bev Dodds as a spider, her parlour a web.

ON MONDAY MORNING, Rebus took Jean's press cuttings in to work. Waiting for him on his desk were three messages from Steve Holly and a note in Gill Templer's handwriting, informing him of a doctor's appointment at eleven o'clock and saying she'd be spending the day at Gayfield Square. Rebus reached for his cigarettes and lighter and headed for the car park. He had just got one lit when Siobhan Clarke arrived, carrying the laptop.

'Any luck?' he asked her.

She looked at his cigarette. 'Soon as you finish that foul thing, come upstairs and I'll show you.'

The door swung shut behind her. Rebus took one last puff and flicked the cigarette to the ground.

By the time he got to the CID room, Siobhan had set up the laptop. An officer called over that there was a Steve Holly on the line. Rebus shook his head. He knew damned well what Holly wanted: Bev Dodds had told him about their trip to Falls. He held up a finger, asking Siobhan to wait a second, then got on the phone to the museum. 'Jean Burchill's office, please,' he said. Then he waited.

'Hello?' It was her voice.

'Jean? John Rebus here.'

'John, I was just thinking of calling you.'

'Don't tell me. A reporter called Steve Holly wants to talk to you about the dolls?'

'He's been onto you too, then?'

'Best advice I can give, Jean: don't say anything. Refuse his calls, and if he does get through, tell him you've nothing to say.'

'Understood. Did Bev Dodds blab?'

'My fault, I should've known she would.'

They said their goodbyes and he walked over to Siobhan's desk and read the message on the laptop's screen.

This game is not a game. It's a quest. You'll need strength and endurance, not to mention intelligence. Do you still wish to play?

'I got this last night. I sent back an email saying OK and at midnight this arrived.'

There was another message on the screen. *Seven fins high is king. This queen dines well before the bust.*

'I was up half the night. I don't suppose it means anything to you?'

Rebus shook his head. 'You need someone who likes puzzles. Doesn't young Grant do cryptic crosswords?'

'Does he?' Siobhan looked across to where Grant Hood was making a phone call. When he came off the phone, she walked over and handed him a sheet of paper. 'I hear you like a puzzle.'

He took the sheet, but didn't look at it. 'Was Saturday night OK?' he asked.

She nodded. 'Saturday night was fine.'

And it had been, too: a couple of drinks and then dinner at a decent, small restaurant in the New Town. They'd talked shop mostly, but it was good to have a laugh, relive a few stories. Grant had been quite the gentleman, walking her home afterwards.

Now, Grant nodded back and smiled. 'Fine' was good enough for him. He looked at the sheet. '"Seven fins high is king",' he read aloud. 'What's it mean?'

'I was hoping maybe you'd tell me.'

He studied the message again. 'Could be an anagram. Unlikely though: not enough vowels, it's all i's and e's. Maybe it would help if you told me a bit about it.'

Siobhan nodded. 'Over a coffee, if you like,' she said.

Rebus watched them leave the room, then he picked up the first of the cuttings. His eyes narrowed. There was a sentence he must have missed first time round. It was the 1995 clipping: Huntingtower Hotel near Perth, a dog finding the coffin and scrap of cloth. Three-quarters of the way through the story, an anonymous member of the hotel staff was quoted as saying, 'If we're not careful, Huntingtower's going to get itself a reputation.' Rebus wondered what was meant by that. He picked up the phone, thinking maybe Jean Burchill would know. But he didn't make the call, didn't want her to think he was . . . well, what exactly? He'd enjoyed yesterday, and thought she had too. He'd dropped her at her home in Portobello, but had declined the offer of coffee.

'I've taken up too much of your day as it is,' he had said.

She hadn't denied it. 'Maybe another time,' was all she'd replied.

His hand was still resting on the receiver. He picked it up and got a number for the Huntingtower Hotel, asked to speak to the manager.

'I'm sorry,' the receptionist said. 'He's in a meeting at the moment. Can I take a message?'

Rebus explained who he was. 'I want to speak to someone who was working at the hotel in 1995.'

'Well, I've been here since '93.'

'Then you might remember the little coffin that was found.'

'Vaguely, yes.'

'I've got a cutting from a newspaper at the time. It says that the hotel might have been getting a reputation. Do you know why that might have been?'

'I'm not sure. Maybe it was that American tourist who disappeared.'

REBUS WENT to the National Library annexe on Causewayside. When he'd shown his ID and explained what he needed, he was taken to a desk where a microfilm reader sat. Even though he told the staff that today's was 'a rush job', he sat for the best part of twenty minutes before a librarian arrived with the film boxes.

The *Courier* was Dundee's daily paper. Rebus's own family had taken it. He wound the tape of its archives forward until he was four weeks shy of the date the article appeared. There, on an inside page, was the headline TOURIST'S DISAPPEARANCE A MYSTERY, SAY POLICE. The woman's name was Betty-Anne Jesperson. She was thirty-eight and married. She'd been a member of a tour party from the USA. Her husband, Garry, said she was in the habit of waking early and going for a pre-breakfast walk. No one in the hotel had seen her depart. The countryside was searched, and police went into Perth town centre armed with copies of her passport photograph. But as Rebus wound the film forward a week, the story was cut down to half a dozen paragraphs. A further week along, and there was just a single paragraph. The story was in the process of vanishing as completely as Betty-Anne had.

Rebus copied the details into his notebook, then put in a request for more papers: the *Dunfermline Press*, *Glasgow Herald* and *Inverness Courier*. Only the *Herald* was on microfilm, so he started with that. Nineteen eighty-two, the doll in the churchyard . . .

It had been found in May. He started at the beginning of April. Problem was, Glasgow was a big city, more crime than a place like Perth. He wasn't sure he'd know if and when he found something. And if it was a Missing Person, would it even make the paper? Thousands of people disappeared each year.

By the time he'd searched April, he had no reported MisPers, but six deaths, two of them women. One was a stabbing after a party. A man, it was stated, was helping police with their enquiries. The second death was a drowning. A stretch of river Rebus had never heard of: White Cart Water, the body found by its banks on the southern border of Rosshall Park. The victim was Hazel Gibbs, aged twenty-two. Her husband had walked out, leaving her with two kids. Friends said she'd been depressed. She'd been seen out drinking the previous day, while the kids fended for themselves.

Rebus walked outside and got on his mobile, punching in the number for Bobby Hogan at Leith CID.

'Bobby, it's John. You know a bit about Glasgow, don't you?'

'A bit.'

'Ever heard of White Cart Water?'

'Can't say I have.'

'What about Rosshall Park?'

'It's in Pollok, southwest of the city centre.'

Rebus looked at the cutting in his hand; the one from the *Herald*.

'Thanks, Bobby,' he said, ending the call. He reread the article. CHURCH CONDEMNS SICK JOKE FIND: the coffin found in the churchyard. The church itself located on Potterhill Road. In Pollok.

'I DON'T SUPPOSE you'd care to explain yourself,' Gill Templer said.

Rebus had driven to Gayfield Square and asked her for five minutes. They were back in the same stale office.

'That's just what I want to do,' Rebus told her.

'You were supposed to be attending a doctor's appointment.'

'Something came up. You're not going to believe it.'

She stabbed a finger at the tabloid newspaper open on her desk. 'Any idea how Steve Holly got hold of this?'

Rebus turned the paper so it was facing him. Holly couldn't have had much time, but he'd patched together a story that managed to mention the Arthur's Seat coffins, a 'local expert from the Museum of Scotland', the Falls coffin, and the 'persistent rumour that more coffins exist'.

'What does he mean, "more coffins"?' Gill asked.

'That's what I'm trying to tell you.' So he told her, laid the whole thing out before her. In the musty, leatherbound sets of *Dunfermline Press*es and *Inverness Courier*s he'd found exactly what he'd known and dreaded he would find. In July 1977, a scant week before the Nairn beach coffin had been found, the body of Paula Gearing had been washed ashore four miles further along the coast. Her death could not be explained, and was put down to 'misadventure'.

In October 1972, three weeks before the finding of the coffin in Dunfermline Glen, a teenage girl had been reported missing. Caroline Farmer was a student at Dunfermline High. She'd recently been jilted by a long-term boyfriend, and the best guess was that this had led her to leave home. Her family said they wouldn't rest until they'd heard from her. Rebus doubted they ever had . . .

Gill Templer listened to his story without comment. When he'd finished, she looked up at him. 'It's thin, John.'

Rebus jumped from his seat. 'Gill, it's . . . there's something there.'

'A killer who leaves coffins near the scene?' She shook her head slowly. 'I just can't see it. You've got two bodies, no signs of foul play, and two disappearances. Doesn't exactly make a pattern.'

'Three disappearances including Philippa Balfour.'

'And there's another thing: the Falls coffin turned up less than a week after she went AWOL. No pattern again.'

'Can I at least follow it through? Just one, maybe two more officers. Give us a few days to see if we can convince you.'

'We're stretched as it is.'

'Stretched doing what? We're whistling in the dark till she comes back, phones home or turns up dead. Give me two people.'

She shook her head slowly. 'You can have one. Who do you want?'

'Give me Ellen Wylie,' he answered.

She stared at him. 'Any particular reason why?'

He shrugged. 'She'll never make it as a TV presenter, but she's a good cop.'

'OK,' she said. 'Go ahead.' She tapped the newspaper. 'I'm assuming the "local expert" is Jean?' She waited till he'd nodded, then sighed. 'I should have known better, bringing the two of you together.'

IT TOOK HIM two hours to type up all the dates and page references for the newspaper stories, and arrange with the library for copies. Ellen Wylie hadn't looked thrilled at the prospect of working a two-hander with Rebus, but now she was busy on the phone, begging favours from police stations in Glasgow, Perth, Dunfermline and Nairn. She wanted case notes if any still existed, plus pathologists' names. Whenever she laughed, Rebus knew what had just been said to her: 'You don't ask for bloody much, do you?' Hammering away at his keyboard, he listened to her work. She knew when to be coy, when to get tough, and when to flirt. Her voice never betrayed the set features of her face as repetition made her weary.

'Thank you,' she said for the umpteenth time, dropping the receiver into its cradle. She scribbled a note on her pad, then lifted the handset again and made the next call.

Rebus was intrigued by the long gaps in the chronology: 1972, 1977, 1982, 1995. Five years, five years, thirteen years. And now, just maybe, another five-year gap. The fives made for a nice pattern, but it was broken by that silence between '82 and '95. There were all sorts of explanations: the man, whoever he was, could have been away somewhere, maybe in prison. There was another possibility, of course: that he'd gone on with his spree right here, but somehow hadn't bothered with the coffins, or they hadn't ever been found. A little wooden box . . . a dog would chew it to pulp; a kid might take it home; someone might bin it, the better to be rid of the sick joke. Rebus knew that a public appeal would be one way of finding out, but he couldn't see Templer going for it.

'Nothing?' he asked as Wylie put down the phone.

'No one's answering. Maybe word's gone round about the crazy cop from Edinburgh.'

Rebus crumpled a sheet of paper and tossed it towards the bin. 'I think we're getting a bit stir crazy,' he said. 'Let's take a break.'

Wylie headed off to the baker's for a jam doughnut. Rebus decided to head into the warren of narrow passages between St Leonard's and Nicolson Street. He wondered if maybe his imagination was putting in some overtime today, seeing connections where none existed. He got out his mobile and rang Jean Burchill.

'Jean?' He stopped walking. 'It's John Rebus. We might have struck gold with your little coffins.' He listened for a moment. 'I can't tell you about it right now. I'm on my way to a meeting. Are you busy tonight?' He listened again. 'That's a pity. Would you be up for a nightcap?' He brightened. 'Ten o'clock? Portobello or in town?' Another pause. 'Yes, town makes sense if you've been in a meeting. I'll drive you home after. Ten at the museum then? OK, bye.'

He looked around. He was in Hill Square, at the back of Surgeons' Hall. According to the sign on the railings, the door in front of him was the entrance to the Sir Jules Thorn Exhibition of the History of Surgery. He checked his watch. He had about ten minutes before it closed. What the hell, he thought, pushing the door and going inside.

He found himself in an ordinary tenement stairwell. Climbing one flight brought him to a narrow landing. As he passed the museum threshold an alarm sounded, alerting a member of staff that there was a new visitor, but she left him to it.

The main museum display was well presented. The exhibits were behind glass and well lit. He stood in front of an apothecary's shop, then moved to a full-size dummy of the physician Joseph Lister, examining his list of accomplishments. Beside Lister was a plaster cast of Burke's head—the marks of the hangman's noose still visible—and one of an accomplice, John Brogan, who had helped transport the corpses. Next along was a portrait of the anatomist Knox, recipient of the still-warm cadavers.

'Poor Knox,' a voice behind him said. Rebus looked round. An elderly man, dressed in full evening attire—bow tie, cummerbund and patent shoes. It took Rebus a second to place him: Professor Devlin, Flip's neighbour. Devlin shuffled forward, staring at the exhibits. 'There's been a lot of discussion about how much he knew.'

'You mean, whether he knew Burke and Hare were killers?'

Devlin nodded. 'For myself, I think there's no doubt he knew. Yet it was never proven that he was complicit in the murders. Poor Knox .. . the man was possessed of a kind of genius. But the Church was against him, that was the problem. The human body was a temple, remember. Many of the clergy were against exploration—they saw it as desecration. They raised the rabble against Knox.'

'What happened to him?'

'He died of apoplexy, according to the literature. Hare, who had turned king's evidence, had to flee Scotland and ended his days blind and begging on the streets of London.

'Seventeen murders,' Rebus said, 'in a confined area.'

'We can't imagine it happening these days, can we?'

'But these days we've got forensics, pathology . . .'

'Exactly,' said Devlin. 'And we'd have had no pathological studies at all had it not been for the resurrectionists and the likes of Messrs Burke and Hare.'

'Is that why you're here? Paying homage?'

'Perhaps,' Devlin said. Then he checked his watch. 'There's a dinner upstairs at seven. I thought I'd arrive early and spend some time amongst the exhibits.'

'I'm sorry, Professor Devlin,' the curator called. 'It's time I was locking up.'

'That's OK, Maggie,' Devlin called back. Then, to Rebus: 'Would you like to see the rest of the place?'

Rebus thought of Ellen Wylie, probably back at her desk by now. 'I should really . . .'

'Come on, come on,' Devlin insisted. 'You can't visit Surgeons' Hall and miss out on the Black Museum.'

The curator had to let them through a couple of locked doors, after which they entered the main body of the building. The corridors were hushed and lined with portraits of medical men.

'The dinner guests like a stroll after their meal. Most of them end up here.' He stopped at an imposing set of double doors and tried the handle. The door opened and they entered a large hall.

'The Black Museum,' Devlin said, gesturing with his arms.

'I've heard of it,' Rebus said. 'Never had cause to visit.'

'Off limits to the public,' Devlin explained. 'Not sure why. The college could make itself a bit of money, open it as a tourist attraction.'

It wasn't, to Rebus's eye, as grisly as its nickname suggested. It seemed to consist of old surgical tools, looking more fit for a torture chamber than an operating theatre. There were lots of bones and body parts and things floating in hazy jars. Paintings, too, mostly from the nineteenth century: soldiers with bits blown off them by cannonball or musket.

'This is my favourite,' Devlin said. Surrounded by obscene images, he had found a still point, the portrait of a young man, almost smiling for the artist. Rebus read the inscription.

'"Dr Kennet Lovell, February 1829."'

'Lovell was one of the anatomists charged with the dissection of William Burke. It's even likely that he pronounced Burke dead after the hanging. Less than a month later, he sat for this portrait.'

'He looks pretty happy with his lot,' Rebus commented.

Devlin's eyes sparkled. 'Doesn't he? Kennet was a craftsman too. He worked with wood.'

Rebus studied the portrait. Lovell had deep black eyes, a cleft chin and a profusion of dark locks of hair. He was a handsome man.

'It's interesting about the Balfour girl,' Devlin said.

Startled, Rebus turned to him. 'What is?'

'The caskets found on Arthur's Seat . . . the way the press have brought them up again.' He turned towards Rebus. 'One notion is that they represent Burke and Hare's victims.'

'Yes.'

'And now another casket seems to be some memorial for Philippa.'

Rebus turned back to the portrait. 'Lovell worked with wood?'

'The table in my dining room.' Devlin smiled. 'He made that.'

'Is that why you bought it?'

'A small memento of the early years of pathology. The history of surgery, Inspector, is the history of Edinburgh.' Devlin sniffed and then sighed. 'I miss it all, you know.'

'I don't think I would.'

They walked away from the portrait. 'Working in pathology was a privilege, in its way. Endlessly fascinating, what this animal exterior can contain.' Devlin slapped his chest to make the point.

There was silence for a while, then Rebus had an idea. 'I need a second opinion on some old post-mortem results, Professor. Could I ask a great favour of you?'

'I know I've been retired a good few years, but I don't suppose the theory and practice have changed,' Devlin replied.

'Actually the most recent case is 1982.'

'I was still wielding the scalpel in '82.'

Rebus would have preferred someone with a bit of clout, someone like Gates, but he knew the current Professor of Forensic Medicine was rushed off his feet. Devlin would have to do.

SIOBHAN CLARKE was sitting on the sofa in her living room with her legs tucked under her, staring at a notepad. She'd gone through dozens of sheets of paper, working out possible anagrams and meanings. Seven fins high is king . . . and mentions of 'the queen' and 'the bust': it sounded like something from a card game.

The phone rang. 'Hello?'

'It's Grant.'

'What's up?'

'I think maybe I've cracked it.'

Siobhan swivelled her legs so her feet were on the floor. 'Tell me.'

'I'd rather show you. I'm right outside your flat.'

She walked over to the window and looked out. Sure enough, his Alfa was parked in the street. 'My buzzer's second from the top.'

'Sorry it's so late,' he said a minute later, as he followed her into the living room. 'But I couldn't keep it to myself.'

He sat down next to her on the sofa, reached into his jacket pocket and pulled out a London A–Z.

'I went through all the kings I could think of from history, then anything else to do with the word king.' He held up the book so its back cover was showing. A map of the London Underground.

'King's Cross?' she guessed.

He nodded. 'Take a look.' He slid across the sofa, his finger tracing the light blue line which went through the station. 'Go one stop north of King's Cross.'

'Highbury and Islington?'

'And again.'

'Finsbury Park . . . then Seven Sisters.'

'Now backwards,' he said, practically bouncing on the spot.

'Don't wet yourself,' she said, then looked at the map again. 'Seven Sisters . . . Finsbury Park . . . Highbury and Islington . . . King's

Cross.' And saw it. The same sequence, but abbreviated. 'Seven . . . Fins . . . High Is . . . King.' She looked at Grant. 'Well done you,' she said, meaning it. Grant leaned over and gave her a hug.

She squirmed out of his grip and slid across the sofa a little, making some space between them.

'"This queen dines well before the bust."' She looked at him. 'All these underground stops . . . what do they mean?'

He just shrugged. 'They're all on the Victoria Line.'

They stared at one another.

'Queen Victoria,' they said in unison.

Grant booted up the computer and did a search on the Internet.

'Could be the name of a pub,' he suggested. 'Like in *EastEnders*.'

'Yes,' she said. 'Or the Victoria and Albert Museum.'

'"Bust" could mean a drug bust, could it?'

'More likely it's a statue,' she said. 'Maybe of Queen Victoria, with a restaurant in front of it.'

They worked in silence for a while after that, until Siobhan's eyes started to hurt and she got up to make some coffee.

Bringing the mugs back through from the kitchen, she asked if he'd found anything.

'Tourist sites,' he said, hunched over the computer. He took the mug from her with a nod of thanks. 'You wouldn't believe how many Victoria Roads and Victoria Streets there are in London, and half of them have restaurants.' He leaned back, straightening his spine.

'And that's before we start looking at pubs.' Siobhan ran her fingers through her hair. 'The first bit of the clue was clever. But this . . . this is just looking at lists. Does he expect us to go to London, visit every restaurant and café in the hope of finding Queen Victoria's bust?'

'He can whistle if he does.' Grant's chuckle was empty of humour.

Siobhan looked at the screen. 'Why London?' she asked. 'Why not somewhere closer to home? There's a Victoria Street here. And I think it has a couple of restaurants.'

'Any statues?'

'Not on the outside.'

He checked his watch. 'They won't be open now, will they?'

She shook her head. 'First thing tomorrow. Breakfast's on me.'

REBUS AND JEAN sat in the Palm Court. She was drinking a long vodka, while he nursed a ten-year-old Macallan.

'So they might all have been murdered?' she said, when she'd heard

Rebus's story. The lights in the lounge had been turned low, and a pianist was playing.

'It's possible,' he admitted. 'It needs to be investigated.'

'Where on earth will you start?'

'We're waiting for the original case notes.' He paused. 'What's the matter?'

There were tears in her eyes. 'All this time, I had those cuttings . . . Maybe if I'd given them to the police sooner . . .'

He took her hand. 'All you had were stories about dolls in coffins.'

'I suppose so,' she said.

'Meantime, maybe you can help. I need to know who has shown an interest in the Arthur's Seat exhibits. Going back as far as 1972. Can you do some digging for me?'

'Of course.'

He gave her hand another squeeze. 'Thanks.'

She gave a half-hearted smile and looked around her. 'I was here just last week, to celebrate Gill's promotion. Such a happy occasion . . . It seems a long time ago. Do you think she's coping?'

'Gill's Gill. She'll tough it out.' He paused. 'Speaking of toughing it out, is that reporter still giving you grief?'

She managed a thin smile. 'He's persistent. Wants to know what "others" I was talking about in Bev Dodds's kitchen. That was my fault, sorry.' She seemed to have regained some composure. 'I should be getting back. I can probably find a taxi if . . .'

'I said I'd run you home.' He signalled for their waitress to bring the bill, then they walked back to his car.

 **Chapter Four**

Tuesday at 11.00am, Siobhan Clarke and Grant Hood started working Victoria Street. They found a parking bay in the Grassmarket, and Grant dropped a couple of coins into the machine.

Victoria Street was a steep curve up to George IV Bridge, lined with bars and gift shops. They walked the length of the street, then doubled back. Three restaurants this side, and a cheesemonger. Pierre Victoire was first. Peering through the window, Siobhan could see that it was fairly empty with little in the way of decoration. They went in anyway, but ten seconds later they were back on the pavement.

'One down, two to go,' Grant said. He didn't sound hopeful.

Siobhan repeated the clue. '"This queen dines well before the bust."' She shook her head slowly. 'Maybe we've got it wrong.'

Grant shrugged. 'Next stop, can we at least have a coffee? I skipped breakfast this morning.'

Siobhan tutted. 'What would your mum say?'

'She'd say I slept in. Then I'd tell her it's because I was up half the night trying to solve this bloody puzzle.' He paused. 'And that someone had promised me breakfast would be on them . . .'

Restaurant Bleu was next. It promised 'world cuisine' but had a traditional feel: varnished wood, small windows, cramped interior.

Grant pointed towards a winding staircase. 'There's an upstairs.'

'Can I help?' the assistant said.

'In a minute,' Grant assured her. He followed Siobhan up the stairs. One small room led to another. As Siobhan entered this second chamber, Grant heard her say, 'Bingo,' in the same instant as he saw the bust. It was Queen Victoria, two and a half feet high, in black marble. It sat on a low plinth, pillars either side.

'Bloody hell,' he said, grinning. 'We cracked it!'

Siobhan looked all around, but couldn't see anything.

'I'll tip it,' Grant said, easing Victoria from the plinth.

'Excuse me,' a voice said behind them. 'Is something the matter?'

Siobhan slid her hand under the bust and drew out a folded sheet of paper. She beamed at Grant, who turned towards the waitress. 'Two coffees, please,' he instructed her.

They sat down at the nearest table. Siobhan held the note by one corner. 'Think we'd get any prints?' she asked.

'Worth a try. What does it say?'

'See for yourself,' Siobhan said, using a knife and fork to turn the sheet of paper in his direction.

B4 Scots Law sounds dear.

He reached up to scratch his head. 'Not much to go on, is it?'

He took the cups from the waitress, who had returned. Siobhan watched him stir sugar into his coffee. 'If Quizmaster placed this clue here . . .'

'He knows this restaurant,' Grant said, looking around. 'Not everyone who ventures in would bother coming upstairs.'

'You think he might be a regular?'

Grant shrugged. 'Look at what's nearby, on George IV Bridge. The

Central Library and the National Library. Academics and book-worms are great ones for puzzles.'

'That's a good point. The museum's not far away either.'

'And the law courts . . . and the parliament . . .' He smiled. 'Just for a second there I thought we might be narrowing things down.'

'Maybe we are,' she said, placing the paper in an evidence bag.

Grant was studying the clue again. 'Could be part of an address.'

'Or a coordinate . . .?'

He looked at her. 'From a map? Maybe that's what the rest of the clue tells us. How's your Scots Law?'

'The exams were a while back.'

'Ditto. There's always the library,' he suggested.

REBUS WAS AT HIS DESK, five sheets of paper spread out in front of him. Five lives. Five victims, possibly. Caroline Farmer the youngest. Just sixteen when she'd disappeared. He'd finally got through to her mother this morning. Not an easy call to make.

'Oh my God, don't tell me there's news?' That sudden blooming of hope, wizened by his response. But he'd found out what he had to. Caroline had never come back. There had been unconfirmed sightings in the early days, but nothing since.

'This may seem a strange question, Mrs Farmer, but did Dunfermline Glen have any significance for Caroline?'

'I . . . I'm not sure what you mean.'

'Me neither. It's just that something's come to our attention, and we're wondering if it might tie in with Caroline's disappearance.'

'What is it?'

He didn't suppose she'd take the coffin in the glen well; resorted instead to cliché: 'I'm not at liberty to disclose that at present.'

There was a silence. 'She liked to walk in the glen.' Then her voice caught. 'You've dug her up, haven't you?'

'Not at all.'

'What then?' she shrieked.

'I'm not at lib—'

She'd put the phone down. He sighed and did the same.

A member of the station's civvy staff arrived with a large card-board document-box. Rebus lifted the top off, peered inside and pulled out the topmost folder, labelled *Paula Jennifer Gearing*. The Nairn drowning. He started to read.

About twenty minutes in, Ellen Wylie arrived.

'What have you got?' she asked.

'Our friends in the north came good.'

'Paula Gearing?'

Rebus nodded. 'She was twenty-seven. Married four years to a husband who worked on a North Sea oil platform. No kids. She had a part-time job in a newsagent's . . .'

Wylie came over to his desk. 'Was foul play ruled out?'

Rebus tapped his notes. 'Nobody could ever explain it, according to what I've read so far. She certainly didn't seem suicidal.'

'Pathology report?'

'It's in here. Can you get onto Donald Devlin, see if he can spare us some time?'

'Professor Devlin?'

'I bumped into him yesterday. He's agreed to study the autopsies for us. His number will be on file,' Rebus said. 'He's one of Philippa Balfour's neighbours.'

'I know. Have you seen this morning's paper?'

'No.'

She fetched it from her bag, opened it to one of the inside pages. A Photofit—the man Devlin had seen outside the tenement on the days preceding Philippa's disappearance.

'Could be anybody,' Rebus said.

Wylie nodded. 'We're getting desperate, aren't we?' she said.

It was Rebus's turn to nod. Releasing the Photofit to the media, especially one as generalised as this, was an act of desperation.

She took the newspaper with her, sat at a spare desk and picked up the telephone, preparing to make the first call of another long day.

'THIS IS HOPELESS,' Siobhan Clarke said.

They'd spent the best part of three hours in the Central Library, followed by nearly fifty quid at the bookshop next door, buying maps and touring guides of Scotland. Now they were in the Elephant House coffee shop, and Grant Hood was staring out of the window at the view of Greyfriars Churchyard and the castle.

Siobhan looked at him. 'Have you switched off?'

He kept his eyes on the view. 'Sometimes you have to clear your mind for a while, start again from scratch.'

She glared at him. 'Are you saying we've just wasted half a day?'

He shrugged.

'Well, thanks very much!' She pulled herself out of her chair and stomped off to the toilets. Inside, she stood leaning against the wash-bowl. The sod was, she knew Grant was right. But she'd wanted to play the game, and now it had drawn her in. She wondered if Flip Balfour had become obsessed with the game in the same way. If she'd got stuck, would she have asked for help? Siobhan had yet to ask any of Flip's friends or family about the game. No one had mentioned it in the dozens of interviews, but then why would they?

Gill Templer had offered her the Press Liaison job, but only after engineering the ritual humiliation of Ellen Wylie. It would be nice to feel she'd rejected the offer out of a sense of solidarity with Wylie, because everybody at St Leonard's knew how much she had wanted, and pressed for, that job. But that had had nothing to do with it. Siobhan herself feared that it was more the influence of John Rebus. She'd worked beside him for several years now, coming to understand his strengths as well as his faults. And when it came down to it, she preferred the maverick approach and wished she could be like that. But there was room for only one maverick like Rebus. So she'd follow orders, back her boss up, never take risks. And she would be safe, would continue to rise through the ranks . . . Detective Inspector, then maybe DCI by the time she was forty. She saw now that Gill had invited her to dinner that evening to show her how it was done. You cultivated the right friends, you treated them well. You were patient, and the rewards came. One lesson for Ellen Wylie, and a very different one for her.

Back out in the café, she watched as Grant Hood completed the crossword in his paper and threw the paper back down.

Grant looked up at her approach. He reached out and touched the crossword. 'Know what a homonym is?' he asked as she sat down.

'No, but it sounds rude.'

'It's when a word sounds like another word. There's one in today's crossword, and it got me thinking about our latest clue: "sounds dear". We were thinking of "dear", meaning expensive or cherished. But it could be a homonym, signalled by "sounds", meaning that the word we want isn't d-e-a-r but d-e-e-r.'

She frowned. 'So we end up with "B4 Scots Law deer"? Is it just me, or does that actually make less sense than before?'

'Don't be like that. Now, there's a story about how Holyrood got its name. One of the ancient kings, David the First, was out hunting when a stag pinned him to the ground. He reached for its antlers only to find that it had vanished and in its place was a cross. Holy rood means holy cross. He saw it as a sign and built the abbey of Holyrood right there.'

'So you think it might have something to do with the Palace of Holyrood. Perhaps part of Scots Law relates to Holyrood—it would make another royal connection, like Victoria.'

'All we have to do is find ourselves a friendly lawyer.'

'Would someone from the Procurator Fiscal's office do?' Siobhan asked. 'If so, I might know just the person . . .'

THE SHERIFF COURT was in a new building on Chambers Street, just across from the museum complex. Grant dashed back down to Grassmarket to feed the meter, while Siobhan asked around the court until she'd located Harriet Brough. The lawyer was wearing a tweed two-piece with grey stockings and flat black shoes.

'My dear girl, this is splendid,' she said, taking Siobhan's hand and working her arm as if it were a water pump. 'Are you here for a trial?'

'No, I just had a question and I wondered if you'd help.'

'I'd be delighted to.'

'It's a note I've found. It might relate to a case, but it seems to be in some sort of code.'

The lawyer's eyes widened. 'How very exciting.' Siobhan watched as Brough read the note through its polythene jacket, her brow creasing.

'I'm sorry,' she said at last. 'Maybe the context would help.'

'It's a Missing Person inquiry,' Siobhan explained. 'We think she may have been taking part in a game.'

'And you need to solve this to reach the next stage? How curious.'

'B4 doesn't mean anything in Scots Law?' Siobhan looked towards the lawyer. 'Some paragraph or subsection?'

Brough laughed. 'There could be several hundred examples, though they'd more likely be 4B rather than B4. We use numerals first, as a general rule: paragraph 4 subsection B.'

'The first clue had a royal connection. The answer was Victoria. We wondered if this one might have something to do with Holyrood.'

'Well, you're cleverer than I am,' she conceded. 'Maybe my lawyer's mind is too literal.' She made to hand the note to Siobhan, but then snatched it back again. 'I wonder if the phrase "Scots Law" is there to put you off the scent.'

'How do you mean?' Siobhan asked.

'Something I learned from my hill-walking days,' she said, 'is that "law" is the Scots word for a hill . . .'

Rebus was on the phone to the manager of the Huntingtower Hotel. 'The person who found the coffin says he left it at the hotel and thought no more about it. So might it be in storage?'

'I'm not sure,' the manager said. 'It could have been thrown out during a refit. I won't make any promises . . .'

'Let me know as soon as you find it,' Rebus said, repeating his name and phone number. 'It's a matter of urgency, Mr Ballantine.'

'I'll do what I can,' the manager said with a sigh.

Rebus broke the connection and looked across to the other desk, where Ellen Wylie was with Donald Devlin, trying to track down the autopsy notes from the Glasgow drowning. By the look on Wylie's face they were having little luck.

Rebus got back on the phone. The Glasgow coffin was more awkward. The reporter who'd covered the story had moved on. Nobody at the news desk could remember anything about it. Eventually he was transferred to personnel, where he was given a forwarding address for the journalist, whose name was Jenny Gabriel. It was a London address.

'She went to work for one of the broadsheets,' the personnel manager stated. 'It was what Jenny always wanted.'

So Rebus went out and bought coffee, cakes and four newspapers: *The Times*, *Telegraph*, *Guardian* and *Independent*. He went through each, studying the by-lines, but didn't find Jenny Gabriel's name. Undaunted, he called each paper and asked for her by name. At the third attempt, the switchboard asked him to hold. The sweetest words Rebus had heard all day.

'Jenny Gabriel, news desk,' a voice said.

It was time for the spiel again.

'My God,' the reporter said at last, 'that was twenty years ago!'

'Just about,' Rebus agreed. 'You don't still have the doll, do you?'

'No, I don't.' Rebus felt his heart sink a little. 'When I moved south, I gave it to a friend. He'd always been fascinated by it.'

'Any chance you could put me in touch with him?'

'Hang on, I'll get his number. He's in Edinburgh actually,' Jenny Gabriel said. 'His name is Dominic Mann.'

'Many thanks,' Rebus said when she'd given him a number, and he cut the call.

Dominic Mann wasn't home, but his answering machine gave Rebus a mobile number to try. The call was picked up. 'Hello?'

'Is that Dominic Mann?' And Rebus was off again, this time getting the result he wanted. Mann still owned the coffin and could drop it into St Leonard's later on in the day.

'I'd really appreciate that,' Rebus said. 'Funny thing to hold on to all these years . . .?'

'I had planned to use it in one of my installations.'

'Installations?'

'I'm an artist. Just as well I didn't end up using it. It might have been wrapped in paint and bandages and sold to some collector.'

Rebus thanked the artist and put down the phone. The Nairn coffin was easier: two calls got Rebus the result he wanted. He was told by a reporter that he'd do some digging, and was called back with the number of someone in Nairn, who then did some digging of their own and found the coffin stored in a neighbour's shed.

'You want me to post it to you?'

'Yes, please,' Rebus said. 'Next-day delivery. I'll see you get a refund.'

Rebus put down the phone and looked across to Wylie's desk. 'Anything?' he asked.

'Getting there,' she said, her voice tired and irritated.

Devlin got up and walked over to Rebus's desk. 'I can't tell you how much I'm enjoying this.'

'Glad someone's happy, Professor.'

The pathologist prodded Rebus's jacket lapel with a finger. 'I think *you're* in your element.' He beamed, and shuffled out of the room to find what he called the 'facilities'.

By the time he came back in, Rebus was on the trail of the Dunfermline coffin, but nobody—local press, police—seemed to know what had happened to it. Nearly thirty years had passed; unlikely it would turn up.

At the other desk, Devlin was clapping his hands silently as Wylie finished another call. She looked across to Rebus. 'Post-mortem report on Hazel Gibbs is on its way,' she said.

Rebus smiled. 'Well done.' His phone rang. It was Huntingtower. They'd found the coffin in a cellar used for lost property. They would post it next-day delivery. Rebus hung up and took a gulp of coffee.

The phone went again. This time it was Siobhan. 'I'm going to talk to David Costello,' she said. 'If you're not doing anything . . .'

'I thought you'd paired up with Grant?'

'DCS Templer has snared him for a couple of hours.'

'Has she now? Maybe she's offering him your liaison job.'

'I refuse to let you wind me up. Now, are you coming or not?'

COSTELLO WAS IN HIS FLAT. When he opened the door to them, he looked startled. Siobhan assured him that it wasn't bad news. He didn't seem to believe her.

'Can we come in, David?' Rebus asked. Costello nodded slowly. To Rebus's eyes, he was wearing the same clothes as on his last visit, and the living room didn't seem to have been tidied in the interim.

Siobhan handed him a sheet of paper.

'What's this?' he asked, slumping onto the futon.

'It's a clue from a game. A game we think Flip was playing.'

Costello looked at the message again. 'What sort of game?'

'It's run on the Internet by someone called Quizmaster. Solving each clue takes the player to a new level. Flip was working on a level called Hellbank. Maybe she'd solved it, we don't know. You've never heard of it?'

Costello shook his head.

'Was she interested in games at all?' Siobhan asked.

Costello shrugged. 'Dinner-party stuff. You know: charades and the like. Maybe Trivial Pursuit or Taboo.'

'But not fantasy games? Role-playing?'

He rubbed the bristles on his chin. 'You're *sure* this was Flip?'

'We're pretty sure,' Siobhan stated.

'And you think it has something to do with her disappearance?'

Siobhan glanced in Rebus's direction, wondering if he had anything to add. But Rebus had picked up a poetry book and was busy with his own thoughts. He was remembering what Flip Balfour's mother had said about Costello, about how he'd turned Flip against her family. And when Rebus had asked why, she'd said: *Because of who he is*.

'Interesting poem, this,' he said, waving the book. He recited a couple of lines:

> '*You do not die for being bad, you die*
> *For being available.*'

He closed the book, put it down. 'I'd never thought of it like that before, but it's true.' He paused to light a cigarette. 'Do you remember when we talked, David? I asked you if Flip might have met someone, and you said she'd have told you. You said she couldn't keep things to herself.'

Costello was nodding.

'And yet here's this game she was playing. Not an easy game either, lots of puzzles and word play. She might have needed help.'

'She didn't get it from me. She never mentioned it.'

Siobhan lifted the toy soldier from the shelf. 'This is a gaming piece, isn't it?'

Costello turned to look. 'Is it? I'm not sure where it came from.'

'Been in the wars,' Siobhan said, studying the broken musket.

Rebus looked over to where Costello's own computer—a laptop—sat. 'I take it you're on the Internet yourself, David?' he asked.

'Isn't everybody?'

Siobhan forced a smile, put the toy soldier back. 'DI Rebus here is still wrestling with electric typewriters.'

Rebus saw what she was doing: trying to soften Costello up, using Rebus as the comedy prop.

'To me,' he said, 'the Internet is what the Milan goalie defends.'

This got a smile from Costello.

Because of who he is . . . But who was David Costello really? Rebus was beginning to wonder.

'If Flip kept this from you, David,' Siobhan was saying now, 'might there be other things she kept secret?'

Costello nodded. 'Maybe I didn't know her at all,' he conceded.

'What about her other friends?' Siobhan asked. 'Do any of them like games, puzzles?'

Costello was thoughtful. 'No one I can think of,' he said at last.

Afterwards, Siobhan drove Rebus back to St Leonard's. They were silent for the first few minutes. Traffic was bad. The evening rush hour seemed to start earlier with each passing week.

'What do you think?' she asked.

'A bit of background on Mr Costello might be in order.'

'He seemed genuine enough to me. When he answered the door, he looked terrified that something had happened. Besides, background check's already been done, hasn't it?'

'Doesn't mean we didn't miss anything. If I remember rightly, Hi-Ho Silvers was given the job, and he's so lazy he thinks sloth's an Olympic sport.'

There was the sound of a mobile. 'Mine,' Siobhan said. She pressed a button on the hands-free phone. 'Hello?'

'Is that DC Clarke?'

She recognised the voice. 'Mr Costello? What can I do for you?'

'I was just thinking . . . about games and stuff? Well, I do know someone who's into all that. Rather, Flip knows someone.'

Rebus got his notepad and pen ready.

Costello said the name, but his voice broke up halfway through.

'Sorry,' Siobhan said. 'Could you give me that again?'

This time they both caught the name loud and clear: 'Ranald Marr.' Siobhan frowned, mouthing the name silently. Rebus nodded. He knew exactly who Ranald Marr was: John Balfour's business partner, the man who ran Balfour's Bank in Edinburgh.

THE OFFICE WAS QUIET. Officers had either clocked off or were in meetings at Gayfield Square. Another day without any sighting of Philippa Balfour, and no word from her, no sign that she was still alive. Credit cards and bank balance untouched, friends and family uncontacted. Nothing. Rebus placed a call to the Big House and asked to speak to Claverhouse or Ormiston in Crime Squad, Number 2 Branch. Claverhouse picked up.

'It's Rebus here. I need a favour.'

'And what makes you think I'd be daft enough to oblige?'

'Let's put it this way: sooner you help me, sooner I can hit the pub and drink myself unconscious.'

'Why didn't you say? Fire away.'

Rebus smiled into the receiver. 'I need an in with the *gardai* in Dublin.'

'Whatever for?'

'Philippa Balfour's boyfriend. I want a background check.'

'I put a tenner on him at two-to-one.'

'Best reason I can think of for helping me out.'

Claverhouse was thoughtful. 'I should say the person you want is Declan Macmanus.' He gave Rebus the number in Dublin.

'Thanks for your help, Claverhouse.'

Rebus put the phone down and sat back in his chair. Then he noticed something across the room. It was the Farmer's old chair. Gill must have turfed it out only for someone to claim it. Rebus wheeled it over to the desk, made himself comfortable. He thought about what he'd said to Claverhouse: *sooner I can hit the pub and drink myself unconscious.* It had always been part of the routine; a large chunk of him wanted that hazy oblivion that only drink could provide. His mobile rang. He fished it from his pocket, put it to his ear. 'Hello?'

'John?'

'Hello, Jean. I was meaning to call you.'

'Is this an all right time?'

'Sure. Has the journo been hassling you?'

'Nothing I can't handle,' Jean said. 'I've been doing a bit of digging, as you asked. I'm afraid I haven't found very much.'

'Never mind. I'll have a look tomorrow. Unless you're free tonight?'

'Oh. I promised a friend I'd go see her. She's just had a baby. I'm sorry.'

'Don't be. We'll meet tomorrow. Can you come to the station?'

They agreed a time and Rebus ended the call. He got the feeling she was pleased that he'd asked to meet this evening, that she'd been hoping for some hint that it wasn't just work for him.

Or he could be reading too much into it.

He picked up his phone and dialled the number Claverhouse had given him. His call was answered after half a dozen rings. 'Can I speak to Declan Macmanus, please.'

'Who shall I say is calling?' The woman's voice had that seductive Irish lilt. Rebus imagined raven hair and a full body.

'Detective Inspector John Rebus, Lothian and Borders Police.'

'Hold, please.'

While he held, the full body had become a pint of slow-poured Guinness, the beer seemingly shaped to fit its glass.

'DI Rebus?' The voice was crisp, no-nonsense.

'DI Claverhouse gave me your number.'

'That was generous of him. What can I do for you?'

'I don't know if you've heard about this case we've got, a MisPer called Philippa Balfour.'

'The banker's daughter? It's been all over the papers here.'

'Because of the connection with David Costello?'

'The Costellos are well known in Dublin, Inspector.'

'I want to know a bit more about the family.' Rebus started doodling on a sheet of paper. 'I'm sure they're blemish-free, but it would put my mind at rest if I had some evidence of that.'

'As to "blemish-free", I'm not sure I can give that guarantee. Every family has its dirty laundry, does it not?'

'I suppose so.'

'I could send you the Costellos' laundry list?'

'That would be fine.'

'Do you happen to have a fax number there?'

Rebus recited it.

'And how confidential would this information remain, Inspector?'

'As confidential as I can make it.'

'I suppose I'll have to take your word then. You sound honest, and that's a start. Goodbye, Inspector.'

Rebus put the phone down. When he looked at the sheet of paper in front of him, he found he'd drawn half a dozen coffins. He waited twenty minutes for Macmanus to get back to him, but the fax machine was playing dead.

HE HIT THE MALTINGS first, and followed it up with the Royal Oak, before making for Swany's. Just the one drink in each pub, starting with a pint of Guinness, good but filling. He knew he couldn't do too many, so switched to IPA and finally a Laphroaig, then it was a taxi to the Oxford Bar, where he demolished the last corned beef and beetroot roll on the shelf. He was back on the IPA, needed something to wash down the food.

Rebus had come here in a vain attempt to flush all those little coffins out of his mind. Arthur's Seat and Falls and Jean's four. He kept seeing them as the work of one killer . . . and wondering if there were any more of them, rotting on barren hillsides perhaps, or turned into macabre ornaments.

When the door opened, everyone turned to examine the new arrival. Rebus tried not to show surprise. It was Gill Templer. She saw him immediately and smiled, unbuttoning her coat and taking off her scarf. 'Thought I might find you here,' she said.

'What can I get you?'

'Gin and tonic.'

Harry had heard the order and was already reaching for a glass.

Rebus noticed that the other drinkers had shifted a little, giving Rebus and Gill as much privacy as the cramped front bar would allow. He paid for the drink and watched Gill gulp at it.

'I needed that,' she said.

'Rough day?'

'I've had better.'

'So what brings you here?'

'A couple of things. As usual, you haven't been bothering to keep me up to date with any progress.'

'There's not much to report.'

'Then there's the small matter of your doctor's appointment.'

'Yes, I know. I'll get round to it, promise.' He nodded towards the pint. 'This is my first tonight, by the way.'

'Aye, that'll be right,' Harry muttered, busy drying glasses.

Gill smiled, but her eyes were on Rebus. 'How's it working out with Wylie?'

'I've no complaints.' Rebus felt awkward. He didn't like Gill being here like this, dropping in and catching him off-guard. He didn't like that the regulars were listening to every word.

Gill seemed to sense his discomfort. 'I should be going. This was just a quick one before home.'

'Same here.' Rebus made a show of checking his watch.

'I've got the car outside . . .?'

Rebus shook his head. 'I like to walk, keeps me fit.'

Behind the bar, Harry snorted.

Gill wrapped the scarf back round her neck. 'See you tomorrow then.' She gave a little wave which seemed to take in the whole bar, and was gone.

SIOBHAN SAT in her living room, staring at the message on the laptop.

I forgot to tell you, from now on you're against the clock. In twenty-four hours' time, the next clue becomes void.

Siobhan got to work on the keyboard: *I think we should meet. I have some questions.* She hit SEND, then waited.

Quizmaster's reply was prompt. *The game will answer your questions.*

She hit more keys: *Did Flip have anyone helping her? Is anyone else playing the game?*

She waited for several minutes. Nothing.

She was in the kitchen, pouring a glass of Chilean red, when she heard the laptop announcing a message. She dashed back through.

Hello, Siobhan.

She stared at the screen. The sender's address was a series of numbers. Before she could reply, the computer told her she had another message.

Are you there? Your light's on.

She froze. He was here! Right outside! She walked quickly to the window. Down below, a car was parked, headlights still on.

Grant Hood's Alfa.

He waved up at her. Cursing, she ran to the front door, down the stairs and out of the tenement. 'Is that your idea of a joke?' she hissed.

Hood, easing himself from the driver's seat, seemed stunned by her reaction.

'I just had Quizmaster online,' she explained. 'I thought you were him.' She paused, narrowed her eyes. 'Just how did you do that?'

Hood held up his mobile phone. 'It's a WAP,' he explained sheepishly. 'Wireless Application Protocol. Just got it today. Sends emails, the lot. I'm sorry. I just wanted to . . .'

'What are you doing here anyway?' she asked.

'I think I've cracked it.'

She stared at him. 'Again? How come you always wait till late at night?'

'That's when I do my best thinking. Are you going to invite me in?'

'Come on then,' she said.

Upstairs, the first thing she did was check the laptop, but Quizmaster hadn't replied.

'I think you scared him off,' Hood said, reading the on-screen dialogue.

She fell onto the sofa. 'So, what have you got for us tonight, Einstein?'

Hood reached into the bag he'd brought with him and started pulling out maps and guidebooks. 'I got thinking about what that lawyer friend of yours said.'

Siobhan frowned. 'She said hills are sometimes called laws.'

'"Scots Law",' he recited. 'Meaning maybe we're looking for a word that means the same thing law does in Scots.'

'Which would be . . .?'

Hood unfolded a sheet of paper and started to read aloud. 'Hill, bank, brae, ben, fell, tor . . . The thesaurus is full of them.'

She took the paper from him and started reading the list for herself. 'We went through all the maps,' she complained.

'But we didn't know what we were looking for. Some of the guides have hills and mountains indexed at the back. For the rest, we check grid reference B4 on each page.'

'Looking for what exactly?'

'Deer Hill, Stag's Brae, Doe Bank . . .'

Siobhan nodded. 'You're assuming "sounds dear" means d-e-e-r?'

'I'm assuming a lot. But it's better than nothing.'

'But couldn't it wait till morning?'

'Not when Quizmaster suddenly decides we're against the clock.' Hood picked up the first map book and flicked to the index.

After half an hour, she asked Hood if he wanted coffee. He was sitting on the floor, back against the sofa, with an Ordnance Survey map across his thighs. He looked up at her and blinked, as though the lighting in the room was new to him. 'Cheers,' he said.

When she came back with the mugs, she told him about Ranald Marr. The look on his face changed to a scowl. 'Keeping it a secret, were you?'

'I thought it could wait till morning.' Her answer didn't seem to satisfy him, and he took his coffee from her with only a grunt of thanks. Siobhan could feel her anger rising again. This was *her* place, *her* home. What was he doing here anyway?

She picked up another of the map books, *Handy Road Atlas Scotland*. The first page, square B4 was the Isle of Man. The next page B4 was the Mull of Kintyre, and the page after that, when she studied the B4 square closely, her eyes fixed on a small triangle, indicating a peak. Hart Fell. It was 2,651 feet high. She looked at Hood. 'A hart's a kind of deer, isn't it?'

He got up off the floor, came and sat next to her. 'Harts and hinds. The hart is the male,' he said, studying the map. 'It's the middle of nowhere.'

'Maybe it's coincidence,' she suggested.

He nodded, but she could see he was convinced. 'A fell is another name for a law. A hart is a kind of deer . . .' He looked at her. 'No coincidence.'

REBUS AND JEAN BURCHILL were walking on Arthur's Seat. It was a bright morning, but there was a cold breeze blowing.

'Do we know where the coffins were found?' Rebus asked.

'The records from the time are vague. "The northeast range of Arthur's Seat" is how the *Scotsman* put it. A small opening in a secluded outcrop.' She shrugged. 'I've wandered all over and never found the spot.'

She held her jacket round her; Rebus got the feeling it wasn't just the wind making her shiver.

'I'm afraid history's about all I have to offer,' she said suddenly. 'I've asked around but no one seems to remember anyone showing particular interest in the coffins, except for the occasional student or tourist.' She sighed. 'I've not been very helpful, have I?'

'A case like this, Jean, everything's useful. If it doesn't rule something in, it can help rule other things out.'

'I get the feeling you've made that speech before.'

It was his turn to smile. 'Maybe I have; doesn't mean I don't mean it.' He paused, looked out over Edinburgh. 'It's a beautiful city, isn't it?'

They were on the hill's west face. Spread below them were the spires and chimney pots, crowfoot gables, with the Pentland Hills to the south and the Firth of Forth to the north, the Fife coastline visible beyond.

Smiling, she leaned forward, going up on her toes so she could peck his cheek. 'Best just to get that out of the way,' she said quietly. Rebus nodded, couldn't think of anything to say, until she shivered again and said she was getting cold.

'There's a café behind St Leonard's,' Rebus told her. 'I'm buying.'

SIOBHAN WAS WEARING a vest, polo neck and pure wool V-neck jumper. She had an old pair of thick cords on, tucked at the ankles into two pairs of socks. She hadn't worn the Barbour in years, but couldn't think of a better chance to use it, or her hiking boots. Additionally, she was wearing a bobble-hat and carrying a pack containing her mobile, a bottle of water and a flask of sweetened tea.

'Sure you've got enough gear?' Hood laughed. He was wearing jeans, trainers and a yellow cagoule. 'What do you reckon? An hour to the top?'

Siobhan slipped the backpack over her shoulders. 'With luck.'

As they climbed the first fence, Hood gave Siobhan a foot up, then leapt over, his hand on the fence-post for purchase.

'Not a bad day for it,' he said, as they started to climb the steep gradient. 'Reckon Flip would have done this on her own?'

'I don't know,' Siobhan conceded.

'I wouldn't have said she was the type. She'd have taken one look at this climb and got back into her Golf GTi.'

'Except she didn't have a car.'

'Good point. So how would she have got here in the first place?'

Which was another good point. They were in the middle of nowhere, only forty miles from Edinburgh, but the city seemed a distant memory. If Flip had come here, she'd have needed help. 'Maybe a taxi,' she said.

'Not the sort of fare you'd forget.'

Despite a public appeal and plenty of photos of Flip in the papers, no taxi driver had come forward. 'Maybe a friend then. Someone we haven't traced yet.'

'Could be.' But Hood sounded sceptical. She noticed that he was breathing hard. A couple of minutes later, he'd shed the cagoule and tucked it beneath his arm.

'Don't know how you can wear that lot,' he complained.

She pulled the bobble-hat from her head and unzipped the Barbour. 'Is that better?'

He just shrugged.

Eventually, they were reduced to scrabbling with their hands while their feet sought purchase, the stony soil crumbling and sliding away beneath them. Siobhan stopped to rest.

Hood was ten or so feet above her. She offered him a swig of water, but he shook his head and started climbing again. She could see sweat shining in his hair.

'It's not a race, Grant,' she called out. He didn't reply. After another half-minute, she followed him. He was moving away from her. So much for teamwork, she thought.

The climb was levelling off a little. Hood stood up, hands on his hips, admiring the view as he rested. Catching up with him, she handed him the bottle. 'Here,' she said. He took a mouthful. 'It's clouding over.' Siobhan was interested in the sky rather than the view. The clouds were thick and blackening. She guessed they had another fifteen or twenty minutes to go. Hood expelled breath noisily.

'You OK?' she asked.

'Good exercise,' he said hoarsely. Then he began climbing again. There were damp patches on the back of his dark blue sweatshirt. Any minute now he'd probably take it off and be clad only in a T-shirt as the weather turned. Sure enough, he paused to pull the sweatshirt over his head.

'It's getting cold,' she warned him. The temperature must have dropped three or four degrees, perhaps more.

'But I'm not.' He tied the arms of the sweatshirt round his waist.

'At least put your cagoule back on.'

He seemed ready to argue, then changed his mind. Siobhan had already zipped up her Barbour again.

The rain began, just a smattering of big drops at first. Siobhan put her hat back on and watched Grant pull his hood up. It was getting windy too, gusts cutting across them.

'Do you want to wait?' she asked, knowing what his answer would be: silence. Grant had switched to autopilot, his eyes staring, nothing on his mind except reaching the summit, whatever it took.

As they clambered up the last steep incline, the land levelled off. They'd reached the summit. Already the rain was easing. Twenty feet away stood a cairn. Siobhan knew that sometimes hill-walkers added a rock or stone each time they ended a climb.

'What, no restaurant?' Grant said, crouching down to get his breath back. The rain had stopped, a shaft of sunshine splitting the clouds and bathing the hills around in an eerie yellow glow.

'Hot tea, if you want it,' Siobhan said. He nodded and she poured him a cup.

He sipped at it, studying the cairn. 'Are we scared what we'll find?'

'Maybe we won't find anything.'

He conceded as much with a nod. 'Go look,' he told her. So she screwed the top back on the flask and approached the cairn, walked round it. Just a pile of stones and pebbles. 'There's nothing here,' she said. She got down on her haunches to take a closer look.

'There must be.' Grant rose to his feet, walked towards her. He touched a foot to the cairn, then gave a push, toppling it. Dropped to his knees, running his hands through the debris. Soon the pile of stones was completely flattened.

'Useless piece of shit!' he cried out. She couldn't be sure who or what his words were aimed at.

'Grant,' she said. 'Weather's closing in again. Let's head back.'

'We got it wrong,' he said, almost in tears.

Siobhan knew she was going to have to coax him back down the hill. He was wet and cold and losing it. She crouched in front of him. 'I need you to be strong, Grant. You go to pieces on me, and that's it finished. We're a team, remember?'

'That's all?' he asked hollowly.

'That's it.' He was staring at her hands. He reached out with his own, wrapping them round hers. She started to rise, pulling him with her. 'Come on, Grant.'

They were both up on their feet now, and his eyes weren't moving from her. Slowly he released her hands. Siobhan turned to move away, start the descent. She hadn't gone five paces when Grant flew past her, bounding down the slope like a man possessed. He lost his footing once or twice but bounced straight back up again.

'Tell me those aren't hailstones!' he called out at one point. But they were: stinging Siobhan's face as she tried to catch up.

When they got into the car they just sat there for a full minute, getting their breath back.

'Bloody Scottish weather,' Grant spat. 'Is it any wonder we've a chip on our shoulder?'

'Have we? I hadn't noticed.'

He snorted, but smiled too. Siobhan looked at him, hoping it was going to be all right between them. He was acting as if nothing had happened up on the summit. She took off her Barbour and tossed it into the back. Grant slipped the cagoule over his head. Steam rose from his T-shirt. From beneath the seat, Siobhan retrieved the laptop and plugged her mobile into it, booting the machine up. When she started typing a message, Grant leaned over to watch.

Just been up Hart Fell. No sign of next clue. Did I get it wrong?

She pressed SEND and waited, pouring herself a cup of tea. Grant was trying to prise his denims away from his skin. 'What time's the meeting with Ranald Marr?'

She checked her watch. 'We've a couple of hours. Time enough to go home and get changed.'

Grant looked at the screen. 'He's not there, is he?'

Siobhan shrugged, and Grant turned the Alfa's ignition. They drove in silence, the weather clearing ahead of them. They had reached the outskirts of Edinburgh before a message was announced.

Grant pulled onto the verge and stopped the car. 'What's he saying?'

Hart Fell is all I needed. You didn't need to climb it, she read.

'Bastard,' Grant hissed.

You're two moves away from Hellbank. Clue follows in approximately ten minutes. You have twenty-four hours to solve it. Do you wish to continue the game?

Siobhan looked at Grant. 'Tell him yes,' he said.

But she was already typing: *Continue to next level, but please, just tell me if Flip had anyone helping her.*

Grant sucked in his breath. 'You like to gamble, don't you? We don't want to lose him.'

'What's life without a bit of risk?'

A few minutes later the laptop told them there was a message. Grant leaned over again to read it.

A corny beginning where the mason's dream ended.

While they were still taking it in, another message arrived: *I don't think Flipside had any help. Is anyone helping you, Siobhan?*

She typed 'No' and pressed SEND.

'Why don't you want him to know?' Grant asked.

'Because he might change the rules, or even take the huff. He says Flip was on her own. I want him to think the same about me.' She glanced at him. 'Is that a problem?'

Grant thought for a moment, then shook his head. 'So what does the latest clue mean?'

'I haven't the faintest. I don't suppose you're a Mason?'

He shook his head again. 'No. Any idea where we might find one?'

Siobhan smiled. 'In the Lothian and Borders Police? I don't think we'll have too much trouble . . .'

THE COFFINS HAD TURNED UP at St Leonard's, as had the autopsy notes. There was just one small problem: the Falls coffin was now in the possession of Steve Holly. Bev Dodds had given it to him so it could be photographed. Rebus decided he'd have to visit Holly's office. He grabbed his jacket and walked across to the desk opposite, where Ellen Wylie was looking bored as Donald Devlin pored over the contents of a slim manila file.

'I have to go out,' he explained.

Devlin looked up. 'And where are your peregrinations taking you?'

'There's a reporter I need to talk to.'

'Ah, our much-derided fourth estate.'

The way Devlin talked, it was getting on Rebus's nerves. And he wasn't alone, if Wylie's look was anything to go by.

'I'll be as quick as I can,' he reassured her.

REBUS CHANCED HIS LUCK, parked on a single yellow line outside the offices of the Glasgow tabloid and climbed the three flights to a cramped reception area. A woman was working a switchboard.

'I'm here to see Steve Holly,' he said. 'Is he in?'

'He's out for the day, I'm afraid.'

'Well, I'm here to pick up the doll, if he's finished with it.'

'Ooh, that thing.' She made a show of shivering. 'He left it on my chair this morning. Steve's idea of a laugh.'

'The hours must fly.'

She smiled, enjoying this little conspiracy against her colleague. 'I think it's in his cubicle.'

'Photos all done?'

'Oh, yes.'

'Then maybe I could . . .?' He pointed a thumb towards where he guessed Holly's cubicle might be.

'Don't see why not.'

It was easy enough. There were only four 'cubicles': desks separated by freestanding partition walls. No one was working in any of them. The small coffin was sitting next to Holly's keyboard, a couple of Polaroids lying on top. Rebus congratulated himself: if Holly had been here, there'd have been questions to parry, maybe a bit of grief.

Back at the office, he arranged the coffins neatly on his desk. Wylie and Devlin looked curious as he peered closely at the nails, the undersides, comparing them. 'Whoever made these coffins measured up, marked his outline with a pencil, then cut with a saw.'

Wylie looked puzzled. 'Are you saying it's the same person?'

Rebus didn't reply, simply picked up another coffin. The one from Falls. 'Now this one, the proportions are different. Joints aren't so tidy. Either a rushed job, or my guess would be it's by someone else.'

'A copycat?' Wylie guessed.

'I wouldn't know,' Rebus admitted. 'Which brings us to . . .' He dipped a hand inside a drawer and brought out, wrapped in tissue, one of the Arthur's Seat coffins. Jean had lent it to him. She was putting her job on the line. If it was discovered that she'd sneaked an artefact out of the museum, she'd be dismissed on the spot.

Devlin had risen to his feet and Wylie wanted a better look also.

'My goodness,' Devlin gasped. 'Is that what I think it is? I've never seen one outside the museum. You know, I have a theory as to who made them.'

Rebus raised an eyebrow. 'Who?'

'You remember that portrait I showed you? Dr Kennet Lovell?' When Rebus nodded, Devlin went on. 'He was the anatomist who carried out Burke's autopsy. Afterwards, I think he carried a weight of guilt over the whole affair. He probably bought his share of bodies without asking too many questions. The thing is'—Devlin licked his lips—'our Dr Lovell was also interested in carpentry.'

'Professor Devlin,' Rebus told Wylie, 'owns a table he made.'

'Lovell was a good man,' Devlin was saying, 'and a good Christian.'

'He left the coffins to commemorate the dead?' Wylie asked.

Devlin shrugged. 'I've no evidence . . .' His voice tailed off.

'It's an interesting theory,' Wylie conceded. 'But to get back to the modern coffins. If there's no connection between the four found between 1972 and 1995 and the Falls one, we're chasing a wild goose.'

'You're saying we should ditch the previous cases?' Rebus asked.

'I'm saying their only relevance here is if they connect to the Falls coffin, always supposing *it* has anything to do with the Balfour disappearance. And we can't even be sure of *that*.'

Rebus turned to Devlin. 'What do you think, Professor?'

'I'm forced to agree, reluctant though I am to be cast back into the darkness of an old man's retirement.'

'There's been nothing in the autopsy notes?'

'Nothing as yet. It looks very much as if both women were alive when they went into the water. Both bodies sustained some injuries, but that's not so unusual. The river would have rocks in it, so the victim may have hit her head when falling. As to the victim in Nairn, the tides and sea life can do terrible things to a body. I'm sorry I can't be more helpful.'

Rebus nodded. Perhaps Wylie was right. Four coffins left by the same person, one by someone completely different, no connection between them. The problem was, he felt there *was* a connection. There were times when instinct had to take over.

'Maybe if you could give the notes a final look,' he asked Devlin.

'Gladly,' the old man said, bowing his head.

Rebus turned his attention to Ellen Wylie. 'Maybe you should make your report to DCS Templer. Tell her what we've done. I'm sure there's work for you on the main investigation.'

She straightened her back. 'Meaning you're not giving up?'

Rebus gave a tired smile. 'Just a couple more days. To convince myself it's a dead end.'

DAYTIME DRINKING was special. In a bar, time ceased to exist, and with it the outside world. And when you stumbled back out from twilight into raging daylight, people all around you going about their afternoon's business, the world had a new shine to it.

Vodka and orange: not his first choice, but it didn't leave a smell. He could walk back into St Leonard's and no one would know. When his mobile sounded, he thought of ignoring it, but its trilling was disturbing other drinkers, so he pushed the button. 'Hello?'

'That was a bit naughty.'

'Who's this?'

'Steve Holly. We met at Bev's house. And I'm glad we did meet that day, or I might not have been able to place you from Margot's description.' Margot: the receptionist. Not enough of a conspirator to resist grassing Rebus up . . .

'What do you mean?'

'Come on, Rebus. The coffin.'

'I heard you'd finished with it. I was going to return it to Ms Dodds.'

'I'll bet. Something's going on here.'

'Bright boy. That "something" is a police investigation. In fact, I'm up to my eyes in it right now, so if you wouldn't mind—'

'Bev Dodds said something about other coffins . . .'

'Did she? Maybe she misheard.'

'I don't think so.' Holly waited, but Rebus wasn't saying anything. 'Fine,' the journalist said into the silence. 'We'll talk later.'

BALFOUR'S BANK wasn't much like a bank at all. For a start, it was sited on Charlotte Square, one of the most elegant parts of the New Town, and inside there were thick carpets, an imposing staircase, and a huge chandelier. Transactions were dealt with by three members of staff seated at desks so far apart that discretion was assured.

'Reckon anyone here has an overdraft?' Grant asked.

'The staff might. Not so sure about their clients.'

A middle-aged woman walked towards them. 'Mr Marr will see you now,' she said.

The woman led them up the staircase and at the end of the first-floor hall she knocked on a double set of doors and waited.

'Enter!' At which command she pushed open both the doors, gesturing for the two detectives to walk past her and into the room.

It was huge, with three floor-to-ceiling windows covered by pale linen roller-blinds. Ranald Marr was standing behind his large, antique walnut desk, his tan looking as though it had its roots in the Caribbean rather than a sunbed. He deigned to come forward to greet them.

'Ranald Marr,' he said. Then, to the woman: 'Thank you, Camille.'

She closed the doors after her, and Marr gestured towards a sofa. The two detectives made themselves comfortable while Marr settled into a matching leather chair.

'The reason we're here, Mr Marr,' Siobhan began, 'is because it looks like Philippa was involved in some sort of role-playing game.'

'Really?' Marr looked puzzled. 'What's that got to do with me?'

'Well, sir,' Grant said, 'it's just that we've heard you like to play those sorts of games, too.'

'"Those sorts of . . ."?' Marr frowned. 'Oh, you mean my soldiers. But Flip never showed any interest . . .'

'This is a game where clues are given and the player has to solve each one to reach a different level.'

'Not the same at all. What I do is called war-gaming. I re-enact battles with model soldiers on a board,' Marr explained. 'You figure out where the defeated side went wrong, and you try to alter history.'

'Do you play against other people?' Hood asked.

'Sometimes. I find that it relaxes me, helps me think.' He broke off. 'You think it a childish hobby?'

'Not at all,' Siobhan said, only half truthfully. 'Ever play any other way?' she asked casually. 'I've heard of chess players sending their moves by post. Or how about the Internet?'

He shook his head. 'I'm not the most technically gifted of people.'

Siobhan turned her attention to a bookcase stacked with books. 'Ever heard of a character called Gandalf?'

'Which one? I know at least two. The wizard in *Lord of the Rings*, and the rather odd chap who runs the games shop on Leith Walk.'

She looked at him. 'You've been to his shop then?'

'I've bought a few pieces from him down the years. But I mostly buy mail order.'

'And over the Internet?'

Marr nodded. 'Once or twice, yes. Look, who was it exactly who told you about my liking to play games?'

'I'm afraid we're not at liberty to say,' she said.

Marr didn't like that, but refrained from making a comment.

'Everything all right, sir?' Grant asked.

'Everything's fine, but it's proving a terrible strain on all of us.'

'I'm sure that's true,' Siobhan said. 'Well, we'd better let you get back to work now, sir . . .'

As they left the building, she said, 'He knows about the Internet, Grant. And playing those war games, he's probably got an analytical mind.'

'Quizmaster?'

She wrinkled her nose. 'I'm not sure. I mean, what's in it for him?'

Grant shrugged. 'Control of Balfour's Bank.'

'Yes, there's always that,' Siobhan said. She was thinking about the broken playing piece in David Costello's flat. Costello had said he'd no idea where it had come from, but then he'd called her and told her about Marr's little hobby . . . She was having trouble focusing on what was important. She kept trying to put herself in Flip Balfour's shoes, to think along the same lines. It was important, she knew, to do the job well, not to piss off Gill Templer. She wondered about the liaison job and whether she'd burned her bridges there . . .

'Meantime,' Grant was saying, 'we're no closer to solving the clue.'

He broke her train of thought. She turned towards him. 'Just promise me one thing, Grant.'

'What's that?'

'Promise you're not going to turn up outside my flat at midnight.'

'OK,' he said. 'I promise.'

Then he turned and gave her a wink.

BACK AT ST LEONARD'S, Siobhan got on the phone to the Farmer.

'I'm after a favour, sir. Sorry to disturb your peace and quiet.'

'There's such a thing as too much peace and quiet, you know.' The Farmer laughed, but she detected something behind his words.

'About this favour . . .?' she began. 'It's sort of a clue to a puzzle that Philippa Balfour was trying to solve.'

'And how can I help?' He sounded interested.

'Well, the clue goes: "a corny beginning where the mason's dream ended". We wondered if it might be "mason" as in "Masonic Lodge".'

'And someone told you I'm a Mason?'

'Yes.' It had been Rebus's suggestion.

The Farmer was quiet for a moment. 'Let me get a pen,' he said at last. Then he had her repeat the clue while he wrote it down. 'I'll need to think about it. Can I ring you back?'

'Of course, sir.'

'Are you any nearer to finding out what happened to her?'

'We're all working flat out, sir.'

'I'm sure you are. I'll speak to you later. Bye, Siobhan.'

She put the phone down. 'He's going to mull it over,' she told Grant, who was sitting on the other side of her desk.

'Great, and meantime the clock's ticking.'

She sighed. 'Are they getting harder?' she asked. 'Or is it that my brain's packing in?'

'Maybe we should call it a day.'

Siobhan glanced up at the clock. It was true: they'd put in about ten hours already. The whole morning had been spent on a wasted trip. She could feel her limbs aching from the climb. The trip to Balfour's Bank . . . she wondered if that had been a waste of time too. Ranald Marr and his war games, the tip-off from David Costello . . . Skulking at the back of her mind was the possibility that this whole exercise was a waste of time, that Quizmaster really was playing with them, that the game had nothing to do with Flip's disappearance . . . When her phone went, she snatched at it.

'DC Clarke, CID,' she recited into the mouthpiece.

'DC Clarke, it's the front desk. Got a Mr Gandalf down here wanting a word.' The speaker's voice dropped. 'Weird-looking bugger.'

Siobhan went downstairs. Gandalf was holding a dark brown fedora. He wore a brown leather waistcoat over the same Grateful Dead T-shirt he'd worn in his shop.

'Hi there,' Siobhan said.

His eyes widened as though he didn't quite recognise her.

'It's Siobhan Clarke,' she said, holding out her hand. 'We met at your shop.'

'Yes, yes,' he mumbled. He stared at her hand but didn't seem inclined to shake it, so Siobhan lowered her arm.

'What brings you here, Gandalf?'

'I said I'd see what I could find about Quizmaster.'

'Have you come up with anything?'

'Not a great deal, except that he may have other names.'

'Such as?'

'Questor, Quizling, Spellbinder, OmniSent . . . How many do you want? We're talking about the virtual world. Quizmaster could have *virtually* any number of names at his disposal.'

'And no way of tracing him?'

Gandalf shrugged. 'Maybe if you asked the CIA or the FBI . . .'

'I'll bear that in mind.'

He shifted slightly, almost a squirm. 'I did learn one other thing.' He took a sheet of paper from the back pocket of his cords, handed it to Siobhan, who unfolded it. A news cutting from three years before—a student who had disappeared from his home in Germany. A body had been found on a remote hillside in the north of Scotland. Identification had proven difficult because the corpse had been lying there many weeks, but the parents became convinced it was that of their son, Jürgen. A revolver had been found twenty feet away. A single bullet had pierced the young man's skull. The police had it down as suicide, explained away the location of the firearm by saying some animal could have moved it. Plausible, Siobhan had to concede. But the parents weren't convinced. The gun wasn't his, and couldn't be traced. The bigger question was: how had he ended up in the Scottish Highlands? No one seemed to know. Then Siobhan frowned, read the story's final paragraph again:

> Jürgen was keen on role-playing games, and spent many hours surfing the Internet. His parents think it possible that their student son became involved in some game that had tragic consequences.

Siobhan held up the clipping. 'Where did you get this?'

'From someone I know. He's writing a book about the perils of the e-universe.'

Siobhan folded the clipping. 'Thanks, Gandalf. Your friend can have this back when I'm finished with it.'

When Siobhan went back upstairs she found Grant Hood scrunching a sheet of paper into a ball and failing to hit the waste-paper bin with it.

'What's up?' she asked.

'I got wondering about anagrams.'

She looked over his shoulder at the remaining sheet of paper and saw that he was working on anagrams for 'mason's dream'.

'Call it a day?' he suggested.

'Maybe.'

He caught her tone of voice. 'You've got something?'

'Gandalf,' she said, handing over the news story. She watched him read, noticing that his lips moved slightly.

'Interesting,' he said at last. 'We'll have to hand it over to the inquiry. We've got our work cut out with this bloody clue.'

'Hand it over . . .?' She was aghast. 'This is *ours*, Grant.'

'Christ, Siobhan. It's an *inquiry*, lots of people all chipping in. It doesn't belong to us. You can't be selfish with something like this.'

'I just don't want someone else stealing our thunder.'

'Even if it means finding Flip Balfour alive?' He stood up to face her. 'This all comes from John Rebus, doesn't it, wanting to keep the whole investigation to yourself, like it's down to you alone.'

Colour rose to her cheeks. 'Look, all I was trying to say . . .'

' . . . was that you don't want to share, and if that doesn't sound like Rebus, I don't know what does.'

'You know your trouble?'

'I get the feeling I'm about to find out.'

'You're too chicken, always playing by the rule-book. Blinkers on and toeing the line.'

'Chickens don't wear blinkers,' he spat back.

'They must, because *you* do!' she exploded.

'That's right,' he said, seeming to calm a little, head bobbing. 'That's right: I always play by the rules, don't I?'

'Look, all I meant was—'

He grabbed her arms, pulled her to him, his mouth seeking hers. Siobhan's body went rigid, then her face twisted away. The grip he had on her arms, she couldn't move them. She'd backed up against the desk, stuck there.

'A good close working partnership,' a voice boomed from the doorway. 'That's what I like to see.'

Grant's grip on her fell away as Rebus walked into the room.

'Don't mind me,' he continued. 'Just because I don't indulge in these newfangled policing methods doesn't mean I don't approve.'

'We were just . . .' Grant's voice died.

Siobhan walked round the desk and lowered herself shakily into her chair. 'Sir,' she said, keeping her voice level, 'I wouldn't want you to get the wrong impression about what happened here . . .'

Rebus held up a hand. 'Nothing to do with me, Siobhan.'

'I think something needs to be said.' Her voice had risen. She glanced over towards Grant, who was looking away from her.

'Oh?' Rebus was asking, genuinely curious now.

I could finish your career right here, Grant. 'It's nothing,' she said finally, her eyes fixed on the paperwork before her.

'Anything happening your end, Grant?' Rebus asked blithely.

'What?' Colour bloomed in Grant's cheeks.

'The latest clue: anywhere near solving it?'

'Not really, sir. How about you?'

'Me?' Rebus tapped a pen against his knuckles. 'I think today I've managed to achieve the square root of bugger all.' He paused at the sound of a dull electronic bleeping. 'Is that mine?' he asked, already reaching into his jacket. 'Hello?'

'John? It's Jean. Are you working?'

'Surveillance,' Rebus told her.

'Oh dear, do you want me to . . .?'

'It's OK, Jean. I was joking. I'm just about to go home.'

'It's just that I'm sitting here with a bottle of wine and the TV . . . And some company would be nice.'

Rebus knew he was in no fit state to drive. 'I don't know, Jean. You've not seen me after a drink.'

'What, you turn into Mr Hyde?' She laughed. 'I had that with my husband. I doubt you could show me anything new.' Her voice strained for levity, but there was an edge to it. Maybe she was nervous about asking him: no one liked a rejection . . .

'I could take a taxi. I should go home and change first, though.'

'If you like.'

'I'll see you soon,' he said.

 **Chapter Five**

It had just gone seven thirty when the phone woke Siobhan. She staggered from bed, padded through to the living room. She'd had a bad night, the last clue ricocheting round her skull, along with a replay of Grant pinning her arms, while John Rebus watched from the doorway. She had one hand on her forehead; the other reached for the handset. 'Hello?'

'Good morning, Siobhan. Didn't wake you, did I?'

'No, I was just making breakfast.' She blinked, trying to get her eyes open. The Farmer sounded like he'd been up for hours.

'Well, I don't want to keep you, only I've just had a very interesting phone call. I phoned some people who know the Craft better than I do, and one of them got back to me. He's in the middle of writing a book about the Knights Templar, connecting them to the Masons. That's probably why he saw it straight away.'

Siobhan was in the kitchen now. She checked there was water in the kettle and switched it on. 'Saw what?' she said.

The Farmer started laughing. 'You're not awake yet, are you? I'm talking about the clue. It's a reference to Rosslyn Chapel. You know where that is?'

'I was there not too long ago.' A case she'd worked with Rebus.

'Then maybe you saw it: one of the windows apparently is decorated with carvings of maize. Yet the chapel was built before maize was known in Britain.'

'"A corny beginning",' she recited.

'That's right.'

'And the mason's dream?'

'Well, the chapel has two elaborate pillars. One is called the Mason's Pillar, the other the Apprentice Pillar. The story goes, the master mason decided to go abroad to study the design for the pillar he was to construct. But while he was away, one of his apprentices had a dream about the way it should look. He got to work and created the Apprentice Pillar. When the master mason returned, he was so jealous he bludgeoned the apprentice to death with a mallet.'

'So the mason's dream ended with the pillar?'

'That's right.'

Siobhan went through the story in her head. 'It all fits,' she said at last. 'Thanks so much, sir.'

'Call me some other time, Siobhan. I want to hear how it all ends.'

'I will. Thanks again.'

She ran both hands through her hair. Rosslyn Chapel. It was in the village of Roslin, about six miles south of the city. Siobhan sat down, chewed her bottom lip. They hadn't needed to go to Hart Fell: the name had been enough. In less than three hours, time would be up. Did Quizmaster want her to go to Roslin? She sent an email:

The Apprentice Pillar, Rosslyn Chapel. Do I stay or do I go?

Then she waited. She wondered if Quizmaster could have gone somewhere. She got the feeling he would take a laptop and mobile with him wherever he went. So what was he playing at?

'Can't risk it,' she said impatiently. She sent another message: *I'm going to the chapel.* Then she went to get dressed.

She got into her car, placed the laptop on the passenger seat. She thought about calling Grant, but decided against it. She'd be all right; she could take any flak he threw at her . . .

You don't want to share. And if that doesn't sound like Rebus, I don't know what does. Grant's words to her. Yet here she was heading off to Roslin on her own, having alerted Quizmaster that she was coming.

She turned the car in the direction of Grant's flat.

IT WAS JUST GONE eight fifteen when the phone woke Rebus up. It was his mobile. He slid from the bed and got his feet caught in the clothes strewn across the carpet. Down on hands and knees, he fumbled for the phone, held it to his ear. 'Rebus,' he said. 'And this had better be good.' He glanced towards the bed. No sign of Jean. He wondered if she'd gone to work.

It was Gill Templer. 'You're late,' she said.

'Late for what?' he asked.

'The big story. Your presence is requested in Holyrood Park. A body's been found on Arthur's Seat.'

'Is it her?' Rebus felt his skin suddenly go clammy.

'Hard to judge at this stage.'

'I'll go straight there.'

'Sorry to have disturbed you.'

'Bye, Gill.'

'Bye, John.'

As he was switching off the phone, the door swung open and Jean

Burchill walked in. She was wearing a towelling robe and carrying a tray: orange juice and toast, a cafetiere full of coffee.

'My,' she said, 'don't you look fetching?'

Then she saw the look on his face and her smile vanished. 'What's wrong?' she asked.

So he told her.

GRANT YAWNED. His hair was standing up at the back, and he seemed conscious of it, kept trying to press it flat with his hand.

'Didn't get much sleep last night,' he said, glancing in Siobhan's direction. She kept her eyes on the road. 'Look, about yesterday . . .'

'Let's pretend it never happened,' she said quickly.

'But it did.'

'Subject closed, Grant.' She turned to him. 'I mean it. It's either closed, or I take it to the boss—your call.'

He started to say something, but stopped himself. He asked her to repeat what she'd already told him about the Farmer's call instead. She did, glad that they were staying off the subject of the clinch.

'Sounds good,' he said when she'd finished.

'I think so,' she agreed.

'Almost too easy.'

She snorted. 'So easy we almost missed it.'

'It didn't take any skill, that's what I'm saying. It's the sort of thing you either know or you don't. How many Masons do you suppose Philippa Balfour knows?'

'What?'

'It's how you found out. How would *she* have worked it out? Do you see what I'm saying?'

'I think so. You're saying it needed specialist knowledge that the previous clues didn't?'

'Something like that. Of course, there is one other possibility.'

'Which is?'

'That Quizmaster knew she'd know about Rosslyn Chapel.'

Siobhan saw what he was getting at. 'Someone who knows her? You're saying Quizmaster is one of her friends?'

'Wouldn't surprise me if Ranald Marr turned out to be a Mason, man in his line of work . . .'

'No, nor me,' Siobhan said thoughtfully. 'We might just have to go back and ask him.'

They turned off the main road and drove into the village of Roslin.

Siobhan parked the car beside the chapel and they walked into the ornate interior. Grant stood in the central aisle, gawping much as she had done the first time she'd come here.

'It's incredible,' he said quietly, his words echoing off the walls.

There were carvings everywhere. But Siobhan knew what she was looking for, and walked straight towards the Apprentice Pillar. It was about eight feet high, carved ribbons snaking down it.

'This it?' Grant said. 'So what are we looking for?'

'We'll know when we find it.' Siobhan ran her hands over the cool surface of the pillar, then crouched down. Intertwined dragons were coiled around the base. The tail of one of them, twisting back on itself, had left a small nook. She reached in with finger and thumb and brought out a small square of folded paper.

'Bloody hell,' Grant said.

She didn't bother with gloves or an evidence bag, knew by now that Quizmaster wouldn't have left anything useful to Forensics. She unfolded the paper and read. *You are the Seeker. Your next destination is Hellbank. Instructions to follow.*

Siobhan turned the paper over. Its other side was blank.

'Bastard!' Grant called out. 'I bet he's having a bloody good laugh, seeing us chasing all over the place!'

'I think that's part of it, yes,' Siobhan agreed quietly. 'He likes to see us being run ragged.'

They went back to the car, and Siobhan sent an email to Quizmaster: *Ready for Hellbank clue.*

'Now what?' Grant asked. Siobhan shrugged. But then the laptop announced there was a new message. She clicked to read it.

Ready to give up? That's a surer thing.

Grant let out a hiss of breath. 'Is this a clue or a taunt?'

'Maybe both.' Another message came through: *Hellbank by six tonight.*

Siobhan nodded. 'Both,' she repeated.

'Six? He's only giving us eight hours.'

'No time to waste then.' She looked at him. 'What's a surer thing?'

He forced a smile. 'It looks like a crossword clue. I mean, it's not quite grammatical, is it? It almost makes sense, but doesn't.'

'Like it's a bit strained?'

'If it *was* a crossword clue . . .' A little vertical crease appeared between Grant's eyebrows as he concentrated. 'Let's say it's an anagram. "Ready to give up . . . that's a surer . . . thing". "Give up" could mean "yield", as in yielding meaning. If you use the letters in "that's a surer", you'll get a word or words meaning a "thing".'

Siobhan could feel a headache coming on. 'Isn't there some computer program we could use?'

'Probably. But that would be cheating, wouldn't it?'

'Right now, cheating sounds fine to me.'

But Grant wasn't listening. He was already at work.

UNIFORMED OFFICERS STOOD around holding rolls of striped tape. There was a line of parked cars on the roadway below: journalists, photographers, at least one TV crew. Word had gone around fast.

Bill Pryde was explaining, as he and Rebus climbed, that a walker had found the body. 'In some gorse bushes. No real attempt to hide it.'

Rebus kept quiet. Two bodies never found . . . the other two found in water. Now this: a hillside. It broke the pattern.

'Is it her?' he asked finally.

'From the Versace T-shirt, I'd have to say yes.'

Rebus looked around. Arthur's Seat was a wilderness in the middle of Edinburgh. 'You'd have a hard job dragging a body up here,' he said.

Pryde nodded. 'Probably killed on the spot.'

'Lured up here?'

'Or maybe just out walking.'

Rebus shook his head. 'I don't figure her for the walking type.' They were getting close now. A cluster of stooped forms on the hillside, white overalls and hoods. Rebus recognised Professor Gates, the pathologist, red-faced from the exertion of the climb. Gill Templer was next to him, listening and looking.

'Better not go any further than this,' Pryde said. Then he called for someone to fetch two more sets of overalls. As Rebus finished zipping up his one-piece, Pryde started forwards towards the corpse.

'Throttled,' Gill Templer informed them.

'Best guess at this stage,' Gates corrected her. 'Morning, John.'

Rebus nodded a greeting back. 'Dr Curt not with you?'

'Phoned in sick.' Gates continued his examination. The body lay awkwardly, legs and arms all jutting angles. The gorse bushes next to it must have hidden it well enough, Rebus guessed. And the clothing helped with the camouflage: light green combat trousers, khaki T-shirt, grey jacket. The clothes Flip was thought to have been wearing the day she'd gone missing.

'Parents informed?' he asked.

Gill nodded. 'They know a body's been found.'

Rebus walked round her to get a better view. He'd seen dozens of corpses over the years; they never got any less sad, or made him any less depressed.

'The fingers have been gnawed at,' Gates stated, more for his tape recorder than his audience. 'Local wildlife most probably. Bit of a bugger, that.' Rebus knew what he meant: if Philippa had fought her attacker, her fingertips might have told them a lot—bits of skin or blood beneath the nails.

'Drag marks on her heels,' Gates went on. 'Not too severe. Lividity consistent with body's position, so she was either still alive or only just dead when she was dragged here.'

'Nothing in the pockets?' Rebus asked.

Gates shook his head. 'Jewellery on hands, and an expensive watch.'

'At least we can rule out robbery,' Rebus muttered.

Gates smiled. 'No signs of the clothing having been disturbed,' he commented, 'so you can probably rule out a sexual motive, too.'

'Better and better.' Rebus looked at Gill. 'This is going to be a cinch.'

'Hence my ear-to-ear grin,' she parried solemnly.

BACK AT ST LEONARD'S, the station was buzzing with the news, but all Siobhan could feel was a dazed numbness. Playing Quizmaster's game—the way Philippa probably had—had made Siobhan feel an affinity with the missing student. Now she was no longer a MisPer, and the worst fears had been realised.

'We always knew, didn't we?' Grant said. 'It was just a matter of when the body turned up.' He dropped his notebook onto the desk in front of him. The page was covered with anagrams. He turned to a fresh sheet, pen in hand.

George Silvers and Ellen Wylie were in the CID room too. Siobhan asked who found the body.

'A woman out walking,' Wylie replied. 'Daily constitutional.'

'Be a while before she takes that route again,' Silvers muttered.

'Was Flip lying there all this time?' Siobhan was looking across to where Grant was busy juggling letters on his notepad. Maybe he was right to keep working, but she couldn't help feeling a certain distaste. How could he not be affected by the news?

Wylie answered Siobhan's question. 'Chief Super seems to think so.' As she spoke, she looked down at her desk, and rubbed her hand along it as though wiping off dust.

It hurts her, Siobhan thought . . . even saying the words 'Chief Super' reminds her of that TV appearance and hardens the sense of resentment.

When one of the phones rang, Silvers went to answer.

'No, he's not here,' he told the caller. 'Hang on, I'll check.' He put his hand over the mouthpiece. 'Ellen, any idea when Rebus will be back?'

She shook her head slowly. Suddenly Siobhan knew where he was: he was on Arthur's Seat . . . while Wylie, who was supposed to be his partner, wasn't. She thought of Gill Templer, telling Rebus he was needed there. He'd have gone like a shot, leaving Wylie behind. It looked to Siobhan like a calculated snub by Templer. She would know *exactly* how Wylie would feel.

'Sorry, no idea,' Silvers said into the phone. Then he held the receiver out towards Siobhan. 'Lady wants to speak to you.'

It was Jean Burchill, asking if the body had been identified.

'Not a hundred per cent. How did you know?'

'John told me, then rushed off to Arthur's Seat.'

Siobhan's lips formed a silent O. John Rebus and Jean Burchill . . . well, well. She looked across to Grant and saw that he was staring at his notepad, as if mesmerised by something there.

'Do you know where on Arthur's Seat?' Jean was asking.

'Across the road from Dunsapie Loch and a bit further east.'

Siobhan was watching Grant. He was holding out the notebook in front of her, but too far away for her to make out much.

'I know where you mean,' Jean said, 'Hellbank, I think it's called.'

'Hellbank?' Siobhan made sure Grant could hear her.

'Quite a steep slope,' Jean was saying, 'which might explain the name, though the folklore prefers witches and devilry.'

'Yes,' said Siobhan. 'Look, Jean, I've got to go.' She was staring at the words circled on Grant's notepad. He'd worked out the anagram. 'That's a surer' had become 'Arthur's Seat'.

'He was leading us to her,' Grant said quietly.

'We can't know that for certain. All he was doing was taking us to the places Flip went.'

'She turned up dead at this one. He killed her.'

'Then why bother helping us play the game?'

'To mess with our heads.' He paused. 'No, to mess with *your* head. And maybe more than that.'

'Then he'd have killed me before now.'

'Why?'

'Because now I don't need to play the game any more. I've come as far as Flip did.'

He shook his head slowly. 'You're saying if he sends you the clue for the next stage, you won't be tempted?'

'No,' she said. 'And anyway, after this there's no way I'd go anywhere without back-up. He must know that.' She had a thought. 'The next stage is Stricture,' she said.

'What about it?'

'He emailed Flip . . . *after* she'd been killed. Why on earth would he do that if he'd killed her?'

'Because he's a psychopath.'

'I don't think so.' Siobhan stood up abruptly. The laptop was in her shoulder bag, still hooked up to the mobile phone. She got it out and set it up. 'Any minute now he's going to hear on the radio or TV that the body's been found. He'll be expecting to hear from us.'

'Hang on,' Grant said, 'we need to clear this with DCS Templer.'

She gave him a look. 'Back to playing by the rules, eh?'

His face reddened, but he nodded. 'We need to tell her.'

Silvers and Wylie, who'd been listening intently throughout, had understood enough to know something important was going on.

'I'm with Siobhan,' Wylie said. 'Strike while the iron is hot.'

Silvers disagreed. 'You know the score: Chief Super'll blast the pair of you if you go behind her back.'

'We're not going behind her back,' Siobhan stated, eyes on Wylie.

'Yes we are,' Grant said. 'It's a murder case now, Siobhan. The time for playing games just stopped.' He rested both hands on her desk. 'Send that email, and you're on your own.'

'Maybe that's where I want to be,' she retorted.

'Nice to have a bit of plain speaking,' Grant said.

'I'm all for it,' John Rebus said from the doorway. Ellen Wylie straightened up and folded her arms. 'Speaking of which,' he went on, 'sorry, Ellen, I should have called you.'

'Forget it.' But it was clear to everyone that *she* wouldn't.

When Rebus had listened to Siobhan's account of the morning's events they all looked to him for a decision. He ran a finger along the top of the laptop's screen. 'Everything you've just told me,' he advised, 'needs to be taken to DCS Templer.'

To Siobhan's eyes, Grant didn't look so much vindicated as revoltingly smug. 'OK,' she said, ready to make a partial peace, 'we'll talk to the Chief Super. Though I bet it's not what you would have done.'

'Me?' Rebus said. 'I wouldn't have had the first clue, Siobhan. Email's a black art as far as I'm concerned.'

Siobhan smiled, but there was a thread running through her mind: black art . . . coffins used in witches' spells . . . Flip's death on a hill-side called Hellbank. Witchcraft?

SIX OF THEM standing in the cramped office at Gayfield Square: Gill Templer and Bill Pryde; Rebus and Ellen Wylie; Siobhan and Grant. Templer was sifting through copies of the emails silently. Finally she looked up. 'Is there *any* way we can identify Quizmaster?'

'Not that I know of,' Siobhan admitted.

'I think it's possible but I'm not sure how,' Grant added. 'The Met has a computer crime unit, doesn't it?'

Templer studied him. 'Think you're up to it, Grant?'

He shook his head. 'This is way out of my league. I mean, I'd be happy to liaise . . .'

'Fair enough.' Templer turned to Siobhan. 'This German student you were telling us about . . . I'd like a bit more detail.'

'Shouldn't be too difficult.'

Templer's gaze shifted to Wylie. 'Can you run with that, Ellen?'

Wylie looked surprised. 'I suppose so.'

'You're splitting us up?' Rebus interrupted.

'Unless you can think of a good reason not to.'

'A doll was left at Falls, now the body's turned up. It's the same pattern as before.'

'But not by the same coffin-maker. Different workmanship altogether, I believe you said.'

'You're putting it down to coincidence?' Rebus asked.

'I'm not putting it down to anything, and if something else crops up in connection with it, you can start back in again. But we're on a murder case now, and that changes everything.'

Rebus glanced towards Wylie. She was simmering—the transfer from dusty old autopsies to a background check on a student's curious demise . . . It wasn't exactly thrilling. But at the same time she wasn't going to throw her weight behind Rebus—too busy working on her own sense of injustice.

'Right,' Templer said into the silence. 'For the moment, you'll be going back to the main investigation.' She tidied the sheets of paper together, then looked up at Grant. 'Can you stay behind for a sec?'

'Sure,' he said.

The rest of them squeezed out of the room, glad of the fresher, cooler air. Rebus, however, loitered near Templer's door. 'Got two seconds, Gill? Something I forgot to mention . . .'

'Forgot?' She produced a wry smile.

He had three sheets of fax paper in his hand. 'These came through from Dublin. I was asking about the Costellos.'

She looked up from the sheets. 'Any particular reason?'

'Just a hunch.'

'We'd already looked into the family.'

He nodded. 'Of course: a quick phone call, and back comes the news that there are no convictions. But you know as well as I do, that's often just the beginning of the story.'

Rebus knew he had Templer hooked. She turned to Grant and told him to come back in five minutes.

'Better make that ten,' Rebus added, winking at the young man.

Declan Macmanus had come good. David Costello had been wild in his youth: 'the result of too much money given and not enough attention', in Macmanus's phrase. Wild meant fast cars, speeding tickets, fights in pubs, smashed windows, verbal warnings issued where some miscreants would have found themselves behind bars.

Later, David Costello had cleaned up his act, Macmanus conceded, pinpointing the turnaround to an eighteenth birthday party, where a friend had tried to leap between two roofs for a dare, falling short, plummeting into the alley below. He wasn't killed. But there was brain damage, spinal damage . . . not much more than a vegetable.

'Bit of a shock at that age,' Macmanus had written. 'Got David clean and sober in no seconds flat, otherwise he might have turned out not so much a chip off the old block as a bloody great boulder.'

Like son, like father. Thomas Costello had managed to write off eight cars, yet never lose his driving licence. His wife Theresa had twice called police to the home when her husband was in a rage. Both times they'd found her in the bathroom, door locked but missing some splinters where Thomas had started attacking it with a carving knife. 'Just trying to get the bloody thing open,' he'd explained to officers. 'Thought she was going to do herself in.'

Twice she had taken overdoses, and everyone in the city felt sorry for her: hard-working wife, abusive and lazy husband who just happened to be hugely wealthy through no significant effort of his own. The two rooms at the Caledonian made sense now . . .

'Lovely family,' Gill Templer commented.

'Dublin's finest.'

'And all of it covered up by police. Your thinking on this is . . .?'

'That there's a side of David Costello we didn't know about till now. And that goes for his family, too.'

'OK, talk to the parents when they get here. They'll be coming over again now that Philippa's been found.'

'And the boyfriend?'

She nodded. 'But not too heavy . . . doesn't look good with someone who's grieving.'

He smiled. 'Always thinking of the media, eh, Gill?'

She looked at him. 'Could you sent Grant in, please?'

'One impressionable young officer coming right up.' He pulled open the door and gave Grant another wink as he passed.

Ten minutes later, Siobhan was getting a coffee from the machine when Grant found her.

'What did Templer want?' she asked, unable to stop herself.

'Offered me liaison.'

Siobhan concentrated on stirring her drink. 'I'm thrilled for you.'

He stared at her. 'You could try a bit harder.'

'You're right, I could.' They locked eyes. 'Thanks for helping with the clues. I couldn't have done it without you.'

Only now did he seem to realise that their partnership truly was dissolved. 'Oh . . . right,' he said. 'Look, Siobhan . . .'

'Yes?'

'What happened in the office—I really am sorry.'

She allowed herself a smile. 'Afraid I'll tell on you?'

'No, it's not that.'

But it was, and they both knew it.

THAT SAME AFTERNOON Ellen Wylie watched Grant Hood's first TV appearance on the office monitors. He was seated next to Gill Templer as she read out a short statement concerning the finding of the body. Bill Pryde was on Templer's other side, fielding most of the queries. Everyone wanted to know the cause of death.

'We're not even in a position to confirm identity as yet,' Pryde stated, his words punctuated with little coughs. Wylie knew the coughs were nervous tics. She'd been the same herself.

Gill Templer glanced towards Pryde, and Hood seemed to take this as his cue. 'Cause of death is also yet to be determined,' he said, 'with a post-mortem examination scheduled for late afternoon. As you know, another conference will take place at seven this evening, by which time we hope to have more details available.'

'But the death's being treated as suspicious?' one journalist asked.

'At this early stage, yes, we're treating the death as suspicious.'

Wylie stuck the end of her Biro between her teeth and ground down on it. Hood was cool, no doubt about it. He'd changed his clothes: the ensemble looked brand new, she thought.

'There's little we can add right now,' he was telling the media, 'as you'll no doubt appreciate. If and when an identification is made, family have to be contacted and the identification confirmed.'

'Looked good in there, didn't he?' someone said when the conference had ended and the monitor had been switched off.

She stared at the uniform who'd asked, but there was no malice apparent. 'Yes,' she confirmed. 'He did all right.'

'Better than some,' another voice said. She turned her head, but there were three officers there, all Gayfield-based. None was looking at her. She turned her attention to Siobhan's notes on the German student. She would make a start, busy herself with phone calls.

Just as soon as she got the words *better than some* out of her head.

Siobhan was sending another message to Quizmaster. She'd taken twenty minutes getting it right. *Hellbank solved. Flip's body found there. Do you want to talk?*

It didn't take long for him to respond. *How did you solve it?*

Anagram of Arthur's Seat. Hellbank the hillside's name.

Was it you who found the body?

No. Was it you who killed her?

No. Do you wish to continue? Stricture awaits.

She stared at the screen. Did Flip's death mean so little to him? *Someone killed Flip at Hellbank. I need you to come forward.*

His reply took time coming through. *Can't help.*

I think you can, Quizmaster.

Undergo Stricture. Perhaps we can meet there.

She thought for a moment. *When does the game end?*

There was no answer. She was aware of a figure standing behind her: Rebus. 'What's Quizmaster saying now?' he asked.

'He wants me to go on playing the game.'

'Tell him to sod off. You don't need him now.'

'Don't I?'

The phone rang; Siobhan picked up. 'Yes . . . that's fine . . . of

465

course.' When she ended the call, she looked up at Rebus and he raised an eyebrow expectantly.

'The Chief Super,' she explained. 'Now that Grant's got liaison, I'm to stick with the computer angle. Find out if there's any way of tracing Quizmaster. And canvass Flip's friends and family again.'

'Why?'

'Because I couldn't have got to Hellbank on my own.'

Rebus nodded. 'You don't think she did either?'

'She needed to know London tube lines, geography, the Scots language, Rosslyn Chapel and crossword puzzles. That's a tall order.'

Rebus was thoughtful. 'Whoever Quizmaster is, he needed to know all those things too.'

'Agreed.'

'And to know she had at least a chance of solving each puzzle.' He paused. 'If you're going to be talking to David Costello, maybe I could tag along. I've got a few more questions for him myself.'

'What sort of questions?'

'Let me buy you a cup of coffee and I'll tell you . . .'

THAT EVENING, John Balfour, accompanied by a family friend, made the formal identification of his daughter Philippa. When it was over, Bill Pryde gave Rebus a call on his mobile to let him know.

He was in the Oxford Bar with Siobhan, Ellen Wylie, Jean Burchill and Donald Devlin. Grant Hood had turned down the offer of a drink, saying he had to do a quick crash course in the media—names and faces. The conference had been moved to 9.00pm, by which time it was hoped the autopsy would be complete, initial conclusions reached.

'Oh dear,' Devlin said. He'd removed his jacket and had bunched his fists into the capacious pockets of his cardigan. 'What a terrible shame.'

Rebus bought the first round and they colonised the back room's top table. The place wasn't busy, and the TV in the opposite corner meant they were unlikely to be overheard.

'Now we're all here . . .' Rebus said, lifting his pint, 'cheers!'

He waited till everybody had lifted their glasses before putting his own to his mouth. Scotland: you couldn't refuse a toast.

'All right,' he said, putting the glass back down, 'there's a murder case needs solving, and I just want to be sure in my own mind where we all stand. Call it an unofficial briefing.'

'With the booze as a bribe?'

He looked at Wylie. 'I've always been a fan of incentive schemes.' He managed to force a smile from her. 'Right, here's what I think we've got so far. We've got Burke and Hare—taking things chronologically—and soon after them we've got lots of little coffins found on Arthur's Seat. Then, connected or not, we've got a series of similar coffins turning up in places where women happen to have disappeared or turned up dead. One such coffin is found in Falls, just after Philippa Balfour goes missing. She then turns up dead on Arthur's Seat, location of the original coffins.'

'Which is a long way from Falls,' Siobhan pointed out. 'I mean, those other coffins were found near the scene, weren't they? And the Falls coffin is different from the others.'

'I'm not saying otherwise,' Rebus interrupted. 'I'm just trying to establish whether I'm the only one who sees a possible link?'

They all looked at each other; no one said anything until Wylie mentioned the German student. 'Swords and sorcery, role-playing, ends up dead on a Scottish hillside.'

'Exactly.'

'But,' Wylie continued, 'hard to tie in with your disappearances and drownings.'

Devlin seemed persuaded by her tone. 'It's not,' he added, 'as if the drownings were considered suspicious at the time, and my examination of the pertinent details doesn't persuade me otherwise.'

'Fine,' Rebus said, 'then I'm the only one who's even remotely convinced?' This time, not even Wylie spoke up. Rebus took another long swallow of beer. 'Well,' he said, 'thanks for the vote of confidence.'

'Look, why are we here?' Wylie laid her hands on the table. 'You're trying to convince us to work as a team?'

'I'm just saying all these little details may end up being part of the same story.' He ran a hand over his head. 'Christ, I don't know.'

'Look, thanks for the drink . . .' Ellen Wylie's glass was empty. She picked her bag up from the bench, started getting to her feet.

'Ellen—'

She looked at him. 'Big day tomorrow, John. First full day of the murder inquiry.'

'It's not officially a murder inquiry until the pathologist pronounces,' Devlin reminded her. She looked ready to say something, but just graced him with a cold smile, said a general goodbye, and was gone.

'Something connects them,' Rebus said quietly, almost to himself. 'I can't think what it is, but it's there . . .'

Devlin checked his watch. 'Actually, I'm afraid I'm unable to tarry.' He seemed to find it painful rising from the table. 'I don't suppose one of the young ladies might proffer a lift?'

'You're on my way home,' Siobhan conceded at last.

Rebus's sense of desertion was softened when he saw her glance in Jean's direction: she was leaving the two of them alone, that was all.

He sat in silence with Jean until they'd gone, and was about to speak when Devlin came shuffling back. 'Am I right to assume,' he said, 'that my usefulness is now at an end?' Rebus nodded. 'In which case, will the files be sent back to their place of origin?'

'I'll get DS Wylie to do it first thing,' Rebus promised.

'Many thanks, then.' Devlin's smile was directed at Jean. 'It's been a pleasure to have met you.'

'And you,' she said.

'I may pop into the museum some day. Perhaps you'd do me the honour of showing me round . . .?'

'I'd love to.'

Devlin bowed his head and started back towards the door.

'I hope he doesn't,' she muttered. 'He gives me the creeps.'

'You're not the first to say that. But don't worry, you're perfectly safe with me.'

'Oh, I hope not,' she said, eyes twinkling above her glass.

THEY WERE IN BED when the news came through. Rebus took the call, seated naked on the edge of the mattress, uncomfortably aware of the view he was presenting to Jean: probably two spare tyres around his middle, arms and shoulders more fat than muscle. The silver lining was: the view could only be worse from the front . . .

'Strangulation,' he told her, sliding back under the bedclothes.

'It was quick then?'

'Definitely. There's bruising on the neck just at the carotid artery. She probably passed out, then he strangled her.'

'Why would he do that?'

'Easier to kill someone when they're compliant. No struggle.'

'Where's the carotid artery?' she asked, as he wrapped his arm around her, kissed her hair.

He placed a finger on his own neck. 'Put pressure on it, the person blacks out in a matter of seconds.'

'Would doctors know about it?' Jean asked, after a while.

'Anyone who's had medical training would,' he answered. 'Why?'

She looked thoughtful. 'Just something from the paper. Wasn't one of Philippa's friends a medical student, one of the ones she was going to meet that night . . .?'

 # Chapter Six

His name was Albert Winfield—'Albie' to his friends. He seemed surprised that the police wanted to talk to him again, but turned up at St Leonard's at the appointed time. Outside the room, Siobhan and Rebus locked eyes and nodded at one another, having left him waiting for half an hour. Rebus pushed open the door forcefully.

'Many thanks for coming along, Mr Winfield,' he snapped. The young man almost leapt from his chair. The window was closed tight, the room stifling. Three chairs—two on one side of the narrow table, one on the other.

Rebus sat down, throwing a bulky folder onto the table in front of him: no names on it. Winfield seemed mesmerised. Rebus rested his hand on the folder and smiled.

'It must have come as a terrible shock.' A quiet voice, soothing, solicitous . . . Siobhan sat down beside her thuggish colleague. 'I'm DC Clarke, by the way. This is DI Rebus.'

'What?' the young man said. Perspiration made his forehead shine.

'The news of Flip's murder,' Siobhan continued. 'It must have been a shock.'

'Y-es . . . absolutely.'

'You knew her well, then?'

Winfield kept his eyes on Siobhan. 'I suppose so. I mean, she was Camille's friend really.'

'Hot in here, isn't it, Albert?' Siobhan paused. 'You don't mind me calling you Albert?'

'No . . . no, that's fine.' He stared down at the tabletop for a moment, then glanced up at her again. But whenever he did his eyes were drawn towards her neighbour.

'Just a few follow-up questions really,' Siobhan was saying.

'Right . . . fine.' Winfield nodded enthusiastically.

'So you wouldn't say you knew Flip that well?'

'We went out together . . . in a group, I mean. Dinner sometimes. At her flat or mine.'

'You live down near the Botanics?'

'That's right.'

'Nice part of town.'

He nodded. 'My father bought it for me.'

'What about Flip's boyfriend?' Rebus asked.

'David? What about him?'

'Just wondering if you consider him a friend,' Rebus said.

'Well, it's a bit awkward now . . . I mean, it *was* awkward. They kept splitting up, getting back together again . . .'

'And you took Flip's side?' Siobhan guessed.

'I had to, what with Camille and everything . . .'

'You say they kept splitting up. Whose fault was it?'

'I just think they had this personality clash. They were similar in lots of ways. They couldn't let an argument lie. There had to be a winner and a loser, no middle ground.'

'Did these disagreements ever turn violent?'

'No.'

'But David's got a temper on him?' Rebus persisted.

'No more so than anyone else.'

Siobhan cleared her throat, a sign that she thought Rebus had hit a wall. 'Albert,' she said, her voice like a balm, 'did you know that Flip liked to play computer games?'

'No,' he said, looking surprised.

'Do you play them?'

'I used to play Doom in the first year.'

'Flip was playing a game online, a sort of variation on a treasure hunt.' Siobhan unfolded a sheet of paper and slid it across the table. 'Do these clues mean anything to you?'

He read with a frown, then expelled some air. 'Nothing.'

'You're studying medicine, aren't you?' Rebus interrupted.

'That's right. I'm in my third year.'

'I'm assuming you know something of the carotid artery then?' Siobhan asked.

'It's an artery in the neck. Actually, there are two of them.'

'I had to look it up in a dictionary,' Rebus told Winfield. 'It's from the Greek, meaning sleep. Know why that is?'

'Because compression of the carotid causes you to black out.'

Rebus nodded. 'That's right. And if you keep on pressing . . .'

'Christ, is that how she died?'

Siobhan shook her head. 'We think she was rendered unconscious, then strangled afterwards.'

In the silence that followed, Winfield looked wildly from one detective to the other. Then he started rising to his feet.

'You don't . . .? For pity's sake, you think it was *me*?'

'Sit down,' Rebus ordered. In truth, Winfield hadn't got very far up; it looked like his knees were refusing to lock.

'We know it wasn't you,' Siobhan said firmly. 'You were with everyone else in the bar that night, waiting for Flip.'

'That's right,' he said, 'that's right.'

'So you've nothing to worry about,' Rebus said.

'Anyone else in your group like to play games?' Siobhan asked.

'Nobody. I mean, Trist has a few games for his computer. Tomb Raider, that sort of thing. But probably everyone does.'

'No one else in your circle studies medicine?' Siobhan asked.

Winfield shook his head, but she could see he was having a thought. 'There's Claire,' he said. 'Claire Benzie. I've only met her once or twice at parties, but she was an old schoolfriend of Flip's. God, that's right . . .' He looked up at Siobhan, then to Rebus. 'Of all the bloody things, she wants to be a pathologist.'

'YES, I KNOW CLAIRE,' said Dr Curt, Gates's grey-faced assistant, leading them down a corridor towards one of the lecture halls at the medical faculty. Rebus had asked if he was feeling better. Gastric problems, Curt had explained. 'Very pleasant girl,' he said now, 'and a good student.' He stopped at a set of doors and peered through the glass upper half. 'Yes, in here.'

The lecture room was small and antiquated: wood veneer on the walls, curved wooden benches rising steeply. Curt checked his watch. 'Only another minute or two.'

Rebus peered inside. Someone was lecturing to a few dozen students.

'It's an old building,' Siobhan remarked.

'Not that old really, in the context of the university. The medical school was based at Old College in earlier times. If you're interested, Devlin's your man. He's the unofficial historian of the medical faculty's early days.'

'I didn't know that. I know he has a theory that Dr Kennet Lovell placed the coffins on Arthur's Seat,' Rebus said.

'Ah, the ones that've been in the papers of late?' Curt frowned in thought. 'Funny you should mention Lovell. Claire told me recently she's descended from him.' There was a sound of movement inside the hall. 'Ah, Dr Easton's finished. Better stand back, lest we're stampeded to death.'

A few students acknowledged Curt as they filed by. Finally, with the hall three-quarters empty, Curt went up onto his toes. 'Claire? Could you spare a minute?'

She was tall and thin with short blonde hair and a long straight nose. Her eyes were an almost oriental shape, like tilted almonds. She carried two folders beneath one arm. There was a mobile phone in her hand. She came forward with a smile. 'Hello, Dr Curt.' Her voice was almost playful.

'Claire, these police officers would like a word.'

'It's about Flip, isn't it?' Her face had fallen, all humour lost to it, and the voice had taken on a sombre tone.

Siobhan nodded slowly. 'We're treating Flip's death as homicide and we just need your help to clear up a few things.'

'I keep thinking maybe it wasn't her, maybe it's a mistake . . .'

'You can use my office,' Curt said.

As they walked back down the corridor, Rebus watched Claire Benzie's back. She was holding her folders in front of her, discussing her recent lecture with Dr Curt. Claire Benzie was interesting, he thought. The morning her friend's murder is announced, and she's able to attend a lecture, talk about it afterwards, even with two detectives right behind her . . .

Dr Curt ushered them inside his office. 'I've got one or two things to do,' he said. 'Just close the door after you when you've finished.'

'Thanks,' Rebus said.

Curt left them. It was a cramped, airless room. Books and documents covered every bit of shelf space.

'So,' Claire said, dropping into the visitor's chair. 'What is it you want to know?'

'You were at school with Flip?'

'For a few years, yes.'

They'd already been through the notes from Claire Benzie's first interview. Two of the Gayfield Square contingent had talked to her.

'You lost touch?'

'Sort of . . . a few letters and emails. Then she started her history of art course and I found out I'd been accepted by Edinburgh.'

'You got in touch?'

Claire nodded. She'd tucked one leg beneath her on the chair. 'Sent her an email, and we met up.'

'You saw her often after that?'

'Not that often. Different courses, different workloads.'

'How did she meet David Costello, do you know?' Rebus knew the answer but was wondering how well Claire knew Costello.

'I think she said something about a party . . .'

'Did you like him?'

'David?' She was thoughtful. 'Arrogant sod, very sure of himself.'

Rebus almost came back with: *Not at all like you, then?* Instead, he looked to Siobhan, who reached into her jacket for the folded note.

'Claire,' she said, 'did Flip like to play games? Role-playing . . . computer games . . . maybe on the Internet?'

She thought for a moment. 'We had a dungeons and dragons club at school.'

'You were both in it?'

'Until we realised it was strictly a boy thing.' She wrinkled her nose. 'Come to think of it, didn't David play at school, too?'

Siobhan handed her the sheet of clues. 'Ever seen these before?'

'What do they mean?'

'Some game Flip was playing. What are you smiling at?'

'Seven fins high . . . she was so pleased with that.'

Siobhan's eyes widened. 'Sorry?'

'She came bounding up to me in some bar . . . I forget where . . . she was laughing . . . and she said this.' Claire pointed to the sheet. 'Seven fins high is king. Then she asked me if I knew what it meant. I told her I hadn't the faintest. "It's the Victoria Line," she said. She seemed so pleased with herself.'

'She didn't say anything about it being part of a quiz clue?'

Claire shook her head. 'I thought . . . well, I don't know what I thought. Has this game got something to do with her death?'

'We don't know yet,' Rebus told her.

Claire closed her eyes. When she opened them, there were tears shining there. 'Only seems like yesterday we were schoolgirls . . .'

'This was in Edinburgh?' Rebus asked. The first interview hadn't gone into her background, except as it related to Flip. 'Is that where your family live?'

'It is now. But back then, we lived in Causland.'

Rebus frowned. 'Causland?' He knew the name from somewhere.

'It's a village, about a mile and a half from Falls.'

'You know Falls, then?'

'Used to.'

'And Junipers, the Balfours' house?'

She nodded. 'For a while, I was more house guest than visitor.'

'And then your family moved away?'

'Yes. My father . . .' She broke off. 'We had to move for his work.'
Rebus and Siobhan shared a look: it wasn't what she'd been about
to say.

'Did you and Flip ever visit the waterfall?' Rebus asked casually.

She smiled, eyes losing focus. 'We used to play there. It was our
enchanted kingdom. Life Never-Ending we called it. If only we'd
known . . .' She broke down then, and Siobhan went to comfort her.

Rebus walked into the outer office and asked the secretary for a glass
of water. But by the time he got back with it, Claire was recovering.

'Thank you,' she said, compressing it to the single syllable *kyoo*.

'I think that's plenty to be going on with,' Siobhan was saying.
'You've been a big help, Claire. We might be in touch again later.'

'Fine, whatever.' Claire stood up, clutching her files to her chest.
'I've got another class,' she said. 'Don't want to miss it.'

'Dr Curt tells us you're related to Kennet Lovell?'

She looked at Rebus. 'On my mother's side.' She paused, as if
expecting a follow-up question, but Rebus didn't have one.

They watched her leave, then Rebus closed the door. 'What do you
think?' he asked, turning back into the room.

'I don't know,' Siobhan admitted. 'The tears seemed real enough.'

'Seven fins high: say Flip didn't come up to her at a bar. Say Claire
already knew what it meant.'

'Because she's the Quizmaster?' Siobhan shook her head. 'Then
why bother telling us *anything*?'

'Because . . .' But Rebus couldn't think of an answer for that.

'I'll tell you what I'm wondering. Why did her family move? There's
something she was holding back.'

'Her old school might tell us,' Rebus said.

Siobhan went to ask the secretary for a phone book.

Rebus made the call, putting the speaker on so Siobhan could
listen. The headmistress had been one of the teachers during Flip and
Claire's time there.

'Poor, poor Philippa, it's terrible news . . . and what her family must
be going through,' the headmistress said.

'I'm sure they've got every support,' Rebus commiserated. 'Actually, I'm phoning in connection with Claire Benzie. It's part of the background, trying to build up a picture of Philippa. I believe she and Claire were good friends at one time.'

'Pretty good, yes.'

'They lived near one another, too?'

'That's right. Out East Lothian way. I believe Claire's father drove them in to school.'

'Claire's father worked in Edinburgh then?'

'Oh, yes. Some sort of lawyer.'

'Is that why the family moved? Was it to do with his work?'

'Dear me, no. I think they were evicted. One shouldn't gossip, but with him being deceased I don't suppose it matters.'

'We'll hold it in strictest confidence,' Rebus said.

'Well, it's just that the poor man made some bad investments . . . lost thousands . . . his house . . . the lot.'

'How did he die?'

'I think you've guessed. He took an overdose of some kind of tablets. It's quite a tumble after all, isn't it, from lawyer to bankrupt? Such a pity, two families torn apart by tragedy.'

'Yes, it is,' Rebus agreed. 'Many thanks for that. Goodbye.' He put down the phone and looked at Siobhan.

'Investments?' she echoed.

'And who would he trust if not the father of his daughter's best friend?'

'Balfour's about to bury his daughter,' Siobhan reminded him.

'Then we'll talk to someone else at the bank.'

Siobhan smiled. 'I know just the man . . .'

RANALD MARR was at Junipers, so they drove out to Falls.

The gates at the house were being protected by two uniformed police officers from St Leonard's.

'Who's up there?' Rebus pointed through the gates to where three cars were parked in the driveway outside the house.

'The parents,' the officer told him, 'house staff . . . someone from the funeral home. And a family friend.'

Rebus put the car into gear, crawled through the gates. He guessed that the black Volvo S40 belonged to the funeral home, leaving a bronze Maserati and a green Aston Martin. He couldn't decide which belonged to Marr and which to the Balfours, and said as much.

475

'The Aston's John Balfour's,' Siobhan told him. 'It's in the notes.'

He looked at her. 'You'll be telling me his shoe size next.'

'I do want to know if he's a Mason.'

'Rebus nodded. 'I'll handle that.'

A maid answered the door. They showed their warrant cards and were ushered inside. The maid headed off without saying anything.

'This place is straight out of Cluedo,' Siobhan murmured, studying the wood panelling, the paintings of Balfours past. There was even a suit of armour at the foot of the stairs. The same door the maid had disappeared through was opening now.

Ranald Marr, in black suit and tie, white shirt, strode towards them, looking upset.'What is it this time?' he asked.

'Mr Marr?' Rebus stuck out his hand. 'DI Rebus. I just want to say how sorry we are that we've had to intrude.'

Marr, accepting the apology, also accepted Rebus's hand. Rebus had never joined the Masons, but his father had taught him the handshake one drunken night, back when Rebus was in his teens.

'Is there somewhere we could talk?' Rebus said.

'Along here.' Marr led them into one of two hallways. Rebus caught Siobhan's eye and nodded, answering her question. Marr was a Mason. She pursed her lips, looked thoughtful.

Marr had opened another door, leading into a large room filled with a wall-length bookcase and a full-size billiard table. Two chairs sat against one wall, a small table between them. On the table sat a silver tray laid with a decanter of whisky and some crystal tumblers. Marr sat down and poured himself a drink. He gestured towards Rebus, who shook his head, Siobhan likewise. Marr raised his glass.

'Philippa, God rest her soul.' Then he drank deeply. Rebus had smelt the whisky on his breath, knew this wasn't his first of the day.

'So,' Marr said, 'what is it you want this time?'

'Hugo Benzie,' Rebus said.

Marr's eyebrows lifted in surprise. He took another pull on his drink. 'You knew him?' Rebus guessed.

'Not very well. His daughter was at school with Philippa.'

'Did he bank with you?'

'You know I can't discuss the bank's business. It's not ethical.'

'You're not a doctor,' Rebus said. 'You just keep people's money for them.'

Marr's eyes narrowed. 'We do a sight more than that.'

'What? You mean lose money for them too?'

Marr leapt to his feet. 'What's this got to do with Philippa's murder?'

'Just answer the question: did Hugo Benzie have his money invested with you?'

'Not with us, *through us.*'

'You advised him?'

Marr refilled his glass. 'We advised him against taking risks.'

'But he wouldn't listen?'

'What's life without a bit of risk: that was Hugo's philosophy. He gambled . . . and lost.'

'Did he hold Balfour's responsible?'

'I don't think so. Poor bugger just did away with himself.'

'What about his wife and daughter? Did they bear a grudge?'

He shook his head. 'They knew what kind of man he was.'

Siobhan handed the sheet of paper to Marr. 'You remember I asked about games?'

'Yes.'

'This clue here.' She pointed to the one relating to Rosslyn Chapel. 'What do you make of it?'

His eyes narrowed. 'Nothing at all,' he said, handing it back.

'May I ask if you're a member of a Masonic lodge, Mr Marr?'

Marr glared at her. Then his eyes flickered in Rebus's direction. 'I'm not going to dignify that question with a response.'

'You see, Philippa was given this clue to solve, and so was I. And when I saw the words "mason's dream", I had to find a member of a lodge to ask what it meant.'

'And what did it mean?'

'That's not important. What *may* be important is whether Philippa sought help along the same lines.'

'I've already told you, I knew nothing about any of this.'

'Any other Masons of her acquaintance, Mr Marr?' Rebus asked.

'I wouldn't know. Look, I really think I've given you enough time. Today of all days.'

'Yes, sir,' Rebus said. 'Thank you for seeing us.' He held out his hand again, but this time Marr didn't take it. He walked to the door in silence, opened it, and walked out. Rebus and Siobhan followed him back down the hallway.

They left the house and got into Rebus's car. He was thoughtful as he eased the vehicle back down the driveway. 'I don't know,' he said. 'Back there, you'd almost have thought Marr had lost his own kid . . .'

'You're not saying . . .?'

'Did he look like Flip at all? I'm useless at that.'

Siobhan thought about it. 'Rich people all look the same to me. You think Marr and Mrs Balfour could have had an affair?'

Rebus shrugged. 'Hard to prove without a blood test.'

'And Claire Benzie?'

'Claire's interesting, but we don't want to rattle her chain. A year or three from now, she could be our friendly local pathologist.'

'Whichever way you look at it, she has every right to feel pissed off with the Balfours.'

'Then how come she was still friends with Flip?'

'Maybe she was playing a game of her own.'

They drove in silence until they'd left Falls far behind.

'Marr's a Mason,' Siobhan said at last. 'And he likes playing games.'

'So now *he's* the Quizmaster rather than Claire Benzie?'

'I think it's more likely than him turning out to be Flip's father.'

'Sorry I spoke.' Rebus was thinking about Hugo Benzie. Before driving out to Falls, he'd rung a lawyer friend and asked about him. Benzie had specialised in wills and trusts, a quiet and efficient solicitor in a large city practice. The rumour was, he'd stuck money into Far East start-ups, guided by tip-offs and his favoured daily paper. If this were true, then Rebus couldn't see Balfour's as culpable. Probably all they'd done was channel the money on his instructions. Benzie hadn't just lost his money, to Rebus's mind, he'd lost something more substantial: his faith in himself. Having stopped believing in himself, it was probably easy to start believing in suicide as an option. Rebus had been there, with the bottle and the darkness for company. But in Benzie's shoes . . . wife and daughter . . . he didn't think he could have done it, leaving behind a devastated family. And now Claire wanted to be a pathologist, a career filled with corpses. Would each body she dealt with be her father's image . . .?

'Penny for them,' Siobhan said.

'No sale,' Rebus replied, fixing his eyes on the road ahead.

'CHEER UP,' Hi-Ho Silvers said, 'it's Friday afternoon.'

'So what?'

He stared at Ellen Wylie. 'Don't tell me you don't have a date lined up. You know: a meal, some dancing, then back to his place.' He started gyrating his hips.

Wylie screwed up her face. 'I'm having trouble keeping my lunch down as it is.'

The remains of the sandwich were on her desk: tuna mayonnaise with sweetcorn. There'd been a slight fizziness to the tuna, and now her stomach was sending her signals.

'Must have a boyfriend though, Ellen?'

'I'll call you when desperation takes hold.'

As Silvers shrugged and moved off, Wylie tried to turn her attention to the story of the German student, Jürgen Becker.

But she felt she'd burned her bridges with Gill Templer, and knew it was all her fault. She'd pushed too hard to be noticed in the hope advancement would follow. She knew she should have kept her head down. That was how Siobhan Clarke worked; she never looked pushy, even though she was every inch the careerist and a rival— Wylie couldn't help but see her that way. Templer's favourite from the start, which was precisely why she—Ellen Wylie—had begun campaigning overtly and, as it turned out, too strenuously. Leaving her isolated, stuck with the Jürgen Becker story.

GRANT HOOD had another press conference to organise. He already knew the names to put to faces, had arranged short get-to-know meetings with the 'majors', these being the more reputable crime reporters of long standing.

'Thing is, Grant,' DCS Templer had confided in him, 'there are some journos we can call our own. They'll toe the line, place a story for us if and when we want them to, while holding back stuff we don't want getting out—but it cuts both ways. We have to give them good copy an hour or two before the oppo.'

'The oppo, ma'am?'

'Opposition. See, they look like a solid mass in the press room, but they're not. In many respects, it's dog eat dog. The hacks who're not in the loop, they're keenest of all, and not likely to be scrupulous. They'll get chequebooks out when it suits, and they'll try to win you over. Not with cash maybe, but with drinks, a bit of dinner. They'll make you feel one of the lads, and that's when you're in trouble, because you might let drop a hint or a teaser, just to show them you're in the know. And whatever you've come out with, you can guarantee they'll print it with knobs on. Never forget which side you're on, or that there *are* sides. OK?' She'd patted his shoulder, and finished by saying: 'Just a word to the wise.'

'Yes, ma'am. Thank you, ma'am.'

Then she'd given him the list of 'majors'.

He'd stuck to coffee and orange juice in each meeting, and was relieved to see most of the journalists doing likewise. Now he was drafting a press release, copies to go to Bill Pryde, Gill Templer and Colin Carswell for their input and approval.

He'd been given his own office at Fettes HQ, for the duration of the inquiry. Carswell, the Assistant Chief Constable, was on another floor in the same building. He'd already knocked on Grant's door and come in to wish him luck. When Grant had introduced himself as Detective Constable Hood, Carswell had said, 'Well, no cockups and a result on this, we'll have to see about doing something better for you, eh?'

Meaning a hike to detective sergeant. He'd have to be careful from now on: careful who he spoke to and what he said, careful who he spent time with, careful what he did.

Careful not to make enemies.

THE CID SUITE at St Leonard's was emptying. Officers not involved in the murder case were clocking off for the weekend.

Siobhan looked at her watch. She'd called the Crime Squad earlier, asked about computers. Claverhouse had said, 'Someone's already on it. We're sending him over.' So now she was waiting. She'd give it another ten minutes then leave. After all, she had her own life, didn't she? Football tomorrow if she wanted it, though it was an away match. Sunday she could go for a drive . . .

'Are you DC Clarke?'

He had a briefcase with him, which he placed on the floor. She was reminded for a second of door-to-door salesmen, cold callers. He was overweight, most of it around the stomach. He introduced himself as Eric Bain.

'I've heard of you,' Siobhan admitted. 'Don't they call you "Brains"?'

'Sometimes, but to be honest I prefer Eric.'

'Eric it is. Make yourself comfortable.'

Bain pulled over a chair. 'So,' he said, 'what have we got?'

Siobhan explained, while Bain gave her his full concentration. At the end of her speech he asked to see the emails on-screen.

So Siobhan booted up the laptop, connecting her mobile while she was at it. 'Shall I check for new messages?'

'Why not?'

There were two from Quizmaster.

Game time is elapsing. Do you wish to continue, Seeker?

An hour later, this had been followed by: *Communication or cessation?*

'Do you want to reply?' Bain asked.

She started to shake her head, then changed it to a shrug. 'I'm not sure what I want to say.'

'Be easier to trace him—or her—if she doesn't shut down.'

She looked at Bain, then typed a reply—*Thinking about it*—and hit SEND. 'Reckon that'll do?' she asked.

'Well, it definitely ranks as "communication".' Bain smiled. 'Now let me have those other messages.'

She hooked up to a printer, and two minutes later she had printed the history of Quizmaster's correspondence.

'See all this?' he asked, pointing to the bottom halves of some of the pages. 'This is the juicy stuff.'

Beneath the word 'Headers' lay more than a dozen lines of extra material: Return-Path, Message-ID, X-Mailer . . . It didn't mean much to Siobhan.

'How come some messages don't have headers?' Siobhan asked.

'That,' Bain said, 'is the bad news. If a message has no headers, it means the sender is using the same service provider you are.'

'But . . .'

Bain was nodding. 'Quizmaster has more than one account.'

'Making him harder to catch?'

'Harder, yes. But he must have set up a payment account with each one. Even if you're on a month's free trial, they'll usually ask for some details first, including a Visa card or bank account.'

'So they can start charging you when the time comes?'

Bain nodded. 'Everyone leaves traces,' he said quietly, staring at the sheets. 'They just don't think they do.'

'So we need to talk to the service providers, get them to hand over his details?'

'If they'll talk to us.'

'This is a murder inquiry,' Siobhan said. 'They'll have to.'

He glanced in her direction. 'There are proper channels, Siobhan. There's a Special Branch unit deals with nothing but high-tech crime. We'll need their help.' He checked his watch. 'And it's too late tonight to do anything about it.' He looked at her. 'Buy you a drink?'

They went across the road to the Maltings. After two drinks Bain said he felt peckish and what about seeing if Howie's had a table. She didn't feel hungry but somehow she found herself unable to say no.

JEAN BURCHILL WAS WORKING late at the museum. Rebus had told her of Professor Devlin's idea that Dr Kennet Lovell had made the coffins, and she had been intrigued. She'd decided to do some investigating of her own, to see if the pathologist's theory could be substantiated. She hadn't come up with much. She knew that she could take a short cut by talking to Devlin himself, but something stopped her. She imagined she could smell formaldehyde on his skin and feel the cold touch of dead flesh when he took her hand.

When her phone rang, she was slow to pick it up.

'Jean?' It was Rebus's voice.

'Hello, John.'

'I was just wondering if you . . .'

'Not tonight, John. I've a lot I want to get done.'

'Fair enough.' He couldn't hide the disappointment in his voice.

'What about this weekend: any plans?'

'Well, that was something I wanted to tell you. I've got two tickets for Lou Reed at the Playhouse tomorrow night. He could be great, could be mince. Only one way to find out.'

'I haven't listened to him in years. All right then, let's do it.'

'Where shall we meet?'

'I've some shopping to do in the morning . . . how about lunch?'

'Great.'

She asked him how the case was progressing. He was reticent, until he remembered something. 'You know Professor Devlin's anatomist?'

'Kennet Lovell?'

'That's the one. I had to interview a medical student, friend of Philippa's. Turns out she's a descendant.'

'Really?' Jean tried not to sound too intrigued. 'Same name?'

'No: Claire Benzie. She's related on her mother's side.'

They chatted for another couple of minutes. Then Jean put the phone down and walked out of her room to the outer office where the secretarial staff sat. Left the door open, so her shadow stretched across the floor. She didn't bother with the lights. Switched the kettle on and rinsed a mug under the tap.

Through the doorway, she could see her desk and the photocopied sheets, all she'd been able to find so far on Dr Kennet Lovell. Kennet. She'd thought the name a misprint at first, but it kept recurring. The initial post-mortem examination of William Burke had been undertaken by Dr Alexander Munro, the Professor of Anatomy. This was followed by a public dissection in the university's packed anatomical theatre. Lovell had assisted. Noisy medical students gathered around like so many vultures, hungry for knowledge, while those without tickets hammered at the doors for entry.

She had worked from history books: some about the Burke and Hare case, others about the history of medicine in Scotland. She hadn't told Rebus about any of this. She was worried that the Arthur's Seat case was a blind alley, and one down which John, with his need for answers, might go careering. This was history—ancient history, compared to the Balfour case. She was conducting this research for her own satisfaction; didn't want John reading anything more into it. He had enough on his plate.

There was a noise in the corridor. When the kettle clicked off, she thought no more about it. Poured the water into her mug, dunked the tea bag a few times, then tipped it into the swing-bin. Took the mug back into her room, leaving the door open.

Kennet Lovell had arrived in Edinburgh from his home in Coylton, Ayrshire, in December 1822, aged barely fifteen. His parents were farming folk, and he had been educated locally, helped by the local church minister, Reverend Kirkpatrick. One historian, in a book about Burke and Hare, speculated that Kirkpatrick had given Lovell an introduction to a friend, Dr Knox, recently returned from overseas. Knox had housed young Lovell for the first year or so of his life in Edinburgh. But when Lovell had started university, the two seemed to have drifted apart, and Lovell moved to lodgings in West Port . . .

Jean sipped her tea and flipped through the photocopied sheets: no footnotes or index, nothing to indicate the provenance of these apparent 'facts'. More frustrating still, Kennet Lovell was a bit-player in the Burke and Hare story, existing only for that one gruesome scene. Three years after the Burke autopsy he seemed to be in Africa, combining much-needed medical skills with Christian missionary work. His reappearance in Scotland came in the late 1840s. He set up a medical practice in the New Town, his clients probably reflecting the wealth of that enclave. One historian's supposition had it that he had been bequeathed the bulk of the Reverend Kirkpatrick's estate, having 'kept in good graces with that gentleman by dint of regular correspondence down the years'. Jean would have liked to see those letters. She made a note to try tracking them down. The parish in Ayrshire might have some record, or someone at Surgeons' Hall might know.

'Monday,' she said out loud. It could wait till Monday. She had the weekend to look forward to . . . and a Lou Reed concert to survive.

Switching off her light, she heard another noise, much closer. The door to the outer office swung open and the lights all came on. Jean took half a step back, then saw it was just the cleaner.

'You gave me a fright,' she said, putting a hand to her chest.

The cleaner just smiled and put a bin-bag down. 'Mind if I get started?' she asked.

'Go ahead,' Jean said. 'I'm finished here anyway.'

As she tidied her desk, she noticed that her heart was still racing, her hands shaking slightly. She often wandered through the museum at night. This was the first time she'd been spooked.

'Heading straight home?' the cleaner asked.

'Might make a pit-stop at the off-licence.'

'Kill or cure, eh?' the cleaner said.

'Something like that,' Jean replied, as an unwanted image of her husband flashed up in her mind. Then she thought of something and walked back to her desk. Added a name to her notes.

Claire Benzie.

'SHALL WE GET A DRINK?' Jean suggested after the concert at the Playhouse. They'd been drinking on and off all afternoon and evening: wine with lunch, then a quick one at the Oxford Bar. A long walk down to Dean Village and along the Water of Leith. They'd considered an early supper, but were still full from the Café St Honoré. Walked back up Leith Walk to the Playhouse. Still early, so they'd gone to the Playhouse bar for one. Now, just gone eleven on a Saturday night, the street was noisy with alcohol.

'Where do you suggest?' Jean asked. Rebus made a show of checking his watch. There were plenty of bars he could think of, but they weren't places he wanted Jean to see.

'Could you stand a bit more music?'

'What kind?'

'Acoustic. It'd be standing room only.'

She was thoughtful. 'Is it between here and your flat?'

He nodded. 'You know the place is a tip . . .'

She laughed, squeezed his hand. 'Are you doing this on purpose?'

'What?'

'Trying to put me off.'

'No, it's just . . . I just don't want you—'

She interrupted him with a kiss. 'I won't be,' she said.

He ran a hand up her arm, let it rest on her shoulder. 'Still want that drink first?'

'I think so. How far is it?'

'Just up the Bridges. Pub's called the Royal Oak.'

'Then lead me to it.'

They walked hand in hand in silence until Jean said, 'Is there a twenty-four-hour shop somewhere on the route?'

'More than one. Why?'

'Breakfast: something tells me your fridge won't exactly be an Aladdin's Cave.'

MONDAY MORNING, Ellen Wylie was back at her own desk in what everyone in the force referred to as 'West End', meaning the police station on Torphichen Street. When they passed her, her colleagues asked about the Balfour case. She was waiting for someone to say something about her TV appearance, but no one did. Maybe they were taking pity on the afflicted, or just showing solidarity.

'Reassigned?' Shug Davidson guessed.

She shook her head. 'I'm following a lead. It's as easy to do it here as there.'

'Ah, but here you're a long way from the big picture, the *centre* of everything.'

'I'm at the centre of the West End,' she told him. 'That's good enough for me.' Earned herself a wink from Davidson and a round of applause from Reynolds. She smiled: she was back home.

It had niggled at her all weekend: the way she'd been sidelined—bumped from liaison and dropped off at the twilight zone in which DI John Rebus worked. And from there to this—a tourist's suicide from years back—seemed yet another snub. So she'd come to a decision: if they didn't want her, she didn't need them. Welcome back to the West End. She felt safe here, and here she could safely reach the conclusion that she was on another wild-goose chase.

Now all she had to do was prove it to Gill Templer's satisfaction.

She'd called the police station in Fort William and spoken to a very helpful sergeant called Donald Maclay, who remembered the case well. 'The upper slope of Ben Dorchory,' he told her. 'The body had been there a couple of months. It's a remote spot. A gillie happened on the scene; could have lain there years otherwise. Nothing in the way of ID on the body. So we talked to the B and Bs and hotels, checked the Missing Persons records.'

'What about the gun? Did you get any prints?'

'After that length of time? No, we didn't.'

Wylie was writing everything down, abbreviating most of the words. 'Gunpowder traces?'

'No. The pathologist didn't find any burning or residues, but then this wasn't like a body, more a scarecrow. The skin was like parchment. There's a hellish wind blows across that hill.'

'You didn't treat it as suspicious?'

'We went by the autopsy findings.'

'Any chance you can send me the file?'

'If we get a written request, sure.'

'Thanks.' She tapped her pen against the desk. 'The gun was how far away?'

'Maybe twenty feet.'

'You think an animal moved it?'

'Yes. Either that or it was a reflex thing. Put a gun to your head and pull the trigger, there's going to be a recoil, isn't there?'

'I'd think so.' She paused. 'So what happened next?'

'Well, eventually we tried facial reconstruction, then issued the composite photo. Nothing very much happened until we got this call from Munich, from the Germans. Next thing, the parents turned up at the station. We showed them the clothes and they recognised a couple of things . . . the jacket and a wristwatch.'

'You don't sound convinced.'

'To tell you the truth, I'm not. A year they'd been looking for him, going out of their minds. The jacket was just a plain green thing, nothing special about it. Same goes for the watch.'

'You think they managed to convince themselves simply because they *wanted* to believe?'

'Wanted it to be him, yes. But their son was barely twenty . . . experts told us we had the remains of someone twice that age. Then the bloody papers went and printed the story anyway.'

'How did all the sword-and-sorcery stuff come into the picture?'

'First we knew about that was when they put it in the paper. The parents again, they'd been talking to some reporter.'

Wylie held the article in front of her. The headline: DID ROLE GAME KILL IN HIGHLAND GUN MYSTERY? The reporter was Steve Holly.

Jürgen Becker was a twenty-year-old student who lived with his parents, both professionals, in a suburb of Hamburg. He attended the local university, specialising in psychology. He loved role-playing games, and was part of a team who played in an inter-university league on the Internet. Fellow students said that he'd been 'anxious and troubled' during the week leading up to his disappearance. When he left home for that last time, he took a backpack with him. In it were his passport, a couple of changes of clothes, his camera, and a portable CD player with maybe a dozen or so discs.

'The backpack and stuff, they never turned up?' Wylie asked.

'Never. But then if it wasn't him, you wouldn't expect them to.'

She smiled. 'You've been a real help, Sergeant Maclay. Thanks.'

STEVE HOLLY WAS STILL on his way into work when his mobile sounded. He lived in the New Town, only three streets from what he'd recently called in print 'the tragic death flat'. Not that his own place was in the same league as Flip Balfour's. He was at the top of an unmodernised tenement—one of few still left in the New Town. And his street didn't have the cachet of Flip's address.

He stopped to answer his mobile. 'Steve Holly speaking.'

'Mr Holly, this is DS Wylie, Lothian and Borders CID.'

Wylie? He tried to place her. Of course! That brilliant press conference! 'Yes, DS Wylie, and what can I do for you this morning?'

'It's about a story you ran three years back—the German student.'

'Would that be the student with the twenty-foot reach?' he asked with a grin.

'That's the one, yes.'

'What's it got to do with Philippa Balfour?' he asked.

Silence on the line. 'Sorry?'

'Last time I saw you, DS Wylie, you were attached to the Balfour case. Are you saying they've suddenly shifted you onto a case that isn't even in the Lothian and Borders remit?'

'I . . .'

'You're probably not at liberty to say, right? Me, on the other hand, I can say whatever I like.'

'The way you made up that sword-and-sorcery stuff?'

'That wasn't made up. I got it from the parents.'

'That he liked role-playing, yes, but the idea that it was some game brought him to Scotland?'

'Speculation based on the available evidence. Highland mountains, all that Celtic myth rubbish . . . just the place someone like Jürgen would end up. Sent out on some quest, only there's a gun waiting for him when he gets there.'

'Yes, I read your story.'

'And somehow it ties in with Flip Balfour, but you're not going to tell me how?' Holly licked his lips; he was enjoying this.

'That's right,' Wylie said.

'It must have hurt when they pulled you from liaison,' he said, solicitously. 'Not your fault, was it? They should have prepared you better. Christ, Gill Templer worked liaison for a hundred years . . . she should have *known*.'

Another silence on the line. Holly softened his voice. 'And then they go and give it to a detective *constable*. DC Grant Hood. Now there's one cocky little bastard if ever I saw one. Like I say, something like that's got to hurt.'

He thought she'd gone, but then heard something which was almost a sigh. Oh, you're good, Stevie boy, he thought to himself. You'll have the right address some day.

'Sorry if I hit a nerve, Sergeant Wylie. But look, maybe we could meet. I think I might just have a way to help, even if only a little.'

'What is it?' The voice hardening. 'Tell me now.'

'Well . . .' Holly angled his head towards the sun. 'Say this thing you're working on . . . it's confidential, right?' He took a breath. 'Don't answer that. We both know already. But say someone . . . a journalist, for example . . . got hold of this story. People would want to know how he got it, and do you know who they'd look to first?'

'Who?'

'The liaison officer. And if a certain journalist—the one in possession of the leak—happened to . . . well, *indicate* that his source was not a thousand miles from the liaison officer . . . I'm sorry, it probably sounds petty to you; you probably don't want to see DC Hood with mud on his new starched shirt. It's just that when I start thinking something, I need to go the whole way. Do you know what I'm saying? I'm free all morning. I've already told you what you need to know about Mountain Boy, but we could talk anyway . . .'

REBUS WALKED into the Caledonian. The 'Caley' was an Edinburgh institution, a red-stone monolith at the west end of Princes Street.

The receptionist smiled at him. 'Mr Costello's expecting you.' She gave him the room number and directed him towards the lifts. A liveried porter was hovering, but one look at Rebus told him there was no work for him here.

How the other half live, Rebus thought as the lift glided upwards.

It wasn't a room after all, but a suite, with a connecting door to the suite next to it. Rebus caught a glimpse of Theresa Costello before her husband closed the door. The living area was compact: sofa, chair, table, TV. There was a bedroom off, and a bathroom down the hall. David Costello was sitting at the table. He had shaved, but his hair was unwashed, lank and greasy. His grey T-shirt looked new, as did the black denims.

Thomas Costello was shorter than Rebus had imagined him, a boxer's roll to his shoulders when he walked. His mauve shirt was open-necked, and his trousers were held up with pale pink braces.

'Come in, come in,' he said, 'sit yourself down.' He gestured towards the sofa. Rebus, however, took the armchair, so the father sank into the sofa himself, spreading his arms out either side of him.

'I'm sorry I have to intrude at a time like this, Mr Costello.' Rebus glanced towards David.

'We quite understand, Inspector. You've got a job to do, and we all want to help you catch the sick bastard who did this to Philippa.' Costello clenched his fists, showing he was ready to do some damage to the culprit himself.

'Well, Mr Costello, I just have some follow-up questions . . .'

'And do you mind me staying while you ask them?'

'Not at all. It may even be that you can help.'

'Fire away then,' he told Rebus.

Rebus took aim and fired. 'David, we've asked you about this Internet game we think Flip might have been playing . . .'

'Yes.'

'And you said you didn't know anything about it, and didn't go much for computer games and suchlike.'

'Yes.'

'But now we hear that in your schooldays you were a bit of a whiz at dungeons and dragons.'

'Who told you I was a "whiz"?' David asked. 'Because I wasn't. The D and D craze lasted about a month.'

'Flip played, too, when she was at school, did you know that?'

'I don't think the subject ever came up.'

'Then how would Flip's friend Claire have got to hear of it?'

The young man snorted. '*She* told you? Claire the Cow?'

Thomas Costello tutted.

'Well, she is,' his son snapped back. 'She was always trying to break us up, pretending she was a "friend".'

'She didn't like you?'

David considered this. 'I think it was more that she couldn't bear to see Flip happy. There was some history between her family and Claire's, and I think Flip felt guilty. Claire was a real blind spot.'

'Why didn't you tell us this before?'

David laughed. 'Because Claire didn't kill Flip.'

'No?'

'Christ, you're not saying . . .' He shook his head. 'I mean, it was just mind games with her, just words.'

'We're keeping an open mind,' Rebus said.

'Davey,' the father said, 'if there's anything you need to tell these officers, get it off your chest!'

'It's *David*!' the young man spat. His father looked furious, but didn't say anything.

'What about Flip's mother?' Rebus asked casually. 'How did you get on with her?'

'Fine.'

Rebus allowed the silence to linger, then repeated the word back at David, this time as a question.

'You know how mothers are with daughters,' David started to add. 'Protective and all that.'

'Rightly so, eh?' Thomas Costello winked at Rebus.

'Thing is, David,' Rebus said quietly, 'we've reason to believe there might have been a bit of friction there, too.'

'I've no idea what you mean.'

'I mean,' Rebus said, 'that Mrs Balfour harboured the thought that you'd somehow poisoned Flip's mind.'

'You must have misheard the lady,' Thomas Costello said. 'Look at the strain she's been under . . . doesn't know what she's saying.'

'I think she knew.' Rebus was still looking at David.

'It's right enough,' he said. 'Jacqueline had some notion that I was giving Flip ideas.'

'What sort of ideas?'

'That she hadn't had a happy childhood. That she was remembering it all wrong.'

'And did you think she was?' Rebus asked.

'It was Flip, not me,' David stated. 'She'd been having this dream, most nights for a fortnight. She was back at the house in London, running up and down stairs trying to get away from something. I told her it might be to do with repressed memory.'

'The boy's lost me,' Thomas Costello admitted.

His son turned his head towards him. 'A repressed memory is something bad that you've managed not to think about. I was quite envious, actually.' They stared at one another. Rebus thought he knew what David was talking about: growing up with Thomas Costello couldn't have been easy.

'And Flip told her mother about the dreams?'

David nodded. 'Who then blamed the whole thing on me.'

'Bloody woman,' Thomas Costello hissed. He rubbed his forehead. 'But then she's been under a lot of strain, lot of strain . . .'

'This was before Flip went missing,' Rebus reminded him.

'I don't mean that: I mean Balfour's,' Costello growled.

Rebus frowned. 'What about Balfour's?'

'Lots of money men in Dublin. You get to hear rumours. Overstretched . . . liquidity ratios . . . just words to me.'

'You're saying Balfour's Bank is in trouble?'

Costello shook his head. 'Just a few stories that they might be headed that way if they don't turn things around.'

Rebus got the feeling Costello wouldn't have said anything, but Jacqueline Balfour's accusations against his son had tipped the balance. He made his first note of the interview: *Check Balfour's*.

'Will that do you for now, Inspector?' Costello said, making show of reaching into his trousers and drawing out a pocket watch.

'Just about,' Rebus admitted. 'Unless there's anything either of you would like to add?'

There wasn't. Costello insisted on seeing him to the door, shook his hand. David didn't get up from his chair.

BACK IN ST LEONARD'S, Rebus phoned a contact on a Sunday newspaper's business pages.

'How sound is Balfour's?' he asked, no preamble. 'I've heard there are rumours.'

The journalist chuckled. 'Ah, rumours, where would the world be without them?'

'Then there's no problem?'

'I didn't say that. On paper, Balfour's is ticking along as ever. But their half-year forecast has been revised downwards; not quite enough to give big investors the jitters, but Balfour's is a loose affiliation of smaller investors who have a tendency towards hypochondria.'

'Bottom line, Terry?'

'Balfour's should survive. But if the balance sheet looks murky at year's end, there may have to be one or two ritual beheadings.'

Rebus was thoughtful. 'Who would go?'

'Ranald Marr, I should think, if only to show that Balfour himself has the ruthlessness necessary for this day and age.'

'No place for old friendships?'

'Truth be told, there never was.'

'Thanks, Terry. A large G and T will be waiting for you behind the bar of the Ox.'

When he put the phone down, Rebus scribbled the name Marr onto his pad and circled it. Ranald Marr, with his Maserati and toy soldiers. *You'd almost have thought Marr had lost his own kid . . .* Rebus was beginning to revise that opinion. He wondered if Marr knew how precarious his job was, knew that the small investors might start demanding a sacrifice . . .

He stood up and walked over to Siobhan who was sitting at her desk. Brains was sitting with her.

'Hello, Brains,' Rebus said.

'His name's Bain,' Siobhan corrected. 'He likes to be called Eric.'

Rebus ignored this. 'It's like the deck of the Starship *Enterprise* in here.' He was looking at the array of computers and connections: two laptops, two PCs. He knew one of the PCs was Siobhan's, the other Flip Balfour's. 'Tell me,' he asked her, 'what do we know about Philippa's early life in London?'

She wrinkled her nose, thinking. 'Not much. Why?'

'Because the boyfriend says she had these nightmares, running up and down the London house being chased by something.'

'Sure it was the London house?'

'What do you mean?'

She shrugged. 'Just that Junipers gave me the heebies: suits of armour and dusty billiard rooms . . . imagine growing up with that.'

'David Costello said the London house.'

'Transference?' Bain suggested. They both looked at him. 'Just a thought,' he said.

Siobhan turned back to Rebus. 'You want the lowdown on Flip's London years?'

He began to nod, then shook his head. 'No,' he said, 'you're right . . . it's too far-fetched.'

As he moved away, Siobhan turned to Bain. 'That's usually right up his street,' she said. 'The more far-fetched, the better he likes it.'

Bain smiled.

After the meal on Friday night they'd said their goodbyes. Siobhan had got into her car Saturday morning and headed north for the football with an overnight bag. Found herself a guesthouse. Good win for Hibs in the afternoon, then a bit of exploring and a spot of dinner. A weekend without Quizmaster: just what the doctor ordered. Except that she couldn't stop thinking about him, wondering if there was a message on the laptop back at her flat. Now the computer sat on her desk. She was almost afraid to touch it, afraid to give in to the craving . . .

'So what do we do now? Get on to Special Branch?' she asked.

'We talk to the Crime Squad. They route our request.'

'Go ahead then,' she said.

So Bain picked up the phone and had a long conversation with DI Claverhouse at the Big House. While he was busy, Siobhan decided to connect to the Net, just to give her something to do.

There were three messages from Quizmaster. The first was from Friday evening, around the time she got home: *Seeker—My patience wears thin. The quest is about to close on you. Immediate response requested.*

The second was from Saturday afternoon: *Siobhan? I'm disappointed in you. Game is now closed.*

Closed or not, he'd come back on Sunday at midnight:

Are you busy tracing me, is that it? Do you still want to meet?

Bain ended his conversation and put down the phone. He was staring at the screen. 'You've got him rattled,' he said.

'New ISP?' Siobhan asked. Bain checked the headers and nodded.

'You really think the game's closed?' she asked.

'Only one way to find out . . .'

So Siobhan got busy on the keyboard: *I was away all weekend, that's all. Inquiry progresses. Meantime, yes, I'd still like to meet.*

She sent the message. They went and grabbed coffee, but when they came back there was no reply.

'Is he sulking?' Siobhan asked.

'Or away from his machine.' Bain shifted his chair towards the desk. 'While we're waiting, maybe we should take a look at Ms Balfour's deleted files.' He saw the look on her face. 'You know you can undelete files?'

'Sure. We already looked at her correspondence.'

'But did you look at her emails?'

Siobhan was forced to admit she hadn't. Or rather, Grant hadn't known it could be done.

Bain got to work on Flip's PC. Soon they were staring at a list of deleted messages, stretching right back to when she first got the computer. It didn't take long to find something more interesting than gossipy exchanges between Flip and her friends.

'Look at this,' Siobhan said, pointing at the screen.

'It's from Balfour's Bank,' Bain said. 'Someone called RAM.'

'I'm willing to bet it's Ranald Marr.' Siobhan read the note.

> *Flip, Great news that at last you are part of the virtual world! You'll also find the Internet a great research tool to help you with your studies. Yes, you're right that you can delete messages—it makes space in the memory, and allows your computer to work more quickly. But remember that deleted messages are still recoverable unless you take certain steps. Here's how to delete something completely.*

The writer went on to explain the process. He signed himself 'R'.

Bain ran a finger down one edge of the screen. 'Explains why there are big gaps,' he said. 'Once he'd told her how to fully delete, she started doing it. Also explains why there are none of the messages to or from Quizmaster. Not even her original message to RAM.'

Siobhan rubbed at her temples. 'Why would she want everything deleted anyway?'

'I don't know. It's not something most users would think to do.'

The phone rang and Bain answered. It was a Special Branch officer called Black. When Bain came off the phone five minutes later, he puffed out his cheeks and exhaled noisily. 'They want copies of all the emails between you and Quizmaster, plus details of Philippa Balfour's ISP account and user names, plus the same for you.'

'Except it's Grant Hood's machine,' Siobhan said.

'Well, his account details then.' He paused. 'Black asked if we had any suspects.'

'What did you say?'

'I said we don't have enough evidence yet. But you think it's Marr, don't you?' he said quietly.

She nodded.

'We could always send him Marr's name. We could even provide his email address,' he suggested.

'Would that help?'

'It might. You know the Americans can read emails using satellites? Any emails in the world . . .' She just stared at him, and he laughed. 'I'm not saying Special Branch have that sort of technology, but you never know, do you?'

Siobhan was thoughtful. 'Then give them what we've got. Give them Ranald Marr.'

The laptop told them they had a message. Siobhan clicked it open. Quizmaster.

Seeker—We meet on completion of Stricture. Acceptable?

'Ooh,' Bain said, 'he's actually *asking* you.'

She typed another message: *There are questions need answering.*

An immediate reply: *Ask, Seeker.*

So she asked: *Was anyone playing the game apart from Flip?*

Yes.

How many? Siobhan typed.

Three.

Did they know who they were playing against?

A thirty-second pause. *Absolutely not.*

Siobhan got to work on her next message: *Can you tell me who they were? Do you know who they are?*

The reply was immediate. *No to both. Stricture clue will follow.*

'I think he's had enough,' Bain said. 'Probably not used to his slaves talking back.'

Siobhan nodded her agreement.

'I don't think I'm Grant Hood's standard,' Bain added. She frowned, not understanding. 'In the puzzle-solving department,' he explained.

'Let's wait and see about that.'

'Meantime, I can get that stuff PDQ'd to SB.'

'AOK,' Siobhan said with a smile. She was thinking of Grant again. She wouldn't have got this far without him. Yet since his transfer he hadn't shown the least curiosity, hadn't so much as called to find out if there were some new clue to be solved. She wondered at his ability to switch focus so completely. And she hoped that when Stricture came through, the busy Grant might spare a minute for his old sparring partner, whether Gill Templer liked it or not.

GRANT HOOD had spent the morning dealing with the press, reworking the daily news release for later in the day, and fielding calls from the victim's father, who was angry that more broadcast time wasn't being given to appeals for information.

He hadn't had time for lunch, and breakfast had been a bacon roll from the canteen, almost six hours ago. He was aware of politics all around him—the politics of Police HQ. Carswell and Templer might agree on some things, but never on everything, and he was poised between them, trying not to fall too fatally into either camp.

He knew he was coping so far, but only by dint of forgoing food, sleep and free time. On the plus side, the case was now garnering interest from further afield: New York, Sydney, Singapore and Toronto. He jotted down the details of each international press agency, with contact numbers and even a note of the time difference.

'No point me sending you faxes in the middle of the night,' he'd told one news editor in New Zealand.

'I'd prefer an email, mate.'

It struck him then that he needed to get his laptop back from Siobhan. He hadn't thought of her in a couple of days. His 'crush' on her hadn't lasted long. Just as well they hadn't taken any further, really: his new job would have driven a wedge between them.

His phone rang again. He leaned back in his chair, taking the receiver with him. 'DC Hood.'

'It's Steve Holly.'

'Steve, what can I do for you?' But the tone was immediately professional. Gill Templer had warned him about Holly, who was definitely not on her list of 'majors'.

'Well, Grant.' Holly managed to get a sneer into the word. 'I was just after a quote to go with a piece I'm running. Women going missing . . . dolls found at the scene . . . games on the Internet . . . students dead on hillsides. Any of it ring a bell?'

Grant thought he'd squeeze the life out of the receiver. The desk, the walls, they'd all gone hazy. 'Case like this, Steve,' he said, attempting levity, 'a reporter will hear all kinds of stuff.'

'Believe you solved some of the Internet clues yourself, Grant. What do you reckon? Got to be connected to the murder, haven't they?'

'I've no comment to make on that, Mr Holly. Look, whatever you think you may know, you've got to understand that stories—true or false—can do irreparable damage to an investigation.'

'Look, Grant, admit it: you're stuffed on this one. Best thing you can do is fill me in on the small print.'

'I don't think so.'

'Sure about that? Tasty new posting you've got there . . . I'd hate to see you go down in flames.'

'Something tells me you'd like nothing better, Holly.'

The telephone receiver laughed into Grant's ear. 'Something this big, Grant, you can never keep it watertight.'

'So who punched the hole through the hull?'

'A whisper here, a whisper there . . . you know how it is.' Holly paused. 'Oh no, that's right—you *don't* know how it is. I keep forgetting, you've only been in the job five minutes, and already you think you can lord it over the likes of me.'

'I don't know what—'

'Those little individual briefings, just you and your favoured poodles. It's the likes of *me* you should be looking out for.'

'Thanks, I will,' said Grant. 'Look, on the record, we don't know that any of the stuff is pertinent to the current case.'

'It's still news.'

'And possibly prejudicial.'

'So sue me. Get in the queue.'

Grant was about to put down the phone, but Holly beat him to it. He got up and kicked the desk, then kicked it again. *I have to go to Carswell with this. I have to tell Gill Templer!* Templer first . . . chain of command. Then *she'd* have to break the news to the ACC. There might even be time for a court injunction.

He picked up the phone, shut his eyes in silent prayer.

JEAN BURCHILL HAD SPENT much of her day trying to trace the correspondence between Kennet Lovell and the Reverend Kirkpatrick. She'd spoken to people in Alloway and Ayr—the parish minister; a local historian; one of Kirkpatrick's descendants. She'd spent over an hour on the phone to the Mitchell Library in Glasgow. Then she'd headed for Surgeons' Hall, where she'd stared long and hard at the portrait of Kennet Lovell. He had been a handsome young man. Often in portraits, the artist left little clues as to the character he was painting: profession, family, hobbies. But the sheer plainness of the Lovell portrait bothered her. Either the painter had had little enthusiasm for the commission, or the subject had given little away. This young man, hardly out of his teens at the time, had assisted in the Burke autopsy. According to one report: 'by the time the lecture was finished the classroom had the appearance of a butcher's slaughterhouse'. Jean stared into Kennet Lovell's eyes again. The black pupils seemed luminous, despite the horrors they'd witnessed.

Or, she couldn't help wondering, *because* of them?

The curator wasn't able to add much to what Jean already knew.

'I'm also interested in Lovell's correspondence,' Jean tried.

'Yes, well, we would be, too.'

'You don't have *anything*?' She was surprised.

The curator shook his head. 'Either Dr Lovell wasn't a great man for the pen, or else they've perished.' He sighed. 'A great pity. We know so little about his time in Africa.'

'Or in Edinburgh, come to that.'

'He's buried here. His grave's in Calton cemetery.'

'I might as well take a look.'

'I'm sorry I can't be more help.' Then his face brightened. 'Donald Devlin's supposed to have some table made by Lovell.'

'Yes, I know, though there's nothing in the literature about an interest in carpentry.'

'I seem to recall reading something somewhere . . .' But try as he might, he couldn't remember what or where.

 Chapter Seven

By the time Assistant Chief Constable Colin Carswell arrived at Gayfield Square on that Tuesday morning, he was out for blood.

John Balfour had bawled him out; Balfour's lawyer had done his damage more subtly, his voice never wavering in its professional tones. Still, Carswell felt bruised, and he wanted some measure of revenge. The Chief Constable was remaining aloof—*his* position had to be maintained at all costs. This was Carswell's mess, one he'd spent all the previous evening surveying.

The best minds in the Procurator Fiscal's office had pored over the problem and had concluded that there was little chance of blocking the story. After all, they couldn't prove that either the dolls or the German student had anything to do with the Balfour case, and so would find it difficult to persuade a judge that Holly's information could, once published, be detrimental to the inquiry.

What Balfour and his lawyer wanted to know was why the police hadn't seen fit to share with them the story of the dolls, or the information about the German student and the Internet game.

What the Chief Constable wanted to know was what Carswell

intended doing about it. And what Carswell wanted was blood.

The briefing room was packed with officers—everyone who had worked or was working on the Balfour case.

'Here he comes,' someone said as Carswell's car drew up outside. There was a sound of folding paper as the fresh tabloids were closed and put out of sight. DCS Templer, dressed as though for a funeral, came into the room first, followed by DI Bill Pryde. When Carswell himself walked in, there was a ripple of movement as officers subconsciously corrected their posture.

'We've got ourselves a mole,' he bawled. No 'good morning', no 'thank you all for coming', the usual protocols forgotten. He nodded slowly, eyes trying to take in every face in front of him. When he saw that there were people at the back, out of staring range, he walked up the aisle between the desks. 'A mole's always an ugly little thing. It lacks vision. Sometimes it has big greedy paws. It doesn't like to be exposed.' There were flecks of saliva either side of his mouth. 'I find a mole in my garden, I put down poison. Moles make everything ugly, and that's why they have to be eradicated.' He walked back down the aisle.

'Someone like Steven Holly, he's lower than a mole on the evolutionary ladder. He's pond life. He's the scum you sometimes see there.' He waved a hand slowly in front of him, as if skimming water. 'I'm going to find whoever talked to him. Don't think I won't. And don't think you can trust Mr Steven Holly to protect you. If you want to stay buried, you'll have to feed him more stories, and more, and more! He's not going to let you rise back up to the world you knew before. You're different now. You're a mole. *His* mole. And he'll never let you forget it.'

A glance in Gill Templer's direction. She was standing by the wall, arms folded, her own eyes scanning the room.

'If the person responsible wants to come forward, that's fine. You can do it now, or later. Think what's at stake if you don't. Not part of a team any more, not on the side of the angels. But in a journalist's pocket. For as long as he wants you there.' This final pause seemed to last an eternity. Carswell slid his hands into his pockets, head angled as though inspecting his shoes. 'DCS Templer?' he said.

And now Gill Templer stepped forward. 'OK, there's been a leak to the press, and what we need now is some damage limitation. Nobody talks to anybody unless they run it past me first, understood?' There were murmurs of assent.

Templer went on, but Rebus wasn't listening. His attention had been mostly on the people around him. Gill Templer and Bill Pryde were distant figures, whose discomfort he could almost ignore. Bill's big chance to shine; Gill's first major inquiry as a DCS. Hardly what either of them would have wanted.

And closer to home: Siobhan, concentrating hard on the ACC's speech, maybe learning something from it. Grant Hood, someone else with everything to lose, dejection written into his face and shoulders. A leak to the press, you looked at liaison first. Even if not to blame, a good liaison officer might have been all that was needed in the way of Gill's 'damage limitation'.

Rebus wondered at the extent of the damage. Quizmaster would now know what he'd probably always suspected: that it wasn't just him and Siobhan, that she was keeping her colleagues apprised. Rebus knew she was already wondering how to handle it, how to phrase her next communication with Quizmaster, supposing he wanted to keep playing . . . The Arthur's Seat coffins connection annoyed him because Jean had been mentioned by name in the story, cited as 'the museum's expert' on the case. Could she have said something to him unwittingly? He didn't think so.

No, he had the culprit in his sights. Ellen Wylie looked like she'd been wrung out. Her eyes had a resigned look. She'd kept staring at the floor during Carswell's speech, and hadn't shifted now.

Holly had got to her, he felt sure.

Wylie had probably seen it as a way of getting back at all of them: Gill Templer, cause of her public humiliation; Siobhan, for whom Templer still had such high hopes; Grant Hood, the new golden boy, coping where Wylie had not . . . And Rebus, too, the manipulator, getting her to do the hard graft on his case.

But now ACC Carswell was reading from a list of names, and Rebus caught his own as Carswell snapped it out. DC Hood . . . DC Clarke . . . DS Wylie . . . The coffins; the German student—they'd worked those cases, and now the ACC wanted to see them. Faces turned, curious. Carswell was announcing that he'd see them in the 'boss's office', meaning the station commander's.

'You've already heard my spiel,' Carswell told them when they'd all settled in the office. 'So I won't bore you again. If the leak came from anywhere, it came from one of you. That little shit Holly knew way too much.' His mouth snapped shut.

'With respect, sir,' Siobhan Clarke said, 'we've had to ask questions, put out feelers. Steve Holly could just have been putting two and two together.'

Carswell just stared at her, then said: 'DCS Templer?'

'Steve Holly,' Templer began, 'not the brightest bulb in the chandelier, but he's as sneaky as they come, and ruthless with it. Some of the other journos, yes, I think they could take what's out there in the public domain and make something of it, but not Holly. And he shouldn't have even known about the gaming connection.'

'There's been outside assistance,' Grant Hood argued. 'A museum curator, a retired pathologist . . .'

Rebus laid a hand on Hood's arm, silencing him. 'It was me,' he said. Heads turned towards him. 'I think it might have been me.'

He concentrated on not looking in Ellen Wylie's direction, but was aware of her eyes burning into him.

'Early on, I was out at Falls talking to a woman called Bev Dodds. She'd found the coffin by the waterfall. Steve Holly had already been sniffing around, and she'd given him the story . . . I let it slip that there'd been more coffins . . . let slip to her, I mean.' He was remembering the slip that Jean had in fact made. 'If she yapped to Holly, he'd have been on a flier. I had Jean Burchill with me—she's a curator. That might have given him the Arthur's Seat connection.'

Carswell was staring at him coldly. 'And the Internet game?'

Rebus shook his head. 'That one I can't explain, but it's not exactly a well-kept secret. We've been shoving the clues at all the victim's friends, asking if she'd asked them for help . . . any one of them could have told Holly.'

Carswell was still staring. 'You're taking the fall for this?'

'I'm saying it could be my fault. Just that one slip.' He turned to the others. 'I can't begin to tell you how sorry I am.'

'Sir,' Siobhan Clarke said, 'what DI Rebus has just admitted could go for any one of us. I'm sure I may have said a little more than I should on occasion.'

Carswell wafted his hand in front of him, quieting her. 'DI Rebus,' he said, 'I'm suspending you from active duty, pending further enquiries.'

'You can't do that!' Ellen Wylie blurted out.

'DI Rebus knows the consequences,' Carswell was saying.

Rebus nodded. 'Someone needs to be punished.' He paused. 'For the sake of the team.'

'That's right,' Carswell said, nodding. 'Go home, DI Rebus. Write your version down leaving nothing out. We'll talk again later.'

HE WAS SITTING in the living room of his flat, staring out of the window, when the call came.

It was Gill Templer. Her opening words: 'You stupid bastard. You could have kept your mouth shut.'

'I just told the truth,' he said.

'*That* would be a first . . . not that I believe it for a minute. Ellen Wylie practically had "guilty" stamped on her forehead.'

'You think I was shielding her?'

'I don't exactly take you for Sir Galahad. You'll have had your reasons. Maybe it was simply to piss off Carswell; you know he hates your guts.'

Rebus didn't like to concede that she might be right. 'How's every-thing else?' he asked.

'Liaison's snowed under. I'm giving a helping hand.'

Rebus bet she was busy: all the other papers and media trying to play catch-up with Steve Holly.

'What about you?' she asked. 'What are you going to do?'

'I haven't really thought about it.'

'Well . . .'

'I'd better let you get back, Gill. Thanks for calling.'

'Bye, John.'

Rebus went to the kitchen to make a mug of tea, and discovered he was out of milk. Without bothering with a jacket, he headed out to the local deli, where he added some ham and rolls to the shopping. Back at the main door to the tenement, someone was trying one of the buzzers. 'Come on, I know you're there.'

'Hello, Siobhan.'

She turned and put a hand to her throat. 'Christ, you gave me a . . .'

Rebus unlocked the door. 'Because I sneaked up on you, or because you thought I was sitting upstairs with my wrists slashed?' He held the door open for her.

'What? No, that's not what I was thinking.' But the colour was rising to her cheeks.

He preceded her up the stairs, opened his front door.

'It's your lucky day,' he said. 'Not only am I not dead, but I can offer tea and rolls with ham and mustard.'

'Just tea, thanks,' she said, finally regaining some composure.

Rebus went into the kitchen and stuck the kettle on, found two clean mugs in the cupboard. He called out, 'So, are you here to check up on me or thank me for sticking my neck out?'

'I'm not about to thank you for *that*,' she said, coming into the kitchen. 'You could have stayed quiet, and you know it. If you owned up, it was because you have some agenda going. So why did you do it?'

'It was the quickest way, the simplest.' He handed her a mug of tea and led them through to the living room, where they both sat down. 'Everything calm at base camp?'

'Say what you like about Carswell, he's a pretty good motivator. Everyone thinks it was that speech of his that made you feel guilty.'

'And they're now working harder than ever? A team of happy gardeners with no nasty moles to bother them?'

Siobhan grinned. 'It was pretty bloody corny, wasn't it?' She reached down to place her mug on the floor. 'I got another message.'

'Quizmaster?'

She nodded, unfolded some sheets from her pocket and reached towards him with them. The first was an email from Quizmaster: *I'm disappointed in you, Siobhan. I'm taking my ball home now.*

Siobhan: *Don't believe everything you read. I still want to play.*

Quizmaster: *And go yapping to your bosses?*

Siobhan: *You and me this time, that's a promise.*

Quizmaster: *How can I trust you?*

Siobhan: *I've been trusting you, haven't I? And you always know where to find me. I still don't have the first clue about you.*

'I had to wait a while after that. The final sheet came in about'—she checked her watch—'forty minutes ago.' She handed it to him: *Add Camus to ME Smith, they're boxing where the sun don't shine, and Frank Finlay's the referee.*

'Well,' he said, handing the sheets back. 'It doesn't mean a thing to me. Take my advice, Siobhan. Give it to Crime Squad or Special Branch or whoever's supposed to be tracking this creep down.'

'Then you don't want to help me do some detecting?'

He laughed. 'You want me in even more trouble with Carswell?'

She looked down at the paper. 'You're right,' she said. 'I wasn't thinking. Thanks for the tea. I must be heading back. Lots to do.'

'Starting with handing that clue over?'

She stared at him. 'You know your advice is always important to me.'

'Is that a yes or a no?'

'Take it as a definite maybe.' She stood up to leave.

'Thanks for coming, Siobhan.' He stood up and followed her out into the hall, opening the door for her.

She was on the stairwell before she spoke again. 'Do you know what Ellen Wylie said after that meeting with Carswell?'

'What?'

'Nothing at all.' She studied him, one hand on the banister. 'Strange that. I was expecting a long speech about your martyr complex.'

Back in the flat, Rebus stood in the hall, listening to her footsteps recede. She'd come here asking for something, and he'd turned her down. How could he tell her that she should learn her own lessons, not his, and that she'd be a better cop at the end of it?

He walked through to the kitchen, poured Siobhan's and the rest of his tea down the sink. Back in the living room he sat in his chair in the living room, took pen and notebook from his pocket, and jotted down the latest clue as best he could remember it.

JEAN BURCHILL'S MORNING had consisted of a series of meetings, and by lunchtime she felt exhausted.

Steve Holly had left two more messages for her, and she just knew that if she sat at her desk with a sandwich, the phone would ring again. Instead, she headed into town down the Bridges. It was all cheap clothes shops and takeaways, with queues of buses and lorries waiting to crawl through the traffic lights at the Tron Kirk.

She purchased some fruit and a carton of orange juice and then paused on North Bridge, staring eastwards towards where the new parliament site showed no signs of progress. Just across from it were the *Scotsman*'s shiny new offices. She took a right into Waterloo Place, munching on an apple. She knew where she was headed: Calton cemetery. As she entered through the wrought-iron gate, she was confronted by the obelisk known as the Martyrs' Memorial, dedicated to the memory of five men who had dared in the 1790s to advocate parliamentary reform. This at a time when fewer than forty people in the city had the power to vote in an election. The five were sentenced to transportation: a one-way ticket to Australia.

Just to the east, over the cemetery wall, was a small crenellated tower. This she knew was all that remained of the old Calton Prison. Closing her eyes, she could almost replace the traffic noises with yelps and whoops, the dialogue between prisoners and their loved ones echoing back along Waterloo Place . . .

When she opened her eyes again, she saw what she'd hoped to find: Dr Kennet Lovell's grave. The headstone had been set into the cemetery's eastern wall, and was now cracked and soot-blackened, weeds obscuring much of the inscription. 'Dr Kennet Anderson Lovell,'

Jean read, 'an eminent Physician of this City.' He'd died in 1863, aged fifty-six. Jean crouched down and started pulling the weeds away. When she had cleared them, she found that Lovell had married no fewer than three times, and that each wife had passed away before him. As she examined the dates, she saw that the wives had died young, in childbirth, perhaps.

His first wife: Beatrice, *née* Alexander. Aged twenty-nine.

His second wife: Alice, *née* Baxter. Aged thirty-three.

His third wife: Patricia, *née* Addison. Aged twenty-six.

An inscription read: *Passed over, to be met again so sweetly in the Lord's domain.*

Jean couldn't help thinking that it must have been some meeting, Lovell and his three wives.

SIOBHAN WAS BACK at her desk, trying to form anagrams from the letters in 'Camus' and 'ME Smith', when Eric Bain came into the office.

'All right?' he asked.

'I'll survive.'

'That good, eh?' He placed his briefcase on the floor, straightened up and looked around. 'Special Branch get back to us yet?'

'Not that I know of.'

Bain walked over to the fax machine, picked up some sheets and sifted through them.

'Bloody marvellous,' he gasped, approaching her desk. 'Don't ask me how they did it, but they did it.'

'What?'

'They've traced one of the ISP accounts already.'

Siobhan's chair fell back as she got to her feet, hands grabbing at the fax. As Bain relinquished it, he asked her a simple question. 'Who's Claire Benzie?'

'YOU'RE NOT IN CUSTODY, Claire,' Siobhan said, 'and if you want a solicitor, that's up to you. But I'd like your permission to make a tape recording.'

'Sounds serious,' Claire Benzie said. They'd picked her up at her flat in Bruntsfield, driven her to St Leonard's. She'd been compliant.

'There'll be a copy for you, and one for us,' Siobhan was saying, as Bain fed tapes into both recording machines. 'OK?'

Benzie just shrugged.

Bain set both tapes running, then eased himself into the chair next to Siobhan. Siobhan identified herself and Bain for the record, adding time and place of interview.

'If you could state your full name, Claire,' she asked.

Claire Benzie did so, adding her Bruntsfield address.

Siobhan sat back for a moment, composing herself. Then she leaned forward, elbows on the desk.

'Claire, do you remember when I spoke to you earlier, in Dr Curt's office, I asked you if you knew anything about the game Philippa Balfour had been playing?'

'Seven fins high is king,' Benzie said. 'I told you about it.'

'That's right. You said Philippa had come up to you at a bar and explained it to you. But you didn't know anything about the game itself?'

'No. I hadn't a clue till you told me.'

'Then how come whoever was sending Flip those messages was using your Internet account?'

Benzie stared at her. Siobhan stared back.

'I want a solicitor,' Benzie said.

Siobhan nodded slowly. 'Interview ends, three twelve pm.' She asked if Claire had anyone in mind.

'The family solicitor, I suppose,' the student said. 'My father.'

When she saw the puzzled look on Siobhan's face, the corners of Benzie's mouth curled upwards. 'I mean my stepfather. Don't worry, I'm not about to summon ghosts to fight my corner.' She added, with quiet confidence, 'I didn't kill her.'

MAYBE THE CENTRAL LIBRARY was the right place for Rebus. Many of the customers today seemed to be the dispossessed, the tired, the unemployable. One old man, toothless mouth gaping, sat at a desk near the telephone directories, his finger running ponderously down each column. Rebus had asked one of the staff about him.

'Been coming for years, never reads anything else,' he was told.

'He could get a job with Directory Enquiries.'

'Or maybe that's where he was fired from.'

Rebus acknowledged that this was a good point, and got back to his own research. So far he'd established that Albert Camus was a French novelist and thinker. He'd won the Nobel Prize and then died while still in his forties. The librarian had done a search, but this was the only Camus of note to be found.

He then asked for dictionaries.

She directed him towards the shelf he needed, and added, 'I did that other check you asked for. There are some books by a Mark Smith, but nothing by anyone called M. E. Smith.'

'Thanks anyway.' He started to turn away.

'I also printed you out a list of our Camus holdings.'

He took the sheet from her. 'That's great. Thank you very much.'

He pulled out the first dictionary he found and opened it at 'stricture'; it meant binding, closure, tightness.

There was a clearing of the throat behind him. The librarian was standing there. 'My colleague, Kenny—' She pointed back towards her desk. 'He thinks he knows who Mr Smith is.'

So Rebus walked over, nodded a greeting at Kenny, barely out of his teens, wearing round metal-framed glasses and a black T-shirt.

'He's a singer,' Kenny said without preamble. 'At least, if it's the one I'm thinking of: Mark E. Smith.'

'Singer with The Fall?' Rebus said quietly, almost to himself.

'You know them?' Kenny seemed surprised that someone Rebus's age would have such knowledge.

Rebus nodded distractedly. 'Saw them twenty years ago. A club in Abbeyhill.'

Then the other librarian, Bridget, gave voice to his thoughts. 'Funny really,' she said, pointing to the sheet of paper in Rebus's hand. 'Camus's novel *La Chute* translates as "The Fall". We've a copy in the fiction section if you'd like one.'

CLAIRE BENZIE'S STEPFATHER turned out to be Jack McCoist, one of the city's more able defence solicitors. He asked for ten minutes alone with her before any interview could begin. Afterwards, Siobhan entered the room again, accompanied by Gill Templer.

'I don't think we need a recording made,' McCoist stated. 'Let's just talk this through, see where it takes us. Agreed?'

He looked to Gill Templer, who nodded eventually.

'When you're ready, DC Clarke,' Templer said.

'Claire,' Siobhan said, 'these clues Flip was getting, one of them came from an email address which we've traced back to you.'

McCoist looked up from his notepad. 'Can I just ask how you came into possession of these emails, DC Clarke?'

'They . . . we didn't really. Someone called Quizmaster sent Flip Balfour a message, and it came to me instead. I was checking Ms Balfour's computer for anything that might explain her disappearance.'

'So this was *after* she'd disappeared?'

'Yes,' Siobhan admitted.

'And this is the message you've traced back to my client's computer?'

'To her ISP account, yes.' Siobhan was noticing that Claire had looked up for the first time: it was that use of 'my client'. Probably she'd never seen her stepfather's professional side before.

'ISP being the Internet service provider?'

Siobhan nodded.

'Have there been subsequent messages?'

'Yes.'

'Very well.' McCoist stabbed a full stop on the notepad with his pen, then sat back thoughtfully.

'Do I get to ask Claire a question now?' Siobhan asked.

McCoist peered at her over the top of his glasses. 'My client would prefer to make a short statement first.'

Claire reached into her pocket of her jeans and unfolded a sheet of paper which had obviously come from the pad on the table, although the writing was different from McCoist's scrawl. She cleared her throat. 'About a fortnight before Flip went missing, I loaned her my laptop computer. She had some essay she was writing. I never got the chance to ask for it back. I was waiting until after the funeral to ask her family if it could be retrieved from her flat.'

'Is this laptop your only computer?' Siobhan interrupted.

Claire shook her head. 'No, but it's linked to an ISP, same account as my PC.'

Siobhan stared at her; still she didn't make eye contact. 'There was no laptop in Philippa Balfour's flat,' she said.

Eye contact at last. 'Then where is it?' Claire asked.

'I'm assuming you still have the proof of purchase?'

McCoist spoke up. 'Are you accusing my daughter of lying?' She wasn't just a client any longer.

'I'm saying maybe it's something Claire should have told us earlier.'

'DCS Templer,' McCoist began haughtily, 'I didn't think it was police policy to accuse potential witnesses of duplicity.'

'Right now,' Templer shot back, 'your stepdaughter's a suspect rather than a witness.'

'Suspected of what? Running a quiz? If you presented this to the Procurator Fiscal you'd be laughed back down the ranks.' He knew she was newly promoted; knew she'd yet to prove herself.

Gill had already regained her composure. 'What we need from

Claire, Mr McCoist, are some straight answers, otherwise her story's looking thin and we'll need to make further enquiries.'

McCoist seemed to consider this. Siobhan, meantime, was busy making a mental list. Claire Benzie had the motive all right—the role of Balfour's Bank in her father's suicide. With the role-playing game, she had the means, and luring Flip to Arthur's Seat would give the opportunity. Now she suddenly invented a loaned laptop, conveniently missing . . . Siobhan started another list, this time for Ranald Marr, who'd warned Flip early on about how to delete emails. Ranald Marr, second-in-command at the bank. She still didn't see what Marr would have gained from Flip's death.

'Claire,' she said quietly, 'those times you went to Junipers, did you ever meet Ranald Marr?'

'Yes. I never really knew what she saw in him.'

'Who?'

'Flip. She had this crush on Ranald. Schoolgirl stuff, I suppose.'

'Was it reciprocated? Did it go further than a crush?'

'I think,' McCoist said, 'we're straying somewhat from the—'

But Claire was smiling at Siobhan. 'Not until later,' she was saying.

'How much later?'

'I got the feeling she was seeing him up until she went missing.'

'WHAT'S ALL THE EXCITEMENT?' Rebus asked.

Bain looked up from the desk he was working at. 'Brought in Claire Benzie for questioning.'

'Why?' Rebus leaned down, reached into one of the desk's drawers.

'One of the emails, I got Special Branch to trace it.'

Rebus whistled. 'Claire Benzie sent it?'

'Well, it was sent from her account.'

Rebus considered this. 'Not quite the same thing?'

Gill Templer burst into the CID office. 'I want Ranald Marr brought in for questioning. Who wants to fetch him?'

She got two volunteers straight away—Hi-Ho Silvers and Phyllida Hawes. When she turned round, Siobhan was standing behind her.

'That was good work in there.' Gill touched Siobhan's shoulder. 'Take a break. We'll let someone else have a shot at Ranald Marr.' She looked around the room. 'The rest of you, back to work.' Her eyes met those of John Rebus. 'What the hell are you doing here?'

Rebus opened another drawer, this time pulling out a pack of cigarettes. 'Just came to collect a few personal items, ma'am.'

Gill pursed her lips, stalked out of the room.

Siobhan approached Rebus. 'What the hell *are* you doing here?'

'You look shattered.'

'I see your silver tongue's as rusty as ever.'

'Boss told you to take a break, and as luck would have it, I'm buying. While you've been busy scaring wee lassies, I've been doing the important stuff . . .'

SIOBHAN WAS STICKING to orange juice, and kept playing with her mobile: Bain was under strict orders to call her if there was news. 'I need to get back,' she said, not for the first time.

'Have you eaten?' Rebus asked. When she shook her head, he came back from the bar with a packet of Scampi Fries, which she began to devour, when she heard him say: 'That's when it struck me.'

'When what struck you?'

'Siobhan, wake up.'

'John, I feel like my head's about to explode.'

'You don't think Claire Benzie's guilty, that much I understand. And now she says Flip Balfour was getting her end away with Ranald Marr. 'It's going to be some conversation, isn't it, when Balfour asks his trusted compadre what the cops wanted him for. Funeral should be a jolly affair.' He lit a cigarette. 'You going to be there?'

'Thinking of it. Templer and Carswell—they'll be going.' She looked at her watch. 'I should head back, see what Marr's been saying.'

'You were told to take a break.'

'I've had one.' She stared at the mobile, then up at Rebus. 'What were you saying about Strictures?'

Rebus's smile widened. 'Nice to have you back with us. I was saying that I've worked out the first bit of the puzzle.'

'I didn't think you were that interested.'

'I changed my mind. So do you want to hear?'

'Sure. I'm all ears.'

'Albert Camus,' he began slowly, 'wrote a book called *The Fall*. And Mark E. Smith is the singer with a band called The Fall.'

Siobhan frowned. 'I think I had one of their singles once.'

'So,' Rebus went on, 'we have *The Fall* and The Fall. Add one to the other and you get . . .'

'Falls?' Siobhan guessed. Rebus nodded. 'You think maybe that's where Quizmaster wants to meet?'

'I think it has to do with the next clue.'

'But what about the rest of it: the boxing match, Frank Finlay?'

Rebus shrugged. 'I didn't promise you a miracle.'

They went back to St Leonard's, but there was no news. Rebus watched Siobhan for a few minutes. She went from one huddle to another, desperate to know things. He could see she was having trouble holding on: a head full of theories and fancies. She, too, needed the breakthrough, the break. He walked up to her, took hold of her arm. 'When did you last have a hot meal?'

'You sound like my mum . . .'

He took her to an Indian restaurant on Nicolson Street. It was dark and up a flight of stairs and mostly empty.

'You know Falls better than I do,' she said. 'What landmarks are there?'

'Well, the waterfall itself, and maybe Junipers. That's about it.'

'There's a housing scheme, right?'

He nodded. 'Meadowside. And there's Bev Dodds's cottage and a few dozen commuters. Not even a church or a post office.'

'No boxing ring, then?'

Rebus shook his head. 'And no Frank Finlay House.'

Siobhan seemed to lose interest in her food. Rebus wasn't too worried: she'd already dispatched a Tandoori starter and the bulk of her biriani. He watched her take out her phone and try the station.

'Eric? It's Siobhan. What's happening there? Have we got Marr yet?' She listened, then her eyes met Rebus's. 'Really?' Her voice had risen slightly in pitch. 'That was a bit silly, wasn't it? . . . OK, Eric. Thanks for that. See you later.' She ended the call, took her time placing the phone back in her bag.

'Spit it out,' Rebus said.

'Well,' Siobhan said, 'they went to pick up Mr Marr at his home in The Grange, only he wasn't there.'

'And?'

'And the reason he wasn't there was, he'd been told they'd be coming. The ACC "suggested" they phone Marr beforehand, as "a courtesy".' She picked up the water jug, tipped the dregs into her glass. 'Looks like Marr did a runner.'

'Better stick one of the napkins in your pocket,' Rebus suggested. 'Looks like some egg needs wiping from Carswell's face.'

'I can't imagine he'll have fun explaining to the Chief Constable,' Siobhan agreed.

'If Carswell's thinking straight, he'll do nothing till the funeral's over. Could be Ranald Marr will turn up there anyway.'

'A fond farewell to his secret lover?'

'If Claire Benzie's telling the truth.'

'Why else would he run?'

Rebus stared at her. 'I think you know the answer to that one.'

'You mean if Marr killed her?'

'I thought you had him in the frame.'

She was thoughtful. 'I had him in the frame for Quizmaster.'

'Meaning she was killed by someone else?'

The coffees arrived, and with them the ubiquitous mints. Without being asked, the waiter had also brought the bill.

'Split it down the middle?' Siobhan suggested. Rebus nodded, took three fivers from his pocket.

Outside, he asked how she was getting home.

'My car's at St Leonard's: need a lift?'

'Nice night for a walk,' he said, looking up at the clouds. 'Just promise me you *will* go home, take a break.'

'I promise.'

They parted on the pavement, Rebus heading back to the flat.

When he got in, he called Jean, but she wasn't at home. He stood in front of some sheets that he'd pinned to the wall, detailing the four women—Jesperson, Gibbs, Gearing and Farmer. He was trying to answer a question: why would the killer leave the coffins? OK, they were his 'signature', but that signature had not been recognised until now. If the killer had hoped to be identified with his crimes, wouldn't he have tried some other method: a note to the media or the police? No, Rebus saw them as little memorials, holding meaning only for the person who'd left them there. And couldn't the same be said for the Arthur's Seat coffins? No one had ever claimed responsibility for them; they'd been memorials, never meant to be found or associated with the Burke and Hare killings.

He tried Jean's number again, but there was still no answer. Stuck a Steve Earle album on: *The Hard Way*.

Rebus didn't know of any other . . .

'YOU'RE LUCKY I didn't change my name,' Jan Benzie said. Jean had just explained how she'd called every Benzie in the phone book. 'I'm married to Jack McCoist these days.'

They were sitting in the elegant drawing room of a three-storey town house in the city's west end, just off Palmerston Place. Jan

Benzie was tall and thin, and wore a knee-length black dress with a sparkling brooch just above her right breast.

'Thank you for seeing me at such short notice.'

'There's not much I can add to what I told you on the phone.' Jan Benzie sounded distracted, as if part of her was elsewhere. Maybe that was why she'd agreed to the appointment in the first place. 'It's been rather a strange day, Ms Burchill,' she said now.

'Oh?'

But Jan Benzie just shrugged one shoulder and asked again if Jean would like something to drink.

'I don't want to keep you. You said Patricia Lovell was a relation?'

'Great-great-grandmother, something like that.'

'She died very young, didn't she? Do you know if it was in childbirth?'

'I've no idea. She had one child, a girl, that's all I know. You say you're researching Kennet Lovell?'

Jean nodded. 'I'm looking for some correspondence between Dr Lovell and his benefactor. Would your family have any of his papers?'

Jan Benzie shook her head. 'None.' She moved an arm towards the occasional table next to her chair, lifted her cigarette packet and eased one out. 'Do you . . .?'

Jean shook her head and watched Jan Benzie light the cigarette with a slim gold lighter. The woman seemed to do everything in slow motion. It was like watching a film at the wrong speed.

'He had several wives, Dr Lovell, did you know that?' Jean asked.

'Three, wasn't it? Not so many, really. I'm on my second . . . who's to say it'll stop there?' Jan Benzie examined the ash at the end of her cigarette. 'My first committed suicide, you know.' She paused. 'Don't suppose I can expect the same of Jack.'

Jean wasn't sure what she meant, but Jan Benzie was studying her, seeming to expect some reply. 'I suppose,' Jean said, 'it would look a bit suspicious, losing two husbands.'

'And yet Kennet Lovell can lose three wives . . .?'

Jean's thinking exactly.

Jan Benzie had risen to her feet, walked over to a window.

'Well,' Jean said, 'I'd better be going. Sorry again to have . . .'

'No trouble,' Benzie said. 'I hope you find what you're looking for.'

Suddenly there were voices out in the hall, and the sound of the front door being closed.

'Claire and my husband,' Jan said, sitting back down, arranging

513

herself in her seat the way an artist's model might. The door burst open and Claire Benzie stormed into the room.

'I don't bloody care,' she was saying. 'They can lock me up if they want, throw away the bloody key!' She was pacing the room as Jack McCoist walked in. He had his wife's slow movements, but they seemed merely the result of fatigue.

'Claire, all I'm saying is . . .' He leaned down to peck his wife's cheek. 'What a bloody awful time we've had,' he informed her. 'Cops crawling over Claire like lice. Is there *any* way you can control your daughter, darling?' His words died as he straightened and saw they had a visitor. Jean was rising to her feet.

'I really should be going,' she said.

'Who the hell's this?' Claire snarled.

'Ms Burchill is from the museum,' Jan explained. 'We've been talking about Kennet Lovell.'

'Not her as well!' Claire dropped onto one of the two sofas. 'Well, wherever you're from, Ms Burchill, why don't you piss off back there? I'm just out of police custody and—'

'You will *not* speak like that to a guest in this house!' Jan Benzie yelped, springing from her chair. 'Jack, tell her.'

'Look, I really should . . .' Jean's words were swamped as a three-way argument started. She backed away, heading for the door.

'You've no bloody right!'

'Anyone would think it was *you* they interrogated!'

'That's still no excuse for . . .'

They didn't seem to notice as Jean opened the door, tiptoed down the stairs and escaped into the street. Walking away, she glanced back. The houses here had walls so thick they could double as padded cells, and it felt like that was just what she'd escaped from.

Claire Benzie's temper had been something to behold.

 Chapter Eight

The village of Falls had no cemetery, but there was a small, little-used church—more the size of a chapel—just off the road between Falls and Causland, which the Balfour family had picked for the funeral.

There were too many people for the church. The doors were left open so that the short service could be heard outside. The day was cool, the ground heavy with dew. Cars lined the main road, the hearse having discreetly pulled away, heading back to Edinburgh. Liveried drivers stood beside several of the vehicles, cigarettes in hands. Rollers, Mercs, Jags . . .

The minister, who was used to seeing the Balfours only at Christmas, was a thorough man. He had checked his script with the mother and father, asking solicitous questions whose answers would help him bulk out Flip's biography, but he was also bemused by the attentions of the media. Being used to encountering cameras only at weddings and christenings, when one was pointed in his direction for the first time, he gave a beaming smile, only afterwards realising the inappropriateness of his action. There would be no photos of the coffin being lowered, or the parents by the graveside. Permission had been granted for one photograph only: of the coffin being carried from the church.

With the pews and side aisles being crammed, the police officers present kept to the back of the crowd. Assistant Chief Constable Colin Carswell stood with hands clasped in front of him, head slightly bowed. Detective Chief Superintendent Gill Templer was next to Detective Inspector Bill Pryde, just behind Carswell. Other officers were further off still, patrolling what grounds there were. Flip's killer was still out there, and so, if the two could be differentiated, was Ranald Marr. Inside the church, John Balfour kept turning his head, examining each face as if looking for someone.

John Rebus was standing by the far wall, dressed in his good suit and a long green raincoat, its collar up. He was thinking how bleak the surroundings were when Gill Templer had come towards him, face set, and had asked what he thought he was doing there.

'Paying my respects. Unless there's a law against it,' he'd added.

Siobhan was about fifty yards from him, but so far had acknowledged his presence only with a wave of her gloved hand. Her eyes were on the hillside, as if she thought the killer might suddenly reveal himself there. Rebus had his doubts. As the service ended, the coffin was carried out, and the cameras began their short work.

John Balfour had one arm round his wife. Some of Flip's student friends were hugging each other, faces buried in shoulders and chests. Rebus recognised Tristram and Tina, Albert and Camille . . . No sign of Claire Benzie. He spotted some of Flip's neighbours, too, including Professor Devlin, who had come bustling up to talk to him earlier, asking about the coffins, whether there'd been any progress. Rebus had shaken his head and moved away.

Rebus watched the rest of the procession. David Costello preceded his parents out of the church, blinking at the sudden light, digging sunglasses from his pocket and slipping them on. Behind him, his mother and father walked their separate and very distinct walks, more like nodding acquaintances than spouses.

But now something was happening . . . A car arriving, door slamming, and a man dressed casually—woollen V-neck and grey slacks— jogging up the road and in through the churchyard gates. Rebus recognised an unshaven and bleary-eyed Ranald Marr, saw Steve Holly's face crease as he wondered what was going on. The procession had just reached the graveside when Marr caught it up. He walked to the front and stood in front of John and Jacqueline Balfour. Balfour released his grip on his wife, hugged Marr instead, the gesture returned. Templer and Pryde were looking to Colin Carswell, who made a motion with his hands, palms down. Easy, he was saying. We go easy.

'For I am the Resurrection and the Life,' the minister was intoning. Marr was standing beside John Balfour now, eyes on the coffin. Off to one side, Siobhan was moving between the graves, as if searching for something. Rebus didn't think any of the reporters could see her: the mourners formed a barrier between her and them. She crouched down in front of a gravestone, seemed to be reading its inscription. Then she rose to her feet again and when she saw that Rebus was watching her she flashed him a quick smile, which for some reason he didn't find reassuring. She moved round to the rear of the mourning party.

Carswell was muttering something to Gill Templer. Rebus knew they'd probably let Marr leave the churchyard, but insist on accompanying him immediately afterwards. Unlike the rest of Balfour's associates and acquaintances, Marr wouldn't be seeing the marquee and the finger buffet.

'Ashes to ashes . . .'

A couple of the reporters were already preparing to head off. Rebus slipped his hands into the pockets of the raincoat, started a slow patrol of the churchyard's perimeter. Earth was raining onto Philippa Balfour's coffin, the last rain the polished wood would ever feel. Her mother sent a cry up into the sky.

Rebus found himself standing in front of a small headstone. Its owner, Francis Campbell Finlay, had lived from 1876 to 1937, a carpenter, probably serving the surrounding farms. He had to suppress a smile. Siobhan had looked at the box in which the remains of Flip Balfour lay, and she'd thought: boxing. Then she'd looked at the grave itself and realised that it was a place where the sun didn't shine. Quizmaster's clue had been leading her right here, but it was only once she'd arrived that she'd been able to work it out. She'd gone looking for Frank Finlay, and found him. Rebus wondered what else she'd found when she crouched in front of the headstone. He glanced back to where the mourners were departing the churchyard, but he couldn't see Siobhan. Carswell was talking to Ranald Marr, who was responding with resigned nods of the head. When Carswell put out his hand, Marr dropped his car keys into it.

Rebus was the last to leave. Siobhan was standing on the verge, leaning her arms on her car roof, in no hurry. Rebus crossed the road, nodded a greeting.

'Thought we might see you here,' was all she said.

'Like I told Gill, it's not against the law.'

'You saw Marr arriving?'

Rebus nodded. 'What's the story?'

'Carswell's driving him up to the house. Marr wants a couple of minutes with Balfour to explain things.'

'Doesn't sound to me like he's about to confess to murder.'

'No,' she said.

'I was wondering . . .' Rebus let the utterance fade.

She tore her eyes away from the spectacle of Carswell attempting a three-pointer in Marr's Maserati. 'Yes?'

'The latest clue: Stricture. Any more ideas?' Stricture, he was thinking, as in confinement. Nothing quite as confining as a coffin.

She shook her head. 'What about you?'

'I did wonder if "boxing" might mean putting things in boxes.'

'Mmm.' She looked thoughtful. 'Maybe.' She took her arms off the car roof, slid her right hand into the pocket of her Barbour.

Rebus noticed that she held the car keys in her left hand. He wondered what was in that right-hand pocket.

'See you back at the ranch,' she said.

'I'm still on the blacklist, remember?'

She opened her driver's-side door. 'Right,' she said, getting in. She offered him a brief smile and nothing more. He took a step back as the car came to life, wheels sliding before finding tarmac.

She'd done just what he'd have done: kept to herself whatever it was she'd found. Rebus jogged to his own car and made to follow.

'YOU THINK I KILLED HER, don't you?'

Three of them in the interview room. An unnatural hush outside the door: whispers and tippy-toes and phones snatched up almost before they could ring. Gill Templer, Bill Pryde and Ranald Marr.

'Let's not jump to conclusions, Mr Marr,' Gill said.

'Isn't that what you're doing?'

'Just a few follow-up questions, sir,' Bill Pryde said. 'Were you having a relationship with Philippa Balfour, Mr Marr?'

'What sort of relationship?'

Bill Pryde's voice was a bear-growl. 'The sort her dad would string you up by the balls for.'

'I think I take your meaning.' Marr looked as though he was thinking through his answer. 'Here's what I will say: I've spoken to John Balfour and he has taken a responsible attitude to that conversation. The talk we had has no bearing on this case. And that's pretty much it.' He sat back in his chair.

'Whether something does or does not have "bearing" on a case is up to us to decide, wouldn't you say, sir?'

Colour rose to Marr's cheeks, but he wasn't going to take the bait. He shrugged merely, and folded his arms to let them know that, so far as he was concerned, the discussion was now at an end.

'A moment of your time, DI Pryde,' Gill said, angling her head towards the door. As they stepped out of the room, two uniforms stepped in to stand guard. Officers were already homing in, so Gill pushed Pryde through the door marked 'Ladies', and stood with her back against the door to deter the curious.

'Well?' she asked.

'They've stitched something up between them,' he said.

'Yes,' Gill agreed. 'We should have brought him straight here.'

'Carswell's blooper,' Pryde said, 'yet again.'

Gill nodded. 'You think Marr confessed to Balfour?'

'I think he probably said something.' He shook his head slowly. 'The more I hear about John Balfour, the less I like him. Bank's looking like going down the toilet, house filled with account-holders . . . his best friend walks up and says that he's been getting his end away with the daughter, and what does Balfour do? He does a deal.'

'The pair of them keeping quiet, keeping the lid on it?'

It was Pryde's turn to nod. 'Because the alternative is scandal, resignation, public fisticuffs and the collapse of all they hold dearest: namely, cold hard cash.'

BACK IN THE INTERVIEW ROOM, Ranald Marr had the look of someone who knew he'd soon be back behind the wheel of his Maserati. Gill, unable to bear such smugness, decided to play her last card. 'Your affair with Philippa, it lasted a while, didn't it?'

'God, are we back to that again,' Marr said, rolling his eyes.

'Common knowledge. Philippa told Claire Benzie all about it.'

'Is that what Claire Benzie says? I seem to have been here before. That little madam would say anything to hurt Balfour's.'

Gill was shaking her head. 'I don't think so. She could have blown the whole secret wide open any time. She didn't do that. I can only assume it's because Claire has some principles.'

'Or she was biding her time.'

'And now we know why you were keen to explain to Philippa how to erase emails.'

Marr tried staring her out, but it didn't work. Gill had interviewed more than a dozen killers in the course of her CID career. She'd been stared at by eyes filled with fire, eyes turned insane.

He dropped his gaze and his shoulders slumped. 'Look,' he said, 'there's one thing . . . I . . . didn't tell the whole truth about the game Flip was involved in.'

'You haven't told the whole truth about anything,' Pryde interrupted, but Gill quietened him with a look.

'I didn't know it *was* a game, not back then. She brought one of the clues to me. The mason's dream. She thought I might know what it meant.' He managed a smile. 'She was always overestimating me. She was . . . I don't think you've been getting anything like the whole picture of the kind of person Flip was. I know what you saw at first: spoilt rich kid.' He was shaking his head. 'That wasn't Flip at all. Maybe it was one side to her, but she was complex, always capable of surprising you. Like with this puzzle thing, she would take these sudden interests, passions in things. For years, she'd been going to the zoo once a week on her own, just about *every* week, and I only found out by chance, a few months back.' He looked up at them. 'Do you see?'

Gill wasn't sure that she did, but she nodded anyway. 'Go on,' she said. But it was as though her words had broken the spell. Marr paused for breath. 'She was . . .' He shook his head. 'I want to go home. I have some things I need to talk about with my wife.'

'Are you OK to drive?' Gill asked.

'Perfectly.' He took a deep breath. But when he looked at her again, tears were welling in his eyes. 'Oh Christ,' he said, 'I've made such an utter balls-up, haven't I? And I'd do it again and again and again if it meant I had those same moments with her.'

'Rehearsing what you're going to say to the missus?' Pryde said.

'My God,' Marr said, almost with a sense of awe, 'I hope and pray I never grow a skin as thick as yours.'

'Compared to me, Mr Marr, you're an armadillo.'

REBUS WALKED THROUGH St Leonard's like the spectre at the feast. He could feel a killer slipping through his fingers. The evidence he'd taken home, the notes pinned to his wall, didn't amount to evidence at all. It was a jumble of coincidence and speculation, a thin gossamer pattern created almost from air. For all he knew, Betty-Anne Jesperson had eloped with her secret lover, while Hazel Gibbs had staggered drunkenly on the bank of White Cart Water and slipped in, knocking herself unconscious. Maybe Paula Gearing had hidden her depression well, walking into the sea of her own volition. And the schoolgirl Caroline Farmer, could she have started a new life far from small-town Scottish teenage blues?

So what if someone had left coffins nearby? He couldn't even be sure it was the same person each time. And with the autopsy evidence, there was no way to prove any crime had been committed at all. Flip Balfour was the first victim who could definitely be said to have perished at the hands of an attacker.

He eased himself into the Farmer's chair, held his head in his hands, felt that if he took them away it might explode. Too many ghosts, too many ifs and buts. Too much pain and grieving, loss and guilt . . . He knew who, at last, he could turn to.

It was a male voice that answered Jean's extension. 'Sorry,' the man said, 'she's been keeping her head down lately, off on one of her little mystery trips.'

'Oh?'

'She gets these projects going from time to time. They could set off a bomb in the building and Jean would be the last to know.'

Rebus smiled: the man could have been talking about *him*. But Jean hadn't mentioned that she was busy with anything outside her normal work. 'So what's she up to this time?' he asked.

'Mmm, let me see . . . Burke and Hare, that period.'

'The Resurrectionists?'

'Curious term that, don't you think? I mean, they didn't do much resurrecting, did they? She seems to be focusing on this doctor who helped carry out the post-mortem on Burke. What's his name?'

'Kennet Lovell?' Rebus said.

'That's right.' The man seemed slightly put out that Rebus knew. 'Are you helping Jean? Want me to leave her a message?'

'You don't happen to know where she is?'

'She doesn't always confide in me.'

Just as well, Rebus felt like saying. If Steve Holly ever managed to contact this guy, he'd have everything he could possibly want on Jean, down to her home phone number, without having to ask.

Rebus told the man there was no message, and put down the phone. Jean was obviously following up Devlin's theory that Lovell had left the coffins on Arthur's Seat. All the same, he wondered why she hadn't said anything.

He stared at the desk opposite, the one Wylie had been using. It was piled high with documents. Narrowing his eyes, he rose from his desk and walked over, started lifting piles of paper from the top.

Right at the bottom were the autopsy notes from Hazel Gibbs and Paula Gearing. Professor Devlin had told him that they should be returned. Quite right, too. They might be lost for ever or misfiled if allowed to be smothered by the paperwork generated by Flip Balfour's murder. Rebus placed them on his own desk, and wrote a note saying: *Could someone please send these on as specified. Cheers, J.R.*

Looking around, it struck him that although he'd followed Siobhan's car into the car park there was no sign of her now.

'Saw her five minutes ago. Said she was headed down Gayfield Square,' a colleague explained.

'Thanks,' he said, sprinting out to his car.

There was no quick route to Gayfield Square, so Rebus took a few liberties with traffic lights and junctions. Parking, he couldn't see Siobhan's car. But when he dashed indoors, she was standing right there, talking to Grant Hood.

Hood made a show of spotting someone across the room as Rebus approached. 'Sorry, got to . . .' And he was off.

'Anything happening?' Rebus asked.

'Ranald Marr's already been released. All we got out of him was that Flip *did* ask him about that Masonic clue.'

'And his excuse for lying to us?'

She shrugged. 'I wasn't there, so I can't say.' She fixed her eyes on him. 'Excuse me,' she said, 'but for an officer under suspension, aren't you spending an awful lot of time in the office?'

'Something I forgot, I came to retrieve it.' As the words came out, he realised he *had* forgotten something: the Falls coffin, still in its carrier bag in his desk drawer at St Leonard's. He had intended to take it back to Bev Dodds. 'Is there maybe anything *you've* forgotten, Siobhan?'

'Such as?'

'Forgetting to share your find with the rest of the team.'

'John . . .' Her eyes were avoiding his now. 'You're off the case.'

'Maybe so. You, on the other hand, are off your trolley.'

'You've no right to say that.' She still wasn't looking at him.

'DI Rebus!' The voice of authority: Colin Carswell, standing twenty yards away in the doorway. 'If you'd spare me a moment.'

Rebus looked at Siobhan. 'To be continued,' he said.

Carswell was waiting for him in Gill Templer's cramped office. Gill was there too, standing with arms folded. 'So, DI Rebus, what can we do for you?' he asked.

'Just something I had to pick up.'

'Nothing contagious, I trust.' Carswell offered a thin smile.

'That's a good one, sir,' Rebus said coldly. He turned to Gill. 'I want back on the case.'

Carswell just snorted.

'Siobhan's playing a wild card. I think she's back in touch with Quizmaster, maybe for a meet.'

'He's sent another clue?'

'At the churchyard this morning.'

Gill was hooked. She narrowed her eyes. 'One of the mourners?'

'It could have been left any time. Thing is, Siobhan's been wanting a meeting.'

'Hang on, hang on,' Carswell broke in. 'How do we know any of this? You saw her pick up some clue?'

'The last one led to a particular grave. She crouched in front of the headstone . . . And that's when I think she picked up the clue.'

'You didn't see her do it?'

Sensing another confrontation brewing, Gill stepped in. 'Why don't we just bring her in here and ask her?'

Rebus nodded. 'I'll fetch her.'

But out in the Inquiry Room, there was no sign of Siobhan. Rebus walked the corridors, asking for her. At the drinks machine, someone said she'd just left the building. Rebus quickened his pace. No sign of her on the pavement; no sign of her car. He went back indoors. Tried her mobile, got a recorded message telling him the phone was in use.

'She's gone,' he told Gill. Catching his breath, he noticed Carswell was missing. 'Where's the ACC?'

'Summoned to the Big House. The Chief Constable wanted a word.'

'Gill, we've got to find her. Get some bodies out there.'

'OK, John, we'll find her, don't worry.' She lifted the receiver and left a message with Siobhan's pager, asking for an urgent call-back. But Rebus wanted more, and eventually she agreed: patrols would be on the lookout for her car.

It struck Rebus that she could be *anywhere*, not just inside the city boundary. Quizmaster had taken her to Hart Fell and Rosslyn Chapel. No telling where he'd choose for a rendezvous. The more isolated it was, the more danger Siobhan was in. He tried her mobile a third time: still engaged. Then, suddenly, he knew what it was: her mobile was hooked to Grant Hood's laptop. Even now, she could be telling Quizmaster she was on her way . . .

SIOBHAN HAD PARKED her car. Two hours yet till the time Quizmaster had suggested. She reckoned she could lie low till then. The pager message from Gill Templer had told her two things: one was that Rebus had told Gill everything; two, that if she ignored Gill's order, she'd have some explaining to do.

Explaining? She was having trouble doing that even to herself. Going out on her own fragile limb like this was the sort of stupid thing she regularly chastised Rebus for. All she knew was that the game—and she knew it wasn't *just* a game; was something potentially much more dangerous—had got to her. Quizmaster, whoever he or she turned out to be, had got to her, to the extent that she could think of little else. She moved in her seat so she was facing the laptop. The line was already open, had been since she'd got into the car. No new messages, so she sent one of her own.

Meeting accepted. See you there. Siobhan.

She shut down the computer and placed it beneath the passenger seat, making sure it wasn't visible: didn't want someone breaking in. When she got out of the car, she made sure all the doors were locked, and that the little red alarm button was flashing.

Just under two hours to go now; a little time to kill . . .

JEAN BURCHILL HAD TRIED calling Professor Devlin, but no one ever answered. So she wrote him a note, asking him to contact her, and decided to deliver it by hand. In the taxi, she wondered what the urgency was, and realised it was because she wanted to be rid of Kennet Lovell; he was taking up too much of her time.

If her research was to progress, she needed some kind of proof of Lovell's interest in woodwork. Without that, she was at a dead end. Having paid the driver, she stood in front of an array of buzzers. On the offchance that Professor Devlin might be back from his wanderings, she pressed the button marked simply 'D. Devlin'.

The intercom crackled. 'Hello?'

'Professor Devlin? It's Jean Burchill from the museum. I'm doing some research on Kennet Lovell and I wonder if I can have a word.'

'Miss Burchill? This is somewhat of a surprise.'

'I've tried phoning . . .'

But the door was already signalling that it was no longer locked.

Devlin was waiting for her on his landing. 'Come in. I'm afraid you'll find my housekeeping somewhat lacking . . .' He led her into the living room, cluttered with boxes and books. 'I am separating the wheat from the chaff,' he told her. 'Selecting that by which history shall judge my small endeavours. So, tell me, what have you found out about Lovell?'

'Not a great deal. That's really why I'm here. I can't find any reference to him having an interest in carpentry.'

'Oh, it's a matter of record, I assure you, though it's many years since I came across it. Perhaps in some monograph or dissertation . . . I really can't recall. Could it have been a university thesis?'

Jean nodded slowly. If it had been a thesis, only the university itself would hold a copy. 'I should have thought of that.'

'But don't you agree he was a remarkable character?' Devlin asked.

'He certainly lived a very full life . . . unlike his wives.'

'Ah, so you've been to his graveside. What did you think?'

'At first, nothing . . . but then later . . .'

'You began to speculate as to whether or not those poor women had been assisted on their final journey?' He smiled. 'It's obvious, really, isn't it?'

Jean became aware of a smell in the room: stale sweat. Perspiration was shining on Devlin's forehead. 'Who better,' he was saying, 'than an anatomist to get away with murder?'

'You're saying he murdered them?'

He shook his head. 'I'm merely speculating.'

'But why would he do that?'

Devlin shrugged. 'Because he could? What do you think?'

'I've been wondering . . . He was very young when he assisted at Burke's autopsy. That might explain why he fled to Africa.'

'And God alone knows what horrors he encountered out there,' Devlin added.

Jean picked up a photograph. It showed a middle-aged woman, dressed for some formal function. 'Your wife?' she guessed.

'My dear Anne. She passed away in the summer of 1972. Natural causes, I assure you.'

Jean looked at him. 'Why should you have to assure me?'

Devlin's smile faded. 'She meant the world to me . . . *more* than the world . . .' He clapped his hands together. 'What can I be thinking of, not offering you something to drink. Tea perhaps?'

'Tea would be wonderful.'

'I can't promise any sense of wonder from PG tea bags.' His smile was fixed.

'And afterwards, maybe I could see Kennet Lovell's table.'

'But of course. It's in the dining room. Bought from a reputable dealer, though I admit they couldn't be categorical about its provenance, but they were fairly persuasive, and I was willing to believe.' He had taken his glasses off to give them a polish with his handkerchief. 'Tea,' he repeated, making for the hallway.

She followed him. 'Have you lived here long?' she asked.

'Ever since Anne passed on. The house held too many memories.'

He was in the kitchen now. 'Won't be a minute,' he said.

'Fine.' She started to retrace her steps back to the living room. The summer of '72 his wife had died . . . She passed an open doorway: the dining room. The table filled almost the whole space. A jigsaw lay on top of it, not quite complete: missing just the one piece. Edinburgh, an aerial photograph. She walked into the room, studied the table. The legs were sturdy, utilitarian, a plain enough design. She crouched down, seeking the missing piece of jigsaw. There it was: almost hidden beneath one of the legs. As she reached for it, she saw that the table boasted one nice, secretive touch. Where the two leaves met in the middle, a small cupboard had been inserted. She squeezed into the narrow confines so that she could open the cupboard. It was stiff, and she almost gave up, but then it clicked open, revealing its contents.

A plane, set square and chisels. A small saw and some nails.

Woodwork tools.

When she looked up, Professor Devlin was filling the doorway. 'Ah, the missing piece,' was all that he said.

ELLEN WYLIE WALKED into the CID suite at St Leonard's, to find it deserted.

Carswell's speech to the troops had cut into her like a knife, not just nicking the skin but radiating pain through her whole body. When they'd all been called into the office, she'd half hoped her silence would give her away. But then Rebus had stepped in, taken the whole thing upon himself, leaving her feeling worse than ever.

Which was why she'd made the trip to St Leonard's. She walked over to his desk. The autopsy notes were sitting on it, waiting for someone to follow the instructions left on them. She lifted the note from the top, sat down in Rebus's chair. Without really meaning to, she found herself opening the first file and starting to read.

She'd done this before, of course; or rather, Professor Devlin had, while she'd sat by his side taking note of his findings. Slow work, yet she realised now that she'd enjoyed it—the notion that there might be some case hidden in the midst of those typewritten pages. Skimming them now, she realised finally why she'd come here: she wanted to apologise to Rebus . . . And then she looked up and he was standing not four yards away, watching her.

She picked up one of the sheets. 'I was just . . . maybe one final look before it all went back into the storeroom.'

He nodded, walked into the room.

'What's wrong?' she asked.

'I was hoping Siobhan might be here.' He walked over to her desk, hoping for some clue . . . something, *anything*.

'I wanted to thank you,' Ellen Wylie said.

'Oh?' He turned from Siobhan's desk. 'Don't worry about it, Ellen.'

'But I got you into trouble.'

'No, you didn't. I got myself into trouble, and maybe made things worse for you too. If I'd stayed quiet, I think you'd have spoken up.'

'Maybe,' she admitted. 'But I could have spoken up anyway.'

The phone rang and he snatched at it. 'Hello?' Suddenly his face relaxed. 'No, he's not here right now. Can I take a . . .?' He put the receiver down. 'No message.'

While he'd been on the phone, Ellen Wylie had started flicking through the autopsy stuff again. As he put the receiver down, he saw her lower her face towards one of the files, as though trying to read something. She pointed to the bottom of the page. 'Can you read this signature?'

'Which one?' There were two, at the foot of the autopsy report for

Hazel Gibbs, the Glasgow 'victim'. One was the signature of the 'Chief Pathologist, City of Glasgow'; the other of the 'Deputising Pathologist'.

'I'm not sure,' Rebus said, examining the squiggles. 'But the names should be typed on the cover-sheet.'

'That's just it,' Wylie said. 'No cover-sheet.' She turned back a few pages to confirm this. Rebus came round the desk so he was standing next to her. 'Was it missing when the files arrived?'

'I don't know. Professor Devlin didn't say anything.'

'Wasn't Ewan Stewart the Chief Pathologist for Glasgow then?'

Wylie flicked back to the signatures. 'Yep,' she said, 'I'll go with that. But it's the other one that interests me. If you take another look, isn't it just possible it says Donald Devlin?'

'What?' Rebus looked, blinked, looked again. 'Devlin was in Edinburgh back then.' But his voice dropped off. The word *Deputising* floated into view. 'I don't get it,' he said. 'Why wouldn't Devlin say?' Rebus was flicking through the other report, the one from Nairn. Neither pathologist was Donald Devlin on that occasion. All the same . . .

'He didn't want us to know,' he said at last. 'Maybe that's why he removed the cover-sheet.'

'But *why*?'

Rebus was thinking . . . The way Devlin had returned to the back room of the Ox, anxious to see the autopsies consigned once more to history . . . The Glasgow coffin, made of balsa wood, cruder than the others . . . Devlin's interest in Dr Kennet Lovell and the Arthur's Seat coffins . . .

Jean!

'I'm getting a bad feeling,' Ellen Wylie said.

'I've always been one for trusting a woman's instincts.' But that was just what he *hadn't* done: all those times women had reacted badly to Devlin. 'Your car or mine?' he said.

JEAN WAS RISING to her feet. Donald Devlin still filled the doorway, his blue eyes as cold as the North Sea.

'Your tools, Professor Devlin?' she guessed.

'Well, they're not Kennet Lovell's, dear lady, are they?'

Jean swallowed. 'I think I'd better be going.'

'I don't think I can let you do that.'

'Why not?'

'Because I think you know that it was I who left those coffins,' the old man stated. 'I can see it in your eyes. No use pretending.'

'The first one was just after your wife died, wasn't it? You killed that poor girl in Dunfermline.'

He raised a finger. 'Untrue: I merely read about her disappearance and went there to leave a marker, a *memento mori*. There were others after that . . . God knows what happened to them.' He took a step into the room. 'It took some time, you see, for my sense of loss to turn into something else.' His hands stroked the table's edge. 'I should never have let slip about Kennet Lovell . . . a good historicist would naturally be unable to resist looking into my claim further, finding disturbing parallels between past and present, eh, Miss Burchill? And it was *you* . . . the only one who ever made the connection.'

Jean was working hard to control her breathing. 'I don't understand,' she said. 'You were helping the inquiry . . .'

'Hindering, rather. And who could resist the opportunity? After all, I was investigating *myself*, watching others do the same . . .'

'You killed Philippa Balfour?'

Devlin's face creased in disgust. 'Not a bit of it.'

'But you left the coffin . . .?'

'Of course I didn't!' he snapped.

'Then it's been five years since you last . . .' She sought the right words. 'Last *did* anything.'

He took another step towards her. She ducked, reached into the cupboard for one of the chisels. Suddenly he had hold of her hair, pulling her back up. She screamed, hands still scrabbling for a weapon. She felt a cool wooden handle. Her head felt like it was on fire. As she lost her balance and started to fall, she stabbed the chisel into his ankle. He didn't so much as flinch. She stabbed again, but now he was dragging her towards the door. She half rose to her feet and added her momentum to his, the pair of them colliding with the edge of the door, the chisel falling from her grasp. She was on her hands and knees when the first blow came, spinning white lights across her vision.

She knew she had to get back onto her feet, start fighting back. He was an old man . . . Another blow made her flinch. She could see the chisel . . . only twelve feet to the front door . . . Devlin had her by the legs now, hauling her towards the living room . . . His grasp of her ankles was like a vice. Oh, Christ, she thought. Not like this . . . not like this . . .

THE AREA AROUND Canonmills and Inverleith was an easy enough beat: no housing schemes, plenty of wealth. The patrol car always made a point of stopping at the gates to the Royal Botanic Garden, it was perfect for the officers' mid-shift break. PC Anthony Thompson always provided the flask of tea, while his partner, Kenny Milland, brought the chocolate biscuits.

'Magic,' Thompson said, though his teeth told him otherwise: there was a dull ache from one of his molars whenever it came into contact with sugar.

Thompson loved American cop films, everything from *Dirty Harry* to *Seven*, and when they stopped for their break he sometimes imagined that they were parked outside a doughnut stand, in baking heat and searing glare, with the radio about to burst into life. They'd have to leave their coffee and burn some rubber, giving chase . . .

Not much chance of that in Edinburgh. A couple of pub shootings and a body in a skip, these comprised the highlights of Thompson's two decades on the force. So when the radio did burst into life, detailing a car and driver, Anthony Thompson did a double take.

'Here, Kenny, doesn't that one fit the bill?'

Milland turned and looked out of his window at the car parked next door. 'I don't know,' he admitted. 'Wasn't really listening, Tony.'

Thompson, however, was on the blower, asking for a repeat of the licence plate. He then stared down at the front of the neighbouring vehicle. 'We're only parked bloody next to it,' he told his partner.

THEY DIDN'T CALL it tea in the Du Thé café. It was a 'herbal infusion': blackcurrant and ginseng to be precise. It tasted all right, though Siobhan was tempted to add a spot of milk to cut the sharpness.

She hadn't meant to walk the entire length of the Royal Botanic Gardens, but somehow found herself at the eastern gate, next to Inverleith Row. Shops and cafés just along to the right, by Canonmills. Still time to spare . . . She thought of fetching her car, but decided to leave it where it was. If she walked back through the Botanics, then drove back here, she'd have missed the meeting time. Besides, she didn't know what parking was like where she was headed.

Her decision made, she headed back towards the Botanics, but passed the entrance, staying on Inverleith Row. Just before the rugby ground at Goldenacre she took a right, the path turning into more of a track. Dusk was fast arriving as she turned a corner and approached the gates of Warriston Cemetery.

NO ONE WAS ANSWERING Donald Devlin's buzzer, so Rebus hit all the others at random until someone responded. Rebus identified himself, and was buzzed into the tenement, Ellen Wylie right behind him. She actually passed him on the stairs and was first at Devlin's door, thumping it, kicking, pressing his bell.

Rebus crouched in front of the letterbox and pushed it open. 'Professor Devlin?' he called. 'It's John Rebus. I need to talk to you.'

Rebus put his eyes to the letterbox. His eyes widened. 'Holy Christ,' he said, getting to his feet. He stood back and launched a kick at the door. The wood complained, but didn't give.

He was about to take another run at the door when Wylie stopped him. 'Together,' she said. So that was what they did. Counted to three and hit the door at the same time. The jamb made a cracking sound. Their second assault split it, and the door opened, Wylie falling through it so that she landed on all fours. When she looked up, she saw what Rebus had seen: almost at floor level a hand had attached itself to the living-room door and was trying to open it.

Rebus ran forward, pushed through the gap into the living room. It was Jean, bruised and beaten, her face a smear of blood and mucus. One eye had swollen and was completely closed.

Rebus dropped to his knees in front of her. He didn't want to touch her, thought there might be bones broken.

Wylie was in the room now, too, surveying the scene. It looked like half the contents of the flat lay strewn across the floor, a bloody trail showing where Jean Burchill had crawled her way to the door.

'Get an ambulance,' Rebus said, voice trembling. Then, 'Jean, what did he do to you?' He watched her one good eye fill with tears.

Wylie made the call, stressing that it was an emergency. Then she saw that Rebus's ear was close to Jean's face. Wylie realised she was trying to say something.

Rebus looked up. 'She says, did we catch him?'

Wylie caught the meaning at once, ran to the window and pulled the curtains back. Donald Devlin was scurrying across the road, dragging one leg and holding his bleeding left hand out in front of him. 'Bastard!' Wylie yelled, making for the door.

'No!' Rebus's voice was a roar. He got to his feet. 'He's mine.'

As he bounded downstairs two at a time, he realised Devlin must have been hiding in one of the other rooms, slipped out while they were busy in the living room. He tried not to think of what Jean's fate would have been if they hadn't interrupted him . . .

By the time he reached the pavement, Devlin had disappeared from view, but the splashes of bright blood were as clear a trail as Rebus could wish for. He caught sight of him crossing Howe Street, making for St Stephen Street. Rebus was gaining, until the uneven pavement caught him, sending him over on one ankle.

He punched numbers into his mobile. When the call was answered, he yelled for assistance. 'I'm keeping the line open,' he said. That way, he could let them know if Devlin suddenly flagged a taxi or boarded a bus.

He could see Devlin again now, but then he turned the corner into Kerr Street. By the time Rebus got to the corner, slowed down by his twisted ankle, he'd lost him again. Deanhaugh Street and Raeburn Place were straight ahead, busy with pedestrians and traffic: the evening trawl home. Rebus crossed the road at the traffic lights and found himself on the road-bridge that crossed the Water of Leith . . . There were several routes Devlin could have taken, and the trail seemed to have stopped. Resting one arm on the parapet, taking the weight off his ankle, Rebus happened to look down at the river flowing sluggishly below.

And saw Devlin on the footpath, heading towards Leith.

Rebus lifted the phone and called in his position. As he was doing so, Devlin looked back and saw him. The old man's pace quickened, but then suddenly slowed. He came to a stop, turned back and stared at Rebus, who was taking the steps down to the path.

As he walked towards Devlin, Rebus saw the scratches on his face, and realised that Jean had been giving almost as good as she got.

'Something struck me, seeing you on that bridge,' Devlin said. 'I suddenly thought: they don't have anything on me.'

'Well, we can always make a start with attempted murder.' Rebus slipped a hand into his pocket, brought out the phone.

'Who are you going to call?' Devlin asked.

'Don't you want an ambulance?' Rebus held the phone up, took a step forward.

'Just a couple of stitches,' Devlin commented, examining the wound. 'I'd nothing to do with young Philippa, you know.'

'Someone stealing your idea?'

'Well, it wasn't exactly mine in the first place.'

'Are there any others we don't know about.'

Devlin smiled. 'Isn't four enough?'

'You tell me.'

'It seemed . . . satisfactory. No pattern, you see. Two bodies not even found.'

'Just the coffins.'

'Which might never have been connected . . .'

Rebus nodded slowly, didn't say anything.

'Was it the autopsy?' Devlin asked at last. Rebus nodded again. 'I knew it was a risk.'

'If you'd told us at the start you'd carried out the Glasgow post-mortem, we wouldn't have thought anything of it.'

He nodded, dabbing at the cuts on his face with his fingers. 'I do hope DS Wylie doesn't get into trouble for not keeping a closer eye on me when I was studying the autopsy reports.'

'I don't think she's the one that's in trouble here.'

'Uncorroborated evidence, isn't that what we're dealing with, Inspector? One woman's word against mine? I'm sure I can find some plausible motive for my fight with Miss Burchill.' He studied his hand. 'One might almost call me the victim. What else do you have? Two drownings, two Missing Persons, no evidence.'

'Well,' Rebus corrected him, 'no evidence apart from this.' He held the phone a little higher. 'It was already on when I took it from my pocket, connected to our comms centre down in Leith.' Glancing back over his shoulder, he saw that uniformed officers were making their way down the steps from the bridge. 'Did you get all that?' he asked into the mouthpiece. Then he looked at Devlin and smiled.

THEY WERE LOADING Jean Burchill into the ambulance when Rebus's mobile started ringing. One of the paramedics was explaining that they couldn't rule out spinal or neck damage, which was why they'd placed braces round her head and neck.

Rebus lifted the mobile to his ear. 'Hello?'

'DI Rebus? It's Eric Bain here.'

As the trolley slid home into the back of the ambulance, Rebus said, 'Any sign of Siobhan?'

'That's why I'm calling. I can't reach her. They think she's in the Botanics. There are half a dozen men out there looking for her.'

'Bain, I'm a bit tied up right now.'

'Oh. It's just that one of the email addresses Quizmaster was using, it traces back to Philippa Balfour's account.'

Rebus was inside the ambulance now, seated across from the trolley. Jean had her eyes closed, but when he reached for her hand, his pressure was returned. He didn't understand: was Bain trying to say that Flip Balfour had been Quizmaster?

'If Benzie did lend her laptop to Flip Balfour,' the Crime Squad officer was saying, 'we've got two computers in the same place, both used by Quizmaster.'

'Yes?' Rebus was having trouble concentrating.

'And if we rule out Ms Balfour as a suspect . . .'

'We're left with someone who had access to both?'

Silence for a moment, and then Bain: 'I think the boyfriend's back in the frame, don't you?'

'I don't know. But Siobhan's gone to meet Quizmaster,' Rebus said. Then he paused. 'She's at the Botanics, you say?'

'Yes. Her car's parked outside.'

Rebus thought for a second: Siobhan would know they were looking for her. Leaving the car in full view was too big a giveaway . . . 'What if she's meeting him somewhere else?'

'How can we find out?'

'Maybe Costello's flat . . .' He looked down at Jean. 'Look, Bain, I really can't do this, not right now.'

Jean's eye opened. She mouthed something. Rebus lowered his head. 'Fine . . .' he heard her slur.

She was telling him she'd be OK; that he had to help Siobhan now. Rebus turned his head, his eyes meeting those of Ellen Wylie, who was standing on the roadway, waiting for the doors to close. She nodded slowly, letting him know she'd stay with Jean.

'Bain?' he said into the mobile. 'I'll meet you at Costello's flat.'

BY THE TIME Rebus got there, Bain had climbed the winding stairs and was standing outside Costello's door.

'I don't think he's home,' he was saying, crouching down to look through the letterbox.

Rebus looked at the door, then at Bain. 'Together?' he said.

Bain stared back at him. 'Isn't that illegal?'

'For Siobhan,' Rebus said simply.

They hit the door together on the count of three.

Inside, Bain knew what he was looking for: a computer. He found two in the bedroom, both of them laptops. 'Claire Benzie's,' Bain guessed, 'and either his own or someone else's.'

The screensaver had been activated on one computer. Bain accessed Costello's ISP and opened the email files.

'No time to try for a password,' he said, almost to himself. 'So all we can read are the old messages.' But there were none to or from Siobhan. 'Looks like he wipes as he goes.'

'Or else we're barking up the wrong tree.' Rebus was looking around the room: unmade bed, books scattered across the floor. Notes for an essay on the desk next to the PC. Rebus limped over, opened the top drawer slowly. Inside: maps and guidebooks, including one about Arthur's Seat. A postcard of Rosslyn Chapel and another guidebook.

'Right tree,' he remarked simply. Bain got up, came to look. Rebus tried sliding the drawer out further. Something was sticking. He took a pen from his pocket and dislodged it: an Edinburgh A–Z.

'Open at the Botanics,' Bain said, sounding relieved. If that's where David Costello was, they'd have cornered him by now.

But Rebus wasn't so sure. He was examining the rest of the page. Then he looked over towards Costello's bed and saw a framed photo of Costello with Flip Balfour, with a headstone just coming into the frame. They'd met at a dinner party . . . breakfast next morning and then a walk in Warriston Cemetery. That was what Costello had told him. Warriston Cemetery was just across the road from the Royal Botanic Garden. Same page of the A–Z.

'I know where he is,' Rebus said quietly. 'I know where she's meeting him. Come on.' He limped from the room, hand already reaching for his mobile. The detectives who were wandering around the Botanics could be at Warriston in two minutes . . .

'HELLO, DAVID.'

He still had his funeral clothes on, including the sunglasses. He grinned as she walked towards him. He was just sitting there, legs swinging from the wall. He slid down and was suddenly standing in front of her.

'You guessed,' he said.

'Sort of.'

He looked at his watch. 'You're early.'

'You're earlier.'

'I had to recce, see if you were lying.'

'I said I'd be on my own.'

'And here you are.' He looked around.

'Plenty of escape routes,' Siobhan said, surprised by how calm he was. 'Is that why you chose it?'

'It's where I first realised I loved Flip.'

'Loved her so much you went and killed her?'

His face fell. 'I didn't know that was going to happen.'

She drew in a deep breath. 'But it happened anyway.'

He nodded. 'Yes. That's what you wanted to hear, isn't it?'

'I also want to know why.'

'How many reasons do you want? Her yah friends? Her pretensions? The way she kept picking fights, looking to break us up just so she could watch me crawling back?'

'You could have walked away.'

'But I *loved* her.' He laughed, as if acknowledging his own foolishness. 'I kept telling her that. You know what she told me back? That I wasn't the only one.'

'Ranald Marr?'

'Since before she left school. And still at it, even when *we* were together!' He stopped, swallowed. 'Enough motivation for you?'

'You vented your anger on Marr by disfiguring that toy soldier, and yet Flip . . . Flip you had to *kill*?' She felt calm, almost numb. 'That doesn't seem quite fair to me.'

'You wouldn't understand.'

She looked at him. 'But I think I do. You're a coward, David. You say you didn't know you were going to murder Flip that night—that's a lie. You had it planned all along . . . You were Quizmaster.' She paused. 'Something I don't understand—you sent Flip a message after she died?'

He smiled. 'That day at her flat, while Rebus was watching me and you were working on her computer . . . he told me something, said I was the only suspect.'

'You thought you'd try throwing us off the scent?'

'It was just supposed to be that one message . . . but when you replied, I couldn't resist. I was as hooked as you were.'

'Are you thinking of killing me, David?'

He shook his head briskly, irritated by the assumption. 'You know the answer to that,' he spat. 'You wouldn't have come otherwise.' He walked over to a low headstone and rested against it. 'Maybe none of it would have happened without the Professor.'

Siobhan thought she must have misheard. 'Which one?'

'Donald Devlin. First time he saw me afterwards, he guessed I'd done it. That's why he came up with that story, someone loitering outside. He was trying to protect me.'

'Why would he do that, David?'

'Because of everything we talked about . . . committing murder, getting away with it.'

'Professor Devlin?'

He looked at her. 'Oh yes, he's killed too, you know. Old bugger as good as said so.' He ran his hands over the headstone. 'I went to his flat once. He showed me these cuttings . . . people who'd disappeared or drowned. There was even one about a German student.'

'That's where you got the idea?'

He shrugged. 'Who knows where ideas come from?' He paused. 'I helped her, you know. She was dead impressed, all those clues . . .' He laughed. 'Flip was never much good with computers.'

'You turned up at the flat, told her you'd solved Hellbank . . .'

Costello nodded, remembering. 'She wasn't going to go with me until I promised to drop her off afterwards . . . She'd just kicked me out again—final this time, she'd piled my clothes on a chair—and after Hellbank she was heading off for a drink with all those bloody friends of hers.' He screwed his eyes shut for a moment, then turned to face Siobhan. 'Once you're there, it's hard to go back . . .'

'There never was a Stricture?'

He shook his head slowly. 'That clue was all for you, Siobhan . . .'

'I don't know why you kept going back to her, David, but one thing I do know: you never loved her. What you wanted was to control her.'

'Some people like to be controlled, Siobhan.' His eyes were staring into hers. 'Don't you?'

She thought for a moment, opened her mouth and was about to speak, but a noise interrupted. He snapped his head round: two men approaching. And two more fifty yards beyond them. He turned slowly back to Siobhan.

'I'm disappointed in you.'

She was shaking her head. 'Not my doing.'

He leapt from the headstone, hurtled towards the wall, his hands reaching the top, feet scrabbling for purchase. Siobhan threw herself after him, grabbed a leg with both hands and pulled. He tried kicking her off, but she held on, one hand reaching up towards his jacket, trying to haul him back. Then they were both flying backwards, his the only cry. He landed heavily on top of her, the air exploding from her lungs. Costello was on his feet and running, but two of the officers had him, wrestled him back onto the ground. He managed to slide his head round so he was looking at Siobhan, the two of them only a couple of yards apart. Hatred filled his face, and he spat in her direction. The saliva hit her on the chin. Suddenly she didn't have the strength to wipe it off . . .

JEAN WAS ASLEEP, but the doctor assured Rebus she'd be fine: cuts and bruises, 'nothing time can't heal'.

'I very much doubt that,' he told the doctor.

Ellen Wylie was there by the bedside. Rebus walked over and stood beside her. 'I wanted to say thanks,' he told her.

'For what?'

'Helping break down Devlin's door, for one thing. I'd never have done it on my own.'

Her reply was a shrug. 'How's the ankle?' she asked.

'Ballooning nicely, thank you.'

He limped along to A&E, where Siobhan was having a couple of stitches put into a head wound. Eric Bain was there. The conversation stopped as Rebus approached.

'Eric here,' Siobhan said, 'was just explaining how you worked out where I'd be.' Rebus nodded. 'And how you gained entry to David Costello's flat. By kicking in a suspect's door without a warrant.'

'Technically,' Rebus told her, 'I was on suspension, so I wasn't a serving officer.'

'Making it even worse.' She turned to Bain. 'Eric, you're going to have to cover for him.'

'Door was open when we got there,' Bain recited. 'Botched break-in, probably . . .'

Siobhan smiled at him, gave his hand a squeeze . . .

 **Chapter Nine**

It was a Sunday afternoon of sharp, low sunlight, the shadows impossibly long and skewed into an elastic geometry. Trees bowed by the wind, clouds moving like oiled machines. Rebus glanced towards Jean, quiet in the passenger seat.

He'd given her the option, but she'd decided to come with him to Falls. Rebus pulled on the handbrake and turned to Jean. 'I'll only be a minute. You want to wait here?'

She nodded. He reached into the back for the coffin, which was wrapped in newspaper, a front-page headline by Steve Holly, and got out of the car. Knocked on the door of Wheel Cottage.

Bev Dodds answered. She had a smile fixed to her face and a frilly apron tied round her waist.

'Sorry, not a tourist,' Rebus said. Her smile faded. 'Doing a roaring trade in tea and buns?'

'What can I do for you?'

He lifted up the parcel. 'Thought you might like this back. It is yours, after all, isn't it?'

She parted the sheets of newsprint. 'Oh thanks,' she said.

'It really *is* yours, isn't it?'

She wouldn't look at him. 'Finders keepers, I suppose . . .'

But he was shaking his head. 'I mean, you made it, Ms Dodds. This new sign of yours . . .' He nodded in its direction. 'Care to tell me who made it? I'm willing to bet you did it yourself. Nice piece of wood. I'm guessing you've a few chisels and suchlike.'

'What do you want?' Her voice had grown chilly.

'When I brought Jean Burchill here—there she is in the car, and she's fine by the way, thanks for asking—when I brought her here, you said you often went to the Museum.'

'Yes?' She was staring over his shoulder.

'Yet you'd never come across the Arthur's Seat coffins.' Rebus affected a frown. 'It should have clicked with me then.' He stared at her, but she didn't say anything. 'Still,' he said, 'brought you some extra business, eh? But I'll tell you one thing . . .'

Her eyes were liquid; she brought them up to meet his. 'What?'

He pointed a finger at her. 'You're lucky I didn't tag you sooner. I might have said something to Donald Devlin. And then you'd look like Jean back there, if not a damned sight worse.'

He turned away, headed back to the car.

On the way back into Edinburgh, Jean asked if they were going to Portobello. He nodded, and asked if that was OK with her.

'It's fine,' she told him. 'I need someone to help me move that mirror out of the bedroom.' He looked at her. 'Just until the bruises have healed,' she said quietly.

He nodded his understanding. 'Know what I need, Jean?'

She turned towards him. 'What?'

'I was hoping you might tell me . . .'

IAN RANKIN

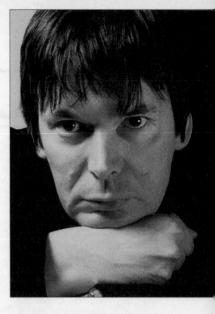

In Edinburgh's National Museum, a series of seventeen tiny coffins some five or six inches long are on display. Inside each is a wooden doll. Found in 1836 in a cave on Arthur's Seat—the hill that overlooks the city—their significance has never been fully explained, but some think they may be connected with the gruesome murders committed by the infamous duo, Burke and Hare.

Rankin, a Scot who grew up in a mining community in Fife but who now lives in Edinburgh, was fascinated. 'It's astonishing, the care that went into them. What struck me was that this is the kind of thing you might look for in a film about a serial killer . . . some kind of a trophy.'

What also fascinates him is the city of Edinburgh itself, and in all his Inspector Rebus novels—*The Falls* is the twelfth in the series—its special atmosphere is felt. 'I came to Edinburgh as a student and I found it a very curious place—very secretive, difficult to get to know, reticent,' Rankin says. He continues to explore, in his writing, the city's contrasts—the outward formality and gentility, the crime and chaos lurking beneath the surface.

Rankin sees himself, too, as a person of stark contrasts. 'There is a kind of Jekyll-and-Hyde thing within me. On the surface I'm a very mild mannered Clark Kent type, but there's a part of me that has a lot of aggression and petty grievances against the world,' he explains. Writing, he finds, is a form of catharsis. 'I palm most of my problems onto Rebus so I can exorcise most of my demons on the page.'

A few years ago, Rankin moved with his wife and two young sons to rural France, so he could afford to support a writing career. He's come a long way since. Having only just turned forty, he's already had one of his novels televised and his sales increase with every new book. Detective Inspector Rebus, whose name, interestingly, describes a type of puzzle, is fast becoming a household name to rank alongside Inspector Morse.

ECHO BURNING. Original full-length version © 2001 by Lee Child. US condensed version © The Reader's Digest Association, Inc., 2001. British condensed version © The Reader's Digest Association Limited, 2001.

FORCE 12. Original full-length version © 2001 by James Stewart Thayer. US condensed version © The Reader's Digest Association, Inc., 2001. British condensed version © The Reader's Digest Association Limited, 2001.

THE OBSERVATORY. Original full-length version © 2000 by Emily Grayson. US condensed version © The Reader's Digest Association, Inc., 2001. British condensed version © The Reader's Digest Association Limited, 2001.

THE FALLS. Original full-length version © 2001 by Ian Rankin. British condensed version © The Reader's Digest Association Limited, 2001.

The right to be identified as authors has been asserted by the following in accordance with sections 77 and 78 of the Copyright, Designs and Patents Act, 1988: Lee Child, James Stewart Thayer and Ian Rankin.

ACKNOWLEDGMENTS AND PICTURE CREDITS: *Echo Burning:* pages 6–8: Illustration by Brian Sheridan. Page 165: Roth Child. *Force 12:* pages 166–168: illustration by Craig White. *The Observatory:* page 292: woman's face: Imagebank; pages 292–293: observatory: Science Photo Library; page 293: couple on beach: Photodisc; woman's face: Telegraph Colour Library. *The Falls:* pages 366–368: Edinburgh skyline: GettyOne Stone; coffins: National Museums of Scotland; photomontage: Shark Attack. *The Falls:* the collection of poetry in David Costello's flat (page 433) is *I Dream of Alfred Hitchcock* by James Robertson, and the poem from which Rebus quotes is entitled 'Shower Scene'.

DUSTJACKET CREDITS: Spine from top: Brian Sheridan; Craig White; Imagebank, Science Photo Library, Photodisc, Telegraph Colour Library; Gettyone Stone, National Museum of Scotland.

Printed by Maury Imprimeur SA, Malesherbes, France
Bound by Reliures Brun SA, Malesherbes, France

214AJ